BLACK OPERA

BLACK OPERA

MARY GENTLE

GOLLANCZ
LONDON

The right of Mary Gentle to be identified as the author
of this work has been asserted by her in accordance with
the Copyright, Designs and Patents Act 1988.

First published in Great Britain in 2012 by Gollancz
An imprint of the Orion Publishing Group Ltd,
Orion House, 5 Upper St Martin's Lane, London WC2H 9EA
An Hachette UK Company

A CIP catalogue record for this book
is available from the British Library.

ISBN (Cased) 978 0 575 08349 3
ISBN (Trade Paperback) 978 0 57508350 9

1 3 5 7 9 10 8 6 4 2

Typeset by Input Data Services Ltd,
Bridgwater, Somerset

Printed and bound by
CPI Group (UK) Ltd, Croydon CR0 4YY

The Orion Publishing Group's policy is to use papers that are
natural, renewable and recyclable products and made from wood
grown in sustainable forests. The logging and manufacturing
processes are expected to conform to the environmental
regulations of the country of origin.

www.orionbooks.co.uk

To Maggie Noach, a much-missed friend

*'The Good guys and the Bad Guys
are both hoping for a miracle ...'*

NOTE

This story takes place in that curious gap in European history, the two decades between the battle of Waterloo and the arrival of the Victorian age; when bel canto opera flourished, and the word 'scientist' was first coined.

I have used the source material regarding the history and royalty of the Kingdom of the Two Sicilics with the same careful and exact attention to detail as the bel canto composers.

Given that Gaetano Donizetti once set an opera in Liverpool and described it as 'a small Alpine village outside London', the reader is probably safe in regarding *Black Opera* as Alternate History.

SINFONIA

10 April 1815 – Indonesia

The water rose up in a wall like the end of the world.

The ship's prow dropped down – down – so far down it seemed impossible it could ever lift again—

Spilling off a monumental weight of water, it began slowly to rise.

The Flores Sea blazed, darker than indigo, every wave crest tipped with crimson and carmine.

Yes, we are a day late. The dark of the moon was yesterday. But perhaps, *perhaps* we will not all be dying for nothing—

Ranieri glanced back through the glass of the steam-ship's wheel-house. Two of his men grappled with the captain: a grey and grizzled man in a salt-worn peaked cap. By his lip movements, he appeared to be shouting.

Protesting where we're taking his ship, no doubt.

The steam-driven paddles made it in advance of all its kind; keel laid down in France by special order. *That alone must make it ours, to do with as we wish*, he thought.

A pain sawed at his waist, from the rope that bound him to the rail.

The wind, hot and abnormally dry, snatched the voice from his mouth. He shouted to the woman:

'Now! – *Sing*—!'

Identical ropes trapped her. The same wind snapped her black hair out in a pennant, and slapped it back in her face. Against the violet sky, she appeared a ghost from Byron or Shelley; her skin visibly white through the skirls of ash and spray.

Her gaze riveted, not on him, but on the child he held.

The girl, her daughter, had no ropes lashing her to the rail. Nothing held the six-year-old safe on the pitching, yawing deck – except the grip he had on her shoulders.

'Ranieri!'

He read it from her lips. Not his real name, but he has been answering to it from Rome to Indonesia.

'Give me Maria Grazia! Anything else is yours!'

The ship's prow strained, lifting towards the vertical. As if the baying of the gale were nothing, he mouthed his order again at the woman. And lifted one hand free of her child.

The woman frantically nodded, her hand shielding her mouth against the snowfall of ashes.

Air cleared unnaturally around her face.

She began to sing.

It should not have been possible to hear her over the storm. That he could hear a thread of sound, no matter how soft, under the ear-battering gale, made his spirits rise immeasurably.

The whole hull thrummed with the straining side paddle-wheel's engines. Barely a dish-rag of canvas high on both her masts kept her facing into the seas.

The ship stood all but upright on her stern at the top of the alizarin and scarlet wave. The prow pitched forward; down. Spray deluged him, tightening the hemp ropes painfully. A hill of water momentarily cut off the wind from his right-hand side.

At one and the same moment, he heard the singer's voice leap up into a spine-shivering soprano, and saw clear across the seething ocean to the island.

Sumbawa Island – at last!

Sumbawa: one among an archipelago of thousands of islets that make up the Lesser Sundra Islands, on the border between Indonesia and the Indian Ocean. Twelve thousand miles from Europe, and fifteen miles away, now, from their foundering ship in the tiny Flores Sea. An island-shape barely visible in the dimness.

4

He could not have seen it at all if not for the single cone of the volcano, Mount Tambora. A lightning-filled pillar of smoke plundered upwards from the volcano: dark violet and deepest black.

Hard to be sure in the spray and detritus-filled air . . . He slitted his eyes, and made out a red spark of lava beginning to snake down from the peak.

'Sing louder!' He shrieked into the momentary lull of the wind, barely audible over the slamming of steam-pistons, and the shrill sound of rivets popping free of the side paddle-wheel casing. 'Sing!'

The woman sobbed a note, reaching out her hands to her daughter.

Ranieri picked the child up. He put a distasteful hand over her mouth to stop her blaring; ignored her kicking, stained legs, and held her out – to the full length of his arms – so that she would fall directly into the glistening slide of the wave's trough, never touching the ship's side.

He did not need to voice the threat. Only the exhortation:

'Sing louder! *better!* than you have ever sung before!'

Terror and desperation gave her voice power.

Ranieri drew in a breath, sour with the volcano's exhaled gases, and sent his own ringing tenor to join her, spiralling upwards in a duet.

Unfortunate that I am the only one of our people with a true voice, he found himself wryly thinking at this last moment, that must be his last moment. *I wonder, will this work?*

His voice reverberated in his chest, as if he sang in the nave of a cathedral, or some pagan amphitheatre; he felt himself join with her and her anguish.

The words sang of love and death.

At the aching zenith of the duet, soprano and tenor went beyond themselves into an apotheosis of sound, barely seeming that of human voices.

Below the sea-bed, below the abyssal rock that strains with the pressure of the subduction zone, the magma chamber reaches breaking point. Liquid rock, fire and gas surge upwards.

The volcano of Tambora is far too narrow a channel to contain it.

The girl-child panicked, spasmed out of Ranieri's hands, and fell, vanishing into spray and coiling water.

It's too late now, even though the mother goes from song to agonised, horribly comic screech. It is done. He thinks desperately, *Will they know, back home, what we have achieved here? That we have succeeded? We are so far away—*

The island of Sumbawa detonates.

The explosion of the volcano Tambora is the loudest sound heard on the planet since the Neolithic age and the super-eruption of Mount Toba. The ancient Plinean rupture of Vesuvius is nothing to it; Krakatoa, decades later, will not outdo it. Twelve cubic miles of rock lift into the atmosphere.

An ash-and-cinder cloud will extend six hundred miles, turning the sky to night. The eruption is heard clearly in Sumatra, twelve hundred miles away, where it is mistaken for artillery.

It is not heard in Europe.

Europe does not take notice of news in the Far East. They are too busy with the upcoming end of their own wars against the Emperor of the North.

They don't hear how it's pitch-dark in Indonesia for two days – and, afterwards, it's discovered that eleven or twelve thousand people died in Tambora's pyroclastic surges, and perhaps seventy thousand in the floods, starvation, and disease that comes after.

But the following year – AD 1816 – is known throughout the northern hemisphere as 'the Year without a Summer'.

A generation-long war is over: a Gallic tyrant has scraped a desperate victory on the field of Waterloo, and consented to an Armistice; and now they desire to enjoy the peace. But in Europe and America, cloud and a persistent dry sulphurous fog cover the sun each month. Storms wrack the winter. Snow falls in June, and a bitter frost comes all year round. The potato, wheat, and oat harvests fail. Livestock die.

The desolation of the wars is barely gone before the resulting extensive famine. Typhus and cholera outbreaks follow hunger. And rioting, looting and arson follow them.

Men look at the skies and talk of the punishment of God.

A very few men do not.

They talk of a ship lost in the seas around Mount Tambora, on that rash and vital voyage.

'Gentlemen, ladies – "Matteo Ranieri".' A man raises his glass to their fellow-conspirator. 'One of the Prince's Men has fallen – but the Prince's Men go on.'

They drink deep, around the table, but do not afterwards smash their crystal glasses. Valuable things are only to be broken when it becomes necessary.

Now their experiment is proved, they can begin to plan.

All that stands between them and success is time.

1

Some years later – Napoli, Port district.

He could not remember the notes.

The sounds fell away from Conrad like tides receding across a beach—

He rose out of what he realised was a dream.

The backs of his eyes hurt. Conrad felt with tentative fingers at the flesh around his right eye-socket, and found it puffy. Pain centred at the retina of the eyeball—

Light!

—drilling its way through his brain as his eyelid slitted open.

The lemon-yellow of Naples' morning sun, rising south and east of Vesuvius, stabbed through his window and roused nausea. Conrad Scalese rolled over – having just time to wonder, *What am I doing in bed fully dressed*? – and made the edge of the mattress.

He vomited onto the bare floorboards.

'Padrone?'

Tullio's deep voice cut through his head, making Conrad clutch both hands back over his eyes.

The man-servant deftly wiped his face clean. 'Too much getting pissed at the after-show party? Or's your head again?'

'Sick,' Conrad managed.

It wasn't that sensible an answer, since it could be equally taken to refer to a hangover from too much celebratory drinking. Tullio Rossi murmured something consoling, however. Conrad clamped his eyelids shut, behind his palms, and listened to the click of spoon against glass; the sound of water pouring.

The remains of his dream fell through auditory memory: dry sand through his fingers. Every note is gone.

But it won't have been mine, he realised. *Not mine – words are my talent, not music. It'll be something I heard at some opera house—*

The cold edge of a glass tipped against Conrad's mouth. He swallowed Tullio's usual remedy by reflex, the touch of laudanum just distinguishable. The residue tasted bitter.

'Sorry, padrone, I thought you were drunk last night.' Tullio's baritone carried the rough edge of his army days even now; too much shouting of orders over the explosion of cannon and screaming of horses. He held the volume of it down to quiet questioning. 'Sick headache?'

If the pain hadn't half-blinded him, Conrad would have sworn violently.

'I don't get "sick headaches". Women get "sick headaches"!'

'Absolutely, padrone.'

Only a man who knew him very well could have distinguished amusement in the ex-rifleman's tone. Conrad knew him very well.

Gritting his teeth, Conrad got out: 'The ancient Greek physicians called it "hemicrania" – "migraine"—'

'Oh. Megrims. My old mum used to get those. Not on the rag, are you, padrone?'

Conrad suppressed what he could of the pain to say encouragingly, 'You're fired, Tullio.'

'Yes, padrone. Third time this month. Drink up, now.'

Pain stabbed from Conrad's first cervical vertebrae, up across his skull. Half his face by now seemed something between numb and squashy. It felt as if the air itself pressured him, squeezing his head in a vice, exactly as it had felt during the very first of these episodes, after a twelve-hour continuous artillery barrage in the war.

Conrad gave the glass to Tullio and rolled gingerly back on the bed, supine, gathering as much dignity as he could be bothered to assume.

9

'If anyone calls, I'm . . . naturally tired after last night's success. They can come back with their congratulations later. '

Tullio eased the shutters three-quarters closed. That cut out most of the early sunlight. 'If anybody calls at this hour, I'll tell them to go fuck a mule!'

Amusement hurt.

Conrad hauled a pillow over his head, wincing as cotton scraped at flesh unaccountably tender. He tensed, restless despite the opiate; hearing his tendons and ligaments stretching with a crack that did not dilute pain. Tullio's laudanum held Conrad on the edge of sleep and waking. Time stretched and contracted oddly. He suspected it had been only a few moments when he heard the quiet noises of Tullio with a cloth and bucket, cleaning up the mess beside the bed. The smell of vomit faded.

'Sorry for that.'

'Shoulda guessed. You had a bad night.' The forty-year-old man voiced sardonic amusement. 'Another master would give his servant a raise, mind you . . .'

'I don't pay you,' Conrad obliged him by pointing out.

'Well, it won't hurt you to agree to the raise, then, will it?'

Conrad made a noise half-laughter and half-groan. 'Please – stop consoling the sick, you don't have the knack of it!'

'Padrone, I was there for *Il Terrore di Parigi, ossia la morte di Dio*—'

Tullio Rossi struck a dramatic attitude, somewhat hampered by the mop.

'—*The Terror of Paris, Or, The Death of God*! That's drama. I think we're finally going to be rich!' He dropped the operatic stance, and muttered. 'You deserve it, Corrado.'

'There might be money for more than second-rate, second-floor lodgings . . . I need this libretto to make my name. I need to finally pay off my debts.'

He did not say, *I need proper wages for a man-servant who consents without argument to subsist on bed-and-board*; but he made a private solemn resolution.

'Sleep, you.' Tullio's rough voice was affectionate. By the sound of it, he took bucket and mop together in one hand; using the other to open the bedroom door.

It closed behind him with a click that made Conrad wince.

Sleep pulled, with a promise of pain gone when he woke.

He pushed dream-thoughts aside, drawing his own success to himself as if he were a dragon hoarding maidens.

People will think I drank myself into a stupor last night, but why would I? I didn't want to miss a minute of it!

Il Terrore di Parigi, put on as the second opera of this Carnival season, just before Lent – since Naples, unlike other Italian states, doesn't close its opera houses at the start of Lent. Set against the background of that Enlightenment September when Robespierre made Paris's famous noxious mud turn red in the streets.

Who can resist heroes and heroines in danger from Madame la Guillotine? Four acts – a good three hours, counting the interval – and the script and staging all Conrad Scalese's.

For a moment Conrad was beyond the pain, luminous with a memory of absolute satisfaction. Music and human voices intertwining with precision and drive, building to a heart-shaking climax, and – after the end of the opera's last act – twenty-seven seconds of pure silence. (He counted each, breath stopped in his throat.)

Every level of the opera house from boxes to pit exploded in applause. *Brava! Bravi! Bravissimo!*

Conrad Scalese, librettist – no – *poet*. Creator of stories . . .

Conrad rolled over, half-burying himself in sheets and blankets.

. . . *Finally successful! Finally* there.

The world broke apart with a shattering, literal, crash.

✦

Conrad sat bolt upright before he was perfectly alert, automatically pushing at the blankets. Cold wind sliced across his body.

Small fangs of pain sliced into his skin.

He got his eyes open, realising all in one moment, *The shutters are fully open – the window is broken! The floor – the bed—*

—I'm covered in broken glass!

'What in hell, *padrone*!'

Tullio Rossi shoved through the bedroom door. The last of the window pane fell to the floor in guillotine-sharp pieces. Rossi wrenched the broken shutters aside, and stumbled, his foot catching against a brick on the floor among the glass.

'*Merda!*' Shards of glass stood out from Conrad's hands, his dazzled attempts to remove them only seeming to drive them deeper.

The red clay brick lay surrounded by dust and brilliant shards on the floorboards. Undeniable and present.

Tullio snapped his fingers. Conrad relinquished his hands to Tullio: army experience would let him remove the splinters more cleanly.

'Corradino!' The voice from below in the street was a familiar clear bass. 'Conrad! What does it take to wake you up!'

'Spinelli – you idiot – I have a fucking front door—!' Conrad clamped his eyes shut. He could not smell smoke, he realised. *So, the building's not on fire, no excuse*!

Being still clothed meant he had his shoes on. Conrad staggered upright, crunching over the glass on the floor. Tullio cursed, following, attempting to deal with his master's injuries.

With no regard for splinters still in the frame, Conrad kicked the glass doors open and put one foot on the balcony, leaning off the side so that he could see down into the street.

Blazing sunlight over the Bay of Naples skewered his right eye. He squeezed his eyelids together, blinking away tears, and snarled with intense quietness:

'JohnJack, I'm going to fucking kill you!'

'Kill me later. Come down here *now*. And get your coat on – you're leaving Naples!'

Before his other eye watered shut, Conrad saw that Gian-Giacomo Spinelli – called 'JohnJack' on occasion, for his having sung at the Theatre Royal in London, God bless the English for their ignorant love of opera – had his own coat pulled hastily on, and a low hat tugged down over his eyes.

He also had the collar of his jacket folded under itself, his crimson cravat badly tied, and every other sign of having dressed hastily (and conceivably in the dark).

A carpet-bag bulged at his feet.

Tullio firmly seized Conrad's hands one at a time, ensuring each was free of glass. The cold February wind made Conrad's mind feel more clear.

'Has everyone in Napoli gone mad this morning?'

'Get to the carriage, I'll tell you on the way!' JohnJack Spinelli glanced left and right, and looked up at Conrad again. 'I had to come round the back – the front of your building's being watched.'

'Watched!'

'Leave this way and you won't be seen. The rest have packed up and gone already. Fanny's on her way to Milan with Persiani. We broke down the door and Barjaba's lodgings are deserted. They say the impresario was seen fleeing over the rooftops, clutching a carpet-bag full of the house takings, on the way to a hired carriage—'

Conrad spluttered disbelief.

'—He's gone!' JohnJack snarled. 'The others have left on the public stage or the first ship they could get out of Naples harbour. I waited to get you. Tullio, get him packed, we don't have any more time!'

Vomit burned in the back of Conrad's throat.

He was aware that Tullio moved away, and a moment later returned with a jacket that he urged on over Conrad's slept-in shirt and waistcoat. And, over top of that, a faded and battered greatcoat, surviving from the war. As if it were still war-time, when a man must up and move without warning and only the vaguest idea of why.

Tullio moved around the room behind him; the sounds unmistakably those of things being thrown into carpet-bags and travelling trunks.

The disparate parts of the morning failed to make any sense.

Conrad opened his eyes cautiously. Below, the tall, skinny coloratura basso stepped from foot to foot, either against the frost on the cold earth, or in urgency. While pale in the face, he did not appear to have a hangover – *Though he should*, Conrad thought. *Given what he drank last night—*

All the previous night overwhelmed him, pushing aside the pain. Five ovations; singers and audience made into the closest of drunken friends after the performance; and Conrad himself in the middle of it, for the first time one of the centres of success.

'No.' He gestured at Tullio to stop packing. 'No, I'm not going anywhere! We had the success of the season last night!'

'Yes.' Spinelli sounded grim. 'And in the early hours of this morning, just before dawn, that same Teatro Nuovo opera house where we had the success? Burned down to the ground! Struck by a lightning-bolt from God.'

2

'Struck by *lightning?*'

'Burnt to the foundations.'

Conrad stared. Shock overrode all questions except *What happens to* Il Terrore di Parigi *now?*

The other implications rushed over him like a storm-wave.

'Is everybody all right? Was anybody hurt!'

'The building was deserted by then. No; no one.'

Spinelli's definitive answer sank in. Conrad heard himself begin to babble. 'Did we lose the costumes? What about the stage-flats? Can we transfer to another opera house? Was it sabotage—'

A chop of the hand cut him off. JohnJack spoke just loud enough to be heard. 'Conrad, the Teatro Nuovo burned down because it was struck by God's lightning . . .'

GianGiacomo Spinelli huddled deeper into his greatcoat than the spring chill in the Port District could justify. As close to whispering as a man shouting up at a balcony can come, he finished:

'By the Wrath of the Lord. Because of the opera's impiety.'

'That's . . .' Conrad struggled between pain and growing astonished anger. '—Bullshit, JohnJack!'

'Now isn't the time to give me your atheist arguments! The Inquisition say the opera house was struck down because of your libretto, Conrad. They can't get the impresario, or the composer, because they're gone. You're still here. The Inquisition is going to

15

arrest and question you for blasphemy if you don't get your arse downstairs and into this coach I have!'

Squinting through wet blurred vision, Conrad made out something large at the dark end of the street; heard the stamp of a hoof, and smelled the soft scent of horse manure.

The silhouette was not a light about-town cabriolet or barouche, but a large, luggage-laden coach. A cross-country traveller: the kind that singers and composers and other artists slog from town to town in, every opera season.

Early light made his eye throb. Conrad felt overwhelmed by a sense of unreality. The intimately sized Teatro Nuovo had become utterly familiar these last six weeks of rehearsal. How to imagine that the ranks of gilded boxes, the narrow cramped spaces behind the stage, no longer exist?

Spinelli added, 'We have space enough for you, Corrado, and your man Tullio can ride with the driver.'

'You're not serious?'

Spinelli threw up his hands. 'Yes, I'm serious! Now—'

'Lightning strikes – let me guess – the opera house's roof? And it's supposed to be our fault? The gables of the Teatro Nuovo are higher than any other building around it! Why wouldn't lightning hit it. *Cazzo!* It's built from timber from top to bottom, and do they believe in lightning rods? No! Of course it would go up like a firework! Haven't they any common sense!'

'Corradino!—' Spinelli hit the heel of his hand to his forehead. 'Signore Giuseppe Persiani at least has the excuse that he writes Church music as well as opera. Fanny Tacchinardi and the rest of us are at risk because we were dumb enough to sing what you wrote, but that's not as bad as actually writing the bloody thing. It's the easiest thing in the world to find blasphemy in words! Now are you coming or not!'

'No!' Conrad drew in a breath. He belatedly realised. 'You waited for me?'

'Are you going to get your arse down here, or do I have to get Rossi to throw you over his shoulder!'

JohnJack's been here a quarter of an hour, at least.

Fifteen minutes, in which he could have been two miles further away

16

from the Inquisition's officers. And two miles here and now will count for a lot later on.

I have good friends.

'. . . All right. We can sort out it with the Teatro Nuovo opera board by letter. Give me two minutes to fill a carpet-bag!' Conrad turned away from the outside world, mind on his desk, his papers—

Sudden loud sound jolted him from head to foot.

Mind and body dislocated; he clapped both hands to his head. Agonising pain blossomed, as if his skull opened along its fissures; laudanum did not touch it. Conrad swore at himself for weakness.

He forced his eyes open. Dazzles hung in the centre of his vision; left him more than half blind.

And again! – the crash of something heavy striking against wood.

'The door!'

'We won't make the back stairs now.' Tullio left off emptying the wardrobe and chests, and called grimly but quietly down from the window. 'Signore Spinelli, you may need to make a run for it!'

Conrad rubbed his fists over his eyes. The corners felt wet with pain. Some of his vision cleared, but left him squinting

Two – three – four more thundering blows of fists against wood came from the lodgings' locked and bolted outer door. *'Merda!'*

Tullio Rossi held a wicked little flintlock pistol in one hand. It had once been the property of the Emperor's gendarmerie, and rarely missed fire. The broad-shouldered man directed a look at him. 'Padrone?'

Conrad instinctively gestured to him not to load it. 'All we need is an accident and a man killed! No. Go! Keep them talking!'

Tullio Rossi was already moving towards the door.

JohnJack's right. It's the Inquisition.

Conrad squeezed his eyelids shut and opened them; more of the shifting dazzles dispersed. Fear of the Church coalesced in his belly and grumbled in his bowels. By some alchemy, it transmuted into anger.

Here I am, yet again at the mercy of the irrational!

Who have law and power on their side. The fury turned on himself.

17

A man who can think himself safe from the righteous if he keeps his head down – and then goes ahead and puts it all on stage in an opera! What a fool I am—

And more than a fool, because I have no intention of changing.

Conrad leaned over the balcony, ignoring the shattered glass. Sunlight crept down the house-walls. He cupped hands for shade, his skin speckled with blood, and ignored the blurred sunlit curve of the Bay of Naples, and the looming, blue-grey broken crater. Because otherwise he might allow himself to think, *Is this the last time I'll see the outside for weeks? Or months?*

The cells of the Holy Office are terrible.

'JohnJack!' He called down urgently. 'There'll be officers coming round the back of here! Go. Now!'

Tullio's voice sounded at the outer door in gruff innocence. Increasingly aggressive voices raised against him, words inaudible but the authoritarian sound clear.

'Corrado—' Spinelli reached up, fruitlessly; the balcony was too high. Jumping down would mean a broken leg, or worse injury.

Conrad forced himself to focus through the pain behind his eye. 'Get your coach out of here. They might let you go if you're on your own. I'll catch up with you later.'

Spinelli's round features were not suited to dark emotions unless in heavy stage make-up, but his stance was telling: shoulders tight and fists clenched. 'Come after us! Try Rome first, it's the last place they'll expect us to be. Be safe!'

Spinelli seized the bag at his feet and turned on his heel. Conrad staggered as he pushed himself back into the room.

Every minute they're here may be one minute they're not following JohnJack.

Conrad walked through the tiny main room of his lodgings. The outer door was open on chaos, Tullio's broad back blocking most of the view. Seven or eight men in dark clothing crowded the landing beyond him. By the volume of noise, every man present must be attempting to out-shout the rest.

Conrad felt a sudden nostalgic desire for his old long-barrelled heavy cavalry pistols. Firing a ball into the ceiling would get instant silence.

18

Although the noise right now might well kill me.

'Gentlemen?' he managed to ask.

The leading intruder shouldered Tullio to one side.

Conrad met furious black eyes in a sallow face.

The man barely referred to the document crumpled in his hand, gazing hungrily up.

'Conrad Arturo Scalese, sometimes known as "Corrado" or "Corradino Scalese", aged twenty-nine years, resident in the Port district of Naples – you are the author of a declared heretical work, namely, *Il Terrore di Parigi, ossia la morte di Dio*. You are hereby placed under arrest in the name of the Cardinal of Naples!'

A shift of cloud above the lodging-house brought dim sunlight into the stair-well and the second-floor landing. It glowed on the black cappa cloaks worn over the white habits of the Dominicans, and on dark hair and white faces. In the uniform, all alike as brothers.

For one moment, in amusement born out of sheer terror, Conrad saw them in terms of opera. *All-male chorus, tenor and baritone, opening Act 1 – these will be the jolly singing Assassins, of course; daggers under their cloaks, and all smiles!*

The brilliant tonal contrast of the blacks and whites pierced his head sufficiently that Conrad clapped a hand over his eye, and bit back a groan.

He saw the arresting Dominican's face almost shining.

—Because I've shown a weakness.

'You are – unwell.' The man's voice held an undertone of satisfied malice, as if he thought some vice had earned the pain Conrad suffered. That was confirmed a moment later. 'So you are the drunkard that rumour makes you out to be. Not that I'm surprised – heretic, blasphemer, and atheist—'

The dark man's attention suddenly shifted.

Conrad caught the noise, too. Doors opening on the landings above, and the creak of stair-rails as his neighbours leaned over them. *In Naples, nobody's business is their own.*

The Dominican smiled.

'Conrad Scalese—' He pitched his voice to be intensely carrying.

Any of the gossiping old women in the apartment building will hear it, deaf as they claim to be.

'You're under arrest – by the authority of the Congregation of the Holy Office of the Inquisition!'

'Perhaps we should speak in private,' Conrad said flatly. Pain half blinded him, but left him even less inclined to be bullied.

He stepped back into the sitting-room before he could be shoved, a pace in front of the Dominican friars, and gripped Tullio's wrist. It might look like an appeal for physical support. In fact, it forced Tullio to keep his flick-knife hidden in his other breeches pocket.

And who knows, it might make them underestimate me.

Releasing the ex-rifleman, Conrad faced the first priest. 'And you are, signore?'

'My name is an unimportant matter, between myself and my God,' the man said dryly. 'More importantly for you, I stand here as a representative of Christ Miraculous and His Church—'

'Let me see your authorisation.' Conrad held out a demanding hand.

A steel cuff snapped shut over his wrist.

For a vital moment he failed to react.

'Brothers, shackle him! Search the rooms!'

3

'Yes, Canon-Regular!'

The first blow put Conrad so far back into agony that he could hardly struggle. If not for the pain's razor edge, he would have screamed like a woman, but it left him literally breathless.

He hit back blindly, powered by fear.

The leader seemed clerically ageless – he could have been any-where from thirty to fifty. All the other Dominican friars were in their twenties or early thirties, and all evidently trained for this. Two men pinned Conrad's arms, and another kicked the back of his knee with a solid boot.

Conrad overbalanced under the hammering blows, and went down with all three of them, rolling on the threadbare carpet and the varnished floorboards. His mind seemed to absent itself, fleeing from sensation, and he found himself hyper-aware of small details – the dusty marks of boot-soles printed on his knee-breeches and stockings; the pattern of the Turkey carpet as the side of his face pressed into it.

Two men knelt on him.

Cloth rucked up against his face – one of the Dominican cloaks, pulled off in the struggle, and now blocking light from his eyes. A seam ripped as he fought; it felt like the under-arm of his shirt. Hands at his wrists and ankles locked the shackles shut.

He strained to get an arm free, or to kick, and found himself rolled over on his back, with their fingers digging painfully deep into his muscles. Three or four men pinned him, discussing in barely breathless voices what 'evidence' might be hidden in the apartment.

'Padrone?' Tullio sprawled a few feet away, flat on his face, a Dominican friar kneeling in the centre of his back. His wrists were tied with plain rope. Unusually, fear showed on his face.

For me as well as him. Damnation.

Conrad coughed, clearing the dust from his throat. 'I see they weren't chosen for their spiritual gifts . . .'

It reassured him immensely when Tullio chuckled, even if the sound was gruff and breathless.

Footfalls jarred his head. One of the friars searching the premises pelted back out of the bedroom, stuttering.

'Canon Viscardo! A rear window is smashed, but from the outside!'

The Dominican Canon jerked his head and two of the junior priests left the lodgings at a run. Conrad heard them clattering down the stairs.

I hope JohnJack and the others are streets away by now!

Conrad couldn't move from his star-fish sprawl. He strained to lift his head, to see what the men holding him did.

Intrusive hands settled over his eyes, from behind.

Before he could pull away, the fingers of the right hand landed with peculiar accuracy over the exact area of puffy flesh that hurt.

'God afflicts you.'

Conrad recognised the Canon-Regular's dry voice close beside his ear. The touch felt harmless.

And that might easily change.

Temporise – placate him—

No! Conrad thought.

No, I'm in their hands, I'm handcuffed, che cazzo!; *they're going to interrogate me whatever I do or say. And—*

Too many memories, too fast, flash past, from the mountains of the north, where in that freezing, gritty, mud-locked campaign they had often occasion to question peasants and supposed enemy spies.

—And I will break, because any man who's not a fanatic does. And some fanatics do, too.

But they will have to break me first.

Conrad snorted at the Dominican he could not see. 'I have an affliction? Yes. I doubt it's from a deity!'

'Of course you doubt. You're an atheist. But . . . He may also intend that you be fit for interrogation by his Eminence Cardinal Corazza . . .' The last sounded like a self-addressed question.

Conrad weighed up the certain pain of trying to fight free. The injury the men might do him for resisting this arrest.

Who can I appeal to? I have no powerful patron if Domenico Barjaba's left—

An abrupt movement wrenched pain through his skull and spine.

Hands dragged at him – lifted him, he realised through the shattering hemicrania; or rather, lifted his head and shoulders off the floor.

He was suddenly immobile, released from the worst of their grip. Gravity pulled his head, neck, and shoulders back against something upright, warm and cloth-covered.

The Canon-Regular's chest.

The man knelt behind him, Conrad realised, supporting his semi-supine body.

'Don't you need the Host?' Conrad provoked, hoping to get the man away from him without physical struggle. 'Blessed wine? Holy water? Some sort of Church paraphernalia for throwing out demons—'

Dry palms covered both his eyes. 'All there needs to be is Faith.'

'And I don't have any!'

The man hummed under his breath. A vibration went through Conrad's body, shivering the pain into splinters of glass.

All Conrad's attention focused on his involuntary closeness to the man behind him; he didn't register the exact moment when he realised that he could spare attention for something beyond his body's blinding pain.

Pain that subsided.

◆

The last of the hemicrania burned out of his vision. A sodden, thick sensation permeated his head. The hangover from hemicrania is worse than that from drink. *But I welcome it, every time*, he thought dizzily. *It means the pain is gone.*

'There.' The Canon-Regular's hands moved away. 'Merciful is God, who will even heal an atheist sinner.'

Conrad blinked against the suddenly bright and painless world. Overturned table – rucked-up rugs – scattered books – sheets of paper, marked with the prints of sandals—

The line of his vision left him staring up, at the one undisturbed object on the mantel over the fireplace.

'Or – it's twenty minutes by the clock since my servant gave me laudanum. And that's how long it takes to work.'

The Canon pushed Conrad upright.

It caused no pain. The relief was an intense pleasure. Conrad sat with his head supported in his hands for a moment, glad almost to tears.

Moving with care, he lifted his head from his hands – to discover Canon Viscardo, kneeling, smiling at him.

It was a disconcerting expression on the knife-sharp features.

'You have Faith,' the Canon announced. 'Somewhere, deep down.'

Irritated, Conrad realised he was afraid again. He abandoned his usual reticence. 'If there's any man I hate, it's one who claims to know more about the inside of my mind than I do!'

A smug expression settled on Viscardo's features. It suited him better than the smile.

'My son. You don't resist the idea so strongly unless, in your heart, you still have Faith. You're just fighting against realising it.'

I am almost too angry to breathe, Conrad realised. *Because I've had this said to me so many times.*

'Canon-Regular, you're so violent against the idea of atheism because, deep down, you know it's true – you're just fighting against that realisation.'

'That's completely different!'

'I thought it might be.'

'Understand me—!' Viscardo's lean face twisted. He reached forward too quickly for avoidance. Conrad flinched, despite himself, cuffed hands lifting in a useless attempt at protection.

The sallow hand flashed past his vision, settled against his scalp, and knotted in a handful of hair.

'—You belong to the Holy Office now.' The Canon-Regular showed strong, broad teeth.

Water ran unexpectedly from Conrad's eyes. He didn't cry out. Viscardo's fist pulled his head forward and down. The pain forced him into a ridiculous, bent over, position. He stared at the floor between his knees, from a matter of inches away. Chest compressed against his thighs, he grunted out inarticulate protests.

'Atheism is one of man's corrupt philosophies.' Above, the priest's voice changed, suddenly suffused with a kind of humble simplicity. 'Faith leads us to God, the true God, who sacrificed His son – His *son* – so that we would be forgiven. Not because we deserve it, but through IIis mercy. You would deny the human race any dignity!'

Cold iron touched the skin of Conrad's neck. Hands gripped his arms and shoulders, professionally immobilising. Viscardo's scalp-pulling increased; he felt hairs tear free, and water ran involuntarily from his eyes. Conrad tried to twist free, and the weight and hard solidity of metal fitted around his neck, under his chin—

The lock of a steel collar snapped closed.

Cuffs and shackles are one thing. Human prisoners are subject to those. *But dogs are collared and chained—!*

A hand thrust him to one side.

Conrad caught himself and sat, jarred but free of physical pain.

The hemicrania, now that he was not experiencing it, slipped out of his memory as severe pain always does. Knowing that fact was no consolation.

Boiling with rage and shame, he snapped back at Viscardo. '"Dignity"? Knowledge is dignity! That's what you'd deny us. You'd rather we go to your god in our thousands from malarial fevers in Naples, say, than have one Natural Philosopher use observation and experiment!'

The Canon-Regular snarled. 'So, what, you'll follow in the footsteps of that abomination Galvani, and his nephew Aldini the shame of Italy? Eviscerating frogs and stealing bodies from fresh graves?'

'I hate to disappoint you, but most of science isn't half so exciting as that.'

Viscardo appeared likely to die of apoplexy, if his complexion was anything to go by.

Conrad pulled at the collar's animal touch. He shuddered, and forced himself to specifically human discourse:

'I did see Signore Aldini perform his "Galvanic reanimation", when I was in London. Aldini did it with wires, and zinc and copper plates, and certainly the eyes of executed murderers opened, and their muscles jerked and twitched like Galvani's frogs before them. But whether this means his theory of "animal electrical fluid" causing life is correct, I can't say. There are sciences that are in their infancy; you can't expect everything to be known as yet.'

'Seeking immortality – twitching severed limbs – creatures in the Arctic!' the Dominican Canon-Regular muttered, quickly and quietly enough that Conrad was not sure he caught the words correctly. 'Infant science, indeed! It should have been aborted! Along with that Shelley bitch!'

Viscardo got to his feet, staring down with an expression best suited to an entomologist. It was a considerable psychological disadvantage not being on his feet, Conrad thought. *I know I'm a few inches taller than he is.*

'Signore Scalese, I would be false to the robes of my Order if I allowed you to walk around free. You are a dangerous plausible man, and the sooner your words are taken out of the public ear, the better.'

'That's exactly my opinion of you!'

Words are shimmering, enticing structures, and Conrad has built such structures in the past. Perhaps for this reason, his belief in them always has reservations.

26

He choked on bitter laughter. 'I may write operas, but I don't pretend they're anything but stories. Theology is just a matter of the mind getting drunk on the power of words!'

Viscardo seemed caught by that, gazing down from between shining black wings of hair. 'Not words, signore. The reality of the power behind the words, that we strain to express . . . Because how can short-lived mortal beings ever really understand the omnipotent God who is, was, and shall be?'

'Now he's the omnipotent deity who can't be understood. A minute ago he was the father mourning the son he sacrificed. If I ask how he can be both incomprehensible and human at the same time, you'll tell me it's a mystery, right?'

'What's a mystery to me,' Luka Viscardo said tensely, 'is how you have the Luciferan pride to think you understand everything about the universe, and can therefore tell me I'm wrong!'

Conrad snorted. He managed to struggle up onto his knees. 'I don't need to know everything to know that a logical contradiction is a logical contradiction!'

'There's your belief – the primacy of human reason. I think . . . that you were right, signore. You don't have Faith. Your reason blinds you to it. I pity you more than I can say. And it makes me furious to admit that a man is beyond saving! – but, to be saved, you'd have to let go of that human reason, and humbly turn to God. And you never will. Complete the binding.'

Light glittered darkly from something coiled and slung over another of the Dominican's arms. The heavy burden crashed to the floor. Sunlight reflected from the metal links of a chain.

The reality of it – here in this room where he is used to the sunlight reflecting off the polished wood of his desk, while he wrestled with metre and rhyme and plot – curdled Conrad's stomach.

He wrenched, but failed to break their grip on him. The priests moved with practised, mundane precision. One of the taller Dominicans bent over and threaded the steel chain through the hasps of the cuffs, that had worked up under the wrists of his coat; and the shackles around his ankles; and – while another two of them held Conrad motionless – through the hasp of the collar around his neck.

Straining, Conrad gritted out, 'Is this what the Church author-
ises for innocent men!'

Canon Viscardo took the free ends of the chain from his junior
priest with a nod. He opened his other hand, and Conrad saw he
had a single open link: shining steel as thick as his little finger.
The Canon's dark eyes seemed more intent than it required as he
threaded the ends of the chain over the open link, and closed his
hand around it.

Without looking away from the steel, Viscardo spoke. 'You're
not innocent, Scalese.'

'Is that decided, then!'

'I was at the Teatro Nuovo last night for your blasphemy. *La
morte di Dio*! The death of God!'

'What do you expect in an opera set in the Enlightenment!'

A capella singing filled the lodgings, suddenly; the Dominicans
beginning at some unseen signal. Loud and beautiful: 'Dominus
Deus – King of Heaven—'

Recognition made Conrad choke. *That is Signore Rossini's 'Little
Mass'!*

*And, no matter how he claims he wrote it as Church music, this part is
exactly the same tenor cabaletta that I heard at La Scala, Milan. I suppose
it was too good to lose . . .*

Canon Viscardo opened his fist. The sunlight that filtered in
through the drawing-room windows gleamed back from the steel
link – now sealed into a closed oval ring.

Momentarily, it was unimportant that the binding was complete – an unbroken chain, running through the hasps of his cuffs,
shackles, and collar, so that he might be chained to a post like a
dog or horse or bull. Conrad stared, hypnotised, at the seamless
surface of that final link.

Nothing visible to prove it had ever been open.

Unbroken, too, to the touch of his bruised fingers.

Is it some metallurgist's trick? Or some conjuror's distraction and switch?

The Canon-Regular smiled with equal amounts of frustration,
smugness and venom.

Hands under Conrad's arms hauled him bodily up. One muscled
Dominican friar steadied him on his feet.

Conrad glanced at that man, just as the friar exchanged looks with a younger, pale-haired Dominican. Both men focused on Luka Viscardo, and for the briefest moment, Conrad saw a wary concern on their faces. And – shame?

So they don't all consider him godly . . . He seems an unpleasant man, full of spite; I suppose he might be exactly the same if he worked for the most revolutionary of societies desiring Atheism and Liberty.

Viscardo, short of breath from the singing, gasped, 'When God desires you bound, you're bound beyond the power of man to escape.'

The barrier between his thoughts and his mouth had vanished, Conrad discovered. 'A blacksmith and a file, or two minutes with a cold chisel, and I think I could prove you wrong!'

A snort came from Tullio's direction.

One friend in the room, at least!

'God is not mocked, Signore Scalese. But there: even daily miracles won't convince an atheist of your calibre, will they? What's your excuse for disbelieving in this?'

Conrad wrenched his shoulders free of the friars' grip. He shook the chain, sliding his thumb over the cold tempered metal. 'You call it a miracle as if that explains it! If something is against the apparent natural laws of science and philosophy, it's no use hiding it under the name of "miracle" – you need to examine it, see what really causes it!'

'You have the truth there in your hand! How much more plain could it be? I ask God to bind the wicked, and He binds you. Holy Mother! can't you see what's in front of you?'

'I see what you see.' Conrad held the compelling black gaze. 'I see the same phenomenon – I just don't accept that it's accounted for by superstitions and dogma.'

Viscardo looked away and signalled. All but two of the friars left Conrad alone as if he were contagious, and commenced packing up the documents and papers strewn across the floor.

Conrad turned the steel links in his hands, fascinated despite himself. 'If I see something that appears to contradict the current explanations of science – if I see steel become plastic at such a low temperature, and without burning my skin – then I want to set up

29

experiments to find out why this is. It demands investigation! Not blind "worship".'

'God Himself comes nowhere into your blasphemous science. You make a false idol of your science: that it holds the incontestable truth—'

'Incontestable! Have you read nothing that's been published in England? Germany? France? Davy! Berzelius! Lamarck! Darwin? The disagreements? If a present explanation is wrong, another theory can be proposed and tested – there's never any shame in saying "I don't know".'

Viscardo's eyes shone.

Because this was a particularly stupid time to speak my mind?
Anger won't make him listen – but will anything?

No one has entry to the cells under the Cardinal's palace except the Inquisition. They answer to no law except their own. They can imprison a man for years if they choose. And they often choose.

Conrad realised, as he stared challengingly back, why the Dominican's gaze was so dark. His irises were a brown colour deep enough that they could barely be distinguished from the pupil.

Like a dog's eyes. What's that old pun about the Dominicans? 'Domini canes'—'*the Dogs of the Lord'. The Hounds of God. This one's a mastiff: he won't let go.*

The Canon-Regular shouldered past Conrad and gave out orders left and right. Conrad trod on the coils of steel chain, and almost fell. A bruised and dusty Tullio – on his feet now – gave Conrad a wry look.

Conrad scooped up an armful of chains, and bundled their chill weight between his cuffed hands. 'Tullio—if you get the chance, run. I don't think I can protect you.'

Tullio attempted a stern glare, but was interrupted.

'Move!' Canon Viscardo's order snapped out briskly enough to have the other Dominicans gathered in a moment, documentary evidence under their arms, and two men each to guard Conrad and Tullio. One man slammed a punch under the ex-soldier's sternum that made him sway in their grip.

'Let Rossi go!' Conrad scrambled for a justification of his protest. 'He's just a servant. He's illiterate!'

'Chosen for his illiteracy, I expect.' Viscardo looked up from a two-year-old libretto from the Paris Opera. 'Because of the blasphemy he might read here. But he still has ears and eyes – at the moment – and he can tell us what he's seen and heard you do.'

Hands hauled Conrad out onto the main second-floor landing. He grabbed up another armful of chain and stopped himself tripping headlong down the stairs.

Two of the Dominicans locked their clenched fists in the shoulders of his coat. A crash made him twist around and look back. A friar efficiently nailed boards across his closed door, fixing the Seal of the Holy Office of the Inquisition to them.

Is it possible this is the last time I'll leave these rooms?

He was unaware he had stopped dead at the top stair until the accompanying Dominicans seized him, forcing him forward and down. A cluster of robed men waited on the next landing, a tall familiar man in their midst.

'Merda! JohnJack, I'm sorry—' Conrad started.

The nearest priest, a Mediterranean-coloured man barely older than a boy, slammed a fist into Conrad's kidney. Conrad gasped for air and collided with the stair-rail, supporting himself on it, breathing hard.

JohnJack Spinelli hauled Conrad up by an elbow, despite his own cuffs. 'We'll sort it out, don't worry.'

Five minutes ago the stairway might have been deserted, full only of cool brown shadows and green Roman tiles, the tenement deceptively barren. Now, the muffled laughter of the two very pretty girls who lived together on the fourth floor echoed down the open stair-well, and Conrad heard a choked-off enquiry by their male guest. Half a dozen wives bundled out together, one floor above, in a cloud of dark eyes gone brilliant for scandal. An old man, who had always had time to talk to Conrad, banged his stick against the hand-rail. The high-voiced, painfully honest enquiries of small children began.

Conrad shut his ears to it, deliberately not looking up the stair-well to see who might be hanging over the railings.

The Canon-Regular raised his voice. 'Bring them. Keep them quiet!'

31

Dominicans hustled Conrad down the final flight of stairs, Tullio Rossi behind him, JohnJack Spinelli in front.

'Have Brother Marcantonio bring the closed coach round—'

A loud, slow knocking interrupted Viscardo.

The whole group of Dominicans shuffled to a halt behind the Canon-Regular. Conrad, stopped on a higher stair, had the height to see over most of the hooded men, but not all.

He leaned out, over the rail, squinting at the foot of the stairs.

The door to the street stood open, sunlight spilling into the foyer of the tenement house.

Against the brightness, Conrad made out a figure in police uniform – a tall, sleek-haired young man with a cockade in his hat, who rapped his knuckles against the lintel of the door.

'It was open,' the newcomer murmured, 'so I thought I'd come in . . .'

The sunlight shifted and his silhouette became recognisable.

Conrad gave a surprised exclamation, his bruised stomach muscles catching him. 'Luigi?'

Luigi Esposito, Chief of Police for the Port district, posed like a tenor given a particularly fine entrance. The sunlight brilliantly sparked off his belt-buckle, gorget, and the hilt of his ornamental sword. He occupied himself in pulling off his white leather gloves, one finger at a time, until every one of the priests there was staring at him.

He looked up with a singular sweetness at Conrad.

'I do hope you're not trying to avoid our chess game, Corrado? How much is it you owe me now?'

Before Conrad could recover from his speechlessness, Canon-Regular Viscardo stepped off the lowest stair, glaring at the younger man. 'Gambling is against Church law!'

If there was a smile of absolute insincerity, the police officer had mastered it years ago.

'Gambling for money? I'm shocked! Corradino and I merely keep a tally of points, and pay them off with a glass or two of fine wine . . .'

Luigi's bow to the churchman was a masterpiece of insolence masquerading as politeness.

'. . . But first we have an appointment.'

Viscardo seemed to gather all the power of the Church to him, the sun on his black hair like the glitter of an adder sliding out from under bracken. 'Out of our way! Signore Scalese is under arrest for blasphemy.'

'Are you really, Corrado? I've spoken to you before about your Natural Philosophy . . . We can discuss it again on our way.'

'You're taking him nowhere! You may have the authority of a Chief of Police, but I have the personal written authority of the Cardinal of Naples!'

'Do you really?' Luigi Esposito shifted himself from the door-jamb with a casual push of his shoulder.

Conrad met his gaze across the crowded lobby.

The Chief of Police for the Port district lazily smiled.

'In that case, it's as well I'm not here on my own authority. I come on behalf of his Majesty King Ferdinand, Second of that name, ruler of the Two Sicilies, who requests and requires Conrad Scalese to attend him immediately at his court. And . . . I do believe that King trumps Cardinal.'

4

Once downstairs and out of doors, Captain Luigi Esposito secured
Canon Viscardo by the elbow and moved him aside, haranguing
him and the group of priests in a confident tone just too quiet for
Conrad to overhear.

Overhead, sharp bangs echoed down the street – wooden
window shutters slamming open.

Conrad caught the Canon's searing glare at Luigi; a contempt
that seemed not to be alleviated by the police uniform.

. . . *Oh.* Conrad found himself nodding. *Esposito: 'the exposed'.*
One of the traditional surnames the Church gives to foundlings,
those nameless children abandoned on orphanage doorsteps:
noble bastards, children of prostitutes and the poor, priests' off-
spring . . . *Evidently this Viscardo thinks he has more than one reason to
despise Luigi.*

'Peacock!' JohnJack muttered, his gaze on the police captain,
but he sounded relieved.

Conrad found his mouth still dry. 'Wait and see.'

He fumbled at the back of his greatcoat collar, turning it so that
it cushioned his metal collar, and folded his thick felted wool cuffs
under the steel shackles.

Tullio's eyes narrowed as if he watched for skirmishers. His gaze
flicked up and down the oddly deserted street, identifying gossips
at windows. Even Naples quietens for the Holy Office. 'Them

34

dumb god-botherers didn't think about transporting a prisoner weighed down so he can't walk.'

Conrad yanked his hands apart with the chain taut, hoping to split the links or the hasps on the cuffs. Nothing happened except bruises. 'This will do wonders for my public reputation! First I'm a drunkard, because hemicrania knocks me out. And now I'm a criminal in chains! No one's going to wonder when I get shipped out to the prison on Ischia, are they?'

A coach rattled up the narrow street towards them.

Conrad blinked. *Some signal was given and I missed it.*

The sunlight flashed back from tack and plumes, and the shining polished rumps of the team of horses. The royal arms stood out clearly painted on the door. A dozen or so of Luigi Esposito's constables followed. Their uniforms at least had the effect of keeping back the now-emerging, curious – and loud – neighbours.

'Impossible!' Canon-Regular Viscardo's frustrated hiss echoed across the street. The grooms looked at him with amusement. The man's black brows pulled down over equally black eyes in a frown of cold power. 'You can't stand in the way of Mother Church! God Himself is King over Kings!'

Viscardo's hand slammed against Luigi Esposito's chest. Conrad saw a sheet of paper sideslip down to the cobbles. One of the officers picked it up and gave it to his Chief.

Luigi wiped the paper with a silk handkerchief, inclining his head politely. 'Thank you, Luka. I'll certainly pass your message on to his Majesty.'

The Canon choked.

Luigi Esposito stepped past him, taking Conrad by the elbow.

Conrad collected himself, halting at the coach door. 'What about Spinelli, and my man?'

The Chief of Police rocked back on a heel, one of his now-stained fingers grasping the scroll. He didn't look over his shoulder, but a flick of his eyes directed Conrad's gaze.

Two of the attending police officers stood either side of John-Jack Spinelli, and – as he looked – another two arrived either side of Tullio Rossi.

'I don't believe there's cause to worry.' Luigi held the coach door open, waiting until Conrad gave way and climbed in.

'I hope you're right – *uff!*'

Conrad sat down abruptly on the forward-facing seat, having enough trouble balancing himself and an armful of chains without the dip of the carriage's springs.

Luigi Esposito stared at the growing crowd in the chilly spring morning. The group of Dominicans began to break up. Esposito swung himself into the opposite seat and called up to the coach-man, 'Move off!'

Conrad peered out through the cramped window, raising his voice over hollow hoof-beats and the creak of tack. 'It looks as if they've let them go?'

'I may—' the police chief had a fine air of innocence '—*may* have heard some rumour of the Church being involved this morning. And if I had heard that, I would surely have brought the on-duty shift with me, even if you don't presently see them all. They might be waiting by the friars' coach, to relieve them of any prisoners for which they don't have specific written authorisation . . .'

Conrad took the stained paper Luigi held out, and scanned it hastily. 'This is their official Order of Arrest? No one's mentioned here by name except me.'

'Er – exactly.'

The Chief of Police wedged his shoulder into one padded corner of the coach, and crossed his legs, enabling himself to take on an attitude of careless aristocratic inefficiency. Viscardo would only be the latest in a long line to be fooled by it.

'By the time they come back with a revised warrant, I believe your man and your friend will know enough to be elsewhere . . .'

Conrad sat back on the carriage seat, relief unstringing him. 'I think you can trust Tullio and JohnJack for that.'

He rested his chains down in his lap, wrenching his badly tied cravat loose enough that he could breathe. In the sunlight as they drove across the city, he could see that his knee-breeches were dusty, and one wool stocking was badly laddered.

'I can't attend a court occasion looking like this!'

'No time to sort you out, unfortunately.' Luigi winced and

offered another clean silk handkerchief. 'You're still in knee-britches from the opera last night, and it's before noon . . . But never mind the social niceties. It's an informal audience, not a full court presentation.'

Dabbing at his clothes didn't make them look any less like he'd been rolling around on the floor in them, Conrad decided.

Luigi demonstrated an apparent expertise at reading the physical signs of tension. 'His Majesty was anxious enough to get hold of you this morning that I don't think he'd notice if you turned up stark bollock naked . . .'

Conrad snorted. He held himself back from too-relieved laughter with an effort. The wind brought the scents and sounds of Naples as they rattled down a hill: a great conglomeration of breakfast cooking on street-sellers' booths, and beasts of burden being loaded for the day, and the citizens – as usual – loudly conducting all their business in the street, no matter that the morning had no more than a touch of spring in it.

'I thought your *Parigi* went off particularly well last night, Conrad.'

Approbation for his opera made Conrad breathless with happiness. All the same . . .

Luigi's fishing.

Predictably. Nine-tenths of his police work seems to be gathering gossip. Or making it up, for dissemination.

'I have no idea why the King would take me away from the Inquisition. Why he wouldn't leave a blasphemy charge to the Church.'

Luigi's chess-playing expression disappeared. He looked faintly disappointed.

'How often have I told you, Corradino? Never volunteer information; make the other man pay for it with information of his own.'

'You don't have any more information about this. You would have told me.'

'I would? I'm going to have to start watching myself around you, I can tell . . .'

Between Luigi's amused, deliberate bickering, and Conrad's

effort to coil his chain neatly over one arm while answering him back, the crowded streets between the Port and the Palace passed easily. Conrad was grateful.

They dismounted from the coach at the Palace. A strong salt wind blew off the Bay.

Luigi led him through the opulent Byzantine corridors, on his way to a formal audience with one of the most powerful monarchs in the Italian states. A handful of police officers and courtiers trailed them, until Luigi's offhand wave dispersed everyone.

They passed the last door, entering an anteroom empty except for servants. Luigi clapped Conrad on the shoulder.

'That door over there. The King is waiting.'

Conrad frowned. Two months of living back in Naples has been enough to remind him how King Ferdinand divides his time between his two capitals, Naples on the mainland, and Palermo on the island of Sicily – and remind him, too, that this is a monarch who, amazingly, kept his country intact during the recent revolutionary uprisings and wars with the Emperor, which ravaged every other Italian state.

What follows from that?

That Ferdinand II isn't a stupid man.

That I need to be very careful. Because I have no real idea why I'm here.

Luigi Esposito regarded the door to the King's reception rooms with visibly frustrated curiosity. 'I do hope to see you for chess or backgammon soon, Corrado. I'm sure you'll have a lot to tell me . . . Better not keep his Majesty waiting.'

How do I demand that a King tells me what he wants?

Is this just a quarrel over whether the King or the Holy Office gets the atheist to chastise?

Conrad nerved himself to walk in, and dredged up a confident smile.

It faded as the door opened.

✦

A servant ushered him through, announced him, and effaced himself as only the excruciatingly well-trained can. And made it wordlessly clear that he thought a man who wore no hat, and had no money in his pocket for the traditional tip, was even less of a gentleman than a man in shackles.

Conrad didn't bother to tell him that no member of the opera world – '*la feccia teatrale*', as they call it; the dregs even of the demi-mondaine, with its claques, back-biting, scandal, and calumny – would ever be regarded as socially acceptable.

At the far end of the sunlit chamber, French windows stood open to the air and the Bay of Naples. Conrad felt unreasonably glad to smell the February morning as it warmed. *Not imprisoned yet.*

'Signore Scalese.'

A man in a blue cut-away coat and white breeches turned away from watching Vesuvius. The sea air had slightly disturbed his brown hair, cut short and brushed forward in the new Classical Roman fashion. His neck-cloth was crisp and spotless, and his coat bare of all orders except the Lion and Hawk of the Sicilies. Conrad thought the man only a handful of years older than himself – thirty-five at the most. Ferdinand's round, amiable face gave the impression of plump prosperity without intelligence.

Which history and current circumstances argue against.

Conrad met the King's eyes and was pinned by an unwavering, amiable, but surprisingly keen gaze.

This could be as dangerous as the Dominicans.

A formal bow was difficult, chains clasped to his body. Conrad thought he managed it without looking a complete fool, although his face heated. 'Your Majesty.'

'You'll forgive this not being a formal audience.' The King visibly came to some decision. 'Walk with me, Signore Scalese.'

King Ferdinand Bourbon-Sicily stepped through the outer door. Conrad followed, emerging onto a stone terrace above the sea.

He blinked at the muted sunlight – and realised that a canvas awning was stretched above, shielding the walkway from the light. It was made of ship's canvas, Conrad noted, after the ancient Roman style, with slits cut throughout so as not to become a sail in reality. Sun and shadow cast hieroglyphic patterns on the pale flagstones at their feet.

'Your family is from the Two Kingdoms, signore.'

'My father was court musician severally in Bavaria and the Prussian territories, your Majesty. But I have some claim through my mother's family, who own property in Catania.'

Ferdinand dragged his gaze back from clouds racing inland towards the mountains, as if the sight of the Bay were magnetic. He gave Conrad a frankly speculative look.

'I'm told you may settle in Naples, given your professional success here.'

'I had intended to stay, your Majesty.' Conrad let his tone make it a reference to the burning of the Teatro Nuovo, if the King should care to interpret it that way. 'My mother lived a lot in Naples in her youth, though her family's from the other Sicily. I spent some of my childhood here, your Majesty.'

'Call me "sir" when we're private.'

'"Conrad", then, sir, if you wish.'

I'm not yet certain that Tullio and JohnJack are safe; I need to know what's going on!

Conrad spoke bluntly but politely, ignoring the etiquette that says one does not question a king. 'Sir, may I ask: what do you want from me?'

Ferdinand's inoffensive smile sharpened. He spoke mildly. 'Do I want something?'

'This morning I appear to have been saved from the Church, sir, only to fall into the hands of the State. I wonder what the State wants of me.'

The King inclined his head, evidently not offended. 'The State wants a private conversation. As to the nature of it . . . Come with me, Conrad.'

Conrad, bare-faced about the necessity, scooped up his chains more securely, and walked beside King Ferdinand down the awning-shaded terrace. He could see past the old royal Angevin palace, Castel Nuovo, square and granite and grim; to the curve of the Bay and Naples harbour. Spring clouds scudded up the sky, casting shadows on early, crowded streets.

They passed another set of French doors. Ferdinand glanced inside the palace.

Ah, this is why we're walking out here!

The air might be only just warm, but the sound of the breeze, as well as the noise of the waves, meant no servant indoors stood a chance of overhearing them.

Conrad's hands sweated, carrying the steel of his chains.

'You're an atheist,' Ferdinand said.

'Yes, sir.'

'Why?'

Conrad deliberately abandoned the ideas of prevarication, or tact.

I'm deep enough in, in any case! Let a monarch have the undecorated truth told to him.

'Because I never believed, sir. I don't know why.'

Seeing Ferdinand's expression, he made the effort to give a wider picture.

'I remember when I was six, believing in *die Großmutter* who brings coal on St Stephen's Day for bad little boys. And the next year, I didn't believe, being too old for fairy tales. I don't know if I ever had any such belief in the Holy Virgin and Mother Church . . .'

Conrad frowned, struggling for memories too far back, and too well-handled, to be certain.

'If I'm remembering correctly, I never had to disbelieve in God. By the time I was nine, I had been in heretic churches—'

Impolite to call them Protestant, here.

'—And I remember listening to them sing of the all-seeing, all-punishing Deity, and thinking they sounded the way mice would sound, if mice worshipped a cat.'

Ferdinand's eyebrows shot up, his bland expression surprised into keen intelligence. 'Rather an Old Testament view . . . So you've been exposed to heresies as well as the true Faith. Your opinion of the Holy Father and the Church is—?'

Conrad closed one fist around the chain-links, tight enough to leave marks.

Tullio always tells me I don't have the brains for a convincing lie.

'I don't deny the Church's miracles, sir. Or rather, I don't deny that, by the singing of Mass, the sick are healed, daily, and ghosts are laid to rest, and the walking dead appeased. I've seen this.'

'But?'

'But—!' Conrad gestured, and restrained himself at the sound of clinking metal. 'I do deny that this has anything to do with a Deity! Nothing about it demands a god in explanation. Why aren't these things regarded as a part of the natural world which we don't yet understand?'

Ferdinand's pace slowed. He clasped his hands behind him as he walked. His bright gaze appraised Conrad. 'The natural world? Do you hold with Dr Schelling's ideas of *Naturphilosophie*, then – that all of nature is a single organism, aspiring upwards to a more spiritual stage, no matter how low it may be? A speck of dust, a weed, a reptile; all aspire to rise and become part of the single great World-Spirit?'

Conrad couldn't help an impolite snort. 'I rather think that's religion under another name! Wasn't Schelling a poet as well as a professor of philosophy, sir? Poets often have a difficult time telling science from mysticism.'

Conrad could have sworn the King of the Two Sicilies momentarily looked highly amused.

'And this from a man who writes poetry for a living!'

'I don't write poetry, sir. I write librettos.'

'And the difference?'

'The English poet Mister Lord Byron doesn't have to take his poem back during rehearsals and turn one stanza into one line – or one line into six lines on a different subject altogether.'

'Ah . . .'

Man-sized Roman amphorae stood against the palace wall. Vines grew up from urns, curling around the stanchions that held the awning. The sun cast coiling shadows on the flagstones, at which the King tilted his head, appearing thoughtful.

'No God, only material nature. That sounds very much like "denying the Church's miracles".'

'Sir, the Church claims miracles are caused by a deity rewarding and punishing us according to the condition of our immortal souls . . . But even a glance shows virtue often isn't rewarded, and sin isn't punished. Besides, I met during the war a Monsieur Xavier Bichat, a physician, who developed an analysis of human tissue types. He found no "soul" there, no matter how deeply he dug.'

Conrad glanced away off the terrace, at where the bare masts of merchant ships rocked rhythmically; crews rowing between them and the shore. One warship – an English frigate, from the flags – cut white water at her prow, running down towards Sorrento. Flocks of bum-boats, lateen-sailed feluccas and dhows, and fishing boats (all equally full of traders) disconsolately tacked back towards the harbour.

'Bichat theorised there might be some vital Galvanic force of life that arises purely from our material bodies – a vital force which may be capable of things we don't yet understand – a force which produces our conscious souls. Yes, I've attended Madame Lavoisier's salon, and heard other natural philosophers claim Monsieur Bichat is wrong! But they won't go to Church doctrine when they seek to disprove his findings. They'll theorise and experiment. *Porca vacca!*, these aren't amazing speculations – even the Mister George Lord Byron has written about them! And Madame Shelley, too. My ambition, sire, one day, is to adapt her "creature given life by man" to the opera stage.'

Better the King have it all now, Conrad decided. *Along with a chance to throw me out, rather than explode at me later.*

'All these unexplained phenomena – miraculous healing, the Returned Dead and the like – they should be investigated. Nothing should be sacrosanct! I was for example in London when Signore Buckland himself showed off the bones of his Megalosaurus, which he discovered in their southern quarries. The bones of an amazing saurian sixty or a hundred feet in length, never yet found alive by explorers anywhere, and discovered in fossils that make the world hundreds of millions of years older than the Church Fathers tell us!'

'Mines and canals are a more reliable gauge of the earth's age than the generations of "begats" in the Old Testament?' Ferdinand suggested the blasphemy with gentle humour.

But then, he's a king. He can.

'Signore Conrad, doesn't it require faith to believe that this Earth is hundreds of thousands of years old? Or billions?'

'Logic and reason can be applied to fossils and strata. I don't believe or disbelieve it. I think it's a hypothesis with some compelling proof. But I'm perfectly capable of swapping to a later theory, if it's well supported. The advances we could make in Naples if we had an *Institut* here, as in Paris, or a Royal Society like England's!'

Conrad broke off, too late to avoid implying a lack in the kingdom.

Ferdinand stopped walking. 'All things ought to be made the subject of experiment, you mean, by Natural Philosophers, and examined to see if they're miraculous or secular in their operation?'

'Yes!'

'I don't disagree.'

Conrad, caught off his stride, almost tripped as he stopped and turned.

Ferdinand appeared to be enjoying Conrad's expression. 'If God is all-powerful . . . An omnipotent God ought not to be frightened away by Natural Scientists and their investigations, should He? If He made the Earth and the Heavens for us to study and learn from, I can hardly imagine He wouldn't expect us to turn that learning eye on the Divinity.'

Conrad struggled for a word – polite or impolite – but found nothing.

The King of the Two Sicilies laughed out loud, with no malice. 'I know, I know! There are men among his Eminence's Inquisitors who would happily put Ferdinand of the House of Bourbon-Sicily on the rack for such opinions . . . But really, this *is* the nineteenth century.'

Ferdinand unclasped his gloved hands, and waved south, towards the promontories and islands and the sails of distant ships.

'When Signore Darwin the younger from London stopped here, on his voyage back from South America, I all but kidnapped him to start just such an Institute as you describe.'

'Signore Darwin was in Naples?' Envy flooded Conrad. *And I wasn't here!*

'I discovered that Gabriele Corazza, our current Cardinal, has the greatest objection to being told he's the heir of an ape – a mere soulless animal arisen by chance – and so an Institute is currently impossible. I think sometimes the Church is the greatest obstacle to religion!'

Not all men are kings who can say what they please in private conversation. Perhaps he just wants to hear me condemn myself out of my own mouth.

But the Inquisition could have discovered all this, and put a report on his desk. This man is head of the Church in his kingdom. Why is he taking the trouble to conciliate me?

Conrad spoke with challenging coolness, ignoring the wrenching apprehension in his belly.

'I find the Church an obstacle primarily to knowledge, sir. Suppose Darwin's beloved wife, for whom he would do anything, had not been a notorious free-thinker after Madame Wollstonecraft's mode? Suppose he had married that cousin of his instead: a demure, ordinary, religious woman? How long might we have had to wait for Signore Darwin's theory of life evolving through natural selection, if he faced the concern that his wife thought he might end in Hell? It might have been another twenty years . . .'

Now – am I a dead man walking?

'Sir, the Dominicans have everything well in hand. I expect my trial for blasphemy can take place by this afternoon!'

It came out more intractable than he intended.

Conrad didn't back down.

The wind ruffled at Ferdinand's carefully cut hair. He was otherwise completely still. His pale eyes focused, and rid Conrad of any idea that the man's quietness meant weakness.

'Think of the power it shows you invoked, Conrad, if you got the Teatro Nuovo struck down. Blasphemy . . . Yes, I suppose they would charge you with that.'

Would. Not will. Conrad's mouth dried up with hope.

'It may be the nineteenth century, sir, but I have no doubt the Church will call it the Devil's power!'

'Would you?' The King's smile held iron. 'What do you think of the fact that you got a building struck down?'

The canvas awning rippled above, sending a wave of shadow and sunlight across the terrace. The morning air felt cool, and then warm. Without quite knowing why he knew it, Conrad instinctively realised: *This is the question I'm here to answer.*

A quarter of an hour with this man and he's exposed every religious and scientific belief I have. He hasn't done that for nothing. If I want to know why I'm here – there's nothing for it but honesty.

'I can't explained myself without offence to "your Catholic Majesty"; I'm sorry.'

Ferdinand nodded a qualified acceptance.

Conrad searched for words, apprehensiveness driving him to choose with precision. *Who knows how important this might be?*

'Sir, the Church is – threatened – if there's a causal connection between *Il Terrore di Parigi* and the Teatro Nuovo fire. The Church regards opera as profane. It regards its own Sung Mass as sacred – as the sole producer of miracles. To me . . . they're the same thing. Both are musicodramma. Both music and the sung word, used together to create – *something* – by the power or projection of dramatic human emotion.'

He let out a breath.

'The Church makes use of musicodramma. The Mass is one passion. Every man and woman praying at a Sung Mass or other liturgical rite is feeling the suffering Passion of Christ as if those emotions were their own. As if every dark Station of the Cross gouged their own flesh, and the rock that rolls away from the Tomb releases each of them to their own resurrection . . . And opera – opera is the pure extreme of *secular* passion. Love, revenge, triumph, grief, all as expressed by voice and music . . . In the opera house, they feel it as their own emotion, too. They love and they hate, oh, just as strongly.'

Ferdinand made a gesture, indicating they should walk on down the long terrace. Conrad found his knees were not quite steady.

The King's expression was blandly stupid again. 'So, if I ask you why the Teatro Nuovo burned down, you'll give me one of two answers . . .'

'Coincidence, sir. Many operas feature the most extreme transgressive emotion, and yet few opera houses are struck by lightning.'

'That would be the first answer.' The skin around Ferdinand's

46

eyes tightened. 'The second answer, Conrad, is, "a miracle". You won't deny that something happens at a Sung Mass, when a man's healed?'

The brush of Canon Viscardo's fingers against his closed eye felt immediate as the warm wind; Conrad tasted Tullio's laudanum. 'Something happens. Yes, sir. Undeniably something. I think no one as yet knows what.'

'But something, is the point. You'll agree that there have, in the past, been occurrences at operas that would – if they'd happened in church – been called miracles.'

'I agree, sir. With the reservation that some of these occurrences will have been mistakes, some hysteria, some just rumour, and some not caused by anything about the opera itself.'

Ferdinand Bourbon-Sicily looked rueful. 'You were reported to me as a man who might have reservations! . . . I agree, on the whole. Let me re-phrase. If you magnify – intensify – the emotions of a crowd, whether with community passion in Church, or individual passion in the opera house, then, some of the time, something will happen.'

'Yes. Therefore it's possible *Il Terrore* is responsible for the Teatro Nuovo fire. But also reasonably likely that it isn't.'

Conrad felt himself pinned under the analytic gaze of the King.

Ferdinand broke into a rich chuckle. 'You are a Natural Philosopher! You won't commit yourself to anything being certain.'

It felt more like praise than mockery.

'I'd hate to disappoint your Majesty.'

The amused look Ferdinand gave him made Conrad's gut lurch with hope.

'Sir – why am I here?'

Ferdinand stopped, resting his hand on the granite sea-wall. The lapping water below sounded surprisingly loud.

'I've been given a transcript of the libretto for Il *Terrore di Parigi, ossia la morte di Dio*. Also, the royal library has your libretto of two years back, from Paris. *Les Enfants du Calcutta, ou, Le Problème de Douleur. The Children of Calcutta, Or, The Problem of Pain*. For an atheist, you think much about the contradictions of religion.'

Conrad let loose his usual frustrated reply to that. 'Perhaps that's why I'm an atheist. Sir.'

Ferdinand's mouth twitched. Whatever emotion he contained, Conrad saw it fade as the King's gaze went eastward, to the blue glass of the horizon, and the double-peaked hill that is the illusion produced by the crater of Vesuvius.

The thronged streets of the port were dwarfed by the mountain, blackly close at hand. The Palace, at sea's level or only a few yards above it, left Conrad gaping across water at the green foothills. He remembered, from his own ascent, furrows, vine-sticks, loaded wagons, donkeys kicking up white dust.

For all it was spring, a covering of snow shrouded the defunct volcano. A very little haze at the summit might have been cloud, or the volcano breathing.

Conrad tensed, waiting for a verdict.

'You'd imagine,' King Ferdinand said quietly, 'that for what I need, I need a believer. A man of Faith. I think I need a man with a proven affinity for opera – and a mind that will reject nothing when it considers what to write.'

'You need me?'

Conrad's stunned thoughts escaped his mouth.

'You need me as a librettist?'

✦

The shadow of the awning made it difficult to read Ferdinand's face. His cultured voice said, 'Someone to write an opera for me, yes.'

The high facade of the Palazzo Reale echoed back a shout of laughter. Conrad belatedly realised it was his.

He slapped his hand over his mouth and stuttered into silence, little spurts of half-hysterical mirth escaping his control.

'Sorry— I thought— I've been expecting a pyre! Twenty years in an Inquisition cell—!' He found it hard to hold back the avalanche of words. 'You want me to write an opera . . .'

Ferdinand's shoulders, that had gone regally stiff, relaxed. Tension left him on a released breath. Lines showed worn into his plump face as he smiled – he looked as if he must govern his country, as well as reign.

'I'll certainly leave you the option of the Holy Office, if what I offer is repugnant.' The King folded his hands behind his back and looked unreasonably content to wait for Conrad to recover himself.

'Sir?'

'I don't share your atheistic views, Conrad. That doesn't mean I decry them. On the contrary. I believe that you may be exactly the man to write my opera for me.'

Sunlight off the sea below made Conrad flinch, caught between scepticism, hope, and misgiving. He prompted, 'And?'

'And I need an opera written with the same kind of power that was generated by *Il Terrore di Parigi.*'

Conrad fidgeted with his chain, seeking the link that Luka Viscardo had sealed, running his thumb over the smooth surface of the steel. The King of the Two Sicilies watched him with a hawk's gaze.

Be honest. No matter what it may cost.

'I'm . . . not sure I could do it again.'

King Ferdinand did not immediately jump up and summon a detachment of riflemen, or a palace aide to shove Conrad out of the front door and into the hands of the Inquisition.

'Sir, I don't say this to spread guilt away from me. I say it to give credit where it's due. I didn't get the Teatro Nuovo struck down. It took a whole company of singers and musicians and stage crew to achieve that, as well as Giuseppe Persiani as composer and myself as librettist.'

The King said, 'A company, yes. Every man's words, music, and voice create the opera together. But as things stand, your composer and the singers appear to have left Naples. I have the librettist left.'

The complexity of Ferdinand's expression was startling, on a man who at first appeared bland. He spoke with a direct, dignified, intent excitement, restrained by absolute control.

'Conrad – you were a part of something powerful enough that it called down fire out of the heavens. Something born of Aristotle's catharsis in drama – the purging of pity and terror in the human heart – coupled with the *magia musica,* that Pythagoras knew connects us with the heavenly spheres above. That is power. Yes, music and the singers and everything else is part of it. Your words give it shape. They create those situations which draw people in, make them cry, laugh, feel love or hatred, indignation or sorrow. If you assisted in causing that once, Conrad – I believe you might do so again.'

The smalt blue of Sorrento and the southern Bay blurred in Conrad's gritty vision, as if on a watercolourist's palette. He hadn't blinked as the King spoke, he realised.

'Conrad, I need a man who will write me a particular kind of opera. The Two Kingdoms needs this. So, it seems that I need you.'

'Because I'm an atheist.'

Ferdinand's amused smile made a reappearance. Along with his tension.

'Precisely because you're an atheist!'

'And . . .'

Conrad pulled his thoughts together. *Now we come to it.*

'. . . If I'm understanding you, sir – you want me to attempt to cause another "opera miracle"?'

Ferdinand of the House of Bourbon-Sicily shook his head.

'Not exactly. No. I want you to stop one.'

5

'Stop a miracle.' Conrad fumbled his chains. Coils of metal slithered and crashed to the paving stones, bruising his feet through his shoes. 'How—! What—? Stop?'

He forced away panic, striving for rationality.

'A miracle, caused by a Mass – or by another opera? *Porca miseria*, this is different! Stop a miracle! But who—? Why? Has that even been done before?'

Ferdinand's look was both sympathetic and reproving. 'On rare occasions. A sufficiently intense outpouring of emotion has been known to overwhelm something lesser.'

Just how magnificently written must an opera be, to produce a reaction 'sufficiently intense'?

'Sir . . . when I woke up today, I was expecting it to be the start of my successful opera career. Finally – *finally*! – I'd written a libretto that made the opera shine – instead of the words and story being a silly adjunct to the music and singing. The audience cheered themselves speechless. Angelotti and the stage crew joked that the noise would shift the roof-beams.'

Conrad rubbed the heel of his hand over his eyes, feeling the last sensitivity of hemicrania in the right socket. The migraine seemed centuries in the past.

It must be . . . less than two hours.

'And this morning – this morning, the opera house is a ruin. I'm arrested for blasphemy. And, apparently, I need to be an atheist to write a libretto for his Majesty of the Two Sicilies. To prevent a miracle.'

The urge to drop down and sit with his head in his hands was very strong. Conrad straightened up.

'Forgive me, sir, I think I must be still asleep and dreaming!'

Ferdinand's wry smile was joined by a crisp tone. 'Then I suggest you wake up and seize your opportunity with both hands. This is an important decision for you.'

He broke off, looking grave.

'I apologise. There are only certain other things I can tell you, before you must come to that decision.'

Conrad opened his mouth to object. He found himself conceding. 'I do realise one thing, sir – if you were going to summon me, it ought to have come from your Master of Music by a letter to my lodgings; or by a servant if it was urgent. Not from your Majesty yourself, privately, with Captain Esposito's help. If this is a secret State matter, then – until and unless I agree to this, the less I know, the better.'

Ferdinand Bourbon-Sicily looked mildly impressed.

The first time I've ever been grateful to my father for lecturing me on the ins and outs of courts.

Conrad shoved his linen cravat under a painful edge of his steel collar to pad it. His business frame of mind came to him; the one in which he usually dealt with impresarios. It sat oddly out of place with the Bourbon King, but Conrad felt doggedly determined to show responsibility. The more so since his loss of control – however brief, he felt hot behind the ears recalling it.

'The things I can know, before I need to commit myself to this, are these. You want me to stop an "opera miracle"—'

He had no better word to describe it.

'—By means of another opera. To do what I apparently helped to do at the Teatro Nuovo, but this time not to cause, but—' Conrad searched for an adequate term. '—To overcome – no, to counteract what another opera is doing. At the same time when this other opera attempts their miracle? I don't see how else it could be done . . .'

52

Ferdinand inclined his head. 'Exactly so. We should move on, in case of gossiping ears.'

Isn't this end of the terrace secure enough?

Conrad swept up the remaining loops of chain and followed the King. They stopped where the area between palazzo and terrace wall was much wider. It overlooked the curtain walls and round towers of the Old Palace, grimly reflected in the Bay. *No one can approach anywhere near, without being seen.*

Ferdinand Bourbon-Sicily frowned. 'You're hardly the only means by which I intend to stop . . . the people responsible. If nothing else is successful, however, I'll need an opera strong enough in every way to wipe their hope of a "miracle" out of existence.'

Conrad realised he must have looked at a loss.

He said hastily, 'And the subject?'

'It hardly matters on what subject you choose to write, except that it should be fresh – not the same tired old mad heroines and jealous brothers. And yet it should be broad enough that most men and women will sympathise with it. I need strength of emotion; subject matter is irrelevant. Create a tragedy or the *lieto fine*, the happy ending; have your hero atone, or be dragged off to hell – I give you complete freedom. Just give your audience no option but to feel.'

If it were that easy to write a success—!

Conrad imagined the reality of writing without censorship, and without an impresario's interference. If no one else had been present, he thought, he might have disgraced himself with a triumphant yell, or a war-dance of joy.

'Conrad, a warning before you do decide. I know organised crime has its fingers in the opera house business. The Local Racket, here. Some influence from the Honourable Men on the other island.'

Conrad nodded, no more willing to say *Camorra* and *Mafia* overtly, and rubbed his thumb across his fingers.

'Then you also know their methods.'

Ferdinand's words woke memories of being pushed behind his mother's skirts, gazing up at sharply dressed young ruffians as they demanded both his father's presence and money – neither easily to be had. Holding his baby sister, who could not yet walk; so Conrad must have been only six or seven himself.

'. . . Blackmail. Extortion. Violence. Murder. Those are the same dangers you'll run, Conrad, if you involve yourself with this.'

Conrad made an awkward, automatic bow. Questions scurried around his mind, but nothing would come into focus. He glanced across at Ferdinand Bourbon-Sicily, who gazed down at the ever-moving waves.

Conrad frowned.

'Sir . . . Are you trying to scare me off?'

The King of the Two Sicilies looked at him cheerfully.

'Why, yes, Conrad. If it's possible that you can be scared off, I am. But what I've told you is true. Think seriously.'

'And if I refuse, I would go—?'

He couldn't voice it. *Back to the Dominicans and the Holy Office?*

'Into exile from the Two Sicilies, to a place of my choosing. With sufficient funds to establish yourself in your career. After you'd sworn a solemn oath to speak of none of this, ever, even on your death-bed.'

'You'd send me away, rewarded with money, just for listening to you about this?'

'Certainly.' Ferdinand momentarily sounded amused. 'I'd thought of settling you in Istanbul.'

'Istanbul!'

'It seems an ideal city – you could be atheist to the Turks, Conrad, instead of to the Holy Father.'

Conrad gaped.

For the first time since the brick had smashed through his window, he laughed in pure delight.

'Perhaps I could take over from Signore Donizetti's brother, sir, as Instructor General of the Imperial Ottoman Music at the court of Sultan Mahmud . . .'

But whether I'd be Master of the Sultan's music or not, I'd be too far from the Italian opera houses. And the King will have agents there who'd make sure I didn't try to come back.

Conrad took a breath deep enough to bring him, under the

54

smell of the sea, the scent of smoke from innumerable chimneys. A few hundred yards away is brawling, bubbling Naples, outside the walls of the Palazzo Reale. Even here, he could hear the calls of the sellers of pollanchelle – Indian corn attached to the stem and boiled – and the vendors of iced water and aniseed candy. And the shouts and insults of some quarrel that will not quieten down until long after both parties (and their families, and their friends) are back in their own houses.

I've hardly been back long enough to consider it home.

That's not to say I'd welcome permanent exile.

In the mountains of the north, Conrad found that men don't, on the whole, fight for great causes. They fight for the man next to them. JohnJack Spinelli risked the Dominicans for no better reason than rescuing one Conrad Scalese's skin. Tullio Rossi will look askance at him if he turns down a challenge.

But Tullio will kick my arse if I don't find out all I can before I accept. I survived the war and 1816. If it comes to being frightened off, I can weigh a danger as well as anyone.

Conrad found the King of the Two Sicilies surveying him with a bland gaze that gave away nothing, for an uncomfortable period of time.

'And now, Signore Conrad – we come to the difficulties with your oath.'

Without pausing for any response, the King strode back down the terrace to one of the French doors. It was immediately flung open from the inside, and a well-dressed footman bowed. 'Sire?'

'Summon a blacksmith from the royal stables. Inform Major Mantenucci that I desire to speak with him at his earliest convenience in the map room.'

'Immediately, sire.'

The King began to pace, his gaze apparently on the flagstones. Conrad didn't think he saw them.

The blacksmith arrived.

Ferdinand ordered, 'Strike off those chains.'

The smith – local, by his dialect – put down a kind of miniature anvil set into a wooden block, that smelled of oiled metal. He busied himself examining the chains, close enough that black smuts from his hands rubbed off on Conrad's coat, along with cinder-dust from the forge, and orange rust. Conrad looked away as he picked up a hammer.

The strikes made the anvil and chains ring, vibrating through the bones of Conrad's arms.

It was loud enough that he missed what additional orders the King gave to the footman. From the gestures, he suspected it was an order that the man in the leather apron should be paid off well.

Cuffs released, hinges pivoting open. Ringing coils of chain fell down on the flagstones. A final blow knocked apart the hasp of the collar, jarring Conrad's head and neck. The man opened the collar and removed it.

Conrad stood, stepping back.

His whole body felt light, not just his neck and shoulders. The sea-wind blew salt against him as he breathed in. He made fists and stretched his arms, muscles cracking.

Write a libretto? Right now, I could fly!

The terrace door closed behind the blacksmith.

Ferdinand Bourbon-Sicily turned away from looking, once more, at Vesuvius.

'The oath, sir.' Conrad managed to sound reasonably respectful. 'Let me guess. The same atheism that makes me suited for what you want, also presents a problem? I'm an atheist, and therefore automatically a moral monster. How can I be trusted to keep my word if I don't have God standing behind me with a big stick?'

A quirk tugged at the corner of Ferdinand's lips.

'You're not a stupid man, Conrad. That's good to know. I suppose you'll say that men give their oaths on sacred relics every day of the week, and then break them?'

Conrad flexed his neck, his spine welcoming the freedom from the iron. 'If you want me to keep silent about what you tell me, I'll give my word. You'll have to judge my moral character for yourself, sir, and see if you think I'll keep it.'

Conrad didn't say, *Exactly as you have to do with any other man you want to trust, atheist or religious!*

He nevertheless saw recognition in Ferdinand's gaze.

'Conrad, it might be considered dangerous – it seems dangerous, to me – to have only a sense of personal honour to protect one against the very tempting proposals of evil?'

Conrad said agreeably, 'It would be nice if there was something else.'

Ferdinand pushed his hand through his hair, ruffling it more comprehensively than the wind, and did not quite laugh. 'I find it's the pressures of society that keep most young men from more than the approved vices. Without them ever thinking of religion or ethics . . . You're a philosopher, Conrad. I'm told, from other sources, that you live much less well than you might, given your earnings. And that this is because you insist on paying off the debts your father left when he died – although at that time you were not of age, and therefore the responsibility was not yours, and should have fallen to the family's oldest male relative.'

Conrad bit back terms one should not use in front of Majesty.

Cazzo! Shite! I'm going to kill Luigi! Shameless gossip.

'One of the temptations of royalty is to rely always on one's own judgement. I try not to. In your case, it seemed reasonable to make enquires of the police chief where you live. Captain Esposito thinks highly of you. Apart from a despicable ability – I quote the good captain – to win at games of chess, he had no complaints to make about your time in his district.'

Conrad managed to raise a barrier between his brain and his mouth, before he gave an opinion that Luigi wouldn't object to Conrad's chess or backgammon skills half so much, if he didn't have a foolish conviction he should keep betting money on his own.

I suppose it's Luigi's duty to tell, if King Ferdinand is shrewd enough to ask.

Conrad muttered, 'Uncle Dario – my late father's brother – told me my father's creditors could go hang. They're all small tradesmen. It seemed an injustice.'

'At another time, I should much enjoy debating the basis of natural or theological justice with you, Conrad . . . You've been warned, and told everything possible, I think.'

'Yes, sir.'

'This is an urgent matter. How long will you need to decide?'

'You mistake me.' Conrad couldn't repress a cheerful reckless smile. 'My answer – is yes, sir.'

✦

The King took a few hasty steps, and swung around. 'Don't be so quick. You're not – you can't be – fully aware of the dangers!'

He's torn, Conrad realised.

The King's expression vanished into blank politeness, but Conrad retained that glimpse. A man in the position of wanting simultaneously to encourage and discourage . . . *Because he thinks I'm too rash?*

Because this is hazardous?

'Sir, at this point, I'm as aware of the dangers as I can be. If I hear nothing after this that I find I object to as a matter of principle, I'll write your libretto. You have no idea how much I want to do it! Respectable people – don't employ atheists. The opera industry keeps me in bread and olives, but where it rubs up against the respectable world, I'm reminded again and again what I am. Censors, patrons, impresarios . . . the noblemen on local opera boards . . .'

Conrad Scalese wouldn't have been allowed into the army, if not for the wars against the Tyrant. Even then he was promoted no higher than lieutenant.

'You're offering me the opportunity to practise my skills as a librettist, and perhaps do something that no one in opera has ever done . . . Whatever else you have to tell me, it's almost certain I'll agree. I can't promise success. Only that I'll put everything I can into the attempt.'

Conrad was aware of the smell of his own sweat. To be sticky, hot, ill-dressed, and the clear victim of a scuffle wasn't the way to come before a king.

He waited.

The King reached out and laid his hand on Conrad's shoulder, ignoring the coat's scuffs and dirt superbly.

'Conrad Scalese. Nothing you hear after this can go beyond you and I, unless I give explicit permission. Do you swear – affirm – that you will keep silent about what I tell you? '

'I affirm it, sir.'

Conrad paused.

'Except – my servant.' The term did not sit easily in Conrad's mouth. 'Tullio Rossi will find out what's happening, no matter what I do. But if he gives me his word, I know he'll keep it.'

'Will you put your life on his discretion?'

'Always.'

His tone must have conveyed that this wasn't a rash or rapid judgement. Ferdinand gave an accepting nod.

'Very well. Inform this Rossi of what you must. And tell him, not that I'll hang him, but that he'll get you hanged if he's lax. If I know the type of man, that will keep him silent more than a threat to himself.'

Conrad nodded, quietly impressed.

'Tell as few as you can, as little as you can – and if you decide at any time that you want nothing to do with the employment I offer you, I need you to affirm you'll never speak of any part of it afterwards. Never, to anyone. Will you affirm those things?'

'I affirm that I'll keep silent.'

Conrad frowned.

'—Unless anyone will come to harm by my doing so. In that case, I'll do my utmost to consult with you first, sir, but I won't keep quiet if it means someone will be hurt or killed.'

'. . . Has anyone ever told you you're a difficult man, Conrad?'

'Yes, sir. Almost everyone.'

Something in that evidently appealed to Ferdinand. The King shook his head ruefully, with a mercurial smile that Conrad realised was much more characteristic of the man than his banal public expression. It did not detract from his sincerity.

'Very well, I accept the reservation. I accept your word. In turn, I swear I'll tell you all of this matter that I can, except where reasons of State mean I cannot.'

Ferdinand offered his hand. Conrad took it. The King's grip felt surprisingly strong.

'I'll guarantee your safety as much as is humanly possibly. In fact your defiance of the Church is useful, Conrad. I can make you seem just a bone of contention between Cardinal Corazza and myself – our views are known to differ . . . But, if you were in the Neapolitan forces during the northern campaign, you'll know that not all dangers can be avoided. There are powerful men involved. They won't like being opposed.'

Powerful men – but not the Camorra or the società onorata?

The same kind of powerful men.

The old helpless fury spilled into Conrad's memory, and this time goaded him. 'I'll need you to provide safety on the other Sicily for my mother, Agnese, and the family. I can undertake this with a clear conscience, but I don't want them dragged in.'

'That's reasonable. Yes.'

Ferdinand turned on his heel, making restlessly for the end of the terrace.

He's not relieved that we've made an agreement. If anything he's more tense. What is it he has to tell me?

Conrad rapidly moved up, and fell in the half-pace behind a monarch that good breeding requires.

Ferdinand beckoned him forward, to his side.

'I'll arrange for your family to be watched and guarded, and if it becomes necessary, moved to a safer place.'

The King paused, and rested his hands on the sea-wall's sun-bleached stone. He stared at the Amalfi coast. The fingers of his right hand drummed a tattoo.

'As for you . . . I intend, first, to hide you in plain sight. Nothing attracts attention like guards. We'll attach you to the Master of Music here at the Palace; say, as a copyist. If it's discovered you're writing a libretto, describe it as a one-act summer comedy in Neapolitan dialect, or a replacement opera to go on if another production fails.'

The world fell into one of those moments of silence. It brought Conrad the lap of waves, and the cries of sea-birds over in the harbour. The wind shifted inshore, carrying the faint odour of umbrella pine over the smell of the city.

'Tell me, Conrad. Have you ever heard of a society that calls itself "the Prince's Men"?'

6

Now we begin to get answers! Conrad scraped at the barrel-bottom of his memory. *With a jackdaw-mind that snaps up every shiny thing to store for opera librettos, have I ever . . . ever—*

'No, sir.' Conrad pushed away frustration. *The first thing I'm asked, I don't know!* 'Maybe I've been away from Naples too long.'

'Being elsewhere in Europe need not necessarily preclude you coming across their activities. From St Petersburg to Madrid; from England to Egypt . . . The Prince's Men are woven into the world like ivy.'

'Not unlike those other organisations we suffer from in the Two Kingdoms, sir?'

'They differ in key respects.'

Ferdinand clasped his hands again behind his back, letting his turning movement carry him around to face Conrad. His gaze swept the Palace walls and windows in a natural way. It wouldn't tell any outsider he was checking to see if they were spied on.

In his own Palace.

'The Prince's Men resemble the Lodges of Freemasonry more than they do the cells of organised Sicilian criminals. They recruit by word of mouth, they meet behind closed doors, and their membership and existence is kept secret. If they are heard of, at all—'

Here a brief amusement showed on Ferdinand's face.

61

'—It's as men who meet for "philosophical and scientific debates"—'

The King continued to turn on his heel. Conrad noted this allowed Ferdinand to survey all the Palazzo Reale, and what of the small royal dock was visible from this terrace.

Doubtless we're observed. But not overheard.

Ferdinand shifted his attention back to Conrad.

'—Naturally, this is believed to be a cover for a revolutionary political society, devoted to overthrowing European monarchies by violence. They're hardly the only such society. I believe, however, that the Prince's Men do have the widest and most heterogeneous membership. Everybody from wagon-drivers and charcoal-burners to magistrates and noblemen. Financiers, courtiers – in my court, I don't doubt – and certain men of the Church . . . *Lazzaroni* . . . It appears that, as a society, they're not interested in making money – their upper ranks largely have it, and donate it to the cause. Ostensibly, they do claim to desire the removal of reactionary ministers of state and kings.'

Conrad couldn't help his brows going up. 'Ostensibly?'

'As a "philosophical position". None have been caught in any illegal activity. I'll assume you know this Kingdom has its own force of agents, spies, and secret police. Apart from organised crime, Europe is now riddled with political associations that are radical, revolutionary, or plain anarchist – most of whom are devoted to political change by way of terror, murder, and assassination. It took a number of years for us to discover that the Prince's Men are – very different.'

He turned towards a door into the Palazzo Reale. 'I intend you to meet with the two men who can best explain the situation.'

Conrad started forward.

He nearly walked into Ferdinand Bourbon-Sicily.

The man remained motionless, his back to Conrad. Conrad felt that he shouldn't move forward. Ferdinand didn't want his face seen at this moment.

'Conrad— After this point, there's no going back. Be sure. Are you sure?'

Conrad folded his arms, marvelling at the easiness of moving without fetters. 'I've had time to think, sir, now the Inquisition aren't wrestling with me . . . As far as managements are concerned, no impresario's going to want the man who got the Teatro Nuovo burned down by lightning. Too dangerous. It's a fortnight to the end of the month. My payments to Father's creditors will be coming up. I need this job.'

The King rasped an interruption. 'You need *a* job.'

'Yes. I can leave Naples, change my name, flee to Rome . . . Or, I can take your offer, sir, which means keeping my name and spitting in the eye of anyone who thinks I'm atheist scum. Even if I can't claim it's more than a petty royal sinecure, it's still connected with the court. Gossip can't say I ran off like a yelping dog and Giuseppe Persiani found me a job out of charity!'

The other man took an irresolute step towards the French windows. Conrad glimpsed servants behind the glass. They looked uncertain whether to open the doors or not.

'Conrad, at this moment, I still know more about this business than you do. I'm warning you. Be certain.'

Is this business so terrible that he thinks I'll refuse anyway, once I know?

Is it something in which King Ferdinand of the Two Sicilies has qualms about involving another man?

'Sir, you have a guaranteed place in life.' Conrad considerately did not add: revolutions and foreign Tyrants aside. 'As for me – there are always more poets besieging impresarios, offering to write librettos at half the price! I value my reputation. It's hard-won, and I worked for it. I don't see why a random lightning-bolt should take it away!"

Ferdinand glanced back. Conrad met his gaze. He felt ashamed of his attempts at humour.

The King regarded him with a long considering stare. 'Very well.'

Ferdinand walked forward, and the doors opened for him.

As unwritten law demanded, Conrad did not raise the subject again while they walked into the royal palace. The usual gadfly crowd of gentlemen-in-waiting, aides, officials and servants congregated around the King within moments. Ferdinand curtly waved them away. He took what Conrad later understood must have been short-cuts through the warren of a building.

The Palazzo Reale was two quite different palaces, it became apparent: one all grandiose white space, grand marble staircases, and frescoed barrel ceilings, and the other, behind the scenes, being full of dusty passages and green baize doors, and wood-panelled rooms too small to keep a cat in, never mind swing it.

They emerged from one such door, Conrad treading almost on the King's heels so as not to become lost, and turned a sharp corner into a long gallery.

The ceiling rose up high and pale. Every few yards on their left hand side, the outer wall held a tall sash window. The glass was cunningly offset to cast light into every corner of the long gallery. Together with the white gauze curtains that veiled the row of windows, it gave an impression of mist shot through with sunlight—counteracted by the right hand wall, that was all solid colours.

'The map room,' Ferdinand announced.

Whatever I expected as a 'map room' . . . this isn't it!

His eyes adjusting to the dim light, Conrad made out that every section of the long wall was painted with maps. The images shone bright on the plaster, blue and green and ochre and gold. To look was to have the odd sensation of flying, like a hawk, above Naples or France or the Adriatic shores.

Most of the maps were of Europe, and some of the Americas; one at least of the South China Sea, another of Indonesia, and the coastal lands of Australia. The ochres and greens of Europe were here and there brighter, where new paint changed the boundaries after the end of the Emperor's War.

An eight foot long map-chest stood against the wall, by one of the windows. Servants had just finished setting up a linen cloth incongruously on top of it, with chairs and bright silver place settings, and were bringing out coffee.

Conrad realised, *My mouth is dry as a furnace!*

The King instructed a nearby footman. 'See we're not disturbed.'

Absently watching the last man's back as the footmen paced away, Conrad realised, *This is another place one can't be spied on.*

No furniture to hide behind. No one can approach without being seen – or eavesdrop through a retaining wall. Or spy by clinging outside the window like a fly.

The King seated himself on a baroque chair beside the map chest, and gestured for Conrad to take one of the others.

'Ah—' Ferdinand glanced past Conrad's shoulder, and gave a welcoming smile. 'Major Mantenucci!'

✦

Precipitated into remembering his manners, Conrad stood up again. *This must be one of those two men he mentioned; the ones who can best explain this situation.*

A lively spare-bodied man came down the gallery, moving with alacrity. Mopping his forehead free of the sweat of his energetic movement, he took off his hat, showing himself crop-haired, iron grey still present in his hair and moustaches.

'I forwarded the request, sire. An answer will arrive when it can.' His bow to the Majesty of the Two Sicilies could be charitably describable as perfunctory. All his attention focused on Conrad himself.

Conrad noted that the man had police insignia on his uniform. *A Commendatore. That will make him Luigi's boss; the overall Chief of Police for Naples.*

'Sire, I heard that you were directly interrogating the criminal responsible for burning down the Teatro Nuovo.'

The King gave Mantenucci a look of long acquaintance, and considerable amusement. 'And so you hurried here, hoping to see that the King isn't messing the case up through direct intervention?'

'Wouldn't dream of saying that, sire . . . If I were to remind your Majesty that police investigations are my purview, rather than your Majesty's . . .'

The King's look was far more friendly than the man's words seemed to justify. 'Really, Enrico, I have absolutely no desire to take on the Chief of Police's job along with my own. Any more than you would choose to be King.'

'Too right I wouldn't.' Mantenucci snorted.

They spoke to each other, Conrad thought, like a general and his most trusted officers, with the humour of shared experiences, good and bad, and with the air of men who will fight.

Conrad remembered etiquette sufficiently that he waited until after the Major seated himself. Enrico Mantenucci served himself coffee, that smelled quite wonderful, and drew up a chair to the end of the map chest. A glance at Ferdinand assured Conrad the King had begun to drink from his own bone-china cup.

Conrad brought his cup to his mouth and drank, just as the Major turned and raked him with an assessing glance.

'So this is our atheist pyromaniac, is it?'

Conrad managed, superbly, not to sneeze his coffee out of his nose.

He rose from his seat again and bowed. The police chief did the same.

Ferdinand waved them both to sit down.

'I've asked you here, Enrico, to introduce Signore Conrad to what we know of the Prince's Men.' He turned with perceptible authority to Conrad. 'I have few men who are more knowledgeable.'

'Know your enemy!' Mantenucci helped himself to more coffee. His tone of voice turned gruffly apologetic. 'You won't find a police officer in Naples who thinks highly of humanity in general; we see too much of men at their worst. So I dare say I hold these scum in too much contempt. You must judge for yourself, Signore Scalese.'

Mantenucci visibly collected his thoughts.

'I will say one thing. The beliefs of the Prince's Men are dangerously strong. And, as with any madmen, if their recruits spend a lot of time around them, they come to believe the same things by a kind of contagion. We've had a few of their runners and messengers for interrogation, and it's always the same. They're serving God, and they won't let any of us sinners stand in their way.'

Conrad startled. 'They're a religious association? His Majesty described them as a radical political conspiracy.'

Ferdinand demurred. 'Not just that. I've said I think them like the Freemasons.'

Mantenucci ejected air from his nostrils sharply. 'Oh aye! Or the Rosicrucians, Alchemists, Zoroasters, Hospitallers, Knights of St Gaius, and the rest. I say they're as much a religious order as the Dominicans or the Franciscans. They just happen to be utter heretics.'

Ferdinand, catching Conrad's eye, murmured, 'Good Catholic,' with a tilt of his head towards Mantenucci that appeared more amused than anything else.

The Commendatore of Napoli's police gave his King the look of a man both long-suffering and sharing an old joke. 'If I might continue, sire . . . These Prince's Men. Religious, yes, because of their belief in God. But Devil-worshippers, too, because for them the universe is arsy-versy—'

'Devil-worshippers?' Surprised into interrupting, Conrad put his tiny cup loudly down onto its saucer. 'Are you certain? Not just worship of the wrong deity?'

Mantenucci's expression warmed, briefly, as if to someone scoring a hit in fencing. 'I see you're not to be frightened by a few heresies.'

Conrad found his own smile equally ironic. 'I am a heresy, I'm told, signore.'

The police Commendatore set his elbow on the map desk, and subjected Conrad to a closer scrutiny than was comfortable. Finally he gave an amiable nod. 'All right, signore. Let's put ourselves in their position. For the sake of argument, suppose that we're Prince's Men—'

The King raised a quizzical eyebrow.

'Not you, sire,' Mantenucci qualified. 'You're too good a son of the Church. Now Signore Scalese—'

'Conrad.'

'—Conrad, here,' the police chief echoed, good-humouredly, 'is a damned atheist, and I'm equally damned for what I see every day among the scum of Naples. So let's say that he and I are Prince's Men. Here's our first question. Who made the world?'

'No one?' Conrad offered, having no idea of his theoretical role. 'It began by natural processes, developing from – Leucippus's atoms? Heraclitus's fire?'

Ferdinand interrupted, enthused. 'Ah! The old pagan

67

philosophers before Plato! Pythagoras, Anaximander; with their perennial search for first causes . . . You're one of the physiologoi, Conrad!'

It was impossible not to respond to the other man's intellectual delight. Conrad smiled. '"Physiologoi", "Natural Philosopher" – it's only another word for scientist, sir.'

Enrico Mantenucci glowered briefly at his sovereign, cutting the interruption short, and turned back to Conrad. 'We're supposed to be Prince's Men, the two of us, and their answer is, God made the world—'

'Of course,' Conrad remarked.

'But.' The Commendatore ticked off a point on an upraised forefinger. 'It's not the God of good Catholics like his Majesty here. It's the Watchmaker God of English Signore Newton and the French Deists. God made the world, gave it universal laws to tick and function – and then ran off somewhere, never to be seen again. So, if we're Prince's Men, who's now in charge of the world?'

Conrad allowed himself a hopeful note. 'No one?'

'You'd think so, wouldn't you? But, no—' Mantenucci checked off a second point on his fingers. 'Devil-worshippers, remember? As Prince's Men, we hold that the Creator God's nature was evil. He set up a universe in which everything that lives suffers pain. The penalty for original sin is visited on every head, even babies too young to do more than breathe and blink.'

Conrad caught a glimpse of pain in Mantenucci's expression, and wondered what accounted for it.

Mantenucci took a breath and regained enthusiasm. 'Fortunately, in the moments after Creation, before He departed, He left a deputy in charge – known as Satan, or the Devil. But this isn't a good Catholic Satan, but what we Prince's Men call "the Prince of this World".'

Ferdinand, as if he continued a long argument, interjected, 'Which is the Manichaean heresy of the Albigenses!'

'Yes, sire, but I doubt they've been in Naples that long.' Mantenucci prodded the map-chest with an arresting finger. 'The Prince of this World, hence the name of his followers—'

'You don't consider,' Ferdinand Bourbon-Sicily interrupted, his tone melancholy, 'that we're creatures of the Fall, and need pain to teach us morality? Or, at best, that pain's an inescapable accompaniment to free will?'

Mantenucci shook his head. 'As a Prince's Man, I wouldn't consider it. Pain is evil.'

'I could have some sympathy with that view,' Conrad said aloud.

He found the police chief aiming the next question at him:

'Signore Conrad, who's responsible for good?'

It felt as if he discussed a libretto with a composer, rather than the censor; one of those moments when all the possibilities of a story present themselves for due consideration.

Conrad mused. 'I'm a Prince's Man . . . So. Let me turn it around. I don't attribute responsibility for evil to the "Prince of this World". He didn't create it. Has he even been given enough power to prevent it? Evil must be inherent in the Creator-God, since it was one of His first principles. So good, which opposes evil, has to come from . . . Satan? The Prince of this World?'

Mantenucci nodded like a professor whose pupil advances.

'Exactly! The God that created us all quickly abandoned us all. The Devil, the "Prince of this World", is the only hope we have for good in the world; hence his followers, the Prince's Men—'

He interrupted himself to add, 'I know you have different ideas, Majesty, but I see no possible origin of the name except the Gospel of the Sainted Apostle John!'

Ferdinand gave a wry smile. 'Having read the good Signore Niccolò di Bernardo dei Machiavelli, and his treatise of government, I merely wonder if *The Prince* is not a model for how they plan to govern all Italy. That would make them "Prince's Men".'

Mantenucci snorted, under his breath, and pushed fingers through hair too short to ruffle. It shone like iron in the morning light through the gauze curtains.

We must make an odd picture. Opera writer, police chief, and King!

'We'll be lucky if they're only after Italy, Majesty.' The Commendatore drained his Turkish coffee at a gulp. 'Now. I've been able to piece together their talk of the Devil. They speak in the way the old Hebrews and Muslims do – he's an Adversary, a Tester, to make sure that men are kept as moral as God intends 'em. That's what the "Prince of this World" was to do originally: test men to see they'd be strong, like metal in the forging. But the God who created us left, and the world was left in the Tester's hands.'

Conrad made to speak.

Mantenucci held up an arresting finger. 'As a Prince's Man – I have to say the Tester's hands are tied. The Adversary can't change the way the universe is set up: God laid down universal laws, as strong as Time and as steady as bedrock. The Prince of this World might be able to mark every sparrow which falls, but he can't do a damn thing about it.'

Under the man's iron-dark brows, a light sparked.

'That's where the Prince's Men come in. They see themselves as acting for him. Man has free will.'

'As if an all-knowing God could create true free will—!' Conrad stopped himself, seeing it was plainly not the time for that discussion.

Enrico Mantenucci waved it off sternly. 'Man's free will is the one exception to those universal laws. What are miracles, but mankind's free will requesting God to make an exception to the laws of Creation?'

'Commendatore, you do realise that's not a rhetorical question?'

'Gentlemen!'

Mantenucci inclined his head to the King. 'As Prince's Men, we see there are tiny chinks in the universal laws. However they come there. Miracles. So. What do we choose to do?'

Conrad closed his eyes against the bright stimulus of the wall maps, and rested his chin on his joined hands. 'As a Prince's man, I choose . . . to exploit that in some way?'

He opened his eyes to find the grizzled police chief looking almost mischievous.

Mantenucci said, 'Absolutely. Miracles are made by the Prince of this World, to help Mankind. But also suppose . . .'

Conrad allowed himself to follow the internal logic of Mantenucci's proposition. '—Suppose that it can go both ways. That mankind can help the Prince of this World . . . ?'

It spread itself out instantly in his mind, like a logic problem

70

a tutor might present, or any difficulty in solving how an opera might finish.

'—Help the Prince. By doing . . . something that he can't do for himself. By bringing about a miracle? An opera miracle?'

Ferdinand Bourbon-Sicily and Enrico Mantenucci exchanged glances, expressions between smug and rueful.

'I have every confidence in my atheist pyromaniac,' Ferdinand said.

Mantenucci barked a laugh. 'O, very well, sir. Grant you that one.'

He leaned an elbow on the map desk and turned back to Conrad. Seen with the morning light full on him, Conrad thought him closer to fifty-five than forty-five, but he was full of a contained fierce energy.

'That's it exactly.' Mantenucci visibly dropped his stance as Devil's advocate. 'According to everything our spies have gathered, the Prince's Men need to request – or create – a miracle, to bring about a change that the "Prince of this World" can't.'

Conrad thumbed his right eye-socket. The merest spectre of pain haunted him as he sifted the flood of information. 'If there's a real danger, won't it come from this conspiracy and how much political and religious unrest they might stir up?'

Enrico Mantenucci looked mildly affronted. 'A "real danger"?'

'Apologies. My secular assumptions coming to the fore.'

Ferdinand drained his cup and set it down. 'You're an atheist, Conrad Scalese, in a world where God is only too prone to granting religious miracles in church, and secular miracles when opera reaches its sublime heights of passion. You don't deny they can occur, and I'm grateful – I can talk with you freely about the nature of the Church, and the danger of the Prince's Men, alike, without you fleeing in horror. I know you'll remain impartial towards every matter of theology, if only because you have no use for theology as an explanation.'

Conrad filled his small coffee cup again, and slipped sugar into the thick black liquid. 'I hardly know if I'm being accused or complimented!'

Mantenucci chuckled. 'Take it as whichever pleases you!'

Conrad faced the King, where Ferdinand sat against a background of blue, green, and gold. 'Sire—It's hardly every opera, or every Mass, that produces a miracle. Suppose these Prince's Men manage to burn down a few buildings like the Teatro Nuovo? There are some that would cause disruption, I suppose; this Palace, or the Duomo—'

Ferdinand lifted his hand. 'We would survive that. Their opera miracle is reported to be on a much larger scale.'

The map gallery fell so silent that Conrad could hear the wind outside the sash-window panes, and a maid singing as she crossed the public square, two floors below.

'Sire, what exactly is this miracle intended to do?

Enrico Mantenucci looked to his King. 'You're authorising him to be told state secret information?'

'Oh, I think we can trust our atheist's oath . . .' Ferdinand's playfulness dissolved as he turned a grave expression on Conrad. 'I'm sorry to burden you.'

The King of the Two Sicilies leaned forward, folding his arms as if he shielded himself from the cold.

'Conrad, do you remember the Year without a Summer?'

Conrad failed to suppress an involuntary shiver.

'I remember . . . I don't think I saw a clear sky after the end of the war, not for fourteen months. It rained every day. I remember trudging home after being discharged, through fields of drowned seedling crops—'

—Tullio Rossi hulking at Conrad's heels, bitching the more as his wounds mended, his rifle never off his shoulder and never unloaded—

Men scrabbled to make a living after the devastation of troops marching through cities, and killing each other on fields forever afterwards difficult to put to the plough. Even a handful of quarter-ripened corn could be cause for a bloody scuffle. The sky turned overcast and stayed that way, day after day. As the year went on, cloud and mist thickened, with often little enough to tell the day from the night except a searing aurora of red and green guttering down in the west.

'Spring never properly came.' Conrad spoke soberly. 'It snowed

72

the July after we fought the Emperor. The peasants ate grass. Every morning in the city there were corpses in the road, frozen overnight.'

He remembered the bodies clearly, although he put effort into forgetting them. Elbows and knee-joints so much wider than the shrunk curved thighs and withered biceps . . .

Every step of the way from the North back to the Sicilies, he pictured his mother and sister too poor to do more than end up open-eyed under the rebellious sky.

Enrico Mantenucci observed grimly, 'They say a civilisation is only ever three failed harvests from barbarism.'

'I believe it, given the effect of just one failure on my kingdom, and in the rest of Italy, and Europe . . .' Ferdinand unconsciously mirrored Conrad, rubbing at his forehead.

Eventually the clouds parted. The sun reappeared, and the earth turned warm enough the following spring for corn to send up tentative green stalks. It was not so many years in the past. Conrad unambiguously recalled the craving for a full stomach that goes with a constant subsistence-level diet.

'They say it snowed in America all that summer . . .'

Conrad pulled himself out of the past with difficulty, swallowing down his hot cup of coffee to anchor himself in the present. The chairs were placed closest to the wall maps of Italy and southern France, Austria and Turkey; all lands touched by that blight.

That time is over. I'm here.

And Ferdinand is speaking of the Year without a Summer because—

Conrad felt his mind lock up.

Because the opera miracle is on a larger scale—

Silence caught in Conrad's throat like dust.

He managed, finally, to speak.

'Something of that scale – *that* was an opera miracle?'

7

Conrad shook his head, not in disbelief but in rejection. 'No man who lived through that could want to see it again. Surely?'

'This would be far better explained by Adriano.' Ferdinand shifted on his chair. 'We can't delay now. If you have questions that Enrico or I can't answer, we must hope Adriano arrives before you leave, or that you can meet him later.'

'It's not as if he can just leave at any time without suspicion, sire. They'll be watching him as a matter of course.'

Conrad, listening to Mantenucci, became aware of Ferdinand's gaze on him.

Without alteration of his bland, slightly worried expression, Ferdinand remarked, 'We have our own spies and agents – some of them honourable men, whose names would be blackened if they got out, since they appear to be dedicated to the cause of our enemies.'

'A double agent has a thankless task.' Conrad refrained from adding what had become obvious in the war: trusted by neither side, and killed off by either pretty quickly. It must have been obvious in his expression.

Ferdinand leaned back, the shifting sunlight blazing ultramarine across the rich cloth of his uniform jacket, catching his white breeches and cavalry boots. He said quietly, 'I have only one spy who's grown to a power in the inner ranks of the Prince's Men.

He's called "Adriano", since it's one of his many baptismal names, and there are plenty of men similarly called. It's from him I have most of my information – there would have been no warning, otherwise.'

The King's eyes were momentarily blank with reflected light. Conrad felt a sudden cold in his belly, and recognised it. *The morning of battle, before the first exchange of shots.*

Enrico Mantenucci leaned forward. 'Signore Adriano was by luck present at the beginning of this particular conspiracy. He finally succeeded in infiltrating the heart of the Prince's Men a few years ago.'

'And that was not by luck.' Ferdinand smiled. 'When I met him, Adriano was already skilled in looking a fool and being a very clever man. He said it put him at an advantage when people underestimated him. I knew him first as a junior member of the Diplomatic Corps, dealing with the Emperor of the North. I tracked him through a nest of his superiors, in fact, so that I could meet the man who was actually keeping the Two Sicilies from the Emperor's influence – by a mixture of distraction, subterfuge, and a highly intelligent mind that could think on its feet.'

The King's mind was clearly not on the painted wall maps. His gaze focused miles and years away.

'Had you been privileged to watch Adriano's diplomatic dances with the Emperor . . . He has a fool's face, beautiful as a woman's, with black hair and the most remarkable blue eyes— If he had been a woman, you could only have called it flirting. And then he dropped that manner completely when he infiltrated the Prince's Men. They were impressed by dangerous men, so he kept that aspect of himself to the fore. At my request, he has allowed himself to be drawn deeper and deeper into their affairs. Adriano used to be regarded by society as a dilettante. After much contact with the Prince's Men and their associates – I suppose there are very few now who don't think him some kind of criminal.'

Mantenucci nodded silent agreement.

'Adriano has never complained to me about the loss of his public reputation,' Ferdinand said. 'I've never condemned what he has to do to maintain his position. How can I, when I demand the information he can bring?'

Conrad caught the King's deliberate glance.

This is also a warning to me. Whatever reputation I end up with, I can never tell anyone the truth.

Conrad swallowed down another hot coffee. He dared to serve both Mantenucci and the King from the pot, while Ferdinand's mood remained so abstracted. The Commendatore nodded silent agreement not to call the servants.

Ferdinand Bourbon-Sicily stood.

Chairs scraped as Conrad barely managed to follow Mantenucci, rising as protocol demanded.

The King started off down the map gallery with a measured pace, speaking into the silence.

'A number of years ago, Adriano made contact with the inner circle of the Prince's Men. He passed invaluable intelligence to me . . . When it came out that a covert journey was being planned, supposedly to the Dutch East Indies, I authorised him to travel as a high-ranking member of the conspiracy. Their exact destination was not known, but by then Adriano had a theory about what they intended to do.'

Ferdinand stopped. He put his finger against the painted wall. Conrad craned his neck to look at the vast crescent of island-chains running on a slant from the desert browns of Australia, green New Guinea, up to Malaysia and the China coast. Indonesia.

'He was taken to a ship that immediately set sail for the Far East. He was accompanied by six men and two women, all of whom were only known to him by false names. Their leader was one Signore Matteo Ranieri. At the end of many months, they reached the vicinity of the Indonesian island of Sumbawa. There they divided into groups; some to stand further off from the island, and some to go in close. Adriano tried to board the ship of those latter men and women who would be close to the island, but failed. He did discover that they were expected, when they got there, to sing.'

Conrad, social manners abandoned, demanded, 'Did he hear it?'

'Adriano heard them rehearse. It was bel canto at its most glorious; a fragment of an opera that no man can trace. Neither he nor I have been able to find the composer. Perhaps it's a young man just out of some conservatoire. I doubt a known composer could disguise his style so as to be unrecognisable.'

Enrico Mantenucci put in gruffly, 'Adriano's no singer, but he has some of it memorised, he thinks, Conrad; he'll let you hear it on the forte-piano.'

Ferdinand Bourbon-Sicily reached back, without looking, and Enrico Mantenucci put his coffee cup into his hand. The King swallowed the black brew down, and with his free hand traced a course of the wall map.

'The two ships separated . . . On Sumbawa there is a volcano called Mount Tambora. Tambora erupted. It killed tens of thousands of the native peoples. Terrible waves devastated the nearby islands. Adriano and the surviving conspirators only stayed alive because they were aboard a ship that could reach deeper waters, and ride out the cataclysmic tidal waves. The inciting singers and their ship were lost.'

The Mediterranean may be calm, but Conrad has experienced Atlantic rollers and the Baltic. It's nauseatingly easy to imagine men and women swept away among the detritus of a manic sea. *Who knows how truly violent a Far Eastern ocean might be?*

The gallery was quiet enough that the infinitesimal rub of skin against paint became audible. The King's finger tracked to the next map, which was of the world, ticking off North America, Spain, France, the Slavic countries.

'Millions of tons of pulverised rock and lava were blown into the sky. My Natural Philosophers, here, tracked the clouds that spread – well, spread as far as we had people to observe them, and further. The world had a year of refulgent sunsets. And the average temperature, recorded here and in Palermo, was several degrees lower, both winter and summer. Hence, the Year without a Summer.'

Ferdinand abandoned the maps, and sank back down in his chair.

Conrad followed, relieved to be able to sit. He leaned his elbow heavily on the map-chest for support. *A year without summer is, in reality, a year – and more – with endless winter.*

Ferdinand held up a warning hand. 'My people are divided on whether that was the intention of the Prince's Men, or whether Tambora's eruption was what they desired, and the year 1816 an unintended consequence of their true objective. You must listen and judge for yourself.'

Conrad couldn't help snorting. 'Sir, if that was an unintended consequence, what the hell is it they do want?'

Conrad became abruptly aware of his tone – a *faux pas* bordering on *lèse majesté*. Ferdinand Bourbon-Sicily only seemed amused.

To hear the atheist swearing by Hell, Conrad realised.

Ferdinand added lump after lump of brown sugar to a treacly cup of Turkish coffee, replaced the tongs, and took a testing sip. Not changing his thoughtful expression, he said, 'It's conceivable their Sung Miracle was only intended to cause Tambora and its immediate consequences.'

The Commendatore nodded easily, despite the tension suddenly present in the gallery. 'And of course, if laying waste to a few islands in Indonesia was all they could claim – to be honest, it would be of no consequence to us.'

Conrad glanced up. *Does Mantenucci's expression match his tone?*

Enrico's lined face was cynically compassionate. 'Men tend to their own back-yards. But, unfortunately, the Prince's Men are now in ours. There's . . . reason to suppose that Mount Tambora may have been a test.'

'A test,' Conrad echoed.

King Ferdinand said quietly, 'To see if such an eruption were possible. As Enrico suggests, so far as Europe's concerned, Indonesia is a collection of savage islands, of no conceivable importance. If tens of thousands of people die on and around Sumbawa, that's soon heard and sooner forgotten. It's only by luck that we've discovered it has implications for us.'

Conrad collected himself. 'And those are?'

Ferdinand rose to his feet and beckoned. 'Look over here.'

Being on his feet relieved Conrad's need for action only a little. Approaching the wall, he was overwhelmed by blue, green, gold, and in places white, where the artists had painted cumulus clouds casting a shadow on otherwise featureless sea.

Green hills, gold corn, pale castles . . . The panel closest on his right was a topographic map of the peninsula of the Italian states, hill-shadows defining the mountainous spine. The panel on his left showed a closer map of Naples itself, and the Golfo di Napoli.

The shaded relief map showed up how very vastly the volcano dominated the area, and how far its foothills extended across the face of the earth.

Conrad saw momentarily not the green mountain of classical history, the landscape-view that defines the city of Naples, but a hollow black scab, tendrils of infection spreading out into the body.

Cold to the base of his spine, Conrad remembered, *On the terrace, the King couldn't take his eyes from Vesuvius.*

'Sir,' he said. 'Do they mean to make us a Tambora?'

No, surely not; Vesuvius has been dead since the ancient Romans—

'I think they must.' Ferdinand's tenor sounded beside him. The King rested his hand on Conrad's dusty shoulder, not far from where the metal collar had marked his coat. 'Look at the Two Sicilies.'

He moved his other hand, drawing it lightly down the face of the map.

'Ætna, on island-Sicily, the most restless of mountains.'

Ferdinand's finger traced the Aeolian Islands.

'Here is Vulcano, Vulcan's Forge. And Stromboli, a volcano reliable enough in its eruptions that men call it "the Lighthouse of the Mediterranean".'

Enrico Mantenucci shifted lightly on his feet beside Conrad. 'As for the whole Tyrrhenean Sea – I lose count of how often ship's captains report the growth of new volcanic reefs as "unknown dangers to shipping". From the Straits of Medina up to Marseilles, it's notorious!'

Ferdinand pointed to Naples.

'And mainland Sicily. Even ignoring Mount Vesuvius for one moment – west of us, here in Naples, is the Phlegraean Peninsula, also called the Campi Flegrei and Campi Ardenti: "the Burning

Fields". There are over forty craters, though none mountainous except little Monte Nuovo. My Natural Philosophers speculate that the Burning Fields may ultimately conceal more lava than Vesuvius does.'

By the map-maker's art, Conrad saw it as if from the heavens. Sulphur pools and volcanic splits in the earth ran westward from Naples, past the vent called Solfatara, all the way to the little port of Pozzuoli.

Every cultured man reads Pliny; every man of a certain class in Naples knows how in AD 79 the mountain Vesuvius erupted in smoke and lightning, and surging flows of clouds that scalded hotter than a furnace. All give a moment's thought to it; the majority then bury it down deep where it can never trouble them.

Conrad remembered being a small child in Catania, under the shadow of Mount Ætna. Lulling himself to sleep by watching the bright threads of lava edge down the mountain's slope . . . By day, the winding cracks in the black ash gave off smoke and fumes. By night, they were a winding, spitting track of red fire; the red reflecting up into the vapours and illuminating them Hell-coloured.

He had walked far enough up the mountain as a boy to feel how hot the cracks in the earth are, and see the slow push of lava. Coming to Naples, he remembered feeling glad that he would live in the shadow of the dormant Vesuvius, rather than grumbling and semi-waking Ætna.

Well, that didn't work out.

Conrad took a step back so that he could survey both maps. Down the mountainous spine of Italy, and then from the Adriatic in the east to the Mediterranean in the west . . .

'Tambora's in Indonesia,' he thought aloud. 'Why Europe? Why here?'

Enrico Mantenucci snorted indelicately, as if Conrad were being dense. 'If they could use Church music, then, yes, their geographical location wouldn't matter. The Mass can take place anywhere!'

The King restrained the police chief by a raised hand. 'Adriano reports they deduced that their Manichaean heresy isn't suitable for a Sung Mass. Therefore they must use the other form of musicodramma – opera. So, as to why Europe and why here? . . . Here, because – although there have been notable contributions from the Germans and the French – Italy is the heart of opera. And Napoli is the heart of Italy. Since the Prince's Men desire the best possible chance of a musicodramma miracle, where else could they come?'

Conrad can think of composers in Vienna and Paris and St Petersburg who would quarrel with the King's assessment – but much as he enjoyed his own time in Paris, and despite how he values the German blood he inherits from his father, he has no intention of arguing with the King. Never argue with any Italian state about the supremacy of their women or their own opera.

Ferdinand Bourbon-Sicily sighed, clenching and unclenching one fist as if he were unaware of his own tension.

'And as for why this one of the Two Sicilies – I believe the Prince's Men aim at us here because, although Ætna is more unstable, we in Naples alone have two volcanoes.'

Conrad looked wordlessly at innocent paint. At the image of the towering, snow-covered black walls of the crater of Vesuvius. And the sulphur pools and fissures of those Phlegraean Fields that ancient Roman philosophers believed opened down into Hades.

'The danger is not to the Two Sicilies alone. My Natural Philosophers say that if the Campi Flegrei and Vesuvius suffer a sufficiently large eruption, then that may trigger the other volcanoes – may rip up the bed of the Tyrrhenean Sea as if it were merely the skin on a pan of milk, in one single detonation.'

Ferdinand brushed points to east, west, north and south on the painted map, as if he drew the Church's cross over the Two Kingdoms.

'It could destroy Italy, southern France, half the Mediterranean Sea; Istanbul, the Holy Land, North Africa . . . before we even think of the besmirched sky. How many "years without summers" might that make?'

Conrad slammed his mind shut on the frighteningly real visualisation of rock, gas, fire, and air, conspiring in one moment to wipe Naples and the Two Sicilies from the Italian earth. His mouth dry, he jolted out, 'But why?'

The King turned away from the wall maps. 'Simply put, signore? Flood and famine and disease cause a greater number of deaths over time – but for sudden mass deaths, I don't believe humanity yet knows a weapon more violent than the volcano.'

Conrad sat back down heavily on the Baroque chair that the servants had set out by the map-chest.

Sitting without permission in the presence of the King was against every rule and custom. Ferdinand Bourbon-Sicily did not rebuke Conrad for ignoring protocol.

'Sir.' Conrad said it clearly enough to re-establish a respect for royal authority. 'Suppose you do know that's what these Prince's Men intend to do. That only answers "how". It says nothing about why they should want such an absolute devastation!'

Ferdinand Bourbon-Sicily appeared amused. It was not a cruel expression. 'The Sicilies lost a scholar in you, Conrad.'

Enrico Mantenucci thrust another hot coffee at Conrad and briskly took his own seat. 'Use that famed atheist mind of yours to speculate, Scalese!'

Conrad drank down scalding liquid, shakily. 'Signore, you're the Prince's Man, you tell me!'

Ferdinand walked back from the maps, leaning his hands on the back of Mantenucci's chair. 'He has you there, Enrico! I suspect this next part is not best handled by Socratic dialogue.'

'No, sire.' Mantenucci's lips quirked, under his grey moustache. He glanced apologetically at Conrad. 'Very well, let's say we're not Prince's Men . . . I don't know what's keeping Adriano, but I can summarise his reports. What we deplore about the Tambora eruption – the wholesale loss of life – is, to them, the point of what they did. They may be heretics, but throughout all of human history, even heretics have understood the power of making a sacrifice to the Deity.'

Conrad spluttered.

Ferdinand cut in. 'The ancient Greeks sacrificed a holocaust of bulls; the Jews, lambs; and the Celts burned their human sacrifices alive.'

The King's eyes appeared haunted.

'Even Christians, throughout history, have sacrificed the

innocent to the Devil at a Black Mass, in the hopes that it will be the payment for what they want.'

Scientific inquiry – or natural bloody-mindedness – reasserted itself. 'That may be their belief,' Conrad began.

'What else powers a miracle except belief?' Enrico Mantenucci folded his arms across his chest. 'I throw your own arguments back at you, Signore Conrad. Does it matter who or what the Prince's Men are, or what they believe in, if the methods they use have been known to work?'

Conrad could only shake his head in agreement.

Ferdinand paced a restless few steps on the tiled floor. 'They intend to perform a blood sacrifice. Their black opera—'

'"Black opera"?' Conrad blurted.

'—A name I coined, by similarity with the Black Mass.'

Ferdinand halted, staring into invisible distances.

'At first we assumed they desired to compel the attention of God. That they intended their "sacrifice of innocents" to rouse the attention of the Creator-God, and so bring his attention back to his world here—'

'Cazzo!' Caffeine, strain, and the last several hours obliterated any trace of Conrad's court manners. 'Don't the Prince's Men believe we exist in the world of an evil Creator? You say their absent God was perfectly aware of human pain when He created this universe – He had the power to omit it, but chose not to! Who in their right minds could want to resurrect an evil God!'

Ferdinand straightened, his poise that of a man militarily trained since youth.

Conrad glared back, waiting for a rebuke.

The King gave him a look of satisfaction.

'I see I chose the right man to challenge them on their own terms. Yes. We failed to think that way because the Creator is of supreme importance to us. The Prince's Men . . . their Creator-God is gone, and they're happy to have it so.'

Conrad frowned. 'What is it they do want?'

'We were right in assuming that the Prince's Men believe a blood sacrifice – of sufficient scale – can compel a deity . . . We mistook which God.'

The King stepped closer to the map gallery's closest window. He reached out and slid one sash window up. Conrad felt his skin prickle with alertness as the live wind of spring blew in.

Ferdinand said, 'What the Prince's Men plan to do, with their black miracle, is to alter the constraints that have been in place since the Universe was created.'

The breeze blew the gauze curtains out and around Ferdinand, almost obscuring the intent gaze he fixed on Conrad.

'They want their Prince of this World released from those chains, to rule the world as it should be – with all the senseless pain healed, and the waste restored and made good. This is the future they believe in, beyond the flames of their blood sacrifice . . . They will use their black opera to summon up the Prince of the World.

'And, by their miracle – they will free Him, to reign over us all.'

8

'In short,' Enrico Mantenucci grunted, 'they want to set their Devil up as our God!'

Conrad rose without seeking permission. His thoughts whirled, and physical movement eased that. He paced the length of the gallery and back. The open window allowed a warm wind through; a welcome contact from the world outside.

His mind fought against accepting the idea of such a miracle – or so he thought. When he listened to his thoughts, he heard them chattering: *There isn't a god – there might be a god if they succeed – what would the world be like if someone added a god to it now?*

'Of course,' Mantenucci added grumpily, 'as their heretical ideas are false, all they'll succeed in doing is killing a million men, if we're lucky. If we're unlucky, they'll succeed in raising up the real Devil.'

Conrad felt his pulse hammer in his ears. 'Theology is bunkum! As to "miracles" . . . I'm willing to allow Tambora could have been man-caused.'

Therefore, so might Vesuvius be, one day.

Conrad drew a breath and let it out, tension finding resolution in a sudden black humour. 'After all, it isn't the first time someone's had the idea of using a sacrifice to get God's attention.'

Enrico Mantenucci raised prompting brows.

'The Crucifixion?' Conrad pointed out.

Both the Commendatore and the King developed an identical, absently-shocked, expression. It was wholly familiar to Conrad from other men.

They'd forgotten what I am. Drifted into assuming that I must share their beliefs, because 'everybody does'.

'I apologise for my levity, sir.'

'Don't apologise.' Under Ferdinand's bourgeois exterior, a sharp humour gleamed. 'It's a quality that will give your opera power to counter theirs.'

Conrad dropped back into his chair. 'It's truly possible they can alter the world.'

Mantenucci nodded, slowly. 'Yes – but even his Majesty's Natural Philosophers can't be sure how it would work, or exactly what it would do. It's the Prince's Men who have the confidence it'll do what they want.'

Ferdinand, hands clasped behind his back, turned away from the windows and the view of the plaza below. 'I would suppose that, from their point of view, it's simple enough. If "the Prince" can do miracles to help us, but not to help himself, then Man can likewise bring about a miracle to liberate the Prince from the Laws left behind by creation.'

'Even if the change were only a minor improvement,' Enrico Mantenucci put in. 'Say, allowing the Prince of this World to administer justice. The Men would consider that morally preferable to what we have now. No more suffering three-month-old babies, dead before their time. No lives lived in sickness and crippling injury. If we were Prince's Men, we might think a Just universe the ideal. The old Greek philosophers did! If suffering can't be eliminated, then at least undeserved suffering can. Only the criminal, the immoral, and the vicious would suffer. The good would not.'

Drawn in to something so involving, it took Conrad a full minute to ground himself.

Very dryly, he said, 'That very much depends on who you define as the criminal, the immoral, and the vicious.'

Mantenucci grinned and applauded, one finger tapping the opposite palm.

Ferdinand sounded whimsical. 'I still hold out for my Mach-iavellian Prince of this World. He'd be less arbitrary than your Just God – would reward those who strive and succeed, no matter what methods they use, and punish only those who are feckless and lazy. A God of *virtù*.'

Caught between his various mother tongues, Conrad appreci-ated the point. 'Virtue' has a moral dimension. *Virtù* only denotes ability.

Enrico Mantenucci muttered 'Blasphemy!' under his breath, but looked grimly amused.

'Perhaps,' Ferdinand agreed. 'But I think the point is, as we judge from our intelligence, that unless something is done, the Prince's Men will succeed.'

'The Prince's Men are insane!' Conrad muttered.

Ferdinand sat back, sounding oddly wistful. 'Neither mad, nor evil, reportedly. It would be easier if they were.'

Major Mantenucci sounded grudging. 'Sire, for some men, or some acts, I can only use the term *wicked*.'

'We must look at this through their eyes. Otherwise we have no hope of defeating them. By all means, gentlemen, speculate.'

Conrad exhaled, purging tension deliberately from his body. *Think of it like a libretto.*

I can't.

'Sir, if I see unscientific alterations to the world, that doesn't mean I'm going to label them "miracles"!' Conrad couldn't help a wry grin. 'When people talk about magicking up Satan, I tend to leave the room.'

Light and shadow swept the gallery in quick succession. Outside the tall windows, clouds raced from the west across the now-higher sun. Conrad shivered at the ghost of the Year without a Summer and its thousands of deaths.

Major Mantenucci muttered under his breath, and reached to top up the King's coffee cup. Conrad silently took the pot when the police chief relinquished it.

Ferdinand said, 'We may disagree on the nature of God, and whether or not His nature is subject to change by Mankind. But do we agree on this, Conrad? That there is every likelihood that the Prince's Men can repeat what they did to Mount Tambora, here in the Two Sicilies.'

Conrad scowled and thrust his fists into his coat pockets, slumping down in his chair. 'I want to talk to your Signore Adriano about what he witnessed . . . I know there have been significant miracles connected with opera in the past. If you're right, and the Prince's Men used Tambora as a test, I agree, we can't leave it to chance that they'll fail with Vesuvius. But I come into this on the grounds that what we call a "miracle" is something as yet unaccounted for by science, not an expression of the will of a Deity. If I agree that these lunatics can trigger a volcanic eruption, I don't agree that we'll find God at the end of it!'

'With all respect, Signore Conrad, does that matter?' Ferdinand steepled his thumbs and index fingers. His eyes met Conrad's. 'Your business will be the black opera. It will require inhuman excellence on their part, to provoke what they want it to provoke. We must have the counter opera. If you can work without needing to think of the theology – I have no difficulty with that.'

Conrad clenched and unclenched his fists. 'All right, sire, yes.'

Ferdinand rummaged among the papers and small maps on the map-chest. He selected what Conrad saw was an almanac. The King thumbed through it. '. . . Adriano reports that the Prince's Men must choose a dark phase of the moon to give their black opera.'

Conrad raised his brows. 'Very superstitious, sir.'

Ferdinand put paper in the almanac to mark his place, and put it down. 'In fact, my Natural Philosophers confirm the fact. It seems volcanic eruptions tend to occur at that time when the sun and moon both pull at the earth from the same side.'

'Ignoring astronomy, Signore Conrad?' Enrico Mantenucci blandly commented.

Conrad felt his ears blush hot.

The King set three of the cups in a line on the map-desk, ignoring the police chief's amusement. 'The sun – the moon – the earth. Like so. Apparently there's a strain on the earth with such a direct line. They tell me the sun's and moon's gravity affects, not just the tides of the sea, but the "tides of the earth", if you like. Lava and magma become unstable, under the earth. It was at such a high earth-tide that Tambora erupted.'

Conrad examined the cups carefully. 'Would a solar eclipse be better? Worse, that is, from our point of view?'

Ferdinand nodded, clearly pleased. 'A direct line-up would provide more stress on the Earth. It seems that the Prince's Men have known since Tambora's eruption that they needed to wait for a suitable eclipse, or partial eclipse. If you were to look in any Almanac, you'll find there are precious few this side of the next half century. Only one is suitable.'

He opened the almanac and turned it around to face Conrad.

'The path of a partial eclipse crosses Italy's southern states, including both Sicilies, on the fourteenth of March. All the evidence points to that being the date they've chosen.'

Conrad frowned. 'March?'

He looked closer.

Ferdinand Bourbon-Sicily raked his fingers through his Brutus-cut brown hair, reducing the fashionable style to a street-brat's crop. 'I'm afraid so.'

'But it's—' Conrad stared at the entry. 'February now. And— This March? Not next spring? It would be— That's six weeks from now!'

The King of the Two Sicilies laughed out loud.

It might be the release of tension.

Or again, I may just look completely fish-smacked.

Ferdinand murmured an apology.

Conrad hardly heard it. 'I thought a year, at least! No book, no score, and— You need an opera in six weeks.'

'Of course, that would be the thing, out of all, to disconcert you . . .' Ferdinand's humour changed to a grave regard. 'Conrad, to be clear, I'm asking you to write the libretto for my opera. You'll have six weeks to put on a first night. I'll let you have the Teatro San Carlo. I know that you gave me your decision – but the options are still open. Now's the time to change your mind, if you desire to.'

The dazzle of being a librettist at Naples' premier opera house blinded Conrad for a moment. The ligaments and tendons of his knees felt loose. Conrad bit back the words of immediate acceptance. He suppressed that part of himself that wanted to shout, *Yes, I'll do it, I'll write your opera!*

He regarded Ferdinand Bourbon-Sicily, attempting to clear from his mind any remnants of deference for royalty that might be influencing him. And the fact that he liked this man.

'Six weeks is a short time for an opera to be composed, rehearsed, and staged,' Conrad said, mildly as he might.

'True.'

'And you've known about the black opera for – some time?'

'Also true.'

Conrad collected his wits. *I can't let this slide.*

'Normally,' he said, 'any man, if asked, would jump at the chance to write an opera for the King of the Two Sicilies. But in all this time, apparently, no one has. Therefore I have to ask, sire. What's the catch?'

✦

King Ferdinand exchanged an indecipherable glance with Enrico Mantenucci.

'I'd want you to oversee the production in general,' Ferdinand said blandly. 'You'd handle the staging and manage the singers, as is normal for a librettist, but since I can't appear as the impresario, you'd have to take that on, too – at least, in name. I'm told you have many contacts in the opera world – singers, stagehands, costumiers, builders of effects . . . I'll put as much finance in your hands as you need.'

Am I supposed to notice that he hasn't answered my question?

The impulse to simply agree pulled at him like gravity.

Even if the Prince's Men are nothing more than a gang of lunatic revolutionaries lurking in corners – even if the Tambora volcano was a fluke – if they're wrong about the threat . . . I'd still be staging my own libretto at one of the greatest theatres in Italy!

In six weeks.

. . . Barely six weeks.

Conrad forced himself to speak as calmly as possible. 'If I were a King, with a King's resources, and I needed to counter the "black opera", I'd be looking for Felice Romani, the premier librettist of Italy, to write my arias and cabalettas and strettas. And I'd ask Donizetti and Mercadante, Bellini and Pacini, maybe even Rossini, to compose the music. I'd bring in every famous singer that I could hire, no matter the cost and inconvenience. Rubini and Duprez and Domzelli for your tenors! Tamborini and Luigi Lablache as basses; Caroline Ungher as contralto; sopranos of the class of Giulia Grisi, Giudita Pasta, Adelaide Tosi, Malibran—'

Conrad broke away from the image of what a production under royal command might truly be like.

'I certainly wouldn't wait until only six weeks remained! . . . And yet, sir, that appears to be what you've done.'

Ferdinand watched him with quiet interest.

'I'm not as good as Felice Romani,' Conrad admitted brutally, 'even if I may be, one day soon. Is this something designed to counter the black opera? Or is the "counter opera" a diversion of some kind, to keep the agents of the Prince's Men busy, and draw them out, so that when they attack this opera, they can be caught?'

The King of the Two Sicilies beamed. 'You're not a stupid man, are you?'

Conrad's heart gave a galloping lurch, as if his body had not been aware until then how much he was risking by interrogating a king.

He sounds . . . as if he approves.

Ferdinand spoke with a pleased air. 'Well, then, it's true that I won't object if the opera does function as a lure, and I manage to finally arrest any of the members of the conspiracy. Everywhere my people look, delays are put in our way, agents are turned aside, men give alibis to each other . . . There are "men of the Prince" in every country, including mine. But—'

Conrad suppressed his almost-voiced interruption.

Ferdinand's voice held the bite of conviction.

'—If it were that, I wouldn't have needed to tell you the truth about the black opera. Or trust your oath – your affirmation. This is the truth. If we fail to find and disrupt the site of the black opera before the partial eclipse, then our only method is to fight fire with fire – we stage a counteracting opera, at the exact same time as theirs. An opera of our own, written and composed to be everything that the black opera is not. And the power and passion behind our words and music will – *must* – counter the effect that the Prince's Men wish for.'

Ferdinand paused, looking soberly at Conrad.

'You're no dupe or diversion. We must have the counter-opera, and it must succeed.'

Conrad hesitated, and then gestured at himself. 'And the reason Felice Romani isn't sitting in this chair?'

'Oh, that's simple enough.' Ferdinand waved expansively. 'When all this was finally confirmed beyond doubt, I did approach those men whom I considered to be the best composers and librettists in the field. At the beginning of last year, after I was sure we would have until the following spring's eclipse, I hired the finest singers I could. The Teatro San Carlo workshops were filled with craftsmen night and day, constructing settings for the scenes—'

'That production at the Teatro San Carlo was you? Sir,' Conrad added, softening his interruption. 'I know a lot of people who worked in the San Carlo rehearsals that summer. And stagehands and crew. I heard before I came here that it was supposed to be for a big production, but it . . . got the reputation of being unlucky . . .'

Conrad could only stare at the King.

Ferdinand confirmed, 'It was unlucky. There were fires set. That might have been saboteurs. There were bad dreams, and ghosts seen in the opera house, and the dead walked. We had an exorcism performed, but it didn't stop them. Letters arrived, with threats that the recipients began to keep to themselves.' He frowned. 'You will have heard of the death of the celebrated tenor Monsieur Adolphe Nourrit.'

'Yes . . . I understood that he came to Naples to learn the chest-voice high C under Signore Donizetti's teaching. And couldn't master it, and therefore committed suicide.'

'That story was put about. In fact, it was a gruesome accident in the theatre that was no accident, and proved the last straw for the other principal singers, all of whom fled Naples before the day was out. In case another such accident should happen.'

The King's expression took on a sardonic humour.

'Nine months from the time we began, the famous impresario I had hired fled, with his belongings in a carpet-bag, under cover of darkness, to a hired carriage. Donizetti left for Rome, Bellini for Catania, neither of them having written the music for their scenes – and Gioacchino Rossini fled to Paris, and flatly refuses to come out. Or compose a note.'

Ferdinand stood again, and began to pace the map corridor.

'That production completely collapsed. In the past few weeks I've found no professional opera-house composer willing to work for me. I will, however, find one . . . The reason you're being given such a short amount of time to succeed in this second attempt is because the first failed so disastrously.'

He turned, and Conrad unconsciously found himself straightening under the King's gaze.

'I'm a judge of men's character, Signore Conrad. I don't think you a man to fear this secret society overmuch – though you will doubtless take the necessary precautions. The House of Bourbon will give you as much freedom and help as possible. Will you have the job?'

The unflattering knowledge of being second choice, the self-evident difficulties with the production, the danger of the Prince's Men – *Even if they are only an association of religious madmen!* Conrad's stubborn scepticism asserted – all of the obstacles seemed nothing, compared to the weight of this man's trust.

Conrad pushed back his chair and stood up. 'I've made my decision. This doesn't change it.'

Ferdinand Bourbon-Sicily shook him by the hand. The painfully hard grip conveyed everything of urgency.

'We do still have six weeks.' Conrad glanced around the map gallery, noting that Enrico Mantenucci remained comfortably seated. 'I've known winter season operas, due for an opening on the twenty-sixth of December, that didn't start rehearsals until the eighth or tenth of the month. Some of them became classics . . .'

Ferdinand's grin was suddenly boyish. 'Though I dare say that was with the music composed, the book already written, and the costumes sewn and stage sets built?'

'And better not mention,' Mantenucci completed with gusto, 'that some of those same classic operas – Signore Bellini's *Norma*, for one! – started off with vile reviews – being sung by a cast rehearsed into exhaustion until four in the morning of the opening day!'

It lifted Conrad's mood, oddly enough. The stubbornly wilful part of his character woke. 'Oh, people put on operas in six weeks every day . . .'

Ferdinand Bourbon-Sicily gave an amused chuckle. 'Those sound like words that will haunt a man!'

Conrad stretched each muscle where he stood, still cramped from the absent weight of his chains. More seriously, he said, 'We'll need to tell the singers and stage-crew something, sire. If only to account for the dangers, and the guards.'

Ferdinand's expression told him that he had been correct about the presence of guards.

Conrad said, 'If I could make a suggestion? We tell them that the Camorra or the other Sicilian group, are determined to stop this opera. We don't have to say why.'

Ferdinand began slowly to nod assent.

Conrad concluded: 'They'll make up their own rumours. If the singers, musicians, and stagehands have courage enough that they're prepared to stand up to the *società onorata*, we needn't feel too badly about putting them in danger from the Prince's Men.'

'Because their methods are the same.' Ferdinand hit his fist into his palm. 'That's well thought of! The necessary few, you may need to tell the exact truth. Avoid that if you can—'

Enrico Mantenucci came alert, like a grey-muzzled gun dog.

'—Enrico?'

Distant sharp words sounded. Servants – close at hand.

Conrad heard a scuffle approaching outside the map corridor.

An officer in police uniform stumbled, making a precipitate entry into the gallery. The matt light showed his features pinched and white. He had no attention for any man but his superior officer.

Ferdinand nodded permission. 'Go.'

Mantenucci muttered a superficial apology and strode off up

the gallery. The interchange when he and his subordinate met was too quiet to be overheard.

Conrad felt embarrassed, out of place. 'Should I leave, sir?'

'Not yet. It may be nothing.'

Mantenucci slapped his junior officer on the shoulder, in rough encouragement, and sent him off.

The Major glanced back at the King.

Conrad heard the chair scrape beside him.

Ferdinand stood. Conrad scrambled to his feet as protocol demanded – feeling, too, that Mantenucci's suddenly drawn expression required it.

His gaze snapping with comprehension, Ferdinand demanded, 'Adriano is – more than late?'

9

Mantenucci shot a look at Conrad.

He assumes the King will order me out if he wants me gone.

'I'm sorry, sire.' The Commendatore spoke to Ferdinand. 'My men have discovered Signore Castiello-Salvati's body. It's on the steps going down to the royal dock – someone on the *Guiscardo* spotted it.'

Conrad's unwelcome imagination painted the King's dock, familiar to every man of Napoli; the masts and cat's-cradle ropes of the moored royal yacht *Roberto il Guiscardo*, the steps running up to the Palazzo complex . . . A knot of gathered men who stand, look at each other, look down, look away . . .

'You're sure he's dead?' Ferdinand demanded.

He's dead, Conrad thought. *Or the Commendatore wouldn't refer to a code-named 'Adriano' by his family name.*

'Yes.' Mantenucci flinched. Lines on his face momentarily deepened. 'They made it look like a criminal's death – as if the Camorra or Mafia had killed an informer.'

Conrad kept himself still by an effort. Two years ago he was in Rome, and present by sheer accident when an informer's body was found on the Isola Tiberina. The memory was still strong. Someone had dropped a sun-bleached sail-cloth over the body, and it was patched and sodden with blood. Spreading edges of the stain showed black where blood was older and drying, vibrant scarlet where it was barely out of the vein.

Flies clustered in blue-green humming armour over one exposed foot.

The odour permeated everything – the fresh stench of blood, that ought to go with sawdust in a clean butcher's shop. A smell of blood and tissue, not decay . . .

'It's also a warning, sire.' Mantenucci broke the silence. 'They've left him still recognisable.'

'A warning to me.' Ferdinand Bourbon-Sicily strode away down the map gallery. His languid stride camouflaged quite how fast he moved. He halted at the end window. After a moment he opened it and leaned his hands on the sill, gazing out over the piazza.

Cumulus clouds sailing up from the west passed directly over-head, casting shadows that ran up the palace walls, and through the gallery. Conrad, alternately chilled and warmed, could not have spoken if challenged at gun-point. He felt grateful for the cool wind. His stomach roiled.

Other memories threatened – the damage done by bayonets, rifles, artillery shells, cavalry sabres.

I was a soldier: I ought not to mind.

Living next to a knacker's yard in London had failed to make him used to any of its sights and sounds. *But if the English Mister Darwin and the others are right, we're all animals.*

It isn't the bloodshed, Conrad thought, dimly aware that Mante-nucci's voice still reported to his King. *It's the deliberate cruelty.*

On that island in the Tiber, the supposed informer had been left, at dawn, on a piazza not far from both the Hospital and the urine-reeking river. Two years ago, and Conrad still remembers how some curious fool pulled the cloth away.

The dead man lay face-up, in still-wet blood that pooled four yards around him. It took Conrad a moment to realise the body was naked—blood covered over every inch of its skin.

The man's lips were sewn together, over and over, with saddle-makers' black thread. Spider-webs of leaking blood marked his cheek and chin. Conrad's experience of war let him know, *He was alive long enough that his mouth moved and tore against the thread. Long enough to know that if he could scream, he might be saved.* But—

A razor's cut sliced round from left to right through the man's throat, without snagging or catching. A second mouth, opened in lieu of the sealed one, but this one would never speak.

That it had spurted and gushed was obvious by how blood ran away down the cracks between flagstones, and pooled in rounded ancient stone gutters. It was tracked away on careless boots and shoes. Between that smell, the river, and Conrad finding his own shoes leaving bloody footprints, he finally found a private corner and vomited.

This is how the people of whom we don't talk signal that they've killed an informer – a spy.

Ferdinand stood at the window with his head down, weight on his supporting arms.

Conrad involuntarily pictured blood-soaked black hair flopping over well-shaped brows, as the King had described them, and blue eyes dry and dull. *Is this what Ferdinand imagines now?*

Ferdinand Bourbon-Sicily leaned out of the open window and emptied his stomach in a businesslike manner onto the balcony.

I would suppose he's seen bodies like this, too.

Beside Conrad, Enrico Mantenucci rumbled in an undertone that didn't carry. 'Kings don't have friends at court. Everyone in this poison viper's pit has their own interests. I suppose, as an educated young man, you'll have heard of the Varangian Guard?'

Conrad pushed back visceral shock, ransacked his memory, and discovered they were speaking of history. 'The Byzantine Emperors' bodyguards?'

'From the Scandinavian countries. No Byzantine Emperor could trust his countrymen, so he brought in warriors from Norway and Sweden and Denmark – who were, of course, a world away from their native lands, and dependent solely on the Emperor. That made thcm loyal.'

The King, with the curtains blowing around him, remained utterly still. Enrico watched him with a keen, sympathetic gaze.

He gave a grim smile.

'Adriano was an uncommon man. He loved what he did. He had no other desires – his family were rich enough for him to tell every one of the courtier-rats in this palace to fuck themselves.

He wasn't just his Majesty's Varangian Guard; he was his friend.'

One of Conrad's childhood languages flashed up *Doppëlganger!*

Shadow-brother. Fated twin.

That's why this fascination. Kinship. In another world I might be him, or he, me.

Omen. Abject warning.

Ferdinand suddenly moved. He strode back down the gallery, stopping by each window and throwing the sash up, opening each to the air. It reminded Conrad of how peasant women open every window in the house, after a death, so the soul won't be held captive.

Superstition is harder to shift than religion!

The angle of the unobstructed sunlight as it struck into the gallery was itself a shock. *It's not even midday!*

Wind brought the smell of the sea, and smoke from innumerable chimneys, and sea-weed, and hot tar boiling in the distant shipyards. Ambushed by sensation, Conrad took a deep breath.

Ferdinand halted beside both of them. 'Who found him?'

Mantenucci spoke with blunt honesty. Only the lines on his face indicated he wished he might temper the truth.

'Sailors from the *Guiscardo*, sire, when it came in. No one else saw anything, apparently – those steps are an ideal place to meet and exchange information; my own men have used it. No spy can approach from the direction of the palace without crossing wide courtyards and exposing himself to you, and from a distance, on the dock, it would be assumed it was men or officers of the *Guiscardo* there, or men who had business with them.'

'You've given orders.'

'Yes, though I think a search will be useless. The blood has been dry long enough that he was killed before dawn.'

'I want the murderer found.' Ferdinand spoke in a grim, undone voice, as if this was not the first subordinate's death for which he took personal responsibility. 'You know what they'll say here. Signore Adriano Castiello-Salvati, murdered in a brawl over a harlot . . .'

'It's too late to redeem his name now, sire.'

'I— Yes. Yes, you're right.'

Conrad found his nails digging into his palms. Not for the loss of a brave man, he realised. The part of him that was artist felt only a cold-blooded regret for what had been lost. No chance, now, to speak with the man who heard what was sung at Sumbawa. *And if someone has noted down an approximation of the score, without Adriano Castiello-Salvati's experience the true sound is lost.*

'Warn your men against gossip, Enrico. Report it as a robbery turned murder. I know he has – had – no close family. Put up a stone in one of the respectable churchyards, but I'll have him interred in the royal mausoleum here, with a Sung Mass. My confessor will keep it confidential. Adriano's service to my kingdom has been invaluable.'

Conrad did not have the heart to say, *It doesn't matter what honours you give him; there's no one there now to hear it.*

Ferdinand suddenly swore. 'I have no idea how men do this in the name of any God!'

Out of respect, Conrad bit down on his tongue, and let the small pain remind him not to be contentious. Not to say, *Ask the Inquisition how many Jews and heretics and witches they've judged,* or, *Ask the Muslim Barbary pirates how they convert Christians at the point of the sword!*

Ferdinand apparently caught his look. He said nothing. Mantenucci removed a flask from one of his coat pockets and passed it to Ferdinand. Conrad smelled brandy.

The King shook his head, like a horse with a troublesome fly; then upended the silver flask and drank it down with no more reaction than if it had been water.

Will *this be me, one day?* Conrad suddenly thought. *With Major Mantenucci reporting to the King how the Prince's Men have murdered me?*

I knew there was this chance when I agreed. I just didn't expect it to come so close, so soon.

'There's no doubt of who and why . . . ?' Ferdinand's lips twisted sardonically. He gave Mantenucci a deliberate echo of the earlier conversation: 'Suppose that we're Prince's Men, Enrico – what would you do?'

'If I'm a Prince's Man, and I suspect the Two Sicilies still oppose us, after we sabotaged their first counter-opera? I suppose . . . Sire, I suppose I should take care to find out the most important spy the other side have in our organisation, and I should murder him.'

Ferdinand Bourbon-Sicily gave a snort, and emptied the silver flask. His reactions remained coldly sober. Conrad remembered nights on which he had finished a bottle of brandy and gone to bed no less sober than before; most of them in the Alpine wars.

Ferdinand looked up from the silver flask, full into Conrad's face.

'Conrad— Enrico will have to brief you further, now that we don't have Adriano. Assuming that you still wish to work with us.'

'Yes.'

There was nothing more he could say and not have it sound like bravado.

The King inclined his head.

'Enrico. Get Conrad safely out of here.'

Under Ferdinand's abruptness, Conrad glimpsed concern.

He cares for the Two Sicilies first – but for his men, too. And this is why Adriano, and doubtless others, keep faith with this man.

Mantenucci stroked his moustache thoughtfully. 'If you take my advice – yes, I can huddle him out the back way, with a dozen of my men to make sure he isn't spotted. But he's just as likely to be spotted because he's protected.'

'Enrico—'

'Sire, if you want Signore Conrad here safe, have him walk out of the Palace in an hour or two, with the other disappointed petitioners, when the time for audiences is over. He'll vanish into the crowds in Naples and no one will even know he's important.'

'Ah. Yes. Very well. Conrad—'

Ferdinand rested his hand on Conrad's shoulder, his grip secure.

'—I'll have my Master of Music appoint you to some sinecure, to account for your comings and goings here . . . A copyist in the library, perhaps. That should enable you to communicate with us incognito. I leave you with the responsibility for the libretto, and the work of an impresario until I can give my attention fully to that. I look to hear from you how the counter-opera develops – as soon as you can. We have much less time than we need.'

10

Conrad walked back up the long central Roman road of Naples at a rapid stride.

He threw his head back, drawing in a breath. Inexpressibly pleased to be smelling horse dung where carriages passed and brackish harbour mud, instead of musty tapestries and beeswax polish. *The outside world, at last!*

The two hours in the Palazzo Reale, waiting until the time for the levee should be past, left him with an incalculable energy now. He turned off into the many little streets of the Port quarter, elbow to elbow with loud-voiced crowds. Evergreen trees ruffled leaves in the sunlight, casting cool shadows. He kicked up dust in the narrow roadways, automatically manoeuvring around slower-walking groups. Men in high-crowned hats, with walking sticks in one hand and wife on the other arm. Mother and nurse and baby, and two children walking . . . No one who looked like a murderer, or a Prince's Man, even supposing either could be recognised on sight.

Conrad found himself finally on the edge of the market quarter, among flowers and vegetables and jabbering women with voluminous aprons. Lower class and younger men went without hats or shoes, only wearing knee-breeches and a waistcoat open over a shirt.

A loud cheer almost sent him across the road in shock.

They're only playing mora . . . !

I feel as exposed as a butterfly pinned to a board!

Conrad waited for his heart to stop thumping, watching the teams outside a tavern exclaiming specific loud numbers and holding out their hands with (naturally) a different number of fingers extended. Another roar went up when the captain on one team outguessed the other – a man in a pair of vertically striped trousers that were an affront to any eye.

Conrad absently stepped out of the way of two or three younger men, walking with women in high-waisted dresses and complicated hair. He straightforwardly envied them for a moment. Just to be able to swagger and impress a girl, with nothing else hanging on it . . .

Walking helped him think.

Not to rid his mind of images.

He gave it up after another hour or so, approaching his lodgings by circuitous ways.

He found his steps slowing. *Hiding in plain sight from these 'Prince's Men' . . . And then there's the power of the Church . . .*

A broad-shouldered, brutal-looking man shifted from where he leaned on a shadowed wall. And, as he reached the sunlight, visibly became Tullio Rossi.

'They're gone,' he grunted.

Conrad couldn't help a smile. *I can rely on Tullio relaying the essential piece of information.* 'You and JohnJack, you're all right?'

'Signore Master Spinelli's up there setting your room to rights. I let him do it.' Tullio's bruiser-face dissolved into a smile that was mischievously wicked. 'Told him, he knows more about where ornamental knickknacks go than I do . . .'

Conrad ignored the suspicious looks and semi-audible comments from his neighbours as they approached the lodgings. None of them quite dared question him openly after a visit from God's Hounds.

At least I can let it slip I'm working for his Majesty King Ferdinand II, no less.

Rumour will get about, and most people will assume it to be an exaggeration of an even more low-ranking post.

Tullio rubbed his large hands together. 'So what we doing, padrone?'

Conrad clapped him on the shoulder, if only to be reassured that the man was here and in the flesh. 'We're writing a libretto.'

'And there was me thinking the Church wanted to put a stop to that . . .'

Tullio had the expression of a man who expects to hear a satisfying explanation.

'So. Whose wine are we pissing in today, padrone? Not Holy Church, not the King . . . the Honoured Men?''

'Close.' Conrad couldn't help a wry grin. 'You'll get all the details. About the opera, too. But first – first, we become an impresario.'

'Blessed Saint Jude, Apostle and Martyr!'

✦

The first twenty-four hours went past so quickly Conrad barely had time to breathe. The business of being an impresario, even in name only, involved a lot of footwork – at least for Tullio, since Conrad decided it was better he settle down to work out an overall composing and rehearsal schedule, while Tullio ran about all over Naples, ferreting out who had fled the city and who had merely gone into hiding for a tactful amount of time.

'. . . We have Signore GianGiacomo Spinelli,' Conrad found himself reviewing, some time later in the auditions, for the benefit of a man who appeared surprisingly younger than his known forty years. 'You will have heard him; a stunningly good comic or tragic bass. And if we have yourself—'

Giambattista Velluti waved a pale, long-fingered hand. It was the only sign of his status as a castrato singer, other than his androgyne dark good looks. Not for Velluti the tall obeseness of many castrated singers. He smiled with the confidence of a man who knows he can insist on working with the best.

'You cannot tell me anything at all about the libretto? Or what my role will be?'

Conrad managed not to look like a man who knows only two certain words of his libretto – 'Act One'.

'I realise that you're used to being the primo uomo in any company, signore. There's no question but that you'll be First Man and have the hero's role. However, at the moment this is only a preliminary agreement. When we hammer out contract details, we can of course take note of any special requirements you may have . . .'

A surprisingly amiable discussion settled the draft agreement. Conrad thought himself lucky to get away without 'entrance, up-stage, riding a white horse and wearing a plumed helmet', or 'dis-embarks from on-stage warship while a grateful crowd cheer the victor wearing laurels' enshrined in the castrato's contract, but decided against mentioning this. Rumour said Velluti had little sense of humour about such things.

That settled, he sent the castrato on for a social audience with his Majesty King Ferdinand, without letting Velluti know that that was the second and more important audition.

Conrad found himself dreaming of Castiello-Salvati's death, in the grey hours. He put it out of his mind after the second time, with the finality he had practised during the war.

Ferdinand Bourbon-Sicily, in his character as an impresario, drafted more letters to be sent out to Milan, Venice, Pesara, Rome – letters that showed him to have paid surprisingly close atten-tion to the mechanical details of producing an opera during his patronage of the Teatro San Carlo. Conrad forged a signature that matched the handwriting and posted them on.

By the third day he found himself reduced to vulgar southern profanity.

Minchia! but the contracts are a bitch to write! Half the singers he wants are attached to other opera houses. But I suppose he is a King . . .

Conrad lost four days of the first week before he knew it. Nor-mally, the usual chaos of an opera in progress would begin to be reported back – he was familiar enough with that from Barjaba's bitching, before the man fled. Once the impresario summoned, contraltos and basses set out by carriage from towns the length and breadth of all Italy, complaining to a man (and woman) about bumpy interminable mountainous journeys and bed-bugs in inns. Sopranos would travel with their mothers in tow – and nothing is

105

quite so terrifying as the mother of a seconda donna who thinks she ought to be the mother of a prima donna – and musicians from town bands and church parades would make a foot-sore way to Naples (the carriages being mostly beyond their means) to compete with the locals.

This time there was an ominous lack of reply. And of those that did, almost all were chorus singers and musicians for the orchestra, not opera stars.

Knowing he must still be ahead of their arrival, even assuming that roads and tides were good, Conrad took the advantage of the following twenty-four hours to secure any as-yet overlooked Neapolitan singers, whether with Teatro experience, church choir, chorus, or merely sitting on the sea-wall singing folk-songs. With the good ones secured, he was left with a succession of weak tenors and mezzos whom Conrad would cheerfully have pushed into Vesuvius – too many opera plots featured that already, unfortunately. It was a great relief when the next knock on the door announced Sandrine Furino.

'Back from Rome? I thought you'd abandoned me like the Persianis. I swear, Sandrine, if I weren't an atheist I'd say *Thank God*!' Conrad kissed her hand and led her to the cherry-striped satin couch that the Dominicans had at least left with all four legs. 'If I need anything right now, I need a stunning mezzo . . .'

'Then you won't mind paying me a stunning amount of money.' Sandrine Furino unpinned her hat and veil. As always, she left her gauze scarf still around her neck. She wore her bodice a little higher than might be expected, but the width of her satin gigot sleeves emphasised her tiny waist. She spoke in the low, slightly breathy tone which fascinated all her young male admirers at the stage door. 'What sort of role would you have for me? Not another britches-part?'

Conrad sighed and threw his quill down, coming to join Sandrine on the couch, and pour tea from the slightly dented service Tullio had brought in. 'But you're so good at playing romantic heroes.'

'And sometimes I'd like to play the girl!' Sandrine smoothed down the set of her gown at her hips, and threw Conrad what he took to be a deliberately smouldering look from under her long lashes. 'Travesti roles are losing their appeal, Conrad. They remind me . . . Well. They remind me.'

'All right. I still wish there was a way to get your amazing lower range on stage . . .'

Conrad braced himself and gave the warning about the supposed Camorra. Making a mental note: *If she does join, she'll certainly be one of the ones told about the Prince's Men.*

'I'm in sufficient danger walking down the street as it is.' Sandrine gave him a somewhat rueful look. 'I don't suppose I care about more.'

'All right, then . . .' *If she says that, I have to accept it.* Conrad reached for the scribbled notes spread over his desk. 'So, JohnJack for the villain, unless a decent tenor unexpectedly leaps out of the woodwork. Velluti's just been signed up, he'll expect to sing the hero . . . So, yes, I could offer you a female role.'

'A role central to the story,' she insisted, looking at him under her lashes again. 'Not the heroine's maid, or the villain's discarded mistress. Something with meat in it.'

As things stood at the moment, she looked fair to be the prima donna, but Conrad bit his tongue in case he had to retract the offer later. *It's only been four days, who knows what the King will say?*

'I swear—' Conrad held up his hand, only to find his notes whipped out of his grasp.

'You're in, Signorina Sandrine,' Tullio observed, shuffling the papers together, and returning her welcoming smile. 'Now go away for a few hours, while my master explains to me just why he appears to have forgotten how to sleep or eat . . .'

'Certainly.' As she passed Tullio on the way to the door, Sandrine Furino stood up on tiptoe in her neat ankle boots, and pressed a kiss to his cheek. 'You look after him so well, you sweet, sweet man . . .'

It didn't take her wink from the doorway to collapse Conrad in choking laughter – Tullio's expression had already robbed him of the ability to breathe.

'I'll bring in the food,' Tullio Rossi managed eventually, with immense dignity. 'Parsley omelette. If you weren't so starved, you'd end up wearing it!'

♦

Conrad had barely finished eating when footsteps trod up the stairs again, and he heard a knock on the door.

Tullio lifted an eyebrow. 'More appointments?'

His caution made Conrad conscious, suddenly, that he himself was wary of an unknown caller. *I don't suppose that's too surprising. Not with the Inquisition and everything the Prince's Men did to Castiello-Salvati.*

'No, I was done.' Conrad watched as Tullio went to answer the door. 'I've hired everybody I know here who are good singers or stage-hands.'

There had been something of a local dearth of the latter, too. The King's first attempt at the counter-opera, secret though it supposedly was, had scared a lot of people off, Conrad's more peripatetic friends among them.

'Well, padrone, I don't suppose the secret society of assassins would knock . . .'

'The Dominicans did!'

He found himself still nervous while Tullio was out at the front door.

'Man to see you,' Tullio reported back. 'Don't know him. Young chap.'

'Show him in.' Conrad moved the short distance from the table to the chairs by the fire. 'If I'm lucky it's a world-famous *tenore di grazia* . . .'

A well-dressed young man in his early twenties followed Tullio back into the room, removing his tall hat. His hair was of that colour neither brown nor blond, he wore narrow white trousers, black boots, and a cut-away dark blue tail-coat with wide lapels; his neck-stock was spotless linen. Conrad found himself frowning.

I know that face . . . do I? Surely . . .

The youth bowed, hair flipping energetically. 'Gianpaolo Pironti at your service, cousin!'

This would be one of Baltazar's sons, Mother's nephews, and . . . my

108

cousin? I know I haven't seen most of my cousins for years, but . . . No. I don't think so. No.

'And you're here because . . . ?' Conrad prompted.

'I've just done two years in the Conservatoire in Catania.' Gianpaolo Pironti beamed. 'Eventually I want to join the opera world as a composer. I have no patronage – so I appeal to nepotism! Can you help me, as a member of the family?'

Conrad went for a delaying action. 'That would depend on how good you are.'

Cousin Gianpaolo looked hopeful.

Conrad gave up and asked directly. 'And, also, on why you're a girl dressed up as a man?'

'Ah.' Pironti looked startled. 'I thought I was good enough not to be spotted.'

The slim figure had nothing to betray her in her body, the slightly padded coat shoulders distracting from any bust. If she looked young to have graduated from a conservatoire, that was the only consequence of her having no facial hair.

Conrad snorted. 'I'm in opera!'

He waved a hand at her male clothing.

'I'm used to seeing women in britches roles, and male castrati singing men disguised as women. Our last production, we had a soprano dressed as a woman singing the heroine, a mezzo dressed as a man playing the hero, and a contralto dressed as a man but playing a woman disguised in male clothing. If I can keep that lot clear while they're singing their trio – and the love-duet – I can certainly spot a woman off-stage when I see one! But you do look like my cousin Gianpaolo . . . like family . . .'

She gave him a fishy eye. 'That's because I'm your sister, you berk.'

Conrad blankly stared at her.

He realised his mouth had fallen open, and shut it. Out of the corner of his eye, he caught Tullio looking slightly relieved. *Was he truly afraid of a visit from the Prince's Men?*

'You are Isaura, aren't you?' Conrad examined her in quiet wonder. 'Isaura . . . I haven't seen you for . . . oh Lord, is it nine years?'

He stood up before he realised he was going to do it. The cross-dressed young woman looked apprehensive at first – and as he moved towards her, threw her arms around him, and hugged him as tightly as he gripped her. Despite being of a height with him, she felt small in his arms.

'Nine!' She sounded as if she were laughing and crying together. 'You came home after Papa died.'

He put her back at arm's length, and she rubbed the heel of her hand across her face, the gesture all boy. Her words brought back the past: coming home, after his father Alfredo had been dead for some months, and finding the house was in the process of being sold to cover a little of Alfredo's debts. Conrad had arranged for his mother Agnese to live in a house her maternal uncle Baltazar could loan her, after arguing that it would disgrace the family for them to be on the streets. And Baltazar Pironti had consented, provided Conrad added him to the list of Alfredo's most pressing creditors.

'I remember it was Cousin Gianpaolo who eventually persuaded Baltazar into a compromise that at least let me eat.' Conrad's mind was still in the past. 'Paolo writes to me every year or so and tells me about our finances. But you . . . I remember you as this dark, withdrawn, fifteen-year-old beanpole of a girl, always standing behind Mother's skirts, and now— '

'It isn't Paolo. It's me. I write to you.'

Conrad opened his mouth to contradict her, and shut it again.

All the minuscule doubts of a decade – *Does Cousin Gianpaolo Pironti have either the talent or the energy to cope with law and finance, never mind any ability to go against his father Baltazar?* – vanished like dead leaves in a fire, supplanted by the instant realisation that this is his sister; his sister, telling the truth.

Isaura Scalese folded her arms. 'Paolo wouldn't touch account books if you paid him! I borrowed his identity. Later on, he wanted to go to Paris, so he was happy to leave me his name so I could go to the Conservatoire. And I wasn't "withdrawn" when you came home! I was off spending half my time as a boy!'

Conrad saw Tullio unashamedly lean his arms on the back of

the striped sofa, so that he could listen in comfort. It made him want to splutter his disbelief.

But I can't. I believe every word.

'You didn't see much of me because that was the first time I seriously dressed up as Gianpaolo. So I could sort out Mother's business affairs. Paolo himself is useless! Uncle Dario will never come back from America—'

Conrad thought that a shrewd assessment of Alfredo's brother.

'—And I wasn't going to let Uncle Baltazar get his hands on anything we still had . . .' She chewed her lip. 'But in the end there was nothing, and I had to appeal to you to come home—'

'That was you? I thought that was Mother.'

'I forged the letter. Anyway, once he let Mother have that house, that town was far enough away from Uncle Baltazar and the rest of the family that I could carry on being "Gianpaolo" . . . One advantage of being in the part of the family in disgrace. And I've studied and written music, and now I want to compose opera!'

Conrad was for one ice-hot moment full of jealousy of her lack of responsibilities.

He pushed the feeling away as unworthy.

It left him regarding his undeniably female sister, at home in coat and trousers, with her gloves, hat, and cane left with careless elegance on the coat-table by the door.

It's not a charade she's playing, he realised. *She'll pass anywhere, for people who don't already know.*

'Why don't you want to run a salon?' he demanded, almost at random. 'You could be a drawing-room composer like Malibran's sister, what's her name—'

'Viardot! Pauline Viardot. I bet you don't forget Rossini's name! Or Donizetti's, or Pacini's!' Familiar grey eyes, very like his own, narrowed in disgust. 'Why would I want to compose an opera for a handful of my friends? Or for some nobleman in his palazzo, and have to bring in a core of "guest" singers from the opera houses because none of his friends can sing a note!'

Tullio's low rumble broke the silence. 'I think your sister wants to be a professional opera composer, padrone.'

'Yes, I did get that impression!' Conrad waved a hand in apology.

'Isaura, this is Tullio; we were in the war together. You might have met him when I came to Catania.'

Isaura had been all outraged youth. At Tullio's interjection, she sat down in the other chair, moving as if men's clothes came perfectly naturally to her, but looking at him with an expression that reminded Conrad forcibly of the little endlessly-talking girl that he had held by the hand in Prussia and St Petersburg and a dozen German kingdoms.

Isaura studied Tullio Rossi with unfeminine directness. 'I remember you. You nearly caught me in Paolo's clothes several times. I borrowed your walk when I went to the Conservatoire—' She moved in illustration. '—From the shoulders.'

Another man might have been bewildered, Conrad thought, but Tullio, having been used to the opera world for at least a decade, grasped the point – and the compliment – at once.

'Glad to have been of help with your role.' One corner of Tullio Rossi's mouth turned up. He set about serving the last of the tea with milk and cream, and went to Isaura first to put the recently chipped cup on her small table.

Conrad took his own damaged cup and sighed. He leaned his other elbow on the arm of the chair, and rubbed at his chin.

'If you want a career – one that women can and do have, as independent businesswomen – why not become a singer rather than a composer? Thousands of women do that.'

Isaura glanced at Tullio, who was now aimlessly clearing the main table and shamelessly listening, and turned back to Conrad. ' "Una voce poco fa qui nel cor mi risuonò; il mio cor ferito è già . . ." '

She broke off.

'That was . . .' Conrad helplessly searched for a word.

'. . . Ouch! My heart is already wounded!' Tullio echoed the aria of Rosina from Il Barbiere di Siviglia, 'never mind my ears! I'll pay money, I swear, if you never, ever, sing again!'

'You know, most people say that . . .' Isaura grinned, clearly not at all insulted. 'I've never had that trouble with instruments – piano and violin, I'm fine. I can carry a tune in my head, and write it down. Just not sing.'

Conrad found himself exchanging glances with Tullio and

knowing precisely what was in the other man's mind. Bellini had an opera produced at seventeen, while he was at the same Conservatoire in Catania: *it's not impossible that anyone might come out of their training with a similar genius . . .*

And I don't recall anyone asking Bellini if he could sing. Conrad indicated the small upright instrument crammed into the far corner of the room. 'I think the piano needs tuning, after our ecclesiastical visitors, but suppose you play as best you can?'

She mouthed 'ecclesiastical?' in bewilderment, but evidently put the question aside in favour of the more-important piano. Conrad found himself assessing her as if she were a stage-role. There was nothing female in how she flipped aside the tails of her coat and sat down, or how she addressed the keys. She took a sheet of music from inside her jacket, presumably of her own composing, and Conrad leaned back, listening to her play.

. . . She has talent.

Enough talent, even, to set some recitatives or other connecting material if the deadline gets short. But as for starting at the top, with a whole opera – especially one sabotaging a secular prayer designed either to compel God's attention, or make active whatever the true natural phenomenon of a miracle is . . . No.

But how do I say that?

Tullio hitched his hip up to rest on the back of the sofa while he listened. He nodded. 'In a few years. Maybe as few as five, if you want it bad enough. And if it's there.'

Conrad tended to freckle slightly in the summer. He wouldn't have been reminded of it had Isaura's face not been pale enough now to show a few sun-dots, dark over the bridge of her nose.

For all that, she was smiling.

'If it's there,' she echoed. 'I wish I knew if it came by hard work, or by being there to be uncovered – like coal . . .'

She nodded an acknowledgement to Tullio, and shot a glance that Conrad caught, which said plainly as day, *Why doesn't my brother say something?*

Because your fool brother doesn't know what to say.

'Gianpaolo' wandered across the small room to the desk, her gaze evidently picking up the gist of those letters he still had to copy and edit for King Ferdinand. Her curiosity was so innocent Conrad found it impossible to resent.

Her head came up; she looked at him brightly.

A woman who can look me directly in the eye, like a man. I wish I could find one who wasn't my sister!

'Here's something I can do for my keep, if you let me stay,' she offered frankly. 'I handled productions at the Conservatoire; I liked it. I could be your secretary.'

He had no heart to turn her away. For all he was looking at a young man about town, the ghost of a fifteen-year-old beanpole kept getting in the way.

'You could,' he said measuredly, 'if I have your sacred promise, on the grave of our father, that you'll keep everything you see secret.'

Isaura blinked. 'It's important, isn't it? I'll give you my promise. But – you know the old fraud would have gambled any information away for money as soon as look at it.'

Conrad was aware of Tullio's stifled choke, somewhere in the corner of the room.

He ignored it. Something of an idea was taking shape in his mind. It emerged out of a mist and became solid.

'I do have a violin, too.' He went to the lockable cupboard and took out the case that had survived the Dominicans' intervention. The deep gloss of Alfredo Scalese's rather-more-than-serviceable violin greeted them. He pushed the case towards Isaura.

After a little preparation, she put it to her shoulder. Conrad closed his eyes, letting the sound take him over. Once not distracted by the silhouette of the slim young man-woman . . .

She finished with a small flourish.

Conrad opened his eyes.

'Now, that you could do professionally. Right now. Today.' The room seemed very bright. 'Your professors must have told you this.'

'Yes.' The stubborn set of her mouth was utterly familiar, transcribed up to the age of five-and-twenty from somewhere near five. 'But I intend to compose opera.'

Conrad made a gesture towards Tullio. 'But not today. And

114

while you're working towards it . . . I do have something you can do for me, as well as help me with those fornicating letters. If you're willing.'

Isaura-Gianpaolo shrugged questioningly, her hands held out from her sides, entirely Neapolitan.

Conrad closed the violin case and pushed it towards her. 'The first attempt to have this opera put on has been – prevented. Consequently, every composer worth paying has left town without, in some cases, waiting to be paid.'

Isaura's eyes opened very wide.

'Whatever composer we get is liable to be – inexperienced.' Conrad reached for the kindest word he could, and saw all the others reflected in her gaze. 'I want him to have all of his concentration on the music. I know the composer usually conducts, perhaps for the rehearsals, and certainly for the first three performances. I want you to do that.'

She protested. 'If not the composer, then it's the first violin who conducts.'

'And I want you to be my first violin.'

Isaura glanced from him to Tullio and back, as if dazed. '. . . Truly?'

'Promise!' Conrad responded as automatically as if he had still been the fifteen-year-old boy crammed into a too-tight-this-year formal coat, holding on to his little sister's hand as she swung on him and gazed in awe at the Prussian kings. 'But there's danger—'

Ignoring that, Isaura threw her arms around him, hard enough to make him grunt, and hugged him like a brother. And, like a much younger sister, gave release to her excitement in a soprano squeal.

'I'll show you a first violin!' she exulted, eventually letting go, looking as if she had vital Galvanic current running through her veins. And before he could open his mouth, narrowed her eyes and dropped suddenly into quite another tone. 'Corrado, what are we involved in? Is it the people we don't talk about?'

Conrad couldn't help a snort. 'In your case, it's the people you don't know about!'

115

He sobered.

'Most of the singers, hands, costumiers, face-painters and the like will be told the Mafia or Camorra are the danger we face. If they won't defy organised criminals, they certainly won't stand up to the people we're up against, so it's better they leave.'

He rested both hands on his sister's shoulders, and looked down into her eyes.

'I'm authorised to brief only those who must know. You're one of the closest to me; it would be pointless not to trust you with what you'll see. I know I can trust you. Make your mind up what you can take an oath on. Swear silence, and I'll tell you what's happening here. If not; if you want to go elsewhere . . . no one would blame you.'

'I would.' Isaura held up her hand as if in court. 'I swear. Now tell.'

It took a while.

✦

'The fire at the Teatro Nuovo was a coincidence,' Conrad finished briskly, 'and whatever these Prince's Men happen to believe, there is no Deity for them to change the nature of!'

'There might be, if they get their opera miracle,' Tullio rumbled.

Isaura looked wide-eyed, which on Gianpaolo's face made her seem twelve years old. 'You still got the opera house struck by lightning, though, Corradino.'

'Say I have—' He jabbed a finger at her. The aggressiveness of the gesture clearly startled her.

Conrad immediately sat down on the couch beside her, giving up the advantage of height, and trying to make himself seem more approachable.

The girl's been here five minutes and I'm already subjecting her to the 'asking a question in the Royal Society' Conrad Scalese. How about Conrad-the-brother? I doubt she's been spending her time lately reading the history of the heretical American Mr Franklin.

'Say it was a miracle,' Conrad went on, more conciliatory. 'What does that mean?'

Isaura watched him carefully, as if he might be an escaped

116

patient from a lunatic asylum. 'People usually say that means God did it.'

'God did it.' *Dear God.*

Conrad stopped himself from laughing at his own thoughts, since that wasn't less likely to make him seem a lunatic.

'All right, but what does that mean? What are the phenomena men call "God"?' Conrad nested his fist in his palm, tapping the one against the other. 'How does miraculous lightning differ from normal lightning? Or are they both God's, and God just performs one at random, and aims one for a miracle?'

Isaura's eyes were even wider, if possible. 'Mother blames you for me not being devout, you know. At least, she said that whenever she was furious with me. That's why I was in the convent school for three months. Do you really think it wasn't a miracle?'

'I think it was a bolt of lightning.' Conrad took her hand, and was relieved that she allowed it. 'Look at how often God strikes down his own places of worship. Even St Mark's in Venice, with their bells consecrated to ward off the artillery of Heaven and the "powers of the air" – until the Church authorities finally decided that Mr Franklin's "iron points" weren't irreligious, and fitted them. And after that, coincidentally enough, lightning's been harmlessly conducted to the earth.'

Conrad stopped, and glared at her. He demanded, 'What are you laughing at?'

'You still lecture.' Her smile grew, and she looked teary-eyed. 'Just like you did when you were thirteen, and I was tiny – it's the first thing I remember about my big brother.'

Tullio, who appeared to have given up cleaning away the tea things entirely, remarked, 'Weren't you sweet, padrone . . .'

'Out on the street, Rossi. Without a penny. I'll even take your shoes.'

Isaura looked uncertain at that, but grinned a moment or two after Tullio did.

'In any case, the Teatro Nuovo didn't have a lightning-conductor,' Conrad finished. 'Though I suspect that has very little to do with the "heresy"' of Franklin's iron points. It's more likely to be the opera board too stingy to pay out.'

His sister smiled. It was not difficult to remember the doe-eyed three-year-old wandering fascinated after her big brother – showing a flawless ability to pass any adult blame on to him, too.

'Three months in a convent school?' he added.

'They didn't expel me!' Isaura protested immediately. 'They asked Mother to withdraw me.'

By the care with which she inflected 'asked', Conrad suspected 'begged' would be the better word.

He felt a constriction in his throat. *I've missed so much of her life. Which appears to have been remarkable, so far.*

'Do you have lodgings?' he wondered aloud.

She shook her head.

'You'll stay here,' he said, at the same moment that Tullio went over to set up the Chinese screen in front of the other, elderly couch; and make a day-bed for his master.

'If I may . . . ?' Her eyes were momentarily bright as she nodded.

Conrad put his arm around her shoulder, where she sat beside him, and gave her a careful hug. 'I know lodging with an atheist might be a social handicap, but at least you needn't worry about being caught in your shirt of a morning . . .'

'I don't think I'm an atheist.' Isaura surveyed him. 'If you listen to rumour, the Conservatoire is a hotbed of revolutionary science and heresy – which isn't quite true, we mostly talk about, well, music. Possibly I'm a freethinker.'

Conrad restrained himself from slapping his own forehead. 'What do you think an atheist is!'

'Judging by my big brother – a heretic who'd like to burn down every church in Italy?'

Conrad ignored Tullio's mutter of, 'Not *every* church . . .'

'Just most of them?' She grinned. 'Are you sure you're not more of an anti-theist than an atheist?'

'When I throw Rossi out, you can carry his bags.'

Conrad caught the slide of her gaze as she eyed Tullio Rossi.

Tullio had his arms folded, and was shaking his head.

'Heretics,' he muttered. 'First one, and now another one, worse than the other one! We're all going to burn . . .'

'You first,' Conrad invited, and watched Tullio's morose expression be succeeded by a broad smile.

After a moment, Isaura's oddly worried look lightened, and she smiled at Tullio.

Conrad let himself ruffle her hair, surprised to find himself disturbed at how short she had cut it. *Conventions have power.*

'I suppose,' he said thoughtfully, 'I should have realised. If you're happy to disguise yourself as a man and work in man's clothes, you're not going to be too worried about other social conventions.'

She shook her hair back into place with a boy's gesture. 'Still thinking, remember? Means I look at things one by one.'

Tullio, having finished with the day-bed, paused with the clean linen he was taking through to the bedroom. 'I've seen miracles, though. Seen it on campaign. Men in the surgeon's tent lived who shouldn't have, because a priest came round, or a hedge-witch.'

Paolo-Isaura visibly hovered between treating Tullio Rossi as a servant or her brother's friend, and enthusiastically settled on the latter. 'Someone they believed could help them. And how do you know these wounded "shouldn't have" lived? A different doctor might have given a different opinion—'

'—Because I know what happens to a man when his guts are laying outside his belly and covered in mud—'

Perhaps by association, Conrad noticed that his wounds had opened again, where the steel had chafed his wrists. Enough to make blood stain his shirt. Since Tullio looked fully engaged with Isaura's argument, he left both of them alone and eased off his coat, and set himself to washing the wounds and gathering bandages. His attention didn't return until, he realised, voices had risen to a steely loud pitch. He looked up from trying to fasten a bandage around his wrist, to see Isaura leaning on her hands on the table, glaring across at a Tullio Rossi who had one boot up on the neighbouring chair, a bundle of sheets balanced on his knee.

'—And I've seen a man with his eye knocked into his skull recover and see again—!'

'—You can try to put me off with gruesome examples as much as you like, Signore Rossi, but these things have to be examined—'

Conrad slammed his hand flat on the table. It made his sore wrist ache, but produced a loud enough sound that both shut up and turned their heads to stare at him.

'Yes. Consider the Returned Dead. Spectres. Ghosts, and other hauntings. Not miracles, but so far inexplicable,' Conrad said to Isaura. He added, 'Tullio, you also know damn well that men died who shouldn't have. Whatever a miracle is, not everybody gets one.'

Both of them subsided – Tullio with a look as though he had just recalled he was arguing, unrestrainedly, with his master's sister.

Conrad studied Isaura, and saw no similar realisation that she had been arguing with a servant as if he were a gentleman.

Because Tullio's closer to being my brother than my servant? Or she could be a social heretic as well as a religious one, and still be sticking to the principles of the Enlightenment.

As if I didn't have enough trouble!

He smiled, nonetheless.

Tullio Rossi dumped the linens and came round the table and took Conrad's right wrist, tutting at the clumsy attempt at a bandage, and picking up a new strip of old sheet to try again.

It took Conrad a moment to realise that his left hand was gripped as well, and that Paolo was cleaning the minor wound with a damp cloth and frowning concentration.

'You can't expect to hide a whole opera production . . .' she observed absently.

'Misdirection is the intended route, rather than trying to conceal us. I'm also given to understand we have our own watchers, spies, secret police, and so on.' Fear made a reappearance in the pit of his stomach. 'I really ought to send you home.'

Paolo ignored the addition as if he hadn't voiced it. She tied the bandage off neatly.

'I'm in!'

✦

Gianpaolo-Isaura proved her worth as a secretary within two hours the following morning: she streamlined the copying of Ferdinand's letters and handled the start of auditions from outside

the city with enviable speed and skill. And all the contract negotiations. Conrad, who had thought he might have to spend a few
days instructing her, realised by lunch-time that she was not
only handling correspondence and interviews, but keeping the
accounts as well.

'Thanks,' Tullio observed, as the three of them ate pasta bought
further down the street. 'It usually takes me weeks to convince
the padrone that he's superfluous; you've done it in a morning.'

Conrad, impelled to a fraternal defence, warned, 'Tullio—'

And realised that Gianpaolo's response had been to stick out
her tongue at the ex-soldier.

She followed that with a cheerful résumé of those gestures she
had learned in Napoli's streets, demonstrating both her attention
to detail and phenomenal memory.

'The padrone isn't useless,' she retorted, twirling pasta on her
fork. 'That's why he shouldn't be wasting time handling the con-
tract-work when he should be writing a libretto!'

'You know,' Conrad said, pressingly aware of his lack of even a
subplot, 'you're right.'

Isaura and Tullio mugged surprise at him with a remarkably
similar humour.

'Of course you'd both join together to bait me,' Conrad observed,
amused. 'I realise I have lackeys, now. It's traditional to harass the
master.'

Isaura-Paolo poked his shoulder with a stiff forefinger. 'Then I
suggest the master gets to work . . .'

Conrad duly sat and meditated an hour or so, knowing better
than to prod his brain for an idea, but letting his thoughts wander
where they might – hoping for something to emerge from the
fog, as it always inexplicably did. Isaura went down to meet a
ship from Marseilles, supposedly carrying the Corsican castrato
Armando Annicchiarico. And a messenger arrived not long before
the siesta, carrying an envelope closed with the royal seal.

Conrad tipped him, broke the wax, and pulled out a sheaf of
papers.

'Not more reading,' Tullio muttered, from where he sprawled in
front of windows in which the glass had been replaced.

'Salvatore Cammarano's notes for the first counter-opera. His libretto got burned, apparently . . .' Conrad was unaware of anything for the next half-hour. When a ceramic edge nudged his hand, he took a mug of wine from Tullio. It didn't improve what he read. 'It's as bad as the King said it was. We do have to start from the ground up. I don't know what Cammarano was thinking . . .'

'Maybe,' Tullio sounded cynical, 'that these Prince's Men would break his knee-caps, if he turned in something decent?'

'Or that his final drafts are much better than his first?' Conrad pushed his chair back and stood up. 'If anyone calls for me, take a message, will you? I'm going down to the Palace library.'

'Do this, do that, take a message.' Tullio's grumbling held a badly disguised tone of amusement. 'It may not be really hot yet, but you know what? I'm taking a nap, padrone. Wake me up when the next catastrophe happens.'

'If there was any justice, Rossi, you'd be struck by lightning!'

'Nah. I leave that to my betters and social superiors. Particularly those who ended the Battle of Maida with a splinter from an artillery carriage in their bums . . .'

'And isn't it a pity we're not writing a one-act Neapolitan comedy.' Conrad couldn't suppress a smile. 'Heroic as that might be, I don't think it's going to carry me through four acts and a whole evening!'

✦

He grabbed up his hat, cane, and gloves, and summoned a carriage, since even in early spring, now, it had turned too warm to walk comfortably down to the Palazzo Reale and Ferdinand's libraries – an enviable collection, and unusually scientific for a European monarch.

As he was jolted over the cobbles, Conrad worried like a mastiff at the idea of a suitable subject for his libretto.

Classical tragedy? The life-story of some historical figure? Rossini and Colbran between them grabbed all the major historical heroines . . .

The coachman reined in slightly, muttering. Four men in double-breasted greatcoats, only two of them wearing their tall hats, and the burliest with a carriage-whip clasped behind him, stood in debate in the middle of the street. There were any number of children over six and under twelve scattering around unsupervised. Four, playing tag, darted across in front of the horse. Conrad caught sight of a groom in a muffler, standing by his master's carriage, who was evidently taking the time to show off the fine points of the dun mare to more of the brats.

The coach swung back to pass three women in shawls and bonnets, with a child in plain blue shift and a white coif.

Here there were no pavements, and groups of people chatting occupied all the road. Approaching the palace, which did have pavements, the couples and groups more reluctantly left the centre of the road clear. The carriage slowed, nevertheless, for a rifleman in a cockaded hat walking with his arm around the waist of a woman – her red dress and bonnet and white shawl of sufficient quality to make her sweetheart or wife rather than whore.

And slowed again, for a trooper wheeling a barrow piled high with ammunition boxes.

Conrad sat back in his seat with a groan. *This is my audience.*

These are the people who will come to every performance and comment more knowledgeably than the Master of Music at a conservatoire. Some come to be a composer's claque and hiss his competition. Most of them come to the Teatro San Carlo with a better ear for voice and music than any house in Italy. And these are the people who have to be seized up into passion by King Ferdinand's opera.

I'm approaching it the wrong way. Any average work won't do it.

So that leaves me looking for a subject that they won't expect, but will love. And Ferdinand wants it done in six weeks.

Conrad opened his mouth and shut it again.

I wonder if it really compromises my atheism to swear by hell-fire and bloody damnation!

He left the carriage and found his way to the smallest of the King's libraries, which was the one best stocked with good translations of the classical Greek and Roman authors. He read omnivorously for hours, only occasionally interrupted as functionaries

123

and courtiers wandered in and out. None of them paid overt attention to the books that piled up by his elbow.

*I'd bet money that the Prince's Men have a paid spy in the Palace. Most
likely more than one. But who'd suspect me, a lowly copyist attached to the
King's Master of Music?*

*And Prince's men or not, I prefer to be considered 'lowly' when it comes
to royal courts.*

Any attention from a King, major or minor, plunges one into
the jealousy and enmity that is court politics. Make a friend, make
three enemies, as the proverb goes.

Of the half dozen other men who occupied chairs in the library,
all had the look of genuine scholars or Natural Philosophers – it
spoke well for Ferdinand Bourbon-Sicily that his court attracted
them, Conrad thought, going back to the passage in Seneca that
he had been puzzling over.

A coil of cold wind snaked over the back of his neck. He felt all
his hairs stand up.

A sepulchral moan echoed through all the bookcases, and the
heights of the vaulted roof.

It swelled into a groan of spiritual anguish.

One annoyed academic voice hissed, '*Sssshh!*'

Conrad was broken rudely out of communion with blood-
drenched love affairs (not to mention incest, patricide, vengeance,
fraternal treachery, and other promising subjects). He looked
wildly around.

An old man in scholar's voluminous robes sniffed, returning
pointedly to his leather-bound tome.

Searching for what had disturbed him, Conrad instantly saw
the translucent shimmering form of a ghost.

The spectre drifted through the main library table, ignoring how
it cut its body off at the waist. The skirts of its formal velvet coat
swirled through the page that Conrad had been reading. White
eyes looked down.

'Conrad. Son!'

11

Conrad marked his place in his book with his finger and regarded his father's ghost.

'Father.'

The apparition wore court dress, as always, as if prepared to give a recital at a moment's notice to some German princeling or Neapolitan count. The ghost of Alfredo Scalese was too familiar a sight to surprise Conrad very much. He calculated that it was a rare year that went past without one or two visits by the man.

Several of the other users of the library gave pronounced harrumphs at the impolite manifestation, and went back to their books.

'I comfort myself, sometimes,' Conrad murmured, hardly above a whisper. 'With the thought that at least you're only a spectre. If you were one of the corporeal Returned Dead, you'd be much more intrusive.'

The ghost laughed. It had a chilling quality, although Alfredo's round face held nothing but amusement.

'I'll never understand how a son of mine could be so fond of work.' Alfredo shook his head, his white hair twisting on an unseen wind. 'The day's done. If you were to walk down by the Mercato, I guarantee you'd meet a dozen pretty girls.'

Bluntly, Conrad said, 'Go away, Father.'

'Oh, you snake's tooth!' His smile was roguish, clearly still dwelling on hypothetical girls. Alfredo's teeth had been a good colour and regular before he died; they were blinding white now. 'I recognise that temper: that's your mother in you. Used to give me hell sometimes . . . Why don't you get out and enjoy yourself, son?'

Conrad wondered how closely his father's ghostly existence allowed Alfredo to examine the lives of others. *Will he know if I lie?*

'It's very simple.' Conrad lowered his gaze determinedly to his book. 'If I don't work, I don't earn. If I don't earn, I don't eat.'

'Oh, you could eat on what you earn in half of the year! Live well, too. If you didn't insist on this ridiculous plan to give your money to other men, when my debts died when I did.'

'The law disagrees with you!'

'Fuck the law, forwards and backwards!'

'SSSSSHH!'

All four of the remaining scholars were glaring when Conrad looked around.

He swept his notes up and crammed them into his pockets, and strode to the far, deserted end of the library, sinking into a wing-backed chair there. It did him no good: Alfredo Scalese's ghost glided effortlessly beside him.

Conrad couldn't help a low snarl. 'There speaks the man who changed his name to avoid his debts! Not that it worked. They still pursued us all round Europe.'

Alfredo's gliding figure shrugged. 'I only changed to an Italian name to get a foothold in the opera business. Many men have done it! Look at Johann Simon – beg pardon, Giovanni Simone – Mayr . . .'

About to cite everything of Mayr's early bel canto from *Ginevra di Scozia* to *La Rosa Bianca e La Rosa Rossa*, set against his father's lack of any produced opera in his lifetime or after it, Conrad fell into an ambiguous silence.

True, Alfredo Scalese ended up in debt and couldn't support a family and died in early middle age, but he could at least compose functional court music, and his son never has . . .

The court dances never brought forth any miracles, either, but Alfredo had the ambition to try writing music for opera. Conrad felt again the suspicion that being a librettist meant he had turned out a disappointment to his father.

'. . . And why not welsh on the rest of my debts – especially those owed to respectable businessmen?' Alfredo cut short his attempts to jolly Conrad into unreliability. 'Only tell me . . . why should my son be wasting his life away in unhappiness, over something as unimportant as money? I promise you, after you die, nothing counts for less.'

It might be the more-than-mortal vision of spectres that allowed Alfredo to perceive his moods, Conrad thought. *Or, despite his comparatively early death, Alfredo might just know his son that well.*

'I have a chance to succeed in my ambitions,' Conrad said quietly, standing and concentrating on the small shelf of books above a solid desk. *Some men can't see ghosts; better not to be seen talking to myself.* 'I'm composing another libretto. For the early summer season, perhaps.'

There was nothing else he was free to say, even to a spectre. He thought it unlikely Alfredo was able to gossip to other ghosts, but a promise of silence is a promise.

'And you need help with a libretto?' Alfredo drifted close enough to survey the books Conrad was taking down at random from the shelf – large travel books and atlases for the most part. He intersected Conrad's arm, and was chill as the wind that sent clouds trailing rain across the Bay.

'Myself, I had once considered a rewrite of *The Vestal Virgin*, but everyone and their mule produces a version of that! Illicit lovers condemned for letting the Vestal flame go out, it's so tempting—' Alfredo checked, and snorted. 'Then again, Venus shows her forgiveness by lighting the altar-fire again with a lightning-bolt. I should suppose you've had enough of lightning!'

Conrad winced.

'I'm sorry, Father.' He deftly avoided a move by the spectre to hook a transparent arm through his. 'I have to work.'

There were a dozen books he would like to have taken home from the library, but only for interest's sake. None gave him an idea.

A gentle, non-spectral cough drew his attention.

Conrad looked up to see Luigi Esposito removing his hat, and smoothing back his hair.

'Intercepted a complaint,' the police captain said.

Alfredo Scalese clapped spectral hands. 'At last! What has my son been up to?'

'A complaint about *you*,' Luigi said, with far less good humour than Conrad had seen him display in a long time. 'You disreputable old ruffian.'

The local police chief prodded in Alfredo's direction with a dusty forefinger, and, despite incorporeality, Alfredo drifted back a yard or so.

'If you were alive, I'd have you in debtors' prison so fast you couldn't blink!' Luigi shot Conrad a shame-faced look. 'I know he's your father. I just wish he was here to pay for his own sins.'

I just wish he was here, Conrad surprised himself by thinking. He didn't voice it, for fear both of seeming weak, and of giving his not-mortal sire ammunition for a later date. *Yes, I know what he's like, but he was my father.*

Luigi, constrained by no such past emotions, said, 'Begone, before I fetch an exorcist!'

A spatter of applause came from the occupants of the King's library as Alfredo Scalese drifted off through one wall.

Captain Esposito elegantly perched himself on the desk, pulling out books at random from the shelves and flicking through them, ignoring the dust on his white gloves. 'I've had occasion to rebuke you for your father in the past. And I dare say I will in the future – the older generation are quite disgraceful in their morals . . . Not your fault, of course . . .'

'I'm glad you realise that—' Conrad, re-shelving books as fast as they escaped Luigi's butterfly-interest, stopped as one fell open between his and the police chief's hands.

He set the large book down on the library table, open at one of a series of full page engravings.

Massive jungle terraces rose to a sky full of brilliant birds . . . Ancient cities crowded with soldiers in feathered head-dresses, carrying obsidian swords . . . Stark step-pyramids stood out against a dawn or sunset sky. Dark serpentine ferns edged impenetrable jungle, and Conrad saw Cortez upon the shores of the Americas, and a volcano new to an Italian audience, because it rises threateningly above an Aztec civilisation—

Conrad exclaimed in satisfaction. 'Got it!'

The last engraving was a close-up. The top of a terrifyingly steep step-pyramid, with a bloody altar on the summit. Dead warriors in jaguar furs sprawled on the steps. A woman in nothing but diaphanous white robes and a crown was tied screaming to the altar. A priest in a man-bird mask raised a stone dagger over her heart. In the foreground, their obvious wounds bleeding, two men duelled, one evidently a native and one a European.

The caption below read *The sacrifice of the Feathered Serpent, Quetzalcoatl.*

Luigi Esposito had finished dusting off his gloves, or given it up as a bad job, and read while leaning over Conrad's shoulder. 'Try rhyming that in a verse!'

Conrad ignored him, staring down at the black and white image.

'Wonderful!' Conrad closed the book, as soon as he had it memorised. 'A tragic romantic triangle between the Aztec Queen, an explorer – Hernan Cortez, maybe? – and one of her subjects . . . her chief General or War-lord, I think . . .'

'And both of them too busy fighting each other to notice she's being slaughtered by the Wicked Priest?'

Conrad snickered and caught himself. 'You wait. You'll take this seriously when it's the climax of Act IV.'

'Oh, Act II, wouldn't you say?' Luigi beamed. 'I'm sure there's a lot of story to go after that fracas. Shame there isn't an Aztec police chief there to put the lot of them in jail.'

'Including the blood-thirsty priest? Don't tempt me.' Conrad closed the book and tucked it under his arm, since there was just room. He nursed the indescribable satisfaction that comes with the emergence of the seed of an idea. 'Not sure if this is *seria* or *semi-seria*.'

Instinct told him that the black opera itself would be tragedy. In some ways, it's easier to arouse acute emotion when the ending is tragic.

But that doesn't mean something with comedic or joyous

129

elements wouldn't work just as well to counter it. There are different acute emotions for the *lieto fine*.

Conrad added, aloud, 'I doubt the censor will let me kill a Queen on-stage, even if she is a foreigner. So I may defy the current trends and manage a happy ending.'

'Really, those are so unfashionable since the censors started allowing us tragic dénouements . . .' Luigi smirked.

'And I've never seen you cheering when the boy gets the girl . . .'

'Absolutely not. *Giulietta e Romeo* or nothing!'

That was more usually a case of the girl getting the girl, the heroine being sung by a soprano, and the hero by a contralto or mezzo, but Conrad didn't point that out to Luigi.

The police captain put his hat back on, dusted himself down, and walked out of the library at Conrad's side. Conrad caught his sideways look that held disguised but deep curiosity. Luigi Esposito said nothing. In the Palace corridor, he checked his direction, glanced back at Conrad, and remarked, 'Chess, Thursday?'

'Of course.'

The police captain sketched a salute, and sauntered off.

Major Mantenucci won't have seen any reason to brief him, Conrad realised. *Maybe he can be brought in under the pretext that we face organised crime? Or as part of the protection for the Teatro San Carlo?*

Because I miss our challenging discussions. And this isn't the first time he's been of use for ideas for a libretto . . .

✦

Most of a sleepless night was spent reading the book of South American history and making note of potential emotional situations. Lost in the beginnings of the words the men and women peopling the story might speak, he walked down to the Palace the following morning, as early as he thought he might find the small library open.

He was intercepted by one of the footmen.

'The King wishes to see you.' The man's casual contempt was accompanied by a lack of any salutation, even plain signore.

Gossip gets around. They already know that there won't be

130

a gratuity with Signore Scalese, lackey of the King's Master of Music, so why bother with him?

Conrad felt hot around the ears.

I really will have to have words with King Ferdinand. I can't blame him for not understanding that I need a salary in advance, or that paying off my father's debts means I have no more than enough to eat and drink—

'Conrad!'

Ferdinand's voice broke cheerfully in on his thoughts, calling him from beyond an open door. He waved a dismissive hand at Conrad's attempt at a bow (this time without shackles).

'Never mind all that – I have our composer!'

12

The King sounded both briskly excited and content. 'I didn't want you to further waste your time writing to lesser-known composers who've already refused – I swear I've been in contact with every composer who's ever written for the opera houses, down to the Ricci brothers—'

'There's nothing wrong with the Riccis' music!' Conrad, indignant on their behalf, remembered to add, 'Sir.'

'Oh, certainly not. But there are rumours that Signore Federico and Signore Luigi recently married twin sisters—' The Ricci being twin brothers themselves. '—And scandal says it's quite definitely a marriage of four. Whether that's true or not, we can't currently afford the attention.'

'They could have written under a false name,' Conrad muttered, but he was almost certain the Riccis had mentioned a run booked in St Petersburg, last time he saw them. Ferdinand was already striding through the anteroom towards the next ones, visible beyond a series of doors.

'I have a composer, Conrad! Come with me.'

Conrad exerted his stride to be half a pace behind the King. 'If all the professional composers of Italy won't do this, sir, who could you ask?'

Has he found some amazing new discovery, fresh from a conservatoire?

Or, more likely, it's a foreigner with a deft hand at Italian opera, a Handel or a Mozart?

Even kings are not above looking pleased with themselves, Conrad discovered as Ferdinand glanced back.

'Once I looked away from the opera houses, it was obvious! I've found you a very-well-thought-of drawing-room composer.'

Conrad halted for a moment as if the breath had been knocked out of his stomach.

He tried to cover it up by making it look like a stumble.

Ferdinand chuckled.

'Don't be so prejudiced, Conrad! There's been some remarkably good music produced by the composers of drawing-room operas.'

I really shouldn't have said that to Isaura. It's enough to make a man believe in cosmic justice.

'A drawing-room "opera" runs an hour, if that!' Conrad huffed out, not quite daring to catch the King's elbow to stop him. 'Not the two-and-a-half or three hours that a professional production runs in an opera-house! And they need only be good enough to please amiable fathers, uncles, mothers, cousins, guests! They don't need to stand the test of an audience liable to hurl down benches from the upper galleries—'

From the wince, Ferdinand had heard of that notorious occasion.

'—Or launch a barrage of cod's-heads at some unfortunate baritone!'

Conrad noted belatedly that a bearded man, seemingly in his mid-thirties, stood in the open doors of an audience chamber. Narrowed dark eyes stared at Conrad.

He obviously heard every word—

The man remarked, 'I suppose, then, I must be sure to compose something unlikely to provoke *fish*.'

Conrad bit back the *oh shite* that seemed the only possible comment.

Ferdinand swept in past the footman who had automatically thrown the final door open at the King's approach, leaving Conrad to follow him in.

'Roberto!' The King of the Two Sicilies raised his voice in a determined cheerful greeting. 'As I promised – a librettist for you!'

Conrad halted not far inside the doors, which closed behind him with a decisive click. Rich carpets and gilded furniture made little impression.

Ferdinand shook the other man's hand, and added, with pointed civility, 'Conrad Scalese wrote the script that brought lightning down on the Teatro Nuovo. Conrad, meet Roberto Capiraso, Conte di Argente.'

The dark-haired man was dressed well enough to be a nobleman. He stiffly held out his hand. Conrad shook it.

'Corrado Scalese,' he said, as he habitually did in Naples; his mind racing to somehow salvage the situation.

But – I know you! If only by sight and reputation.

'You're on the San Carlo opera board, aren't you, Signore Count?' Conrad hazarded, in a conciliatory tone.

Something of the stiffness went out of the Conte di Argente's spine. Roberto Capiraso nodded, looking as if – were he not Neapolitan nobility – he would have allowed himself to seem pleased at the recognition. 'For many years now. I inherited my brother Ugo's box at the San Carlo, and his position on the board.'

One dark brow went up.

'I regret I don't recall any professional dealings we may have had with you, Signore Scalese.'

The tone was still unashamedly snobbish, but this time not malicious.

'No. So far I've been involved with the smaller houses here.'

Every town in Italy has its opera board, in charge of matters pertaining to the local opera house – renting and owning boxes, contributing money, arguing every tedious detail when it comes to deciding what impresario to hire for which season. In Conrad's experience, every nobleman who sits on a town's opera board – and thus makes himself responsible for keeping the opera house up, usually mostly with what proceeds they can wheedle out of the gambling concessions – turned into a petty-minded, obstructive, nit-picking bureaucrat, however genuine their love of the art may have been. Roberto Capiraso, though . . .

Conrad suppressed a grin – and the next comment that his uninhibited mind had been about to blurt out.

134

You're the one Sandrine calls 'Il Superbo'!

If Sandrine Furino had indeed begun it, it had caught on generally. Conrad wondered if it had reached the Count himself yet. Conrad first heard it when Sandrine was singing the title role in *Il cavaliere d'Eon*, the Chevalier d'Eon's life-story. It was an opera much bedevilled by the Board continually wishing to alter everything, including the (vital) terms on which the impresario controlled the opera house foyer gambling concessions.

'Superbo!' Sandrine had commented – she was costumed as a cross-dressing French nobleman, for a rehearsal that the board had decided to oversee, and object to, in minute detail. She sat down with a flounce.

Since at that point Conrad was only back from Bavaria a week and still thinking in German, the mezzo further translated:

'"The Proud Man", or "the Haughty Man". But in his case, I prefer to translate it freely as "the Arrogant Son of a Bitch"!'

Count Roberto was likely five-and-thirty. He looked more. Part of that was his close-cropped pointed beard – *Unfashionable!*, Conrad thought smugly, and then wondered how he came so low as to be taking note of fashion. *I doubt the Conte di Argente worries that clean-shaven chins are required of gentlemen. He looks as if he never does what's required.*

He also looked intimidating, Conrad recognised irritably. That came from his broad long body, and his square-on stance. No slim model of fashion, certainly, but his body spoke of utter assurance.

Ferdinand stepped across the line of sight between Conrad and the Count, and Conrad felt the interruption as if it were a physical snap.

'The Count is a recognised composer of one-act pieces.' Ferdinand Bourbon-Sicily signalled for drinks, ignoring the deft palace servants as if they weren't there. 'And I know that he won't mind me saying that, while his family is noble, he handles a great deal of banking business. Gentlemen, shall we sit down?'

Conrad took a glass from the tray offered by a servant, and seated himself on a solidly comfortable sofa.

I can read the undertones as well as the next man – the King's smart to pick a man financially powerful enough that even the Prince's Men will hesitate to challenge him.

Compelled to further social conversation, Conrad added, 'I didn't know you composed music, Count.'

'No reason you should.'

In another man's voice, it might have suggested modesty. In the Conte di Argente's tone, faintly emphasising the pronoun, it invited Conrad to consider himself so far beneath the social circle of the Count's drawing-room operas that even the echoes wouldn't reach down to him.

Torn between annoyance and amusement, Conrad thought, *Oh hell, how do I rescue this?*

King Ferdinand turned back from dismissing the servants from the chamber. 'I'm sure you'll work well together, gentlemen.'

More of an order than an observation, Conrad reflected.

The Count swirled his brandy and inhaled. 'Give me the libretto and I'll see what I can do.'

'There is no libretto as yet, Count.' Conrad was proud of his level tone.

'Very well: the first Act, then—'

'Oh, can you handle more than one Act?'

The words emerged before Conrad could censor them. He avoided Ferdinand's gaze.

I may be many things, but I'm not a football – to be kicked whenever it's convenient.

Roberto Capiraso shifted his ground. 'I trust the libretto will be of some quality when it is done? I'm used to a sophisticated audience. Who appreciate art, and don't demonstrate their displeasure with fish.'

I suspect I'm going to be sorry I ever mentioned that . . .

'It isn't the sophisticated audiences who make opera,' Conrad found himself saying. 'Not the nobles who own boxes, and close the curtains so they won't have their conversations interrupted by singing. Not the mayors and police chiefs and local civil servants who hire boxes by the season. We need to hook the citizens of Naples, Signore Count. The ones that come in to sit on the lower benches, or stand in the pit, and pay night by night for their place.

They know opera – and they recognise every bit of orchestral fudge, and every note transposed for a weak singer. They come in every night of a run for three weeks, as enthusiastic and intimidating on the last night as on the first. Or they break an opera before its third performance.'

Capiraso raised a dark brow, and spoke with toneless false sympathy. 'I understand many of your works, regrettably, haven't survived the first performance. Without even an electrical storm to blame for it . . .'

Conrad caught sight of Ferdinand's face.

The King's given him Les Enfants du Calcutta *to read . . . Wonderful.*

Conrad managed a careless shrug and returned the shot. 'You'll need to visit the San Carlo, Conte. Check its size. I know your productions will have been held in the drawing-rooms of aristocrats . . .'

Conrad gazed up at the extravagant plaster wreaths on the ceiling, apparently innocently.

'. . . You could hold a one-act opera in the Teatro San Carlo – and a circus too; likely both at the same time.'

Roberto Capiraso blinked, his heavy lids giving his eyes a lizard quality. 'Up until now, signore, I have never participated in a circus.'

'Gentlemen!'

Ferdinand Bourbon-Sicily rose to his feet, signalling impatiently that they should keep their seats. He paced the room agitatedly for some moments.

He turned on them, his back to the bright windows. 'Let me explain, gentlemen—'

'I apologise, sir,' Conrad said, before Ferdinand could continue. He offered a conciliatory nod to the Conte di Argente, who appeared to have some cutting remark just aching to leave his tongue. 'This opera is vital, sire, and no idiot should stand in the way of it. Certainly not the ones who are supposed to be assisting you.'

Roberto Capiraso returned the nod of acknowledgement, his remark left unspoken. 'I – believe I understand what's at stake. I shall be pleased to have an associate who understands the mysteries of a libretto.'

The bearded man's concession warmed Conrad. *Both of us behaving like schoolboys – it must come from having five weeks now to produce an entire opera . . .*

Ferdinand leaned forward on his satin-backed chair. He said crisply, 'We're not here to debate the merits of drawing-room operas versus the cut and thrust of commercial life. Corrado, be aware I've read the Count's scores; you have no reason to fear any lack of talent or commitment on his part. Roberto, you've studied Signore Scalese's libretto for *Il Terrore di Parigi*; I think I need not say more. Can I assume you'll work together? You both know what is at stake.'

Conrad's *yes* came a scant fraction after Capiraso's.

Ferdinand smiled his brilliant, entirely open, smile. 'Good. I understand from Conrad that we have some of the primary singers?'

'Three, sire.' Conrad added reassuringly, 'We have four sets of church choirs who are used to singing in the chorus; we have the San Carlo's notoriously good orchestra; and Michele Angelotti's crew have signed on to do scenery and stage machinery.'

The King nodded, pleased. 'And a first violin willing to take on the business of conducting the orchestra, as I understand it. I assume, Count, you'll want the time to compose, rather than to conduct your own rehearsals? In that case I see nothing more except setting the pair of you to work to produce a libretto and a score.'

It was unwise, and very likely because Roberto Capiraso was frowning and looking likely to protest, but Conrad couldn't resist repeating airily, 'Of course, Highness – people put on operas in five weeks every day . . .'

'I dare say they do, in the commercial sphere.' Roberto Capiraso very evidently had no idea there could be any objection to his remark. 'My last work took me the better part of two years to compose.'

'Don't worry,' Conrad advised amiably, 'I'm sure you'll learn to compose faster now.'

Capiraso gave him a suspicious look.

Just as the man turned back to the King, however, Conrad saw a small quirk of the lip that might have been a restrained smile – as if, having crossed swords and found his attack returned, the Conte di Argente was both challenged and satisfied to have found his opponent not a walkover.

Perhaps this won't be so impossible after all . . .

'Good!' Ferdinand clapped his hands and stood – barely giving his subjects time to scramble to their feet as well. 'I'll show you where you'll work.'

✦

Another trek through endless baroque rooms succeeded.

With a view to being amiable – and, it occurred to him, saving considerably in work and time – Conrad asked, 'Is it absolutely necessary we have a full four act opera?'

Roberto Capiraso's dark brow went up again. 'I know Signore Donizetti has put on some singular one-act operas for court performances at the San Carlo.'

Conrad nodded thoughtfully. 'Luigi – Captain Esposito – recommended me to see his *Elvida* if it was ever revived.'

Although that, Conrad remembered, had been more to do with the striking girl who played the villainous king's sympathetic son, in tight-fitting white breeches.

Ferdinand beamed back at them amiably. 'Court performances can be remarkably stuffy. Don't think I don't know! Nobody allowed to clap until the King applauds . . . Pah! And no composer wants to use his best music, because there'll only be the one performance. Signore Donizetti is a notable exception. All the same, I think to build up the emotional power, we're liable to need a performance open to the public, and a full four acts.' He frowned. 'Given what my astronomers say, it may have to be an afternoon rather than an evening performance, keeping in mind what time the partial eclipse begins. We can't be caught beginning too late . . . but I would sooner have had an evening audience.'

Ferdinand took out a pair of keys from his pocket, and himself let them through one door into an obscure anteroom, and through the next door into what had plainly been one of the Palace's libraries.

This room had windows that opened on the Bay, but was smaller, and the walls were lined with locked cupboards and locked chests. A number of statues occupied crowded shelves, and two huge green-topped desks took up all the centre of the room.

An upright piano stood by the window, incongruously pushed into too small a space.

'I was thinking, since yesterday, how to solve the problem of how confidential your work must be, both of you . . . This will be your place of work, gentlemen,' Ferdinand Bourbon-Sicily announced.

Conrad's gaze focused.

He realised that he was staring at one of the marble statues set out on the shelves. The stone still had the dry remnants of dirt in the crevices, looking as if it had not been cleaned since excavation from some Roman archaeological site. It stood twelve inches tall, and was the figure of a satyr. Conrad at first thought the shaggy figure, half-goat and half man, was holding a tree-trunk.

What projected up past its wicked grinning face was its phallus. Its cock was almost as large as the creature itself, and the carved satyr needed to support it with both hands.

Conrad mouthed an 'oh', which he meant to say aloud, but found himself lost for a voice.

'This is Naples' secret museum,' Ferdinand continued, blasé as any collector of classical artefacts. 'Some years ago the Church made representations to me that having the more – unrestrained – Roman and Greek statues on public display was an incitement to sin. I had them collected and placed in here. These galleries are always kept securely locked, and guarded, in case of theft. It takes two letters from recognised classical scholars for any man to be admitted – and the curator has been given orders to defer any such requests. I had the piano put in here this morning . . . Is this acceptable, gentlemen?'

Roberto Capiraso was not blushing – he had the look of a man who had not blushed since the age of twelve – but he did look a little startled. 'Ideal, sire.'

Conrad collected himself enough to agree. 'Yes, sir.'

Ferdinand gazed at them both with a deliberately cheerful expression.

'I'll see that you both have keys. They are not to be given into the care of any other person, no matter how much you trust them.'

Conrad dumbly nodded.

Ferdinand dusted off his gloved hands, and looked fondly around at the erotica. 'No one will be surprised to find this room locked. Which it will be, gentlemen, when neither of you is here. Please take great care with any of your working documents. I assume you've spent time considering ideas for the libretto and the music we need, and that you're ready to begin? Remember, Roberto, Conrad: we have just under five weeks to our first night.'

The door closed behind the King of the Two Sicilies.

Roberto Capiraso looked around at the numerous man-beasts engaged in acts of fornication – and visibly eradicated them from his notice. He said absently, 'Was it "Corrado", signore?'

I wonder if I shall be free to call 'il Conte' Roberto? Amused despite himself, Conrad said, 'Corrado or Corradino – or Conrad – depending on how Italian you'd like me to be.'

'You're not native to Italy?'

Conrad would not have noted it under other circumstances, but alert as he was, he noted that Il Superbo seemed to relax slightly at that. He put it aside for later thought.

'Born in the other Sicily,' Conrad answered, 'but bred up mostly in the German states. My father was native to the Duchy of Bavaria.'

'Very well, Corrado. I am Roberto.'

He's genuinely intending to be friendly.

He just can't help sounding like he has a broom up his arse.

But Ferdinand's chosen him, and I have to have a better reason than that not to work with him.

'Roberto . . .' Conrad opened the various desk drawers, looking for paper. 'The Argente family is Italian?'

'Now.' The Count took a sheaf of paper marked with staves out of his inner coat pocket, and moved cautiously towards the upright piano. 'But Spanish in origin. We moved here recently, some three hundred years ago, when there was war with the Arabs and Hebrews in Granada, and the Counts of Argente wished to live at peace . . . You and I appear to take in considerable amounts of Europe between us – one hopes, it will spark fresh talent.'

The Wars in Granada were a melange of bright armour and heraldry in Conrad's mind. 'A shame I didn't know about your family history before. It sounds an interesting setting for a libretto.'

Roberto struck middle C, listened, and unexpectedly smiled. 'A good sound considering this is an upright piano . . . I'd thought perhaps something more exotic than wars against the Moors and Jews?'

'Exotic.' Conrad found himself also smiling, at first with relief, and then with enthusiasm. He put down the book of engravings that he still carried with him. 'I think we can contrive something exotic. Look at these plates and tell me if your music thinks them worthy.'

'I refuse to write anything purely for uncivilised flutes, drums, and cymbals!'

'I don't recall Signore Rossini sounding particularly Turkish when he put his Italian girl in Algiers – and Signore Donizetti, when he set *Il paria* in India, didn't—'

Conrad caught the glint in Roberto Capiraso's eye and realised, *I've bitten the bait again.*

He diverted himself smoothly: 'But of course, if you think it's too difficult a setting for an opera . . .'

Il Superbo smirked. 'I'm sure I'll manage.'

Conrad suppressed the urge to throw something at the man, or burst out laughing, or both. 'On reflection, I doubt the censor will let us put a queen on stage at all, so I had thought we might call it *The Aztec Princess.*'

The Count paged slowly through the engravings.

Conrad put out his own papers. 'I've noted down our basic triangle of lovers for the main plot. Our hero, Hernan Cortez, the only European explorer in South America that anyone's ever heard of – who they usefully appear to think may have been a god, whose title was "the Plumed Serpent".'

Conrad shifted the wooden chairs so that he could sit at the table, in the narrow gap between that and the locked cupboards of antiquities. After a moment, the Conte di Argente joined him.

'Our heroine, the Aztec Princess herself, is "Tanis".' Conrad went on, flicking through his notes. 'Of course, she's the betrothed of the Aztec's chief General. Every opportunity for martial music . . . Do you want to stage an actual battle between the Europeans and the Aztecs, by the way? I know the Aztecs are supposed to have been terrified by the appearance of fighting men on horse-back, like centaurs . . . Velluti might get his up-stage entrance on a white horse, but I don't think Angelotti and the stage-crew can adequately manage enough horses for a convincing battle . . .'

'There might be certain practical problems,' Roberto agreed dryly.

The Count reached out for the stack of notes detailing ideas for the plot, with such authority that Conrad didn't stop him taking them.

'Very well. *L'Altezza azteca, ossia La principessa di sangue –The Aztec Princess, Or, the Princess of Blood*. Our Princess—"Tanis"?' He raised dark eyebrows.

'"The serpent lady",' Conrad translated.

'. . . Princess Snake-lady – you have too many princesses in your title, by the way – loves the Spanish explorer Hernan Cortez, but she is betrothed to Lord-General Chimalli, Commander of the Jaguar Warriors. And I suppose his name also translates?' Roberto sounded amused.

'To "shield",' Conrad said absently, busy setting out his ink-well and pen. 'A Jesuit writer made a list of Aztec words; I think they cry out to be used as names.'

Il Superbo gave him the look of an educated man. '"Tanis" would be Greek, surely? A form of the Carthaginian Goddess "Tanith".'

Conrad shrugged, declining to be baited. 'I like the meaning. Her name in the Nahuatl language was originally "Tecuichpochtzin"—'

Even with practice at reading it, he stumbled hopelessly.

'—Which means "Lord's daughter", and we're not using it! If it helps,' Conrad intercepted the Count's visible frustration, 'she was baptised "Doña Isabel" after she converted! But "Isabella" hardly sounds exotic.'

Roberto Capiraso rubbed his hand across his face, with an odd little sigh. 'No; hardly!'

I should show willingness to compromise, I suppose, Conrad thought. 'I did consider calling her "Tayanna" or "Zayanna"; that's a name in Nahuatl, meaning "sunrise".'

He was surprised to see the other man try the names silently on his tongue, in the way that singers did.

'Three syllables, ends in a vowel – easier to scan, surely?' Roberto Capiraso cocked a dark eyebrow. 'I prefer Tayanna. The other version sounds too . . .'

'Soft?' Conrad agreed, before he realised. After a moment's silent contemplation, he drew a thin line with his pen and added 'Princess Tayanna' to the list of characters. 'We can still have a costume of feathers and snake-patterns for her.'

'Mm.' The Count turned back to the papers. 'So Chimalli loves his betrothed, Tayanna. I suggest our Aztec princess was betrothed by her late father to this Jaguar General, she won't look so flighty then when she prefers Signore Cortez.'

Conrad nodded. He took back his first page and – after tapping the steel pen nib thoughtfully for a moment – scribbled industriously. 'Better title?'

The drawing-room composer received the title sheet back and studied it.

'*Il serpente pennuto ossia La Principessa di Sangue* . . . *The Feathered Serpent, or, The Princess of Blood.* Not there yet, but improving.' Roberto Capiraso thumbed through the synopsis. 'So we have a triangle between Princess Tayanna, her Jaguar General, and Signore Cortez . . .'

'. . . And naturally both of them can't have her.' Conrad tapped his pen again. A blot fell on his clean page. 'No one in the audience will spare more than a passing sympathy for the villain, so we have to work on that aspect. Difficult when the hero and heroine obviously belong together.'

Roberto picked the pen out of Conrad's hand to make a note

of his own, and passed it back. 'Even though the Jaguar Knight General is legally betrothed to her?'

'This is opera.' Conrad smiled, very innocently. 'I've often thought that the country of origin might be Catholic, but opera itself is wholly Protestant . . .'

Roberto Capiraso leaned back in the uncomfortable wooden chair, face almost masking his amusement. 'And why would that be, Signore Heretic? There have been many operas on Catholic heroines.'

'The subject of operas might be Catholic – Signore Donizetti's English queens and rebels – or it might not be. Example, the Romans of Spontini, Mercadante, Pacini. But the format of opera is Protestant.' Conrad idly drew spider-legs from his ink-blot. 'Everything is about the individual, not the family or the congregation. The individual's emotional development – their "spiritual" health, if you like. Love, hate, loyalty, guilt, bliss . . . all of it has the highest priority. In the case of our love-triangle – love is the law, and the Law counts for nothing.'

Roberto Capiraso mouthed, 'Protestant!' under his breath, went to get his own pen, and continued making marginal notes on Conrad's papers.

'It gives us a first scene,' Roberto added. 'Chimalli waiting in the palace – they must have palaces! – for his betrothed. His Jaguar Knights with him: bass and high-bass chorus. He confesses his love for the Princess, looks forward to their marriage. A message arrives: she isn't coming, she's giving an audience to the stranger, Cortez – this isn't the first time this has happened. Our Lord-General bursts into a cabaletta of vengeance. Delays the entrance of heroine and hero, which is always good.'

Conrad seized his pen and began to scribble the synopsis down.

All right, maybe there's one drawing-room composer with a grasp of the necessities of opera.

There was little enough of the plot filled in otherwise, so he was not surprised when Roberto didn't comment again until he reached the end.

'So, the finale, Cortez and Princess Tayanna . . .'

The Count read on without further comment, while Conrad

added a beetle to his blot-collection, and gazed out of the window at the sea. Something about the brilliant play of light put him in the frame of mind to form coherent ideas.

The Conte di Argente turned over the last page, sat for a moment staring at the secret museum, and finally said, 'I understand that the end of this opera is particularly important. Do you think that what you have here is adequate?'

The word made Conrad flush hot. 'No. It's a place-holder. Given how difficult it is to see what an adequate *lieto fine* might be, I've sketched in a tragic ending. Now that the censors allow it, such endings are very popular, and the death-scene of two lovers sacrificed on the step-pyramid—'

'—Is very like the two lovers going to Madame la Guillotine together at the end of *Il Terrore*,' Roberto Capiraso pointed out.

'Are you saying I'm not original!'

Il Superbo threw his head back in laughter, short beard jutting.

'Oh, I don't accuse any opera libretto in a thousand of being original!' He caught his breath. 'It's not what's wanted by the audience. They like their shocks to come slowly, two or three times in a decade . . . I merely meant, the end of this opera relies on audience reaction, and it may be a little soon to give them something that was a *succès de scandale* a few weeks ago.'

That was almost tactful, Conrad thought. 'Then we don't sacrifice the main characters.'

He reached for the engravings of step-pyramids again.

'Maybe a tragedy could be our sub-plot? Look, here we have sacrifices of blood with a thousand warriors slain to dark gods. So we don't want a thousand warriors. Far too brutal. One will do. Or three, if we need two tasteful deaths, maybe one by poison . . .'

'Not warriors, either,' Roberto put in, his expression keen. 'Who wants to see males in jeopardy? Sacrificial maiden – no, too obvious.'

Conrad idly sketched with his dip-pen on the back of his notes, playing with designs for step-pyramids as stage-flats. 'I'd thought there ought to be a slave-girl, maybe as our soprano role? Hopelessly in love with Cortez, because he loves the Princess—'

Capiraso prodded the table with a blunt finger. 'Now loves the

Princess. Before that, he loved the slave, promised her marriage, but now . . .'

'Aria of the abandoned lover,' Conrad noted down. 'I wonder if we could get away with her having been married to him? That would give us a very good situation: he's torn between the woman he loves and the wife he doesn't.'

'That means no marriage between Tayanna and Cortez until the slave-girl is dead.' The Count continued tapping his finger on the polished wood of the table. His hand was squarish in shape, not at all the epitome of the aristocrat.

Conrad roused himself from speculations why the hands of a bricklayer might be in the Argente family tree, to hear Roberto Capiraso add:

'Is our heroine villainous? Might she poison her rival?'

'Then she won't deserve her happy ending.'

'*Che cazzo!* Very well, suppose no marriage, but she's now drifting away from Cortez in favour of one of his young captains – didn't you say there was a tenor role there? Leave a loophole for a happy ending with the right people pairing up. Not that most finale pairs would last six months in the real world . . .'

'Cynic!'

The Count made a production out of ignoring that remark. He finally tapped on the engraving, rather than the table. 'We need this high priest, too. But he can't just stand there like a bump on a log until he makes the sacrifices at the end.'

'Perhaps Cortez has a priest with him. A Jesuit, like the one who recorded the word lists. He and the High Priest of the Sun could have a duet of two basses, tearing strips off each other.'

'And trying to convert each other, no doubt? Conrad, do you *want* the censor banning us? Despite what pressure King Ferdinand can bring to bear?'

'Somewhere out there is a Church censor with a sense of humour,' Conrad murmured, sitting back in his chair and giving Roberto a grin. 'One day I'll find him.'

'When you're in jail!' Roberto Capiraso scrolled up his pages of notes, and slapped them down in front of Conrad, while he himself moved over to the piano. 'Write me some verses, poet!'

Forty-eight hours later, Conrad leaned a hand on the desk to read the stretta of Act 1 Scene 6 over Il Superbo's shoulder, frowned, and shook his head.

'The final scene doesn't have enough power. Put as much effort into it as you would the end of the second act!'

Roberto Capiraso looked first bewildered, and then annoyed. He scowled, as if temper might hide any momentary weakness. 'Very well, Signore Professional Librettist – why the *second* act?'

Conrad raked his fingers through his hair, and realised he did not look Romantically dishevelled, like the English Mister Lord Byron, but like an urchin come in from fighting in the street.

'Where does the interval come? The interval!' Conrad persisted. 'When they go out to eat and drink and gamble, and talk to their friends, and maybe don't come back to hear the rest of the opera? True, yes, you want word-of-mouth after the final act, friends telling friends how good the opera is and that they should see it. But if you don't get bums back on benches and bodies back in the Pit after the interval, you'll never make the third day when the run breaks even!'

Roberto Capiraso scowled again. Even if Conrad did note the corner of his mouth turn up.

'Very well. As much effort as would be necessary to nail a professional audience to their benches . . .'

The Conte di Argente dipped his pen-nib in the ink-pot, crossed out half a page, and began to write on the staves again, slowly, with long pauses between phrases.

✦

Two days after that, Roberto Capiraso, Conte di Argente, entered GianGiacomo Spinelli's lodgings, disguised from any observers in soundly middle-class clothing.

He tossed a sheaf of papers on the table. Conrad recognised it as the current synopsis (to Act III) and partial draft of Act I, annotated with suggested remaining voice-roles for the working-titled

L'Altezza azteca, ossia il serpente pennuto –The Aztec Princess, Or, The Plumed Serpent.

Conrad made introductions to Spinelli and the others present, and allowed the Count the pleasure of telling Sandrine Furino that she had a part in *The Aztec Princess*.

'As the Aztec princess,' Roberto confirmed – seeming rather charmed by this slight, dark-haired, well-dressed woman, and the look on her face at the news. 'Princess Tayanna, inheritor of her father's throne, ruler of the Aztec lands. Essentially a mezzo role, but I'm told your tessitura includes a strong contralto?'

'Oh yes . . .' Sandrine beamed blissfully.

JohnJack patted her shoulder as he found his own seat around the ancient parlour-size grand piano. He read with Sandrine, since most of their first duet was in place. Velluti, who should have been present, apparently thought he need not join rehearsals just yet; Conrad resolved to have a word with the man about that.

Conrad also thought he might need to step in between Gianpaolo-Isaura and the Count. However, Roberto graciously allowed the boy to play the piano, on the grounds that he needed to examine the shape of the music without distraction.

'It's the end that's insufficient,' he muttered afterwards, while the rest were engaged in tea. 'What on earth do you call this, Corradino? If you wanted to be a famous writer, you should have stuck with comedy; didn't you write a couple of successful comic operas for the Naples audience?'

Conrad found himself amused that il Conte di Argente had picked up Isaura's nickname for him, and used it without apparently noticing.

'By which you mean, all I can write is low-class Neapolitan dialogue? And Spinelli is "just" a comic bass used to singing in dialect?'

'No . . .'

It was interesting that Il Superbo did not particularly want to insult JohnJack – possibly, Conrad thought, because he made the Count's music sound sublime.

Lightly, Conrad remarked, 'I've said it before, Count. You don't understand how we do it in commercial opera.'

'And what would an atheist writer of bedroom farces understand about art!'

Conrad laughed. *I could like this man.*

'I do write more than one-act comedies,' Conrad said mildly.
'Let me hear it. What's the problem?'

Roberto Capiraso might have been startled, Conrad thought,
at how fast the others crowded back around the piano once he
started playing. He adjusted the position of the lamp, so the light
fell on the score – he had the libretto open at Cortez's entry, with
his men, into the court of the Serpent-Queen. The pages were
thoroughly covered in pencil with the freckles of musical notation.

The Count ran his fingers over the keys, calling up a jaunty
march tune.

'. . . Not bad.'

He nonetheless sounded dissatisfied. Conrad suspected it wasn't
the ancient small forte-piano's overtones he was unhappy about.

'It's not at all bad. But—' JohnJack Spinelli looked wary of outright criticism in front of Il Superbo.

There's that 'but', Conrad found himself thinking; a chill in his
belly.

*Yes. Not that I have the musical literacy to tell him what's wrong,
but . . . There. Some of what I hear from him has the bad habit of – pulling
back from commitment?*

Conrad frowned.

*Is it possible that Roberto Capiraso might be out of his depth? A medio-
cre composer, in fact?*

Or does 'Il Superbo' conceivably suffer from lack of confidence?

The Conte di Argente slammed the piano's cover down, jolting
Conrad out of his listening.

'No damn gravitas,' Roberto muttered, apologetically.

JohnJack said instantly, 'Yes it has. Play it slower.'

'That's the oldest trick in the book and it won't work—!'

Conrad noted that the Count nonetheless opened up the lid of
the piano, and let the fingers of his right hand briskly pick out the
melodic line.

'—You see, nothing! Complete rubbish—'

The basso shook his head. 'No, much slower!'

150

Roberto Capiraso re-seated himself and brought his left hand up to the keys. What had been a seaside banda march tune evolved and slowed under Capiraso's fingers, passing through a haunting aria of love—

Sandrine Furino wrinkled her nose. And got out her mirror to check her maquillage.

'Still clichéd,' she said, apologetically.

—And at its slowest tempo, the music underwent a sudden change into something that shivered the hairs all down the back of Conrad's neck.

'That's an anthem!' Paolo-Isaura whispered.

As silently as he could without disturbing Roberto, Conrad took back his libretto pages from the top of the piano, drew a line through the military chorus, and added four lines of a Hymn for the Aztec Priests:

'We compel our spirits
Out of our earthly bodies;
We ask of the Sun our God,
Who are these strange white half-horse men?'

Roberto Capiraso craned his head to read. With a complete unselfconsciousness that Conrad decided he admired, the Count sung both the High Priest's and Chorus's parts, in a rough tone straining to imitate bass, so that each voice-part overlapped his music and came in on each other like a peal of bells.

'Need a soprano voice part.' Spinelli looked as if he were startled at his own unselfishness. 'Set off the bass.'

Conrad noted 'Seconda donna?' on the page. Roberto alternated the melody between the priests and a la-la-la in falsetto harmony for the soprano – for all the potential comedy of that, the music made Conrad's chest ache. The structure of it came clear: melody stopping to let the voices carry it, and then singers halting to let the orchestra pick it up, and then all together.

The silence in the lodging rooms rang after Roberto stopped and lifted his hands off the keys.

'Write the orchestration down before you forget it!' Conrad couldn't help the grin that stretched his mouth as the other man grabbed sheet-music and furiously scribbled. 'Sounds to me like

151

entrance music! And we could even reprise it as the seed of the end of Act One . . .'

Conrad realised that the quiet was intense. The apartments around Spinelli's had ceased arguing over trifles, quarrelling at meals, and gossiping over hanging their washing. There was an air of people listening, if no one yet went so far as to break into applause.

Because so far we have only snippets, out of context.

Conrad sat back from the gossiping group and made a mental note.

The secret museum's too small, once we get a whole cast. Paolo needs to find us a more out of the way place for rehearsals.

Because we need to rehearse, but the traditional gathering in the composer's or singers' lodgings won't work. 'Hide in plain sight', yes. But not where this quality of music can be easily overheard.

13

Ferdinand Bourbon-Sicily came the following day to JohnJack's lodgings, miraculously without a tail of servants and aides. The elderly piano, tuned, but past its natural lifetime, gamely accompanied the first rehearsals.

The King followed when Roberto Capiraso eventually left the singers and wandered over to the large table where Conrad had spread out his lists for Ferdinand to see.

It's il Conte's business as much as anybody's, Conrad reflected, joining them and turning over the top page.

When he saw the King frown, he said, 'You were right, sire, about how many singers have been scared off. Then again, when there's little to choose from, the casting process happens more quickly. We don't have Signore Rossini and Donna Isabella Colbran, but we're lucky enough that we do have Giambattista Velluti. My cousin Gianpaolo—'

Isaura bowed as Conrad waved a hand to introduce him to the King.

'—Who's acting as our secretary, confirms that he's now signed the contract.'

'Finally,' Roberto muttered. 'Taken over a week.'

Conrad guessed that il Conte di Argente had not spent much of his time on the opera board in contact with actual singers.

Ferdinand, on the other hand, nodded, his expression showing pleasure at the world-class castrato's name.

'And in Signore Spinelli, we have one of the better up-and-coming coloratura basses in Italy.' Conrad unearthed a preliminary cast list, one with roles rather than character names. 'Velluti for the hero, naturally. Madame Sandrine's mezzo, set against his contralto tessitura, will make her an ideal heroine.'

The King didn't blink but, as Conrad was learning, that didn't mean much.

'And naturally enough, Signore Spinelli for the male villain. We have little in the way of capable tenors, so minor roles for them unless one turns up in the next week. We do have a very strong chorus here in Naples,' he interrupted himself, 'and none of them show signs of backing out.'

Roberto Capiraso leaned over and tapped the paper. 'We have no main soprano, and no female villainess.'

About to say something curt, Conrad realised, if only from the tension in the bearded man's shoulders, that he was not wilfully pointing out flaws. *Damn. I think he's trying to prove himself worthy.*

'We may have to have one singer fill both gaps, as things are going. You understand, sir,' Conrad turned to the King, 'Signore Gianpaolo has written to every reputable singer in Italy and the Northern Empire; but word has evidently got around that this production is marked out as dangerous.'

Ferdinand Bourbon-Sicily gave him a look remarkably like Tullio Rossi's, on similar occasions; it plainly meant *Tell me something I don't know . . .*

'This is dangerous,' Roberto Capiraso said bluntly. 'But I recognise that name you have written there, Corrado. Is that wise?'

Damn, I was hoping he wouldn't have heard . . .

Equally bluntly, Conrad said, 'We exhausted wisdom some time back. We're now working with desperate ideas and hoping they pay off. That name is there because it occurs to me that a singer whose career is on a knife-edge might be willing to sing for us.'

He glanced over at the King again.

'As far as possible, sir, I've been choosing those principals that

154

I think will be willing to work as part of an ensemble. No singing over the other partner in a duet just because they can; that sort of thing. Singers who'll be willing to showcase another singer in their star turn, because they'll get their own bite at the cherry – I'm very deliberately writing it in that form. We can't be a company of a dozen prima donnas who sabotage each other all the time.'

Ferdinand demanded bluntly, 'Who is it you wish to contact?'

Conrad interlinked his fingers.

'Estella Belucci. As I think Signore Roberto knows, she's a soprano from the other Sicily, from Palermo. I heard her once; her voice can't be faulted. However, she has a reputation in the business for being quarrelsome in rehearsal and performance. She's been dismissed more than once.'

Ferdinand looked momentarily bemused. 'And you want to offer this woman the place of seconda donna?'

'She'd be excellent for the Aztec slave-girl Xochitl. I know Sandrine and JohnJack. They're perfectly capable of keeping a capricious singer in order. Signore Velluti is reputed temperamental himself; I don't think he's liable to tolerate much dissent either.'

Roberto gave up standing in favour of drawing out a chair in the cramped space around the table, and sitting down next to Conrad. 'Sire, I don't want to quote proverbs about beggars not being choosers, but this work needs a dramatic soprano.'

Conrad caught Roberto's expression out of the corner of his eye. He gave the Count a nod, cementing a growing sense of accord.

'Very well.' Ferdinand did not quite frown. 'We have little enough time for rehearsal as it is. Bring the woman here, see if she can fill the role you have for her without disrupting the rest of the singers. I authorise you to tell Signori Velluti and Spinelli, and Madame Sandrine, as much of our excuse or pretext as you think necessary – erring on the extremely cautious side, even so. Wait before informing Donna Belucci of anything, until we know whether we, also, will have to dismiss her.'

'Yes, sir.'

Conrad searched out another set of notes, and three heads bent over the papers in the sharp sunlight.

The following day being Sunday, and nearly two weeks of their time having expired, Conrad had no idea if he would see the Count.

Roberto Capiraso, however, either did not care for his duty to attend Mass, or was neglecting it at this particular time. He arrived by eight in the morning in the secret museum, and sat experimenting with the upright piano (when he was not swearing at its tone) and the text Conrad had handed over – the castrato's entrance aria with accompanying male and female chorus.

The Count brought out a score apparently ripped from one of his one-act 'private house' operas, and it soon repeated in variations through the grotesque museum.

Conrad found himself unconsciously tapping his finger to the first two lines of the stretta. 'Actually, that's quite good . . .'

'Of course it is.'

Conrad was not wholly sure if that was a joke, or Il Superbo being Il Superbo again.

Count Roberto abandoned the piano in favour of reading Conrad's scribbles over his shoulder. 'I see you're allowing Velluti his entrance . . .'

The latest stage direction read: 'Enter Hernan Cortez, mounted on white horse, garlanded with foreign blossoms, at the head of his victorious army; the Aztecs sing their thanks to him for defeating their traditional enemies, the Amazons.'

Conrad shrugged. 'It's easier than listening to how ill-treatment of castrati singers is going to be the death of bel canto opera – again.'

Count Roberto laughed. 'I truly believe Signore Velluti has no idea how conceited he is.'

Conrad wondered if it was actually possible for restraint to make one swallow one's tongue.

He skipped ahead to work on 'the Aztec Princess Tayanna enters for her solo aria of gratitude and growing love for Cortez . . .'

Five hours, even with refreshments, exhausted his ability to shape verse for that day, after the previous week. He swept his papers together, mentally swore at the prohibition from taking them home, and locked the drawer in which he kept them.

'I'll walk with you, Signore Conrad.' The Conte di Argente put the lid of the piano down, and gave a smile made more open by weariness. Conrad waited while he locked the door, and made for that part of the Palace maze with which he was more familiar.

Poor as he was at hearing a score when he read it, Conrad still had plans for the Count's already existent one-act works.

Which are, to be honest, better than what he's producing now. If that's lack of confidence because of how important this opera is – or maybe Il Superbo not believing that he can write a false note – he'd better find his focus soon.

'We can lift at least the stretta from your *Christina regina della Svezia* for the end of Act One. Take it out wholesale,' Conrad said, as they walked down a high corridor made bright by fan-top windows. 'Just score it for the voices we've got. It would be ideal.'

'If you think so . . .' The Count sounded uncharacteristically diffident.

Conrad almost missed a step as realisation hit him.

You imbecile, you've been telling him for a week that drawing-room operas are rubbish! Cazzo! *Is it any wonder his confidence for this project is lacking?*

If Conrad was quietly amused to find 'Il Superbo' as capable of being nervous as the next man, it was not a joke he would risk *The Aztec Princess* for.

'That stretta,' Conrad confirmed. 'And maybe the first bass aria and cabaletta. It's not Spinelli's voice, but if we get a second bass – a high bass, or "baritone" as they're starting to call them – and we could badly do with one, for the High Priest – it would work very well.'

Count Roberto glanced over as they walked, for one moment looking as if he suspected an ill-timed joke.

'I have no objection.'

He sounded fully as arrogant as ever, but Conrad was not annoyed by it this time. *He's being defensive, nothing more.*

157

Two weeks gone, four weeks to go, and I may just be learning to work with my composer . . .

Roberto Capiraso rubbed briefly at his eyes, and visibly shook off tiredness. 'I'd wondered about the contralto's solo from *I cavalieri di Rodi*; it could be transposed to mezzo without much difficulty.'

'Won't need it. Sandrine really does have a remarkable tessitura.' Conrad smiled. 'I like your *Knights of Rhodes*, I think we could use more of it for Act Three – when I get the book done that far.'

'When,' the Count echoed, deadpan.

'I don't have the benefit of a spare manuscript at the bottom of a drawer somewhere . . .'

Exchanging a glance with him, Conrad met and acknowledged a look of very dry humour.

Guards passed them down the corridor to one of the royal apartments. Conrad heard the King's voice from one of the rooms ahead. Private meetings at different times of the day had become a rule for reporting their progress.

'Sir,' Roberto said as they entered a long chamber. Conrad smiled to himself and let the man make the most of his report.

The room swam as he looked away from the King, outlined against the sunlight of a tall multi-paned window. Conrad rubbed at his eyes.

Not until then did he notice that they were not alone.

The room was shaped as an L, and in the other angle of it, a couch stood before a hearth. A woman sat there, staring into the fire. *Waiting, out of the way of the men's business, of course*, Conrad thought cynically.

The light from another window, behind her, silhouetted her profile, making her features difficult to see. Her dark hair, coiled and braided at the back of her neck, was surrounded by a glowing sun-halo where curling wisps escaped from the pins. The mulberry purple-blue of her morning dress blended with the couch's upholstery, both disguising her presence, and throwing her pale skin into sharp relief.

Something in his silence must have caught her attention. Her chin came up.

Years ago, when the spine of Italy was a place for truly bad warfare, he had come back to camp from a foraging expedition and been ambushed fifty yards from safety. A man stood up so quickly that Conrad had no ability to react. He brought his hand around, holding a chunk of weathered granite, and hit Conrad in the side of the head.

In one extended, timeless second, Conrad had registered everything about the man, down to his dirty chewed nails. And everything about the fist-sized jagged stone. It was a nightmare of paralysis: his mind realised the situation quickly and his body was trapped by slow reaction.

The feeling ended as the rock grazed his head, scraping off a great lump of his scalp.

This paralysis, now, did not seem to want to end.

'Dear God—'

Conrad's voice cut off without his volition.

No, not her, it can't be her—

His thoughts simply stopped. He took one blind step forward, staring far too closely for politeness at her oval face. He could have stood all day, looking at the pale, tall woman with lilac shadows around her eyes.

'Leonora. Oh dear God. *Nora*.'

14

She did not speak or move.

Suddenly cold, he thought, *It could be a mistake – people have like-nesses, doubles – sisters – twins!*

But no woman has ever had quite that endearing mouth of hers, upper lip thin and lower lip full, always looking as if she's hiding a smile.

He knows her face, that shows her thinness. He knows that if she were to stand, she would be too tall for a woman; her head always came up slightly above his chin. But put your hands on her slender shoulders and you will feel a surprising amount of strength there.

'Nora?' he questioned.

Her lips parted as if she would speak. This close, Conrad caught a glint of light. It reflected from a tiny, triangular chip, missing from the corner of one front tooth.

Oh Lord, Leonora!

In opera, everyone on-stage freezes at the moment of exposure and revelation. *Tal momento!*, they exclaim, 'this moment'; *O istante!*, 'what a terrible instant!' Conrad understood it, in his own moment: everything in his memory was present – all in one instant – to his inner eye. Walking around the quarters of Venice (neither of them being flush enough with cash to take one of the black boats) she stumbles on one of the ridiculously hump-backed bridges that crossed a canal. He catches at her wrist but her hand slides through his. Her shoulder hit against the low bridge wall. She comes up holding her mouth. There is no blood. He's never sure if she struck the brickwork, or jarred her teeth together. But ever since, she carries the tiny disfigurement – and sets her shoulders and faces directly up at the galleries when she sings, mutely daring anyone to comment. As if anyone could see it from more than six feet away—!

He came back from five years ago to the present. 'Nora. It's me. Conrad!'

Just for a moment, he thought he saw the leap of shock in her eyes—

Fear, recognition, startled longing.

—and then an utter joy to see him again.

Missing for so long, so long—

All of it vanished, inside the double thump of one heartbeat.

The feelings flashed in her gaze, like fish scales glittering as a Leviathan rolls over and vanishes into the depths. All gone, as she looked past him towards the other men in the room.

Buried under the mask of a respectable woman.

Vaguely conscious of King Ferdinand at his elbow, Conrad said, 'I'm sorry, sir.'

'Conrad—'

He made a stunned attempt at social necessities. 'I didn't know you'd found us a soprano!'

Five years ago, six this spring. She was a whirlwind, a hurricane, a woman who could not be withstood when she made her entrance into any impresario's drawing-room, demanding that they hire her out to La Fenice, La Scala, or the Teatro San Carlo. Not as prima donna, admittedly. When he met her singing in La Fenice, she had a tiny role as Inez, the maid to the Queen of Spain. She made up for this lack of lines by her voice. As a superb dramatic coloratura soprano, she could rivet the whole house's attention with forty seconds of unearthly sound, announcing her lady's death, or introducing the villain to the heroine, or rebuking a wicked poisoner . . . Not only impresarios and aristocrats and bourgeois society began to speak of her, but audiences did.

I fell hard in love; was amazed beyond words when she returned it—

One year and one season in Venice later, after fourteen months, just before Lent, during an opera he cannot now listen to if any house revives it—

'—You disappeared!' Conrad barely noticed how hoarse his voice sounded. 'I went everywhere. Genoa, Milan, Padua – Paris and Dresden and Vienna. No one had heard anything of you— Where have you been!'

Ridiculously, all he can think is that age has not touched her in the years since he's seen her.

As his eyes adjusted to the sunlight, though, he saw violet smudges dark under her eyes, and at her temples – saw that she leant back on the couch with the acceptance of an invalid. *If she's held on to her youth, she has not managed to disguise the fact that illness has touched her.*

It doesn't matter.

Seeing her beauty, unchanged except by the lines of sickness and a certain tiredness, he wondered if perhaps Italy, France, and the German kingdoms were not enough – if he should have pursued a forlorn hope to St Petersburg; if she picked up this weary coldness there.

A rush of protectiveness overwhelmed him: he found himself desiring to wrap her up in his greatcoat and demand a carriage, so that he might take her somewhere without her foot ever touching the ground, and there look after her until she is well again.

'Nora . . .' Conrad repeated tenderly

A hand closed over his shoulder, powerful fingers digging painfully into his deltoid muscle.

Conrad was too surprised to resist as the hand dragged him to one side.

He choked on inarticulate rage as he discovered it was Roberto who had physically removed him. Wrenching himself free, he stepped forward between the Count and Leonora, shooting a fiercely protective glance.

Leonora sat up on the couch. Gold caught the light on her finger as she moved her hand. He had not seen it before: he saw it now.

A ring.

'You will have to forgive me—'

Nothing could be colder or less in need of pardon than the Conte di Argente's tone as he brushed past Conrad to the couch, and sat down on the edge, taking the woman's hands between his own, not looking at anything but her face.

'—My wife no longer sings.'

15

'I perceive, also,' Roberto Conte di Argente stated without the possibility of contradiction, 'that my wife is unwell.'

'Of course,' the King murmured, ringing a small bell beside him. As an aide appeared, he ordered, 'See the lady to her coach, and accompany her home. Count, I will require you for further business.'

The next few minutes passed in a confusion which Conrad did not attempt to follow. Leonora's white face turned away from him, and her husband's hands put her furred cloak around her shoulders, his square body shutting out the view of her.

I thought I'd forgotten – got over it – accepted that I would never find her—

'. . . Gentlemen?'

Conrad became aware someone was speaking to him.

The King, he realised belatedly. He met amiable blue eyes turned cold.

'I know both of you are aware of how crucial this opera is,' Ferdinand said. 'Either you put any personal difficulties you have aside, or else I will have to ask one of you to step down. Now.'

His tone was stern rather than furious, but Conrad had by now enough knowledge of Ferdinand Bourbon-Sicily to hear the unspoken *Damn them for this! There isn't time.*

The Count di Argente looked grim. 'Our business takes precedence over anything else. Obviously.'

I have a hundred – a thousand – questions to ask—!

Before his mouth could get him into difficulties, Conrad said, 'This won't affect the opera,' and shut it.

He made his bow and let the servants show him out.

✦

He said no more to Tullio than, 'I've found her!'

Tullio elicited the relevant facts with half a dozen incisive questions, and finished with one of his own. 'You haven't seen her now for five – nearly six – years—You sure it's her?'

'She hasn't changed.'

Isaura had sat silently listening, evidently picking up the context of her brother's feral excitement. At Conrad's last assertion, she snorted. 'If it's been five years, any woman has changed! This Leonora of yours will be nearly thirty . . .'

Conrad felt brief amusement at Isaura's tone, which clearly held thirty to be the next best thing to a hag. 'She doesn't look a day older than when I met her . . .'

His memories of Venice ought to be rubbed featureless, given how often he'd examined them, but they remained clear. *Nora's face is one of the most definite. Below him, her hair spread out all over the pillow. On-stage, lit only by the candles on the musicians' stands, singing her two lines in the moonlit Lion's Court of Alhambra in Act Two.*

War and its disastrous, pointless fighting have been and gone since then; something jerks in his chest at that memory. *It should leave deeper scars.* But his nightmares about that time in his life never undo him as completely as his dreams that he is left by her – again and again. Or else he finds her. And then wakes up, alone.

Separating out the year and more that they lived together – in the apartment room near the Accademia's colony of feral cats – from the dreams, is less than easy.

Conrad didn't sleep during the night.

The reality of Leonora's existence stunned him into a permanent wakefulness. That, he realised, and a growing dread of going back to the secret museum in the morning, and attempting to pick up work where he and – *her husband?* – had stopped.

Two carnivals passed in Venice while he was in that city. The first saw him have to put a mask on, to have the nerve to approach the young singer – the commedia Plague Doctor's grotesque bird beak, since that was the only mask left that he could afford.

She laughed at me – without any unkindness. And it was that which made me see her as human and approachable.

A year later, they made an arrangement to meet in front of St Mark's Basilica on the hour – a strong wind from the south-east had whipped up the water on the Lido, the sea backed up, and the paving stones of the Square were flooded in part. Conrad picked his way through the waters, buffeted by Carnival crowds around the Campanile, arrived precisely as the bells rang – and she was not there.

He never saw her in Venice again.

Nor in any other town he searched.

From that Tuesday in that February until today – yesterday—

No matter how he turned on the day-bed, or mashed his pillows, he was still left staring into the darkness, open-eyed.

All that surprised him about that was that he did not particularly feel it the following morning.

He made his way through the maze of Palace rooms early enough that the footmen and guards were still yawning. He put his key into the door of the secret museum, opened it, and stepped through.

The lemon-coloured light from the eastern windows outlined the solid shape of the Conte di Argente, standing gazing across the Bay. One possessive hand rested on the upright piano. Conrad hesitated, and the bearded man turned to face him.

The numerous man-beasts, fornications, and phalluses blurred in Conrad's sight.

He couldn't help but tell over the other man's name and titles, like rosary beads. Roberto Capiraso. Conte di Argente. And – Leonora, Contessa di Argente?

Conrad saw the Count inhale, his fists clenching, nails evidently digging into his palms.

'Scalese – just what is your interest in my wife?'

The possessive tone raked claws of irritation up Conrad's back. Anger freed his tongue when, Conrad realised, it probably shouldn't have done. 'She must have told you what I— You owe me an explanation!'

'I owe you nothing, you little upstart!'

'I think you do.' Conrad took several paces forward, between cupboards and desk, until he reached the piano and the window, letting his inch or two of greater height intimidate the heavier man in that crowded space.

Il Conte did not look intimidated.

Roberto Capiraso shot a look from pitch-dark eyes. 'Yes, you met her in Venice. She remembers you. Whatever fantasy you may have woven around a woman you clearly never knew at all – is irrelevant. Leonora D'Arienzo became betrothed to me in Venice, married me, and has been my wife since that day to this!'

The avalanche of his words threatened to leave Conrad speechless. Half-blind with anger, he forced out, 'She was my wife in all but name for over one whole year—'

'And she is my wife by the blessed sacrament of marriage!'

It cut off his breath – cut off, Conrad discovered, anything more he could say.

'We have work, here,' Roberto Capiraso emphasised. 'This is the last discussion I will entertain on my personal life, is that clear, Scalese? You will show my wife the respect owed to the Contessa di Argente by one who is—' The man's gaze swept up and took in Conrad in one glance. '—clearly her social inferior, and inferior in all the ways that matter.'

It silenced Conrad for sufficient time that Roberto Capiraso sat down at one of the green-topped desks, unlocked the drawers, and eventually brought out both a steel-nib pen and sheets of paper ruled with staves.

Leaving me standing here as if I were some farm-hand confronted with his master.

Conrad ignored the locked cupboards and his own manuscript. He opened the shutters to the balcony, looking out over the bright sea, and breathed in the live air.

Was he in Venice, back then? I never saw him! I never heard his name, or anything like it!

There were rumours said she'd gone away with a well-dressed young man. But whatever happened, there would have been a rumour, something like that; it's what people like to think.

I don't know, now, which of the moments I saw her in Venice was the last. Because I had not ever expected her to walk away from me.

But then she was not in his bed when he woke, not in their lodgings, and her name – in the smallest possible type and at the very bottom – had been removed from the bill at La Fenice.

Il Conte di Argente would have been, what, in his late twenties then? A rich young nobleman doing the Grand Tour after the Emperor's wars ended? And I had taken on my father's debts. We wouldn't have moved in the same circles, that's for sure.

He could have been any one of the hundreds of young men who frequented the back-stage at the opera. No names. No idea when their boat had left, or which road they might have taken away from the city of canals.

I had only the acid knowledge that Nora was gone. Alone, or with another man, or . . . How could I imagine? When I had no idea there was anyone other than the two of us in the world.

With his back to the other man, Conrad thought himself isolated – until he caught sight of the composer's reflection in the window-glass.

The Count was not looking at Conrad.

In fact, Conrad saw, he appeared to be gazing at one of the archaeological rescues on the shelves – a statue of a Pan-figure, no more than a foot tall; the satyr depicted as amiably fucking a nanny-goat.

Roberto Capiraso was not seeing what he looked at, Conrad realised. The statuette was one of those difficult to look on without reaction – not for its unabashed pornographic clarity, but because one usually couldn't regard the female goat's blissful expression without laughing.

The Conte di Argente might have been in another world. And it might have been a different man sitting there. Roberto Capiraso had the top of his pen resting against his lip, evidently taken up with his own thoughts to a degree that he was conscious of nothing around him. The lines of arrogance were gone from his features; he looked – Conrad searched for the appropriate word – as if he contemplated one of those things that have men awake at three in the morning, turning in their beds and unable to sleep.

Roberto Capiraso's distanced gaze met Conrad's, in the reflection in the glass.

The Count's expression changed to complete immobility, only a slight sneer lifting his nostrils. He made a small production of returning to his paper, and scrawling an opening phrase of music.

Everything was gone, suddenly, in Conrad's mind, except the burning sole fact: *this man is now married to Leonora.*

Whenever and wherever he met her, whether it was when she and I were together or not, she's his by law now.

Her memory was enough to wipe out any momentary sympathy for Capiraso. Conrad stared out across waves towards the green coasts of Sorrento and the Isola di Capri.

Why did she leave me? Why is she with this man?

Ignoring Capiraso as much as possible, he seated himself at his desk and unlocked his notes. And found himself staring, unseeing, as his pen dripped ink on the page.

I need to see her. And I can't. Not without messing up what chance remains of completing an opera with this man.

He forced himself to write.

Work on the libretto – without a word to Roberto Capiraso – was liberating. It took him away from the uncomfortable shared room, away from Naples, away from everything except the creation (that almost felt like discovery) of situations that would wrench the heart and gut with sympathy. He wrestled with his draft lines for Xochitl, one of the Aztec Princess's many slave-girls.

Two interlocking triangles, here. The slave-girl and Princess Tayanna both love Cortez. Cortez and the Jaguar General both love the Aztec Princess.

Around noon, gazing absently out at the bright day, Conrad found himself staring again past the bowed head of Roberto Capiraso. He immediately looked away.

169

This is an opera. How the hell am I going to work with this man on scenes of love, passion, rivalry . . . adultery?

✦

With some mumbled excuse about needing air, Conrad scrambled papers into the drawer, locked it, and left almost at a run.

I'll have to work on the Principessa and the Slave-girl, first; two women being rivals for one man. Because there's no way I can write two men who are rivals for one woman.

The swift afternoon plated gold over Naples' buildings and streets, and made a glittering dazzle out of the foreshore. Conrad let his feet choose, walking west on the sandy track past Egg Castle, under the trees. *Lazzaroni* on the narrow beach watched fishermen up to their waists, dragging nets through the water.

Conrad halted eventually, not sure why. The sunset dazzled his eyes full of glowing dark spots.

He walked the afternoon away.

He let his feet lead him back north of east to his lodgings, under the hanging branches of new-leafed trees. Twilight came and went. The sea-wind whipped his hair full of salt. He walked tiredly upstairs in the dusk.

'Padrone. Someone called.' Tullio indicated the silver tray by the door for calling cards. 'Said he'd be back later.'

Conrad removed his coat and gloves and let Tullio take them. 'Were there any other appointments for today? Is it one of Paolo's? Maybe it's a tenor who can sing . . . Did he look like a singer?'

Having hung up the coat, Tullio went back to filling and trimming his two prized Carcel oil lamps (undoubtedly looted from somewhere north of the Alps; now proudly fitted with new glass mantles). Their light swelled as he lit first one, then the other; making the room much brighter than candles. He shook his head.

'Well-dressed as a banker. Talked like a nobleman. If he's a tenor, I'll eat my boots.'

Before Conrad could read the card, the sound of footsteps at street-level gave him time enough to step onto the landing and take a look down the stairs, dark as it was.

He pulled the door to and stepped back into the lodgings. 'I don't think your boots are in any danger.'

Could the King have started finding additional patrons?

At the knock, Tullio let in a tall, slender, white-haired man, who handed over gloves, hat, and cane. Entering the area of the lamps' light, he stood revealed as a man in his early seventies, with a hawk-nose that had evidently been broken at least once, but did not detract from the man's aristocratic demeanour.

'Cavaliere Adalrico Silvestri,' Tullio announced, reading off the card after the usual murmur, 'Conte di Galdi.'

'Cavaliere,' Conrad echoed, offering his hand. 'Excuse me, I don't believe we've met?'

The impeccable old man regarded Conrad's hand in the way women in the market regard stale fish.

'I haven't come to be sociable, Signore Scalese. This is purely business.' The man clasped his own hands at his back. 'You are Conrad Arturo Scalese, sometimes known as Corrado or Corradino, is this correct? And your father was Alfredo Scalese, born Alfred Amsel?'

'I— Yes—' Conrad could do nothing but stare. To find himself surprised by his father's name, so soon after the coincidence of being surprised by his ghost—

'You'll have to excuse me,' Conrad blurted. 'My father is one of those who doesn't rest easily in his grave. I was visited by him not long ago.' *Before I met another ghost from the past.* 'Signore, if your business isn't urgent, may I request that we put it off until tomorrow?'

Surprisingly, given the man's harsh demeanour, he appeared for a moment to consider this.

'No,' he said finally, 'it can't wait, Signore Scalese.'

'Very well.'

Conrad suggested they be seated, and offered wine, but the man turned down such social amenities, increasingly brusquely.

'I need hardly ask,' he interjected, 'whether you're familiar with your father's debts?'

Conrad decided on brusqueness of his own. 'No, you needn't

171

ask; I'm perfectly familiar with each amount, and each creditor. I will ask, signore, what business it is of yours?'

The knife-faced old man put one hand inside the breast of his frock coat, and brought out a slim envelope, closed with red wax into which a signet ring had been pressed.

'It's my business,' the Conte di Galdi said, 'because I am now the owner of each. I have bought up all of your father's debts, Signore Scalese.'

Conrad couldn't make sense of the words. 'Bought up . . .'

Some intimation of what this might mean made him sit down, rather unsteadily, on the couch.

The old man shot him an impatient look. 'Do you not understand? I approached each one of your creditors; I have bought them out. What you owed to them, you now owe to me.'

It's . . . possible. Conrad's bemused mind admitted that much.

'Why would you do that?'

The Count di Galdi ignored the question.

'Your father owed five thousand scudi, at his death. There is the amount you have paid off in the past. Then the interest on the various loans . . . You may wish to look over the figures, but the total still owed is in the order of three thousand scudi.'

Conrad's fingers felt cold. *Shock. I remember shock from innumerable men on battlefields.*

'If you have all the details,' Conrad said, a little hoarsely, 'you'll see that I have arrangements with each of my father's creditors, as to how much I pay off every month—'

'Yes, yes.' The old man waved an impatient hand. 'Not good enough, signore! A scudo here, a soldi there . . . simply not good enough. I own these debts, and whatever "arrangements" you may have had with your previous creditors are irrelevant.'

Conrad found himself on his feet again. 'Signore Conte, I have no idea why you've decided to interest yourself in my affairs, but I've spent a decade in paying the debts my father owed, and if I need to spend decades more, then that's what I will do! It's a debt of honour.'

'It's a debt which you've got away without paying!'

Adalrico Silvestri, Conte di Galdi, snapped his fingers, and when Tullio re-entered (still holding the Count's hat and gloves), he took both, and gave Conrad a final scathing look.

'That's the trouble with you young men – you think you can avoid your responsibilities. Very nice lodgings you have here, while your creditors are waiting for their rightfully owed money! But now you only have one creditor to deal with, Signore Scalese. Me.'

The Count di Galdi looked back from the open door.

'And I— I am calling in your debt. All of it. Now.'

16

'Wait!'

Being forty years the old man's junior, Conrad found, meant he could spring into the doorway and block it.

Adalrico Silvestri startled back a pace.

Conrad searched desperately for words to stop the man walking away and making good on his threat. So many sleepless worries about the subject of finance left him feeling now as if the pit of his stomach were ice.

'Why have I never heard of the Conte di Galdi before this, if you know my family well enough to buy up our debts!'

With the elderly nobleman's back to the oil lamps it was less easy to see his face, but it was distinguishable that he sneered. 'You may not have heard of me, boy, but that means nothing. I knew Alfredo; that was enough.'

Something reptilian in the handsome ancient features made Conrad suddenly certain.

He may sound like a crusty old man, but he's not.

This might be an accidental personal feud with my father, from long ago – but I don't believe it for a minute.

Conrad let his gaze fall, as if he were both ashamed and abashed; it allowed him to hide his expression.

If I ever trusted my instincts . . . This is one of the Prince's Men.

Ferdinand warned me there would be attempts at obstruction. And di

Galdi will have me arrested in a heartbeat if I don't pay up . . . I wonder if I'd ever reach the jail?

'Signore Conte—' Conrad managed to speak as if he were only shocked, and not alert in every sense. 'I realise my father must have done you some great wrong. As his son, there's nothing I can say of my father, do you understand, signore?'

Silvestri prodded at the floorboards with his stick, as if that were likely to make Conrad move out of the way. 'I understand this: you owe me, Scalese.'

Conrad swallowed back every word he wanted to speak

What can I do, what will the Prince's Men not expect? Hell and damnation, I don't know!

'Sir, I ask you to grant me a few hours' grace. At the moment I have nothing. Once I've seen my employers—' Conrad made it plural at the last second, to give an impression that he had minor jobs every here and where. '—Then, I may be able to give you a quite different answer.'

The ancient aristocrat met Conrad's gaze, his expression unreadable. 'A few hours will make little difference. Expect my banker to call first thing tomorrow—and he'll bring bailiffs!'

Conrad stood back. The old man humphed, strode past with surprising vigour, and slammed the door behind him.

The front window allowed Conrad to see only a departing coach, with gas-lamps dimly showing the heraldic device on it – presumably that of the di Galdi family.

'It would have been easier if they'd jumped me in a dark alley, like I expected. My damned father! Leaving the family like this? What was he thinking?'

'From what you've said about him, padrone, he was probably thinking "the next one'll make me really rich!" Isn't that what every gambler thinks?'

Conrad clenched his fists and forced himself not to smash everything breakable within reach.

'I should be used to this by now! If I have to eat shit sandwich served up to me by some doddering conspirator, it's because of my father! If I have to pay three-quarters of everything I earn to other people, it's because of— And if— Damn it— Alfredo Scalese, answer for your sins!'

The ancient formula belonged to the Church. Conrad hated using it. Particularly so soon after the ghost had visited him voluntarily.

His one satisfaction, he thought grimly, as he watched a spectre manifest, was that Alfredo plainly believed it compelled him.

The temperature in the lodgings dropped more than could be accounted for by the deepening dark. Alfredo Scalese, or Alfred Amsel, as he had been born, manifested by Conrad's desk, one hip hitched up so that he sat on the desk's edge, and every part of his attitude speaking of the easy-going man-about-town. The light from the oil lamps shone through him.

'So soon, Corradino? How pleasant to see you again—'

'I've been quiet for nine years!' Conrad stepped as close to the ghost as he could without intersecting it, glaring into the translucent eyes. 'You're my father, I've been paying off your debt all my life, and here it is bollocking everything up again. Is there no way to be rid of these debts?'

The ghost tapped his forefinger on his lower lip; a pose so artificial that Conrad would have punched him if it were only possible.

'I suppose you might poison that old man, and burn his correspondence if you can get at it. Deny everything . . .' Alfredo shrugged, his amusement as transparent as his body. 'Really, Conrad. You can't be serious. You should do whatever you want to do. Something will always turn up.'

'You feckless son of a bitch!'

Unmoved, the ghost-image of a man shrugged. 'Being feckless is good. It's duty and honour that have you in danger of the debtors' prison, isn't it?'

Despite his father being immaterial, Conrad picked up his silver-plated ink-well that was weighted with solid lead, and hurled it through the ghost.

Tullio flinched at how close the smash came to the glass chimney of one lamp. Regarding the spray of ink up the scarred wallpaper, he muttered, 'Padrone, I know this has been building for nine

176

years, but tell him without breaking our lodgings up – we had enough of that recently.'

'Yes, Corradino.' Alfredo beamed. 'You shouldn't be so irresponsible.'

'Irresponsible.' Conrad reached blindly for whatever he could find, with eyes for nothing but his father's immaterial fatuous smile. 'So I should be responsible and default on your debt, should I? Refuse to pay? It's the law! I'm your son! Tell me how I can "fecklessly" evade your creditors and still keep the name and reputation I've been making for myself!'

The spectre lounged to his feet, smoothing down his cuffs. 'I'll come back when you've stopped throwing tantrums.'

Conrad turned around and leaned his arms on the window-frame, and his forehead against the cold glass. Rage against injustice, and shame for speaking that way to his father, left him motionless and speechless.

He saw in the window's reflective dark surface how Alfredo Scalese shook his head in apparent sadness, and disappeared.

'*Cazzo!*'

Conrad left the window, and dropped onto the sofa beside Tullio. Urgency pressed in on him.

'Is this too – too little – for the Prince's Men?' he wondered aloud. 'But I don't know who else would be my enemy.'

Tullio snorted. 'I know of at least one man who's a financier and has no cause to like you, padrone.'

'Argente?'

'Keep you out of the way of his wife, maybe?'

Conrad thought it through briefly. 'He wouldn't do it. If nothing else, he won't offend the King. He's a Neapolitan Count; Ferdinand could strip him of his estates.'

A quirk of Tullio's mouth signalled assent. 'That only leaves the Prince.'

'And we don't have much time. I'll be watched. I need you to go to the King. But change your clothes first—'

Tullio put up one broad-fingered hand, his smile sympathetic. 'I got it, padrone. Want me to wear a false nose, too?'

'I don't know about a false nose, but I could certainly give you a black eye,' Conrad grumbled amiably, watching Rossi reach for his army greatcoat, and turn the collar up against wind and spies. 'No – wait.'

Tullio cocked his head, the picture of a man waiting for instruction.

'That won't work,' Conrad said decisively. 'They will have checked these lodgings after what went on with the Holy Office. We have no guarantee they're not still watching. If they take note of servants, your face will be known.'

The ex-sergeant shook his head. 'It's all right, padrone. I understand. These "Prince's Men" – they were just a bogeyman until now. But now you met one of them, and he's smart and dangerous.'

Conrad shifted on the sofa.

Tullio thrust his fists into the greatcoat's pockets. 'I'm not going to be scared off by a gang of amateurs either, padrone. We saw worse in the war. If they was a real secret society, there'd be bodies along the foreshore from the harbour to Castell dell'Ovo, and we'd be worrying about assassination attempts on his Majesty. Right?'

'One body was enough.' Restless, Conrad stood again, and paced the small amount of space in front of the hearth.

'I know who's not so known,' Tullio inelegantly said. 'And how they could be even less so.'

'Who – oh. Yes. Yes . . .'

It didn't take Tullio long to fetch her out of the lower floor of the lodging-house, where she had been gossiping – although they were interrupted by half a dozen conversations on the way up the stairs with other tenants, culminating in the landlady. Tullio finally had to shut the door with his foot.

'Holy Baby Jesus!' Isaura remarked, or rather Paolo, Conrad registered, in smart man-about-town clothes.

Tullio sounded oddly apologetic. 'Padrone needs your help.'

Paolo smirked. 'Nothing new there. Is there, big brother?'

Their confidence buoyed him up, somehow, even if he thought it unjustified. Conrad went briskly through the visit by Adalrico Silvestri, with only a pause for Isaura's opinions of their father's behaviour – not significantly different from Conrad's.

'I need you to take a letter to King Ferdinand – to the Palace, and put it directly into his own hand.'

Gianpaolo's eyes widened, the man-about-town subsumed instantly into the shy beanpole girl. 'They might have seen me come in here. They'll know who I am. They might take your letter!'

Conrad stopped her rush of words with a raised hand. 'Look – we'll disguise you! In a dress!'

There was a pause.

The young woman in man's clothing alternately glared at him, and at Tullio Rossi. The ex-sergeant put his hand casually over his mouth, stifling entirely unmanly giggles. Conrad avoided Tullio's gaze, and the ex-sergeant as assiduously looked away from him.

Very dryly, Isaura remarked, 'Thank you, brother . . .'

Caught between laughing and feeling uncomfortable, Conrad said, 'Isaura, you don't have to do this, because I never want to put you into danger. If you do do it, Tullio will ask a couple of his mates from upstairs to go disguised as your servants – a respectable woman wouldn't be out without a pair of footmen, especially in the early evening. No one will look at you and see Gianpaolo Pironti.'

'If the Prince's Men murder me, I'll haunt you too,' Isaura muttered. 'Judging by the evidence, our family's good at making a spectral annoyance of itself – so you better hope I come back safe.'

'I do.' Conrad hugged her as if she were a young woman and his sister, not the man she was dressed as. He couldn't help the weakness of appreciating the comfort he got when she hugged him in return.

'Damn petticoats! Yes, I understand why I have to!' Isaura snorted. 'Let's get this done, then.'

✦

It was not Conrad's habit to pace the floor, but he made a circuit of checking the view through both windows and the stair-well outside the lodgings. The stairs were dark. The new gas lighting in their one main thoroughfare was not much better.

'I shouldn't have sent her.'

He attempted to sit and listen to the voices of Naples below the front room balcony, and lose himself in the search for incidents among the Aztec and European characters which would spur the emotional drama that is opera.

Ten minutes later, he was on his feet again.

There were only seven paces between the bedroom door and the living room door; he counted them repeatedly. The noise from the street outside did not die down, but he could hear nothing that sounded like violence.

'She's a woman. She's my sister.'

'She's Gianpaolo Pironti,' Tullio said, from where he sat with his feet resting on the brick hearth surround. He leaned forward and carefully placed another lump of coal in the grate, against the chill off the sea. 'And she's spent three years at that Conservatoire in Catania. After that, she either knows what to do with a pistol, or she's expert in getting out of trouble before it starts.'

Conrad halted. 'She has a pistol?'

'I might have . . . loaned her my old infantry pistol. Just the right size for carrying in a fur muff, I thought.'

Before Conrad could challenge that, the outer door banged open.

Isaura walked in with more of a stride than a young woman should.

Tullio went out to talk with his mates on the landing, and Conrad followed Isaura, who went straight into his bedroom and began unlacing her skirts and bodice without ceremony, looking with longing at her shirt and trousers laid out on his bed.

'Damn, I hate courtiers!' She kicked off her shoes. 'They gave me the run-around for hours on end.'

Conrad stepped back out of the room and pulled the door mostly closed in front of him, while she dressed; content to hold his conversation through the gap. 'You did get the message to him? When will Ferdinand see me? Tonight? It's late—'

The door opened. Isaura had her loose shirt pulled on and tucked in, and was unselfconsciously buttoning the fall-front flap of her breeches. Her cropped hair flopped out of the hair-pins that had kept it disguised under a bonnet. She ran her fingers through it, sending a clatter of pins across the floor.

'No.' Her expression was serious. 'I couldn't give him the message. The King's not in the Palace.'

Conrad stared, more disoriented than if she had been speaking classical Greek. 'Not in the . . .'

'I finally got it out of one of his damn gentlemen-in-waiting,' Isaura said. 'He's not even in Naples. King Ferdinand left the city this morning.'

17

'"Left the city".' Conrad considered that for thirty heartbeats.

Tullio's '*Vaffanculo*!' was overridden by his own English-learned: 'Fuck it up the arse backwards!'

Tullio broke the following silence. 'You game to try again, Signore Paolo?'

'Of course.' Isaura lowered her chin, having successfully tied her linen cravat. 'I planned to go back out. It was getting late for a lone woman, even with your friends accompanying her . . . Shall we?'

Conrad stood up, not realising until then that he had sat down on the couch like a sack of meal. 'You'll be recognised!'

'That's a risk we have to take.' Isaura-Paolo got in just before Tullio. 'We need to know, brother. Where the King's gone – if he left – or if that's just a cover-up story, and he's sick or assassinated.'

The enumerating of possibilities was numbing. Conrad reached for his greatcoat and hauled it on, knowing the double-breasted coat and a low-crowned hat would leave him anonymous to all except very bad luck.

Paolo objected, 'They'll see you.'

He echoed her directly. 'That's a risk we have to take . . . We'll split up; that's less dangerous. Let's meet on each hour at Antonio's.'

By mid-evening, Conrad's threadbare patience was nearly worn through. He sat in the ancient tavern, lost to view among other patrons, and saw Tullio close the door as he came in. The broad man braced his shoulders when he glanced across at Isaura, who accompanied him.

Not good news, then.

With all of them seated over wine in the packed room, heads together like every other set of conspirators or criminals in Naples, Conrad began optimistically. 'You found out where the carriages were being packed for?'

Tullio shook his head. 'Had a go at finding out what the gossip is. Think we've got the answer. It wasn't easy . . .'

Tullio held out his hand significantly, as any other disreputable man in a tavern would.

Despite the seriousness of the situation, Conrad couldn't help a grin. 'How many ducats difficult was it?'

'Oh, nine or ten, easy . . .' The ex-soldier regarded the handful of small change Conrad passed over with mild disgust, and began counting the calli and mezzicalli with his hands concealed beneath the table – the calli being the twelfth part of a Neapolitan penny, and the other worth one half of that.

'No carriages.' Isaura's alto was quiet, but not close enough to a whisper to attract attention. 'Our friend apparently didn't leave by road.'

'He didn't?'

Tullio, still counting, spoke with absent gravity. 'Word among his servants – and the people who know, because they packed the baggage – is that he had his wife—'

Conrad's memory supplied the name: *Queen Maria.*

'—And all their children, and his mother-in-law, the Old Tart—'

Ferdinand's probity had been something of a shock to the rather lax court morals when he took the throne. Conrad dimly remembered hearing of it – he himself had been in Prussia at the time. Ferdinand's mother-in-law had a fondness for handsome young guardsmen, which had not endeared her to the new regime, and had gained her any number of unsympathetic nicknames. Having met her briefly at a court-attended opera, Conrad had allowed himself to be charmed by her, and rather felt Tullio would react the same way if they ever met.

'—All packed up and put on board ship with him,' Tullio ended.

Dragging his mind back to the current issue, Conrad demanded, 'So why would he take his whole family on—' *The royal yacht, the Guiscardo, no.* '—his boat? Surely this isn't the time for a relaxing cruise . . .'

'He's not so much taking them on the ship, as by it.' Tullio leaned forward with a huge sigh. He appeared halfway drunk to a casual glance. 'Seems he's taking his family to the other Sicily, to Palermo. As far as I can find out, he'll be back. But not until he's got them all settled in for a long stay. All of his family, not just the heir and spare.'

Conrad met Tullio's shrewd gaze.

'He wants them away from Naples and Vesuvius—' Conrad hesitated, and then let out his own sigh. '—And I can't fault him for that. If I could persuade you and Isaura to leave the city, I would. Things may get very dangerous here.'

Isaura quietly snorted.

Conrad looked at her.

'As if it wasn't hairy enough leaving town ahead of Papa's creditors!' she proclaimed.

Conrad smiled. 'I thought you were too young to remember that. I do remember you prattling on, wide-eyed and innocent, distracting attention from whatever Papa was hiding.'

'I can still be wide-eyed and innocent,' Isaura said, somewhat sourly. 'Which is how we know our friend has gone to Sicily.'

Conrad rallied his thoughts. *How long to Sicily and back? How long will the King stay there? Will he need to call at other ports, if he hears anything about the Prince's Men?*

'We should go back home.' Conrad stood.

Once in their lodgings – in what he knew was a purely illusory safety – he briefly put his arm around Isaura's shoulders, for all she was Paolo at the moment.

Taking advantage of the opportunity to speak freely, she mirrored his own thoughts exactly.

'Ferdinand may also be on the track of some move by the Prince's Men. Clearly, that's important, but it doesn't help us. Without specific instruction, there's no one who will authorise such a large withdrawal of money from the treasury. No one will take your word for it, brother, that the King would want them to pay off your debts.'

Conrad grunted. 'We must know somebody . . .'

Tullio hauled his greatcoat off, movements more suited to the field than the drawing-room, and tossed it at Conrad.

The weight was surprising. Conrad looked questioningly at him.

'Got savings, padrone; they're sewn in the hem. Dunno if they come anywhere near what you need . . . Doubt it; sorry.'

Conrad found it on the tip of his tongue to speak a refusal – and didn't.

'I'd do the same for you,' Conrad said, with absolute honesty. 'But if you've got enough money to outweigh Alfredo's gambling habits, I'd like to know how the hell you've been making it!'

Tullio grinned, and handed over the very sharp small knife with which Conrad trimmed his quills. 'Tips, mostly, padrone. What I can screw out of the nobility. And no, I ain't rich, but that Count di Galdi might take it as a down-payment?'

Conrad slit the thread sewing up the coat-hem, while Isaura held her cupped hands beneath.

'If he was just concerned about money, he might . . .' Conrad snatched one penny out of the air before it bounced off into the shadows. '. . . I think this is designed to put me in jail.'

Isaura estimated the sum in her hands by eye as a hundred calli, counted it out, and proved to be almost correct. Tullio's savings were mostly small coins, with a scudo that Conrad thought it better not to enquire into.

Having stacked the coins into piles, they looked at each other, and Tullio set about threading a needle and sewing his savings back into secrecy.

'Nine scudi total isn't going to get us anywhere . . . The trouble is, people I know here are singers and crew.' Tullio shrugged.

'Moncy comes into opera hands and goes out of opera hands just as fast. Look at Signore JohnJack.'

'Well, we won't let that stop us asking, will we?' Conrad eyed both of them with mock sternness.

'No sir, padrone!' Isaura grinned, her confidence seeming to be restored.

'No,' Tullio agreed. 'You know, it's not every man who has the chance of being arrested for the second time in a week . . .'

'You needn't make it sound like an achievement!'

Isaura kicked off her boots and rubbed at her feet. 'We're too late to do more tonight. Corradino, skip work tomorrow morning – we'll go out early, avoid di Galdi's lawyers for a bit. Catch some people before they're up and out.'

Conrad slowly nodded, and then swore.

When Tullio looked questioning, he added, 'Something so simple, and it's giving us so much trouble!'

The ex-soldier continued on his way to the food cupboard, and hauled out another bottle of wine. He removed the cork and set it down on the table, with a sly smile. 'Drink and you might sleep, padrone. Let's drink to God sending us stupid enemies in future, shall we?'

✦

Sleep evaded Conrad, except for the coldest hour, before dawn. He got up from it and moved around briskly, to stir the blood. The starless grey sky felt as though it shut him in.

When the city was rousing, they put on coats and left without attempts at disguise.

'Too late for that now,' Conrad said, buttoning his coat up to his throat in the damp sea-fog. 'If the Conte di Galdi expects us to be doing anything – this is what he expects. Likewise the other people.'

The swift light came, burning off the mist. Conrad abandoned caution and spent the morning attempting to find someone who might lend him what Tullio dropped into the conversation as 'a ferocious amount of money'.

'That our patron will pay back within the week,' Conrad added.

Sandrine and a number of the other singers had nest eggs squirrelled away, but none were sufficient.

'What about a money-lender?' JohnJack Spinelli recommended.

'No capital.'

Conrad went from there to call in on Luigi Esposito for a game of chess and an appeal.

'I may be offered a considerable number of bribes, but I'm not, in fact, that rich,' the police chief said. 'Do you actually know anyone who is?'

Gianpaolo Pironti and Tullio were shown back in just as Luigi asked. A look flashed over Tullio's face as he heard the question.

'*Porca vacca!*' Realisation made Conrad abruptly choke on the remainder of his wine. 'Damnation!'

Luigi waved the others forward, seeming amused. 'You do know a rich man? And that's not good news?'

'Not considering who it is!' The after-taste of the wine seemed sharply acidic. Conrad shook his head. 'I only know one significantly wealthy man, Luigi, and if I tell you who it is, you'll know why I never even considered asking him.'

'Il Superbo!' Isaura exclaimed.

'Roberto Capiraso. Conte di Argente. Il Superbo. Not only would he not lend me money—' Conrad looked down into his empty glass. '—But right now he wouldn't piss on me if I was on fire.'

'That may be true.' Luigi had effortlessly possessed himself of the gossip about Leonora, Contessa di Argente, and in self-defence Conrad had contradicted it with the truth. 'But I really don't want to have to arrest you again.'

Conrad put his head in his hands.

They always say you should ask yourself what your father would do under these circumstances.

I can't run away from Naples. I honestly can't.

I don't want to.

Paolo interrupted Conrad's thoughts. 'He is rich.'

'I'll have to ask him,' Conrad said, sitting up. 'Il Superbo is one of the few other people who do know what's truly at stake. I'm still not looking forward to it.'

Luigi clapped Conrad on the shoulder as he ushered them out of the door. 'Good luck!'

✦

Conrad took a breath after he was shown into the Conte di Argente's mansion, and the servants left them alone. It calmed him enough to deliver his prepared speech. The importance of the counter-opera. The disaster if it was not completed on time. The absence of King Ferdinand, and their complete inability to reach him before the Count di Galdi's (expired) deadline. A reprise of just how significant the counter-opera is to Naples and Italy.

Conrad concluded with, 'I hope that you'll be reasonable, and forget our differences.'

'No, I don't think so.'

Roberto Capiraso stood watching the harbour from glass doors that opened onto a balcony. Curtains were drawn back – great drapes of linen-backed red silk, ornamented with tassels. The walls were swathed in silk. The drawing-room reminding Conrad more than anything of his father's brief sojourn in Constantinople.

The Conte di Argente had evidently been out riding; he wore spotless buckskin breeches and a topcoat after the English fashion, and high boots that it would take his valet an hour or more to polish. With his back to Conrad, he helped himself to brandy, for all it was still morning. Conrad was not surprised to be offered nothing.

With all the quiet poise he could manage, Conrad said, 'It's no coincidence that this has come up now. This is a first attack by the Prince's Men.'

'Possibly.' Roberto Capiraso put his tumbler on the mantelpiece and turned to observe the room.

Conrad might have been a specimen under glass, hung on the wall, for all the notice in the man's gaze. The barbed companion-ship and dry humour of their working partnership might never have existed.

'Then—' Conrad began.

'Do you know,' Roberto Capiraso interrupted him without apology, 'that I had the pleasure, when your note arrived, of hearing my wife request that I consider helping you.'

His voice was cold and level, but Conrad heard it increase in intensity at the phrase 'my wife'.

Two contradictory emotions flooded him. A reckless gladness – *She actually cared enough to speak in my favour!* – and a cold misgiving, guessing the Count's possible reaction.

The clear morning light through the windows made him wince.

Conrad sat on his exasperation. 'You need the libretto to set, even if I end up giving it to you a scene at a time. We have to work together, after all!'

Roberto Capiraso stood with his back to the fire, legs apart, cognac glass in one hand. He gently swirled the alcohol, inhaling, not looking at Conrad. 'There is absolutely no reason I can think of why I should help you.'

Conrad drew in a breath, preparatory to going through the whole matter again – and caught a glint in the Conte di Argente's eye at that display of impatience.

At this moment, he doesn't care about King Ferdinand, the opera, the Prince's Men. None of that is more than theoretical to him at this moment. What he cares about is that I've had to come here, cap in hand, and ask him.

Because of Leonora.

Conscious that his cheeks must be reddening because of the warmth he could feel in his face, Conrad hoped that it might be put down to the hearth-fire's heat. A glance at Roberto Capiraso's face disillusioned him.

I know what he wants.

That Il Superbo might put his own pride above any emergency was not a surprise. The realisation and the prospect were enough to make Conrad hot behind the ears.

Considering that Leonora spoke for me, it's not surprising he wants to see me crawl.

There was even some small part of him that briefly sympathised with Argente. It was that same part that wrote verse for each character based on their own position and sympathies, rather than his own.

While that emotion buoyed him up, Conrad took the risk, stepping forward to where the Count surveyed the last drops of

189

his cognac clinging to the glass. The gilt mirror over the mantel showed both of them, limned by sunlight, and Conrad wished it was otherwise. He did not want his face to be clearly seen.

'Conte,' he said formally.

Roberto Capiraso's head lifted, dark eyes transfixing him.

Conrad swallowed with a sudden dry mouth. 'I ask you for your help, sir.'

He paused, hoping against hope. *Is that enough?*

Clearly, from Capiraso's expression, it was not. A hunger showed in the other man's gaze.

'I ask for your help,' Conrad repeated.

'Do you?' Capiraso sounded almost bored. 'Do it properly, then.'

Conrad knew he must be either flame-red or stark white; he felt hot and cold by turns. He bit his tongue, suppressing all the threats he might have made with the backing of King Ferdinand.

They're useless. That's not what he wants.

Conrad managed, 'Please.' It was no easier to repeat. 'Please. Will you help me? Will you loan me this money?'

A glint of absolute satisfaction showed in Roberto Capiraso's eyes. He tilted his head as if he listened.

'I beg you,' Conrad said, with as much formality as he could.

The silence stretched out – until Conrad knew he was about to turn and slam his way out of the house, no matter the importance of anything else – or else lay Capiraso out with one punch.

The Conte di Argente put his empty glass down. His baritone voice sounded smooth and untroubled.

'No.'

Conrad found, after a long moment, that his mouth was open. He shut it.

'"No"?' He wanted to sound enraged; his voice came out stunned with shock instead. 'No?'

Roberto Capiraso smiled. '"No". Is that not plain enough? No, I will not help you. No, I will not lend you money to stay out of jail. No. Is that clear enough for you?'

Conrad closed his eyes, unwilling to have Roberto Capiraso witness his scalding and absolute humiliation.

All that, and then he refuses me?

190

Humiliation turned to white-hot anger.

'Conte.' Conrad's voice dripped contempt, and he made no attempt to sound different. 'Is it beyond you to be reasonable? You—'

'I am reasonable. What does it matter to me if you're arrested for debt? It hardly matters if you're in jail, does it? It won't stop you writing the libretto.' The Conte di Argente looked far too amused. 'You can write as well in a debtors' jail as you can in that hovel you call your lodgings. I'll send one of my servants to the debtors' prison every morning, to collect the next few pages of your libretto. This problem of yours won't prevent me setting the lines to music.'

Conrad forcibly and deliberately battened down all the words he would have screamed. Pressure built inside him. His attention focused down – he was conscious of nothing but the point on Capiraso's bearded jaw where his clenched fist would hit.

'If the King doesn't like it,' Il Superbo added, 'let him bail you out. He has no one else to compose his music.'

Roberto Capiraso didn't say 'I'm indispensable', but Conrad read it clearly in the man's expression.

I swear— I swear to the God I don't believe in, I will kill him—

The pressured silence shattered at a soft knock on the door.

One of the Count's servants apologised in quiet tones. Capiraso shook his head, and gave a snort of something that sounded like amusement. 'No, send him in. Let them all come!'

The doors opened fully, and Luigi Esposito appeared, accompanied by two grim-faced officers.

'I apologise, Signore Conte,' the police captain said, 'but my men followed Signore Scalese to this house, during his evasion of bailiffs. I have a warrant for his arrest for debt.'

Roberto Capiraso glanced back into the room. His dark gaze burned, and Conrad did not know for one vertiginous second what the man would do.

Il Superbo smiled.

'Then, Captain, do your duty.'

18

Comedy tended to occur to him at the most inopportune moments, Conrad thought, observing the two officers in square-topped hats with crowning green cockades. They stood either side of Luigi Esposito, evidently not aware that the Two Kingdoms' uniforms had any element of hilarity.

'Conrad Arturo Scalese . . .' Luigi Esposito sounded emotionless, repeating the words of the warrant.

Anger and humiliation dowsed the spark of Conrad's humour.

The Conte di Argente sat down at his desk, pulling a score towards himself, seemingly not aware of anyone else's presence in the room.

Conrad thought calmly, *They're already going to put me in prison. The English have a proverb about a sheep and a lamb—*

As if Luigi Esposito could read minds, the sleek-haired man fiddled with the buttons of his uniform cuffs, and under cover of the movement murmured, 'Debtors' prison, Conrad.'

Meaning that I could be worse off. Make it murder and I could be in chains out on the Isle of Ischia.

And Roberto Capiraso, Conte di Argente . . .

. . . Is right, Conrad reflected, adrenaline urging his body to violence, and only a thin thread of reason holding him back.

That realisation – that Il Superbo is correct, that Conrad *can* write a libretto under those conditions – is bitter to choke down.

Yes, I can write. I can delegate most duties of an impresario. By the time it comes to rehearsals, and they need me present, Ferdinand will have returned, and settled this.

So Il Superbo gets the opportunity to humiliate me, and no one will chastise him for doing it.

It could be worse. Leonora could be here while he lectures me about my 'wastrel ways'.

Conrad felt the police chief's touch on his shoulder. Luigi appeared genuinely uncomfortable. Conrad nodded, praying his face was not as red and hot as it felt.

'Shall we go, then?' Luigi Esposito bowed with the utmost politeness to Roberto Capiraso – which the Count ignored – and took Conrad by the elbow. The two officers fell in behind.

At the foot of the mansion's steps, an unobtrusive carriage waited in the sunlight, horses' breath steaming in the air.

Conrad turned his head, and discovered Luigi tugging at the cuffs of his white gloves again. 'No official coach?'

'It would please some people if you were dragged off in ignominy . . .' Luigi politely gestured for Conrad to precede him inside. 'That wouldn't please me. And, since this is my department, I handle arrests as I please.'

The parchment-coloured curtains were pulled down over the windows, leaving them in a honey-shaded dimness. A soft word from the driver, outside, and the closed carriage dipped and creaked, moving off.

Conrad eyed the two officers sitting one either side of him on the uncomfortable seat, and returned his gaze to Luigi. 'Can I send word to my servant?'

'Rossi should be there to meet you.' There might have been a smile on Luigi's face. 'You're a gentleman, Conrad; you shouldn't spend even one night down in the dungeons.'

It didn't seem wise to talk with the two hulks either side of him, but Conrad gave Luigi a speaking look. *When was the last time you called me a gentleman?*

A sudden splash of reality, like a dose of cold water, ended his amusement. *The jailers will need bribing.*

Conrad leaned forward, ignoring how the officers tensed. 'I don't have a scudo on me!'

'Tullio has a purse. You should be able to have a room above ground – though I can't guarantee it'll be furnished in the very best style. And no leg-irons.'

With the police officers so close, Conrad couldn't say anything without being overheard.

Although I expect Luigi will have looked after this lot – corruption in Naples is the air that one breathes! – but to speak of sensitive matters here . . . no.

The first thing I will do after I get out of prison is talk to Luigi Esposito. Because if Tullio has a purse, I'm damn sure it isn't mine.

✦

The jailers who took him from the police – hustling him with far less politeness down the corridors of the forbidding large building – opened a door and pushed him through.

Tullio turned away from a bare window and took three quick strides across the room. Conrad found himself seized and briefly if intensely hugged.

'Sorry, padrone.' Tullio swept his arm around as he stepped back, indicating the bare floorboards and Spartan room. 'Even with Captain Luigi's help, this was the best we could do.'

Three strides had been enough to cross from window to door, and it was no wider from the wall against which a pallet-bed lay, to the tiny fireplace opposite – currently empty of fire. A bag which Tullio had evidently packed stood by the bed.

'You and Luigi want your heads knocked together! Do you have any savings left?'

Tullio scratched at his shaved head. With the air of a man finding something useful to get him out of a confrontation, he pulled six wax candles out of one of his pockets, and a candle-holder out of the other, and put them down on the room's sole plain wooden table. 'Isaura's bringing some coal for the fireplace, and ink and paper. I guess the faster you write, the faster you get out of this place.'

Conrad lifted his face to the light coming in through the

194

uncurtained windows. He wasn't going to answer questions about money.

'And don't you worry about that Il Superbo,' Tullio added with a growl, as he set kindling ready for the coal. 'There isn't a good bone in that man's body; he wouldn't know natural human feeling if it ran over him in a horse and cart!'

Conrad pulled out the elderly high-backed wooden chair, and all but fell into it. The tension of the past hour instantly dispelled, leaving him feeling like cooked spaghetti. He gripped Tullio's arm and released it.

'I want you or Paolo to keep watch on that place, now.' Conrad saw Tullio mouth 'Palace', and nodded. 'Safely. Without being noticed. I need to get word to our friend as soon as he returns.'

✦

The day passed, hours unmarked by any clock. Paolo brought him a carpet-bag of belongings and vanished again.

Conrad drew the wooden stool up to the table, and began paring down a quill. His hands cut expertly, all the while his thoughts scurried around like a disturbed colony of mice.

'There's nothing we can do. Yet.' He put the quill down and picked up another gull's feather, aware of Tullio's hovering worried form. Conrad didn't look up from trimming. 'Can I rely on you to bring food in? What they serve here would poison a camel.'

Tullio grunted and folded his arms. 'You want me to check for our friend every day. What about— Shall I keep an eye on our composer?'

The jailers in any prison are notorious for listening at spy-holes, in case they should overhear anything to blackmail more money out of their prisoners.

'The composer—' Conrad pronounced that without spoken insult, but in the tones Tullio usually used while cleaning horse-muck off his shoes. '—will be kind enough to send me his musical score, as he completes the scenes. You should ask every day if he has anything for me, when you take what I've written to him.'

'Sure.' Tullio looked about himself. 'Hang on, padrone, there's one more thing I can think of that you need. Let me go put the fear of God into 'em—'

'The fear of Sergeant Rossi is likely to be more effective!'

Tullio Rossi left with a grin. It was half an hour later before the ex-soldier returned. Conrad startled at the opening of the door, having become lost in his thoughts and the mutable light.

'Tullio?'

The man swung one of the objects he carried – another wooden chair, Conrad realised. Tullio plonked it down on the far side of the table, and put down the bucket he held in his other hand, which turned out to be a quarter full of coal.

'They agreed you don't have to be in isolation. You can have a fire.' Tullio sat and dug in his pockets, and brought out a greasy pack of cards. 'And I'll play you at Vingt-et-Un. If Isaura manages to find a cheap enough wine, you can at least be drunk for your first night here. After that, I suppose you will have to work.'

Conrad found he couldn't speak for all of a minute.

'Not Twenty-One,' he finally managed. 'If I ever had any idea I could follow my father as a gambler, you cured me of it! We'll play Gin, since at least I can remember what's in the discards.'

He was indeed drunk for his first night, although the wine Isaura found was sour and of a very dubious colour.

Tullio let himself in and out with a fine disregard for the building's status as a prison, until Conrad had to ban him for the morning hours, while he sat at the table – not lighting a candle until he had to – and found to his chagrin that he could perhaps work better isolated.

Although most of the friends who would have disturbed me socially left town after Il Terrore, *except for Spinelli and Sandrine. But . . .*

He left unthought the realisation that he missed working in such close concert with an opera's composer. Missed the mutual inspiration that words had begun to take from the music, as well as the other way around.

And he pushed out of his mind the knowledge that, arrogant son of a bitch as he might be, Roberto Capiraso was an imaginative man, and, like most composers, could likely contribute as much to the shape of the words and story as Conrad's incessant questioning would to the shape of the score.

Seven days elapsed. The same answer came from the palace every day.

His window looked out on a nearby brick wall. It was not an inspiring view, but the terracotta, ochres, and sanguines of the brickwork – reduced to evening monochromes, or brilliant in the dawn – were sufficient to take a man's mind off his isolation and imprisonment, at least for a short time, and allow imagination free rein. Conrad lost himself in the first and second Acts, only pausing to eat, and demand technical answers of Paolo-Isaura and Tullio which they were ill-suited to give.

'Don't ask me where you should end the scene!' Tullio finally shrugged. 'I just watch operas, padrone; I don't know how they work!'

Conrad broke off his interrogation. 'Sorry. At least in here I'm working faster because I'm so deeply involved.'

And I do not – do not – wish I was working with Roberto Capiraso.

✦

Conrad became used to seeing Tullio half a dozen times in afternoons and evenings – bringing in wine, olives, pizza, and whatever other staples the ex-sergeant could forage, along with all the city and theatre gossip he could remember. It was useless to protest his gratitude that Tullio would do this. The big man merely shot him a look that reduced him to the apparent status of a stumbling recruit, and waved away any thanks.

Along with Tullio, two times out of five, Isaura would turn up in one of Sandrine Furino's second-best gowns, with a shawl over her head, and relate how she was chatting with the prison laundresses with a view to arranging an escape.

'Do you think you may have read too many Gothic romances?' Conrad speculated.

Isaura's amused sneer was practised, and modelled on Tullio's own.

Paolo-Isaura and Tullio brought welcome company, both of them. No matter how sunny and well-lit the cell might be, and how many hours could be lost in the construction of a script for *L'Altezza azteca, ossia il serpente pennuto*, the solitude sapped his energy and his courage.

And I really have no right to laugh at Paolo for reading Gothic novels, Conrad mused, chewing on the end of a dip-pen one morning. *It's ironic: every time I speculate about Leonora and the Conte di Argente, I can't help imagining that he abducted her, or blackmailed her into marrying him, or some such Gothic device.*

The prison, being a debtors' prison, was nearly as busy with visitors as with prisoners. Conrad grew used to seeing masked women visiting those who might be lovers or brothers; and small children gazing with wide eyes at the place Papa found himself in.

To think of all the times I swore I'd never follow my father, Conrad considered wryly. *And at least he managed to stay out of jail . . .*

Towards the middle of that week, Conrad managed to interview two or three borderline applicants for the minor roles, who Spinelli forwarded on the grounds that he was too taken with their charms to judge their voices.

Which I doubt. He just wants me to have contact with the outside world.

Paolo visited his cell again, to report how the opera continued, and brought the news of having found a tenor.

'Enrichette Méric-Lalande – you know, the French soprano who sings here a lot? She's refused us – rudely, actually – but she wrote to say she has a protégé, one Lorenzo Bonfigli, who's a tenor, and he turned up yesterday with her letter of introduction—'

'What kind of tenor? Graceful? Lyric?'

'More spinto than lyric, apparently. He's done a few small heroic roles – and he can do Gilbert Duprez's chest-voice high C.' She grinned. 'Four times out of five, anyway.'

Conrad reflected on the advantages of a male chest-voice C above middle C, in the same cast as Velluti's soaring castrato.

'Better be five times out of five, or he suffers! Hire him. We need a High Priest of the Sun. That could work as a lyric-dramatic tenor. And I'm murdering him at the end of Act One,' Conrad added, with considerable *Schadenfreude*. 'He could double as Cortez's Captain in Act Two . . .'

Isaura cheered up, and continued for some minutes on the initial stages of rehearsal with the material they had.

'Less than four weeks, now,' she concluded, her initial enthusiasm beginning to sound harried.

Conrad smiled, and ruffled her hair.

'Now you understand opera. Work faster!'

✦

His private well-lit cell, away from the crowded and unfumigated main prison hall, was something Conrad would have called a godsend if not aware that he owed it to his friends.

There were also long hours of an absolute solitude. Especially at night.

And since I look to be in here until the King's return . . .

I'll do as much as I can.

He interviewed Estella Belucci when she arrived from Palermo one morning, and proved to look very little like a rebel. She turned out to be a surprisingly subdued blonde woman in a fashionable bonnet, who jolted every time someone in the main part of the prison shouted or screamed.

'This "Zo-sheel",' she eventually got the confidence to say, presenting a well-thumbed copy of what libretto details Paolo had passed on, with Xochitl's first verses circled. 'Suppose she's not a slave girl, or wasn't always a slave girl?'

I'll listen to anybody at this point. Conrad opened the books on South America that Tullio had fetched for him, and showed her engravings of the Aztecs in their native costumes, and the initial drafts of the first trio for Velluti, Sandrine, and Donna Belucci.

'What had you in mind?'

Her finger, with its well-trimmed but evidently chewed nails, underlined Cortez' first entry, and the description of the sopranos' warrior-women costumes. 'He defeated their neighbouring enemy tribe, the Amazons?'

Conrad pointed his pen at the globe Tullio had brought in from the secret museum, and tapped the continent of South America. 'The Amazon River, see?'

Estella Belucci raised her pale eyebrows. 'Geography's not your strong point, signore, is it?'

'I promise you, the Amazon River is in South America.'

'Yes . . .' Her smile gave warning of why managements might find her difficult. 'But I think you'll find the classical Amazons come from Greece.'

Conrad spun the globe to peer at Greece.

He wiped off three thousand years of civilisation and as many miles with a dismissive wave.

'Well, the Greeks were great travellers! Obviously America became the home of the classical Amazons by the time of Cortez . . .'

'Obviously.' Her smile lost out to ambition. Estella Belucci leaned forward where she sat. 'Signore, you write here that audiences want girls in peril, not warriors. But suppose it's both? "Zo-sheel" might be an Aztec slave now because she's an Amazon warrior captured in battle and made prisoner!'

Leave it to a singer to make their part a priority. But . . .

'You know,' Conrad said, 'that's a good idea.'

Tullio, letting himself into the cell in time to hear the last interchanges, grinned broadly. 'Certainly is! Amazons always play well – 's an excuse to have a woman with one tit hardly covered!'

Conrad muttered, 'Philistine!' But having seen Estella Belucci out like a gentleman, he came back and scribbled a note in the margin.

✦

On the eighth day, about the time the slanting sunlight on the opposite brick wall told Conrad it was mid-morning, the metal spy-hole in the door slid back, then forward; and there was an incongruous knock.

'Come in,' Conrad called dryly.

The guard pulled open the door that bolted on the outside. 'You have a visitor, signore.'

His tone was sufficient that Conrad knew the visitor must be a woman. Self-conscious, he touched the stubble on his cheeks where Tullio had not yet been in to shave him.

Another of Spinelli's 'borderline' voices for the Priestesses of the Feathered Serpent or the Amazon warriors?

'Show her in.' Conrad couldn't help smiling at the guard's one-male-to-another look.

If he only knew I am just interested in their voices!

'Here, signorina.' The guard held the door open for a woman in a blue morning walking dress and three-quarter coat, and a deep-brimmed fashionable bonnet, with three frivolous ostrich plumes curving over from the back.

The guard slipped out rapidly; clearly expecting a later gratuity.

The locks clicked as the door shut behind him.

Before Conrad could say anything, the woman pulled at her hat-strings and yanked the concealing bonnet from her head, dropping it down on his half-written page.

His chair squealed on the wooden floorboards as Conrad jumped up, staring at the face of Leonora – once Leonora D'Arienzo, since married, now Leonora Capiraso.

Conrad gathered his wits. He managed a bow.

And, although it stuck in his throat: 'Contessa.'

19

'Corrado!' She ignored formality. Her eyes were shining, beyond what might be accounted for by the weak sun reflected in at the window. The time that he hadn't seen her – every sleep-less night, every unprofitable attempt to lose himself in other women's company – burned up as if it had never been. Her smile wiped it all out. She said, again, 'Corrado!', and her perfect voice broke.

'I never expected to see you again.' Conrad realised, blankly, that it wasn't the best thing to say; that he had better have pro-claimed he always knew they would be reunited. The truth spilled out of him like blood. 'I hoped you were ill, or dead, or emigrated to the New World – some reason why I couldn't find you!'

Pain came through too clearly in his voice.

'We might have been within twenty feet of each other, any time these five years! Except you would have been in a stage box, and I in the pit. Why did you leave me?'

Her hand came up as if it would have touched his, but hesitated in mid-air.

Conrad startled out of the paralysis of her presence. *She won't be alone!*

Her husband will be behind her on the stair.

'You shouldn't enter this cell on your own.' Conrad could only speak in a whisper. 'The San Carlo is as much a pit of gossip as La

Fenice was. One visit to an unmarried man without your husband present . . .'

'Oh, don't be foolish. My maid is only a few steps behind me.'

Her voice wasn't loud, but he heard those theatre-taught reverberations that meant she intended it to carry, and be overheard by any nosy guards.

'Our kind of people do visit the poor, and prisoners, and do good works.' Her voice changed pitch, so as not to be casually overheard. 'I only have to mention it quite openly at church. Everybody knows di Galdi is a spiteful old man.'

The Naples gossip circuit working full-time, Conrad deduced.

The door didn't open again. He wondered if there was in fact a maid. Or if, well-warned, she lurked in the passage outside to give word of any approach.

That means Nora truly intends to speak to me . . .

Leonora Capiraso, Contessa di Argente, sat down without invitation on the cell's other wooden chair. She began coolly to remove her gloves.

A sudden consciousness of the physicality of her hands encased in warm leather, which she loosened finger by finger, made him take refuge standing behind his high-backed chair, so she should not see evidence of his desire.

Not looking at him, she said, 'I need to explain why I left Venice.'

'I looked for you.'

And that's all I'll admit. No need for her to know how I walked all the alleys and little bridges, how I went into every church from the Basilica to the smallest chapel, hoping for the miracle of finding her attending Mass.

She regarded him, suddenly fearless. 'You'll think less of me.'

Contradictory emotions choked him.

'I didn't sleep.' Her hands hovered, lifted from her sides, as if she would have touched him but didn't dare. 'For the first year – I never slept the night through unbroken. Bad dreams. Nightmares. Roberto thought I was ill—'

'I don't want to hear about "Roberto"!'

She nodded as if that were a reasonable request to make.

'I wasn't ill,' she said simply. 'I missed sleeping by your side. Your breathing. Your warmth.'

Pain and loss met together in him, and made cruelty. 'Evidently you didn't miss it enough to come back to me. Or not to leave me in the first place!'

'I had to!'

Conrad dug his fingers into his palms until he was sure they must bleed. *I can't say 'I've missed you', 'I love you'.*

Not yet. Not until I know why you're here now. Not until I know—

'Why did you leave me in Venice?'

She turned her head, giving him only her perfect profile and a perceptible shiver.

'We were very Bohemian—' Her attempt at a social smile visibly fractured. Conrad saw her expression became pure honesty.

'How daring I felt, to be singing at La Fenice every night, and spending every day with my lover in Venice. I warned you I was only a provincial girl from Castelfranco Veneto . . . And coming home to that apartment house, by the bridge with the cats . . .'

'Smelly beasts.' Conrad wondered if he should have sounded more sentimental, but her mouth turned up. 'I remember watching those cats from our window.'

They had ranged from wild veteran Venetian mothers and dusty warriors, to stick-thin fluffy black kits, moving as if they ran on stilts. After love, he would lie shoulder to shoulder beside Leonora in the heated afternoon, watching between scarlet-painted shutters, and giving the beasts stories more melodramatic than the most outlandish libretto.

'You made up names for each of them,' he remembered.

Years since I thought of it – that we were so happy we could be shamelessly silly.

'. . . All the ugly ones had the names of prima donnas.'

'Of course!' Leonora wrinkled up her nose at him, instantly turning a lady in her late twenties into a gamin adolescent.

It hit him like a punch deep into the gut. He felt as if his throat bled, getting the words out. 'To see you like that – in the Palace – with no warning—!'

'I had no idea what it would be like to see you.' Moisture glinted in the corners of her violet-shadowed eyes. 'I couldn't speak, couldn't think.'

'You let your husband speak for you.'

'My husband isn't here to speak for me now.' What had been a glimmer of light swelled, and shimmered on the lower lid of her eye.

The tear did not fall.

'I didn't have a contract after La Fenice. I'd been writing to impresarios, but all they could offer was a lot of travelling and small roles . . . St Petersburg . . . one in Buenos Aires . . .' She twisted at one of her discarded gloves. 'Roberto had been back-stage between acts every night.'

'I stayed away from backstage because you asked!' Conrad hated the rough neediness of his tone. 'On the pretext that you needed to concentrate for your performances.'

Anger choked him.

Leonora spoke so quietly that he had to rein himself in to hear her, over the pounding of blood in his ears.

'I didn't notice any of the other men there, but I noticed him. Oh, don't look at me! You were so happy, so cheerful, like – like sun – and he was the dark to your fair—'

'Enough of the poetry.' Conrad cut through her rapid words. Rather than look at her, he began pacing. 'Did you sleep with him?'

'I didn't want to—'

'But someone held a pistol to your head. I understand.'

His bitterness was a dizzy satisfaction to voice at last, seeing out of the corner of his eye how she flinched.

'Is that what I needed to do to keep you, Nora? Look miserable every moment and pine over you?'

He found himself with clenched fists. *I did all my pining for you afterwards.*

'Was he sad like Mister Lord Byron? So unhappy that you just had to crawl into his bed and comfort him? Did he have some tragedy in his life—'

'Roberto said he knew people.'

Her voice was a shock, so flatly commonplace that Conrad stopped and turned, looking down at her.

Her lips compressed for a moment. 'His family were aristocrats, rich, they had influence . . . And that wouldn't have mattered, but – I'd seen so many young women with good voices missing their chances, ending up as provincial singing teachers at the very best—'

The depth of contempt in her tone sounded surprisingly masculine.

'Roberto told me he could speak to impresarios he knew; that his family were on the opera boards of more than one town—'

'A Neapolitan Count,' Conrad interrupted, biting down on scorn. 'Even some impresarios wouldn't want to offend him. So they might well allow his pet soprano a turn or two on the stage.'

Something flashed in her glance. He felt it in his belly and his balls. *That was the old Leonora!*

'And then, irony of ironies, now he has you, he won't allow you to sing. The wife of the Conte di Argente shouldn't be seen on the public stage—'

'You know nothing!'

'I know you appear to have fallen for a story rich young gentlemen have told singers since the beginning of the opera! And you couldn't succeed even with his influence—'

She shot to her feet, faster than he could react. He had just time to remember that Leonora was not a woman to use that tone to. Her warm palm hit his face with a stunning slap.

He probed with his tongue probed and tasted blood. The inside of his cheek was cut by one of his teeth.

She gasped in a breath, looking up at him with defiance and fear both on her face – one emotion purely hers, Conrad thought, and the other common to all women who have opened the situation to violence with a man present.

'He said he would marry me, Conrad!'

It felt more of a blow than her hand.

'And it wasn't a lie, or a false promise. We were married before I left Venice!'

Conrad found himself holding her upper arms with no memory of taking hold of her, the silk of her close-fitting sleeves crumpled under his fingers. 'You know why I couldn't offer you marriage!

I had my father's debts. How could I support a wife? Still less a family!'

Something about the line of her lower eyelids, taut with keeping back tears, made him release her and step back.

She sank down on the chair and sighed, perhaps with relief at the absence of violence. 'Yes. Yes, you told me.'

'And he was rich.'

'He was rich,' Leonora echoed, without the antipathy.

'And well-connected. And—'

He suppressed the part of him that would have whined 'I knew as many men in the opera world!', because the people that a beginning librettist knows are not the same as those known by a junior aristocrat. A piece of cynical advice thrown by his mother Agnese to his gawky younger sister fell from his mouth:

'—And it's as easy to fall in love with a rich man as a poor man.'

'It wasn't like that!'

He shrugged, in that moment pleased to see that his carelessness hurt her.

'I should have written, at the very least. I know that.' Leonora shook her head. 'I told myself it was Fate, that I was on the road, I ought not to turn back.'

Her teeth closed very gently over her lower lip. He wanted to kiss her until she stopped doing that.

'And so you married him because . . .'

'. . . I could marry him.'

Sudden hope was as painful as splinters of glass. 'Is that all the reason! That you needed to marry, and he was able to? If I could have married, you'd have—'

'You think I'd marry just to have a name, and enough money to get started in my career. You're very ready to think of me as a whore. But what else could you think?'

She stood up again in one sharp movement, all Leonora Capiraso, Contessa di Argente, and not the little Nora D'Arienzo who had been billed (at the bottom) on La Fenice's posters.

Etiquette demanded he should remain standing, since he shouldn't sit when a woman was not also seated. Conrad nonetheless sat down hard, leaning forward with his elbows on his knees, and his forehead against his fists. 'Oh, I'm no better than any other man. I'd rather think of you as a prostitute than think that you're in love with another man!'

Her voice softened. 'You were a better man than many. I don't suppose that's changed over a few years.'

Conrad lifted his head out of his hands, finding her dark lilac-shadowed eyes on him. Her face held a keen, affectionate expression.

Conrad stood up. He couldn't help but grab her hand, despite her immediate effort to withdraw it.

'If you care, then leave him! Oh, hell. I can't even ask you to divorce him, I'm still poor—' The barely furnished room seared into his vision, reminding him every moment, as if he could forget, how he was here in prison for owing money, however unjustly by the spirit of the law.

'Wait a few weeks. Wait until I know how well the run of *Il Terrore* did, and see what impresario will take me onto his books.'

He felt stunned by the familiar features, here in front of him.

'Nora, I don't care if he forbids you to sing! Come and sing the role of the Aztec Princess for me—'

His mind scurried, already planning how her soprano would affect the mezzo role, and what on earth he might give Sandrine to make up for taking this from her—

'—Please!—'

Conrad broke off, aware that he was babbling and gripping her hand too hard. Her mouth made a tight line as she gazed at him. In contradiction her eyes seemed wonderfully warm.

'I never thought I'd see you again.' Her expression altered to pure unhappiness. 'I didn't think how this would be, with things changed.'

'Nora.' He smiled impulsively, at the incongruity of that name applied to this slender and beautiful woman in silk and lace. 'Leonora . . .'

'No – you don't know—'

'Yes, I know. You're married! He's your husband.' Conrad, in sudden panic, demanded, 'You have children?'

'No children.'

208

'I apologise.' Formality was easier. Some atavistic part of himself murmured, *no, not sorry, not sorry at all. Let there be still fewer things to hold them together!*

'No, you don't.' Her voice, if soft, was no less intense.

'How much honesty do you want from me? That I hope he drops down dead in the street today? How can I say that? I want you to be happy.' Conrad tried to control his breathing. 'Does he make you happy? Does he?'

Her voice was almost too soft to be heard. 'You make me happy—'

Conrad's body jerked, as if he were all one musical string reverberating to being struck.

'—He makes me happy.'

She gave him a look that pierced him; that anatomised how his heart leaped and broke in a handful of seconds.

He said, 'And yet you chose.'

Her expression was indecipherable and perturbing. She tried to pull her fingers out of his grip. For all her flustering, her cheeks remained pale, neither heated by exertion or blushing with shame.

'Nora . . .' Conrad brought up his other hand, sliding his fingers into the wisps of dark curls behind her ear, where her hair was gathered up on her head.

Her skin was heated where he let his fingertips slide into the depression of her jaw, seeking every sensation so that he would know her pulse beat as fast as his. *Because she must feel something for me—*

He could feel nothing except delicate skin.

She fought harder to free herself. Conrad gripped her around the wrist, taking the weight of her hand.

Her hand felt heavy.

Heavy like the weight that a human body has, when the life has gone out of it.

Conrad frowned, between anger and panic.

Something is wrong – is very wrong—

'Let me go, Conrad!'

He found himself wondering, ridiculously, *Is she holding her breath?*

A struggling woman breathes harder, her breath comes in pants, and her chest rises and falls more quickly. Conrad gripped Leonora's wrist tightly, and stared at her blue bodice, cut in Empire-style under her breasts, so that her long coat and dress would fall undisturbed to her kidskin boots.

No quiver of flesh disturbed those curves.

No woman can hold her breath for minute after minute. No matter that it's ludicrous: there's no reason she should want to. It's not possible—!

'Conrad!'

He met her dark gaze, letting her yank her wrist against the encircling grip of his fingers. Strong for a woman, yes – singers have to be fit – but he is a man, there is no way that she could escape from him. Except that she is nearly free.

Hearsay and heresy congealed like ice in his stomach.

'You were . . . ill.' Conrad winced, beginning the accusation.

He expected her to be chill. A true dank-stone cold. For his hand not to warm hers: for her to feel as if she had walked out of an ice-store into the sun.

Her skin flushed with a fevered heat that owed nothing to a quickened pulse.

She looked to the side, suddenly, avoiding his eyes.

Ah, no. I hoped I was wrong!

Conrad managed not to swear, and to keep his voice steady.

'You were ill . . . Some time between when I last saw you in Venice, and now. You – what – had scarlet fever? Cholera? Or consumption? Or . . . What was it?'

He slid his thumb under the end of her cuff, although it was cut to lie snugly against her skin. A sea-green bead cut its thread and bounced away on the cell's bare floorboards. Conrad let the pad of his thumb rest against the underside of her wrist. It brought him the feel of the two tendons just up from the heel of her hand. And a sensation of flesh cooled by shadow.

Push against her skin as he might, he felt no heartbeat.

Leonora slowly turned her head to look up at him, eyes full of dread.

Conrad put his other hand unforgivably against the breast of her dress. Unforgivable, because she is a married woman, and not married to him. His fingers at her throat, skin to skin, he feels through his blood, bones and tendons—

Under the weight of his palm, her sternum does not rise.

Her ribs do not expand and contract.

Conrad lifted his knuckles to her cheek, and felt that, close as his skin might come to her nostrils, no in-breath or out-breath of air touched him. Nothing at all, no matter how long he left his hand there.

He spoke barely above a harsh whisper. 'You were ill; doctors were called; il Conte di Argente offered his money – and none of it was any use, was it?'

'No, none.'

'You still died.'

20

Conrad didn't want to say it aloud. His mouth felt arid.

'You're one of the Returned Dead.'

'Yes.'

Leonora stood perfectly still as she answered.

If she had done that before, he thought, *I would have spotted it at once. No living, breathing body can stand as still as that.*

As still as the dead.

'How long – how—?'

'Some time after I married . . .' She sighed – or mimicked a sigh. Conrad remembered seeing others of her kind who kept doing the things they did when they were alive. Perhaps for the sake of the emotions they need to express.

Certainly not for the breath they don't need.

'. . . I heard afterwards that Roberto was distraught. All I knew was that I . . . woke. I woke, I wasn't breathing. I knew what had happened – I knew a Returned woman in Castelfranco Veneto when I was small. There are . . . changes.'

'You're a miracle.' Conrad snarled the word, not sure if that was because he despised the Church's description of the absolutely inexplicable, or because he didn't need to hear anything about how desperately loving and grieving Roberto Capiraso might have been.

No one can ever say what brings one person back, and not another –

but who knows what Leonora might owe to her desperate grieving husband?

'I no longer sing.' She sounded bereft. 'Since I died.'

Like all of her kind, she was slim. He took her hand again – heavier than the hand of the living, though not by much – and clasped it. Her grip felt warm. If the death-weight of her flesh bothered her, he thought between shock and joy, she never showed it.

'Leonora . . .'

He found himself too sick at heart to consider whether it might be Signore Aldini's galvanic energy in her veins, or whether this was another form of life, that only counterfeits having gone through death. *Speculation is useless. The truth of it is, everything about her has changed, and – nothing is different. She feels as warm in my arms as she ever did.*

Thought vanished in the strangeness of touching Leonora, not unresponsive as a corpse would be, but feeling no pulse under her fever-hot heated skin.

As in a dream, he lifted his hand to her throat, fingers pressing down to find the carotid artery, as he has done on battlefields with fallen men.

No heart beat. Her rib-cage only lifted with air as she breathed in, preparatory to speaking.

'Corradino.' Her voice was breathier than he recalled. 'You don't flinch away?'

'Why should I? I always loved your warmth in my bed.' He realised what he had said to a married woman just as she wrinkled up her nose, and smothered a giggle.

'Don't say that in front of Roberto.' She sounded unaccountably cheerful.

Conrad let his other hand delicately smooth her hair back behind her ears. The ash-brown curls were wonderfully soft and sleek.

'I can't help being glad you don't run from me.' She placed her fingers lightly against his cheek. 'Some people think I ought to be a thing of horror – rotten flesh, raw-head and bloody-bones, children's nightmares. I can see in their eyes that some think I am. That this—'

213

Leonora shrugged, inviting his inspection.

'—is all illusion, and that underneath everything is grave-cold and moss-green. But it's no illusion. This is how I came back.'

Conrad took both her hot hands in his own. 'I suppose everybody asks – but I can't help asking, too. Came back from what?'

The hope of getting an eye-witness answer robbed him of any more speech.

Her expression changed from affection to apology. 'The Mind of God; isn't that what the Church teaches us? But I – don't truly remember anything – I wasn't there – I have no answers. You are not the first to ask.'

She massaged her right hand with her left, and Conrad realised she had withdrawn from his grasp. Her face was sad and knowing. There was no accusation in her expression, but guilt tore through Conrad.

She's used to everybody rejecting her; no wonder she doesn't go out in public!

He took her by the shoulders. 'It doesn't make any difference to me!'

The maid's cry and a clatter of footsteps on the wooden stairs only gave enough warning for him to let her go, and step back.

Leonora snatched up her hat and gloves, clutching them to her, plumes trailing.

The door slammed open and Roberto Capiraso strode through it, moving far too fast for the size of the small cell.

'Madame wife.' His voice grated.

Conrad spoke at the same time as Leonora:

'Argente—'

'Roberto—'

'I recognised your carriage outside. This is not where I expected to find you!' The Conte di Argente overrode all other voices, including the guard's outside the cell. 'Come out, madame wife!'

Conrad, in shock, thought, *Strange how often real life mirrors the stage*. Roberto Capiraso's face flushed red, the man blustering like a stage baritone protesting against his wife's betrayal of his honour.

Nora's voice cut in, not at all loud. Icy and intense. 'Don't make a fool of both of us! I have every right to visit the librettist of your opera. My experience in the world of opera itself is a help—'

Roberto Capiraso's hand closed over her wrist. It had none of the gentleness of Conrad's remorseless investigation. It cut her voice off as cleanly as if he had grabbed her throat.

Her shock at the red indentations of his fingers made Conrad think she was not used to being manhandled like this. That sent a spark of joy through his belly – *At least she isn't beaten by him!* – which flashed into anger.

'You have no right to hurt her, Argente!'

'Oh, I apologise, is that your privilege?'

Roberto Capiraso took advantage of Conrad's stunned silence to reach down with his free hand, and snatch the pages off the table.

'I'll set these.' He nodded curtly to Conrad. 'Unfortunately, my wife and I are too busy to pay social calls at the moment.'

Before Conrad could step forward, the Count caught hold of the open door, pushed his wife unceremoniously through it, and, as he followed, pulled it sharply closed behind him.

'*Cazzo!* Wait! Nora!'

The click as the lock's wards engaged sounded an instant before Conrad's fists crashed down and hit the wood.

✦

Three hours later Paolo arrived with the news that the royal yacht *Roberto Guiscardo* was sighted, and expected to dock back in Naples within the hour.

21

The King placed the long, lawyer-written document on the table, gazing up mildly at the others present in one of his private chambers.

'This is agreed, then, gentlemen?'

Conrad blinked. A night of glacially slow hours had passed, when he rivalled the changing guards for sleeplessness. Now, after the sudden rush of officialdom that had Conrad released into the custody of his Majesty at the Palazzo Reale, he found himself hungry – it was well past lunch time – but the more alert because of it.

Conrad heard the timbre of iron as the King added, very patiently, 'If anyone has difficulties, please speak now – once signed, this is settled.'

'I'm content,' Conrad put in, slightly too quickly.

The silver-haired Adalrico Silvestri, Conte di Galdi, held his gloves and cane neatly in one hand. His other hand rested on the arm of a younger man, whom Conrad recognised as one of Naples' young men-about-town who favoured the opera, and guessed him to be Galdi's son or nephew.

The son-or-nephew, much the same age as Conrad, shot him a glare.

A Prince's Man, like his father? Conrad wondered. *Men to steer clear of, in any case.* He could see that the Silvestri, father and son, would love to have him taken back to debtors' prison.

But they're in no position to overtly argue with the King.

'I consent.' Adalrico Silvestri spoke in a perfectly urbane tone that was more frightening than his son's glares. 'Your Majesty, your Treasury will pay the interests on Alfredo Scalese's debts, enabling Signore Conrad Scalese here to stay out of jail to earn sufficient to pay off the principal.'

The faint emphasis on 'earn' held more contempt than Conrad thought it possible to get into one word.

'Precisely: I don't want charity,' Conrad put in, perilously close to interrupting the King. 'I'll pay the debts off myself given time.'

'Signore Scalese, if I had no . . . obligations . . . owed to your sire from the years before I took the throne, your time would still be spent in prison.' Ferdinand shrugged, managing (deftly as an actor) to leave an impression that Alfredo's help had been incurred during youthful self-indulgence which the adult man would prefer to forget.

Ferdinand Bourbon-Sicily held out the quill to the old man, who scrawled 'Adalrico Silvestri' in one long jagged line. Conrad signed his own name, and watched the king and the other man sign as witnesses – the latter being one 'Niccolò Silvestri'.

Ferdinand let them go through the politenesses attendant on farewells with perfect equanimity, and only after the two men had gone did he regard the anteroom's tall doors with a faint frown.

'Both of them in the Prince's Men, I think,' he murmured. 'My spies don't like the look of the older Silvestri at all. I advise you to avoid the son, too, socially.'

'If I don't want to end up in a duel?' Conrad nodded. 'Yes, sir. He looks the type to give out challenges, and if I did find myself in a duel with him, I doubt I'd get away alive. If not shot in the back, then met with by a gang of *masnadiere* on the way home . . .'

Ferdinand gave a smile of appreciation.

It faded to anger.

'And now I believe I need to have a word or two with the Conte di Argente about using obvious plots by the King's enemies to settle his personal grievances.'

Conrad trespassed on his relationship with Ferdinand sufficiently to contradict him. 'Sir, no! Not if you ever want the man to work with me in the future!'

By Ferdinand Bourbon-Sicily's expression, he was imagining Il Superbo after a raking-down like that.

'Very well.' The King gestured for Conrad to sit with him at the table. 'Then, how is our *Aztec Princess* progressing?'

Conrad took his notes and clean copy from their leather folder, together with more of Paolo's correspondence. 'I'm going to need to settle the roles quite soon. La Tachinardi writes that she's not available to sing any role – still afraid of lightning, according to Paolo. We have one tenor, Bonfigli – Giovanni Davide is booked up two years ahead, and Berardo Winter hasn't replied. Donna Belucci is turning out to be quite an asset—'

Conrad showed the King his synopsis for 'Xochitl the Aztec slave-girl', now 'Hippolyta the captured Amazon warrior'; at which Ferdinand looked thoughtful.

'—And this can be as large or small a role as we require, sir,' Conrad added, 'Depending on how she settles in with the rest of the cast. She need only come on to sing her arias at the beginning of Act II and Act III, to give the crew time to work the scene changes, and allow the cast who have sung in the strettas to rest for a few minutes.'

Ferdinand Bourbon-Sicily nodded as if he were an impresario like Domenico Barjaba. His expression altered. Conrad saw the man suppressed embarrassment.

'In fact – as I was reminded on my return – I have another singer for you. She's under contract to the San Carlo, so we must give her something . . . But it could be a small role. Brigida Lorenzani, a contralto.'

Conrad searched his memory for Naples' faces and reputations. *Lorenzani, Lorenzani . . . Yes. Competent but not reputed to be inspired.* Porca miseria! *Just what we needed!*

'I'll . . . think of something, sir.'

'I'm sure you will. Show me the libretto so far,' the King added.

The rest of the afternoon passed in discussion of how the libretto should be staged.

Dismissing him, finally, Ferdinand picked up two or three of the files bound with red ribbon that Conrad recognised as diplomatic dispatches.

'I may be along again later in the week to watch the rehearsals, Corrado, if you think it won't prove disruptive?'

'If they can't put up with you, sir, I have no idea how they'll cope with the pit hurling old fruit when they sing a sour note . . .'

He left Ferdinand chuckling.

✦

Tullio fell in beside him on his walk back from the Palace. The streets of Naples were one of the most secure places to talk of secrets, so long as one appeared to be involved in no more than gossip – every other man and woman being engaged in their own business, at the volume of a shout.

'I went out looking for all the local gossip about why the Donna and the Signore are together.' Tullio Rossi shoved his hands in his greatcoat pockets, sending Conrad a cautious look. 'And if he beats her, that sort of thing. The servants say there are rumours of a child, years ago, but there's no sign of any in the house, so that may be people making up juicy stories.'

The feeling that urged itself on Conrad was, he realised, guilt.

Tullio added, 'There are the usual rumours she is beaten, but her maids have never seen bruises. Some of them say it must be she who can blackmail him – why else would he keep a wife who can't give him a son? Just the usual scandal, padrone. Nothing you could say was true.'

Nora's married to him, why am I asking around to find dirt?

'I told her why I couldn't marry her,' Conrad muttered. 'Back in Venice. I didn't know she wanted respectability so much.'

Tullio shrugged, turning into the steep road that led to the lodgings. 'But he keeps her from singing, that's what they say. They've been married for five or six years. There was a time when she was very ill – servants can't keep it straight how long ago – and then she recovered, but gave up her professional singing career. She continued to sing in a few drawing-room operas, but then gave that up too.'

219

The evening air had a chill touch to it. 'That was the illness she died from, then?'

And that was when she became Returned Dead.

'They all say she's got a "fragile constitution". They don't all know she was dead.' Tullio smiled crookedly. 'You should hear the rumours, padrone. One lot say she suffers from consumption, and if she sings a single note, she'll drop dead in a shower of blood.'

There are times when it would be satisfying to still have a hundred saints' names to swear by.

Conrad muttered, '*Merda! Cazzo!*'

'Yeah. And there's a whole other set of rumours, not so spectacular but more disgraceful, that she's suffering from a "licentious" disease. Opinions differ about whether she contracted it during her singing career, when it's assumed she was a slut – or caught it from Il Superbo. Who, naturally, as a gentleman, patronises whores. Either way it stops her singing.'

Conrad rubbed his forehead hard, as if that could get rid of the beginnings of another bout of hemicrania. 'I should never have asked you to find out.'

'All I've got's rumours. Sorry, padrone.'

Tullio waited until they were nearly at their door before he spoke again:

'What makes someone Returned Dead? Who does it happen to? Why doesn't it happen to everybody?'

'I don't know.'

But I do know Tullio has his own dead, in the cold ground.

'They say it most often happens to those who leave someone bereaved who can't bear their death; who'd truly give their own life to have that person returned. But that can't be the whole of it, or else we'd have cities full of Returned Dead! It's an insult to people whose dead stay dead – as if they didn't love them sufficiently well. I suspect the explanation is very different.'

Tullio Rossi nodded, his gaze on the road ahead. He walked for a while saying nothing, people stepping aside from his route automatically.

'Watch their house.' In the open street, Conrad won't mention

220

the name of the Argente mansion. 'Is the . . . Donna . . . allowed out alone?'

'With a maid and footmen, most times.' Tullio shrugged. 'He's careful of her – like she was made of glass, the attic-maids say.'

'I suppose I don't blame him.' Conrad called to mind every scrap of rumour and knowledge a jackdaw-librettist's mind had collected on the subject. 'It's possible for the Dead to, well, not die, but to be destroyed . . . and the Dead don't return twice.'

Despite the crowded sunny street, Tullio Rossi shivered.

'She must go out alone at some time,' Conrad added, frustrated. 'The market? To meet female friends? Find out! Because I intend to speak to her again. I have to.'

✦

The next day was work, and Conrad put everything else out of his mind. He made his way down the dusty palace corridors out of the public eye, not to the secret museum – where he might be forced into the company of the Conte di Argente – but to the same hushed small library.

'Son.'

The spectre of Alfredo Scalese, otherwise Alfred Amsel, had the blue translucence of wood-smoke. The ghost's eyes were more opaque than the rest of him, which at least meant one didn't have to see the inside of his brain-case.

Conrad stopped in the empty library's entrance. Abruptly he turned and pulled the tall doors closed behind him. 'What do you want, Father?'

'I stayed for you.'

Since Alfredo had been white-haired when he died, and pale with illness, he looked little different as a ghost. Conrad felt his heart wrench.

'Strange.' Conrad deliberately walked through one of the ghost's arms as he claimed a table and set his own notebooks and folders out. 'You were unreliable, Father – unreliable to the highest degree. You gambled, you spent every scudo you promised to the family, you couldn't keep any post longer than six months; I'd seen Europe, Turkey, Russia, and North Africa by the time I

221

was ten years old. And yet . . . and yet. Part of me regards you as a child regards his loved father.'

He spoke with his gaze on his papers, not looking up until he finished setting them in order.

The spectre met his gaze. Its eyes were rimmed with light, as if it could still weep. But Alfredo Scalese coughed and dusted his nose, as certain not to show emotion as in life. 'I've been watching people reading. There are books here – you'll have to come, I can't exactly lift them, can I? You complained the ancient savage ceremonies of tearing a heart out on top of a pyramid were too bloody to put on stage, which is where you need your climax . . .'

Conrad was mildly amused, despite himself. 'I don't remember objecting, so much as being realistic about the Church censor.'

'But there's a tribe who sacrifice their virgin daughters to the mouth of a volcano! In Naples, what better spectacle to watch? They can shiver happily over their own mountain of fire, and get the thrill of seeing it erupt on stage instead of in real life!'

'That's – thoughtful.' Conrad pulled out a best-quality cotton handkerchief, given to him by Isaura, and sneezed, dusting his nose hard, much as Alfredo had done.

Thoughtful, even if it does remind me far too much of the Prince's Men and their damned volcanoes. But Father doesn't need to know about that.

'I suspect every opera house in Naples wants to do volcanoes. It's inevitable.' Conrad added, 'And I have Angelotti on my back enough as it is. I only asked him if we could collapse the entire Serpent Queen's Palace in an on-stage earthquake.'

Alfredo smiled wickedly. 'Some men have no sense of humour.'

Conrad straightened his shoulders, and followed the ghost down into the stacks. Alfredo darted sideways, and re-appeared through the shelves – which made Conrad's stomach turn over, no matter how many times he'd seen it before.

'There's a biography of Signore Cortez two shelves over,' the ghost remarked, 'but this is my find, down here – the autobiography of a woman who travelled through South America with one of the touring opera companies they have down there! You can get every detail of the country correct to the utmost degree. Shall you take notes?'

Conrad pulled out the indicated volume, which was less dusty than most on the shelves, being newer, and took it back to his table.

The afternoon wore away to evening, servants came into the library with lamps, the windows turned first indigo and then black. Conrad found his hand cramping from so much note-taking and sketching. Before he realised it, he was deep in conversation over the opera with his Father.

With an after-imprint of my father, he corrected himself. He leaned back in his chair, gazing down the library aisle to where the smoke-blue figure bent over, searching the spines for another title.

Is a spectre less of a person than one of the Returned Dead? Or are they no more than he is?

In all the years Father's come to me, after he died, have I ever known him learn anything? He'll remember that we spent half a night structuring the entrances and exits for Act I and II of The Aztec Princess. *But can he change his character? Is he capable of being anything except irresponsible and feckless, as the real man was?*

How many people have gone mad, hoping their loved ones will lose their faults and cruelties in the spectral life they have? Could I ever have a proper father in Alfredo?

Conrad found his fist pressing against his sternum, where an acid feeling burned. It tasted like regret.

Rehearsals at the church hall can continue without me for one night. If Isaura-Paolo can play the piano, the singers can scramble through their parts for Act I.

He allowed himself to be imposed on by his father, moving from one book to the next, reading passages to one another – Alfredo leaning over Conrad's shoulder, arm sometimes intersecting his son's as he pointed out pages in an open book.

In the middle of an argument regarding the male castrato voice versus the female mezzo, Alfredo's head came up like a hound scenting a fox.

At the same moment, Conrad saw the windows were no longer black but grey.

A repetitive sound echoed across the streets of the city.

Cock-crow.

Conrad said, 'Father—'

Alfredo Scalese gave a smile of regretful affection, and sifted away on the air, dispersing like smoke.

Conrad sat down, a little suddenly, and gazed at his heaped piles of notes.

He remained for some time sitting, staring at nothing in particular. And then shook himself, and stood up, sweeping up his documents and returning to the secret museum to lock them safely away.

Roberto Capiraso's dip-pen and ink-well were still on the table, but there was otherwise no sign of the Conte di Argente.

The wind outside the palace felt refreshing and cold. The eastern sky turned a tropical-butterfly blue. Conrad pushed his sleep-deprived body into a walk through the harbour district, moving as briskly as he might while obstructed by crowds of the *lazzaroni* of Naples – 'common working people' or 'beggars', according to who one spoke to. The fishing-boats were selling the last of their first catch for a few soldi, and heading out for a second attempt. Conrad bought breakfast from a food-seller, and let the keen air clear his head as he ate.

He made sure his way back to the lodgings took him past St Abadios' church hall. Loaned through the King's influence for the singers' rehearsals, it was out of the way of most passers-by. Conrad automatically glanced down the twisted lane, between five- and six-storey buildings strung with washing, on the off-chance that some over-enthusiastic cast members would be still at the hall.

Movement caught his eye.

Far too much of it.

So many people there – at this hour of the morning?

Shadow between the tall tenements chilled him. Or at least, he hoped it was the shadow. He pushed forward – the closer he came, the more solid the press of the crowd. Shoulders and elbows got him through to the front.

'Shite . . .' He breathed out.

Plaster flaked off the front walls of the building in a gust of heat.

224

Two or three deceptive trails of smoke drifted out of the doors. The planks on one side were burned through completely.

The alley to the south side of the building was blocked – all that side of the brickwork wall collapsed. Beyond, inside, the small hall stood open to the sky, roof burned away, walls blackened.

Beads of fire sparked in the ruins.

22

One of the chorus tenors, a short man whom Conrad had also seen in the Duomo choir, clutched at Conrad's sleeve with both hands.

'Supernatural fire!' The tenor unknotted his fingers with difficulty to point.

A low haze of smoke or mist filled the remains of the hall. Conrad edged closer. At the level of the floor, he saw scattered fires, burning with a peculiar yellow-white glow. His head came up abruptly.

The colour of the flames – that smell—

Ignoring complaints, Conrad grabbed the tenor's arm, dragged the small man back, and dropped him. His mind supplied him with memories of that same yellow-white quenchless fire, on the battlefields, and at the Royal Society of London. An experiment with a substance always kept under water for fear it should burst into flame on contact with the air—

Conrad shoved bodily through the protesting crowd of *lazzaroni*. Police officers and foot-soldiers in the King's uniform were struggling to set up a bucket-chain from the harbour.

'Not water!' He looked around desperately for someone he might know – and saw no familiar face.

He picked on a man with police lieutenant's insignia, who had a well-shaven face and ironed uniform for a man out of bed just before dawn.

'Signore! Listen! Water will only spread these flames!'

The lieutenant frowned but seemed willing to listen. 'You know what this is?'

'In laboratories it's called white phosphorus. The Turks make use of it on the battlefield, calling it "Greek Fire". It doesn't need to be set on fire; it just burns on contact with air.' Conrad waved an arm at the hall, and fell into giving orders: 'Use sand, or earth. Keep it smothered. Keep the air away from it. There's plenty of dirt here and you have enough men.'

The lieutenant responded to the tone and briskly nodded agreement.

Conrad grabbed his arm before he could shout commands. 'The important thing – that garlic smell – the gas it gives off? That's poison. Wear wet cloths over your nose and mouth. Don't breathe it. Oh and tell your men, on no account let any of the fire touch them. It sticks and keeps on burning through skin and everything, and the only way to cure it is to cut the flesh away.'

Realisation made the lieutenant's eyes wide. He recognised the last description, so much was clear.

Somebody already got too close—

The lieutenant gave Conrad's hand a brief shake. 'Come with me, signore. I need all the advice I can get if we're to stop it spreading.'

✦

An hour later – the fire mostly subdued, and the police lieutenant in close conversation with a newly arrived colonel in the uniform of the King's Rifles – Conrad startled almost into the air as a shout exploded behind him:

'Corradino!'

Powerful fingers grabbed his arm hard enough that he would have bruises.

He was swung round roughly enough to lose his balance. Clutching at the man accosting him, he found himself holding by the shoulders a white-faced Tullio Rossi.

Soot blackened Tullio's shirt and face, and he was streaked with sweat. The rising sun illuminated him, making him slit his eyes as he stared at Conrad.

'I thought you – *Porco-giuda*-Judas-pig! JohnJack! Sandrine! He's here!'

Spinelli, likewise in shirtsleeves, all but ran across the paved square, Sandrine half a pace behind in tiny black heeled boots. The seconda donna Estella Belucci made a game third place, blonde hair coming down out of its pins.

Conrad grunted helplessly as Spinelli opened his arms and gave him a bear-like embrace.

'We thought—'

'—the fire started—'

'—the corner where you sit—'

'—you left your books there—!'

Sandrine hugged him to her with an amazon grip. Estella Belucci, her eyes bright with sentimental tears, waved her new *cavaliere servente* the tenor Bonfigli over, and in a fit of joy embraced him and Conrad together.

'We thought you were dead.' Tullio's hand thumped hard into Conrad's shoulder. 'You fucking mule-dick!'

That also brought back memories of war-time. Conrad only grinned as the rest laughed. He found himself touched on the arm or shoulder by most of those present, as if they assured themselves of his survival that way.

A shout echoed from the chain of men passing buckets. The last of the fire died down as the contents of a dozen leather buckets hit simultaneously. *More sand*, Conrad recognised, hearing the thuds as it spattered the floor.

He found himself cold, and not from the early breeze.

'Last night— What happened in there? I was in the palace, in the library. The rehearsal— Who was on guard after . . . ?'

'We went off to eat at ten,' Estella put in breathlessly. 'We worked ourselves as hard as you'd wish – as hard as that slave-driver Count Argente! We agreed we'd go home then; some of us go to early Mass today. We wanted to start first thing after that. The King's riflemen were on guard last night. But then, we arrived . . .'

The remains of the church hall hissed softly in the morning air. Now it was daylight, it looked more like a building site than a building, covered with piles of earth and the skeletons of walls.

Conrad wrenched his gaze away. 'Have they brought any bodies out?'

Tullio snorted again. 'Half of them are too afraid to go right in and look!'

'It's not natural!' the tenor Lorenzo Bonfigli whined.

JohnJack Spinelli slapped Bonfigli hard between the shoulder-blades. 'Get back in there and help!'

'No, not yet.' Conrad pulled on his responsibilities like a heavy coat. 'Wait until the fire's definitely out. You don't want burns from that, trust me. Meanwhile— Has anyone taken a roll-call? JohnJack, you go round here and take the names of any of the company who've arrived. Sandrine, you and Tullio split up, go see who's still at home. Check Signore Velluti.'

'Paolo took him home,' Tullio said.

The sun soared above the horizon in a lemon blaze. Conrad paced here, there, wherever he could; talking with the police and infantry as they were finally recalled out of the blackened build-ing, the fire quenched.

Conrad was not surprised when a rifleman arrived with a subdued summons to the presence of Ferdinand of the House of Bourbon-Sicily.

◆

He met the King on the sea-walk, close by the hall, Ferdinand cloaked and in a respectable gentleman's coat and trousers, with nothing to mark him out from anyone else.

He paced over the damp flagstones towards Conrad. 'You're getting a bit careless with theatres, Corrado . . .'

'Funny, sir. Funny.'

Ferdinand's smile was as wry as his own.

In a voice that, while not a whisper, would not carry six feet away, the King said, 'My people have been interviewing the singers and theatre crew who got here earliest this morning. The

229

report I have is that a group of unknown men infiltrated the building a very short time before the witch-fire burned.'

Major Mantenucci came briskly towards them, and, at a signal from the King, relaxed, removing his hat and running his fingers through his cropped salt-and-pepper hair.

'It will have been the Men,' he grunted. 'Or their lackeys, obviously. There's sufficient damage to the main hall that it's impossible to hold further rehearsals here. St Abadios' aren't pleased.'

Conrad bit his lip until he tasted blood. *Better than swearing in front of the King of the Two Sicilies. Particularly since I might not stop. This on top of everything else!*

'Do we have no idea who's behind it?' he burst out. 'The – Men—' He managed Mantenucci's half-euphemism. '—They must have a local leader! If they're Europe-wide, someone who's come in from the outside—'

Ferdinand held his hand up, though with an expression that said he sympathised with Conrad's frustration. 'Enrico?'

'According to the information my officers have, orders are relayed via several lieutenants. They don't see the leader's face. The inner circle may, but we have no informants there.'

The police Commendatore scowled.

'The low-level men believe the leader is from outside the Two Sicilies. It could be so. Or it could be a bluff deliberately put around. From what information I have, I believe their leader to be a revolutionary – I suspect, raised in poor, violent circumstances, perhaps without family. That the leader hides his identity leads me to suspect he's now in far better circumstances, a well-off man who's welcome as a gentleman in society, perhaps with a wife, and who therefore wishes to avoid any scandal as to his origins or activities. Either he or his minions are remarkably knowledgeable about bel canto and the demi-monde of Naples itself. We've stopped attempts at sabotage that were keenly aimed.'

Conrad groaned. 'Half the well-off gentlemen high up in the Local Racket meet that description! How will you tell the difference?'

Mantenucci gave a shrug that spoke himself disgusted with their lack of success.

'As to rehearsals . . .' The King let his gaze travel in the direction of the smoke, still lazing up into the air from the ruined hall. 'We could move to a small opera house. The Fondo, perhaps. But . . . then we risk losing that house. After your company left for the evening, every one of the men I had watching here was decoyed away in some fashion. Conrad, you didn't come down here last night?'

'I intended to, sir, but I ended up being productive in the library, and stayed there.'

Ferdinand nodded absently. 'Good. We need a complete libretto as soon as possible. I think . . . Conrad, do I have your attention?'

His sight had blurred, staring out at the harbour and the boats going out. The taste of Greek Fire still sullied his tongue.

With difficulty, he managed, 'Sir?'

'Evidently we can't conceal royal involvement now. We tried hiding in plain sight, and the Men found out what you were and where you were rehearsing, without difficulty.' Ferdinand rubbed his hands briskly against the dawn cold. 'Starting today, I'll let people know that our funding should pay workers to do double hours, and also pay for considerable increased security.'

Mantenucci rumbled reluctant agreement. Conrad forced himself to concentrate, wiping both hands down his coat, ignoring the soot staining the lapels.

There's something in my mind, something I can almost see—

Ferdinand gazed about, pleased with the anonymity the crowd brought him. 'Additional men from Colonel Alvarez's regiment will be brought in. Now we only have to think where the company can continue rehearsals without outside interference.'

Still with the back of his mind busy, Conrad shoved his hands in his pockets against the early morning air.

'Castell dell'Ovo. Sir?' He glanced along the shoreline, but they were too far around the headland to see the stark silhouette. 'I know Egg Castle hasn't been much refurbished since Norman times, but it's on a peninsula – just – and a garrison could make it completely defensible. There's bound to be suitable rooms inside for rehearsal. Although the musicians will complain about the damp.'

Ferdinand looked amused. 'Major Mantenucci?'

The Major's upright figure shifted from the balls to the heels of his feet. If Conrad had not suspected Enrico Mantenucci last let the emotion show at the age of thirteen, he would have thought the man was embarrassed.

'I have also been thinking radically.' Mantenucci said it as if it were a confession. 'I hope you don't object, sir.'

'Not at all.' The King spread his hands. 'Continue.'

'Well, then. The trouble with Egg Castle is that it is a castle. Once you're in, you're besieged, and they always know where to find you. On the other hand . . . You know that this city is old, and there are many layers of buildings. We have had cause to investigate catacombs, shrines, old aqueducts, in the past. But more to the point, sire, there are also great stone chambers under Naples, that it appears were carved out in Roman times by men mining for the volcanic rock. There's a lot of room, it's cool, and it's dry.'

The King nodded enthusiastically. 'Surely that would have wonderful acoustics for rehearsals!'

In the east's harsh light, Enrico Mantenucci's face showed deep determined lines. 'There are a limited and manageable number of exits and entrances. All could be protected by armed men. Whereas the singers can be attacked in places like this—' He waved casually at the blackened beams. '—Under Naples, there would be less danger of that. Any trouble and they could be led out by other routes.'

Conrad found himself nodding.

'Assuming all of us can be trusted.' Ferdinand pulled his coat more tightly around himself in the brisk wind. 'But that's always a consideration. Very well, Enrico – can I rely on you to clear out the required spaces?'

'Sir!'

Conrad went to move off in the police chief's wake. The King's hand rested on his shoulder.

'Is there something else? You seem concerned.' Ferdinand's plump, bland expression was surprisingly penetrating. 'Have you, for example, spoken to Roberto Capiraso or his wife since you left prison?'

'No, sir. Yes, there's something, but that's not it.'

I feel fear, Conrad realised. *Because of what my mind has been turning over, while I dealt with hysterical friends and a damaged building . . .*

Everything fits. I just wish it didn't.

'What is it, Conrad?'

'Sir, I think that someone else knew, beforehand, that the rehearsal hall was going to burn last night.' Speech hurt Conrad's dry throat. 'I was decoyed away, like your guards.'

Ferdinand lifted his brows. His voice, if firm, was sympathetic. 'By who?'

'My father.'

23

'Your father?' Ferdinand exclaimed. 'Your father's dead! If he wasn't, you wouldn't have inherited his debts, and I wouldn't have had to twist the arm of the Conte di Galdi!'

'He often appears as a spectre, sir.'

The wind off the sea lifted Conrad's short hair.

'It was done so neatly I didn't notice. Someone knew enough to decoy me in the library with just the books I might want – knew enough to keep me talking, and to delay me until it was too late to be worth going to the rehearsal hall.'

Conrad looked down at his hands. The extremity of his fingers were white, either with cold or dread.

'My father knows me too well. Either he did this deliberately, or he was a dupe who told others about me. I swear, I only talked to Father about the story of the opera. But clearly that was too much.'

Further down the crowded street, Conrad saw Major Mantenucci in conversation with Tullio.

Ferdinand Bourbon-Sicily slipped his arm through Conrad's, and Conrad found himself steered back on the way towards the Palazzo Reale. They ended up on one of the quays.

The King stopped and gazed out over the choppy Bay, and the two blues of sea and sky, rubbing both his hands together. 'Alfredo Scalese – a true ghost?'

Conrad shrugged. 'Difficult to say, sir. He always looks like Father. He knows what Alfredo would say in any situation. Whether it is a remnant of the man I knew, or whether it's just an echo of some sort, I can't say.'

If I decided that, I'd have to decide how I feel about what he says.

'He was very intent on keeping me in the library all night. I don't know if that was to protect me, or to prevent me stopping the fire, or even both.'

Conrad drew a breath.

'But I've had time to think, now. And I should have seen this before . . . It's obvious. There shouldn't have been anyone in Naples who knew about all of Alfredo's debts.'

The waters of the Gulf of Napoli beat on the rocks at the foot of the wall.

Conrad stared at the repeating waves, rather than look at King Ferdinand's face. 'I hadn't spread the news around. I never do. It's my business, and only mine. And yet, Adalrico Silvestri knew exactly what to demand – and from who – down to every last tiny creditor.'

It was on his lips to explain further, to describe how Alfredo Scalese owed gambling debts in Prussia, rent in Westphalia, money for a South American mining scheme in St Petersburg, and fifty others that only a son should know.

The King's expression showed it was unnecessary. 'I should have realised that.'

As for who else knows details – the Pironti family? Doubtful, since it turns out I haven't been communicating with Gianpaolo Pironti all these years . . . Isaura will know.

I trust her implicitly.

Conrad wiped his mouth in a vain attempt to get rid of the taste of smoke, and blurted, 'Therefore – I think it must be true – that my father is with the Prince's Men!'

Ferdinand's hand rested briefly, comfortingly, on his arm.

'I talked to him,' Conrad finished miserably. 'And I don't, in all honesty, remember everything I said. They could have learned anything through me. Sir, I'm sorry.'

'I think few men wouldn't talk to their father, in your place.'

Ferdinand's understanding was almost worse than being shouted at.

'Yes, sir, but I know what he's like! I've always known. He was a loving, wonderfully funny father who couldn't be relied on to remember the smallest promise, or be persuaded to stop doing anything if he felt like doing it.'

The words came away like scabs being picked off. The only consolation was that they were true. *And I should have said them a long time before this.*

'I know my father. If he has fallen in with the Prince's Men . . . He's capable of sabotaging an underground rehearsal, or the San Carlo. Or leading other men – living men – to do it. He won't be stopped if I ask him, or if someone argues – not for logic or threats – he always does exactly what he likes, and opposition only makes him more bull-headed—'

'Corrado—'

'I need to make a request of you, sir.'

Voices echoed from the nearby crowds, but Conrad felt as though he and Ferdinand stood in deep silence.

'I want you to tell me, sir, if there's anything you can do to stop a spy who can pass through any walls, overhear any words, penetrate any locked door.'

Conrad watched the King's face lose colour.

'Then I make a request of you, sire. Will you ask the Cardinal of Naples if he'll exorcise my father?'

✦

The Duomo and Archbishop's Palace had both been built at an earlier age, before the Normans came into Sicily and the mainland, and were based on the foundations of still older buildings. Since the private chapel they entered had survived (among other events) the great medieval earthquake, it had little of the later decorations and alterations of the main church. Squat columns of white stone held up a vaulted roof. Light that managed to slant its way in through Romanesque window-arches turned to champagne. The stone altar breathed antiquity.

It would have been calming, Conrad thought, if not for the

gilded statues of saints, their wounds painted in exact colour, which seemed out of place against the grim original walls. He lost himself in gazing at the racks of prayer-candles. The dazzle allowed him to forget for a time what he was doing here.

A sensation of proximity made him look up.

A man in Dominican black and white rested both hands on the back of the pew.

'Signore.' The voice was familiar.

The low light was clear enough to show sleek black hair and burning dark eyes. Canon-Regular Luka Viscardo gazed forward, apparently watching King Ferdinand and the Cardinal, Gabriele Corazza, talk.

Viscardo spoke quietly enough that his sneering tone wouldn't reach the King or Cardinal. 'I wonder why, signore, if you're an atheist, you believe the souls of the dead haunt the earth?'

'Because I perceive them, Viscardo.' Conrad matched him sneer for sneer. 'Like the Returned Dead, but not corporeal. I doubt they're "souls" in your sense. Just because there's something that appears to be the personality of a dead man, that doesn't mean that it is.'

Conrad paused, and dissected emotionlessly:

'If it is a survival of something after death, that doesn't necessarily mean there's anything religious about it. It could be a non-supernatural echo of a personality. Or it could simply be that our next stage of life, after we appear to die, is as an incorporeal being. None of that implies a "soul".'

Leather shoes squeaking, Viscardo walked around the end of the pew and sat down beside him, leaning forward as if he comforted a parishioner. 'So that's why you're willing to have us kill your father?'

Conrad couldn't hide his reaction. He grunted. The words hurt him like a boot under the ribs.

Is this what I'm doing? Murdering what remains of my father?

Viscardo's tone turned unctuous. 'This is a sad day for you, signore. There is a comfort in having the ghost of a loved one about the place. As if the person is not quite gone.'

Conrad stood up, unsurprised to find the King and Cardinal

within earshot now, walking back from the altar. He found one of his hands balled into a fist. He hid it in the folds of his coat, turning a shoulder to Canon-Regular Viscardo.

'His Eminence agrees with me,' Ferdinand said, his face stern and sad. 'And grants permission for the exorcism, which he himself will perform.'

Conrad nodded respectfully to the Cardinal, aware of irony.

This is the man who would have interrogated me, being Head of the Holy Office as he is.

'Yes, sir. When?'

For all his magnificent robes, Corazza resembled very remarkably certain comic prints Conrad had seen in England, of red-nosed, explosive-tempered fox-hunters. The Cardinal spoke in a powerful wheezing voice. 'Now.'

Conrad choked out, 'Now?'

'If a soul is in danger of damnation, the sooner it's sent on to God the better.' Cardinal Corazza paced on, calling for various churchmen that Conrad guessed would be his most skilled priests.

Conrad sat down hard on the wood of the pew. Under his breath, he muttered, 'Now?'

Viscardo's voice sounded as if he smirked. 'So that's how an atheist asks us for an exorcism . . .'

'Whatever it is that you people do, the method works – mostly – as I understand it.' Conrad met Viscardo's black gaze with unblinking defiance. 'A shame you don't investigate it scientifically, to find out why!'

Conrad found Ferdinand's hand squeezing his shoulder. The King gestured the red-faced Canon-Regular away, and implacably watched him go.

'Might I tactfully suggest you keep the heresy quieter?'

Conrad gave a wan smile, but couldn't keep it on his face. 'Sir, will we – should I – be present for this?'

'His Eminence has been brought to understand that we will. I think there are questions to be asked of Alfredo Scalese.'

The distant choir sang with Gabriele Corazza as he offered the holy sacrifice of Mass; Conrad could not focus his attention even for a Sung Mass, potential cause of miracles.

He couldn't pay attention, either, to the ancient ceremony of exorcism, no matter how good an opportunity it would have been to observe it. He watched the sun-bathed squat pillars of the ancient Norman chapel. They blurred.

The rite of exorcism continued interminably.

'*Vade retro Alfred Amsel!*' Cardinal Corazza's deep voice hit a pitch perfect note. '*Vade retro Alfredo Scalese! Vade retro mundus, exitas mundus—*'

Conrad could not even bring himself to quarrel with their execrable Latin.

The chapel echoed with the screams of the ghost.

Conrad was conscious of Ferdinand stirring beside him. He managed to nod to the King.

'Signore Ghost,' Ferdinand Bourbon called.

The spectre glided across the ancient flat slabs of tombs, and was brought up with a jolt five yards from the altar. There was no visible boundary there now, but Conrad was willing to bet money it was where the Cardinal had aspersed holy water at the start of the ceremony.

All that means is that he's able to perceive it, and that he believes it repels him.

Alfredo's furious distorted face loomed up, suddenly, at Conrad. 'Agnese must have slept with another man! You're not my son, my son wouldn't kill me!'

'My father wouldn't join a conspiracy against the King!'

Even caught between hurt and fury, Conrad managed to keep the name of the Prince's Men to himself.

'And if I did?' Alfredo shrugged with supreme carelessness. 'So what? I died a long time ago. I can't be wiping your arse every day, boy; do you have any idea how boring existence is for me? I would have thought you'd be happy your old father had found some friends, and some things he can do to feel useful . . .'

Conrad looked away from the blue-grey figure, translucent as Murano glass. He slid down slightly on the pew while Ferdinand began his questioning.

Which will be useless – useless! Ferdinand won't make him talk in any detail about what the Prince's Men plan. Why would he? It's obvious they'd keep my father in the dark!

The questions went round in circles.

Ferdinand sat back. 'How certain are you that you let nothing slip to him?'

Conrad rubbed his face, but could not wipe away the weariness or the shame. 'I tried to discuss only the libretto, in terms of a small summer production, but . . . I was used to talking with him when he was alive; it was one thing he always did well. I can't affirm that I told him nothing I shouldn't.'

The King looked stern, but more forgiving than Conrad thought he should. 'He was your father . . . Your dead father. He gave no hint that he knew far more of your business than he should?'

'Not to me, sir.'

Alfredo Scalese stared around the chapel as if he searched for someone not present. The minute he caught the King's eye on him, he said triumphantly, 'There are certainly those close to you who know more than you think! Not just me!'

'Evil spirits speak ill!' Cardinal Corazza crossed himself, puffing even as he walked the short distance to his King. 'Sire, this one is obviously practised in spreading suspicion between those who trust each other, but my experience suggests that he's merely a gad-fly, even if associated with those who do evil.'

Alfredo caught Conrad's eye and moved one finger, mimicking sealing his lips shut.

Conrad let go a word that made the Cardinal start. He glimpsed the King calming the churchman.

'Why would you do this?' Conrad demanded.

Alfredo visibly pouted. 'Why shouldn't I? I became part of il Principe years ago. Along with the Bloody Hand, the Masons, *la società onorata*, the Rosicrucians, the Carbonari, the Camorra – every group I thought might give me something interesting to pass Eternity. You have no idea how time weighs . . . Imagine how surprised I was when the Prince's Men summoned me because they had a suspicion about my son.'

In peripheral vision, Conrad saw Ferdinand speaking urgently to the Cardinal, and Corazza raising his hand as if to swear an oath of silence.

The King looked speculatively at the ghost.

No. My father will say anything to anybody, no matter what oaths he might swear! Conrad just stopped himself yelling, *Isn't it obvious? He can't even be loyal to the damn Prince's Men!*

Alfredo cocked a jaundiced eye at the riches of the chapel, and the rest of the Duomo. He spread the skirts of his frock-coat and to all appearances perched his immaterial body on the back of a pew, facing Conrad.

'. . . If I'd known I'd end up here, I wouldn't have come. They were right about you, by the way, Conrad,' Alfredo continued blandly. 'You were always a secretive boy, listening and not talking . . . and you showed a regrettable tendency to refuse to gossip about any of what you heard. The money I could have made, if you'd been a bit more careless about what you heard at palace doors . . .'

His hard expression softened, in that face that seemed made out of frozen light.

'But you loved your Papa, didn't you? You won't let him be sent off into who-knows-what? I did think that when it came to it, I wouldn't object – Eternity's a long time – but I haven't had enough of it yet. You won't let them make me go!'

Conrad rested his face in his hands, welcoming the dark.

If I just said to him, 'they can only compel you because you believe they can' . . . A few words from me, and he wouldn't be driven out—

Cardinal Corazza's hound-hallooing voice echoed back from the chapel's arched ceiling. 'Be at peace, Alfred Amsel, and return to your Father—'

'I don't want to go!'

The sound of bells swelled and died, and a long chant in Latin echoed back from the maze of pillars. Conrad did not speak, or look up.

But he heard Alfredo Scalese cursing and screaming as he was forced away, until all sign of him finally vanished.

24

Conrad leaned back on a pew in the main part of the Duomo. 'Tullio, I just want to sit here for a time.'

The ex-soldier gave him a sceptical look. 'If you were any other man, I'd say you wanted to pray.'

'The world must be *easier* if it's only six thousand years old, and sandwiched between Heaven and Hell. Surely?'

He closed his eyes, and after a while heard Tullio's quiet departing steps.

He doubted the other man would go far.

Conrad sat in the Duomo di San Gennaro, not thinking of it as a religious house, but as somewhere quiet where he could sit and eradicate the screams of Alfredo's spirit from his memory.

Suppose he was only an imprint, like the mark the printing press leaves on the paper. That doesn't answer the question of whether he could feel his own terror, or whether it was just for show . . .

And I wish I thought it was the latter.

A fair-haired man in clerical clothing seated himself at Conrad's right, with a decorous sweep of his black robes. It was not Luka Viscardo; that was the best that could be said for him.

A priest. The last thing I need is a comforting priest—!

'Have you considered,' the priest asked in a low murmur, 'that if your debts to the late Alfredo Scalese's creditors were paid in total, you would be free to leave Naples? Perhaps to a place as a respected librettist in, shall we say . . . St Petersburg?'

Conrad studied the man beside him.

The disguise – or possibly it was not a disguise – looked flawless. An ordinary ordained priest. But unlike the Dominican Canon-Regular Viscardo, with his burning single-minded faith, this cleric was apparently one of the Prince's Men.

Since I can't think of anyone else who would pay to get rid of me.

Never mind how they found me, or how they knew it was me they should approach . . . Is there nothing Alfredo didn't tell them?

Conrad felt unsure if the chill in his guts was disquiet, or overwhelming anger at the proposition. 'So you're offering me – what?'

'To pay off all your debts.' The anonymous man in his anonymous clerical black lifted a faint blond eyebrow. 'Surely you understand? Every debt that your father Alfredo owed, to be paid off by . . . the end of this week?'

I suppose . . . I suppose, if they decide that they can do this, they can.

'After all,' the Prince's Man added, 'you may have made some agreement or other, but it can hardly be considered binding. Who'd give up happiness for a philosophical point?'

'Is it philosophical?' Conrad muttered, trying for time. 'I thought we were speaking of money . . .'

And every gentleman knows that money is something not worth talking about. Knows that old money is better than the nouveau riche variety, because it comes from the invisible labour of servants on the land, and not from embarrassingly visible industry. Money, according to scholars and philosophers, is beneath a man.

'Think what you could do with all of what you earn,' the man said, 'were you not paying nine tenths of it to Alfredo Scalese's creditors.'

Conrad felt his expression alter, and, in a panic, realised he did not know what it gave away. 'I could get married . . .'

He realised he had spoken aloud.

The Prince's Man leaned forward, alert. 'There's a lady in the case? Yes, I see why you would hesitate to engage yourself in marriage, and a family, with your prospects so poor. But if your debts were gone . . .'

Conrad did not bother to correct the man's misapprehension.

There is only one woman I would ever marry, and this comes too late for that.

I wonder what I would have done in Venice, if this offer had been made to me then? If I could have said to Leonora, marry me, have my children, I will spend my life making you happy?

I suppose I would have spent my life as a lap-dog of the Prince's Men. For much the same reason men end up obliged to la società onorata *and the other people we don't talk about.*

'Of course—' The man's unexpectedly harsh voice interrupted his thoughts. '—this is not an offer that will be open for all time.'

First the cheese and then the trap, Conrad thought sardonically.

It would have amused him more if he couldn't feel the steel teeth biting. To be free of a burden he has borne these ten years— What does he owe the King of the Two Sicilies, really?

I haven't lived here since I was a child. Even the Neapolitan dialect is strange to my ear now. I have almost no memories of the place, since Alfredo dragged us off round the cold German courts to earn his living. King Ferdinand is making use of me, the King admits as much— I wasn't even their first choice. So why not take what the Prince's Men offer?

The tempting thought emerged from the back of his mind:

Once it's done, it would be done.

If they pay off my debts, and then I do nothing, they can hardly recall their money.

I suppose my life wouldn't be worth a single soldo. *But then, it isn't now.*

This is why his Majesty Ferdinand wanted some big philosophical statement from me about my ethics, since I'm not constrained to morality by a god. I could have referred him to the old pagan philosophers . . .

I need to believe in myself as a certain kind of person, and therefore I need to act appropriately.

Apart from that, it's the small threads hold him. Human ties. Knowing how Tullio would look. How disappointed JohnJack would be. And being aware that Paolo-Isaura would never look up to her big brother again – but would understand why he did it.

244

At the back of his mind, he doesn't want to give Il Superbo another chance to sneer – or give his beautiful wife cause to think of Conrad as a traitor.

'You are an atheist, Signore Scalese,' the man in black urged, his white hands clenched on the back of the pew in front. 'There's no God to make you keep your word.'

Conrad smiled toothily.

I suppose it doesn't matter who they sent with the offer, since it's so tempting . . . but this man is something less than tactful.

'Thank you for your generous opinion of me, Father,' Conrad said, not without irony. 'Please don't send anyone else with this proposition. There's no point. If I choose to give my word, I choose to keep it. The answer is no.'

✦

'Conrad?'

Ferdinand's hand on his shoulder brought him out of his tomb-cold thoughts. He lifted his head, surprised to see that the Cardinal and his priests had left.

A single set of footsteps rebounded back from the walls. Tullio came to stand beside the King.

Carefully putting the logic together, counting off the points on his fingers, Conrad said, 'An exorcism destroys . . . whatever it is . . . that makes the appearance of the person. Whether it is that person or not. I feel – as if Father has died all over again.'

At Ferdinand's gesture, Tullio's strong grip brought Conrad up onto his feet.

'He died at my request.' Conrad looked away, not able to meet either of their gazes. 'It's all the worse because I could never respect him.'

Before he could formulate an objection, he was being walked smartly towards the church door. A swirl of black and white robes might have been Luka Viscardo, but if it was, the man never spoke.

'I'll take him round by way of the taverns this afternoon, sir, in places we won't be recognised,' Tullio said as they came out into the open. 'So at least he can sleep.'

'I approve.' Ferdinand absently patted Conrad's shoulder. It was intended to be comforting, Conrad thought, though it made him feel more like a Labrador retriever.

Conrad allowed himself to look at King Ferdinand, weighing himself intently for any sign of resentment.

No. It was my choice to get mixed up in this. And . . . it was Father's, too.

Sunlight shone on the opulent doors of the Duomo, and the women in bonnets, and men removing their top hats, filing in for their prayers to the loved dead. He and the King and Tullio – two gentlemen and their servant – were anonymous in the crowd.

Ferdinand murmured, apparently idly, 'I made the voyage to island-Sicily recently. While I was there, I saw unusual amounts of smoke and steam issuing up from the crater of Mount Ætna.'

'Are you sure it was unusual?' Conrad felt his face heat, and added apologetically, 'Ætna's always a lively mountain, sir.'

'I know.' Ferdinand smiled like a boy. 'I'm sure. My advisers were in hysterics – I insisted on climbing some distance up the Valle de Bove.'

The King's smile faded, giving way to determination.

'There are earthquakes continually shuddering along the slopes of the mountain. Although the mountain-top is snow-covered, snow and ice have melted away from the actual crater. I saw minor eruptions. In places the earth is coloured yellow with sulphur. The air stinks.'

Conrad was for a moment back in the house owned by his Uncle Baltazar, where his mother and sister now live, watching the open cracks high up the mountain, that emit veils of smoke by day, and spitting lava by night.

'It was bound to happen.' Ferdinand looked at him as though he were missing the obvious. 'As soon as the black opera began their preliminary rehearsals.'

◆

Conrad could find nothing to say for several minutes. The King broke the silence between them, speaking under the low murmur of the collecting congregation.

'Come in to see me tomorrow morning, Conrad. You and I must talk.'

Regret went through Conrad for the possibility of a day out with Tullio, and likely Paolo, lost to a sense of responsibility. He pushed it aside.

'Don't you think, sir, it would be better to discuss anything new now?'

Ferdinand at last nodded. 'It's becoming apparent that we don't have much time.'

He summoned servants, ordering a carriage for Conrad and Tullio alone. Conrad did not object.

We need a truly private discussion, I think.

The carriage fought its way through Naples' crowded, narrow streets; between high buildings strung with washing between balconies and open shutters. They climbed a long hill almost too steep for the horses, coming to eventual clear ground with palms, cypresses, and buds growing to excess.

Conrad recognised the half-built building site on the hill-top, and pointed it out to Tullio. 'Vomero hill's new museum and observatory.'

Tullio Rossi looked under-impressed.

Conrad followed Tullio down from the carriage, Tullio having pulled down the steps to let him descend, and found himself wishing he had his boots instead of his shoes, and a heavier coat on.

The view gave them the Gulf of Naples from Sorrento and Capri over to Vesuvius. The brisk wind in this exposed place would carry any speech away. Conrad caught sight of Tullio looking about himself with a pleased expression – not so much at the sea wind, and the scent of sulphur drifting from the Burning Fields over to the south-west, as at the distance they were above Naples' roofs, and how unlikely it was, therefore, that anyone could overhear them. Some fifteen minutes later, King Ferdinand arrived in a coach with no royal coat of arms on the door.

'I trust you as your master does,' Ferdinand said to Tullio as he approached. 'What you might hear, you'll keep silent. And it would be advisable, I think, were you to patrol these slopes, just

247

in case there are enemies who would take advantage of us being here. Go.'

Tullio caught Conrad's eye.

He's got used to Paolo-Isaura and the opera people, and we don't treat him as a servant.

Conrad was relieved to see amusement rather than resentment.

Tullio Rossi dropped the King a salute. 'Yes, sire!'

Conrad felt an arm link through his as Tullio sloped off, the very picture of a skiving servant.

The King led Conrad towards the green top of Vomero Hill. He released Conrad's arm and lifted his finger, pointing to the south, and traced an imaginary path out from the harbour, west of Sorrento and Capri, south into the Tyrrhenean Sea. It was evident he was not concerned with the shimmering Mediterranean blue, or the light here, which Conrad thought painters would avidly die to have.

'I want you to leave Naples for a while, signore.' Ferdinand's tone was equable, not condemning.

Conrad felt awkward nonetheless. 'I haven't finished the libretto—'

'You've completed enough of the first two Acts that il Conte di Argente will be busy for a week setting it, and the cast rehearsing it.'

Ferdinand looked at him suddenly, his expression sympathetic.

'You need to grieve for your father. As for this business between you and the Count – I want you out of here while both you and Capiraso calm down. You must reach a point where you can agree to work together: that won't happen in the thick of all this. Additionally, I desire you out of the way of the Prince's Men – and if I can smuggle you out of the city quickly enough, today, you will be. When you return, I'll have defensive measures in place here, and for your family in Catania. For the moment . . . I would rather you were safe.'

Conrad was warmed despite himself.

'Then . . . where do I go?' He frowned, having a sudden suspicion. 'What do I do?'

'Ah.' Ferdinand Bourbon-Sicily looked very bland. 'Politicians always have more than one motive . . . Yes, there is something I would like you to do, Conrad. If you have no objection, I should like you to act as my . . . diplomatic aide, shall we say? . . . and take a message from me to a man in exile.'

I'll have to agree or disagree based solely on this much information, that's obvious.

'I don't blame you for not trusting me, sir,' Conrad said frankly. 'Since I can't tell you if I did reveal anything to my – to Alfredo.'

There was an odd hardness in the King's gaze. 'I trust you, Conrad. A man doesn't have two fathers. It's not likely that circumstance will arise again.'

Conrad found it difficult to accept the understanding in the man's gaze.

Would it be so bad if I were gone for a day or two?

If I know Roberto Capiraso, the next thing 'Il Superbo' is likely to do is flaunt the fact that he's married to Leonora – bring her to rehearsals, invite us all to social dinners, offer to let us use his horses to ride . . . and all so that it's plain she's at his side, and no one else's.

'How long will I be away from the opera, sire?'

'I would say . . . less than a week.'

When I get back, we'll likely be too close to deadline for Il Superbo's stupid games . . .

Conrad did not choose to think about Alfredo Scalese at all.

'All right – yes, sir,' Conrad corrected himself. 'I'll take your message. Where am I to go?'

'You'll have sealed orders, to be opened once you're aboard ship. However, I can tell you the general nature of what you'll be doing.'

Conrad nodded. As the thought occurred to him, he added, 'Will I be able to take a servant with me?'

The King looked wry. 'Yes, you may bring Tullio Rossi.' The unspoken end of the sentence seemed to be *As if either of us could stop him coming with you!*

'Thank you, sir.' Conrad reached up and settled his hat before the wind could send it bowling. 'What am I to be doing, then?'

'We have a chance to avert another move by the Prince's Men

249

– but this one is on a much larger scale than the attack on the rehearsal hall.'

Conrad's stomach twisted.

How did I come to be responsible for so many people's safety? Oh yes – I volunteered.

'It concerns matters outside Naples itself.' Ferdinand glanced around, and Conrad found himself gripped by the elbow and steered towards a large rock in the lee of the half-built walls.

Without so much as looking for servants, Ferdinand dusted off the granite with his gloves. 'Sit.'

The slab was a reasonable substitute for a bench. Conrad eased himself down – caught himself sitting in the presence of the monarch and half stood up – and felt Ferdinand Bourbon-Sicily's hand pushing on his shoulder. The King seated himself on the same slab of rock.

In the lee of the new stonework, the wind was cut off. It felt warm enough that Conrad could feel his body unconsciously relaxing from its clenched stiffness. The sound of the wind through the bushes, and the feel of the sun on his face, somehow made it easier to regain his composure.

'Please continue, sir.'

The outdoor light made the King's round face look pallidly unhealthy. It gave Conrad cause to wonder how long the man had been in meetings and conferences, aimed at fighting the threat to his kingdom.

'I visited more than Ætna when I was absent,' Ferdinand remarked, on an apparent tangent. 'On the return voyage, I also called at the island of Stromboli.'

The southern volcanic islands were not visible from here, all of them – Vulcano, Stromboli, Salina, Lipari, Alicudi and Filicudi, and the rest – being a short distance north of island-Sicily.

Conrad found his gaze straying to mainland-Sicily's volcano, where Vesuvius breathed a haze into the upper atmosphere. 'And the Stromboli volcano?'

'There was volcanic upheaval, as ever, from the Lighthouse of the Mediterranean. That's not why I went. I was . . . summoned.'

Startled, Conrad turned his head. Ferdinand seemed as if he

tasted something bitter, as if he didn't like the implications of force, but couldn't omit them.

'In some ways, I owe this throne to the Northern Empire.' The King's mouth twisted as he gazed down on Naples. It was possible from here to pick out Egg Castle, and further along the shore, the roofs of the Palazzo Reale and the Teatro San Carlo. 'You're aware of my father's . . . erratic politics in the last war?'

'Yes, sir.' Since Ferdinand appeared to require some confirmation, Conrad added, '"Erratic" is one of the kinder terms for a man who'd sign treaties and break them before he finished the carriage-ride home . . .'

Ferdinand winced. 'Despite that, I managed – after his death – to persuade the North to leave the Two Sicilies alone. It wouldn't have been difficult for France to put in a puppet governor in my place, or leave us to the Hapsburgs. They did neither, but they still could. So, when they give me commands, I have to agree . . . Shall we walk on?'

Conrad rose and dusted himself off, following the King's lead in walking around the half-risen walls of what would in time become the new museum.

'I would like to ask you for further assistance, Conrad. How much do you know about the situation in the North, after the end of the war?'

'Not much.' Since it seemed to be an afternoon for honesty, Conrad added, 'After the fighting I was in, a man steers clear of the thought that it was all for nothing.'

Ferdinand snorted, but it was a noise of agreement, not derision.

Conrad pieced his knowledge together. 'After the Armistice at Waterloo . . . The fighting ended, and later I heard the Emperor of the North was still on his throne. I gave up following political affairs.' *In disgust*, went unspoken. 'Word has it, he's given up foreign conquest, and is concentrating on building up trade so the Gallic Empire won't fall behind Britain and the Americas. Is that true, sir?'

'True enough. He needs prosperity. Or else the people might start remembering his amazing run of victories, and how that's now over.'

251

Ferdinand began to walk back along the cleared earth before the new building. His restlessness might have been physical, but Conrad – treading in his wake – thought it was not.

The King said, 'Signore Castiello-Salvati helped with the diplomatic negotiations between Sicily and the North . . . I don't know how much he told the Prince's Men before he died. As little as he could, I expect. But they are ruthless in what they do.'

There was a moment's silence in which Conrad felt plainly how the King missed the man with whom he had worked closely.

He's lost a friend, and one of the few who know him as a man, not a king. It will take him years, if not longer, to decide whether another man is trustworthy.

The slow illumination came. *And I suppose it begins with trusting them to work for him.*

Conrad put the momentous thought aside for consideration. As gently as he could, he said, 'I don't yet understand what you're telling me, sir.'

The King of the Two Sicilies walked on, leaving the new building behind, and Conrad followed him past evergreen groves of holm oak, palm, and the stark trunks and penumbral clumps of umbrella pine. If not warm, the day was nonetheless brilliant, and if there was snow on the black of Vesuvius's crown, there were buds in the bushes here, spring well under way.

The King at last stopped at the top of a bluff. Naples lay below. His shoulders straightened.

'It appears—' Ferdinand clasped his white-gloved hands behind his back. '—that there has been a secret coup. The Emperor of the North has been deposed, and sent into exile.'

'What!'

'Oh, you won't have read this in the *Giornale*.' Ferdinand turned his head and pinned Conrad with a no-nonsense gaze. 'Most of the councillors of the Empire have been confidentially told that the Emperor is dying. That includes all his old generals, who most certainly wouldn't allow him to be put out of power if they knew he wasn't dying – isn't even ill.'

The King frowned.

'This is a long-laid plot. It plays on the fears of the generals and

Council members that, without the Emperor, the North will fall into ruin, and therefore the passing-over of power must be strictly orchestrated. The heads of the Council have long planned that, in such a case, they will make graded announcements, over some months – the Emperor has had a riding accident – an injury – from which he recovers – relapses – is ill – is dying . . . And by that time every position of power will be filled with staunch Council supporters, there'll be no dissent, and the only thing to be arranged will be the State funeral.'

Conrad found himself quite literally open-mouthed.

He blurted out, 'He's been sent into exile?'

'Oh, quite. Where could he be sent? Who could – would – take him, and be trusted to keep quiet about it?' Ferdinand snapped off a pine twig and began stripping the short needles from it, one at a time. 'As things stand, the Emperor has been anonymously exiled to the island of Stromboli. And, since that's part of my territory, I'm his prison governor. Hence my visit, to see him properly imprisoned.'

Ferdinand held up the skeleton twig just as Conrad would have spoken.

'One move from me that's sympathetic to his Highness the Emperor – one word – and the secret cabal of Northern councillors who executed the coup can have my throne. We escaped takeover during the war only due to expert diplomacy. Now, unfortunately, that cabal has reason to desire unrest in the Sicilies, to allow them to take control.'

Conrad blinked. His mind abruptly supplied him with the connection. 'That cabal of councillors are Prince's Men?'

'Didn't I tell you, Conrad, that they were everywhere? That includes the Council of the North.'

The King threw down his twig and started on another, ignoring the green stains on his gloves.

'We expected a move against us, after they examined our strength. We've challenged them with the counter-opera; their spies will have told them that by now. That challenge was always going to be answered. I thought it would be local sabotage. But no . . . This is on a larger scale than I expected.'

Conrad fought to settle with the concept that his viewpoint had just shifted from Naples to Europe.

The figure of Tullio Rossi emerged from bushes further down the bluff, gave Conrad a casual salute, and followed a grassy slope off into another stand of pines.

'But . . . If you do everything to keep the Emperor a prisoner . . .' Conrad frowned. 'Then when he escapes, and he will, and re-takes his throne – he'll take over the Two Sicilies.'

'Oh, he'll escape.' Ferdinand gave a dry little nod. 'I would prefer to place my bet on the man who won Austerlitz and Boro-dino, rather than a clutch of politicians, no matter if they have the power of the Prince's Men at their heart. But as it stands now, it does mean the Prince's Men in the Empire can twist the screw down on us at their pleasure . . .'

'Why not kill the Emperor?' Conrad suddenly asked. 'Why just depose him?'

Ferdinand showed his teeth in a smile. 'Too much awe. The "Great Emperor"? There are too few of the Prince's Men as Coun-cillors. If they'd used the knife on the Emperor, every other man's hand would turn against them – or, if they weren't known to be the murderers, the court would tear itself apart to find guilty men. So, a compromise: his Imperial Majesty is sent away to where he'll ultimately die of "sickness" – poison.'

Conrad reached over and took the stripped, bark-less twig out of Ferdinand's hands and tossed it away – only realising afterwards that this probably amounted to severe *lèse majesté*.

But it would be worse if I'd strangled him out of sheer irritation!

'Any way the Two Sicilies comes out of it, the King ends up looking guilty. That's their plan, sir?'

'I think that if they leak the plan in advance, so people learn of the Emperor's imprisonment on one of my islands, they can have me deposed before our counter-opera ever sees the stage.'

'*Che cazzo!*' Conrad added, in English, with feeling: 'Shite.'

'Indeed. And I can't be seen to do anything. However.' Ferdi-nand smiled crookedly. 'I have no intention of letting this attack remove me. In some ways, this latest attention by the Prince's

Men on Naples is fortuitous. I want you to help me arrange a secret escape for the Emperor from Stromboli. One I can reasonably claim that I don't know anything about.'

25

And I'd been thinking I was used to shocks.

All Conrad could manage was an embarrassing squeak.

'Me? I'm not a diplomat! I'm a librettist!'

'I believe you capable. As I said, a day or two out of the city, just now, will ameliorate some of our immediate problems. I ask you because of the nature of the planned escape,' Ferdinand said, 'and because I judge I can trust you.'

The King might be thinking of blackmail: of Alfredo Scalese, of the ever-present difficulties with the Church. *But he's not*, Conrad was startled to realise.

There are things which would give Ferdinand a hold over me, and he's not stupid enough to ignore them. But he's made an assessment of my character. An atheist's character.

And I must have made an assessment of his: I'm trusting that I won't be set up.

Taken aback, Conrad was not aware until the King waved a sheet of paper at him that it was an annotated calendar. A neat hand had drawn maps in the margins. The King's finger traced down the paper to March, and to the fourteenth, re-folded it, and gave it to Conrad to put away in his coat.

'We can get him off Stromboli easily enough if he agrees. You'll be inviting the exiled Emperor to the Teatro San Carlo, for the first night of *L'Altezza azteca, ossia il serpente pennuto.*'

'Good – grief!' Conrad opened his mouth to protest, and shut it without another word.

'It won't seem unusual for the Emperor to attend such a great social gathering. That can be glossed by me to his masters as "keeping the Emperor content in his gilded cage". Give him seats in one of the boxes with easy access. Then, in the general confusion of the counter-opera's success—'

Ferdinand spoke over the rustling ilex leaves with audible optimism:

'—a carriage can spirit the Emperor away, and take him to the northern border. There, the ordinary soldiers will rally to him as he marches to the capital, and he'll depose the Council composed of the Prince's men.'

'And the King of the Two Sicilies will gain a powerful ally against any future attacks by the Prince's Men.' Conrad turned his shoulder as the brisk wind changed to another quarter. It brought the scent of early-flowering camellias. He sought Ferdinand's gaze, pale as the sky. 'Sir, I'm convenient for this – but I'm not convinced I'm competent.'

At the far end of the copse, the bushes shivered and gave birth to Tullio Rossi, greatcoat opened to the breeze. Fists in his pockets, he strolled idly down to meet them.

I'll give him one thing: no one could ever imagine he was here to greet the King of the Two Sicilies!

Ferdinand exchanged a nod with the ex-sergeant. He made no move to urge him away.

'In fact, Conrad, there is a problem I do think you'd be best suited to solve.' Ferdinand turned to him with a small smile. 'The Emperor doesn't trust his "jailer".'

Tullio's eyebrows shot up.

Ferdinand continued. 'Someone in the Prince's Men evidently thought ahead. The Emperor has been informed by men he trusts that the King of the Two Sicilies has been paid to assassinate him. So if I offer a helpful escape – he'll think it's a trap to get him shot.'

'And you want me to think up a way around that?' Conrad couldn't help sounding incredulous.

'I've met your servant, here,' Ferdinand said, dryly regarding Tullio. 'It appears that if I trust you, I trust him. Put both your minds to work on this. You have the whole voyage down there. After all, you only need to make his Imperial Majesty trust you, Conrad. And you're a trustworthy man.'

✦

Conrad did not remember the words in which he consented. He did recall politely refusing the offer of a seat in the King's carriage.

'I'll walk down,' he said. 'Clear my head.'

He followed the footpaths down Vomero hill, the new walls of the museum vanishing behind him. His view was clear across the city and the Bay to Vesuvius's crater, bathed in golden afternoon light. Down in the town, the haze of cooking smoke rose up.

Tullio Rossi slid into step beside him.

Conrad found himself waving his hands. He held his shriek down to a whisper. 'I don't think up diplomatic excuses, I think up opera plots!'

'Wouldn't worry about it, padrone. It's obvious we're the visible distraction for whatever's really going on.'

Conrad shut his mouth, since it appeared to be open.

King Ferdinand didn't say that wasn't the case . . . Perhaps he thinks I'm qualified to understand the implications of an absence?

'Anyway, big boss is right,' Tullio added. 'You need to be out of Naples for a bit, right now, for more reasons than I've got fingers. And possibly toes.'

'I think I'm getting a headache . . .'

Tullio grinned at that, as Conrad had hoped he might.

'We should find Paolo, while I pack, padrone. She's going to love this.'

The knowledge that they would leave on this evening's boat gave Conrad a curious feeling of freedom. *Even if we are being sent to do the impossible.*

'If Paolo didn't need to be here in Naples for rehearsals, she wouldn't let us go alone.' Conrad added lightly, 'No romantic voyage on a boat for you with your master's sister . . .'

Tullio's stubbled cheeks turned a hot pink.

Now that's a surprise— Oh.

Memory came to Conrad as he spoke. 'When Paolo turned up, and we found out she was my sister? You looked relieved. I thought you'd been afraid he was one of the Prince's Men, but that wasn't it, was it?'

The shaven-headed man in the greatcoat, who looked as though he might break bottles with his teeth, turned redder still.

'You were just glad he was a woman,' Conrad concluded.

Tullio managed to look sardonic, despite embarrassment. 'Always more trouble if you fancy a man.'

Conrad refused that bait trailed across his path.

'You like your master's sister.'

'Yes. All right? Yes. I like Paolo. Isaura. I like her.'

'Good.'

Tullio raised eyebrows, and silently mouthed *Good?*

Conrad said frankly, 'She could do worse.'

Before Tullio could interrogate him, he added, teasing, 'Never mind the sea voyage. You'll have other chances to impress her.'

Tullio Rossi fell into a mood that, in less imposing men, would have been termed a sulk – and after the few moments in which it was genuine, played it up for Conrad's amusement.

He does like her, Conrad thought. *I wonder, does she like his company because he doesn't treat her as if she were an ordinary woman, or is there more to it than that? Uncle Baltazar and Mamma Agnese would have fits . . .*

The walk down into the centre of Naples brought them back to the lodging-house, where they found Paolo-Isaura looking equal parts amused and annoyed.

'The show goes on . . . Donna Belucci's part,' she announced, waving a visibly much-pencilled set of libretto pages. 'Passed back to you with all the changes she'd like you to make so she can sing this – and I quote – "tongue-twister of a role" . . . I think she objects to her name, too.'

Conrad bristled. 'What's tongue-twisting about "Hippolyta"?'

Tullio reached over and acquired the thumb-marked sheets. '"Hippolyta, Amazon warrior, prisoner of the Serpent Queen; now known as the slave-girl Xo – Zosh—" You know, she's right! . . .

259

Padrone, looking at this lot, it'd be shorter to say what words of yours she does like!'

Tullio smiled down at Isaura. '. . . Then again – what can you expect from a woman in britches acting like a man?'

Isaura promptly took the script back, rolled it up, and rapped Tullio Rossi hard across the head.

Conrad shamelessly snickered.

That certainly shows interest. It's up to him if he can turn it into something serious.

'We have news, also,' he said, and nodded at Tullio's offer of tea.

He told Paolo of the King's request, not so much because he thought she would abandon her responsibilities as first violin and conductor and come on the voyage, but because he wanted to get the shape of it clear in his mind.

'The Prince's Men have decided that local sabotage, bribery, and intimidation aren't the easiest way to get them what they want. We already thought they must be like most of the radical political secret societies, with members all through the governments which they oppose. The ones in the Prince's Men turn out to be a bit more highly placed than that – about thirty per cent of the Council of the North, Ferdinand estimates. And they have no scruples about de-stabilising that government because it makes it more likely they can take over the Two Sicilies.'

Paolo's eyes widened, which made her look no more than twelve. 'War, again?'

'I doubt it. All of the Emperor of the North's armies against one Italian state? It wouldn't even need to come to shooting.' Conrad, aware he was sounding bitter, added, 'Not that I think it should. One war was plenty for me.'

An echo came from where Tullio was boiling the kettle on a spirit lamp.

Conrad took Isaura's hand. Elegant and long-fingered, he thought it one part of her that wouldn't pass as male, once she grew older. She interlinked fingers with him as she had as a child, and smiled.

'So,' Isaura summarised, when he'd done, 'the Emperor is a

prisoner on the island of Stromboli. He believes the King of the Two Sicilies has been paid to poison his prisoner. You need some way to seem trustworthy. King Ferdinand needs him here in Naples to put an escape plan into operation—'

'I've been thinking about that.' Tullio put tea down for Isaura and his master, and this time waited an awkward moment until Conrad signalled him to join them.

'And?'

'A coach out of Naples, yes.' Tullio's finger traced a route across the table. 'But all the way to the northern border? It's hell travelling north by land. Impassable roads, bridges wiped out by storms, bandits in the mountains . . . Take forever. The Emperor must still have allies. We want somebody with a ship, a couple of hours' drive north of here, to take his Imperial Majesty on board. Then he can go back, maybe by way of Marseilles, and sort out his Council and all the other little traitors.'

'That's sound. I'll suggest it to Ferdinand.'

Conrad drank his tea, which was strong and bitter as he liked it, and then pinched at the bridge of his nose. Paolo squeezed his other hand encouragingly and released it.

'So,' she summarised. 'You sail to Stromboli, and hope not to be recognised by any Prince's Men. All you need now is a way to persuade his Majesty the Emperor that it's perfectly safe to come to Naples, and that he wants to attend *L'Altezza azteca*.'

Tullio frowned. 'Padrone—'

'Got it!' Paolo sprang up and started to make a furious search of the escritoire.

Conrad looked at Tullio, who shrugged.

'Here!' Paolo-Isaura thumped a sheaf of paper down on the table.

Conrad recognised it – Dominican sandal-mark and all – as the libretto of *Il Terrore di Parigi, ossia la morte de Dio*.

Paolo put her arms around his shoulders from behind, as she did not often do now, possibly because it was so recognisable as sisterly.

'You have to capitalise on your talents, Corradino. The North was at the heart of the Enlightenment! It's a fair portrayal of events – give or take a few alterations because it's opera. You can say you'd like to present a copy of the libretto of *Il Terrore* in his honour. Even if he just flicks through it, I bet it'll get you past the door.'

✦

The small boat they sailed on anchored here and there to take soundings, as they approached the Aeolian Islands. Conrad, engaging the ship's master in conversation, discovered that new reefs were rising in these waters almost weekly, and shrinking away as quickly.

He may not think it that unusual, but I think it's disturbing. What are the Prince's Men stirring up under the earth?

The two days on ship accustomed Conrad to the movement of the sea. He staggered when he stepped ashore on Stromboli's small dock. It went unnoticed. The few other travellers either gazed, stupefied, at the stark high crag shooting a jet of flames into the noon sky, or else stared around for what the ship's master described as 'the house of the famous secret prisoner'.

The Council of the North may be unaware of what's happened to his Imperial Majesty, but word's getting around among the common people. Do we have *weeks before this scandal breaks?*

Conrad stretched himself, and took off his muffler. Out of the sea wind, the island was warm. Its low ground-cover seemed more advanced towards spring than Naples, being further south.

'I'll see if there's any carriages.' Tullio glanced about. 'I doubt it.'

He had been uncomfortable and grumpy on the ship; the result, Conrad thought, of his confession about Isaura, combined with being sent on a mission that had almost no chance of succeeding – and perhaps was never intended to.

Tullio's a very private man. And he doesn't like to fail.

Then again, nor do I.

They had landed on the flatter northern tip of the island. Otherwise, it was little more than a huge cone jutting from the sea. Conrad felt himself glad to be at the opposite end of the island to the volcano's stark crater.

I don't see roads – only footpaths – so I'd guess Tullio's right . . .

The big man was back in a few minutes, shaking his head.

'Believe it or not, those men over there are guards.' He made a jerking movement towards the few men in uniform – or, given that most of them had shed their jackets and were sitting smoking pipes, half in uniform.

'"Prison" guards,' Tullio added with a snort. 'Seems they're used to locals coming in to gawp at the ex-Emperor. For a few soldi – which you owe me, padrone! – they'll point out the way to the house where he's kept.'

Conrad dug in his waistcoat pocket. 'Give them a few more soldi. Say I want to view the Emperor without the general public pushing and shoving me, so they're to hold the rest back on some pretext.'

'Good idea, padrone.'

That settled, they walked alone down a dusty trail that ran between hedges of prickly pear, and occasional moorland, and – like all footpaths – seemed to take forever to tread. Conrad caught sight of churches hidden down in the rocks, and residences every so often. It was a shock, finally, to find himself facing a white house almost entirely hidden by old olive trees and realise he was there.

A soldier in uniform jacket and trousers (though he had taken off his neck-stock, and didn't carry his rifle) ambled over. 'Ten soldi to see the great man; twenty to speak to him – once in a life-time experience!'

'But we already paid . . .' Conrad winced at Tullio's knuckles landing squarely in his kidneys.

He smiled and handed over the extra coins. The soldier waved them through.

All the green shutters stood open along the front of the house. Two storeys tall, it was a pleasant mansion, and its occupants, Conrad saw, were taking advantage of the early good weather. Adjutants and aides and servants all crowded round a camp-table set up on trestles on the veranda, under the spreading branches of the olive trees. Two or three high-ranking soldiers sat over cigars and brandy, listening to a stocky figure in white and blue.

'Oh, hell!' Conrad decided that was not too religious a curse. He gripped the libretto in its thick paper wrapping. 'When this doesn't work, I'm going back to Naples and telling Paolo exactly what he can do with it!'

'Confidence, padrone. Confidence!' Tullio muttered, comfortably close enough that he bumped his shoulder against Conrad's. 'Pretend you're a character in an opera!'

'Why do I suspect it would be one of those comically inept and stuttering tenors that infest Neapolitan one-act comedies . . . ?'

At the head of the table, the stocky man in his forties waved his companions aside, and leaned back in his chair.

'Signore,' he said, still with the vowel sounds of a Corsican accent. 'Welcome to my humble home.'

There are too many servants and guards, Conrad thought. *Even if I speak evasively, and he understands me, the story will get out to too many others, and the Prince's Men can't know about this.*

Conrad launched into a sentence regarding the distinguished history of the Emperor's nation, and his own poor attempt to render some of it on the stage and, after a few minutes of this, successfully lost the interest of the military comrades and hangers-on around the table.

He placed the libretto of *Il Terrore di Parigi* on the table, and as he leaned forward, risked saying, in a low voice, 'If I might speak with your Imperial Majesty privately?'

One of the Emperor's brows went up.

'If you're polite enough to give me the rank I won by the sword . . . you're probably an agent provocateur, here to trick me into speaking something to my disadvantage.'

'No, sire, I'm not. I assure you.'

Hopeless! No wonder he thinks that anything that comes from the King of the Two Sicilies is a poisoned chalice – that's all he gets from anybody else.

Conrad muttered something evasive, aware that he was losing the short man's interest, and beginning to panic. He shifted uncomfortably.

The Emperor's dark gaze went past him.

The man sat up in his chair, utterly alert.

264

'Imperial Highness—' Conrad began.

The Emperor ignored that. He stood up, took four or five paces forward on the veranda, Conrad scrambling out of his way as he went past—

The Emperor threw his arms around Tullio in a fierce embrace.

26

'What,' the Emperor demanded, 'is this famous war hero doing as a servant?'

Conrad stared at the spectacle of the tall, shaven-headed Tullio Rossi being ferociously hugged by a man a foot shorter than he was.

I am . . . more than bewildered by this!

The short man in the blue coat, orders and medals still on his chest, spun around and jabbed a finger at Conrad. 'What?'

Let nobody say I can't seize my opportunity—

'If we could speak privately to you, sire . . .'

The exiled Emperor grunted. He turned on his companions and servants, hand sawing at the air, vocabulary that of the military camp. Before a minute passed, there was a clean cloth and light food set out, and no man was closer to the table on the veranda than the servants at the house windows – banging the shutters closed at a furious gesture – and the soldiers out on the path.

Nobody within earshot.

Conrad surveyed the olive trees, aware that Tullio matched him in that.

Not enough cover to hide a man. This is as good as I'll get.

'You'll excuse me,' the Emperor said, 'if I summon back those two.'

He indicated two of the older men, in Northern uniform, who were hanging about somewhat obviously with the guards.

'They have long wanted to meet Signore Tullio here.'

Conrad couldn't help wincing. 'Do you trust these men with your life, sire?'

Dark curved brows snapped down. 'Does Signore Tullio likewise trust you?'

'Yes, sire.' He did not even have to think. Tullio Rossi, putting his coat collar straight where the vehemence of the Emperor's greeting had ruffled him, only gave a jerk of his head as if to say *Of course.*

I suspect this is non-negotiable, Conrad concluded.

'Sire, I'll trust to your judgement.'

The trusted companions – introduced only as 'Philippe' and 'Étienne'; two colonels, by their insignia – joined their Emperor at one end of the long table. Both surveyed Tullio, standing at Conrad's shoulder.

Conrad caught a glimpse of Tullio's throat over the greatcoat collar. It began to glow pink.

'Sit down, Signore Tullio; all.' The Emperor waved Tullio Rossi to the chair between himself and Conrad. 'No – you will not serve. I will. A brave man deserves it.'

It's not every day one is served tea by a deposed Emperor, Conrad reflected, drinking the strong brew. He bit down on his curiosity as much as he might, but finally failed.

'What did he do?' The words burst out of him. He looked apologetically at the Emperor. 'I apologise, your Majesty, but in my country, he's said nothing of this!'

'Well, perhaps that's understandable. He is modest, to a fault.' The Emperor leaned back, loosening his stock. The shadows from the olive tree branches played over features famous on coins, if now a little fleshier. 'As for what happened . . . Tullio Rossi is a hero!'

Conrad saw 'Étienne' and 'Philippe' lean forward.

'You remember Borodino.' The Emperor's voice sank, a sensuous bass. He moved his hands as if he could shape it from the air. 'Snow, mud, clouds from artillery fire, so many brave men suffering; the screams of horses, the trumpet calls of orders seeking victory, the stench . . .'

Letting his gaze slide sideways, Conrad saw an almost identical depth of memory in Tullio's eyes.

'And this man – this hero—' the Emperor leaned forward, putting his hand on Tullio's shoulder, 'not only saved one of our Eagles in the battle of Borodino – no! That would have been enough – but he also saved his Emperor's life! He found us wounded on the battlefield, and carried us over his shoulder. When the rescue party of generals found us, he had wrapped the flag about us both, and taken refuge from the ice and snow in the way that only an old soldier can – in the warmth of a horse's slit-open belly!'

Conrad looked greenly at his tea.

'He'd put my naked body furthest inside.' The Emperor reverted out of the imperial plural. He seemed to recall being a soldier again. 'Tullio Rossi! Giving me his warmth, as well as the heat of the horse of my slaughtered enemy. And saving me, potentially at the cost of his own life.'

Tullio stared down at the tablecloth, even pinker. Conrad felt positive that Tullio was not only attempting to look modest, he was avoiding Conrad's gaze.

'I never suspected him of being so heroic,' Conrad managed without a trace of sarcasm.

The Emperor spread his hands wide. 'I thought he died in the following battle, since he disappeared. But no! I would know you anywhere, my friend.'

'I was captured.' Tullio looked hunted – although Conrad suspected he was the only one who knew him well enough to see that. 'By enemy soldiers. They were going to shoot me.'

'Shoot you!'

More confidently, Tullio added, 'But the building they were using as a prison caught fire. Cavaliere Conrad Scalese here rescued me. I've been acting as his servant since then.'

'An honourable man! My brave soldier Rossi! And so you live!' The Emperor stood up, and again threw his arms around Tullio (who had automatically stood when someone considered his social superior did). The two colonels joined in.

Conrad took advantage of the – to his mind, quite unnecessary – embracing and manly kissing that followed, to gather his scattered thoughts.

'Signore Tullio can explain why we're here,' Conrad said, as things calmed down. 'You'll see we mean you no harm. Just the opposite.'

Tullio Rossi staggered through the explanation. Conrad, smiling encouragingly, saw the Emperor was already convinced – had been, in fact, as soon as his brave soldier Rossi appeared.

'If you accept the invitation,' Conrad added, 'Tullio will guard you at the opera house, and drive the coach that takes you up the coast.'

'Of course!' the Emperor agreed. 'I think I have loyal men who can arrange a ship. I might have known it would be my good friend who saves my life again!'

There was no getting away, even with their business done. The deposed Emperor suggested they have dinner there – which turned out to be a five course meal – and only the plea of urgency in planning the escape got them back to the ship before it left the island.

Conrad leaned on the ship's rail, on deck, waiting to see if his dinner would survive the choppier sea.

When he was sure of it – and the cigar-and-brandy haze had worn off – he went seeking Tullio Rossi.

✦

He found him on a coil of cable towards the prow, faking sleep.

Conrad joined him there, out of the way of the sailors, and watched the island vanish behind them, the red column of its fire reflecting on clouds long after they had sailed north.

Before genuine sleep could intervene, he poked a solid finger into Tullio's ribs. 'Right. Now let's have the real story!'

The big man sighed and rolled over on his back, so that he lay next to Conrad, looking up at the emerging stars.

'You don't think I could be a hero?'

'I know you're a hero. This, though – it's fishier than a three-day-old cod's head.'

'You know I was a deserter from the army.' Tullio's tone was as embarrassed as when he had first made the confession to Conrad that he was a wanted man.

Conrad punched him lightly on the shoulder. It seemed to cheer him.

'But,' Conrad frowned. 'I assumed you deserted from our side – the side fighting against the North . . .'

Naples had been, at that time, fighting against the Emperor as a nominal subsidiary of the Allies. They had afterwards fought for him, for a confusing few months, and reverted to neutral status a year or so later.

'I did desert.' Tullio stared upwards at the Pole Star. 'Eh . . . Twice. At least twice.'

Conrad rested his head back against the rope coils with something of a thud. 'Tell me!'

The big man smiled at his clowning, but only a little. Tullio pushed himself into sitting upright on the rope coil. He rubbed his hand across his forehead. 'Borodino! That was a lot worse than he made out.'

Conrad nodded. 'If you're not an Emperor, things usually are worse . . .'

Tullio's answering grin was wry.

'I deserted from the Allies since we were losing, there wasn't any doubt of that. There was a blizzard blowing, the battlefield was knee-deep in snow, waist-deep in places. I wrapped a fallen flag around myself to keep warm. Had no idea whose flag it was; didn't care.'

Conrad, remembering Maida, said, 'I can understand that.'

Tullio's eyes were distant. 'Then I tripped over. For the fiftieth time, at least. When I scraped some snow off him, it turned out to be an unconscious man in a Northern uniform. I couldn't tell much about the insignia through the snow except he looked like an officer. But I thought that if I took the uniform and wore it, it'd allow me to escape through the Northern lines. By that time, I didn't give a damn about either side.'

The swift twilight gave way to darkness, and the constellations of spring above them. Conrad unconsciously shivered, thinking of

270

the Russian winter. He leaned up on an elbow beside Tullio. 'And then?'

'I stripped the unconscious man, and shoved him, naked, inside the split belly of a horse. So that no one would find the corpse while I was putting the uniform on and blame me.'

Tullio Rossi took a deep breath.

'Then I heard the shouts of a search party, very close in the snowstorm. Wasn't nothing else to do. And nowhere else to hide. So I climbed inside the horse after him, and hauled the cloth over us so we wouldn't be seen. Only they did discover us – but they said he was the Emperor and I was a hero . . .'

Tullio shrugged.

'His Emperorship gave me a battlefield promotion for it, when he came round. Said he wanted to make an officer of me, and lieutenant wasn't good enough, so he made me a captain. I did have a medal, too, but I pawned it.'

'Of course you did.' Conrad blinked. '*Captain* Tullio?'

Tullio Rossi did the closest thing to shuffling that a man can do when he's sitting down.

'You out-rank me.' Conrad couldn't hold back a spluttering laugh. 'Captain Rossi out-ranks Lieutenant Scalese of the Cacciatore a Cavallo!'

'Padrone – shut up.'

'Yes, sir!'

Tullio looked at him from the corner of his eyes.

Conrad gave him a smile.

Tullio lay back and put his hands behind his head, gazing at the stars. 'I knew I'd be found out before long, even if they did love me for getting their old flag back almost as much as they loved me saving their Emperor. So I took my chance in the following battle and deserted back. Got a long way, too, only the Allies arrested me for having left 'em in the Russias. They were keeping a bunch of us in that barn you dragged me out of. Me, I wonder if they didn't set it on fire to save the cost of the cartridges to shoot us . . .'

Up until a few years ago, Conrad could still distinguish the white scars where red-hot metal farmyard implements fell against his hands, as he and another soldier rescued the prisoners from their inferno. *Now those scars have vanished into the general wear and tear.*

'What you did at Borodino was quick thinking – and war.' Conrad tried to make out Tullio's expression in the gloom. 'And I'm not sorry I got you out of that barn, if that's what you're thinking. No matter how many Emperors you saved. Captain Rossi!'

A sailor passed, hanging lanterns at intervals down the rigging, and making it, if not light, light enough to see each other. Tullio, by the turning of his head in the semi-darkness, shot a glance at Conrad that seemed to ask for reassurance, even if not willing to admit it.

If I treat him any differently I confirm his fears, whatever they are.

Conrad prodded Tullio Rossi's shoulder.

'I do have one question. Which is very easily asked . . . What were you *thinking*?'

'Padrone—?'

'—You let me go into this, knowing I had to persuade the Emperor, without telling me any of this?'

Tullio froze, and gave Conrad a pitiful 'oops?' look. 'I was sure he'd never remember my face!'

Conrad grinned. 'Who could be lucky enough to forget you!'

Tullio snorted. 'Thanks, padrone. Thanks. I think.'

✦

They stayed out on deck both nights, talking, and spreading their coats over themselves against the dew.

Before Naples, they had a reasonable framework for the Emperor's escape from the Teatro San Carlo on the fourteenth of the next month.

'Once the lights go down, no one's going to look at his box – with the curtains half closed, he can be out of there before the Sinfonia's finished, and on his way by the time the first aria ends.'

Conrad nodded. 'He'll only trust you to drive the coach, that's obvious. You ought to take another man, it's a job for more than one. I'd say, take Paolo—'

'Except she won't come.' Tullio leaned over the ship's rail, gazing at the rushing green water. 'You don't realise, maybe, but

272

she's convinced she's the only one can conduct *The Aztec Princess* and make it work. Don't like the idea of leaving you both there if there's danger of an eruption . . . I wish we could just take her. Except I know what she'd do to the man who did that.'

The wavelets slid down the side of the boat like silk, taking the dawn's light. Conrad breathed in the scent of salt, which is like nothing else. 'The Emperor won't trust anybody but you. As for Isaura . . . I could tell her the Conte di Argente insists on conducting his own first night. Il Superbo's pushed himself into conducting enough of the rehearsals that she'll believe it.'

Tullio glanced up from the luminescent sea. 'She might. He won't. Put him in front of the pit and the galleries, throwing things at him, and he'll freeze.'

Because that's not the way it is in salons or drawing-rooms . . .

'*Che stronzo!* You're right . . .'

Full light brought green land, and towering cliffs, and the sea becoming a hard blue, as if the foundations of all were utterly secure.

'And what will you be doing, padrone?'

'I'm staying with *The Aztec Princess*.'

Tullio's gaze sharpened and he frowned. Conrad looked at him with more attention as the man seemed to brace himself, physically and mentally.

He's going to say something I don't want to hear.

At least things haven't changed between us; he'll still speak his mind—

'I know why you're staying, padrone, besides the libretto.'

'Tullio—'

'You asked me to find out when she goes out. She doesn't. She pays private calls to bored wives of the local nobles for morning tea – but that's ladies only. She doesn't go to dinners or anywhere else unless she's with her husband.'

The big man squared his shoulders.

'Do me a favour – and the rest of us. Leave the composer's wife alone until after the first night?'

27

A coach met them at the harbour, and took them to a closed meeting with Ferdinand Bourbon-Sicily. It lasted a bare half hour. The incumbent of the throne of the Two Sicilies listened with increasing joy – there was no other word for it – and then shook Tullio Rossi's hand as well as Conrad's.

'I'm well content with the arrangements for the Tyrant's visit,' Ferdinand said as they stood to take their leave. 'Amazed, but content. Well done! Commendatore Mantenucci will be in charge of rumours and dissimulation, closer to the time; make sure you speak with him.'

'Yes, sire.' Conrad heard Tullio's acknowledgement half a beat behind.

The King rested his hand briefly on Conrad's shoulder. His expression was cheerful. 'You'll find we've been busy here while you've been gone, gentlemen. One of Enrico's men will take you where you need to go. Remember – we have less than three weeks to be word- and note-perfect.'

'On my honour, sir.' Conrad, recovering his court manners, managed a creditable bow.

Outside the Palazzo Reale, a second coach waited. Luigi Esposito, in a snappy black civilian coat and cravat and tall-crowned hat, ushered them inside. At the driver's whip-crack, the team of horses moved off in a swift trot.

'It falls to me, on the King's now comprehensive orders,' the police chief of the Port district said, smugly, 'to brief you about where rehearsals have been moved to.'

Conrad slumped back against the seat. 'You're on board, now? Good! Now I can stop biting my tongue round you . . .'

'And I'm sure it was difficult,' Luigi purred.

Conrad gave him a look.

He was not certain where they would go first – certainly not to the San Carlo, since it was next door to the Palazzo Reale; perhaps to his lodgings – but he was startled when the coach slowed to pick a way through crowds, and then drew up outside a baker's shop in the back streets of the Mercato district.

Luigi had a glint in his eye.

Conrad refused to ask for information. 'I didn't realise that you were hungry . . .'

'They bake very well. But they are, for the moment, closed. Come; I'll show you.'

The shop door had an ill-lettered piece of paper attached: Closed owing to family illness. The police chief let himself in with a key, and led them through the shop. For all that the ovens had been allowed to cool, the place still smelled deliciously.

'It's surprising what secrets people hide.' Luigi opened the door to what was obviously a bedroom, at the back of the establishment. The bed had been pushed aside. The police chief bent down and gripped a rope, hauling on it. A trapdoor some four feet by three feet lifted up from the floor.

In the darkness exposed, there were wooden steps going down. As Conrad leaned to look, a light came up.

'Captain Esposito?' The voice from below was familiar. Iron-grey hair became visible. Enrico Mantenucci came into view, stooped from climbing the steps. 'Ah, there you are, Conrad!'

'Caves under the cellars?' Conrad guessed.

'Close. Ancient mines, from the times of the Roman Emperors.' The Commendatore didn't emerge further. 'We can guard this place expertly. There are only two other exits from the mine-system: one in a domestic house at the base of Vomero hill, and the other far out in the countryside on the way to Posillipo. My

275

men are occupying the Vomero house. Colonel Alvarez has his troops taking care of the Posillipo entrance, disguised as a camp of thieving antiquarians digging up the soil . . .'

The man turned around on the steps, and held his lantern aside, so as not to be dazzled going back down.

'Come on, Signore Conrad; no lazing about now you're back from your little holiday!'

Conrad opened his mouth as he was faced only with Commendatore Mantenucci's back, caught a stern look from Luigi, and shut his mouth without letting the indignant protest out. *Holiday, indeed!*

'Let us show you the rehearsal halls,' Enrico Mantenucci's voice floated up. 'And where you'll be working from now on.'

The wood that made up the steps was ancient. Conrad concluded they had been here some centuries, at the least. Aware of Tullio and Luigi behind him, he stepped down into a slanting tunnel in volcanic rock. Lanterns were hung at intervals on the walls. The temperature seemed constant.

'The King had my people mapping all the places under the city. Catacombs. Quarries. Sewer-channels.' Mantenucci slyly shot a smile past Conrad at his subordinate. 'I'll let Esposito show you those.'

Luigi Esposito looked down with distaste at the mud that smeared the tunnel floor, and muttered something, audible only to Conrad, that might have been *Charmed, I'm sure*.

'Sewers,' Luigi added, with a lop-sided smile, 'Wells. Old aqueduct junctions. Ossuaries. Burial mounds. Catacombs – ideal rehearsal spaces. You may get complaints that the audience are unappreciative . . .'

Conrad gave that the quietly profane answer it deserved, and followed the other men into the gloom.

'. . . I'll show you your quarters,' Luigi finished.

Tullio, who had automatically moved ahead, surveyed the slanting tunnel. 'We're living under Naples now?'

'There's been activity by the Prince's Men. Separate lodgings and rehearsal rooms above-ground can't be adequately protected. We sorted out which sectors of the underground network could be isolated by the use of fewest guard-points, and truly made safe.'

Away from the entrance, now, the tunnel walls were smooth rock. A cool but not cold gloom was lit up by intermittent lanterns – few enough that they would not significantly eat up the air. Between the shadows, Conrad saw odd sigils carved here and there into the rock-face.

The messages of miners to each other, eighteen hundred or two thousand years ago?

'Bloody waterways!' Tullio Rossi muttered, shaking one of his boots.

Conrad guessed that the stream running down the channel carved in the rock-floor meant this part of the maze was an underground aqueduct; one of the Roman ones that still supplied the public fountains in the city.

He walked forward briskly, catching up with Major Mantenucci. 'Say we're Prince's Men – how likely is it that we could already be in occupation under Naples?'

'We're Prince's Men? I'd say we hate the Chief of Police and his officers.' Enrico's lips quirked, under the grey moustache. 'Colonel Alvarez's rifle troops, too. If it helps, we rounded up two separate mundane smuggling gangs, both with connections to the Camorra. We questioned them intensively. None had knowledge of other men besides their rivals using these underground tunnels; not for the past year or more.'

By the steel in Mantenucci's tone, there had been no squeamishness in the questioning of those men.

'Wherever it was possible there might be other ways into this part of the underground system, we collapsed them with blasting powder. We can open up more mines here if you need more room. It only remains to ask, is this sufficient for your rehearsals? I guarantee it free of enemies.'

Conrad nodded. 'We'll need to keep the place warm. Well-lit. Oil lamps, not candles: smoke won't help the singers' throats . . . I suppose a bullet in the back will help them less. If this is a prison, at least it's a spacious one.'

Mantenucci and Luigi Esposito shared almost identical wry smiles.

The square-cut passages drove down under Naples with mathematical precision. From time to time Conrad saw that side-chambers led off, and there were carved steps descending further. The atmosphere smelled here and there of wet stone. Lanterns diminished down a slope ahead, and Conrad felt a constant shift of air. It would at least be impossible to suffocate.

Along with the air, he detected sound beginning to move in the tunnels. It was as if argumentative Naples had not been left in the world above. Voices resounded, both raised and singing. Conrad picked out the rough yells of men working – hammers – running footsteps – the slow click of a woman's heeled boots – laughter – and one violin playing phrases of music recognisable from the Conte di Argente's score.

I'm back in Naples!

'This is one of the main rehearsal areas.' Enrico Mantenucci waved a hand as they walked out onto great beams and boards. They formed a stout floor above shattered stone debris that filled the bottom of the great cavern. Conrad recognised Angelotti's work.

Oil lamps glowed. The stone roof narrowed as it went up high into darkness, sloping into an immense bottle shape. Conrad visualised miners hanging down on their ropes, hacking out the tufa rock by oil lamp, seventy generations ago . . .

One clear note sounded.

'Uomo perfido!'

Giambattista Velluti's voice flew up in brilliant, effortless trills, soaring from alto to soprano, his larger chest cavity giving more power behind the high notes than any woman could achieve. The sound of a boy's unbroken voice grown to manhood without changing thrilled through the cavernous mines: Hernan Cortez, denouncing the Aztec Lord General Chimalli—

'Perfidious man, you betray your land of
Obsidian mountains and the scarlet bird . . .'

In the centre of the cavern, a dozen figures stood around Spinelli's forte-piano.

Conrad automatically lowered his voice so as not to interrupt the rehearsal. 'How did they get that underground?'

Mantenucci shook his head, amused. 'Not easily . . .'

'Corrado!' a voice exclaimed. Conrad turned.

Passages led out of the main cavern. Off these, there were smaller chambers and caves, furnished incongruously with desks and chairs from above ground. In the nearest, Luigi Esposito had his hand on Paolo's shoulder, pointing her at Conrad.

Tullio Rossi stiffened.

Isaura sprang up – visibly (to Conrad's gaze) recalled herself as 'Gianpaolo Pironti' – and ran out of the chamber, grabbing Conrad's hand and wringing it like a cousin would. 'You're back!'

'I told you he would be.' Luigi sat himself elegantly down on the corner of Paolo's desk. 'The wind was in the right quarter.'

The rock-walled chamber with the desk and many oil lamps made a surprisingly homely place. Paolo's desk was piled with unfolded sheets of paper. There was a tell-tale chess board set up on the far side.

Conrad embraced Paolo and put her back at arm's length. 'How are things going now?'

Paolo threw up her hands. 'The principal singers can't remember their lines, the chorus rehearsals are dreadful – they're imbeciles! – half of Signore Angelotti's stage crew don't even speak the language, the costumes are late, the set designs need a Leonardo to complete, and the orchestra! Don't even talk to me about the orchestra!—'

'In other words,' Luigi put in, 'about as one would expect.'

Paolo grinned at the police captain. Her eyes were far too warm.

Conrad became conscious of a gap where for the past few days he had been used to find Tullio. His ear brought him the older man's footsteps stalking off across the smooth-hewn boards.

Enrico Mantenucci gave Conrad a nod. 'I'll let Captain Esposito and your cousin show you your own quarters.'

Conrad didn't get two steps before Sandrine pounced on him.

JohnJack Spinelli (whose fingers had been moving in the eternal manipulation of a man telling his beads) abandoned the sacred for the secular, and barrelled through the crowd.

What looked like a delegation from the tenor section of the chorus joined the crowd.

Conrad was submerged in loud demands to correct this, that, or the other verse in the unfinished libretto. The twenty-seventh day of February, he reminded himself, as he took their scribbled-over scripts. Sixteen days to deadline.

And there's one thing I have to do, very soon. Because this isn't the normal opera, where there's time for the librettist to compose the whole script and send it to the composer to set, in advance of deadline. Not even one of those occasions when the composer squeezes the libretto out of the poet by post, a verse or a scene at a time. Time's so short that this will have alterations and additions and subtractions going back and forth, right up to the finish.

And therefore I have to speak to Roberto Capiraso, Conte di Argente.

For the first time since I was in jail.

✦

Catching up with where the counter-opera now stood took a surprising amount of time. Nothing changed, underground. That it advanced on midday was indicated only by the clocks.

Tullio – still sniffy about the police captain's presence – brought a meal from outdoor food sellers, vouched for by Fabrizio Alvarez's soldiers. Conrad shepherded JohnJack, Sandrine, and Velluti out of his own side-cavern (which was presumably a dry cistern), and took advantage of their absence to eat.

He found it disconcerting to discover old furniture from the lumber rooms of the Palazzo Reale set up so closely resembling his lodgings above ground. Isaura had mentioned that she did it, with Luigi Esposito's help, to give some aura of familiarity, and hopefully enable Conrad to bear the underground location better.

Tullio Rossi cursed under his breath as he finished unpacking their travel-cases.

'Don't suppose he knows she's not a boy,' Tullio grumbled. 'Don't suppose he cares!'

Conrad put his knife down, and rested a sympathetic hand on Tullio's shoulder. 'If we're really unlucky, there's somebody devout from the crew or chorus watching, who doesn't realise

Paolo's a girl. And if they're still going to confession . . . and happen to mention the possibility of sodomy . . .'

The older man straightened. 'Bollocks! The Inquisition again!'

'We could ask Paolo to just let the company know,' Conrad suggested.

'—Or she could just stop flirting with that whore Esposito!'

Conrad bit the inside of his lip. It enabled him to use a serious tone. 'She's twenty-five, marriageable, and in opera; you can't expect her to live like a nun.'

Tullio stalked out past the hanging curtains that partitioned off their 'rooms', sounding very much as if he missed the ability to punctuate his departure with a slamming door.

Conrad finished his cheese and olives, and made his way through the lantern-lit maze of tunnels to his cousin's chambers. There was nothing to knock on. 'Paolo?'

'Come in, Corradino!'

He swept aside the faded green velvet curtain. Her chambers also looked as if they had been furnished from the palace lumber-rooms and attics. Conrad glanced at the lamps – four in number. 'You miss windows.'

'Oh yes. And balconies. Breakfast outside on the balcony . . .' She shot a grin up at him. In dark trousers and unbuttoned waist-coat, her white shirt and stock picking up the lamplight, she looked a dissolute young man-about-town. The room only lacked the abandoned stockings and forgotten garters from ladies of leisure.

His own words came back to him with violent impact: *You can't expect her to live like a nun.*

I want to protect her! But . . .

Isaura-Paolo sank into one chair, and shoved another his way with her foot. Reaching down, she rescued a bottle of wine from some corner of the floor.

Conrad sat and rested his elbows on the table. He couldn't help smiling affectionately at her. 'If I act the older brother with you, you'll hand me my head, yes?'

'I thought you were going to hand me mine!' She seemed to collapse into a relieved smile. 'I didn't have anyone telling me what to do while I was at the Conservatoire, and I haven't been

281

told to behave as a woman for three years . . . I wasn't sure you'd understand.'

'I'm not sure I would, if I hadn't met you wearing trousers. What?' Conrad shrugged at her expression of pique. 'It's true. You don't look like a girl. Not that you aren't perfectly attractive as a woman— I mean— That is— I'm sure men who aren't your brother will tell you that!'

He continued over her snicker:

'In fact, that's close to the problem . . .'

Isaura-Paolo showed more than male intuition. 'This is about Luigi? And Tullio?'

'I do wish I believed in a deity,' Conrad muttered. 'Because now, of all times, I'd like to be able to say, Dear *God*, why do I have to be involved in conversations like this!'

Paolo laughed affectionately.

Conrad raked his fingers through his hair. 'I was beginning to think you had a partiality for Tullio. Now there's Luigi. He's a philanderer – but he might change, people do. Or Tullio might be better suited to another woman . . . And I'm talking gibberish!'

Isaura poured wine into two chipped cups, and grinned with the expression of someone taking pity on him. 'Corrado, I'm not planning to get married yet!'

'Oh, thank God!' Conrad stopped. 'You made me say that!'

'I'm a bad influence.' She sobered. 'Corradino, I love you dearly, but when I do decide about someone . . . I'm not sure I'll come to you for advice.'

That stung.

Conrad passed it off with a sardonic comment. 'Given that I'm in love with a married woman, I don't think I'm the person to give you advice . . .'

'Oh, that gilded parasite!' Paolo slumped back with an exasperated huff. 'If it's her you want, spending all her time painting her face to go to teas and dances and salons, you'll end up as her poodle!'

It hurt enough that he winced.

Almost as fast as that reaction, realisation came.

'Paolo?'

282

The woman looked up from under her shaggy short hair, face set. 'What?'

'You—' A glance beyond the green curtains showed them isolated for the moment. '—Will always be my sister. You will never come second in my family affections. No matter who I may otherwise love.'

Shock momentarily gave all her emotions place on her features – jealousy, shame, hope, fear.

Conrad added, 'I'm sorry I never came for you.'

It hurt him that this realisation was new.

'I shouldn't have left you to get out of the Catania house on your own. You'd think meeting independent businesswomen in opera would make it all clear to me, but I . . . forgot . . . you might not like staying at home with Mother.'

'I missed you – even though I wrote to you, you didn't know it was me—!' Paolo-Isaura scrambled up out of the chair, all elbows and knees, and threw her arms around him, holding him far too tightly to be a brother. Conrad hugged her as hard, patting her short hair as she shed tears that soaked into the lapel of his coat.

'I'm sorry!' She awkwardly fell into the chair next to him, as he manoeuvred them to sit at the table. Conrad kept his arm around her shoulders. There were dark smudges under her eyes, as well as the red rims from weeping; it was obvious how hard she must be working.

Quietly, Conrad added, 'Nora's no parasite. She was one of those singers who lived as independent businesswomen. If she'd lived, Nora would have been better than Maria Malibran—'

Isaura raised her head, sounding dumbstruck. 'If she'd lived?'

'*Cazzo!* Well . . . It's not a secret as such, I suppose – Leonora is Returned Dead. So it's hardly her fault if she can't have the singing career she was working towards.' Conrad pushed memories away, but couldn't escape. 'She was working so hard . . .'

'I'm sorry.' Isaura was white. 'I didn't know. Losing it all like that and being left here. Oh God. Poor girl. I'm so stupid!'

'It's forgiven.'

'But, Conrad—'

'Forgiven,' he emphasised firmly.

They sat together for some time, Conrad feeling the rock-hard muscles of his neck and spine gradually relax. He realised he had forgotten the comfort a sibling could give. *When we're not screaming at each other, or having tantrums*, he thought wryly. *Who'd imagine that would continue outside of childhood?*

'I won't abandon my sister just because I have a lover,' he repeated, hoping that would drive it home. 'Do I worry about you and your beaus?'

Isaura banged her forehead on his shoulder before she looked up again. 'I keep putting my foot in my mouth . . . I didn't mean I wouldn't ask for your advice, Corrado. Of course I will! I just meant, I won't ask the family's permission to get married. If I get married, and don't just take lovers.'

Conrad glanced down at her in the curve of his arm. So close, she felt a very slight, small figure.

With utter determination, she said, 'I'll make up my own mind about who I want.'

Conrad brushed her shaggy hair out of her eyes with his free hand, and couldn't help a smile. 'Given that you don't seem Sapphic, I suppose I can take it that will be a man?'

He took advantage of her muttering about how he hardly knew her well enough to say *that*, to add:

'In which case, I'd be obliged if I can put it about to the company that you're not in need of the Church's strictures against perversion?'

'You mean, tell them I'm a woman?'

Isaura tilted her head on one side, considering.

He saw the moment that she seized on an idea with the design of amusing him.

'Why don't you just get Sandrine to put it about that I'm not a sodomite? And I'll run a book with Captain Luigi on how long it'll take one of them to guess why?'

Conrad had the impulse to throw his hands up dramatically, after the fashion of Barjaba. 'No wonder Signore Rossini says that every impresario in Italy is bald by the age of thirty! If they didn't tear their hair out, it would fall out from worry! You have definitely been in bad company – and don't tell me the police are the custodians of public virtue; Luigi Esposito wouldn't know a virtue if he found one on the bottom of his shoe!'

Isaura snuffled back a giggle. She leaned out of his hug, across the table, fetching the wine bottle. 'Since Luigi's a friend of yours, I suppose you ought to know! '

She sighed, and was as suddenly serious.

'Corradino, can I help you, at all? I'd like to. I . . . know you and Il Superbo don't get on – for very obvious reasons – but you have to work together now. Can I do anything?'

Conrad raised an eyebrow. 'You mean to say il Conte has actually spoken to his first violin?'

Paolo-Isaura grinned crookedly, and then sobered. 'He's come down here almost every day, adjusting the score when we rehearse. We still call him "Superbo", but . . . it's become less unkind.' She hesitated. 'I think he may have been trying to make up for his bad behaviour. He's working himself into the dirt on *L'Altezza*, like the rest of us. I know he was a swine to you, Corrado, and I know the situation you're in, but – he'll work professionally with you if you let him.'

'Hn. Maybe.' Conrad shook his head. 'I don't think there's anything you can do to help. But thank you. And for reminding me I can't put it off much longer, if *The Aztec Princess* is going to be finished.'

He stood, and realised she had caught the cuff of his coat. He looked down at her.

Paolo said slowly, 'When you said Leonora was Malibran standard, was that the lover speaking, or the opera aficionado?'

'Before she died, she went on at La Fenice. The opinion was not just mine.'

The disguised woman tapped her fingers together. 'I just thought . . . We desperately need another good voice tutor. Granted she can't sing, but – could she teach? Not down here – the Argente mansion is very well guarded – she could see the chorus singers in her drawing-room?'

Leonora, close enough for any excuse to visit her . . .

'Dear God!' Conrad muttered, breathless.

Paolo-Isaura gave him a much-recovered smile. 'And there you go again! I am a bad influence.' Her expression turned serious. 'I'll go talk to her, since I'm in charge of rehearsals. But . . . you're my brother.'

Conrad read the unspoken *And I won't do it if you can't bear the temptation* in Paolo's determined gaze.

'Go ahead, brat. This collection of divas needs an expert coach. Do what the counter-opera needs.'

She glanced around once to see they were unobserved, and sprang up to give him a hug.

And since the day's already gone to hell . . .

He ruffled her hair out of all order, breaking the heavily charged atmosphere.

'I ought not to talk to Nora,' he said ruefully, 'and I have to talk to Il Superbo. Not the way I'd have it. Where is he?'

'Up at the Palazzo Reale.' Isaura frowned, and put her hands on Conrad's shoulders. 'I know you told me, when I was little, that you were determined to be nothing like our father . . . You do some admirable things, Corrado. I just want you to know that I notice that.'

Being still among the living, there was no physiological reason to prevent him from blushing.

Conrad went off to find an escort from one of Alvarez's men, feeling himself burning hot to the tips of his ears.

I'm obliged to be professional with il Conte di Argente for many reasons. One of which is, because my sister thinks me a considerably better man than I am.

◆

The ever-quickening clock made it mid-afternoon when he left the underground passages of Naples. His eyes, accustomed to lesser light, flinched back from the bright sky. Dazzled, he followed the escort from Alvarez's Rifles into the Palazzo Reale. He dismissed the troopers before he made his way to the museum of archaeological erotica.

Between Leonora and the counter-opera, Conrad found his thoughts not able to settle. Like a set of scales, pressure to remove one subject only made the other rise up into his mind.

The Palace building jolted.

It was a distant bang, as if from a quarry or a pile-driving team at work – but too far off to be that. It gave the impression that something had taken hold of the world and given it a sharp diagonal knock. Conrad felt it at the same time peculiarly disconcerting – his animal nature insisted the earth should always be solid; should not move – and wholly mundane. Live in Naples and one becomes used to a tremor or two from Vesuvius.

Is Ferdinand correct? Should I attribute that to the black opera in rehearsal?

No evidence either way.

Conrad unlocked the door of the secret museum, entered, locked it again, and threw his coat and hat over the cabinet containing a satyr in congress with two wood nymphs.

At the far end of the room, Roberto Capiraso was silhouetted against the bright, seaward-facing windows. He leaned with one arm on the upright piano, looking down at the keys, picking out the line of a melody which now tapered off.

Conrad took a breath. 'Signore Conte.'

28

In the silence, Conrad unlocked the drawer and took out his folders. He had a strong impulse to leave, taking them with him, below Naples. Only necessity – and the thought that it would be a retreat – prevented him acting.

The expectation of a jeer set his teeth on edge. Nothing came. Looking up, he saw the Conte di Argente's expression was vaguely constipated. Conrad finally identified the man's stifled emotion.

He's embarrassed.

He deserves to be!

'I suppose this must be awkward for you.' Conrad broke the silence. 'When you sent me to prison, did you think about when we'd have to work together again? Or didn't you think ahead?'

Roberto Conte di Argente glared from under heavy brows.

'I suppose,' he said stiffly, 'that I took some decisions that were – unwise.'

Hardly a grovelling apology.

But then again, it's Il Superbo.

Remembering asking – begging – for help against di Galdi stuck in Conrad's throat like an immovable bone.

He considered what he could safely say, and hurled caution through the window. 'Tell me – what exactly did I do to earn your hatred?'

Other than it being easier to hate me than to hate Nora?

The Count shifted his gaze. He stared out at the sea.

'Apparently,' Roberto Capiraso broke the longer silence, 'after six years – she still remembers your name.'

It momentarily overwhelmed Conrad.

She does? My name? More? Everything she and I went through, does she still recall it, no matter that she's been through death . . . ?

Roberto Capiraso said sternly, 'Do not pity me.'

Startled, Conrad reflected, *He can read what I think quicker than I can.*

The feeling had only just begun to come clear in his mind that, if their positions were reversed, he would not find being in il Conte di Argente's place very enviable.

The melodic line of the priests' hymn to Cortez as Quetzalcoatl, the Feathered Serpent god, meandered on the warm air. From Capiraso's fingers, it came out more melancholy than Conrad had envisaged.

'Polite hypocrisy won't solve this,' Capiraso said.

'Nor lies.' Conrad added, 'Please don't suggest that you regret your actions.'

'No, indeed.' The other man had a glint in his eye.

'So?'

Roberto Capiraso straightened up from the forte-piano. Silence fell. 'So . . . You didn't point out to the King that his composer, too, might just as well create his music in one of his Majesty's cells?'

Perfectly truthfully, Conrad said, 'I might if it had occurred to me.'

'Ah. My thanks to . . . your inadequate sense of vengeance, then.'

And there's that dry sense of humour again.

Conrad felt himself oddly wistful that it was not possible to fall back into their old relationship. *No matter that we dislike each other,* L'Altezza azteca *is better when we co-operate.*

'Working white-knuckled is not the best way to produce an opera,' Conrad mused aloud.

The Conte di Argente made a short bow, as one gentleman conceding an argument to another.

He has at least made some offer of apology, Conrad thought. *And he's polite. Has Ferdinand spoken to him? Or Nora? Or does Capiraso consider himself honour-bound not to upset the production of the counter-opera . . . ?*

'I made my own decision, not that of the King or my wife.' The Count's tone was amused, but oddly unmalicious. 'You might as well write what you think on your forehead; it's as easy to read.'

'Thank you,' Conrad said ironically.

He found himself exchanging an unspoken and perfectly understood look with the other man.

Everything can wait for two weeks. What I need, desperately, to say to Nora— It can wait until after the first night of L'Altezza azteca. *What I still owe this man after di Galdi and the prison . . . Two weeks is not a long time.*

Roberto Capiraso drew in a breath and let it out.

'I have questions regarding some passages . . .' He took from his jacket what looked like one of Paolo's endless scruffy lists. 'We have gaps all the way through, that we must now fill in, and hardly any of the necessary verses for the end of Acts Three and Four.'

'Give me your notes,' Conrad said. 'Why don't you play me the new material while I look over your queries?'

Roberto Capiraso lifted a folder that rested on top of the upright piano, and extracted a sheet of paper with the staves scored by quick slashes of a pen. Conrad's own words were scribbled over the top, with many alterations.

'First . . .' Capiraso separated and threw a section of the score across the green-topped table. '. . . I've tightened your friend Spinelli's entrance in Act III.'

Capiraso's spiky handwriting marked cuts, Conrad saw, but Il Superbo had not attempted to make revisions to the actual verses.

'I altered the setting, since Velluti complained,' Roberto Capiraso continued, his tone business-like. 'It appears only the primo uomo can have an entrance being praised by his soldiers . . . So General Chimalli is now in the Jaguar Warriors' military camp; enters up-stage after the chorus.'

'We can re-use some of the flats,' Conrad thought aloud. 'Background of tents, palm trees, mountains.'

290

'Baritone and tenor drinking chorus from the soldiers.' Roberto Capiraso drew an ink-line down the page. 'Then I suggest we merge these two separate arias of Chimalli's. Give him half a verse in the major key, proclaiming that all the lands from the Amazon to the sea submit to his armies and to his will. Then the other half of the verse in the minor key, done as an aside to the audience: there is only one thing he can't subdue – the heart of Tayanna, the Aztec Princess – and he would give up all his military conquests if he could conquer that one heart.'

Il Superbo's tone faltered on the last words, despite his deliberate self-composure.

'That's – actually, that's very good.' Startled, Conrad glanced up from the paper, and met Capiraso's dark eyes. 'I'll revise the verses. Roberto . . .'

He was surprised to find himself automatically using the man's first name.

'It's opera,' Conrad said simply. 'Unrequited love and illicit passion are staple subjects. The Aztec Princess can't be different – not if it's to succeed.'

The secret museum was quiet for a long moment.

'I agree.' Roberto Capiraso's tone was flat.

That's the best I'll get.

The urge to question the Count about Leonora – how they met, when they met – was very strong.

And he must want to make the same demands of me.

Roberto Capiraso raised his manual-labourer's hand and pointed towards the museum's door. 'I believe I can work with you if we avoid certain subjects. If, once those doors are closed – or, once we are below Naples in rehearsal – neither of us knows such a person as Leonora D'Arienzo.'

'Very well: I won't speak to you about Nora.'

Conrad opened his mouth to add, *I won't speak to Nora, except where the opera is concerned.*

He cut himself off, immeasurably tempted.

It will be unconscionable to make a promise that only sounds honest because of its wording.

Conrad seated himself at the large table, his gaze staying on

Roberto Capiraso. 'I should mention . . . Signore Paolo suggested today that he ask Nora to help out under Naples as a voice tutor and recitateur.'

Roberto Capiraso's shocked expression salved a number of the wounds to Conrad's pride.

'Help with the counter-opera?' Il Superbo sounded flatly disbelieving.

'No need to speak as if it were ridiculous.' Conrad frowned. 'Before she gave up her career, she knew the business of an opera-house from top to bottom. If she wants to help, let her.'

Roberto Capiraso, for the first time in Conrad's acquaintance, looked as if he had no idea what to say.

And I don't even know if I can bear to speak to Nora.

'Assuming that she agrees,' Conrad said, 'I believe all of us are capable of leaving private business outside of rehearsals. After the first night, then yes – because we must talk about this, soon – but not before. Is this acceptable?'

'Acceptable.' The word came just too quickly from Capiraso's mouth.

The composer went back to the piano. Conrad sketched out a couplet, his gaze on the man. The Count's expression changed a number of times and finally relaxed.

'After all . . .' Roberto Capiraso spoke as if he mused aloud. The whimsically amused glint was back in his eye. '. . . Anyone can put on an opera in sixteen days . . .'

Conrad momentarily put his hands over his face. *I take it back. It's going to be a long two weeks!*

✦

'It's taken us eighteen months.' the King looked grim. 'My men have checked every opera house in Catania. And they've found nothing.'

Conrad met with Ferdinand Bourbon-Sicily again on the Tuesday, the twenty-ninth; ridiculously grateful for the leap year that gave them an extra day of February to work with, even if it was an illusion of the calendar.

'Without any great stroke of fortune,' Ferdinand added, 'I think we won't discover where the black opera is being sung. Not in the next two weeks.'

In England, three public houses (and a heretic church) qualify as a village, Conrad knows. In the Italian states, it's three churches, a campanile, and an opera house, not always in that order. The King's forces have spent a summer and two winters searching every provincial rat-hole village and town, in both the Two Sicilies and beyond.

Conrad made a face. 'Meaning they have to be singing it as a drawing-room opera?'

Ferdinand gave him a tired but approving smile. 'Precisely! I've been assuming that as a possibility for the last six months. There are palazzos with halls large enough to have a full production put on. Ask Signore Conte di Argente! But as for which of them might house it . . .'

A surge of choral singing echoed up the ancient walls, reverberating from the rehearsal-mine. Conrad noted that Ferdinand waited until it faded before he spoke again.

'We're seven miles from Vesuvius here. And Pozzuoli is seven miles west of us. Say the black opera must be within, what, ten miles of the volcano? That gives us half of the Burning Fields, all Naples, then Pompeii, and all the way to Sorrento, Salerno, and the Amalfi coast.'

Conrad bit down on his frustration. 'The black opera they sang in 1815 needed to be close to Tambora. Assume that it has to be somewhere large, for the audience they'll need . . . And that's assuming they need more of an audience than they did for 1815, which was no more than the crew of a boat!' He paused. 'How many private palazzos would be suitable?'

King Ferdinand smiled crookedly. 'Given that they could be rehearsing anywhere in Europe and bringing their singers here at the last moment? Dozens. Hundreds. Even here, if you add up which of the nobility are rich enough to own a palazzo that would put Tiberius to shame, and then might also belong to the Prince's Men . . . and who must be questioned with kid gloves on, because their business affairs are not completely respectable . . . My spies and officials have been searching, but even the King's name doesn't open every door.'

Conrad looked levelly at the King.

He didn't come here just to unload himself of his frustrations.

Ferdinand stood, resting his hand down. Conrad felt the warmth of it heavy on his shoulder.

'Conrad, I don't wish to put still more of a burden on you . . . but I believe we need to face this. *L'Altezza, azteca ossia il serpente pennuto* must be as excellent as fallible human beings can achieve, because – unless something miraculous happens within the next two weeks – the black opera will go forward. The only defence we have against it will be our counter-opera.'

29

March opened with fine weather but Conrad didn't see it. The cast members of *L'Altezza* besieged him with so many requests and suggestions that he spent more time writing underground than in the secret museum. It was impossible not to feel homesick for the tall buildings and narrow streets of Naples above; for the spring sun shining on worn and peeling orange-red plaster, and women leaning on the black-painted rails of their balconies to speak with their neighbours, gossip curtained off by rows of flapping washing.

Roberto Capiraso co-opted Spinelli's forte-piano and did most of his own work down in the ancient mines, since he also was much in demand.

Conrad missed climbing the rickety outer wooden stairs to Sandrine's lodgings, for rehearsals – or to the wooden-railed flat roof above Spinelli's apartment, where they could sit with bread and onions and wine, the Gulf of Naples spread out to their view. In the tunnels, nothing changed. The light came only from oil lamps.

But the whole underground complex was full of echoing sound. And from time to time he would look up and catch distant sight of Leonora.

Roberto did not speak to him unless Leonora was absent. Leonora stayed with the singers – displaying an iron will in rehearsals. Conrad Scalese might as well have been transparent air.

Work was his only palliative.

'Act Three, Hymn to the Sun!' Paolo's summoning of the chorus rang through the chamber. Conrad distinguished her touch on the violin, as strings and woodwind came in, in accompaniment.

He leaned back in his chair – one at the table set up in the main hall – and scribbled two more lines, adjusted a word, crossed one line out, and then scribbled over the other.

'Conrad . . .' Roberto Capiraso sat down in a nearby chair, a sheaf of papers in his hand. He absently signalled one of the servants for wine. 'Some revision's needed for the end of Act Two.'

'Act Two? I thought we had that sewn up!'

'Much of it.' Roberto sounded civil enough. 'The charming L'Altezza Sandrine herself is pleased with her aria of unwilling love – her duet with Cortez – her duet with the Jaguar General —and the 'jealousy trio' between all three that leads into the end of that scene. The High Priest's invocation of vengeance is fine. Although if you're having Lorenzo murdered at the end of Act Two, we may have to move that back.'

Conrad nodded. He found himself pouring wine, since it was unlikely Il Superbo would lower himself. 'And so?'

'Tell me where we stand for the end of Act Two.'

Conrad searched his heaps of paper, and found his notes on the back of a sheet. 'Here we are. Act One, the first love triangle: Cortez and General Chimalli both love the Aztec Princess. Act Two, we introduce the second love triangle: Hippolyta the Amazon slave-girl and Aztec Princess Tayanna both love Cortez. The surprise reveal for the end of the act – the slave-girl has had a child by Cortez. Cat among pigeons, shock and horror from the chorus, Hernan Cortez astonished, the Jaguar General triumphant, L'Altezza herself furious, exits the stage; all ends in confusion!'

The Conte di Argente sipped at his wine, looking as if he concealed amusement.

Conrad added, 'We may have to placate the censor and make the slave-girl Hippolyta into Cortez's native wife. Is there any problem with that?'

'Not with the staging.' Roberto gazed off absently in the direction of the chorus rehearsal. 'An older child, though, not a baby! Any child is bad enough – although a member of the chorus or

296

orchestra will likely have a six- or seven-year-old we can train to be led around stage by his Amazon mother – but can you imagine Signore Velluti holding a baby while wearing any of his usual white costumes?'

Conrad couldn't help laughing. 'I can imagine the disaster if he does!'

'Quite . . .' The Conte di Argente looked at his glass, as if surprised to find it empty. 'We do have some difficulties with the prima donna and seconda donna. Madame Sandrine feels the "slave girl secondary plot" in Act Two is in danger of swamping the true romantic heart of the opera – by which she means Cortez, Chimalli, and Tayanna – and Madame Estella doesn't appear to think her role falls into the category of "secondary plot".'

'*Che stronzo!*' Conrad divided the last of the bottle between their two glasses. 'All right, I'll talk to them – or Paolo will.'

'And may I point out, I have yet to compose anything for our contract singer from the San Carlo? I hear Donna Lorenzani is due back from South Africa shortly.'

Roberto Capiraso's expression held considerable *Schadenfreude*, but also a degree of unmalicious amusement.

'If all else fails, she can have a role as a junior Priestess—' Conrad glanced up, aware that the chorus's voices had ceased at some point while they were debating. Paolo and Lorenzo Bonfigli came to the table.

'Signore Conte!' The diminutive tenor thumped a set of much-annotated music in front of Roberto Capiraso, and launched into a diatribe. Conrad found it amusing that, within forty-eight hours of his presence, the company had taken to badgering their composer quite as much as they did their librettist.

Paolo hitched a hip onto the stout wooden table. 'Need you and Il Superbo to listen to Velluti's run-through.'

Roberto's brusque 'Of course!' cut across whatever answer Conrad would have given. The Count swept up Bonfigli's score and pushed it back into his hands, with what might have passed for an apologetic look.

Paolo winked – and was gone back to the musicians before Conrad could react.

297

I think Il Superbo may actually enjoy composing on the spot, Conrad reflected. *Even if he has no patience at all . . .*

The tenor was not so easily disposed of, drawing il Conte aside and putting his point, with the tenacity of a small dog.

'Cortez's big aria on the step-pyramid.' Paolo patted Velluti's shoulder. 'Time to wrench everybody's heart, so we have to keep rehearsing!'

Surprisingly obedient, Velluti waited for the piano's introduction.

'"*Mio figlio! Mio patria! Mio amore!*"' The castrato voice thrilled up into the spaces of the great cavern. *My child! My country! My love!*

Roberto dumped himself down in his chair, four bars after the beginning of the aria, seemingly at the end of wits and patience. He cast a look at Velluti. '*Gran Dio!* Thank God that man can sing!'

'I can't lie.' Conrad muttered. 'He wasn't hired for his thespian talents . . .'

Roberto unmistakably stifled a laugh.

Giambattista Velluti was not in any meaning of the term a 'singing actor'. He stood on his mark on stage and sang. If necessary, he moved to his next mark and sang again. He showed his better side to the audience. If severely nagged to act, he would place his right foot carefully forward, and extend his right arm towards the audience – usually towards the general region where the boxes owned by the local nobility were situated. Four bars later, he would bring his arm back and place his hand flat on his breast, over where he fondly imagined his heart to be. He struck these two attitudes no matter what role he might be playing. It was the context of the opera that made him seem tragic or comic.

And his voice, which conveyed every nuance that his acting did not.

'When he sings, he's a genius,' Conrad added, in an undertone, 'and we have JohnJack to act.'

Roberto Capiraso took a folded page from an inner pocket and weighed the paper in his hand. 'I've taken a rather unusual step, with that in mind. The traditional "Heroine's Mad Scene" . . . there really isn't any place for it with Donna Sandrine's Princess Tayanna. If I give it to Estella Belucci's Amazon, the prima donna will shoot me.'

He said this with sufficient gravity that Conrad had to choke off a guffaw.

'Giambattista has the best voice,' Roberto continued, 'but the acting ability of a sheep. With your co-operation, therefore, I propose to give the Mad Scene to a man – to the bass. To Signore Spinelli.'

Conrad spread the synopsis out on his knee, reading while he spared an ear for Velluti.

'That is . . . ideal.' He dug in his pocket for a pencil, marking the paper. 'We'd need a repeat verse, here – JohnJack sings brilliant coloratura bass; let him show it off!'

'I suggest it for Act Four, scene two.'

The suggested melodic line sounded so powerfully in his mind, Conrad lost track of what the musicians were actually playing.

'So . . . we have our complex villain being driven mad by the loyalties pulling him apart . . . On the one hand, he's promoting rebellion with the aid of the Priests of the Sun—' Conrad made another pencil note. 'Have them on-stage with him here. He must get rid of his rival, the false Quetzalcoatl, Hernan Cortez – the Feathered Serpent must die! But this means fighting against his love, Princess Tayanna . . . You'll want to bring his warriors on somewhere . . .'

As if there had never been a rift between composer and librettist, Conrad looked over at Roberto, Conte di Argente, without any constraint.

'We might have to choose between a hymn and something military. With what you've got here, a march would suit better. Let's see: JohnJack tells the priests he'll marry Tayanna afterwards, to legitimise his reign as King Chimalli. But he's torn – and suddenly he's tormented by the image of the old King, who was his shield-brother, and whose beloved daughter Tayanna he promised to support! He hallucinates the old warrior-king, and begs his pardon – embarrassing himself in front of his own warriors – then recovers himself,' Conrad scribbled *cabaletta!* in the margin of the score. 'Because he knows that, if the white men aren't driven off, they'll take over the whole Aztec kingdom. His motives for wishing Cortez dead are mixed – but his aim is right. He gathers

299

his followers, exits to martial music, close scene, and we don't need to see him again before the climax of Act Four! *Bravissimo!*'

Roberto leaned back in his chair, apparently observing Velluti, but in reality attempting to see the pencilled notes. 'A true martial march, or town banda martial?'

Conrad tapped his fingernail on the paper, not so much debating the question but wondering that il Conte di Argente should think to ask it.

'Start off with a park bandstand march,' Conrad suggested. 'Segue into the true melancholic march of men going off knowing they're going to die.'

Roberto Capiraso nodded. 'I'll write you the cabaletta to lead into it.'

Before Conrad had even been old enough to name the parts of opera, he had always preferred those faster, change-of-gear sections at the end of long arias – 'cabaletta' for one or two singers, 'stretta' for the whole cast on-stage. To his ear they were the apotheosis of opera.

Conrad folded the already-creased paper and slipped it into his coat pocket, while he applauded Velluti. He leaned over to Argente.

'You know what? Since you've given JohnJack the Mad Scene, and Estella's got her nose out of joint – give her the bravura aria of the slave protesting against the loss of his freedom with a call-to-arms for *Libertà!* The one that usually goes to the tenor. I'd pay money to see Estella singing the Amazon warrior-made-slave who yearns to be free, to fight to liberate her homeland from the Aztec invaders . . .'

Roberto's eyebrows climbed into his hairline. 'You mean an aria of the kind that caused a riot in Signore Donizetti's *Gemma*? And set up a republic in the Netherlands when Monsieur Auber's *Muette de Portici* began a revolution?'

'To be fair, I think it was the signal for revolution, rather than the cause of it.' Conrad smirked. 'I did hear rumours of his Majesty King Ferdinand belting out an aria of young Signore Verdi's on the palace balcony, the day the Two Sicilies became free of the North's power – despite the fact that he can't sing.'

'Write me some verses,' Roberto, Conte di Argente, said, with a somewhat put-upon air that didn't disguise his enthusiasm.

Thirteen days.

✦

With the curtain drawn back, there was no door as such to his chamber. Interruptions came frequently. He was not surprised, as he walked back in from a rehearsal, reading the score he carried in both hands, to realise someone was waiting. Glancing up from the pages, Conrad caught a glimpse of brown kid boots and embroidered white muslin skirts, and saw Leonora putting her fur muff down on his desk.

His heart stuttered and jumped. He came to an undignified sudden halt.

'Leonora! Contessa!'

She wore a short green pelisse over the morning dress, buttoned to the throat, and her hat was a velvet fantasia based on a horseman's steel helm, also sea-green.

His mind gibbered. *The first time I've seen her close enough to speak with—*

An odd calm came over him. Conrad put his score down on his desk. He was near enough to touch her, if that had not been absolute stupidity, and he was not afraid.

She's not the monster my imaginings have made of her. She's just Nora.

Her voice was quiet and direct. She did not quite look him in the eye. 'I want to apologise to you. I know Roberto never will. I apologise for the prison. This is my fault. If it wasn't for me, he wouldn't have any trouble working with you – and he was enjoying it.'

She did meet his gaze, then. Her eyes were dark.

'At first, he didn't tell me the name of the "damned commercial librettist" he was working with, but he quoted me parts of your discussions, and arguments . . . It isn't always easy for Roberto to make real friends, being on the opera board—'

'—Being a stiff-rumped son of a bitch!' The callow, schoolboy insult fell out of his mouth without consideration.

'Roberto is always sure of his opinions.' Leonora's chin came up. 'And always ready to change them. It's just that he's very – thorough – in his arguments, and he rarely meets anyone who can stand up to him.'

By her expression, she did not like being put in a position of defending her husband to him. Conrad let it pass. *Because this is Nora, finally speaking to me . . .*

'In any case,' Leonora said, determined, 'you and he wouldn't have quarrelled if it wasn't for me. Therefore I apologise. I am sorry. Truly.'

Conrad found himself unable to concentrate on anything but her face. 'Thank you.'

'It seemed ridiculous for both of us to be part of *L'Altezza azteca*, and for me not to speak to you . . .'

Her gaze fell. Conrad realised that, before he came in, she had been reading Paolo's daily report where it lay on his desk, deciphering the smudged inky handwriting of their progress.

'I'm sorry, I didn't intend to pry, Corrado; I was . . . I'm hearing the verses now, as a recitateur, and Roberto talks about his composing just enough that I want to know more. It's as if he forgets I was a singer!'

Conrad pushed the report towards her. 'Look at it all you like. One of us will need to add your progress with the singers to it.'

He watched her closely, seeing her expression change as her gaze flicked across the notes. Concern, amusement – at Paolo's terse nagging of his 'cousin', perhaps – and then worry – and finally her intense Delft-blue gaze rising to meet his eyes, full of whatever he dared not hope for or name.

'What I need to say to you,' Conrad murmured, 'can wait until after the fourteenth of the month. Do you understand?'

She bit at her full lower lip – which so automatically made him want to kiss it that he had moved forward before he stopped himself.

'Yes, Corrado, I do understand.'

In his more cynical moments, these past few years, Conrad had thought love was only pain. He understood viscerally, now, why poets speak of love being felt in the heart. It felt as if something physically pierced him through the ribcage. It might have been unselfish empathy for Leonora, going through her life so misunderstood – or an entirely selfish satisfaction that Roberto Capiraso should so prove it: he doesn't understand or deserve her.

'Well then.' He spoke with a forced brightness, that – as she looked up, curiously – became oddly genuine. 'I have a copy of the score; you can give me your expert opinion. If you've forgotten how an opera's put together in the last five years, I'll be very surprised!'

A slow smile grew on her face.

It changed her, he thought. The polite facade that she or any other gentlewoman must keep up in society vanished. The smile was a lot closer to the orphanage brat's grin that Nora had used to have, shortly before she suggested some plan or other that would get them into trouble.

She unbuttoned her pelisse, and unpinned her hat, removing both, and gave him a grandiose gesture. 'Show me your verses, poet! Let's see if I can give you any inspiration.'

Conrad couldn't help a smile.

'I'm not a complete fool. If you won't look after your good name—' For the next two weeks. '—I will. Tullio will make us tea, and . . . Angelotti's wife Maria can act as chaperone, while she's sewing costumes.'

Leonora looked wistful. 'I've never understood why a woman can't have friends who are men. But yes, it will silence rumour.'

Conrad studied her for a long moment. 'You can have friends who are men. Just . . . not me. If we have no chaperone, I'm going to find this place as familiar as our lodgings in the Accademia. And that means I'll kiss you, and touch you, and . . . Forgive me: I don't want to find out whether you will stop me – or you won't.'

Leonora Capiraso said nothing. She gave a small nod.

He turned away to call Tullio.

The large man brought wine, and bread, and olives. He put the cups down with a speaking look at Conrad. If vocalised, Conrad thought, it would have mentioned something along the lines of playing with fucking fire when you're sitting on top of an ammunition wagon!

He's not wrong, Conrad thought, as he helped Angelotti's

seamstress wife set up her sewing in a corner of the stone cell. But it's Nora.

Paolo joined them, during a break in orchestral rehearsal, helping herself to Conrad's olives and reading the new verses over his shoulder. She greeted Leonora with a charming smile (that Conrad thought it would be entirely too confusing to be jealous of).

'I appreciate you taking the chorus through their roles,' Paolo said. 'We still can't get understudies for threats nor money, so groom any one of them you find talented. Just in case. Contessa, we need all the help we can get! And I'm sure my cousin will agree that he needs it . . .'

Conrad gave her a stern look.

He was met by the stubborn set of her lip that meant any protest was useless.

Nora, with demure mischief, said, 'Signore Pironti is correct, obviously.'

'"Paolo",' the disguised girl said cheerfully.

'Please call me Leonora, then.'

Conrad made a mental note to ask – when the next twelve, eleven?, days were over – why a sister and a sweetheart will invariably combine their forces to persecute the relevant male?

✦

Roberto Capiraso took the orchestra through the revised Act III, which echoed through the tunnels. Conrad glanced up from his scribbling as Leonora entered his stone cell again with two of the women who sang mezzo in the chorus, currently on their break, and the carpenter's wife – apparently today's chaperone. Since Tullio appeared to be elsewhere, Conrad went over to the cupboard for wine, and served all. Leonora left the other women chatting, and took the other chair beside Conrad's desk.

'Well?' Conrad indicated the sheets of paper she had brought, rolled up inside her fur hand-warmer, 'suggestions?'

'Oh, certainly . . . I'd make the same suggestions if it were to Roberto,' Leonora murmured aloud, musing over a sheet of paper over-written with so many crossing lines of script as to be indecipherable. 'I did try, when he first started this opera. He told me it "wasn't women's business".'

Conrad snorted. Leonora's head came up, eyes fixing him with a glare that failed to be effectively icy.

'Corrado, if you tell me that you agree . . .'

Conrad glanced across the tunnel at a stone cistern, now dry, that formed a smaller rehearsal room. Paolo sat playing at the cribbage board with a scene-painter's wife, theoretically overseeing Sandrine and Estella in their duet. '. . . I wouldn't dare. We have some remarkable women here. And I know you. You're remarkable, Nora.'

She tossed her head, ash-brown hair flying, in imitation of a fashionable young lady in a pout. 'I know that!'

'Well, then.' Conrad pushed the pen-stand across the green-topped desk. 'Feel free to be extraordinary and help me out!'

'I did have an idea, in fact, Corradino. Our missing contralto, Donna Lorenzani—'

'—Who's ship is due in from Cape Town any day now; yes, yes—' Conrad sighed. 'Believe me, I do know!'

Leonora's smile was wide and warm.

'I think we can do better than a tiny role as a Priestess, Corrado. Suppose we give our captured Amazon slave-girl Hippolyta a mother!'

Conrad gazed at her features in the lamp's white glow. '*Cazzo!* A mother?'

'Call her "Thalestris".' Nora beamed. 'Good classical name. Thalestris . . . Queen of the Amazons! She can be searching for her lost daughter. What do you think? The audience can see her first disguised as a traveller in the Aztec lands – we can put that aria in anywhere that the other singers need a break—'

Conrad drained his glass and seized scrap paper. His dip pen splattered ink across the wood of the table top, but he ignored it, too busy writing to clean up.

'Thalestris . . .' He tried the name on his tongue. 'A warrior-mother . . . Who, when she finds her daughter, will make Hippolyta choose between love and her duty to the Amazon nation! Ideal! . . . "Brigida Lorenzani, contralto, as Thalestris, disguised

305

Queen of the Amazons",' Conrad read aloud as he wrote. He contemplated his own spiky handwriting of the cast list.

Nora pushed her glass forward as the returned Tullio came over to re-fill all of them. 'Queen Thalestris . . . which makes Hippolyta an Amazon warrior Princess! Aren't you tempted to call this opera *Le Due Principesse*?'

Conrad held his thumb and forefinger a quarter-inch apart. 'Thalestris is a small part! Sandrine's already feeling besieged by Amazons. If I get too involved with Hippolyta's family, we're going to lose track of our main love triangles.'

Paolo-Isaura waved from the corridor, not willing to interrupt their train of thought. She would be taking over the orchestral rehearsal. *And that means il Conte will be at leisure soon.*

Leonora sat back in the chair, interrupting his thoughts. She held up her hand in acquiescence. 'Even so, one more thing. Hippolyta's child should be a boy.'

Conrad frowned. 'It makes a difference?'

'I do read in my husband's library,' Nora said mildly. 'Traditionally, the Amazons only raised their daughters. If they had sons, they left them behind with whoever fathered them. Imagine how that would make Hippolyta's choice between love of Cortez and love of country even harder . . . I don't think Estella will complain if she's given that to sing!'

Conrad shook his head, amused. 'You have a streak of cruelty I never suspected.'

Leonora reached to turn the lamp down, since the wick grew sooty and the flame high. Her eyes had a gleam from more than the light. 'Now you think you're flattering me. Either that, or your memory of Venezia is very poor.'

'I do remember you were able to be cruel to fictional characters.'

Conrad could only look at her fondly. Her frank friendship seemed somehow more of a barrier between them than her absence, he realised.

He tore himself away from contemplating her features, and paged through his notes. 'This means revising the Act Four opening yet again.'

Nora pushed back her chair and stood, preparing to leave. Her smile was mocking, but not cruel. 'Of course it does. This is opera. It always does.'

✦

In the mine-shafts and caverns, it was easy to lose track of the hours passing above, and whether they were dark or daylight. Conrad lifted work-blurred vision from the paper. He found his pocket watch very little help in remembering whether the hands indicated twelve midday or twelve midnight.

He suspected the latter.

'There should be a trio for the "white voices" in Act Three.' Roberto Capiraso yawned. And looked astonished that he had done anything so gauche in company.

Conrad managed not to laugh at him. 'Velluti, Sandrine, and Estella? Castrato, mezzo, and soprano . . . Yes.'

'I wondered about three cavatinas. However, I like the idea of changing between all the possible duets in turn, and then the trio, so that all the scenes run on from each other, like Signore Rossini's gran terzetto . . .' Roberto yawned again.

'Take one of the spare beds and sleep.' Conrad pushed his chair back and stood. 'I'm not sure which day it is – Thursday? – but you've been awake for a day and a night. I have to write lines for your new Act Four romanza. Paolo can take care of the rehearsals.'

It was possible to gauge how tired the Count was by the fact that he didn't object, only muttering something as Tullio Rossi led him to one of the other stone cubicles.

Conrad seated himself back at his table, to play with the rhyming scheme. His next sensation was of pain in his shoulder and elbow, and Tullio's voice in his ear – encouraging him to wake, he realised, as the man guided him to sit upright.

Muscles spiked and jolted with pain. His eyes opened. Ink had starred the page where he fell asleep on it. A glance at his watch told him eight or nine hours had passed.

'Is it morning?' He winced as he stretched his arms.

'Think so.' Tullio visibly worked it out. 'Thursday. I think. Maybe Wednesday. Friday? Sorry to wake you. We have trouble in the hall.'

Conrad shook the stiffness out of his bones, and followed the big man along the duck-boards towards the central large mine.

There was certainly nothing wrong with the acoustics of the underground mine used as the main rehearsal hall. Both Sandrine Furino and Estella Belucci were busy proving that as Conrad walked down the long passage towards them. Unfortunately, neither of them was singing.

'—Liar!'

'Abomination!'

'Whore!'

'Thief!'

Conrad, attention on the two women facing off against each other on Angelotti's makeshift stage, shot Tullio a brief querying look.

Tullio murmured, 'Started when Donna Estella insisted her part isn't a comprimario role, and Sandrine disagreed . . .'

'Oh dear.'

On-stage, the two of them matched poses as if it had been scripted. The small, fair-haired Estella Belucci and the brunette, tall Sandrine Furino nonetheless glared eyeball to eyeball – fists clenched, yelling just not quite hard enough to strain their voices.

'And how did you get out of the chorus, hm?' Sandrine hissed. 'On your knees with your mouth full of cock?'

'Better than seeing all of Italy on my back, like you do!'

'At least they come to hear me sing, not look at my tits!'

'Nobody can *see* your tits, you dried up old witch!'

'Why isn't Paolo putting a stop to this?' Conrad muttered.

Tullio jerked his chin. Looking in the desired direction, Conrad saw his sister leaning dopily up against Luigi Esposito's chest, a hand-print plain red on her face. From the diminutive size of the print, it was Estella's.

As he turned back, Conrad caught Tullio scowling.

'Far too friendly with the Captain,' Tullio muttered.

Oh really? Conrad prevented himself from saying, with a sudden onset of common sense.

'I don't think we need our mezzo and our soprano to rip each other's faces to pieces. You take Sandrine, I'll take the Sicilian.'

308

'Good luck with that!' Tullio Rossi shifted off the wall and shouldered his way through the entertained crowd of chorus singers and stagehands.

Conrad, following behind, startled almost out of his boots at a high-pitched squeal of anger. It had all Estella Belucci's voice-trained projection:

'Bitch!'

Her insult bounced back from the bottle-neck roof of the mine, and echoed down the passages.

Sandrine's reply had less power, but far more penetrating intensity:

'Common prostitute.'

'Fish-wife!'

'Slut! Future mother of bastards!'

Estella's mouth opened, shut, and Conrad saw the hitch in her throat where she bit back tears.

She snarled, 'Man!'

The audience was instantly divided into two, from where Conrad stood; those who winced, and those who looked bewildered.

Sandrine Furino drew herself up. 'Congratulations – of the two of us, you are the true cunt.'

✦

Sandrine's high heels echoed on the wooden boards as she walked off stage.

She stopped just as she came level with Conrad.

'I won't quit.' A harsh note of arrogance sounded in her voice, for the first time. 'You need me too much. But you hear me, Corrado. I won't sing in any scene in which that whore is on stage!'

Less than a fortnight to go, Conrad's mental ticking clock reminded him.

'Sandrine—'

The tall slightly-built woman strode out of the rehearsal chamber without any attempt at an answer.

'*Che cazzo!*' Conrad moaned under his breath.

'Don't worry, padrone.' Tullio gave an assessing glance.

His elbow nudged Conrad, dispelling the first blind panic.

'I'll talk to Donna Sandrine. You fix the other one.'

309

30

Conrad turned, saw Paolo still indisposed, and beckoned to Estella Belucci as if decisiveness could solve his problems.

Why isn't Il Superbo here? Nora? Why do I have to attempt to patch up singers' quarrels?

The woman turned white and red, and lifted her chin belligerently as she came to him. Conrad gripped her shoulder, steering her away for a private warning. Finding somewhere confidential was a difficulty, in the stone maze.

He settled for a long straight corridor that housed one of the ossuaries, where he would at least see anyone coming before they got to him.

'Sir . . .' Estella Belucci shivered as she gazed around, her breathing erratic.

Neatly stacked thigh and arm bones were piled on one side of the corridor, brown skulls stacked on top, from the deaths of some ancient plague. Niches in the walls held saint's pictures, and candles, and small statues with their features rubbed bare from fingers touching the sacred.

Conrad, still disorientated from being wakened, looked down into her face. This close, he could see her eyes were sea-coloured, flecked with gold.

'I understand the instinct. You push for more time on stage, more time in front of the audience, more emphasis on your role. It's natural. But you can't sabotage other singers here.'

The defiant set of Estella Belucci's mouth spoke *Why not?* without her needing to frame the words.

'In the first place, Sandrine has done nothing to you; you shouldn't repay her like that. Even if you're ready to trample every other singer underfoot, friend or not—'

'I don't have any friends here!' Estella coloured a hot pink. 'And if I did, they have their careers and I have mine; they'd do just the same if things were the other way around.'

'Your career doesn't matter; this opera does!'

Estella Belucci snorted, more like a street girl than a gentle-woman. 'You're just like any other management—'

'Estella!' Conrad put his hand up in a gesture for silence.

She unmistakably flinched.

He lowered his hand, pricklingly aware of how her eyes followed each physical action he made. There are women who have cause to be scared of anger in men. The blonde seconda donna backed up in a slow but inexorable push, until her back was against the catacomb wall.

Conrad sighed, and rubbed at the socket of his right eye, where hemicrania incubated.

'You have one chance. There are powerful men who wish this opera to succeed. They'll reward you. There are powerful men who wish this opera to fail. If you appear to be a liability – I'll give you over to them myself. Do you understand?'

The shifting lamp light showed her face alive with fright and concentration. 'This company is my last chance. Nowhere else will have me. I have to be seen as a success in this!'

'No, you have to *succeed* in this.'

'Because you have powerful patrons; yes; you said.'

'Because you succeed or fail as the company does!' Conrad reined in his morning-irritated temper, but the catacomb echoed. 'I swear, the Conte di Argente will compose to your strengths. I'll write you the best verse I can. But, understand this – you fail or succeed as this whole opera fails or succeeds. Am I clear?'

311

Estella thickly managed something that might have been, 'Yes.'

'Stop bullying her.'

Conrad startled from head to foot. Sandrine's voice. The concealing echoes battered him. The tall mezzo strode forward, as proud as if she had never walked out, and put her arms around Estella's shoulders.

The soprano collapsed into her embrace, shaking with tears and apologies.

'You were bullying her, weren't you?' Sandrine demanded coldly.

Torn between her unnoticed approach, and the injustice of being accused, Conrad could find a hundred responses, but not a single one – and so found himself stammering into silence.

'We all know each other from before, except Estella.' Sandrine patted the soprano gently on the back. 'Except Velluti, but Signore Prouder-Than-Il-Superbo doesn't need anybody's company except his own. It's difficult to be the newcomer in something like this. Go away now.'

Conrad searched desperately for something to say that wasn't *What!*, and – having failed – backed off down the passage and away.

◆

He went for breakfast – utilitarian, since the cooks of Alvarez's Rifles were used to serving the army – and took his notebook to the mine-chamber reserved for eating, to sketch out the emotional progression of the fourth and final act.

Something isn't right with it.

Eleven days now, if Tullio's right and it's Friday . . .

Towards midday, Tullio took his elbow while Conrad was walking down the underground passages towards his study, and Conrad found himself wordlessly steered towards a smaller rehearsal chamber.

'Costume fitting rehearsal,' the big man murmured, under the sound of Paolo playing something that Conrad didn't recognise on the piano. 'And Il Superbo wants your help with an addition to the libretto.'

Conrad absently nodded, taken with the first view of Sandrine Furino and Estella Belucci under the lamp-light. Sandrine was queenly in la Principessa's green and gold robe, ornamented with dyed ostrich feathers and embroidered serpents, being pinned up even as she moved by two harried seamstresses. Estella's Amazon breastplate, over her short leather Roman centurion's skirt, shone brilliantly.

'Armour looks very convincing,' Conrad observed.

'And so it should,' Tullio muttered. 'It's a medieval one from Egg Castle. His-Imperial-Majesty-our-Composer had me polishing the damn thing all morning!'

'Let me guess, you'd given him Sergeant Tullio's speech on how there's nothing will move rust off a gorget like a little elbow grease?'

'. . . Might have.'

'Self-inflicted injury, then.' Conrad shut himself up as the piano stopped doodling about with an introduction and launched into a spirited cabaletta that he didn't recognise.

Someone's going to have to write an aria to go in front of that – oh well, I did promise Estella.

Sandrine waved her seamstresses away.

Estella experimentally put her fists on her hips. She grinned, evidently finding this supported some of the breastplate's weight. She tossed her hair back – and was the very picture of the captive Amazon Hippolyta.

'*Va, Superba!*' she sang at the Aztec Empress.

Conrad, remembering an earlier remark of Sandrine's, mentally translated his second language into his first as 'Bugger off, you Arrogant Bitch!'

Sandrine, regal and equally amused, came in with her own, '*Va, Superba!*', and the two of them began to prowl around each other, exchanging musical insults.

'And people say he doesn't have a sense of humour . . .' Tullio murmured.

'Only Il Superbo would set a cat-fight to music!' Conrad muttered. 'Damn, where is he? Words are my business. And he's missing an opportunity for some really clever insults!'

The singers and crew, adapted to rehearsals at all hours of the day and night, showed little interest in breaking off to go to Sunday Mass, although a few faces were missing. Conrad decided he could achieve a moment of tact, and didn't raise the subject with them afterwards.

JohnJack, Spinelli and Estella, still in her armour, cornered Conrad after a costume rehearsal, when it must have been Sunday afternoon up in the real world.

'Some brat shied half a brick at Sandrine's carriage, after church,' Spinelli said flatly. 'It nearly hit her. Granted she gets that anyway, but . . .'

Estella's agate-green eyes caught the lamp-light as she interrupted. 'It's fine down here! We have riflemen enough to keep the chorus women happy! But above ground, in the streets, in our lodgings? We're starting to have accidents—'

'—Except they're not accidents, of course,' JohnJack capped her. 'We've been talking. Are we going to have to move down and live in here until the performance?'

'It would only be for, what, nine days?' Conrad's mind yammered at him in panic, *Nine days!*, but he managed to ignore it. 'I think you're right. I'll get Paolo to spread the word.'

His sister-turned-cousin was not particularly happy at being stuck with that job. Conrad left her to it, to go prowling through the occupied tunnels and mines under Naples. The company had settled in remarkably quickly, adjusting themselves to lantern-lit dimness all the hours of the day and night, not to mention the constant company of the dead. It couldn't be easy.

It may be easier than being afraid of the Honourable Men and the Local Racketeers.

And very soon – I'll have to tell them it's worse than that.

The oil lamps cast a softening light over the old brown bones; over skulls, and the rounded ends of femurs. It was easy to imagine the ghosts of ancient monks down here. Or Dominicans. Or more mortal intruders, sent by the Prince's Men to do more than cause minor accidents.

Stacks of bones lined the long corridors. Interspersed among them were tiny chapels or icons, some with withered flowers still drying around them. Conrad knelt and picked up a camellia, scarlet petals brown-edged.

Decay had eaten into the petals. Other, older blossoms had been swept aside into the corridor. It argued someone who regularly visited, but had not been able in the past few weeks, or else the blossoms would be fresh.

Glancing at other shrines, their offerings were in a similar state. It was reassuring.

If the lazzaroni *can't get in here to pay their respects to the Sainted Dead, I doubt any others can get in past Mantenucci and Alvarez.*

I don't want to see any one of the company end up like Adriano Castiello-Salvati.

We have so short a time, now, that we need to keep safe. Surely we can?

Conrad stepped up his pace, preferring it where he emerged out into high-chambered spaces that had once been mines. Ancient Romans or Greeks had left the volcanic rock walls perfectly smooth behind them, and the air was scented by the pine planks Angelotti's team used to construct the flooring.

Conrad walked in at the base of one great bottle-shaped chamber, realising that he must be coming in through an air or drainage channel.

Three dozen voices rose in the opening to Act II.

The chorus sang praises to the Sun.

Opera is a great engine, Conrad felt; reminded of nothing more than those great cathedrals of work in the northern parts of Inghilterra, where looms replaced pews, and a man could not hear himself speak for the rattle of shuttles.

He paused in the shadows, watching Robert Capiraso conduct, and the various awkwardly placed orchestra members produce an echoing celestial sound.

The celebratory passage ended. On stage, the singers would parade off to a martial hymn; but here Roberto Capiraso cut that short and dismissed them, all but the two main singers, who would remain behind to sing their latest conflict.

JohnJack and Velluti began the bass-castrato duet.

Their voices prowled around each other in the orchestral rehearsal, the way their bodies would as soon as they undertook the staging. The music was oddly lyrical, Conrad thought. *Considering they're swearing vendetta, and making arrangements for a duel to the death . . .*

It held him unable to move. Hernan Cortez's triumph ascended like bells, inhuman as the notes of a glass harmonica. Jaguar General Chimalli's rhythmic bass insults undermined Velluti's vocal acrobatics with the gravity that only a deep voice has. Spinelli dropped to a note that Conrad thought a Russian bass could be proud of – sprang up into the rhythm of their dual cabaletta—

The Conte di Argente rapped his knuckles on the candle-stand attached to his piano, and pointed into the gloom. 'No! Again!'

The orchestra rearranged itself, taking their cue from Paolo playing first violin. Capiraso stood listening with closed eyes and a pained expression.

'Stop!' Capiraso slammed his hands down on the top of the piano. Paolo's bow skidded, ended everything in a discord. 'Signore GianGiacomo Spinelli, oblige me by not coming in late—'

Conrad stepped out of the shadows. 'I heard no one out of time.'

'No?' Capiraso, even in the warm gold light, managed to give a chill look that was all Il Superbo. 'No.'

There was a distinctly implied *No, I doubt you would.*

'Signore Scalese, when you are in charge of rehearsals, you may—'

Temper getting the better of him, Conrad snapped, 'In fact, I believe I am in charge! And Paolo is supposed to be conducting them—'

'That boy!'

'—That boy has done three years more in a conservatoire than you have—'

It was a sheer and absolute relief, Conrad discovered, to allow himself to yell at Roberto Capiraso. The tenseness of past days exploded out of him. It might well have been the case for Il

Superbo, too. With his face distorted by light and shadows it was difficult to tell.

'—If you spent less time destroying the morale of the singers,' Conrad finished, loud enough to carry over the Count's bitter protest, 'and more time actually setting my libretto, we might have some chance of getting this opera finished before the first night!'

An anonymous voice from the direction of the rehearsal stage remarked, 'A week and a half is long enough to put on an opera; people do it every day . . .'

'Yes. Thank you!' Conrad bit off his next remark. 'If you've got nothing better to do than bitch—'

'No, nothing.' The voice turned out to be Sandrine, who beamed. Despite the heavy make-up, designed to be seen at a theatre's highest gallery, she had a remarkably subtle expression of mischief that Conrad could plainly see.

'This is not the time! Go rest, all of you.' Conrad pulled a rolled sheaf of paper out of his pocket, and slapped it against the Conte di Argente's chest. 'The new Act Four, Scene Six. Perhaps we could have some good music for it?'

It was touch and go what Roberto's temper would make him do. Thirty heartbeats ticked past.

The composer silently snatched at the papers, and stalked off through the chamber. Conrad watched him go.

'Corrado?'

His whole body suppressed a startle. Not because he was seeing the assassins of the Prince's Men down every tunnel, this time, but because he would recognise the voice anywhere.

He blushed violently. 'Nora!'

He turned around, realising she had been standing behind him all through his quarrel with her husband.

31

That went out of his head – along with the rest of the world – as soon as he saw her face, pale as the white rock walls. He found his mouth dry and wordless.

Five weeks since this began. Less time than that since I've known she was here in Naples.

Whatever her name is – whatever she is – nothing in my feelings has changed!

He was not alone in most senses. The singers and instrument players collected in small groups, under the vast ceiling that the lamp-light barely showed; but they were far more interested in the break from work than in anything else.

Leonora's dark shapely brows came down in a frown. Even that was a beautiful expression on her.

'I'll be speaking to Roberto later. Conrad . . . Do you want this opera to be finished? I foresee one or other of you walking out if you don't stop quarrelling!'

Conrad winced, a twelve-year-old schoolboy caught in a misdemeanour.

La Fenice in Venice is no different from any other opera house. Leonora will know, from there if nowhere else, about quarrels between prima donna and second soprano, between the composer and the orchestra, between anyone and anyone else, in fact. Even if she had never set foot backstage since Venice, she would recognise what damage a quarrel between the librettist and the composer could do.

'We do work together. He can be a good composer.' Conrad was suddenly speechless, as she moved further out into the light of the oil lamps, and he saw her fragile appearance. 'Are you . . . I can't even ask, are you well? What would that mean? Can you be ill?'

'I'm not ill. Just tired.' She smiled, more resigned than sad. 'Corrado, we haven't had time to speak . . . Because you're a man, I suppose you must be wondering whether you had anything to do with this?'

Her unobtrusive gesture took in her fever-warm skin and still-ness; her general differences as Returned Dead.

'Of course I wonder!' Conrad was startled to find his tone so rough. He looked down into her blue-violet eyes, wishing he had the right to brush the wisps of ash-brown hair back from her face. Desperate to show himself rational, adult, he said, 'I can't find any evidence as to why some people Return and most don't. You . . .'

'Me?' Leonora gave him an amused look. 'I've been thinking it over since we spoke – I knew you'd have more questions for me, Corradino! There truly was . . . nothing. Or, I suppose there was nothing but me – or else I wouldn't remember it.'

She shook her head dismissively.

'But it was just . . . being. All I could think of was how much I wanted to be alive.'

'Is that it?' Conrad stared at her and stumbled over his words, barely keeping up with his own mind. 'The Returned Dead come back because they want to?'

Does it have nothing to do with the bereaved? So many of those who die are loved by the ones they leave grieving but still stay dead. If we've had the wrong idea all along . . .

'I don't know, Conrad.' She tilted her head on one side, like Venice's thieving brown fluff-ball sparrows.

'Then it wouldn't depend on those who are left alive; how much they love you. Just on how much you love—' Conrad bit off the word he would have finished with.

Him. Him, not me. She won't have come back for me.
But he said she remembered my name.

Conrad used the silence to gather up courage.

And when he found it, asked a different question entirely. 'I must know. Am I in any way responsible for your death?'

Leonora shook her head. 'I think this will be painful for you to hear, but I died in child-birth, with what would have been mine and Roberto's first child. It seems I have too narrow hips to ever safely bear a child.'

Thinking of her pregnant, thinking of her in the Conte di Argente's bed—

'Yes, it's painful to hear.' Conrad held her gaze for long enough that she understood how many ways he meant it. 'Nora, I thought of you often—' *Every day!* '—over the years. I want to think that might have had some influence on your Return, even if only the smallest.'

'Who knows? ' Leonora reached up with her fingers and gently brushed his cheek. 'Don't let Roberto's temper drive you away, Corradino. Your friendship is valued here, I promise you.'

Her touch scalded him.

'I had achieved some . . . balance of mind,' he whispered, 'while I was away from Naples, and then working down here. Now that's scorched up in flames! How I was, before I left – sending Tullio to ask questions of your servants, wondering if I could find a way to see you when your husband was out . . . It makes me sound like some shabby conventional adulterer!'

Leonora made to speak but he pressed on, in an intense whisper.

'This isn't a case of a woman I once had, and I wonder if I can have her again, in the teeth of the marriage laws!' Conrad watched her features, responsive to his crudity, and all he saw was her wonder. 'Every time I think of you, I think, "this is Nora, Leonora D'Arienzo, who is the other half of my soul. If we never saw a priest in Venezia, that doesn't make us any less married. I know she's faithful to me."'

'Corrado—'

'And at the same time I know you left Venice with Roberto Capiraso, and married him to become Contessa di Argente; I know you lay with him. And now you tell me that you died in birthing his child—'

She gazed up at him in the golden lamp-light. It was impossible to believe he no longer had the right to take her hand, or hold her body close up against him, or kiss her. He clasped his hands behind his back to force himself to remember.

'Nora, I know I asked before – men always ask – but, does he make you happy?'

'Not so many men ask in that tone.' Her lips curved, as if she were remembering small things: the everyday currency between a husband and wife. 'And, yes. I won't lie to you. He does.'

Happier than with me?

As if she could read his mind – or, as her husband had told him, because his emotions are so clearly decipherable from his expression – Nora said quietly, 'I didn't choose him over you just because he made me happy. You made me happy.'

'I know: you told me: you married him because he could marry you.'

A plausible account of events tumbled into his mind like dominoes falling. That she married the Conte di Argente, that she died in child-bed; that suppose – only suppose – she married him because she learned she was pregnant . . .

Because little Nora from the orphanage in Castelfranco Veneto knows what orphanages are like, knows the half-slavery of children fostered out, and would never subject any child she might have to that.

And in that case, if she were pregnant in Venezia, it might have been his, or mine—

Either of us might be responsible for Leonora's death.

'Was it my child?'

'No.'

Clearly, she had expected this question.

'We'd been gone from Venice two years before I fell for a baby. Corrado, I want to talk to you – we will talk, when the opera's safely launched – because there's so much for us to say.' She paused. 'It's just over a week; try to bear with him until then?'

It was not the question he wanted to have asked of him. But since it was Nora, he said, 'Yes, I swear.'

She stepped back, inclining her head in a polite nod.

The Conte di Argente was visible across the chamber, Conrad realised; talking with the second violin. As Conrad watched, Roberto shot a glance at Leonora.

Leonora walked away, gracious, exchanging words with all of the cast during this resting period.

Not mine, never mine, she went through death and came back and she still chose Il Superbo over anyone else.

He saw Nora approach her husband. This time he tried to watch and see, rather than be overcome by jealousy. Leonora smiled up into her husband's face. Roberto touched her hand gently, for such a squarely built man, and then swirled an errant lock of her hair around his finger.

She swatted mock-angrily at his hand and swept off, talking to the seated members of the cast, until Sandrine held up a mirror so that the pale woman could take out the pins and rearrange her hair.

Conrad waited until the composer was standing alone, between conversations; strain momentarily creasing his face.

'Signore.' It was difficult to expose his sincerity to the other man's possible acid. He nonetheless finished. 'I have only just heard. I would like to offer you condolences on the passing of your child.'

Contracting lines showed at the corners of the Roberto Capiraso's eyes. The Conte di Argente was taken aback, evidently. He weighed Conrad with a long look.

His narrow glance relaxed.

'Thank you,' Roberto said soberly.

A chord sounded from the piano. Conrad glanced across to see Paolo playing the first phrase of Cortez's aria of love for the Princess Tayanna. Giambattista Velluti had taken Leonora's hand. Now he sang to her with self-assured passion. There were comments from the other singers and musicians gathered around, but not distinguishable over Velluti's warm contralto notes.

'Vulgar exhibitionist!' Roberto Capiraso sighed.

It was an almost cordial sigh. Il Superbo had evidently become used to the castrato's foibles.

Surveying the crowd around the piano, under the oil lamps that barely touched the gloom high in the bottle-shaped roof, Conrad found himself saying, seriously, 'The time's coming when we have to tell them.'

The Conte di Argente swung on his heel, bringing him around to face them. Sandrine's mezzo sounded as she joined her voice with Giambattista, both of them now serenading a laughing Nora.

'That it's not organised criminals they have to fear.' Roberto raised a brow. 'Do we need to tell them?'

'The essential people, yes – they've noticed the attacks that are feeling out our strength. We owe them.' Conrad met il Conte's gaze. 'If any of them are going to crack, and need to be replaced, the sooner we know about it the better.'

Roberto Capiraso nodded. 'I . . . yes. I suppose you're right.'

Conrad thought, momentarily, of Adalrico di Galdi, and the nameless priest in the Duomo. 'I imagine that the Prince's Men themselves may spread rumours about their presence in Naples – because they'll know that, if we haven't told the company, our people will see that as a betrayal.'

Roberto made a very unaristocratic grimace. 'Yes. The cast have new material to adapt to, today and tomorrow; shall we say, tell them in three days' time?'

'Monday,' Conrad compromised. 'Make it tomorrow evening.'

'Very well.'

There was a pause.

'I suppose, under different circumstances—' Roberto Capiraso evidently braced himself. '—You are a man for whom I might have developed a slight respect.'

There was no doubt, looking at him, that the man was genuine. The mixture of old pain, embarrassment, anger, and relief at having spoken his mind was too complex for any actor.

Under different circumstances, Conte di Argente, you and I would have been friends.

'"A slight respect"?' Conrad echoed, giving the other man a chance to hear what he had said, and decide how he intended it to be taken.

Roberto Capiraso perceptibly winced.

Conrad offered his hand. He couldn't help a smile. 'I suppose that's the best I'll ever get out of Il Superbo.'

The Conte di Argente choked back a snort.

They shook hands, and went to break up the impromptu duet in favour of actual rehearsals.

◆

Morning came and made it Monday, March 6th: eight days left until the deadline. *Somewhere in the Empyrean,* Conrad thought, *Moon and sun and earth are drawing together according to the inexorable Laws of Motion. Moving towards a line that will pull with massive strength at the crust of the world.*

He put together a picture of Naples above, but now only from men's reports. Tremors of the earth had become a regular occurrence; they sounded as hollow dull thuds in the caverns. Campania had minor quakes so often, without visible result except an occasional rock-fall, that even in the mines people ignored them.

There was talk of extra vents opening on the mountain. Colonel Alvarez reportedly sent some of his men up by donkey, plodding the slow and tortuous rise from the base of the volcano, to the edges of the ash-field bordering the fathomless crater. The air was startlingly cool on the way up, but turned scorching hot near to crevasses that vented out smoke stinking of sulphur.

'Be reasonable, padrone,' Tullio said. 'If Vesuvius went boom every time there were earthquakes and smoke-vents, people wouldn't have got in the habit of ignoring it, would they?'

Conrad muttered about Pliny.

Much of the libretto of Act IV was composed and scored in record time. Rehearsal in the catacombs took place in three shifts, over eighteen hours a day. Hearing his words sung transformed them.

'But not enough,' Conrad muttered, where they sat at the back of the main rehearsal mine, passing a bottle.

'It's . . . not a bad opera,' Tullio offered. He took the bottle and drank in his turn. 'In places it's fucking spectacular. But there's long patches where . . . none of it's surprising, know what I mean?

Patchwork Donizetti pretending to be Bellini, with a bit of Rossini crescendo thrown in.'

Conrad winced. 'We have eight days during which we can kick Il Superbo's backside and make him compose up to his full potential.'

Tullio leaned one elbow on a music stand, and squinted up an upturned empty bottle.

'No one knows how good their black opera is.' He gave the bottle up for empty and lowered it. 'Padrone, you know, maybe this doesn't have to be the best thing ever put on at the San Carlo – it just has to be a better opera than theirs.'

'I disagree. We have this one chance. We have to make it the best that we possibly can.'

Conrad put his head in his hands, raked his fingers across his scalp, and emerged energised but (he suspected) unkempt.

'And even if that's not the case – can we really risk everything on that chance?'

✦

With the end of the self-imposed deadline approaching, during frantic rehearsal, the only violence in the catacombs had come from Captain Alvarez's regiment, and the Naples police officers detailed to assist them in guarding the opera rehearsals.

And Tullio Rossi.

And Luigi Esposito.

It only came to Conrad by report, which caused him to curse himself for working so hard.

'You should have seen it!' Isaura was all Paolo, seemingly oblivious as to why the police chief and the ex-soldier might be fighting. 'Luigi put him on the floor without even getting his white gloves dirty! I thought Tullio was a soldier?'

'Now I think about it, he's been out of the army a few years.' Conrad shrugged. 'Luigi's the police chief of a rough district, and he came up through the ranks.'

Which apparently Tullio didn't know.

Or that Luigi is a devious smart bugger who is not above brass knuckle-dusters.

'We had a short discussion afterwards,' Tullio reported, when Conrad finally persuaded him to speak. 'He admits I've got the right to first go, because I met her first. But he reserves the right to flirt.'

'No, really?' Conrad stopped himself snickering.

'I agreed. Because he can't not, padrone; it would kill the ponce!'

Conrad burst out laughing.

The ex-soldier wandered off to Estella and Sandrine, to further contaminate the gossip-well at source, so that it wouldn't be known what he and the police chief might have been fighting over.

Conrad caught Roberto's gaze across the rehearsal hall and found himself coming to unspoken agreement with the composer.

They can wait one more day to be warned about the Prince's Men; let them enjoy their freedom from it while they have it . . .

There were still territorial and administrative differences between the police and the army. Conrad took care to be in the small catacomb he reserved as his study when scuffles occurred – usually late in the evening, after drink.

'You leave me the hard work,' Luigi complained, coming in on Tuesday, the following morning, uninvited; throwing down his hat and gloves on a pile of femurs.

'I leave it to the man who knows what to do!' Conrad cut short a gesture with his writing hand and still left a blot of ink on the end of Act IV scene 3. 'If there's another way into this part of the tunnels, you're the man who knows about it. And your men, too. Not that I intend to hint anything about illegal gambling operations.'

'Good.' Luigi raked his hand through his hair, looking rather less spruce when he had done. 'What is it about rifles? You were in the army. Why do they immediately turn any man who carries them into a dumb brute?'

'Don't ask me. I was Horse, not Foot. Ask Captain Tullio. If you dare!' Conrad grinned at him. He wiped his pen clean on a cloth. 'Any more snoopers?'

'We've managed to successfully keep all intruders out of this area. There are still one or two men coming in to have a look at what's going on – some are local criminal gangs, and a few are obviously hired men.'

'Hired by the Prince's Men?'

Luigi Esposito elegantly shrugged. 'One would imagine so. Either way, they haven't got past the picket line, never mind the inner guards. I may think Fabrizio Alvarez wears the silliest hat this side of Catania, but he does know his job.'

A yawning Tullio wandered in, evidently picking up the last words. In the spirit of his new truce with Luigi, he remarked, 'You never saw padrone here in his cavalry helmet, did you? Now that was silly.'

Conrad essayed plaintiveness. 'I am sitting here . . .'

'It had leopard-skin on it. And a crest, and a plume.'

There was no use in attempting to defend his Horse regiment; the Two Sicilies' comic-opera uniforms were notorious throughout both the Allied and Northern armies, and the only adequate method of defence was a startlingly effective showing in battle.

'Angelotti wants to see you,' Tullio added, after he and Luigi had mocked all they could think of regarding Alvarez's soldiers.

'*Che cazzo!*' Conrad succumbed to the urge to put his head in his hands. He heard Luigi Esposito let loose his tenor laugh.

'I wouldn't have your job for all of the King's treasury!'

Conrad flipped through his notes, finding the instructions to the stagehands and construction crew. 'Come in, Michele.'

It was somewhat superfluous, since without a door to the stone study, men walked in and out much as they wished. The dusty blond figure of Michele Angelotti was no exception.

Angelotti stepped forward and fixed his gaze on Conrad with more dignity than a man usually has when his hands and clothes are covered with plaster of Paris. 'Master Rossini he once told me, all impresarios are bald before they are thirty, from tearing out their hair. All masters of works crews in opera, they are bald before the age of twenty! From impresarios and scriptwriters asking the fucking impossible!'

He spoke strongly accented Neapolitan, and unlike JohnJack Spinelli – who sang it well in one-act Neapolitan comedies – rarely used a purer Italian. On the occasions when Angelotti did, as with

327

his last few words, his tenor voice penetrated clear to the back of the excavated mine, and echoed off down the dry aqueduct tunnels.

Conrad managed to interrupt him. 'Tullio, could you get us some more bread and wine? Michele, you'll have breakfast with me while we talk?'

Angelotti folded his arms over his leather apron, and then evidently realised that an ancient stone mine was not a boss's drawing-room. He gave a curt nod.

'Get enough for all of us?' Conrad dug in his pocket and handed Tullio a fistful of calli.

'I'll bargain 'em down!' Tullio vanished off into the lamp-lit gloom outside the chamber, heading for the ancient wooden steps that climbed to the bedroom of the baker's family, in the Mercato district. The shaven-headed man automatically touched his forehead as he passed one of Alvarez's officers.

'We'll only need one full staging rehearsal,' Conrad said optimistically.

'*Cazzo!*' Angelotti worked himself up to full flood again. 'You want a stage for a horse to enter up top; we manage it. You want balconies, banda – two different banda, seen offside the stage – and we manage that. We build the beginnings of your volcano!'

Conrad opened his mouth to say that he had seen the wooden framework, with metal braces bolted to it, and it swayed unnervingly. He didn't get the chance.

'You want a volcano for the pretty lady maybe to throw herself in, and then the man-like-a-lady to throw himself in after. That's what you say! That's what you get. Now you want a pyramid, only's not a pyramid, but a tower of steps. And you want this upstage without blocking the god-fucking-damn volcano!'

He reached piercing levels of sound again, and Conrad couldn't hold back a wince.

Paolo-Isaura wandered in, presumably drawn by the noise. She raised her eyebrows at Conrad, but didn't get a chance to interrupt the gang-boss.

'—And you want a volcano she erupts! Smoke, fire, lava, boulders, collapse! You get collapse, I'm telling you.' Angelotti reached forward and poked Conrad's waistcoat, leaving a plaster finger-print. 'You get more than collapse, when the stage it catches fire!'

'Someone must have passed along the wrong instructions,' Conrad cut in, and stepped heavily and surreptitiously on Paolo's shoe. He astonished himself with the easiness of a bare-faced lie. 'The decision's still in committee. As to whether we have the erupting volcano, or the step-pyramid struck by lightning in a thunderstorm . . . I'll get back to you by five o'clock today.'

Meaning we have to commit ourselves to the end of Act IV's staging.

Paolo cut in with bubbling enthusiasm. 'That's why the King was determined to get you and your stage crew for this, Signore Angelotti! He knew you're the best to handle this work at the very short notice we have.'

The fair-haired man snorted, but less confrontationally than Conrad thought he might.

'My assistant here, Paolo, will take notes on your plans for each spectacle.' Conrad bowed, and moved away, not catching Gian-paolo's eye as he went. *If he wants to be in opera, she can take the good with the bad!*

Conrad made fists of his two hands and stretched out his arms, muscles cracking; shoulders back, scapulae almost touching. He gave a *wuff!*, felt himself more awake, and took the opportunity of Luigi wandering out after Isaura to sit down to uninterrupted work.

It was quite some time before Conrad realised that Tullio hadn't returned.

Conrad found Isaura in the main rehearsal cave.

'Probably found a mate to drink with,' she remarked. 'I haven't seen him since this morning.'

The police chief, who had been showing a keen interest in Paolo-Isaura's conducting of Act IV Scene II, picked up his bicorne hat.

'I'll go find him, shall I?' Luigi offered. 'I ought to check the patrols are doing their work properly and not sitting around in taverns gambling.'

'Take one of the dumb riflemen with you,' Conrad advised Luigi.

The man's departing mutter would have made him laugh on another day. It did not penetrate the fog of fear that Conrad felt settling on him.

Roberto Capiraso shouldered in past Luigi, deaf to nuances of atmosphere. 'What's this about confirming the staging today?'

Isaura fixed him with a confrontational eye. 'You mean when it should have been confirmed two weeks ago? If we didn't have a crew as good as Michele's they'd have quit!'

It took a quarter hour to calm the composer down.

Conrad caught sight of Luigi striding back through the mine-caves.

The police chief was pale, some emotion shrouding his features like snow covering a landscape. All Conrad could think was, *Something has happened*.

His mind made lightning connections. The piano-stool scraped the stone as Conrad shoved past it, grabbing Luigi Esposito's arm. 'Where is he?'

'The soldiers have rushed him to their surgeon.'

Luigi reversed the grip and caught Conrad's sleeve. Conrad, surprised, was brought to a halt.

'Listen, first, Corrado! He went out with an escort. The rifleman was found dead, knifed, in the alley leading to the baker's entrance. They didn't get a chance to use their pistols; no shots were fired. I found Tullio, unconscious, propped up against the shop-front. He had this note pinned to his coat.'

Conrad took the dirty piece of paper.

The lights were too dim, or Conrad's eyes too blurred.

He held the paper up into the beam of an oil lamp.

This could be Giambattista Velluti – or any one of the cast of your opera. Stop while you still can.

32

Conrad folded the paper, creased it along the folds, and passed it back to Luigi Esposito. 'Show it to the King. First, take me to Tullio.'

Barely conscious of being up out of the tunnels and into a bright morning – as the time turned out to be – Conrad sat for what seemed hours beside Tullio's bed in the infirmary of the Little Sisters. Waiting for a doctor, for anyone, to tell him if Tullio would live.

✦

Luigi Esposito returned later in the morning, pulling up another chair and sitting down, and studying the bruises and stitching on Tullio Rossi's face.

Deliberately encouraging, Luigi said, 'He's had worse some Saturday nights. He'll be fine.'

Conrad ignored that, although the doctor had concurred. 'We got careless. Despite the escort, he was almost beaten to death because he was recognised as "one of the servants" who go in and out of the catacombs. The Prince's Men—'

He took a breath, conscious of the oppressive silence of the infirmary, along with the stink of faeces and sickness.

'—The Prince's Men saw him as just another servant, a thing they could use to deliver a message to us.' Conrad steadied himself with difficulty. 'I could almost forgive them if they attacked him because he's Tullio Rossi and invaluable to putting on the counter-opera! If he dies—'

Luigi grasped his elbow. Conrad forced his voice to quietness, holding down the rage and pain so as not to disturb the unconscious man.

'—If he dies, I'll finish this opera, and then I'll start with Adalrico Silvestri, and after that, I'll take any one of the Prince's Men I can reach. And I'll make them hurt.'

✦

Isaura came quietly into the infirmary before midday, and stood beside Conrad, gazing down at Tullio's unconscious body.

'We need you.' Her tone was unapologetic, but Conrad heard the slight crack in her voice. 'Corradino . . .'

It was, he realised with some surprise, still Tuesday. The seventh day of the month. Seven days left before the first night.

He left his chair without making a sound, and stood beside his sister.

'Tullio would slap me if I messed this up because of him.'

'He would—' Paolo-Isaura broke off.

An infantry sergeant of indeterminate age wandered up to the unconscious man sprawled in the hospital bed. Ignoring Conrad – clearly of too high a social station to be concerned with the patient – he leaned over, and muttered, 'Rossi, you bad-tempered bastard, what are you up to now?'

Conrad drew Isaura aside by her elbow.

'It's one of the island-Sicilian regiments of Foot.' Conrad recognised the insignia. He knew the Teatro San Carlo backstage area was almost ready, final stage furnishings having been added daily, and stood under heavy guard, now. Ferdinand had brought in two new regiments.

'And?' Paolo glowered.

Conrad made an effort to explain that Tullio Rossi was protected by the infantry's informal 'he may be a bad-tempered bastard but he's *our* bad-tempered bastard'. *Which is as good as most men's sworn court oath.*

After that, it was not such a strain to leave for a few hours.

And the time has come, Conrad realised, *when people have to be warned.*

◆

Below ground, the cast was at the stage of hair-pulling hysterics.

Isaura elbowed into the scrimmage, and bellowed with surprising penetration at Giambattista Velluti. 'How many times must I tell you? You sing plain on the syllables people need to hear to make sense of this! You make ornaments on the extraneous syllables, or you wait until the repeat verse which is what it's fucking for!'

Conrad tiptoed past the scrum, to where Roberto Capiraso stood at the entrance to his cell-like library, watching with anxiety.

'This is normal.' Conrad couldn't tell if he reassured himself or Roberto.

Hardly listening, the dark man stroked his cropped beard. 'We're telling them today.'

Velluti shied his shoe at Isaura. Conrad winced, even though the throw deliberately missed. It battered the forte-piano still further.

'We can't put it off,' Conrad agreed. 'But let's at least let them eat first.'

Tuesday's midday brought a scent of dust and horse-dung and the early-flowering camellias, sifting down through the tunnels and aqueducts. The singers and musicians sat together on chairs or Angelotti's makeshift wooden stage, regardless of rank (except for Velluti, who preferred to be surrounded by his acolytes), and ate bread and olives, and drank watered wine.

Conrad's stomach clenched up sufficiently that he couldn't eat.

Roberto's voice, behind him, said quietly, 'There's no way of warning them about the eruptions to come, unless they know about the men behind this.'

'I know . . .' Conrad made sure by eye that he had singers and chorus together in the echoing smooth-walled chamber. The second violin led in the few missing musicians, with a nod to Isaura-Paolo. Conrad had been careful to make sure every key role had a man who could step into it. Michele Angelotti and his crew and apprentices noisily joined them. Conrad waited while they ambled up in a group, and sat down on spare chairs and benches.

'Wish we had these acoustics in the San Carlo,' Armando Annicchiarico muttered. More than one voice agreed with the second castrato.

Conrad snorted. 'I've considered staging the whole opera under Naples, don't think I haven't! If it wasn't for needing an audience, I'd do it!'

'Safer down here,' the diminutive tenor Lorenzo Bonfigli observed. He looked up at Conrad with eyes bright in the eternal lamp-light. 'Corrado, why do we need an audience, again?'

There was general laughter at that. Conrad caught Roberto's eye, where Il Superbo leaned against the wall. The man shrugged. *So you have no better idea of how to handle this than I do!*

'We may not in fact require an audience—' *As the Prince's Men apparently didn't at Tambora.* '—but I think we're stronger for one. They give adulation; we give them everything we have; the stronger they are, the more they give us, and so on, back and forth. Certainly everyone's seen it work the other way, when the Pit aren't interested in anything but gambling, and you can't hear the singing for the conversation from the boxes.'

There were audible winces.

Conrad waited until the singers and crew grew quiet again.

'I need to speak to all of you,' Conrad said, letting his voice and the atmosphere of seriousness project through the mine.

He immediately held his hands up to stem the tide of questions.

'Well?' Sandrine looked at him expectantly.

Conrad leaned back against the ancient forte-piano. 'To begin with the key point. We're going to face more than ordinary sabotage while we rehearse and stage *L'Altezza azteca*, particularly up in the San Carlo. As you all know from what happened to Tullio Rossi, this could be personally dangerous to you.'

The clear acoustics of the mine shaft bounced each proclaiming voice back from the tufa rock. Conrad didn't attempt to disentangle the cacophony.

They fell silent out of necessity.

'It's time to tell you why,' Conrad said. 'I won't be naming names, yet. That's so that if any of you want or need to leave, you can do it in relative safety.'

Conrad paused, thinking carefully what he could and could not say.

'You know the Local Racketeers and the Men of Honour don't want this opera put on. In fact, they're now taking a particular interest in us – with all that that means. We face more than usual sabotage. It could be hazardous, perhaps fatal.'

'Why?' Lorenzo Bonfigli demanded.

'I'll be telling you all the details – but not before I've had an oath of silence from you. It's difficult, I know, but you have to choose now whether you'll quit or stay.'

Some dissatisfaction showed on Bonfigli's face, and on others.

Conrad straightened up. 'You already know that this is dangerous. If you didn't think before about what that can mean, think about it now. It's also true that we have powerful royal protection. You need to weigh it up for yourselves – and make the choice.'

'You're admitting that they'll deliberately target more of us?' Armando Annicchiarico demanded. The second castrato's chubby features took on a shrewd look. 'That they attacked your servant to send us a deliberate message?'

Conrad silently nodded.

'And the mountain?' Armando glanced around. 'I'm not local to this city; when it looks like Mount Vesuvius will erupt and take the Burning Fields with it—!' He made a cutting gesture with the side of his hand. 'I'm out. I have a family to think of.'

Sandrine cut in, with audible amazement, 'You have a family?'

'My brother's widow and his daughters. I'm not staying in Napoli if there's a chance of an eruption. They have no one to support them except me.'

Conrad wrenched his mind away from his mother, Agnese, in the house in Catania; snow-capped Ætna looming over the city. 'You don't have to make excuses, Armando. Anyone can leave. Especially if you have responsibilities. There will be no recriminations.'

'No one would leave unless they were a coward!' Sandrine snapped. 'People who were willing to face the Honoured Men only when they were just a name. And now that someone's been hurt . . . .'

'It's not a sin to be scared.' The newcomer, Brigida Lorenzani, lifted her head out of her score. She was a round woman who dressed flamboyantly to illustrate it – today in a gold velvet gown and green turban – and having arrived late for her San-Carlo-contract-assured part, she lost herself in studying it. Now she observed, 'Only a fool or a brave man crosses the Honoured Men. It's not foolish to decide that one's family take priority.'

Conrad kept his annoyance off his face. Merda per merda! *I really don't want to write Thalestris out; she and Estella have voices that work together.*

'And you, donna?' Conrad asked politely.

'My husband and children are – quite coincidentally – visiting our other relatives in Cape Town.' Brigida adjusted the feather on her turban, and caught Conrad's gaze with eyes that were searingly ambitious. 'I don't scare particularly easily.'

More voices sounded. Some of them were crew; others from the chorus. Conrad sat back to let them talk. Estella nudged John-Jack, and Conrad saw her draw his attention to the situation with a look. If it were not so serious, it would have been amusing to note how spines stiffened among the main singers, and jaws set.

Conrad let the wave of argument break and become repeating surf. He occupied the time with working out how Annicchiarico's roles could be taken over by other singers or dropped completely. Since he had emergency plans for most singers, it took less time than it might. The composer agreed to drop a small scene that couldn't be worked around. Conrad stood with his face away from the centre of the chamber, and wished his eyes were in the back of his head.

Roberto, with an air of incredulity, murmured, 'You're more agitated than they are!'

'That's an exaggeration . . . I want this opera to succeed.'

It was true, Conrad found, and for more reasons than self-preservation.

A quarter-hour by his pocket watch and he asked, 'Well? Decide now.'

Half a dozen of the chorus singers signed off the books, and one man from Angelotti's crew. To Conrad's surprise, there were no more.

He nodded to Luigi. The police chief, by the openings of the tunnels, signalled to his men. They escorted those who were leaving away, and faded into the gloom. Others would assure privacy here.

Conrad drew a deep breath, looking out over the faces turned towards him. He clasped his fingers behind his back, hoping it looked authoritative, and not that he was stopping his hands from shaking. 'You've been told that you face the Local Racketeers, or the Men of Honour. That would be bad enough. In fact, we used their names to hide a similar but worse thing.'

Sandrine looked sceptical.

The effervescent Estella Belucci shrank into herself, clearly afraid.

Conrad allowed himself a look at JohnJack, hoping the bass wouldn't regard him with betrayal.

Spinelli smiled and shrugged. 'Well, if not who, at least tell us what we're up against.'

Buoyed up with relief that he still had one friend – for the moment – Conrad asked, 'Who here has ever seen a miracle at a Sung Mass?'

More than a dozen hands went up.

Before they could begin exchanging stories, Conrad went on. 'Who here has seen anything at an opera performance that you would class the same way – as a miracle?'

He counted nine hands, only two overlapping with the prior group.

This is going to be easier than I thought.

Somewhere between two thirds and three quarters of our people won't need to have opera miracles explained to them.

JohnJack said wryly, 'Count yourself in there, Corrado – you're the one that hit the Teatro Nuovo with lightning!'

'Well, at least you blame me now, and not God!' Conrad muttered.

337

Roberto Conte di Argente moved forward, his eyes hooded. Conrad saw wary hope in his expression. The bearded man sketched the situation in a few words. Conrad was not surprised when none of the singers or musicians, even those without personal experience, queried the possible power of an opera miracle.

No wonder, really, I suppose. They eat and drink notes and music more than they do the Host and wine at the Mass. They make opera happen. They know.

He watched Sandrine sit back down, decorously smoothing the ruffles of her afternoon gown. That action – and the curious but unafraid look with which she invited Conrad to continue – did a lot to restore confidence. JohnJack drew out one of the chairs for Estella to be seated; Paolo-Isaura sprawled on her piano-stool, chin on her hand; Giambattista Velluti clasped his hands behind his back, graciously conferring his attention.

Conrad caught Roberto's gaze. The Count gave a small nod back, clearly indicating *You continue*. Conrad withheld the snort of amusement he might have given. *Trust me to get stuck with doing this . . .*

Conrad reached for one of the wooden chairs and turned it about, sitting with his arms resting on the back of it. 'This afternoon, we're going up to the San Carlo for the first of the dress rehearsals up there. Before we do that . . .'

He felt his smile slip, but he managed to look determined.

'Before that, let me tell you what we know about a political and revolutionary secret society who call themselves "the Prince's Men".'

Brigida Lorenzani raised a plucked, painted eyebrow. 'Another secret society?'

'It's more than just a change of name.' Conrad steepled his fingers. 'The Camorra and the Mafia are crooks. Widespread or not, what they want is to be rich and feared. The Prince's Men have far more ambitious aims – they'll overturn the government of the Two Sicilies if they have to, or any other state. We know that.'

Conrad gave a nod towards Roberto Capiraso, letting the others know that the Conte di Argente was in the King's confidence.

'The Prince's Men are deeply rooted in the Council of the North, and the governments of other countries. They have spies every-where, and they'll kill to get what they want. They have members from every part of society – the woman who sells you fish could be a Prince's Man; so could a count or prince; so could your landlady, your local police officer, your brother.'

Lorenzo tilted his head quizzically. 'That's not so different from the Men of Honour. Why is opera so important to these Prince's Men?'

Estella Belucci chimed in after him. 'What miracle is it that we're trying to achieve? And why are they against it? What will L'Altezza do?'

Conrad nodded as if he had wanted to be asked just those questions.

'King Ferdinand put it best, when he recruited me. We're not trying to bring about an opera miracle – we're trying to stop one.'

That gave rise to complete hubbub.

Roberto Capiraso shouldered through the assembled company to lean down beside Conrad's chair. 'Will you tell them everything?'

'It's bound to come out once we start. Better to volunteer the information.'

Il Conte di Argente slowly nodded.

Conrad clapped his hands once, loud as a shot, and let the echoes from the great bottle-shape of the Roman mine make a silence for him.

'This is it, in brief. The Prince's Men are putting on an opera. We know nothing about their singers, or what theatre will put it on – we suspect a private performance. We do know what the black opera will do. The activity of Vesuvius and the Campi Flegrei are only the start.'

Conrad shivered, aware of the cavernous darkness above him, and the dark maze of passages that were the only way back to the light. He looked from one man's face to the next, and likewise the women. He drew on memories of briefing his troop, in the moun-tainous north, to speak without his voice shaking.

'Most of you here will remember the Year without a Summer. The snow. The starvation. If the King's Natural Philosophers are correct, it wasn't God's punishment for the war. It was the natural result of a volcano in the Far East, which erupted powerfully enough to cloud the skies with dust for a year.'

'But— And Vesuvius—' JohnJack's dark eyes met his, quick mind clearly having made the connection.

'The effect of that volcano, Tambora, may have been natural, blocking off the sunlight and prolonging winter. The eruption itself was not natural.'

There was silence enough that Conrad could hear water trickling in the underground aqueducts, and boards creaking underfoot as people shifted. He wished for help from Roberto, but a glance made it clear that Conrad would be the King's only interpreter as far as natural philosophy was concerned.

He sketched a blunt account of what the previous black opera had brought about in Indonesia – and what the current one might do to Italy.

'Motives and causes are not so important,' he said grimly, 'compared to the extent of the expected catastrophe. Ætna, Stromboli, Vulcano, Vesuvius. The sea-bed of the Tyrrhenean Sea may not be safe either.'

Estella Belucci leaned into the arm that Sandrine put around her shoulders. 'Why do they want to destroy the Two Sicilies?'

'It's not that way around.' Conrad leaned back. The wood of his reversed chair gave a creak, under his wrenching grip. 'The Two Sicilies are in danger because we have volcanoes here – and opera. Not because the Prince's Men wish to destroy us particularly. As far as we can understand, the local destruction we'll see here is irrelevant—'

A crash of voices objected, Sandrine's loudest. Conrad waved her to silence.

'—Except that it is destruction, yes!' He took a breath. 'The Prince's Men want to make a blood sacrifice to raise God.'

Few of the company were Free-thinkers, and most were glad to go to Mass. Conrad saw that where his first question had been 'how can you wake what doesn't exist?', it would not be theirs.

JohnJack glanced around for support. 'A blood sacrifice. Like a Black Mass? If they do that, won't it summon the Devil rather than God?'

'I'm not the expert to speak to.' Conrad caught amused looks, since his views were no secret. 'Truly? I don't think it matters whether you call it God or the Devil. They call it the God they worship. King Ferdinand calls it Satan. Whatever they call up or create, last time it wiped out an island in Indonesia, and starved the world for a year.'

In the white illumination of gas lamps, the silence was charged with fear, speculation, awe, excitement.

'Most revolutionary secret societies would change the world if they could.' Conrad spoke into the silence. 'If the black opera succeeds, and they get their miracle, the Prince's Men *will* change it.'

He did not find it necessary to say that they might not like the result. That emotion was clear on every face.

'Tambora was an experiment, to see if they could do what they wanted. They can. And now they will. If *L'Altezza azteca* doesn't counter what they're doing. If we don't stop them.'

Conrad stood, abandoning his chair, and paced across the boards.

'You can still back out.'

He stopped and swung around, confronting them.

'If you do, King Ferdinand will put you into safe custody until after the fourteenth. You won't be allowed to see or speak to anyone until then, but after that, you'll be free to go. I think it extremely important—' Conrad hit his hand into the opposite palm. '—Extremely important that no one is compelled to sing in *L'Altezza azteca*. If we're to counter the black opera, we have to be whole-hearted about what we do. This— This is for volunteers only.'

He looked around, meeting their eyes.

'Whether you're singing a star role, or painting scenery, you're just as important to the opera. Because every separate thing has to work, to make the whole thing work. Look into your heart and decide whether you can give everything to this opera. If you can't, please, don't stay here out of fear or ambition or misplaced loyalty. If you can, then say so, because we need you!'

Conrad broke off, the rush of words abandoning him because he could find no more that needed to be said – and voices shouted, hands beat together, and the great cavern echoed with applause. He was stunned.

Roberto appeared at his side, holding a hand up as the volume of applause began to diminish. He projected his voice. 'You have an hour, now. Then we'll hear individual decisions. Colonel Alvarez will escort anyone who chooses not to stay to a safe place. The rest of us will go up to the San Carlo, and begin on rehearsing there.'

33

Conrad slipped away, strolling alone without aim along a Roman drainage channel that had served street-fountains in its day, and was tall enough to walk in without bending his neck. Reflected light from inhabited catacombs was dim. Two or three times Alvarez's men checked him, and, on discovering the stranger in the catacombs was Conrad Scalese, let him continue his peregrinations. He kicked at pebbles, like a schoolboy.

When he finally re-entered the main mine, Paolo was ticking off names on a list.

Is that people quitting or staying?

Luigi Esposito's white-gloved hand came down on Conrad's shoulder.

'Message from up top,' Luigi murmured.

Fear thumped cold in the pit of Conrad's belly. 'And?'

Luigi's glance strayed to Paolo. His grin was a mixture of glad and rueful.

'Word from the infirmary. Rossi's awake. They beat him like a drum, but apart from the bruises, he's fine. The doc says you can go up and talk to him as soon as you want.'

✦

Tullio Rossi, conscious and bitching all the way, was brought on a stretcher under the streets of Naples, and settled in their cave-lodgings.

'I won't answer for it if he's kept in this foetid air,' the Royal Physician remarked, ignoring his patient in favour of casting a gaze around the dry aqueduct tunnels and the smooth-sided quarries. 'Surely you haven't been sleeping here yourself, sir?'

Conrad winced as the man audibly dismissed the servant in favour of worrying about the master.

'There's no other option.'

At least, no truly secure option.

The King's physician frowned. 'Then air the place out at least once a day. If not, you may fall ill yourself, owing to the noxious vapours of the earth . . . Your man should be up and capable of work in a week. No need to coddle him; working men have much more crude vitality than gentlemen.'

I'd like to put you away from the 'vapours of the earth', Conrad thought. *Exposed on the upper battlements of Egg Castle, maybe?*

He held his tongue because an insult to the royal servants was an insult to the King.

Drawing the thick heavy curtains that served as the door, after the entourage left, Conrad muttered, 'Stupid motherfucker!'

Tullio looked bad-tempered after suffering his day with the physicians, but that made a few of the stress lines in his face relax.

''S good doctor.' His voice was not strong. 'Just a poor excuse for a man. Alvarez's lot?'

Conrad realised that Tullio had noted the troopers of the King's Rifles guarding the passage outside.

'Don't think you have an advantage,' Conrad said carefully. He knew having guards would make Tullio see himself as weak. 'The rest of the cast and crew have the same arrangement now.'

He set the kettle on the brazier.

'You're right, I've got no facility with invalids or sick-beds. But I can at least make tea.' Absently, while he poured, Conrad added, 'The best thing I can say about the San Carlo dress rehearsal today is that Sandrine didn't break her ankle, she severely sprained it.'

'That good?' Tullio's scratchy voice was amused. 'The English

344

say it's an omen. Bad dress rehearsals, good performance. Now would be a really good time to become superstitious.'

'I'll get you a black cat.'

Conrad brought the tea across. Tullio sat up in the bed.

'Listen,' Conrad said. 'We have less than a week. The sun-moon-earth line up happens on the fourteenth, and we open then, ready or not. As for you . . . You're staying in that bed until I say you can get up!'

Tullio chuckled and groaned all together. 'Gimme a day or two. It's all bruises, padrone. I ache from head to foot; I can take that out on any of the Prince's Pricks that show. Only this time they're not getting behind me with a cosh.'

'Maybe.' He was determined to watch Tullio's head-wound himself. 'I'll find us something to eat.'

Conrad went out to arrange food. On coming back in, he surprised Isaura helping the ex-sergeant into his shirt and breeches.

'Oh . . . Conrad.' Paolo stepped back, cheeks pink. She looked less like a boy when she blushed, unless it was one of the Renaissance's androgynous cherubs.

Tullio finished easing his shirt down over his bandaged ribs, and shot a challenging look at Conrad. 'Paolo, you want to run along for a bit? I want to talk to your brother.'

Gianpaolo looked the most stubborn that Conrad had ever seen her.

She scowled, suddenly, as if something was decided in her mind, and whirled on her heel and stalked out.

'So.' Tullio folded his arms – although the fact that he was sitting propped up in a bed, and that he winced at the action, lost it some of its belligerence.

Conrad became aware he was still standing just inside the room. He closed the curtain fully, and sat down on the end of Tullio's bed.

Tullio said flatly, 'Does the Master want to stop Isaura from nursing his servant?'

'You mean, am I going to pull the head of the family act, and object to some servant courting my sister? Protect my only sister's virtue?'

'She'd bust the bollocks of any man she didn't want near her virtue,' Tullio muttered, 'and we both know it. All the same, I can't see any of your family happy about Paolo spending long hours in the sickroom with an unmarried man.'

Conrad leaned his spine up against the bed-post. He surveyed the ruffled, bandaged form of Tullio Rossi.

'Let's think about that, shall we, Tullio? Let's consider my late father Alfredo, who was – I admit – completely feckless. My mother Agnese, content to depend entirely on my Uncle Baltazar's charity while whining that I don't send her more money. And Isaura herself, who's far more comfortable dressed as a man than as a woman, and likely to stay that way. Not to mention her brother, the librettist, with his staunch atheist beliefs . . . Should I ask if you want your virtue protected?'

Tullio laughed and groaned together, one arm going to support his ribs. 'Padrone, you know what I mean!'

'I know what I mean, yes. I mean that I know you. If it looks like she's going to be hurt, you'll let her down gently and back away, no matter how much you might care for her.'

It was not often he got to see total shock on Tullio's pugilist-face; he couldn't help enjoying it.

'Make sure you don't back off just because you think she might suffer socially,' Conrad added. 'She'll suffer in any case, given what she's like, and she doesn't care. Just . . . Remember she doesn't take well to being protected.'

'She doesn't.' Tullio shook his head. 'Dear God – if Paolo finds out we've been talking about this without asking her, we'll both need protection!'

The laughter was healing, Conrad found. Or that might have been the relief.

Conrad stood up, and turned out the travelling chest that stood locked at the foot of the camp-bed. His hands sifted through spare shirts and found a flat wooden box with brass clasps.

'I intended to do this before . . .' Conrad took out one of a pair of Manton flintlock duelling pistols, state of the art, with an octagonal barrel and the bore scratch-rifled. Deadly up to twenty yards. 'You can take this.'

For the first time in a long time – years, perhaps – the older man looked outright startled. 'That cost a mint! I can't take that! It's one of a pair!'

'And so are you.'

Conrad watched emotions play by lamp-light across Tullio's weathered face.

'Yes, I saved your life in the war. I've lost count of the times you did the same for me. You're far more of a brother than a servant. Take the fucking pistol and practise with it. Brother.'

Tullio stretched out a hand and weighed the pistol that Conrad lay flat on it.

'Seen these shoot,' he observed shortly. 'Take off a fly's bollocks. Are you sure?'

'I'm sure.' Conrad closed the lid on the remaining pistol. 'Are you sure?'

Tullio gave a slant, weary grin. 'I would say this is just to get out of paying me . . . if you'd ever paid me! Sure I'm sure. Find me a powder flask and some moulds, will you?'

The ancient mine-shafts resounded to the painful cracks of pistol shots all that afternoon. Conrad's ears developed a high-pitched whine, and powder gritted between his teeth. The scent of hot metal permeated the carved chambers as Tullio poured melted lead into moulds to make his own ammunition. Conrad found himself grinning at unlikely moments.

It says sad things about a man's life when he finds the smell of gunpowder reassuring.

The smile didn't leave his face while he made out a new codicil to his Last Will and Testament in Tullio Rossi's favour.

If this goes wrong, I've nothing to leave him. If it goes right, but I don't survive, he'll have Ferdinand's reward. And my debts will be paid off by the King. Paolo – Isaura – gets everything else. And won't that make the Pironti family spit blood.

✦

The dark of the moon came remorselessly closer.

The Teatro San Carlo had final stage-flats and props finished and added day and night, under heavy guard. The second dress rehearsal took place on the Wednesday, on the stage of the San Carlo.

It turned into what a limping, grunting, newly up-and-about Tullio termed 'a complete cat's ear-hole'.

'Four hours of singing.' Roberto looked grey around the mouth. 'And the interval lengthened by thirty minutes for set-changes.'

Conrad made a stalwart effort to be reassuring. 'We only need to get used to this theatre. And we can make cuts.'

JohnJack Spinelli, in the gorgeous feathers and gold armour of the Jaguar General Chimalli, gave Conrad a lethal stare. 'Have I ever mentioned that you're hopelessly optimistic?'

'Usually you stick with "hopeless".'

'And we're not yet complete . . .' Roberto Capiraso, ignoring the by-play, gave Giambattista Velluti a pacifying glance, and rummaged through the clutch of papers he held. 'Conrad! Act Four, our primo uomo is in prison, awaiting execution, and have you got any verses for his Hymn of Death yet?'

'The Hymn of Death is going to be the death of me!' Conrad made an attempt to dispel the man's tenseness. 'How do you expect an atheist to write a hymn?'

'Quickly!'

Conrad caught the flash of dark humour. He thought it disturbing to find that the man King Ferdinand foisted on him by royal fiat – the man who had stolen Leonora and married her – was also a man remarkably easy to work with.

'I'll do that next,' Conrad promised. 'And we might pick up some time if the Act III stretta was faster than the aria. Places for sextet, please!'

He clapped his hands for attention and turned to his sister.

'Paolo, convince the orchestra this isn't a dirge. Brisker, please! Pretend you have a cabriolet waiting outside and you're paying the driver by the minute . . .'

That cheered the musicians up enough to undertake yet another run through.

The San Carlo's auditorium, when empty, was overshadowed by its tremendous chandelier. There were no finely dressed people to take attention from the Bourbon blue and gold of the boxes, all six tiers of them. Standing in the pit, eyes closed, Conrad felt as if he stood in the focus of a chambered sea-shell or the ear's canal.

The sextet ground through.

'It wasn't any worse with Annicchiarico,' Tullio's voice muttered.

Conrad opened his eyes to see the big man limping over to what was theoretically the best spot to hear the sound.

'There's nothing wrong with it, padrone. Conrad. The tune just doesn't stay in the mind. Not even while they're singing it.'

Conrad was almost glad to find one of the King's aides at his elbow, and to be summoned across to the Palace.

Mist hid all of Naples, and the sea-fog brushed wet and welcome over Conrad's skin as he crossed the piazza. He turned his face up, and exhaled in relief at being under an open sky.

Something made a sound, as if thunder growled out to sea.

Conrad slowed his steps as he walked along the front of the Palazzo Reale, glancing to the east. It was not thunder. The sea-fog did not break. There was no glow of lava. The grinding together of rocks was unmistakable, however.

Vesuvius's long, slow grumbling and minor tremors excited no notice among the Palace soldiers or the people he passed.

He was shown up to the fourth floor of the Palace, to a suite that he guessed was one of Ferdinand's private offices. The King sat at a vast green-topped desk, folders and files spread out open before him.

'The Prince's Men are giving us largesse . . .' Ferdinand waved Conrad to sit with a thoughtful hand.

'I don't understand, sir.'

'You'd think, this close to the first night, that their people would have to be coming in to Campania with the black opera?' Ferdinand had lines on his plump face that were not there a week ago. 'Enrico and his men are covering the borders. I doubt any of them have slept more than three or four hours a night.'

Conrad had sufficient knowledge of the various states' secret police and blacklists of undesirables from personal experience. No one loves an atheist. 'Has anyone been caught?'

Ferdinand gave a tight-lipped smile.

'That would be the problem . . . Something on the order of fifteen hundred people have entered Campania in the last week alone, all of whom we have solid cause to suspect. The week before, it was just over a thousand. None of them are their inner circle – so far as we know. Each must be interrogated.' He sighed. 'It seems the Prince's Men have sent in sufficient of their minor agents that we have to run ourselves ragged following and questioning them.'

Conrad blinked. 'And meanwhile, the important men quietly take their places?'

'I would imagine so. They come in – or emerge if they're already here. Enrico and his people are swamped taking care of the people we know to suspect. The closer we get to the fourteenth, the more decoys are coming in.' Ferdinand turned over pages in a file. 'So, yes, the more men who cross our borders openly with suspicious notes against them on their files, the more chance that those who cross borders secretly won't be taken.'

Conrad thought it went without saying that some of those might be double bluffs, and therefore no man could be ignored. 'The ones you have. We don't know where they're heading for?'

'I don't ask Enrico and his men what methods they use.' Ferdinand scowled, rubbing at his forehead. 'For which I suspect I shall answer, some day. But even so, they have no useful confessions. Those who are Prince's Men are zealots, fanatics . . . Those who are innocent take up our time and are harmed despite themselves.'

'They have that many people willing to be sacrificed – to be interrogated, to go to prison . . .' Conrad frowned and slipped, speaking without tact. 'I suppose it's obvious now why they killed Signore Castiello-Salvati. He would have been able to help you at this time.'

Ferdinand paused.

After that moment, the King said, 'Enrico is also watching over those residents that Adriano suspected of being Prince's Men. A fair number of the nobility have vanished over the last week. We can't just imprison their relatives or connections. How would we choose which? All have reasons for why they might be absent – business, time spent back at their estates, tours of foreign countries . . . I don't know what excuses the common people make.'

The slow grinding of abyssal rock vibrated through the floorboards and walls.

Conrad stayed silent until it faded away. 'They're still rehearsing.'

'High earth-tide is certainly coming.' Ferdinand pushed a paper chart of the Tyrrhenean Sea across the desk. It was heavily marked in pencil. 'A merchant captain brought me this, from his soundings north of Sardinia. New volcanic reefs, dangerous to shipping. And over here, through the Straits of Medina, something that might be a whole new volcanic island.'

'An island?'

'Only a few inches above sea-level as yet. I had it claimed for the Kingdoms. It was either that or have the damn English get it. I'm calling it "Ferdinandea".' Ferdinand Bourbon-Sicily had a very crooked smile. 'It will probably sink back down. They usually do.'

The King's smile faded as he put his finger on the tiny port inlet of Pozzuoli, a few miles west along the coast from Napoli itself. 'The Campi Flegrei is full of sulphur steam, boiling mud pools, new small ash cones, craters.'

'I don't suppose we have to worry about sulphur pools if Vesuvius blows,' Conrad said bleakly.

'My Natural Philosophers finally think they have a calculation of how much volcanic lava might lie beneath the Burning Fields. They think it comparable to another whole Vesuvius . . .'

Conrad said weakly, '*Cazzo.*'

Other pencil marks on the map annotated Ætna, Vulcano, Stromboli, the Aeolian Islands. It was not difficult to see what that portended.

Ferdinand rolled up the map and looked at Conrad with brisk enquiry.

Conrad detailed a report. He concluded, 'I'm staging another full rehearsal tomorrow.'

'Good. Your new adaptations work? Ah—' The King sat back. 'I had Armando Annicchiarico followed, as I promised. He travelled home to his brother's family in Corsica; that was all. You can be relieved about your judgement of character. He has no connection with the Prince's Men.'

A call for a servant had wine served to both of them. Only when it made Conrad's head swim a little did he realise how many hours it had been since he ate.

Too many rehearsals, too many slashing cuts in the score, too many re-writes of singer's lines to match the new music. This is not the state we should be in a few days before opening.

Halfway down the glass, Ferdinand said, 'No matter where the black opera is, if we can't identify their singers and musicians in the next few days, we have no way of stopping it going forward.'

Conrad felt chills down the hot skin at the back of his neck. They were not caused by the open windows and the swirling sea-fog.

Ferdinand finished: 'I wish I thought Naples might be as lucky as Tambora.'

'Lucky?' Conrad couldn't help but be appalled.

The King looked both sad and amused. 'Remember: Tambora was not sufficient. Tens of thousands of deaths were not a large enough blood sacrifice to rouse their God as they desire. If it had been, we wouldn't be here now.'

Conrad bowed his head, and accepted another glass of wine.

'And Signore Rossi?' Ferdinand turned brisk. 'Is he recovered enough to escort the Emperor north from Stromboli?'

'He says he is, sir.' *But that's Tullio. The idiot.*

Cautiously, Conrad added, 'I've been wondering, sir. Would it be wise to have *L'Altezza*'s first night on the thirteenth, instead of the fourteenth? We could just manage it. Then the Emperor's escape could be facilitated twenty-four hours before we have to handle the rest of this. He'd be gone before high earth-tide, when it comes down to the counter-opera against the black opera.'

When we finally discover if what we're doing is sufficient to stop them.

'No,' Ferdinand said.

The King stood and made his way from behind the desk. Conrad followed a bemused half pace behind.

Glass doors stood thrown open, leading to a balcony that Conrad thought must overlook the old Angevin Palace and the centre of Naples. The sea-mist hid everything but bare masts and round

Norman towers. The city, with its narrow lanes and monumental tenement houses, might never have existed.

Ferdinand stepped out onto the balcony, fine moisture clinging to the gold silk epaulettes of his coat. He stared out at the Bay as if he could pierce the cloud that lay on it.

Muted by the fog, his voice did not carry.

'We can have one first night, Corrado. Naples is full of double and triple agents. The Palace leaks intelligence like a sieve. The only secret we still have is how *L'Altezza* plays in front of an audience. Frankly, that's because, so far, even we don't know that.'

Conrad rested his hands on the stone of the balustrade, the cool dampness welcome. 'But, sir, you want the Emperor to escape safely.'

'In fact—' Ferdinand Bourbon-Sicily gave an amiable and rather more weary smile than before. 'In fact, Conrad, the sole and only reason I'm allowing his Majesty the Emperor to come here is, so that everybody who should be watching us is watching him.'

Conrad stared. 'Sir?'

'—And so that everybody who might be running around chasing us, is running around after him.'

Ferdinand turned, his back to the Bay, his blue eyes fixed on Conrad.

'As long as his Imperial Majesty arrives in Naples and causes sufficient stir that he takes all attention away from *L'Altezza azteca*, I don't care if he gets shot in the middle of the San Carlo foyer! Just so long as the counter-opera goes on.'

I've been thinking of Ferdinand as a man, Conrad realised.

And he's not.

He's a King.

Ferdinand Bourbon-Sicily's tone softened, but not by much. 'While I hope that the Emperor does escape, I hope even more that he flees north pursued by every spy, informer, and paid murderer in Naples. And that, while they're all running around like beheaded chickens, they severely inconvenience the agents of the Prince's Men.'

A gust of wind left the King's hair wet and ruffled. He might have been any man in his thirties, except for the fine lines around his eyes.

'If all the various revolutionary societies and secret services are chasing an Emperor returning as Nemesis . . . Then they're not looking at the opera he should have attended.'

The fog, withdrawing slightly, coiled in visible granular streams at about the level of the Palace roof. Conrad felt the fine wetness on his skin. He did not look away from the King of the Two Sicilies.

'I know you thought the mission to Stromboli a little frivolous.' Ferdinand's gaze warmed. 'Believe that I did have more reasons than placating imprisoned royalty.'

I must tell Tullio.

The worst of it is, it won't change his mind about going.

Conrad realised he was staring. And that he should say something.

'Sir – I wouldn't like to have to take the decisions of a king.'

'No.' Ferdinand's expression quirked. He made his way back inside, to his desk; Conrad following.

'I suppose I need not ask,' Ferdinand murmured, seating himself. 'The minor sabotage continues?'

'Yes, sir. Even though we made all our precautions more stringent after the attack on Alvarez's man and Tullio Rossi.'

The King's thumb tapped on the green leather top of the desk. His intelligent gaze seized on Conrad.

'Give me your view of this. We have a murder, yes. A beating. Singers and musicians frightened; Greek Fire used; stage machinery sabotaged; decoys flooding over our borders.'

Ferdinand slammed his hand suddenly flat.

'The Honoured Men would do more than this! The *lazzaroni* in the Port District could cause more harm! The Prince's Men deposed an Emperor! That they've done nothing to the monarch of the Two Sicilies . . . Nothing yet . . .'

Conrad felt dread collecting under his breastbone.

'Is it that we're well guarded, sir, and the Prince's Men truly can't do anything?'

Ferdinand gave a ferocious, unkingly oath. His face drew into lines that made him look fifteen years older.

'I'd like to think so. Fabrizio Alvarez does . . . Enrico suggests the Prince's Men are so confident we'll fail that all they need do is distract us, and I wish I thought that was just the Commendatore's usual pessimism!'

Ferdinand sighed, his expression complex. Conrad read brief amusement, determination, despair – he thought the older man looked both haunted and hunted.

'Corrado, I'd like to think the army and the security forces make us sufficiently safe. I just can't help but feel we've been running around after the Men's harassment like a kitten after a ball of string! Is this just pre-battle nerves? Or are we missing something – someone – inside the Palace – inside the counter-opera . . . that makes the Prince's Men absolutely sure that we can't succeed?'

34

Conrad delayed returning underground.

The sun began to burn off the fog. Heated and damp, he brushed at the lapels and breast of his cutaway coat, flicking away droplets of rain. That gave him the excuse to pick up spare clean clothing from his lodgings, and to check the rooms, since they were now deserted much of the time.

It's too easy to suspect anybody! Conrad corrected himself on the instant. *To suspect everybody!*

Even isolated by his escort of Luigi's plain-clothes men, walking through Naples' crowded streets – elbow to elbow with other men's arguments – still gave him the feeling he had come back into the real world. The key fit into the door of his lodgings, the lock undamaged. Entering the empty rooms already felt strange. He packed his gear quickly.

Who among us doesn't have a weakness?

It was, Conrad thought, *the same as trying to ask oneself who might be a connection with the Honoured Men or the Local Racket.* The Prince's Men would think that, say, Captain Luigi and Commendatore Mantenucci both knew the police not immune to corruption – and therefore a cynic would say either of them could be bribed, if the price was high enough, having that example in front of them. It was difficult to see what weakness Colonel Fabrizio Alvarez might have, but he would hardly be immune. Gambling debts, perhaps?

The green-painted stair-well echoed to his footsteps, as it had to those of the Dominicans of the Inquisition. Conrad followed his escort towards the baker's that hid the entrance to underground Naples.

Thoughts crowded into his brain, whether he wished or not.

They could offer, say, Sandrine the life of a lady of society, when she isn't singing . . . Isaura might wish for an assured post as the conductor of some opera house's orchestra. JohnJack, Estella, Bonfigli, Lorenzani – they're opera singers, the Prince's Men could make each of them darlings of some particular house in Rome, Vienna, Paris . . . Face it, the librettist Scalese and the composer Argente might both be thought susceptible to contracts with Barjaba or some other of the most powerful impresarios. Me for my debts, or position in society as an atheist. Roberto because, whatever he might protest, the experience of professional opera has got into his blood. Nora because she's his wife, and will go where he goes . . . If I were a Prince's Man, Conrad thought in sardonic pain, I would see that even Signore Tullio Rossi might be tempted by sufficient money that he could forget being a servant and ask Isaura Scalese to marry him. *Cazzo!* If it comes to being ridiculous, King Ferdinand might be suborned, if the Prince's Men promised him they'd somehow lessen the damage to his kingdom.

Imagine a sufficient source of power and corruption, and Diogenes' search for an honest man is over before it's started!

His footsteps echoed back at him as he made his way to his own stone chamber. He pulled the curtain closed behind him.

A disturbance in the air had him turning, pistol out of his pocket, before he could think.

He froze.

A woman in a green coat and walking gown pushed up the veil of her bonnet, where she stood by his desk.

'Nora? Why . . . ?'

'I mustn't be recognised – I couldn't even risk coming as your recitateur. If anyone asks, a church singer volunteered for the chorus, but she wasn't good enough. Let them think she was your whore. I had to see you—'

Leonora laughed, tone self-mocking.

'—Isn't that what every woman says? *Cazzo!* But Conrad, this isn't what you think. I have to warn you!'

◆

Conrad took her by the arm, feeling her over-warm flesh through the velvet of her pelisse. He led her over to sit on the satin-upholstered couch, and sat down beside her, knees weak.

'You're not making any sense.' He slid his hand down to her wrist, and let that be the excuse to take her hand between both of his. He chose the right hand, not wishing to be reminded of the ring on her left. 'Does Roberto know you're in here with me?'

'Oh *Dio*, I hope not!'

Conrad's heart gave a jolt in his chest.

That's too frightened for common or garden adultery.

'Nora . . . Do you need to come away with me?'

She made no direct answer, only avoiding his eye. With her, that might have meant yes, no, or maybe.

'Leonora?'

'I have to warn you.' She sounded as though she were trying to convince herself.

Her hand grew no hotter in his, but it was as warm as if it had lain in the summer sun. He could not help stroking it, chiefly that web of skin between the thumb and forefinger. He wondered idly, *Do the Returned Dead came back with anything of interest to those who read palms? Is there an imprint of death on them?*

Stop thinking. Delaying. Find out what brings her here in such secrecy!

Conrad asked directly, 'Warn me about what?'

The crease of flesh between her brows was her familiar frown. His hand moved to smooth it away with the pad of his forefinger, and he had to force it to remain still at his side. *Because it's no longer my place.*

'It's Roberto. I've been afraid for a while now – a long time, if I'm honest—'

'Does he hurt you?'

She blinked in the light of the oil lamps, as if the question took her completely aback.

'Oh, no. He doesn't hit me. Roberto would never hurt me! But . . .'

Say 'But . . . I want to leave him'. Say 'But . . . I made a mistake, I want to come back to you'.

'There were always rumours about Ugo – Ugo was the Count of Argente before him. ' She seemed to realise she was rambling and visibly pulled herself together. 'He's a rich man – Roberto, I mean – and one doesn't move in those circles and meet completely honest men. I thought in the beginning that he was content to receive his rents and run his enterprises with that money. But I started to think . . . to look . . . I think that Roberto might be a member of— Well,' she finished in a rush, 'of a criminal society.'

'What?' Conrad stifled an uncontrollable laugh. 'He what? You're serious.'

Leonora nodded, head lowered, chipped white tooth nipping at her lower lip. 'I'm almost certain that Roberto is a Man of Honour.'

Her voice was a whisper.

'He has too much money. His competitors, they go out of business. No one talks of such things to a woman, socially, but because I'm what I am, they excuse a strange question here and there. Some of his dealings are not honest.'

Shocked, Conrad thought, *If true, surely the King would have discovered this when he took him on?*

But Roberto is the only composer he could find.

And if Il Superbo has connections with crime that don't directly interfere with the counter-opera . . .

Ferdinand would be prepared to ignore that.

Ferdinand would ignore anything. Mafia, Camorra, Carbonari, Freemasons, Knights of Malta, Order of the Golden Fleece – you name it! Roberto can be anything he wants, short of being one of the Prince's Men, so long as he composes for the Two Sicilies!

Or is this just Nora being naive about how business works?

Conrad picked up Leonora's other hand and held both of them together. It would have been so easy to put his arms around her.

She looked up, white lamp-light catching in her great blue-violet irises. Her black pupils were wide enough almost to swallow up all the colour. Conrad felt that look from his sternum to his groin. In the past, everything had been abandoned at that look, to be dealt with later, after they had gone to bed with each other.

'Nora, if you've suspected this for some time, why does it worry you now?'

'You need to leave Naples.' Her hands closed hard on his, her grip as strong as a man's, though her hands were slender. 'Corrado, please. Listen to me. You've done what the King wanted you to do. Roberto told me you've all but finished the book. Go. You don't need to be here when the opera goes on. Roberto won't be, I've heard him say so; nor will I.'

'He won't?' Conrad made an abstracted mental note that choosing Isaura as the conductor had been the right decision. He was numbly aware of a feeling of betrayal. *Roberto Conte di Argente should at least stay and see things through, not take his wife and flee the town—*

But then, if I were Nora's husband, I'd want to keep her safe above all else.

'The end of Act Four isn't done,' he protested. 'The finale. I'm still doing alterations for just about everybody. My cousin Paolo's staying to conduct.'

Leonora stood, swiftly. 'Never mind your cousin! She can take care of herself—'

Conrad goggled up at Leonora. She stared back, the Nora of the Accademia quarter, both fists on her hips.

'Was I supposed not to notice? Never saw a more obvious Sapphic in my life! She's more or less said she doesn't want to be looked after, Corrado. I'm here to talk to you. For God's sake, leave Naples – come with us, if you wish; we have a coach, and I'll persuade Roberto! Or take a ship. Do whatever you want, but leave.'

'Why?' he demanded.

'Because I don't know what my husband is mixed up in, but if he's so determined to leave Naples by the morning of the performance, then you shouldn't stay! For all I know he's a revolutionary. It won't be the first time an opera's been the sign for an uprising! The *lazzaroni* are a mob waiting to happen, you can hear it in the harbour and the market.'

Conrad put out a hand to stop the flow of her words. 'Why me?'.

She stood with an unearthly stillness, in the empty stone room, but now it had a poised quality as if she only awaited the right moment to run.

'Roberto . . . has too much money. Too many friends. He had you put in prison.' Her lower lashes glinted, a fine film of moisture gathering there. 'He used his friends and had you put in prison without even thinking about it! I asked him not to, Conrad. He said if I ever asked him for anything else on your behalf, I wouldn't like what he would do. If he thinks the opera doesn't need you . . . I know what the Honoured Men are like! Suppose they have you killed?'

'Then I'll come back Returned Dead and you'll never get rid of me.'

'*Che stronzo!*'

The slap of her hand disrupted his attempt at a smile. Her flesh was heavy, as well as heated; he realised his cheekbone would bruise.

All her orphanage heritage was in her flashing eyes and her voice, lowered to a hiss.

'You stupid bastard! What do you think I am, some lady who knows nothing of the world? The Honoured Men took young women and boys every year from the house where I grew up; we all knew they went to rich men. We knew why. Those are people who care nothing for others and I am so afraid I was mistaken, and that Roberto is one of them—'

The Returned Dead do not cry. This is what received wisdom says.

Conrad put that information with the rest of received wisdom and stood up, enfolding Leonora in his arms. Her body quivered with anger, and she bowed her forehead against his high collar and cravat, but hardly rested there. Hot fat tears rolled down her cheeks and dripped onto the lapel of his coat.

'Roberto is a jealous man.' It seemed as if she put her life in those few words.

Her hair smelled of sunlight, where he buried his face against it.

'I don't want him to be part of something like that. I don't want him to hurt you.' Her eyes were shadowed as she moved back. 'I

361

don't know what's truly happening in Naples. I just know that Roberto thinks it's dangerous. He's sending me away the morning before the opera opens. You can think what you like about Roberto, but he loves me, he'd never put me in any danger. If he thinks I should leave – then I know you should leave, Corrado.'

'Because you loved me once.' He couldn't stop himself sounding bitter.

'You complete idiot!'

She grasped the fabric of his coat as if she lacked balance.

'You can leave Naples now. Leave.'

Conrad felt as if he physically swayed where he stood. Their breathing echoed in the confined space. He fought to collect himself.

'Nora, the libretto isn't complete. I can't leave.'

Her fingers straightened his coat lapels, as if the precision needed for those movements could rein in her temper. 'Corrado, I am trying to . . . Will you please listen? I think . . . I think Naples will just become more and more dangerous for you.'

He put his hands over hers, stilling them. To have her adjusting his clothing with her own fingers while he remembered Venice . . . *Too much.* 'I'll leave when I can. If there's anything I learn of your husband that you should know – I'll warn you. '

Nora made a fist and used it to push herself away from him, swaying where she stood, face still wet. The heat of her flesh dried her tears more quickly than would have happened with a living person.

'I don't know why I tried.' She shook her head.

I can't believe I'm not permitted to touch her. This is Nora: my Nora.

Conrad moved forward at the exact moment that she did.

He slid his palm over the fine curls at the nape of her neck, under her bonnet; tilting her head so that she looked up at him.

She stood up on her toes, quickly, and kissed him on the mouth.

'Oh, *Dio*, no!' She stepped back. 'I can't— I shouldn't—'

She slipped out, veil pulled down, the curtain barely moving at her passing.

✦

He found Enrico Mantenucci in a confluence of dry aqueducts, in conference with the Spaniard-looking Colonel Alvarez. He waited until the two men had finished their business before approaching the Commendatore.

Enrico listened quietly.

'We checked Argente out,' he said, Conrad having told all that he remembered. 'There are some Sicilian connections, yes, if you follow me. A few less than honest business connections in his banking, left over from when the previous Count Argente died – his brother Ugo.'

'So, not honest, but honest enough for us?'

Mantenucci clapped him on the shoulder. 'Exactly! And since neither the Camorra nor the *società onorata* support the Prince's Men in any way that we can discover, I think you can stop worrying.'

'I'm in opera; I never stop worrying!' Conrad muttered.

The iron-haired police chief gave him a slow look of appraisal, taking in the bruise under his eye.

'I do commend your strength of will. I know men who would be halfway to Rome in a fast carriage by now – with the woman who warned them.'

Poised to protest that he was not afraid of the criminal societies, the last comment caught him entirely unaware.

'She didn't intend to come with me!' As raw as the honesty felt, Conrad managed a sardonic smile. 'It isn't the first time Nora's wanted to see the back of me. Even if this time it is for . . . for old times' sake, I suppose.'

Enrico gave a bark of laughter. 'If you suppose that . . .'

The grey-haired man's incredulous amusement turned to sympathy.

'Conrad, women don't defy their husbands, secretly, just to beg a man they no longer care for to go into safety. I imagine if you were willing, her next offer would be to take you there personally. So I commend you that you can hold off for the week more that we need. What you do after that – is between the three of you and God.'

35

Hours passed, neither day nor dark. Conrad took refuge with Tullio while the older man healed. That gave Tullio a guard as he slept, and spared another man for the outer entrances to the underworld.

Count Roberto was for once ahead of Conrad in composition: sketches of music easily suited to quatrains or couplets. Conrad threw himself into the libretto and was not surprised when Act IV's finale refused to come into shape.

How can it, when I've blocked off the parts of me that feel?

It would be easy to create a tragedy by the numbers. Hernan Cortez is stabbed by a jealous rival and dies; General Chimalli is poisoned by the treacherous High Priest; they are buried in twin monuments in a joint funeral, and Princess Tayanna sings a finale in which she begs to be laid to rest between the two men who loved her, and drops dead of heartbreak as the curtain falls. United in death.

Tragic cliché is always easier.

I need a satisfying resolution that is not tragic.

He couldn't have said what made him so sure. The instinct had grown stronger the more he heard about the Prince's Men.

Emerging in the San Carlo allowed him to discover it was Thursday, five days before the deadline – six, if the day of the performance counted.

I can see us rehearsing into the early hours every day!

He sat in one of the stage-side boxes, scribbling notes as Velluti set the stretta into motion. Two verses, and then Sandrine and JohnJack picked it up in a flawless duet—

Paolo rapped her violin bow against the tin candle-shield on her music stand, and launched into an enthusiastic debate over another – *another!* – possible change. Conrad leaned back, gazing up at the overhead rails and flats behind the proscenium arch, closing his eyes against the creak of the stage boards as the chorus seated themselves on the base of Angelotti's step pyramid.

'Corrado?'

Conrad sat up, mildly annoyed at being taken by surprise – and aware that if he had more sleep and less trauma, he would have been very annoyed.

Enrico Mantenucci closed the box door behind him. His footsteps were soundless as he came to gaze out at the stage and the empty auditorium.

'What is it?' Conrad rubbed his eyes. 'It's not going to be good news, is it?'

'His Majesty thought you should know, and decide how to tell them—' A tilt of the iron-grey head towards cast and crew. '—Before they read it in the *Gazette*.'

Conrad pushed himself to his feet, the padded chair scraping back. He moved to the back of the box, where he could be sure of not being overheard. The Commendatore joined him.

'Well?'

Mantenucci plainly put his brusqueness down to strain over the opera. 'Conrad, there's no good way to say this. First – first, Signore Vincenzo Bellini has been found dead in France.'

'Bellini, dead?' Conrad felt himself pierced through by unexpected pain. 'Dead. How?'

'Under circumstances that may or may not be suspicious.' Enrico Mantenucci's expression voted for suspicious. 'It's taken time for the news to be made public. It appears he was staying with local minor nobility in Puteaux, as a guest, a month ago, and came down with cholera-fever. No physician was called to the house. I think his hosts panicked, and ran away. What's certain is that they abandoned Signore Bellini in the house for two or perhaps three days, and when it was finally investigated, he was found dead.'

'Such a waste!' Slowly, stunned, Conrad said, '*I Puritani* will be his last opera. And he'll be what, thirty-four, thirty-five? *Dio!* We should all end with such a master-work . . .'

'There's more.' Mantenucci's expression darkened. 'The timing of the news is coincidental, since it came through the diplomatic bag and has been two weeks on the way. The report is from his Majesty's ambassador in England. Maria Malibran suffered a riding accident outside Manchester. She is now dead.'

'. . . Are you sure?' Conrad's head swam. 'I apologise, you will have checked; that was stupid!'

Sombrely, he gazed across the stage at Paolo and the singers. The vast space of the San Carlo auditorium made the singers and musicians seem small. The stage lighting singled them out.

'Your army and police guard have been doubled,' Enrico said gruffly. 'I don't envy you, telling the cast.'

Conrad nodded, numb. 'Both Malibran and Bellini . . . Wait – is this just human stupidity? Do you think— Is it possible that Signore Bellini may have been composer to the black opera?'

The police chief gave him a sharp look of approval. 'Almost certainly. His death, therefore . . . It argues they no longer have a use for him. Any final alterations to the score will have been done.'

They're ahead of us, Conrad realised.

'And Malibran?' he questioned.

Enrico shrugged. 'I can't imagine even the Prince's Men killing a principal singer on the eve of a production. But, they will have been preparing longer; they'll have understudies for each role. If she was trying to get out of being involved? She knew important men socially. She may have threatened or blackmailed the Prince's Men with that fact. It may have been necessary to make a lesson out of her . . .'

The cold reminder of the way the Camorra and Mafia operated served to focus Conrad's mind. He shuddered.

'Or this may be a coincidence.' Enrico didn't sound too confident. 'I'm co-operating with the English authorities to look into it.'

The police chief folded his arms, gazing at the bright costumed singers, his eyes taking on a distant look.

'Murder can serve multiple purposes. What better way to send a warning to us? What we're doing can't be a secret by now. What can be more undermining than knowing these criminals are willing to assassinate one of the first singers of the age, and a premier composer, to show that nobody is safe?'

'It may frighten them.' Conrad heard himself sound harsh. *I'm shooting the messenger.* 'That doesn't mean they'll give in to fear. They've already proved they're brave. If you ask me what the company will think – they'll think that, no matter what the Prince's Men might intend with the black opera, this is a senseless shattering of things that are irreplaceable.'

Conrad vaulted over the front of the box onto the stage, walking towards Paolo.

He did not soften the news. Or soften the likelihood that it was a warning. He only tried to pass on to the others his absolute disgust at men who did not care who or what they hurt.

'Or care when what they destroy is unique,' he finished, looking around at appalled faces. 'I'm starting to think that the black opera won't have any truth to it, no matter who they got to compose or perform it.'

He left them trying to bribe the guards to bring in copies of the *Giornale*.

'Conrad.' Roberto Capiraso stepped forward, score under his arm.

It was the first time Conrad had been unable to avoid speaking to Argente since the man's wife kissed him.

I'd feel better if I didn't understand him.

'Conrad, do you think . . . Am I in competition with something written by Vincenzo Bellini?'

Once again when expressing strong emotion, Roberto sounded operatic – this time like a bass throwing up his hands in horror at some haunting spectre or Gothic graveyard.

He's as bad as an Englishman at expressing his feelings! Conrad snorted inwardly. He had the urge to ease the man's fears. Whether it came from guilt or sympathy, Conrad didn't know.

'It doesn't matter,' he said.

'You think not?'

'I suspect Felice Romani authored their libretto,' Conrad countered grimly. 'We can only do what we can do. But it has to be the best we can do.'

He made his way back to the stage box, corrected the verses for Act IV, and, ironically, found them flowing easier.

Either because my emotions are now raw, Conrad thought. *The scab ripped away. Or else because rhymes and poetic images are a refuge . . . from fear over when the next attack will come.*

✦

Outside the San Carlo, the sun set.

Inside, the great chandelier had its candles lit, as well as the lamps and candles by the stage, for a lighting rehearsal.

The continual shouts of men moving the stage flats into place finally sent Conrad and the singers below ground, to the mine where Paolo-Isaura commandeered the forte-piano.

'Act Three, final scene.' Conrad slapped the written and much amended pages down on the rickety table. He announced, 'Cuts.'

The singers drifted up to cluster around the table, like bees around a hive: apparently lazy but in fact obsessed with collecting their own honey.

'So few lines?' Lorenzo Bonfigli whined, mock-pathetically.

Paolo's alto snort sounded from where she uncovered the piano keys. 'You have a good male role and you're a tenor! Listen, it's only a couple of decades since your sort was confined to singing old men and nurses!'

Conrad overrode Lorenzo's mutterings about how the chest-voice high C was the note of the future. And Isaura's comment that if she had another good mezzo, she'd cast her as the hero, as is proper.

'I've taken out the evil Priest wanting to sacrifice the Amazon's son,' Conrad began, 'since we don't have Armando any more.'

Roberto Conte di Argente gave an absent nod. 'Those verses are considerably shortened. I suppose I can adjust the score . . .'

368

He sounded doubtful. Conrad just prevented himself from screaming.

Any cut, with an over-run of fifty minutes, must be good!

Co-opting one of the wooden chairs, Conrad sat and spread the papers out across the folding table. 'I've also cut the Jaguar General Chimalli bribing the High Priest to give a false prophecy—'

JohnJack muttered something unintelligible.

'—But we can keep Chimalli's message to Cortez – that, on the condition that Cortez refuses to marry Princess Tayanna, his child will be spared evisceration on the step-pyramid.'

Roberto waved a dismissive hand. 'The music's agreed for that, and for the Amazon wench when they take her child away. And for Thalestris throwing off her disguise and proclaiming herself Hippolyta's mother and the Queen of the Amazons.'

Conrad nodded agreement, trying desperately to frustrate those parts of himself that were at war. One part fervently wished that he might enjoy working with his horse's arse of a composer, since – for all he deserved the name Superbo – Roberto was also a man for whom one might feel some slight respect. Every other part of Conrad's mind replayed Nora's impulsive kiss.

He could convince himself he regretted it had happened.

We have five – four? – days. Can I not wait that long!

Glad that only one lamp remained lit on the table, hiding his face in shadow as he leaned back, Conrad turned over pages of the brightly-lit score.

'We have to lose the Princess's aria confessing that if she doesn't do what her High Priest demands, there'll be a revolt by the superstitious mob. Sorry, Sandrine. So we go straight to the chorus preparing the ceremonies for the wedding day. The Amazons and the child are brought out of jail in chains. Tayanna enters with flowermaids. And then – new verses – the shock entry for the ending of Act Three—'

Conrad, pleased with himself, couldn't help sounding so.

'—The wedding ceremony begins, but is cut short. All of a sudden, we hear trumpets! A ship has landed. Visitors are proclaimed. A splendid parade of armed European soldiers enters—'

Conrad leaned forward into the circle of light that illuminated the singers' faces.

'—And that's going to be made up of every warm body that isn't actually singing in this scene in the procession, right? Right down to Angelotti's apprentices! So, the procession of men in armour, with banners, and at their head is none other than Charles the Fifth, Holy Roman Emperor and King of Spain! Who is Hernan Cortez's King and master.'

Paolo interrupted from where she sprawled on the piano-seat. 'Because people nip across the Atlantic every day . . .'

'There's nothing to stop Cortez's King arriving.' Conrad made an expansive gesture, the chair creaking. 'We need that impact on the audience! The great King-Emperor Charles, Carlo Quinto, *il Re* Carlo, has arrived to ask why Cortez hasn't yet conquered the Aztec lands as the "New Spain of the Ocean Sea" . . .'

Conrad turned the annotated score around so that Il Superbo could read the alterations.

'So *il Re* Carlo immediately bans the wedding. And we here have another verse on love and duty. The King tells Cortez he must choose between being the King's Viceroy in the New World, and marrying the native princess, and it's clear which option he expects Cortez to pick. Cortez begs for pardon from his liege lord on his knees—'

'I beg your pardon?' Roberto sat up. 'Hernan Cortez wouldn't!'

Conrad lowered his voice, so that Velluti would not break off his argument with Bonfigli. 'But Giambattista would! Anywhere he can slip it into a performance. I know he can't act, but he can sing "*O mi perdono, Re Carlo!*" so that the pit will weep.'

The Conte di Argente fumbled among books and scores and came up with a pencil to scrawl across his copy. He added something under his breath about vulgar mobs that Conrad chose to ignore.

'So, here is where we shorten Act Three.' Conrad reached over and turned two pages of the Count's score. 'We can lose Thalestris telling Hippolyta that she must choose between duty to her nation and her love for a man. Lose Cortez agonising over whether he can marry Tayanna. There's yet another love-and-duty verse not

370

much further on . . . Here! It was High Priest Mazatl, but we killed him off before that scene, so it's just General Chimalli warning Princess Tayanna that Cortez is worming his way into her confidence so the Europeans can take over the kingdom. She must marry a strong man of the tribe immediately; Chimalli tells Tayanna he loves her; she sings that she must choose between love and duty.'

Roberto's dark brows lifted. 'So?'

'So—' Conrad thumbed over another page. '—Look, you have everybody on stage here. I have a suggestion. Take all the love-versus-duty out of everywhere else in the last half of the Act, and put it here. Make the end a sextet.'

'*Che momento!*' Roberto leaned over the pages, his expression keen as a hound's. 'General Chimalli, Queen Thalestris, and *il Re* Charles on the side of duty – bass, contralto, and tenor. Princess Tayanna, Cortez, and Hippolyta singing all for love mezzo, castrato, and soprano. Yes . . .'

Conrad leaned his chair momentarily forward on its front legs to read what Roberto scribbled on the libretto. The oil lamp cast sufficient light to make that possible, although it only accented the darkness of the tapering ceiling of the mine. He pushed away momentary claustrophobia in favour of watching the Conte di Argente rapidly adapt the melodies he had written.

Paolo-Isaura snatched the pages away almost as soon as they were altered, ink smearing her thumb, and was soon one of a circle of heads at the piano bent over the new version. Voices tried a proposed line or two, with insufficient power to strain any vocal cords.

'I never realised that was in there.' Conrad listened to a fragment of melody, compulsive now that it was not drowned by counterpoint. 'I'm going to be hearing it all day . . . night . . .'

He pulled out his watch, which was uninformative.

'. . . Whichever it is now. I'd give money to see what *Il Giornale del Regno delle Due Sicilie* would write in a review of *L'Altezza*!'

Roberto Capiraso, who had his head tilted while he listened to the piano, shot a glance that chilled Conrad. 'It occurs to me, sometimes . . . That we do all this for something that will, at best, have one performance.'

371

That silenced Conrad for a moment.

'One significant performance,' he countered. 'If we succeed, more of them later on.'

Il Superbo's gloom turned sardonic. 'Very well. Shall we hear some of this significant sextet?'

Conrad stood and clapped his hands for attention.

'All right, let's try it, shall we? Sextet end of Act Three, on the one hand, in support of love, Hernan Cortez—' It was always wise to mention the primo uomo first. '—And Princess Tayanna, and Hippolyta. And on the side of stern duty, Brigida, Amazon Queen; JohnJack, and Lorenzo. Lorenzo, you're the King of Spain and Holy Roman Emperor, could you remember that, please?'

The tenor responded to Conrad's exasperation with a grin. 'Act One, High Priest Mazatl – and corpse – Act Two, Captain Diego – and corpse! . . . Acts Three and Four, *il Re* Carlo, who might even survive! Why would I have any problem remembering that?'

Conrad sorted out copies for the recitateurs and passed those over.

The unsubdued racket that followed sent him retiring to his stone chamber for wine and olives, no matter what time of the day or night it might be.

✦

He slept an hour, and chatted with Tullio, and came out into the mine refreshed.

The new sextet, in its variously good and bad attempts, had temporarily ceased to echo through underground Naples. Conrad found no one present but one of Mantenucci's guards, deep in conversation with Luigi Esposito, and Roberto Conte di Argente picking out notes on the piano.

Luigi had the look that meant he was engaged in business; Conrad therefore didn't disturb him.

'I have a death aria for General Chimalli – or Hernan Cortez.' Broad brick-layers' fingers moved over the keys, and Roberto hummed a solo piece.

Conrad meandered across to the forte-piano. He thought for a moment that the composer was humming brokenly in places for lack of verses to set. Then – the orchestral accompaniment filled in by his mind – he could hear how Cortez would sing as he died, the music filling in the gaps in his broken lines, until at last he would fall silent for ever, halfway through a phrase, and only the violin and flute would finish the achingly-sad wordless aria . . .

Silence followed. It took effort for Conrad to shake himself free of the music's power.

'Cortez is not going to die.' He met Roberto's shadowed eyes. 'He's the Feathered Serpent, Quetzalcoatl; the Aztecs think he's a god!'

Luigi Esposito spoke up, from the other side of the piano; evidently having concluded his business with the guard. 'Corradino, you of all people ought to know how irrelevant that is!'

Conrad couldn't help a spurt of amusement. He nonetheless glared at Luigi, where the police captain rested his elbow on the forte-piano, reading the pages of the score that were spread out on top of it.

'Whether it's relevant or not, I want this opera to have the happy conclusion. The *lieto fine*.'

'How?' Roberto Capiraso's interruption sounded waspish. He scrubbed his fingers through his hair in a way that he wouldn't have, in the days before he was permanently short of sleep. His dark hair flopped back over his forehead, the lamp casting shadows to make his expression unreadable. He gave the police chief no attention at all.

Luigi, turning over the pages of the score, matching lines to music, glanced up. 'This doesn't work.'

'Luigi . . .' Conrad began a warning.

'"Finale, Act Four!",' Luigi read, tilting the paper towards the lamp. '"Princess Tayanna gives her decision in her rondo finale" . . . Here: "Tayanna calls on Quetzalcoatl and sacrifices all love except that of her country, swearing to live as a Virgin of the Sun, thus placating the angry volcano".'

Luigi cupped his chin in his hand, where he leaned his elbow on the piano.

'That's . . . No. Really, Corrado! No. That's bathos. That isn't going to work. It'd be better if they all died!'

Conrad waited for the wrath of Il Superbo to descend on Luigi Esposito.

'No,' the Count acceded. 'It isn't good.'

'*Cazzo!* It's what we agreed!' Conrad protested. 'The volcano that's been bubbling in the background – if Angelotti's done it right – is appeased by the Principessa sacrificing both her love of Cortez and of Chimalli. Instead of lava, the volcano erupts with tropical flowers.'

The silence that greeted that was not one Conrad wanted to hear.

Conrad snapped his ink-smeared copy of the libretto shut, hearing it echo through the Roman mine. 'We can be reasonably sure that the black opera will end in tragedy. It's the easiest way to generate high emotion. We can't guarantee to do tragedy better, particularly when we don't know what they're doing. We can try for reconciliation, peace, and sacrifice; repentance, joy – all emotions which carry a charge, and which I don't think the black opera will bother with.'

Luigi shrugged one shoulder. 'I just give a warning. This'll leave people cold.'

'I wrote the verses! Signore Capiraso set them! We both agreed this, in the synopsis, weeks ago!'

The piano seat scraped back over bare boards. Conrad glanced around to find Roberto Capiraso standing, closing the lid over the keys.

'The police hireling is correct.'

Conrad would have taken a moment to enjoy Luigi's expression of outrage, if he hadn't been contending with one of his own. 'Roberto!'

'It looked simple and right in the synopsis. Things change in the writing.' Roberto swept papers off the top of the piano, into his leather folder. The taut line of his shoulders slumped. 'The counter-opera will work only if it gives the truth of human passions. Otherwise the black opera will erase what we do. Corrado . . . You can't cheat to attain the *lieto fine*. Cortez has to lose either the woman he loves, or the mother of his son. Hippolyta must choose her son or her people. Tayanna loses Cortez or she loses her country to the invaders. The potential for a happy ending for all isn't present in what we've set up here!'

The Count shook his head.

'We would need to rewrite from the beginning . . .'

Half a week. Four days, and a little more, and L'Altezza azteca, ossia il serpente pennuto *is on stage.*

Roberto Capiraso slapped the pages of his score closed, the sound echoing through the cathedral-spaces of the mine.

Conrad groaned under his breath, and gave in. 'Very well: it doesn't work. I admit it. And the final scene is vital – but it is just one scene. Eight minutes! We can revise one scene. We have time. We'll make time.'

Luigi Esposito abandoned his lazy pose, drawing himself up as if he were prepared to assist in any way possible. 'Paolo can take over your rehearsals, Corrado. While Tullio's ill, I'll detail off a couple of my men, to make sure you get fed. We can make this right.'

Roberto Capiraso rubbed at insomnia-marked eyes. 'Conrad, I'm at your disposal for discussions on the music.'

His frank look made Conrad all but blush.

Member of the società onorata *or not, you've been honest with me, and I . . . allowed Nora to do what she wanted.*

'We can find the truth of this,' Conrad managed to say steadily.

The Conte di Argente gave a formal bow. 'I must hope, must believe, that we can. Because I fear that, if the last scene fails to catch the audience's emotions, all the rest of the counter-opera will go for nothing.'

36

Conrad battered his mind against the problem of the finale until the backs of his eyeballs hurt.

Emerging for food, he discovered it to be Saturday morning.

'It's been four days since they clobbered me.' Tullio didn't look up from packing. His bruises were green, yellow, purple; and he had ignored Sandrine's offer of stage make-up. 'I'll be fine.'

'You will.' Conrad realised he spoke more as though it were an order. 'This is Saturday; I'll expect you back by Monday at the latest.'

'Can't guarantee his Emperorship won't mess about and keep us from getting back here until the day itself . . .'

Conrad reached over and took his second best coat from the big man, brushing off the shoulder-capes. 'If it weren't for other factors, I'd stop you going.'

The *Oh would you?* was written as plain as print on Tullio Rossi's battered face.

As Conrad suspected, curiosity overcame bloody-mindedness.
'What "factors"?'

'I'll be happier if you're out of Naples, and . . . if you choose not to return here with the Emperor, then understand that I won't blame you for that.'

Conrad laid the coat down neatly in the travelling trunk, and straightened.

Unsurprisingly, Tullio's dark eyes were fixed on him.

The silence prompted speech. Conrad snapped, 'I told you the Emperor's only here as a diversion! Everybody will be chasing him, not the counter-opera.'

The big man folded his arms and raised his eyebrows, which conveyed his point economically.

'Exactly!' Conrad fought exasperation. 'If you're with the Emperor, you're one of the people who'll get that dangerous attention.'

Tullio shrugged.

After a moment, as if he added the comment for Conrad's benefit, he said, 'Not much choice between being chased by the Prince's Men, or being chased with the Emperor, is there?'

'Maybe not much choice – but you have it.'

Tullio smiled. 'I'm not about to point the Emperor at Naples and catch a ship going in the opposite direction, if that's what you mean.'

'That's what I mean.' Conrad had a feeling of grinding frustration. And pushed it aside on the grounds that Tullio Rossi was an adult, and capable of taking his own decisions—

Even if he is acting like a fool!

Tullio returned to his packing, pondering over a pair of clean but worn boots.

Conrad dug out a pair of his own that were marginally better and passed them over. 'Ferdinand said a while back that returning the Emperor to the north will damage the power of the Prince's Men. Half his councillors will go to the guillotine, apparently. Ferdinand's willing to risk whatever might happen to the Emperor with other countries' secret police, informers, assassins and hired murderers . . .'

Tullio polished a boot absently on his sleeve, and looked at Conrad from under his eyebrows. 'Makes one thing easier.'

Conrad obliged him by asking, 'What's that?'

'Paolo.'

Conrad gave him a querying look.

Tullio smirked. 'You don't know if she's in more danger here, or in more danger if he came with me. So you won't be tempted

377

to lay down the law to her. And he won't be tempted to punch you.'

Conrad pinched the bridge of his nose. 'Tullio . . . Just think on the level of strategy for a moment. It's necessary that the Emperor gets back to the north. It isn't absolutely necessary that he leave Naples in your company with a trail of pursuers, assassins, *banditti*, and secret police behind him. You take my point?'

Tullio finally gave way to the grin that had been visibly building for minutes.

'His Majesty the Emperor's not as innocent as you, padrone, so I dare say he's got that worked out ahead of time. He won't march in with flags flying and guns blazing. I expect he'll be happy if barely anyone notices he's in Naples before he's out of it – and no matter who our Ferdinand tips off, that's the way I'm going to play it.'

Conrad sighed, and shook Tullio by the shoulder. 'And I would warn Ferdinand of that. Except that, since he's sent you to fetch the Emperor, he'll already have taken account of it. Just . . . be careful.'

This time Tullio's smile had teeth. 'Oh, I intend to.'

They went above ground. Conrad walked with Tullio to the harbour, and the *S. Gennaro*, a small two-masted schooner loaned by a Neapolitan nobleman implicitly trusted by Ferdinand, who could bring the Emperor back from Stromboli to Naples with proper dignity, without at the same time disclosing his Imperial Majesty's identity, or the hand of the King of the Two Sicilies in the matter.

'Too fond of the brandy, that Emperor,' Tullio muttered, before he boarded. 'Expect you'll need to pour both of us into the San Carlo when I get him back here . . . Listen. Take care of Paolo.'

Conrad acknowledged his change of tone with a nod. No protestations needed to be made.

The white sails faded into sea-haze.

Conrad dismissed his escort, despite their protests, and they at least fell back to a decent distance. He walked the crowded streets for a while, luxuriating in the infinite blue sky over his head, instead of rock, and the smell of fish, cooking meat, human sweat, and the camellias that burst open with the spring.

The loaded duelling pistol was heavy in his coat pocket.

If the Prince's Men catch up with me – so much the worse for the Prince's Men!

It was not self-indulgence, or not completely. The chance to breathe, before going back into the San Carlo; the chance to walk under an open sky, and hear the drama of the streets; all of it stood a good chance of releasing some answer to the conclusion of *L'Altezza azteca*.

Certainly there's enough drama on the streets to supply a man with a hundred opera plots.

But I don't have a hundred, I have this one. Damn it.

Returning inside, the loud orchestra rehearsal in the San Carlo's pit rattled his concentration. Roberto Capiraso snorted at the suggestion they should go under Naples, but conceded a retreat to one of the stage boxes. He stood, periodically, and conveyed instructions across the auditorium to Paolo in a near-shout.

Conrad stripped off his coat and wrapped it around his head, muffling the noise. He had the score of *L'Altezza azteca, ossia il serpente pennuto* open in his lap. The ink dried on the nib of his pen.

'How difficult can it be?' Il Superbo demanded rhetorically, taking the seat beside him. He opened his copy of the score at one of the love duets, scribbling a note of the coloratura ornamentation he was devising. 'We know the score forward and backward – except where there are more cuts to be made – therefore the ending must be apparent to us.'

Conrad muttered his favoured curses under his breath, and pulled his coat closer over his ears.

'It must be appropriate – your word – and yet surprising; it must satisfy the emotional expectations of the audience, and for preference not be a tragedy. And yet we don't know the black opera is a tragedy, we only guess that it is!' Conrad dug the heel of his hand into the socket of his right eye, light blooming into dazzles. 'What happens if the only possible resolution of the counter-opera is tragic?'

Roberto Capiraso stopped scribbling. His dark eyes blinked. 'It's not.'

The Conte di Argente vaulted over the front of the box before Conrad could formulate an answer that was not *vaffanculo!*, and strode over to upbraid Paolo and the strings.

Three days. Four, including the performance. I can be in the same room with Roberto Capiraso that long without killing him, even a little . . .

The words and events grew tangled, intricate, and meaningless. Conrad stared at ruined pages, wishing for something to cut through the mess like a sword, and bring him the simplicity the finale of *L'Altezza* demanded.

As ever, with work in this state, hours inched past. It was still Saturday when he gave up, if past sunset.

Enough!

He ripped up the spoiled pages. Roberto had left him notes, he saw – a dozen minor improvements that the composer wanted to make to the body of the opera, now he had heard the orchestral rehearsal, each of which demanded a shift in the libretto. Conrad put them off, too.

Out of curiosity, he wandered over to the singers on the stage.

Sandrine Furino, sitting on the stage's edge, leaned on Estella Belucci's shoulder, reading a revised duet. Conrad knelt the other side of the blonde.

'Damn, this is good. Look at those trills and runs—' Sandrine caught Estella's expression, and gave an apologetic shrug. 'I grant you, the leaps he's asking for . . . Almost impossible to sing.'

Estella looked unsure whether she was being complimented or undermined.

'Your range?' Conrad checked.

Estella sounded put out. 'The usual dramatic soprano – A below middle C to the C two octaves above middle C. He wants more than that, never mind my tessitura! The jumps! Chest voice to head voice with nothing in between, and back the same way. It's a soprano-killer. And if he writes anything else that's good, it's in my passaggio!'

She wouldn't be the first soprano to leave the business for good after a role strained her voice too hard, Conrad reflected. *And while I don't know if that actually matters, in terms of what we're doing here, she needs to think it does.*

'I'll have a word with Il Superbo. Remind him he's showing off a dramatic voice, not slaughtering it on the first night.'

'And I'll just have to try harder, won't I?'

The fair-haired woman scrambled up from the edge of the stage and walked over to the piano.

Sandrine stood up automatically. It was a gesture that had been ingrained at an early age, and Conrad knew – from Isaura, if for no other reason – that these things resisted eradication.

'Are you jealous of her role?' Conrad teased.

'Of course I am. One line more for any other singer is one line less for me!' Sandrine gave him a look from under her eyelashes, that returned his teasing with interest. 'You should write another aria for the mezzo . . .'

'A new aria with three days to go? *Cazzo!*' Conrad rubbed his aching head. 'The finale's enough of a bitch.'

Sandrine chuckled, but tactfully didn't ask every other member of the company's question: *have you finished yet?*

Over by the piano, Estella Belucci's soprano soared over its notes.

'"*Occhi come chiaro di luna*"—'

She put a wrenching sorrow into the aria devoted to her hope-lessness over her Aztec rival's beauty:

'Your eyes of moonlight,
Skin of milk and snow;
Your heart made of disdain—'

Estella reached for the final note and lost power.

Isaura coached her again through the note that fell in her pas-saggio where chest voice transitioned to head voice. Conrad made his way back to the box, and read and re-read the libretto, marking where the most effective music fell, seeing if that would hint at how he might finish the finale.

Nothing.

He took notice of the world again in JohnJack/Chimalli's 'Mad Scene', when the coloratura bass was encouraged to float an extended note – at the very top of his tessitura – over eight bars from the orchestra, before seamlessly picking up the reprise of the cabaletta with the chorus.

Conrad applauded. So did the stagehands who had stopped to listen.

There must be an answer: what happens to these roles – these people – *in the end?*

Conrad slid into the shadows at the side of the stage. He caught Paolo-Isaura's elbow, when the short break came.

'I need the last hour of rehearsals tonight.' He continued, before she could protest, 'Just the principal singers. I need to solve this.'

She raked her fingers through her short hair, cravat half undone, the picture of a bashful young man. 'All right . . . I'll tell them.'

Conrad nodded. *I should give her more*, he thought, and spontaneously added, 'I'm glad you're conducting on the opening night. You've earned it.'

'But – il Conte—!'

'I understand he has plans to leave early, but, in any case, Il Superbo makes the orchestra too nervous. And too murderous.' Conrad caught the acknowledging gleam in his sister's eye. 'You bring out the best in them. I don't care if you're discovered and doing it in a skirt, "Gianpaolo Pironti" is going to conduct for us!'

The gleam turned into a grin. 'If I am discovered, it won't be by the Conte di Argente.'

Unless his wife tells him. Conrad shook himself free of the thought. In a different tone, he said, 'We truly need you here. I know you'd rather be with Tullio when he leaves for the north with our friend from Stromboli.'

Her blond-brown eyebrows rose. 'And I know you'd rather leave Naples with our composer's wife . . . But we both have our jobs here, no?'

Conrad glanced around, checking they had not been overheard. 'So we'll both be here on Tuesday afternoon.'

'We both will.'

Conrad rested for the hour or so before he would be needed, watching the further rehearsals from the back of the box.

He found it analgesic, he realised, that Roberto Capiraso remained stubbornly blind to Paolo's gender. He treated her as an upstart boy from the Conservatoire. Whether it was watching Isaura bite her tongue, or exchanging a comment with her afterward ('Damnation, if he keeps looking at me like that, Corradino, I *swear* I'll just stand up and strip off my shirt!'), it kept Conrad able to be in the same theatre with his composer.

I can do this, he realised. *Somehow. Surely?*

We're all together under pressure here, we know we need each other to succeed, and we grow a certain *esprit de corps* between us, no matter what our personal opinions are.

Blindsided, he realised he was thinking of Nora again. Of other things that could never be.

The mourning I feel for the loss of that voice to death . . .

What would L'Altezza azteca *be like if Nora could have sung Princess Tayanna?*

I have Estella and Sandrine and JohnJack. If I could only give them an ending that lives up to their voices! *There must be an answer. What is it?*

The guards changed shift, and Mantenucci's temper seemed unpredictable (if 'Let me do my damn job and protect you!' was any indication). Conrad settled for returning to underground Naples with the singers for the last hour of rehearsal time. The walk back through Naples streets set Conrad's nerves on edge.

'We're all turning into a lot of old women!' he muttered. Unfortunately just as Angelotti's mother passed, bringing bottles of wine in for her son.

Red-faced, he escaped from her scolding by scuttling into the middle of the crowd of singers. Paolo sniggered.

The odour of the evening meal cooking sifted through the aqueducts and passages. That section of the tunnels had been taken over by the work-crew, who drowned out other sound with incessant hammering, and the shouted gossip, friendly banter, and threats of vengeance that was Michele's crew at work.

The answer came to him out of nowhere – or out of whatever place the seeds of story come: perhaps the same mind that dreams at night. Conrad stopped dead.

Spinelli trod on his heels and swore.

Conrad ignored the dramatic complaining from the other

singers who piled into their backs. 'Come with me. No, the food won't be ready yet. Here.'

He led the primo uomo and prima donna – knowing the rest would follow – into his own stone chamber, and drew two thick velvet curtains across the entrance, muffling the noise to where it was bearable.

He gave Velluti his own seat – a gilded, velvet-padded monstrosity brought down from the Palazzo Reale by some over-enthusiastic servant. It was deceptively comfortable. Sandrine and Estella sat down on the satin couch, JohnJack between them, each with an arm linked through one of his. Brigida Lorenzani glanced about and chose a stout dark wooden chair, throne-like, and suitable for her weight. She looked in her silks like a pagan queen; Lorenzo, on a padded stool at her elbow, like an intelligent vizier.

'Very well.' Conrad looked around at them all. 'I've been going about this exactly the wrong way.'

37

That brought about complete cessation of their conversations.

Conrad met their eyes, each person in turn. 'It's all very well for il Conte to specify the counter-opera by classification – *seria, semiseria,* comedy – but that isn't the heart of it.'

JohnJack smiled and leaned back between his two ladies. Conrad didn't give him a chance to interrupt with any *I told you so.*

'You know your roles. You know them as characters, as people.' Conrad paused, watching their faces for recognition. 'What I need to know, to write the verses for the finale, is what you will or won't do, as that role.'

A moment of silence. The basso broke it.

'Oh, si . . .' JohnJack's expression turned introspective. 'I will insist on paying court to the Princess – and repenting my crimes, when faced by the memory of the old King. But Tayanna needs a steady male influence while she rules, and who better than I, one of her own people, who loves her?'

Sandrine gave a curt nod, with an edge of regality to it. 'I won't give up my throne. But I want my lover.' Her large, elegant hand waved in Velluti's direction.

'And Cortez—' Giambattista corrected himself. '—I will not give up the Princess. Pagan though she may be. Or bow my head to *il Re* Carlo, when Spain is so very far away.'

Conrad stayed on his feet, orchestrating the gathering. In fact he had no need to do much except nudge and listen, as they argued in their stage roles. He did not interrupt until after a half hour of back-and-forth, when he pounced on Estella.

'Repeat that,' he demanded.

Estella lifted a dazed expression from where she had been haranguing Velluti. 'I said, "I know you no longer love me, you love Tayanna".'

'And you'll be prepared to leave a man whose affections have gone elsewhere?' Conrad spun around and pinned Brigida Lorenzani. 'Suppose your daughter wants to return to the Amazon lands—?'

'Dear daughter, I welcome you, but not your son.'

Estella Belucci's eyes narrowed. Conrad recognised her expression as the one that made managements tremble.

'You're my Queen and my mother,' Estella said. 'And if you wish to make an exception to that law, it's in your power. Because, otherwise, I will certainly take my son and become a wanderer – leaving the Amazon lands for ever, and abdicating my place as your successor.'

Conrad caught a broad grin on Brigida's round face.

Demurely, she said, 'Then an exception will be made. Something as insignificant as a boy-child should not interrupt the succession.'

Conrad bent to scribble triumphantly on his copy of the score. 'And that resolves Hippolyta, her son, and the Amazon Queen! This is exactly what I hoped for . . .'

'*Semi-seria*, then?' JohnJack questioned.

Conrad straightened up from the pages on his desk. 'It's the best I can do, I think. Not everybody can have a happy ending.'

The coloratura bass snorted. 'I've had the short end of the stick before in Signore Rossini's *semi-seria* comedies! Can I take it that Jaguar General Chimalli will be meeting a bad end when he raises the rebellion?'

'If you're volunteering.'

'Deh! I get to threaten Signore Cortez, I hope, before I perish? And fight him?'

Giambattista Velluti's eyelids lowered. 'The body to be dragged off by the heels, I would suppose, before the Princess and I have a happy duet?'

The bass grumbled, but waved an accepting hand.

Lorenzo Bonfigli coughed. 'And what's *il Re* doing, while you're singing, Cortez?'

Sandrine beamed, before Conrad could make any suggestions.

'Being bribed,' she said happily. 'We Aztecs have gold enough to fill a ship or two for King Carlo. We can arrange a tribute every five years—'

'Two.' Lorenzo flirted his eyebrows at the mezzo.

'—Three years,' Sandrine corrected herself gravely. 'Which will keep Spain content. I assume that Signore Cortez will in any case want to continue with his heroic deeds, and explore all of South America for Spain, in between returning home to his new wife?'

Velluti gave a thoughtful nod. 'I'd hardly retire from conquest.'

Il Re Carlo addressed his new Viceroy. Sandrine caught Conrad's eye, murmuring too quietly to disturb them. 'And I'd hardly retire from ruling my Aztecs . . .'

'Too unfeminine a line to include,' Conrad muttered. He grinned as Sandrine made a face also unsuitable for a princess.

Another half-hour passed, the characters *of L'Altezza azteca* wrangling for position. Conrad wrote as fast as he could to keep up – from time to time there was something worth jotting down as a verbatim line.

When it devolved into mere repetition, he stopped them.

'Enough. This is exactly what I need. And now dinner – before we discover if it's the Aztecs or the Amazons who practise cannibalism!'

The principal singers left – JohnJack and Estella both embracing him – and Conrad collapsed in his chair, the suddenly empty chamber a balm to his thoughts. He ran over the notes that he had made, conscious that his own stomach grumbled.

This is it.

The realisation made his spirit soar. Or whatever part of the human mind that the common reference of 'spirit' means. *This is it, I can mine all the material I need from this—*

Saturday night, now.

Sunday.

Monday.

A few hours of Tuesday morning, should we be utterly desperate. And then we're out of time.

Conrad got to his feet, not sure if he was seeking a meal, or Il Superbo, or both.

The cuts give us eight minutes for the rondo finale, he mused. *Twelve, if we end with a stretta. Most of the music exists in the score – I think – it just needs to be adapted. If Roberto can do it right.*

✦

Work at such intensity brought him to the state that, when he should have lain down to snatch sleep for a few hours, he could only sit and watch his fingers shaking.

The right middle finger had an ink-stained callus.

He licked his left index finger and rubbed at the ink, failing to remove most of it.

I am afraid to sleep. Afraid that if I relax this ardent state of mind, I won't be able to retrieve it when I need it – in four hours' time.

Thinking of similar occasions in the past, sleeping four-hour watches in the war, didn't help. *I should take a job as a ditch-digger,* Conrad berated himself fiercely. *Since it was always easier to go out and dig trenches than think. And at the moment, I would much sooner be shifting mud . . .*

He pushed aside the inner curtain and sprawled down on his camp-bed, staring up at the chiselled roof.

It was an odd thought that brought him sufficient peace to sleep.

I've seen enough of Roberto; Il Superbo is – to give him credit – doing everything he can to assist the conclusion of L'Altezza.

I've seen nothing of Nora.

I suppose, at the moment, that's her way of helping.

✦

Sunday passed too quickly. Conrad swore openly at the stupidity of those singers and musicians who went to Mass, and weren't there when he needed them for rehearsal. Some of Alvarez's soldiers muttered and made the sign to avert the evil eye.

'It won't work,' Paolo stated, noting it happen backstage in the San Carlo. 'You've got as evil an eye as any I've ever seen, cousin!'

Conrad fixed her with it. 'Forty-eight hours, cousin. Then we're done.'

Isaura grinned at him. 'I'll be conducting, and you'll be curled up in the back of one of the boxes, sleeping like a baby . . .'

Conrad nearly let out precisely what he thought of impudent sisters, superstitious cast members, and the entire organisation of the Prince's Men in general and in particular. Fortunately, perhaps, Giambattista called him over, complaining that one of Conrad's favourite new lines was impossible for anyone human to pronounce, and so he let out some of his temper on Velluti's impervious hide.

Sunday and Sunday night saw the most part of the new verses written.

✦

The early part of Monday morning was lost to Il Superbo protesting that he wouldn't violate his music in accordance with this new libretto, and another hour when – instead of giving the Conte di Argente a blunt response – Conrad fell asleep at the table listening to him.

✦

The rest of Monday made Conrad think of Sunday as a slack and indolent twenty-four hours. Between the recitateurs taking the singers through the new verses, and perfecting the new stage blocking with Isaura, and delegating someone to inform Michele Angelotti that his volcano was reduced to mere exotic scenery – Princess Tayanna would take refuge from danger (and sing) some way up the step-pyramid . . . Conrad was not surprised to find himself eating standing up in one of the underground mines, hounding Roberto Capiraso into making his music as breath-taking as possible.

He fell asleep again for an hour in the afternoon. The singers, chorus, musicians, and stage-hands all had their scheduled breaks, so that they should not arrive at tomorrow stumbling with exhaustion and sung-out, but Conrad oversaw all of them, sequentially.

When the curtain goes up tomorrow, I'm done; I don't have to sing, play, or conduct.

One of Alvarez's men took him down into underground Naples at some later time; it was not clear under whose orders. Conrad didn't care. He fell fully-dressed onto his camp-bed and slept – too tired to dream – and woke with his pocket watch telling him it was eleven.

'Eleven o'clock Monday night, sir,' the next one of Alvarez's men said as he arrived.

Conrad's stomach warmed up from icy, which it had become when he feared that he would find it eleven on the morning of the fourteenth.

Still Monday. Still a few more hours we can use.

He got himself an escort back up to the San Carlo.

Abandoning the musicians and chorus to Paolo, Conrad stayed with the principal singers, easing them through rehearsal after rehearsal of the new last twelve minutes, until the words began to come by instinct rather than a panicked search through memory.

Sandrine, Giambattista Velluti, JohnJack, Lorenzo Bonfigli, the Amazons (albeit with Hippolyta's son fast asleep in the care of his father, a tenor from the chorus) . . . all passed in order. Again, they took rest where they could – though there was not much of that, the finale scene requiring all of them on stage.

'Death can be quite relaxing,' JohnJack Spinelli murmured, dozing off in a chair after the fifth time of being dragged away after Chimalli's rebellion failed.

Conrad looked up automatically, and only slowly realised that he was looking for the figure missing from the San Carlo: the composer's Returned Dead wife.

He would have punched JohnJack for a joke in bad taste, if the man hadn't instantly slid into sleep, and Conrad doubted he'd even thought of Leonora when he spoke.

At three in the morning, Conrad called a halt to rehearsals.

'It was *Norma*!' Sandrine sounded thick-voiced with sleep, but triumphant. 'I asked around. Started life with singers dazed by rehearsals up to six hours before the curtain . . . Bellini's *Norma* . . . Ah! *And* Signore Rossini's *Cenerentola*!'

Lorenzo Bonfigli laughed. 'Maybe it's as well we're not doing this for the reviews in the *Giornale*.'

The Giornale *should be the least of your worries*, Conrad thought, but stopped himself from saying out loud. *If they've got their confidence, no need to undermine it.*

The Conte di Argente went as far as to offer Estella Belucci his arm, since the blonde woman swayed where she stood. 'If all goes well, we can revive *L'Altezza azteca* in the future.'

'With a cast that need not be awake at three thirty in the morning . . .' JohnJack stifled a massive yawn, which Conrad thought was ironic seeing the bass had had the most rest during the evening.

Of course, back in his underground dry cistern, Conrad found himself unable to fall asleep.

He was too tired to make sense of the fears and imaginings that turned his mind to an Arctic cold, knowing only that they concerned the Prince's Men.

Ferdinand is right. There's something we haven't seen; some danger from the Prince's Men that we don't yet suspect—

Something is wrong.

Something more than the possibility that the black opera is better, more polished, more effective than L'Altezza azteca?

Conrad found his eyes closing despite himself.

I'm at the heart of a citadel. Even if it isn't visible.

More than this underground sanctuary—there are two or three regiments on duty at any time; there are Enrico's police. And secret police, agents, spies. We have every possible protection. The members of the opera are guarded beneath earth and stone, kept away from danger. Will be guarded, again, when we go up to the Teatro San Carlo in the morning . . .

Danger still manages to get through. Ask Tullio.

Something's wrong.

And I don't know what it is.

Conrad sat down to eat with Luigi Esposito, finding that his early waking on Tuesday coincided with the end of the captain's shift.

'Anxious for the performance?' Luigi mumbled over the rim of a cup of Turkish coffee.

Anxious, Conrad admitted to himself.

But not as much as when I'm beset with night-terrors.

'I'm concerned about Tullio,' Conrad admitted. 'No report of the ship?'

'Did you ever know a count, lord, king, or emperor who could make an appointment on time?' Luigi waved a careless hand, slopping his thick black coffee. 'We wait for them, that's their view.'

'Well, there's that.'

And won't his Imperial Majesty be shocked when L'Altezza *starts exactly on time? We can't afford to miss high earth-tide.*

Conrad finished eating, and was escorted back up to the theatre by a squad of Luigi's men. It was not quite six. The sun was not up, outside. A few gas-lamps glimmered in the dark, on these populous high-class streets. The rest of Naples was a heaped sleeping beast. On the flank of Vesuvius and the eastern hills, only the slightest difference between land and sky showed.

The back-stage area of the San Carlo was currently more draughty than stifling. Conrad didn't bother to take off his greatcoat as the escort ushered him in. He signalled his gratitude to the departing officers, and pushed one of the doors closed behind him; heavy, and felted on the side that faced the stage. The singers had formed loose groups, apparently idly talking or examining the stage-flats that represented Princess Tayanna's serpent-decorated boudoir.

In fact, Conrad abruptly realised, every eye was fixed on Il Superbo.

Roberto, Conte di Argente, stood downstage; head thrown back, cropped beard jutting, his voice raised to Giambattista Velluti. 'You insolent lackey!'

Velluti drawled, 'You amateur!'

Conrad folded his arms and snickered.

At his elbow, Paolo muttered, 'Let them sort themselves out!'

It was an argument with no malice, Conrad saw. Both men relieved their tension and the previous forty-eight hours of frustration by shouting.

'. . . Everybody says "let Paolo do it",' his sister continued to rant under her breath. 'I say, let them hog-tie Il Superbo and dump him on a ship bound for New York or Buenos Aires! Signore Velluti can go to the bottom of the Tyrrhenean Sea, or the top of Ætna!'

'You need a few minutes away from here,' Conrad observed.

He took Isaura by the arm and left the theatre, walking down to the royal dock with a corporal and four men of one of the island-Sicilian regiments with them. The sky was just distinguishing grey from black when they left the Palazzo Reale. By the time they stood on the white stone dock, the eastern sky had a glow of pure lemon light, deepening with the oncoming sun that was still below the horizon.

Behind the round bulk of the earth, Conrad thought, trying to adjust his concept of it so as to be prepared for later in the day.

As if she read his mind – or his glance at the luminous sky – Paolo said, 'We've done it. We start in nine hours.'

'No.' He looked down apologetically at her. 'We've brought ourselves to the position where we might do it.'

A glance showed him the corporal and his troopers spread out along the dock, making enquiries from sailors and fishermen, and not within earshot.

'The counter-opera begins at three, and the black opera must start close to the same time, or miss the line-up of sun, moon, and earth. It's the two or three hours after three o'clock that'll tell us if we've won, or they have.'

Paolo-Isaura gave a thoughtful nod. She might have said more, but the approaching corporal distracted her.

'No news yet, signore. None of the sentries on the islands or headlands have signalled back any sightings, so it's doubtful you'll see the *Gennaro* much before midday,'

Conrad slipped the man a few calli and nodded. He and

393

Paolo-Isaura stayed for a quarter hour more, while the sky fluoresced into an aureate glow, and the sun rose, too bright to look at without eyes watering.

Paolo walked ahead as they came back to the San Carlo, visibly anxious to get inside and prevent the last run-through of difficult verses from turning into a bloodbath. Conrad let her go, one of the soldiers with her.

The air smelled fresh. It was too early for more than the lazzaroni to be out, eating, arguing, gambling over games of *mora*. Many of the poor wore no more than shirt, breeches, and waistcoat. The sun put rising gold over the tops of buildings, beginning to be warm. Summer opera season was common in Naples, if not necessarily elsewhere in the opera world (which mostly conducts its business between the Feast of St Stephen – on 26th December – and Lent). Soon there will be breath-snatching inescapable heat, and a city that only truly awakens morning and evening, and the doors of the opera house will stand open to mitigate the heat of a gathered crowd. And backstage will be so stifling that it's no difficulty to imagine ladies in short-stays or long-stays fainting.

A shouted order halted his escort. Conrad sighed, leaning against the San Carlo corner wall, while the corporal loudly debated orders with another man from the same regiment.

The corner gave Conrad a view both of the unpaved piazza in front of the Palace, and the long straight road that ran past the theatre and off into the city. Only conscience kept him waiting – and both Paolo and Tullio's promise of what they would do if he went off anywhere without a protective escort.

A shine of light caught his eye. Silk and lace of a morning dress turned his head—

The woman in the blue dress moved with a brisk stride from the Teatro San Carlo, to a closed coach. A long Indian shawl covered her shoulders. Her bonnet allowed him only a glimpse of profile.

I would know her walk among a thousand.

Nora!

It hit him with the force of a punch. *Roberto will be sending his wife away the morning of the performance – which is this morning—*

The soft clop of hooves sounded down the street. The coach

disappeared, out of sight. Going back to their mansion, judging by the road taken.

Without sufficient thought to call it a decision, Conrad let himself drift back between a woman and her child, then two men arguing over a horse, then a group of much younger men . . .

Out of sight of his escort, he walked fast; choosing a direct route to the Argente mansion through winding streets too narrow for anything but men on foot.

He put the King out of his mind, and his duty to the counter-opera. *This may be the last time I'll be able to speak with her.*

So I must.

✦

A servant took his name, and returned with an expression of muted surprise. 'La Contessa will see you.'

A confusion of emotions overwhelmed him. Conrad was barely aware of anything until he found himself in a richly furnished study, with a desk, and a long mahogany table that would sit twelve or fourteen. Some of the musicians had left their scores scattered across it at an earlier meeting. He walked mechanically around the table.

Leonora Capiraso stood up from the antique Versailles sofa where she had evidently begun reading. More than one book stood open on an Emperor-style military desk, or had a marker paper in it.

'Corrado?'

'At least we don't have the hypocrisy of "Signore Scalese".' His smile felt false. 'I'd give ten scudi to hear what your servants are saying in your kitchen right now . . .'

She had evidently taken off her bonnet when she came in, but still wore the rest of her morning walking dress; a full-sleeved under-dress of muslin, and over that a silk tunic *à l'antique* in deep blue with a high-waisted bodice, from which the tunic fell in long drapes, giving her a look of austere Roman determination.

Her frown was also severe. 'What is it you want?'

'The book's done.' He shrugged. 'Nothing left that someone else can't tinker with in rehearsal, before the curtain goes up.'

Leonora put down her book, her fingers just brushing the surface of the desk, and stood poised. The light shone through the velvet drapes, full on her face.

Conrad felt an airless dizziness. 'You said I should leave Naples.'

'I said that, yes.'

'I'll leave on one condition. That you come with me.'

Her voice sounded stifled. 'Corrado . . .'

'Leave your husband. Come with me.'

He could not put it more directly.

He felt his hands shaking, and clasped them behind him. Waiting for her reply sucked even more air out of his chest. He thought he came nearer to fainting than at any time since he had been in a surgeon's tent.

'No.'

And that is utterly direct.

He risked himself enough to say, 'You love me. Why else would you try to get me out of Naples? Yes, I know it's dangerous; yes, your husband's right to get you away! But you love me, still, the way you always did. I don't believe you can look me in the eye and say you don't.'

Her lashes lay dark on her cheek for a moment, before they lifted and she met his gaze.

'No, I can't tell you that.' Her defeated voice remained direct. 'If I said I didn't love you, it would be a lie. Corrado—'

She spoke over his attempt at an interruption:

'Wait. If I said I didn't love Roberto, that would be a lie!'

'Then you're going to have to choose. Again.' He felt himself being brutal, perhaps because he did understand her predicament. 'The poor man or the rich man? The old love or the new?'

'You don't understand!'

From any other woman, it would have been a wail or a whine. Leonora let loose the words with a blast of frustration, plainly angry at herself for the inability to explain.

'Make me see, then.' Conrad made the mistake of stepping up to her.

Her eyes were dark blue; so dark, as she looked up at him, that shades of violet showed there. They were her one true point of beauty, Conrad was not ashamed to admit. For the rest, her thick brown hair was no better and no worse than any other woman's, and her body was a little on the thin and tall side.

But her spirit glows out of her face.

Not a supernatural spirit – but whatever it is about her that makes her Leonora. Nora, who glowed like a Russian icon on-stage when she sang . . .

The light from the window caught a semi-circular gleam along the bottom of her eyelid. A tear, he recognised, as it swelled and broke and ran down her cheek.

He leaned down and kissed it from her heated skin, moving his mouth from her cheekbone down to the corner of her lips. It was a strange kiss, with her warm skin, and her body leaning against him with the heft of mortality, but it left him breathless. She pulled him to her fiercely, like an eagle at the stoop.

'It's me you love.' Conrad barely got it out for kissing every part of her mouth, her neck where it curved down to her shoulders. 'You know I never stopped loving you. It's nothing to me that you're one of the Returned Dead. You're still Leonora. Leave here – with me, now – before he tries to send you away and I lose you!'

Conrad pushed his fingers into her hair, the soft coils falling out of hairpins and tumbling over his wrist. He cupped her cheek with his other hand. Her grip around his body was strong; she clung as if she might fall for ever if she lost her hold on him. Her deliberate breath smelled sweet, like honey and fire. He ached, erect, to feel the skin of her thighs against his; to lay belly to bare belly, with her soft flesh heated against him. He slid one hand down her shoulder, down the vee of her trapezoid muscles where they dropped to the flare of her buttocks; bunching the soft cloth of her dress and shift in his fist and pushing her body hard up against his.

Her thigh slid between his, only thin cloth obstructing skin against skin. He felt the vibration as she whined in her throat.

He broke free as far as he could, which was only to take his mouth from hers and straighten up. 'You have to choose. I swear I'll go mad.'

She was half a head shorter than he; it meant she needed to

stand high up on tiptoe to reach his mouth if, as now, he didn't lean down.

Her hand knotted in his cravat and she pulled the linen until he gave way and leaned forward.

Their foreheads touched.

'How can you still love me, Corradino? So much time has gone by. We're different now. I'm . . . what you see I am.'

'That doesn't matter—'

'Not the Return from death! You don't know me!'

Conrad ran the back of his knuckles down her cheek, down her neck, until his hand rested on the unmoving heated swell of her breast above her bodice. 'I know you're ambitious, passionate, reckless, vulnerable; has death changed that?'

Her hair was loose now, falling to her hips; the mass of it rested scented and soft over his wrist. He took hold of her, forcing himself close, as she fought closer; kissed; and finally freed her honey-mouth with a gasp.

'Marry me,' he got out, 'if you need a ceremony; if you need the Church, I don't care! I give you my word, I will stay with you. Married or unmarried, living or dead, I want you with me.'

A faint draught touched his hand and face – and had been doing so for some moments.

It was a warning, Conrad realised, far too late.

'That,' Roberto Capiraso said from the open door, 'will not be happening.'

38

The weight of the single Manton pistol weighed down Conrad's pocket.

No! I shouldn't kill him—

Roberto Capiraso ignored him as if there were only empty air in the study.

Il Conte must have left the San Carlo after the spat with Velluti – perhaps to see off his departing wife, perhaps travel with her out of Naples – but by his face, all that was forgotten. He stared at Leonora with a burning focus, padding forward over the carpet with absolute determination.

Leonora stepped back and abruptly sat down on the blue-upholstered Versailles couch. She fumbled with the tiny buttons of her bodice. Some had been torn loose. Conrad realised it must have been by his hands.

Roberto loomed over the sitting woman, his expression blood-shot. 'You whore.'

Conrad took the pistol out of his pocket. He pointed the muzzle at the Conte di Argente's chest. 'Never threaten her.'

Conrad felt a sudden weight, as of something unspoken, in the room.

Both Roberto and Leonora had ears and eyes for no one but each other.

'You've betrayed me . . .' Roberto Capiraso sounded banal, shocked, unbalanced. 'Liar. Liar and ungrateful whore!'

The bookcase was within arm's reach.

Through red anguish, Conrad felt very grateful. He could not have stepped aside to put the pistol down. But he could stretch out his arm and place it on the pale polished oak, in front of the glass doors protecting the valuable volumes, and let go of the metal that could make him a murderer.

That done, he stepped forward, grabbed at the side of Capiraso's throat and caught his linen stock, and gave it a strong twist. As the man choked, hands going harmlessly up to his neck, Conrad swung him round and freed his right hand.

Old habits from army brawling informed every cell of his body. He brought the punch up from his feet, or so it felt. Punched through his target – as Alfredo had taught him when he was twelve – and felt his knuckles bruise on Roberto Capiraso's jaw.

The stocky man staggered back a pace, not able to get his legs under him. He half-turned – caught his heels against each other – and measured his length, smashing down onto the desk behind him.

The writing desk was nothing solid; nothing to break bones, or a spine, or crack a man's skull open. It had been made to appear – or perhaps was – a souvenir of the war; some general's camp-desk from a command tent, constructed light for travel. It shattered under the dark man's weight.

Roberto Conte di Argente slid, on his face, down the now slanting top of the desk.

He ended on the floor, files and sheets of paper sliding down to bury him in the wreckage.

'Shite!' Conrad tucked his right hand up under his left armpit, hoping the warmth would take some of the swelling sting out of his knuckles. '*Merda!*'

Leonora had both hands over her mouth. She made a sound. It might have been either of their names.

Conrad took a step forward and knelt down, feeling for Roberto Capiraso's pulse. It beat steadily at his carotid artery. The man was not quite unconscious. He gazed up with nothing but confusion in his eyes. Conrad forced himself to unbutton the man's coat and undo his stock and waistcoat. Rage made him breathless.

For me, he can die in his own vomit, but not in front of his – wife. No – not in front of Nora.

Conrad stood up out of the chaos, absently scooping up a fallen stack of bound scores, and loose pages with notes doodled on them. He looked for somewhere to set the stuff down – found the desk not a choice – and placed them on the Versailles sofa. They slid into a heap. Nora stood and stepped back, out of the way. A bound score fell open as Conrad fumbled to keep the stack under control—

His eyes automatically took in what was written on the page within his view.

Music sounded in his mind. Comprehension came instantly. The familiar black spidery handwriting on the staves put the notes into his head, and the orchestration, and the vocal line. It took him scant seconds, in which Leonora did not move, and the Conte di Argente only breathed thickly where he lay.

'This is the aria you were struggling to complete for us yester-day.' Conrad frowned. 'Except that this is scored for a soprano, not a mezzo, and is complete. I don't understand.'

Yesterday, Count Roberto had agonised over the melody and given it up as 'good as it can be in the time'. Here it sprawled across the page in great confident notes and chords – marked for an *Isabella, regina di Castiglia*: Isabella, Queen of Castile – full, and complete.

The aria in *L'Altezza* stumbled, showing flashes of brilliance.

'This is brilliance itself . . .' The document in his hands had been bound some time ago, Conrad realised. The corners of pages were curled, where it had been read and re-read.

Other names dotted the page – a tenor aria for a 'Ferdinand, *il Re* di Aragona', which Conrad had never heard, and would have killed to have for Lorenzo. A bass aria and cabaletta for 'Moham-med, Muslim King of Granada'—

'This is JohnJack's cabaletta for his Mad Scene! Only this version is better!' As if he had not just knocked Roberto down,

401

Conrad demanded, 'Is this another one of your one-act operas? Why didn't you say this was finished?'

Roberto Capiraso made a choking sound. 'Put that down—!'

Conrad hefted the thickness of the score. *Not a one-act opera. Too long and complex to be anything but a full four- or five-act work.*

'If you had this, why not give it to us?' Conrad closed the bound pages together, and then opened the front cover to look at the title page.

Il Reconquista d'amore, ossia la Moor di Venere. The Reconquest of Love, or, the Moor of Venus—

He snorted at the outrageous trap of the subtitle, presumably laying in wait for wherever *Il Reconquista d'amore* might have a London run, close by Shakespearean theatres.

'Put it down, Scalese!'

Conrad shook his head, caught between laughter and anger. 'When did you write this?'

He thumbed through the bound manuscript to the back, and the end of the final act. Aria, stretta . . . and the rondo finale for the soprano. Familiar fragments of melodies teased his mind, and stage situations and confrontations—

Roberto blinked up owlishly, and scowled.

'This final scene has all the music of *L'Altezza azteca*.' Conrad heard himself as if from a stunned distance, and could not tell if he sounded amazed or appalled. 'The same music. But with their melodies just different enough, the arrangement superior enough, that this score is . . . infinitely superior to *The Aztec Princess*.'

Roberto Capiraso muttered something, sounding partly conscious.

Conrad looked up from the staves. 'Why would you do less than your best when you can do this? This is better than anything you've written for us! This is a whole opera you could have given us . . .'

Conrad felt his body tensing to fight.

'The score you've been "composing" and "developing" for us – is complete. Has been complete for some time. Look at it! And this is yours; I know your style well enough by now!'

He met the dark eyes of Roberto Conte di Argente, where the stocky man sprawled on the carpet.

'You've lied to us from the beginning. You had no fear that you couldn't write a full opera. You'd already done it!' Conrad heard himself sounding more bewildered than appalled. 'Tell me one reason why you would pretend to compose an inferior version of what you already have!'

Dread twisted in Conrad's stomach.

Dread as well as anger, he realised.

Despite everything, did I want to believe that Roberto was honest? Because he and I have worked side by side like brothers?

The other man spoke a thick, unintelligible curse.

Conrad hefted the score of *Il Reconquista d'amore*.

An unknown and fully complete new opera. In Naples. At the time when the Prince's Men are here.

Intuition and evidence came together.

'—This is the black opera.'

39

Roberto Capiraso looked as if he went to nod but was stopped by pain.

In a breathless, cracked voice, he muttered, 'Yes.'

The implied *you idiot!* did not need to be stated aloud; it was clear in his tone.

'You've been composing for both operas—'

Conrad couldn't help staring. *I must look like a gawking idiot!*

'—*L'Altezza azteca* and . . . this. Counter-opera and black opera. Both of them.'

This time the other man managed the smallest nod of assent. A flinch of pain creased his face.

A confession. But with the evidence right here in my hands, there'd be no point in denial.

'Major Mantenucci thought their composer was Bellini . . .'

Roberto Capiraso gave a sardonic grimace that was not quite a smile. 'Signore Bellini's death was a convenient chance to spread rumours, as I understand it.'

'And you—'

'*Il Reconquista* was done before I came to Naples,' Roberto Capiraso muttered tightly. 'When I needed to compose music for the key points of *L'Altezza*, to handicap it, I used the earlier, inferior drafts of *Reconquista*.'

As if it were a small image in clear glass, Conrad recalled

speaking to il Conte di Argente on the day they first met. The wars in Granada making a colourful frieze of armour and heraldry in his mind.

Conrad quoted Il Superbo's words back to him. "Something more exotic than wars against the Moors and Jews'?'

Roberto Capiraso flinched.

Conrad suspected it was not through pain.

Conrad let the score drop. '*Cazzo!* Ferdinand had it right! He just couldn't find the right man.'

He drove his bruised fist into his palm.

'It's obvious, isn't it? The Prince's Men have never truly harmed us. Never irreparably. Why would they? It wasn't in their interests. With you in the heart of the counter-opera, writing to fail . . . They had nothing to be afraid of! Our composer is one of the Prince's Men.'

The immensity of the realisation left him stunned.

'I should knock you down again,' Conrad realised, head swimming as if he were the one who had been punched. 'All the time, while we were giving everything, you—'

Roberto Capiraso spat blood onto the carpet. 'You – we – are a diversion to keep the King of the Two Sicilies happy! That's all!'

The Count got the words out with effort, gasping between them. His dark eyes flashed. His broad hands fumbled for a place to brace, behind him. He pushed himself up into a sitting position on the rich Turkey carpet.

Conrad's thoughts moved faster than he could have spoken.

Roberto Capiraso was behind the Silvestri family and the arrest for debt. For revenge, yes. And because he's one of the Prince's Men.

Using my imprisonment as an excuse to drag his feet with composing the music for the counter-opera. Sabotaging even as he wrote.

Disrupting rehearsals – Il Superbo!

Persuading the King that all's going well—

He spent his true energy beforehand, on composing the black opera.

He's told the other Prince's Men everything, everything, they could ever need to know.

405

Hatred echoed down Conrad's muscles and nerves. 'You fucking son of a bitch.'

Roberto snorted, and flinched at the pain it caused. 'You realise how much you've benefited from the unofficial protection you had? If I hadn't been composer for both operas— Would you rather have had Tullio Rossi and, say, Signore Velluti, returned in the same condition as Adriano Castiello-Salvati? And note that it was your rehearsal hall burned down, empty, when the San Carlo is the same as every theatre, an inferno waiting to happen? And it might have had every one of you in it?'

The note of superiority brought Conrad's hackles up.

'Don't even try to justify—!' He kicked the bound score at his feet. 'Who did write this libretto?'

'Felice Romani.' Roberto Capiraso looked as nauseous as if he rested on a swaying deck. 'Last year. After the first San Carlo attempt. Not willingly.'

Well, that finally answers my question of 'Why isn't Signore Romani sitting in this chair?'

Conrad searched the other man's blank features for any sign of guilt, or even regret. 'This is why we could never find the composer for the black opera. This is why you never committed yourself heart and mind to *L'Altezza azteca*, why you always got to a point and then pulled back—'

Roberto Capiraso made as if he would stand up. It was difficult to tell, red-faced from the blow as he was, but his skin might have flushed.

The temptation to kick him down on his back in the wreckage again was strong. Conrad found his vision narrowing, identifying the point on Il Superbo's jaw where a boot would need to land.

Roberto Capiraso scraped up sheet music in uncoordinated hands, pages all dotted with his sharp writing, and attempted to wave it in Conrad's face. 'There are places I wrote supremely well for *L'Altezza*!'

I remember so many occasions in the secret museum and under Naples, watching him speed to get down the notes he heard in his head . . .

Conrad pushed the memory away. He grabbed up the betraying score of *Il Reconquista*. 'This is what you do when you're utterly

406

committed to doing your best. Not holding back, and sabotaging the opera. This— That I could have written the libretto for this—'

Il Superbo pushed himself painfully slowly up onto his knees. Pages slid to the floor. Swaying as if he were about to fall, his hands gripping his thighs, the composer forced himself up onto his feet.

Conrad looked down the couple of inches in height that separated them. Roberto Capiraso stood precisely like the loser of a brawl – neck-cloth untied and coat open, hair dishevelled, his breath coming harshly.

'And what did I write for?' Conrad demanded. '*The Aztec Princess* – flashy, daring, parts of it stunning . . . But with all those subtle, subtle faults, that will show up in performance. You wrote the counter-opera to fail.'

Roberto barely spared him a look. 'Of course.'

For one desperate, conscienceless moment, Conrad could only think, *Roberto's sabotage means arrest and imprisonment for him!*

And that means Nora is free of him. Free to be with a man who has not betrayed his King.

'Nora hates traitors,' Conrad said hoarsely. 'Or did she never tell you that? Too many people betrayed her trust as a girl. If she ever wants to visit you in jail, I'll be amazed!'

Something like absolute misery flashed across Roberto's face. Conrad saw something odd in it, but dismissed it, given how urgent things were.

'We're going to Ferdinand now.' Conrad took a step back, keeping his gaze on the Count, and felt on the bookcase for his pistol.

His fingers skidded over polished oak, encountering no obstruction.

Conrad glanced back.

Leonora Capiraso stood several paces away from the bookcase, his Manton flintlock duelling pistol in her hands. The black muzzle pointed precisely at his heart.

40

'Why are you protecting him!' Conrad exclaimed. 'Didn't you hear him confess?'

But I don't need to ask.

He's her husband; she has a longer history with him than she does with me; of course she's loyal to him.

It still hurt.

As gently as he could, considering Leonora's temper, Conrad said, 'Keep the pistol if it makes you feel safer. But we're going to King Ferdinand right now.'

Leonora said clearly, 'No one is going to King Ferdinand.'

'What?' The bald exclamation made him sound like a village idiot. 'Just because your loving husband has dragged you into this mess—'

Leonora took a precise step to the side. Conrad realised it allowed her to see both himself and Roberto without interruption. And it put her the other side of the long table in the centre of the room – in effect, safe behind a barricade.

He stared at her across polished mahogany and an expensive English lead crystal decanter and its attendant glasses. The pistol muzzle didn't waver from the trunk of his body. The weight of the flintlock pistol was supported by both her hands. The hammer was drawn back and, as he observed that, she brought it back to full cock with a satisfying, terrifying click.

This isn't the first time she's handled a gun.

Four yards away, behind an obstacle – I can't simply grab her.

He learned in the war, at this point there's nothing to do but wait. If – when – the trigger is pulled, there'll be the fraction of an instant between the flintlock mechanism striking the pan, and the flash travelling down the touch-hole and igniting the main charge. Men have thrown themselves aside from the lead bullet and lived, in that instant.

Some irrational, irreverent part of his mind supplied, Tal momento! O istante!

In a voice more distant than the stars, she said, 'Please don't move.'

Conrad could do nothing but gaze, stupefied, at her – at warm scented flesh into which he wished to sink, and obliterate all the world except the two of them. *Except that . . .*

'It's both of you? He forced you to join him?' Conrad added instantly: 'Nora, we can give you sanctuary from the Prince's Men—'

Leonora snorted.

The sound of contempt went clear through him.

'Corrado, when did you ever know anyone make me do anything?'

Conrad stared into her determined, willing face. 'You can't be a Prince's Man. Him, yes; but not you—!'

Roberto Capiraso leaned forward, his hands braced on his thighs for support, and grunted with bitter amusement. 'Oh, she is.'

Conrad couldn't help staring at Leonora, in her high bodice and flowing tunic, with her fallen hair rippling down to her hips and below. Dishevelled, and with a pistol, she might have been the mad-woman in an opera. *Although on-stage it would more likely be a dagger.*

'I told you my husband was a member of a criminal society,' Nora said lightly, as if she ignored the weapon she held. 'I just didn't tell you which one.'

'*Che cazzo!* And what was the point of— Oh. To divert suspicion from him if he made any mistakes.'

'Yes.' Leonora's gaze stayed fixed on Conrad. 'Also . . . I did want you to leave Naples. I forgot how pig-headed you are when it comes to threats.'

Roberto Capiraso's baritone drowned her out. 'You warned him? You treacherous bitch!'

Leonora moved from stillness to swiftness. The pistol came up so that she looked straight down the duelling sights at Conrad. Her fingers tensed, a fraction from fully pulling the trigger.

He flinched.

Her hands stayed steady. She turned her head, gazing at Roberto. 'You have no reason to accuse me! I loved you before and after I died, Roberto, and now, just because I've kissed one man – because it was necessary – you accuse me!'

Contempt and self-contempt tore at Conrad's heart.

Necessary.

Pain flooded in on him, drowning him. He dragged himself free of it sufficiently that he could think. *She must have a reason for saying that—*

That she might be trying to drive him off for his own safety, he put out of his mind as a self-serving fantasy.

Roberto Capiraso spoke thickly, as if he had bitten his tongue. 'It was necessary, was it?'

Conrad could have echoed him: the word stabbed deep. He moved forward a pace. He did not care that the pistol's muzzle shifted with him as he did. 'Why? Why was it necessary for me to love you?'

Leonora didn't take her gaze from the Count. 'Oh, I would have gone much further than love and one kiss. If I were a man, Roberto, and I slept with someone's wife because it was necessary for the cause, you wouldn't think twice about it.'

'You're a woman: it's different!'

Her voice sang with scorn. 'Do you say I can't have principles?'

Conrad flinched back from the zeal shining raw in her eyes.

She took another pace back, towards the door; the mahogany table still between her and both of them.

She doesn't want to be disarmed by me or her loving husband, Conrad recognised.

But she still only has one shot.

Wanting to spring forward, he forced his body to wait.

The slender woman, uncannily motionless, stared at the bruised face of Roberto Capiraso. 'Let me tell you that you have nothing to forgive! I did what was right to keep this man's attention occupied—'

Every small brick of knowledge fell into place, building the edifice before he was consciously aware of it. *She's been decoying me, she doesn't love me*— He framed that with brutal honesty in his thoughts. *Then*—

'Only one thing makes me different from any other man in Naples,' he stated aloud. 'The libretto—'

'Corrado!'

'—For the counter-opera—'

'Conrad!' Her voice bounced back off the ornamented plaster ceiling. 'I've been distracting you, yes! But—'

'But I can't trust anything you've ever said to me.'

Roberto cut in icily. 'Nor, apparently, can I. This is not a matter of playing out a scene of jealous husband and pure wife in the debtors' prison! Leonora, we agreed you would not be further involved in this—'

'It was necessary. I told you it would be.'

'Was it? I think you always intended to find it necessary—'

'Roberto—'

'What have I heard since we came here? Nothing but Conrad, Corrado, Corradino! Tell me how you broke your word, Leonora. Tell me how you planned every step of this to bring him back to you—'

The pain in his voice provoked contradictory emotions in Conrad. Both sympathy, and a blazing hope that he was right. *Right that it's me she's been looking for, as I looked for her!*

Leonora had the stillness of the Dead as she stood with Conrad's pistol raised. All her attention on her husband, she exclaimed fiercely, 'I was as shocked as you were when Bourbon-Sicily presented him as the librettist! The idea that he would be writing the book for us—'

'—Is just too coincidental!' Roberto Capiraso's hands shook as he pulled off his untied neck-cloth. He wiped his face with it, and pushed it into a pocket. Scorn made his voice razor-sharp. 'You mean to tell me, with all your connections among il Principe, that you had no idea where Signore Scalese might be?'

Conrad snorted. 'Unless she has some way of divining where lightning will strike, it must have been a shock seeing me in Ferdinand's opera!'

Two heads turned as one. Both glared at him as if he interrupted some private thing, not his business.

But it is my business! No matter how close they seem to be.

Roberto Capiraso absently tested his swollen red and blue jaw under his clipped beard. 'Leonora, believe me, I know your rank among il Principe is far higher than mine. I refuse to believe you didn't gain access to, say, the police lists of "undesirables" in the Two Sicilies—'

'Yes!' Her eyes seemed to take in all the light from the great sash windows of the mansion. They flashed. 'Yes! Very well! I hoped I might see Conrad privately—'

Conrad's heart lurched.

'—While we were here; it would not have interfered with the mission. I had no idea he would be chosen as the King's librettist – I so swear!'

Conrad went to speak and found his mouth too dry. *I have no idea what I can say to her.*

His body tensed as the pistol's muzzle shivered.

Roberto Capiraso wiped his mouth with his hand, this time. A thread of carmine – *from where a tooth had cut the inside of his cheek?* – ran down his chin, visible through his beard. He spat blood in Leonora's direction. 'You claim that? Am I stupid? Cornuto? Even I can see that you'd spread your legs for him in front of me if he asked you to!'

'Never doubt what I feel for you—' she began.

'I killed you.' The Count sounded almost reflective. 'I've been aware that you would, eventually, exact payment for that.'

'Oh, stop playing the martyr!' Leonora's voice shifted down the social classes. Her chin came up, and she glared at the dark man. 'I've told you before, you were not responsible for my death!'

'You died in attempting to give birth to my child.'

412

Her voice snapped like a coachman's whip. 'I was hardly forced to conceive it!'

Conrad saw her expression change.

He only then realised that he must have given an indication of the rip of her words.

'It couldn't be helped.' Her gaze sought his for one moment, before it went back to Roberto. 'Not by you or any other man. My body wasn't meant for child-birth.'

Conrad's responsibility to the King of the Two Sicilies felt a very distant memory. Even the opera was no more than a fever-dream of work and messa di voce: those bel canto voices that swell up and sink down under perfect control.

Battered by feelings that were just the opposite, Conrad stated, 'I'm finished here.'

'Corrado—'

'No more!'

It made his skin shiver to ignore a weapon, but he gave Nora his shoulder and turned to look directly at Roberto Conte di Argente.

'Tell me one thing. Before I leave this house and go to King Ferdinand and we have no private business.' Conrad drew breath, and managed to get words out steadily. 'Before the child. Before Leonora died. In Venice, she was my wife in all but the church ceremony. How did you get her to love you and leave me?'

Roberto's head snapped around, his expression open and shocked.

'What do you mean, leave you? Scalese, a few assignations don't make a wife! She was never with you!'

41

'Nora and I lived together as man and wife,' Conrad repeated, with as much dignity as he could manage. 'Under the same roof in Venice, for over a year.'

'You did not.' The dishevelled figure of Roberto Conte di Argente stared back, apparently honest in his confusion. 'She would have told me if she had ever been mistress to another man. I was her first lover.'

'Her first?' Conrad choked on words that would be half-venom, half-glee.

No! Since I must disillusion him, let me at least not make Nora sound worse than she is.

'It was three years after the Armistice,' Conrad stated calmly. 'We met. We were together fourteen months. Then along you came . . . and offered her marriage, I understand. It seems that's all it took to entice her away.'

'No.' Roberto Conte di Argente shook his head with perfect sincerity. 'No. Three years after the war ended, she and I were in Venice for that year. I met her there.'

The silence in the richly decorated room stretched out to breaking point.

Have I mistaken the year?

'The first season at La Fenice, when I met her, she sang in *I*

414

Borgia,' Conrad managed. 'Through December and January. Then in *Riccardo Cuor di Leone*.'

Roberto Capiraso inclined his head as if he were not battered and bruised. 'Also small roles in Paer's *Sofonisba*, and Donizetti's *Pietro il Grande*.'

The world might have cracked in two and Conrad would not have heard it.

'The following winter season, a year later,' Conrad said, voice beginning to scratch and dry, 'she sang in *Armide*—'

'Gluck's *Armide*.' Roberto Capiraso sounded like a man in a nightmare – calm because, if he were anything else, he would shriek. '*Riccardo e Saladino*, and *I Virtuosi*—'

'Fioravanti's *I Virtuosi ambulanti*,' Conrad echoed involuntarily.

'—*Ambulanti*, and Mayr's *Rosa Bianca e Rosa Rossa*. She then left Venice with me.'

Conrad swallowed. 'Those two seasons, and the year between . . . yes, we are speaking of the same year.'

The Conte di Argente's face twisted. 'I don't know what sordid little trysts you might have imagined with her during that time. But she was never with you. She was with me.'

Conrad's mouth felt as dry and unwieldy as if it were full of dust. 'Ridiculous!'

Am I going mad?

There was no comfort in that thought.

'Nora lived with me,' Conrad insisted feverishly. 'In my lodgings in the Accademia quarter! We were together each day and night, except when her singing and her jobs as a recitateur and singing-teacher elsewhere didn't allow it. We lived as man and wife.'

The silence grew so intense the noise of the advancing early morning became audible; children and horses in the street outside.

'Nora—' Conrad turned, as if this were any conversation, to bring Leonora in to confirm his side of things.

I'd forgotten she has a weapon.

Clearly, so had she. The wooden stock of the pistol was still in her two hands' grasp, but it sank down, the slanting aim pointing the steel barrel a yard or two in front of her.

Her expression was open and devastated.

Roberto Capiraso spoke as politely as if he were making conversation at a dinner party. 'I had rented a palazzo on the Grand Canal that year. I courted and won the company of the woman whom I desired as my wife. She lived in a respectable boarding-house for singers, which naturally did not allow single gentleman callers. But still, as her betrothed, I had those nights which she spent with me, and those days – every day, when her rehearsals, her singing, and her post giving lessons to others permitted.'

Bile jolted in Conrad's stomach.

He wondered idly if he had been shot. A strong nausea flooded through his abdomen. A crushing sensation constricted his chest.

Daylight illumination from the sash windows exposed every part of Leonora's expression. She watched without blinking.

Conrad inhaled sharply. It felt as if he couldn't get sufficient air.

'You lied.' Conrad spoke to her as if begging to be contradicted.

She said nothing.

Seconds ticked past.

It became obvious she would not respond.

Conrad felt his gut tighten with bitterness. 'So, all the "voice training", the parties I didn't attend, the nights at your friend Rosalba's house, your jobs . . . You must have thought me a complete fool.'

Roberto Capiraso stared at his wife as if she were a woman he had never seen before. Sound wrenched out of him. '*Fessa!*'

Leonora gave the Count a look that reminded Conrad she was brought up in a foundling house and on the streets, and would know the southern Italian slang for the female genitals.

'Neither of you understand,' she said sharply.

Roberto Capiraso wiped blood from his mouth. 'All of this is irrelevant to you, isn't it? Nothing matters except for what il Principe requires!'

Conrad found himself speaking louder to drown the other man out. 'Nora, tell me that you didn't love me. That you don't. Look me in the face and tell me that!'

'Corradino . . .'

She glanced from him to Roberto.

'Neither of you know what happened in Venice that year!

Roberto – Conrad—' Leonora lowered the pistol until it was almost hidden in the silk folds of her tunic *à l'antique*. For all she did not need to breathe, she looked as if she asphyxiated. 'I met you both within two weeks of each other.'

'Two weeks!' Conrad snarled.

Her long hair hid her expression as her head tilted down. It made him more angry.

'Both of you, within fourteen days . . .' She closed her eyes, delicate violet-shadowed lids quivering. 'And I delayed – delayed – I put it off. I knew I had to tell one of you to go . . . And I didn't.'

Roberto stepped forward, hit the edge of the heavy wooden table, and leaned his hands on it as if he needed that to stay upright. 'You have the bald-faced nerve to confess this? He was your lover?'

'You were never faithful to me?' Conrad tried to piece it together. 'You were always fucking both of us?'

'None of this is important.'

Her pale complexion had no pink flush, no redness of anger, but her voice erupted from her motionless body.

'Roberto, you should know this is unimportant! Ugo Capiraso *died* in the cause of the Prince's Men! If your brother could have a grave-marker, the name on it would read "Matteo Ranieri, Prince's Man, faithful unto death". He gave everything for this, gave up being an aristocrat's spoiled older son, gave up his life. It's due to your brother that we stand where we do today! What would he say to see you this disloyal?'

Roberto's peasant hands made fists at his sides. 'You dare mention loyalty! *You* were my cause. They killed Ugo, but I put myself into their hands because they promised me you! Promised their Prince could give you back to me after you died—'

'—Then you're a fool.' Conrad's voice sounded unsteady even to him. 'Because according to her, the Dead come back only when they want to.'

'Is that so?' Roberto might have been listening to a paper at the Royal Society. 'Did I waste everything, then?'

Scorn gave his voice all of Il Superbo's bite.

'I'd lay a bet that she didn't come back for you, in that case,

417

Conrad. And she didn't come back for me. Did you, Leonora? If you did come back yourself, you came back for il Principe, for the Prince's Men!'

'And they needed you.' Conrad felt the pattern lock together. 'Because where else can the black opera have been rehearsing, except in one of the palazzos of the nobility? Ferdinand's men couldn't find it anywhere in Campania. But you could have told him, couldn't you? The Argente family's country estate?'

Roberto's lips showed white. 'Correct. I wanted the Prince's opera to succeed, for her sake – my wife's sake . . .'

The Conte di Argente snorted, thickly.

'My wife! Now . . . *Vaffanculo!* I've changed my mind. I don't want her world, or her Prince! Who cares what God you'd put over us, when we're all irrevocably corrupt!'

'The innocent will be saved.' Leonora's face was unable to be more pale, but she looked as if she had lived a century of terrible years, and every one had left its mark on her. All her attention was on the Count. 'Roberto! No! You're betraying us!'

Conrad stepped to one side, towards the end of the table, to come around and cut her off from the door.

She raised her arms.

The duelling pistol lifted.

It pointed between the two of them – but would only need to move a fraction to shoot either man.

Lead bullets expand in flesh. Even a shot that barely scrapes a limb will tear clothing, burn flesh; or leave a cut through muscle that takes a year or more to heal. In the cavity of the body, a belly-wound will leave a man infected and dying. Conrad judged that Leonora aimed for a shot that strikes under the sternum (avoiding the ribcage) and would fatally clip the heart.

He realised he was free of fear. He felt only irritation – *That is my Manton duelling pistol and I want it back!* – and a suffocating pain in his chest where he did not dare consider Venice, now that none of it is what he thought.

Conrad took another step; not caring if she shot him.

'You have to come back with us now, Nora. Don't be worried. No one will get hurt.'

418

'Oh, I wouldn't say that.' Leonora brought up the flintlock pistol.

Conrad had a moment to regret the weapon's superb balance. The *pazzo inglese* – English crazy person – who sold the pair to him in London had said cheerfully, 'A twelve-year-old boy could hit his mark with this!' Leonora's wicked aim looked far more experienced than that.

The pistol's sights targeted him for a brief, unmistakable moment.

Before he could react, she lowered the muzzle and pulled the trigger.

The hammer fell.

Conrad twisted away, arms up to protect his face, in all the old reflexes learned from being in trenches facing mortars and artillery. He was already throwing himself down when the flint scraped and powder ignited, and fired the half-inch lead ball.

In a corner of his vision he glimpsed Roberto ducking away.

The room exploded in high-pitched ricochets.

Something hard clipped his skull. Conrad's teeth jarred together.

A hard surface hit his shoulder. *The floor*, he realised, sprawling down on the carpet. The stink of burned powder, smoke, and alcohol made him choke. Small objects rained down on his back like a shower of hard hail.

Nothing penetrated his coat.

His head rang and his ear stung. He rolled back up onto his feet, and swayed.

He put his palm to his stinging ear, and brought back a handful of blood.

Conrad surged forward before the shot's echoes in the high-ceilinged room faded. He flung the door open. The vestibule was empty. Two maids clung together on the stairs, hands over mouths, eyes wide.

The front door was closed.

Conrad waved the servants away and stepped back into the main room.

Roberto Capiraso's blood-speckled face was turned away from him. 'She's gone.'

419

Following the man's gaze, Conrad saw a door in the corner of the room that stood open. The flat exterior of the door was covered with the same wallpaper as the room. Closed, it would be invisible. *A servants' door.*

Leading to a labyrinth of dark passages.

'We won't find her now.' Conrad blinked against pain in his head. 'She's Nora; she will have had a way out planned.'

Something ground under his boots. He looked down to see the carpet covered in shattered, glittering debris. Conrad recognised one of the larger lumps. It was the broken base of a lead crystal decanter.

'That accounts for the smell of port . . .'

A fragment had evidently clipped him. Conrad unwrapped his neck-stock and pressed the linen against his ear, to stem the bleeding, and wiped his wet hands.

One of the scientific Institutes has probably done research on why the result is so much worse when one shoots a full bottle or decanter, rather than an empty one. All Conrad's experience comes from bored evenings in the Mess with three-quarters drunk officers. *Empty bottles break or shatter. Full corked bottles explode like grenadoes.*

For a moment he surveyed the wreck of the mansion's room – shattered desk, glass, spilt port – and it could be one of those houses commandeered to billet army officers.

Roberto Capiraso turned away from staring at the servants' door. The movement penetrated Conrad's mental fog.

Conrad met the man's fathomless dark eyes.

Without warning or change of expression, far more quickly than Conrad had reason to suppose he could move, Roberto Capiraso jabbed a short, brutally-effective fist.

Pain exploded in Conrad's ribs, compressing his chest and stopping him breathing. A white flash jolted behind his eyes. He sucked in air – and stumbled back from a glancing blow high on his cheekbone. The wall hit him between the shoulder-blades.

He stayed on his feet, though he swayed. It seemed to take him an unmeasurable moment of time to realise, *Roberto hit me!*

Roberto Capiraso collected up the scattered pages of *L'Altezza azteca, ossia il serpente pennuto*, moving with a slow deliberation that gave away his own physical pain.

The discharged pistol lay a few feet from the door.

Conrad bent, wincing, and recovered it, using his bloodied neck-cloth to wipe the soot off the steel barrel.

The Count rummaged in the wreckage of his desk and picked up the bound score of *Il Reconquista d'amore*.

His hand only shook a little as he held out the black opera.

'Keep hold of that, signore,' Roberto ordered harshly. 'You will now take me to the King.'

42

Conrad placed the bound score of *Il Reconquista d'amore* and the hand-written pages of *The Aztec Princess* on the King's desk.

He bluntly repeated, 'Signore Roberto has been composing for both operas. The black opera is better.'

'This is impossible!' Ferdinand's voice broke with shock and anger. 'And even if it weren't— The time! Past eight in the morning, the day of the performance! We have six hours – less than six hours – to do anything! And what can we do?'

Ferdinand Bourbon-Sicily rose from his chair, pacing agitatedly in front of the floridly ornamented fireplace. He snapped his fingers at an aide. 'Being me maps. Find me Major Mantenucci!'

The young cavalry officer turned from a map table, arms loaded with charts of the local area. 'The Major isn't on duty until nine this morning, sire.'

'Find him! You,' the King beckoned a second aide, 'summon Colonel Alvarez. Order a detachment of the Rifles to the Palazzo Argente, outside the city, with orders to search and seize.'

'Sir!'

The two men left.

'Sit.' Ferdinand gestured to Conrad, and after a moment extended the gesture to il Conte.

Folding wall-panels had been pushed back, opening the King's office up to take in all the sea-ward side of the Palace's fourth floor. Walls shone jager green. Sunlight caught the ceiling that was painted in eighteenth-century pastels. At the further end of the chamber, a flock of aides and military officers commanded other tables covered in maps and charts. Paper unrolled onto the floor. Conrad was vividly reminded of his own days in the north, in muddy tents, at officers' meetings.

He pushed Roberto firmly towards one of the carved upright chairs by the King's desk. The Count sat, and leaned back in his similar chair, one leg negligently crossed over the other, and his hands interlaced in his lap as if he did not wear handcuffs.

Getting in to see the King himself had entailed explanations with the royal guard that left Roberto wearing cuffs connected by steel chain-links, not able to move his hands more than six inches apart. Conrad spent a few seconds fighting back *Schadenfreude* as he took his own seat.

If I came before the King in chains first, then that makes the two of us equal now . . .

If one knew Roberto well – as Conrad was startled to discover he did – one could detect the faint tremors that ran through shoulders and spine. The cold rage that had brought them here still ran in his veins, Conrad guessed. *The Count must want nothing better than to seize Nora and shake her; to scream* Why did you do what you did?

Or perhaps that's just me.

'Sire,' the Conte di Argente ventured.

Ferdinand choked him off with a look. 'We would have known nothing! I would happily have accepted that our composer and his wife took a travelling carriage to Rome, because you were too afraid of violence by the Prince's Men to attend the actual performance today . . . And instead you would have gone to— Where? Where is the black opera! You must know!'

Roberto Capiraso attempted an air of dignity, Conrad saw, despite the bloody cuts and grazes peppering his face.

'I was sent in to be a saboteur.' Roberto spoke with bleak, self-castigating amusement. 'To work side by side with the men that il Principe wanted defeated – destroyed. Do you think I was trusted to know anything, when I could be taken and interrogated at any moment?'

'As their leader,' Ferdinand began.

Conrad saw sweat shine on the Count's forehead, under the now-tousled black hair. Roberto glanced over at him. Their gazes met. Conrad could almost read the man's thoughts. *Better I should tell him than you.*

'I don't lead the Prince's Men in Naples,' Roberto Capiraso confessed quietly. 'Leonora does.'

'Leonora?'

Ferdinand's expression moved rapidly through confusion to realisation and disbelief. 'Leonora Capiraso? The Contessa di Argente? You can't mean—'

'He can,' Conrad said.

Roberto sounded more co-operative, as if he had begun to realise he was in the King's custody.

'Donna Leonora came in as the highest-ranking member of the inner circle in Italy, at the moment. There are other highly ranked men here, but not superior to her.'

He stroked his short beard. Conrad was not certain if he hid a smile or a grimace.

'I know few enough names. That was intentional. I met a few of Nora's lieutenants – the stage properties and costumes for *Reconquista*, for example, have been stored in Gabriele Corazza's palace, until they should be needed.'

Ferdinand summoned another pair of aides, and gave sharp, quick orders.

Conrad surreptitiously watched their lips. The King will waste no time sending men to search the palace and confirm Roberto's story.

Ferdinand leaned back in his chair as they left, gazing at Roberto Conte di Argente. 'All of what you say will be very carefully investigated. It's not difficult to imagine the Prince's Men implicating our own people deliberately to handicap us.'

Roberto shrugged broad shoulders in a surprisingly plebeian gesture.

'I have no reason to lie. My reasons for telling the truth . . . Signore Conrad will have briefed you on those. As for Cardinal

Corazza . . . I think he's the only man in Naples whose rank in Il Principe is close to Leonora's.'

'Gabriele Corazza himself? Gabriele Corazza!' Conrad muttered, his voice high. 'The Cardinal of Naples – the man locally in charge of the Holy Office of the Inquisition!'

Ferdinand's head came up. A frown resolved itself, and his impassive features looked keenly intelligent.

'Astonishing! Corrado, do you realise what that means? If not for Signore Captain Esposito, the Prince's Men would have had you in their power within – what? – four hours of lightning striking the Teatro Nuovo?'

The narrowness of that escape, even more than a month ago, made Conrad sweat into his crumpled linen shirt.

'And nobody would have heard of me ever again!' he muttered.

Roberto Capiraso snorted, hooded lids closing down over his dark eyes. 'You can send police or soldiers, but I imagine the Archbishop's palace will be deserted by now.'

'They may have left information behind.' Ferdinand frowned, gazing at the Count. 'If the costumes and properties have been stored in Naples itself, that must mean the performance is either in the city, or very close to it. But my campanile spies have seen nothing.'

Those will be the runners, Conrad realised, glancing down the long chamber at the continual coming and going of messengers there. Observers, high in town and village bell-towers, that can command a watch over all the roads for signs of movement. Because surely the Prince's Men must be moving now?

'Argente.' Ferdinand Bourbon-Sicily addressed the Count. 'I will keep you out of prison for as long as I have use for you. You will first write me, to the best of your knowledge, a list of those members of the Prince's Men that you are certain of in Naples.'

Conrad reached across the desk and pushed an ink-well and paper toward Roberto.

The King began to work swiftly through the bound score of *Reconquista*, as the Conte di Argente wrote. Clearly he thought it might contain more clues to the location of the opera itself. Roberto Capiraso scribbled quickly, despite his handcuffs.

Conrad shuddered, his gaze drifting towards the tall sash windows, and the unclouded morning sky over the Gulf of Naples.

New awareness prickled down his skin.

Being underground made him shut the constant tremors out of his mind – because, really, who wants to think that at any moment the earth may close up these man-made tunnels, or leave the human interlopers blind and trapped in buried medieval catacombs? And the San Carlo seemed such an extension of this that Conrad expunged the shaking ground from his mind there, too.

A rumble shook the floorboards under his feet, four storeys above the ground. All the newly leafed trees along the foreshore road suddenly shook back and forth in unison. Conrad watched haze grow into existence around the top of Vesuvius.

He found he could not convince himself that random clouds had snared themselves there. The throat of the mountain exhaled vapours.

It does this often; it doesn't have to mean—

Earth, moon, and sun are lining up, he admitted to himself. *It means Ferdinand's 'high earth-tide' later today, if nothing else.*

'*Il Reconquista d'amore* . . . !' Ferdinand slammed his hand down on a page. 'This is so much superior to *L'Altezza azteca*. Conrad! How did we not notice that we were being given failure?'

Pinned under the man's sudden gaze, Conrad stuttered for an answer.

Roberto Capiraso didn't look up from scribbling his long list of names. 'It was designed that way. For example, I wrote Giambattista's arias on the very top edge of his tessitura. I set all Sandrine's crucial notes in the passaggio that she finds most difficult.'

He glanced up, catching Conrad's eye.

'You therefore had to concentrate on bringing them up to that standard. You had little enough time to consider whether the opera could work if they did sing.'

Conrad folded his arms, hiding his hands that shook with anger.

Ferdinand turned the score so that it was possible for Conrad to page through it with him. 'I'm one man. Describe me your opinion of this, Corrado. Is it a danger to us?'

Finally, the chance to look at it properly!

Conrad thumbed anxiously to Felice Romani's synopsis. 'Background – Spain, AD 1492. "The Emirate of Granada, the last kingdom of medieval Spain still ruled by a Moor, King Muhammad the Twelfth (bass). . . . The Christian forces are at their gates, under command of Ferdinand of Aragon (tenor). Here . . . During the Sinfonia, we hear behind the stage curtain the cries of invading Christian knights, and the alarm and counter-attack of the Moorish soldiers beating them back." This is effective.'

Ferdinand Bourbon-Sicily nodded unhappy agreement.

Conrad turned the pages of the score, the notes bringing sound into his mind. A solo lyric soprano aria – an angry romantic duet – the Moorish King's bass lamenting the fall of Muslim Al-Andaluz in Spain – a heroic mezzo (en travesti, as a priest) leading a magnificent Christian anthem for which there was no other word but hymn.

'You wouldn't have got this past a censor!' Conrad exclaimed – and realised that he addressed Roberto Capiraso as if he were still co-worker on their opera. He turned back to Ferdinand Bourbon-Sicily. 'Yes, it's a danger, sir.'

He read on, careful to pay attention to his own reactions. *One doesn't encounter a work of art for the first time twice.*

'"Queen Isabella of Castile, coming to join her husband the King of Aragon, is captured by Barbary pirates, and sold in the slave market to King Muhammed." That could unintentionally be comic – but this score makes us believe her fear, her pride, his sudden lovestruck infatuation, his desire to make her not a slave but a wife . . . "Isabella escapes and returns to her husband and co-monarch, Ferdinand of Aragon. She finds him unwilling to allow her full power as a Queen in her own right. He accuses her of unfaithfulness with the Moor. To prove her good name, and bolster her precarious political power, she is forced to announce a new crusade against Granada – although, heartbroken, she realises at that moment that she loves the Moorish King Muhammad." That has to be the end of Act Two!'

The King of the Two Sicilies smiled with wistful irony. 'In opera, we go to war for love . . .'

He stood, signalling Conrad to keep his seat, and stepped aside to talk to his returning aides and Colonel Fabrizio Alvarez of the King's Rifles. A few police uniforms were visible among the military around the map tables, but Conrad couldn't see Enrico Mantenucci or Luigi Esposito.

Luigi would pay money to go to this opera.

Conrad flicked over further pages, searching for the build-up to the finale ultimo.

'Here we are, sir'. He glanced up as the King returned from giving orders, 'The last Act. Granada falls, all except the central citadel, which is the city garrison and powder store. From the tower, the King's vizier Osmino threatens the Christian knights and their King and Queen that he will fire the powder store, and blow them all to hell. *All'armi!* But Muhammed himself emerges on the tower. He begs Isabella to come away with him, to North Africa, and he will hand over the city to Aragon. She is desperate to accept, but with all their eyes on her, can't. Aria. Desolate, King Muhammad abdicates.'

Conrad broke off, glaring at the scribbling Roberto Conte di Argente.

'One verse in the major key, celebrating his great love for Isabella; one verse in the minor key, his racking grief that she will never be his. JohnJack will recognise that.'

The Count shrugged, not looking up.

Conrad returned his attention to libretto and music:

'"Christian celebrations start, but they're premature. Aria. Queen Isabella foresees that, despite his race and religion, Muhammad will offer her more freedom to rule than her husband Ferdinand ever can. Besides, she loves him. Duet. She conspires with the vizier Osmino. At the height of the celebrations, when Ferdinand of Aragon is about to have the imprisoned Moor executed, Queen Isabella warns her husband that there are Muslim and Jewish saboteurs in the garrison powder store. Ferdinand heroically enters the tower to attempt to prevent this – aria and cabaletta – but fails. He is blown up, as Isabella planned. The widowed Queen Isabella pardons the Moor and takes Muhammed as her consort. She announces no one need leave Granada – there will be peace and community now – she herself will rule a united kingdom of

Christians, Jews, and Moors, according to rational, Godly principles." Then rondo finale, soprano . . .'

Conrad stopped himself, suddenly. Clumsily, tearing the edges
of paper in his haste, he went feverishly back over what he read.

'But this—'

Conrad stood and slammed the bound score open in front of
Roberto Capiraso. It smudged the pages of the man's endless list.
Conrad smacked the open pages, glaring.

'—This is pointless! Your sabotage of our opera, pointless!'

Men turned to listen at the end of the war-room. Conrad
ignored that. He saw nothing but the annotated score, heard only
flute and oboe, horns and trumpets, strings and drum – and the
ardent, searing power of the soprano's final aria.

'Corrado.' Ferdinand spoke with firm authority. 'What have
you found?'

Conrad lent both hands on the desk, close enough to jostle the
seated Conte di Argente. 'Hopeless! I can read a score as well as
the next man! What is this? Is it some sort of fake document,
intended to throw us off?'

Roberto Capiraso sat back. He folded his arms across his body as
much as he could with the short chain between his cuffs. It was an
oddly protective gesture.

'I assure you, Scalese, you have your "black opera" there in
your hands. Orchestration, voice roles, all as we in il Principe have
rehearsed.'

'Impossible!' Conrad snarled, relief and triumph making him
dizzy. 'Who can the Prince's Men have who could possibly sing
Isabella of Castile? Look at this ultimo finale, the soprano's
rondo— Ridiculous!'

The pages of the score brushed past his fingers as Ferdinand
Bourbon-Sicily seized it up.

The King made a choking sound. 'But it's worse than *der Hölle
Racht*! Who could possibly—'

Conrad didn't take his eyes off Roberto Capiraso.

'For all I know, the Prince's Men have kidnapped a dozen
principal, professional singers.' Conrad shook his head, disbelief
building up to fury. 'You may have Giuditta Pasta or Giulia Grisi

tied up in a palazzo somewhere! It doesn't matter! The tessitura of this is inhuman! Middle C to the F two and a half octaves above is a lyric soprano – low C is a tenor range – and here, here!, the A below low C! One singer is supposed to span the range down to a baritone? As for the two-octaves jumps – the succession of high Fs! – yes, I hear it would work as something tremendous. If it were a duet! A trio! . . . An aria— This is impossible for one singer!'

Ferdinand slammed the score down in front of Roberto Capiraso. Ink spilled off the desk, running across leather and wood and down to the priceless carpet. The King ignored it. 'I don't understand! I can't understand, Argente. You've crippled your opera, worse than you have done ours!'

Silence filled the vast chamber.

Roberto Capiraso , Conte di Argente, laid down his steel pen. For a long moment, his gaze went past the shining morning windows, contemplating the shivering sea – or perhaps some memory known only to him.

'I always hear her in my mind as both, you know.' His voice slid into a quietly confiding tone. '. . . Isabella, Queen of Castile. Princess Tayanna of the Aztecs . . .'

Ferdinand opened his mouth, plainly to snarl. Conrad rested a restraining hand on the King's arm. He shot a warning look.

Don't interrupt.

If he could have spoken aloud, Conrad would have said *I heard that tone all too often around army campfires, after we'd been fighting for too long . . . From men who would shatter the next day.*

I think he's realised what he's done in the last hour.

Ferdinand shot a tense glance, signalling Conrad to proceed.

Aware of the potential for fracture – and loss of information from this one source – Conrad prompted gently:

'"Her"?'

'*Il Reconquista*'s soprano will have no need to strain her voice in the part.'

Roberto's secretive smile turned mirthless with regret.

'The role of Isabella was written for her alone – for the only woman who could ever sing in il Principe's opera.'

The Conte di Argente raised his head. Conrad found himself pinned by the dark, penetrating gaze.

Roberto said softly, 'The first of many lies that you were told – is that something in Death destroys the human voice.'

43

Conrad stared, wide-eyed.

'Leonora?' he choked out.

The Conte di Argente gave an odd smile. 'She lies, my wife . . .'

Something inside Conrad, deeper than the everyday, made him feel on the instant that he should have known.

Because Nora, Leonora, could never be separated from her voice! That voice which I've heard in front of thousands at La Fenice, and nakedly private between the two of us.

Not separated by death, or anything else. Why did I allow myself to believe that she was mute?

Because when I knew she was lost to me, and with Roberto, I couldn't bear to think of her at all.

He repeated it aloud, wondering if it would make more sense. 'Leonora still sings.'

The look in Roberto Capiraso's eyes was almost sympathetic. 'She learned, after her death, that the Prince's Men were planning an opera. It took a few years, but she worked her way up to become their leader in that arena.'

'I used to say, she never lies . . .' Conrad gripped his temper hard, ignoring whatever it was that swelled in his throat and behind his eyes, and might have burst out in weeping.

'That she'd keep silent, or she'll let people believe what they

432

want – or she'd allow other people to lie for her – but she doesn't lie—'

—To me.

Conrad stood up from his chair, stumbling across to the open balcony doors, so that no one in the room could watch his face. So that the only thing before him was the innocent sea, air fresh, sky bright, morning rising towards heat.

He smelled salt water, and something acrid. This side of the Palace was away from the crammed roads and houses of Naples, overlooking the Bay, so that very few human voices rose over the noise of distant waves.

Conrad realised that no birds let loose their song. No gulls skimmed the waves. The dogs in the royal kennels were silent.

The marble steps four floors below, going down to the small enclosed royal dock, must be the ones on which il Principe had deposited the body of Adriano Castiello-Salvati.

They— She—

Furious, too choked to speak, Conrad gripped the iron balcony railing hard enough that flakes of paint came away embedded in his skin. He thought he detected a faint, continuous tremble, reverberating through the metal.

All of it's a swamp. I have no firm footing! Because I have no idea what was truth and what was a lie. She's il Principe's leader here, is she? Then everything she's done will be to benefit them . . . to benefit her.

He felt a desperate desire to have his hands on her. Shake the truth from her.

He rested his weight down through his arms, letting the early blue of the Bay fill his vision, ease his pain.

Roberto Capiraso's baritone sounded, not far behind him.

'I think that if Leonora herself did have a choice to Return, instead of the Sung Mass compelling her to come back, she Returned to sing.'

Conrad turned. Ferdinand Bourbon-Sicily was giving urgent instructions to officials and aides, at his great desk. Evidently the man had chosen to let the Conte di Argente – *of all people!* – approach him.

'That we've had traitors and spies with us from the beginning—'

Conrad ignored the handcuffed man's flinch. 'I can be at ease with that. I'm not a fool: these things happen in war-time, and this is a war. But that she came back – came back as she is – and never even considered telling me the truth—'

He cut himself off before he could complete it, aloud:

—*Never considered offering me a place, with her, in the Prince's Men.*

Conrad was used to assuming that when he gave his word, he would keep it. That this was a part of his character. Now . . .

He released the balcony rail and shoved his hands through his hair, aching for some physical outlet for his pain and confusion.

Would I have abandoned his Majesty the King of the Two Sicilies if she offered me a place with her?

I should at least be able to answer that question one way or the other!

Roberto, sounding as if he had overcome his moment of breakdown, said, 'You – even I – were not her first concern.'

Conrad stepped back out of the early sun, into the cool of the room. He heard himself sound strained.

'You and I are the only two men here who could know that truth. Because only you and I have heard her seize the attention of fifteen hundred people with a single passionate note.'

Roberto Capiraso gave a rueful nod.

The King handed off another list of instructions to a page, and walked over.

'Inform me. Aside from the book and music, what do you know of the black opera? About the function of this *Il Reconquista*?'

Roberto frowned. 'I know only as much as was necessary for the structure of the opera. You could tell as much from studying the score, sire. The main climaxes are the stretta at the end of Act Two, and the soprano's rondo finale at the end of Act Four. I assume the latter is what brings about the "sacrifice", as Nora calls it.'

'And how long have you known that the "sacrifice" would be a Plinean eruption of Vesuvius?'

Ferdinand Bourbon-Sicily couched the question almost primly in scientific terms. Conrad saw it hit home.

'The finale ultimo is Leonora, alone,' the Count said. 'Because no other singer could do what she does. I assume that's that part intended to "wake the God of this world". I don't believe Leonora told any but her closest inner circle what that will involve. I . . . Truthfully, I never asked. I neither know nor care about il Principe's theology!'

Conrad saw Ferdinand give the composer his bland, weighing glance, which concealed everything the intelligent monarch might be thinking.

Roberto Capiraso added, 'I knew of the Prince's Men only through my brother Ugo. Ugo was sufficiently older than I that he seemed more of an uncle or father to me, rather than a brother and equal. He died overseas, some years ago. Until recently, I thought he did no more than fund the Prince's Men.'

'I was told Leonora Capiraso came back by way of a Sung Mass,' Ferdinand said. 'Which you organised.'

'Which I asked the Prince's Men to organise,' Roberto corrected, his tone still automatically respectful. 'As far as I could tell, sir, it was an ordinary liturgical Mass, done by a common parish priest. Il Principe added their own elements into the ceremony, but to tell the truth, I was in no state to pay attention to them.'

The Count was lost to memory, his stare unfocused.

'Leonora died. There was nothing the Church, or the Prince's Men, or any man, could have asked in return for bringing her back that I would not have given.'

'But presumably your wife believes in the Prince of this World?'

'She may.' Roberto Capiraso's tone took on sardonic amusement. 'Sire, the antique Aegyptians worshipped cats and crocodiles. The black man of Africa has a thousand gods. The heretic Protestants have One, and say we have Three. Perhaps a Mass sung to any of them would produce a miracle?'

The King's diplomatic expression momentarily failed. He winced.

In lieu of challenging the theology, he ushered the Count back towards his desk. Conrad followed, taking his chair.

'She came back,' Conrad said, aloud, and looked at Roberto. 'And decided on doing this. Why this? Just because it involves singing?'

'She had been intrigued by il Principe before she died. She grew more so, afterwards. *Il Reconquista* is written for a voice not hampered by mortal restrictions. Breath control, sustained notes, pitch, reach, messa di voce . . . The difficulty is in restraining her to something the human ear can believe! Leonora will sing Queen Isabella because only one of the Returned Dead can handle its technical demands.'

Roberto hesitated, and added, less certainly, 'It may be that only someone who has passed beyond death, and returned, can sustain an emotional intensity that surpasses the living.'

'*Che cazzo!*' Ferdinand seemed to bite back frustration and amazement. 'Then it appears our only hope is the impossible – to find someone who can out-sing Leonora Capiraso! We had better hope we can find the Prince's opera singers, to arrest them.'

Roberto Capiraso inclined his head gracefully. For all his dishevelled clothing and bruises, Conrad thought, he still held the poise drilled into Neapolitan nobility.

'You must consider my advice tainted, of course, but, yes – the Prince's opera cannot be countered. No human voice can out-sing Leonora. To counter the Prince's Men, you must find them, and stop . . . them.'

The almost imperceptible hesitation let Conrad know that the Count could not bring himself to say *stop her*.

Ferdinand Bourbon-Sicily's chin lifted. He had the expression of a man who accepts a challenge without hesitation.

He signalled to the army officers and police at the far end of the chamber, and handed one man the Conte di Argente's list of names.

'Arrest these for questioning. Include the servants, and anyone else in the houses; every man, woman, and child. Argente, what's this, here, at the end?'

'Our rehearsal rooms in Naples.' Roberto took the paper back, struggling in the cuffs to write an address more clearly. 'It's a common house in the Via Anticaglia, that has access through the cellar to an isolated part of underground Naples. One of il Principe, an antiquarian, suspects it to be part of that theatre which Nero anciently had built in Napoli for his "performances".'

'Nero!' Conrad couldn't help snarling the obvious question. 'And you didn't tell us this before?'

'It was abandoned at least ten days ago, after the final dress rehearsal. There may be some evidence left.' Roberto's neck showed pink. 'I'm afraid that rehearsal space was my fault. I suggested that, if we were overheard, you'd assume it came from any other of your mine-chambers.'

Conrad muttered. 'We probably did! *Minchia!* What a mess!'

'A mess we will mend by finding the black opera.' King Ferdinand gave out comprehensive orders. A quarter-hour of furious activity succeeded. Aides, officers, and courtiers rushed into and out of the room – plainly now a war-room – and the pace of the ongoing search for the black opera stepped up to something frantic.

Ferdinand stood, arms folded, as his men extended the trestle tables to have maps of all Naples set out, and the countryside around the city. Police officers pinned scraps of paper to each district, noting when each had been thoroughly sifted; suspicious doors hammered on, and buildings entered.

The search grew in intensity.

'Sir!' Enrico Mantenucci shouldered in through the crowd of officers, jacket barely buttoned, holding up a bundle of papers. 'Here's the first list of arrests. We got pitifully few of 'em – either they were planning to go today, or they've been warned.'

Nora will have warned them, Conrad thought miserably. *Because I couldn't stop her from leaving the Argente mansion.*

He caught sight of Roberto's expression, where the Count sat. His chair now had a pair of Alvarez's troopers behind it, too brutish-looking for their blue and burgundy uniforms.

He's thinking the same of himself, Conrad realised.

'And Corazza?' the King demanded.

'The Archbishop's Palace is deserted.' Mantenucci shrugged, dumping the papers on the King's desk. 'But it's plain that they stripped the place bare last night, or early today. Even with inside information, my men failed to find any trace of preparations for the opera in any of the other mansions named.'

Ferdinand sat down in his gilded chair. 'Undoubtedly it will be clear who else is a member of the Prince's Men in Naples, this

437

afternoon, when certain boxes at the San Carlo remain deserted – but that's too late to be useful.'

The police Commendatore greeted that with a wry smile.

'Enrico, I want the *Guiscardo* to go out on a patrol—'

Conrad found himself confronted by the King.

'—Corrado, can you think of anywhere else they might sing? On board a ship as they were at Tambora, or a palazzo, or – what?'

'Some place that could be fortified, so they couldn't be interrupted?' Conrad picked a name from the air. 'Castel dell'Ovo?'

Ferdinand greeted the suggestion with a snort. 'Don't think I haven't had the garrison there checked!'

Conrad watched as information came in to the men at the trestle tables. Name by name, opera houses were crossed off the map.

'We've had the teatros under guard for weeks,' Colonel Fabrizio Alvarez muttered, joining the group of aides around the King's desk, and bringing his own map.

The smaller theatres were slashed out with the stroke of a pen. Halls, palazzos, churches, Bohemian lodgings . . .

Word came back from Pozzuoli, Ischia, Sorrento, the Amalfi coast – the search had evidently begun early in the day, Conrad saw. He guessed the army had fast relays of horses set up; perhaps heliographs, too.

Troops in the streets, men in watch-towers, paid informers skulking at the back of the market district—

'Nothing!' a disgruntled Enrico Mantenucci summed up.

'Gentlemen,' Ferdinand said briskly, 'they can hardly have vanished off the face of the earth!'

'Perhaps they're not here, sire.'

'Maybe they're in the other Sicily—'

'—Or at sea—'

'They're close to that.' Ferdinand flung out an arm, pointing towards the window and Mount Vesuvius beyond. 'Gentlemen, I thought you commanded enough men to assure me that nothing – no one – could be hidden here!'

A frantic debate broke out.

Somewhere they can't be seen, Conrad thought.

'Would they have the nerve to stay underground?' he found himself saying aloud.

Enrico Mantenucci gave a snort at the idea. 'It would be like them! But no, my men have searched underground Naples backwards and forwards.'

The Colonel of the King's Rifles reached to rummage among the maps on the King's desk, flattening down the various sheaves of paper. Fabrizio Alvarez, seen close to, was a thin, dark man, an inch or two taller than Conrad himself, with a drooping moustache that disguised a sensitive mouth for a soldier.

Leaning over the desk, Alvarez ran a finger over a map; west, along the coast road from Naples to the Phlegraean Peninsula. 'Think I've got something, sire.'

The faint spoor of a memory appeared in Conrad's mind.

'You have underground Naples guarded, sir.' Alvarez acknowledged Mantenucci. 'But I can think of one place, underground and above ground. None of the bell-tower spies could see inside. The Grotto of Posillipo.'

Conrad's skin involuntarily shivered between his shoulder-blades.

I'm remembering stone-cold chill, he realised.

He had been four or five. It was before Isaura was born, and Conrad was glad of that later. Alfredo urgently had to leave Naples and the docks were watched . . .

Rock increasingly rose up either side of the coast road, like walls. 'Mined by the ancient Romans,' Alfredo told a fascinated small boy. 'They didn't care to have their direct route from Naples to Pozzuoli interrupted by hills, and when they didn't care for something, they altered it.' The deep cutting became a tall tunnel, high as a cathedral before the roof-arches curved together. But so narrow! A slot, barely room for two carts to pass each other, with the weight of the hills pressing down. The constriction felt so overpowering that the child Conrad embarrassed himself, crying with fear.

Ferdinand Bourbon-Sicily frowned down at the map. 'Surely someone would have seen something.'

'We checked the road this side. We can't be everywhere, sire.'

Enrico Mantenucci gave a tired shrug. It was obvious the small, brisk man had been not so much off-duty, as on unofficial duty and without sleep.

'Pusilleco—' Enrico used the Neapolitan name for Posillipo. '— It's not on the road to anywhere important. If they wanted to go to Pozzuoli, say, they'd take a boat from the harbour here. If they wanted to travel north up-country, they'd have taken the direct route out of Naples. Besides, we'd have seen them go in.'

'Not if they planned ahead,' Conrad suggested. 'It's – possible – to spend the night there. A number of people, carriages, baggage-carts, could all move into place there and not be seen.'

Roberto, in the corner of his vision, didn't react suspiciously; he seemed sunk in misery.

Ferdinand's expression sharpened. 'Fabrizio, send a squad of your cavalry along to scout; that'll be quickest . . . There's nowhere else that we aren't searching, is there, gentlemen?'

The King brushed off the confirmations from Mantenucci's officers as if they were expected. Alvarez sent off one of his aides-de-camp, presumably to brief a cavalry squad. Ferdinand sat on the corner of his desk, much more the desperate man than the king.

'If they are hiding there, they surely can't be planning to sing there?'

'I've been hearing singing underground for weeks now!' Conrad rebelliously muttered.

Enrico Mantenucci snorted. 'Well, they might sing. It's as high as a Gothic church inside. They might not be close to Vesuvius – but they're on the Burning Fields.'

'I can hardly believe the black opera will work any miracle in a tunnel!' Ferdinand sounded affronted.

'The tunnel is a defensible site, sir,' Fabrizio Alvarez put in. 'If they blocked off the road at both ends.'

Conrad leaned back in his chair while Ferdinand and Alvarez exchanged opinions on how susceptible a fortified Grotto di Posillipo might be to men with muskets and grenades.

'Bastards will have a few rifled weapons with them,' Mantenucci grunted. 'Every gentleman hunts . . .'

Servants brought round olives and bread, and a fine wine.

Conrad felt the painful bruises on his ribs, now. He found he could feel little else.

He ate nothing. He sat watching the light on the glistening fruit, unable to make a connection between hunger and satisfying his appetite.

Shock had been hovering since he turned and saw Nora with his Manton duelling pistol.

It descended now.

Nora . . . where are you? What are you doing?

He mindlessly picked up a glass of wine, not tasting it as he drank it down in one go.

Sleep came on him so strongly and suddenly that he couldn't speak, or stand up, or protest to himself that he was in the private apartments of a monarch.

Men's voices slid away into a buzz.

Slumped in the chair, he sank into the inexorable gravity of sleep, desperate not to dream.

Nora . . . Have I really seen you for the last time?

Is my last memory to be your face staring at me over the sights of my own gun?

✦

A hand closed over his shoulder, firmly shaking him.

He opened his eyes to a different light.

A quick glance at the clocks told Conrad it was now closer to nine in the morning than eight.

Only five-and-twenty minutes asleep? It feels like a year!

Enrico Mantenucci patted him again on the shoulder, with a wry smile. 'Fabrizio's patrol sent word back. No Prince's Men at Pusilleco, but people had obviously been there. Judging by the remains of food, they stayed there overnight.'

The police Commendatore frowned.

'I don't trust soldiers to have questioned witnesses properly, but according to what their lieutenant says, there weren't any baggage carts, just coaches. One woman thought she saw a cello case, of all things . . . So I suspect singers and musicians went that

441

way, but as for stage scenery and props – could the black opera be a concert performance?'

'If they want to be as powerful as something staged at the San Carlo, with an audience of over three thousand? No.'

The sleep made Conrad freshly alert, but he felt the antipathy to direct light that was his early warning of hemicrania. He turned his back on the windows, to avoid triggering it, and gave Enrico a nod as the man was summoned back to Ferdinand's side.

Beside him, Roberto Capiraso spoke in a hard voice. 'Congratulations.'

Conrad poured out more wine for himself, and, after hesitation, for the other man. 'In your place, I wouldn't know what to want, either.'

'Throw her into jail, her and all her radicalist friends!'

Conrad realised that Roberto Capiraso had opened the score of *Il Reconquista d'amore* on the King's desk, and was using his steel pen to make alterations.

He couldn't help a prod. 'Revising that finale ultimo?'

'Not at all.'

The Count sounded as much Il Superbo as if he were in a drawing-room, not in handcuffs. You would have to know him well to sense his inner frantic turmoil. Conrad realised that he did.

'It occurred to me,' Roberto said, eyes still fixed on the paper. 'I had the better part of two years to write this. I wrote several careful drawing-room pieces during that period, to see how various arias would sound in public . . . A few months ago, when I was told I would also be composing the counter-opera, I thought I hardly needed to sabotage anything. What kind of an opera can any man write in six or ten weeks?'

Conrad almost choked on outrage. 'Donizetti! Pacini! Mercadante! Meyerbeer! Signore Rossini's comedies! Even the new men, Signore Verdi and Herr Wagner!'

Roberto Capiraso sat back in his chair, ignoring the two troopers behind him. Clearly, he distracted himself from thinking of what was going on. But, clearly, he also meant what he said.

442

'I wasn't then so familiar with the inner workings of opera. Here, creating *L'Altezza azteca* . . . It was exhilarating. That I might bring music forth at such speed, and of such quality. It had to be inferior to the black opera, but I could add that afterwards – subtle mistakes in structure and ornamentation at key points, and stretching voice control to destruction. The rest of *L'Altezza* is – is good. And then . . . I realised that, although I thought *Il Reconquista* finished, it could be so much better.'

By the look on Roberto's face, realisation tasted like sucking a lemon.

'You and I were working together, Corrado. I rehearsed your singers with young Paolo. Every day I could see a way of doing things better. Those I could, I added into *Il Reconquista*. A few got past my guard and into *L'Altezza azteca*. It is very hard to cripple something short of being sublime.'

Conrad opened his mouth – and shut it again.

Il Superbo is very nearly entitled to that. No matter who he is or what he's done.

Roberto added, 'Your cousin and the rest of them, they have an instinct for when something could be better. I hadn't foreseen that I would be unmercifully badgered . . . For a better aria for themselves, yes, perhaps! But last week I actually had Estella Belucci accost me to demand that I strengthen Signore Velluti's part in the finale!'

Conrad suppressed a snort. 'The magnitude of that miracle!'

Roberto Capiraso bowed his head. The early morning light showed bruising and swelling along his jaw. 'Perhaps I'll be allowed the scores, after they imprison me.'

Without looking up at Conrad, he crossed out a phrase of the music, and wrote a different one in the margin.

How is it possible to want this man not to end in Ischia prison?

Conrad shook his head.

Doors clicked open. King Ferdinand strode in, from a further room. He spoke with Enrico Mantenucci, and Conrad didn't interrupt. *If there was news, we'd be told.*

Through the still-open doors, he glimpsed a mass of people. Unsurprisingly, there were numerous clergy, and in the mass of black, he could see priests from all the city's churches, Dominicans; no sign of Cardinal Corazza.

Conrad took the rest in in a glance before servants closed the double doors. A family – *grandfather, father, and son?* – with a definable air of wealth and danger. Their faces had in the past been pointed out to Conrad, as they rode Spaccanapoli Street in fine carriages, with the warning 'Camorra'. A very Borgia-looking family of two brothers in early middle age, and a younger sister, who had similar rumours attached in Catania, in island-Sicily. Spoken of in undertones as 'Honoured Men'.

Uncomfortable beside them, a colonel in Hussar uniform was plainly not from any of the Italian kingdoms. He might have been German, or English, and was speaking to a Turk in uniform jacket and baggy breeches. Conrad recognised faces familiar from Neapolitan salons and opera boards. One man – by the close presence of Ferdinand's royal guard, he might have been under arrest – Conrad knew as a writer from the *Giornale*.

Key men that he keeps under control, or needs as allies. Friends. Enemies. Neutral parties who may become either.

Insistent thoughts of Leonora threatened. Distracting himself, Conrad pulled the maps of Naples and the countryside across Ferdinand's desk, and leaned down to study them.

The map of the Phlegraean Peninsula came first to hand. Conrad traced with a forefinger the road from Naples to the Grotto. West, through the Grotto itself. The road beyond, across the Campi Flegrei, the Burning Fields, to the small thriving port of Pozzuoli, protected by its own cliff-top fort.

He let his fingers trace the maze of small roads and tracks around Pozzuoli. *Lake Averno, one of many volcanic pools. The cone of Monte Nuovo. Solfatara's sulphur springs . . .*

One of the more defined roads ran across Campi Flegrei, from the western end of the Grotto of Posillipo towards Pozzuoli, and made a cross-roads with a north-south road that had existed – Conrad's spotty classical education reminded him – at least since Hellenic settlers in Magna Graecia founded Napoli as 'Neapolis', 'new city', nine centuries before Christ, and long before even the Romans.

444

It must be an antiquarian map that Ferdinand has, Conrad realised. Classical ruins were marked, dotting the landscape—

'What is it?' Roberto Capiraso's voice spoke at his ear.

'What?'

'What have you seen?'

Conrad, startled out of concentration, realised he had frozen with one finger on the map. 'You said you rehearsed in Nero's theatre?'

The Conte di Argente looked very humanly puzzled. 'Under the Mercato. What has that to do with the Campi Flegrei?'

Ferdinand emerged from a group of Mantenucci's constables and strode towards his desk.

He seemed to catch the tension in the air. 'Conrad?'

The ormolu clock on the mantle, above the carved arms of the King of the Two Sicilies, chimed the hour. Conrad startled, as if it had been cannon-fire. *Nine in the morning, on the fourteenth of March.*

Conrad's spine shivered and pulled his shoulder-blades tight with tension. 'We . . . were talking about antique ruins. It's likely nothing – but I went there as a child. And once as a young man – when I thought I might take up watercolour—'

'Corrado!' Ferdinand exclaimed, not unkindly. 'You have something that will help?'

'A ruin of pagan Rome, sir.'

Conrad slid his finger back an inch on the map, uncovering the detail that seemed to burn into his retina.

A small oval.

Small on this scale map.

'On the road out from Posillipo, sir, going towards Pozzuoli. That port would mean it could be reached without needing to enter Naples. I know much was excavated – stone and brick and concrete survives – tiers of seats, and an arena—'

Ferdinand looked down at the map, and then blankly up at Conrad.

Conrad used his nail to underscore the words printed on the map beside the small oval.

'"Anfiteatro Grande." The Flavian Amphitheatre.'

He lifted his head, to meet Ferdinand's blue gaze, and finished: 'It once seated forty thousand men. And – sir, what's the best substitute for a theatre? A theatre.'

44

'On the Burning Fields?' Enrico Mantenucci sounded flatly incredulous. 'You think they'll use a ruin as a theatre, in volcanic fields? When they know to expect an eruption! Are you telling me the Prince's Men are planning to blow themselves up?'

Roberto Capiraso interrupted harshly.

'Leonora's dead.'

Pain twisted his face, and for a moment it seemed he couldn't speak. Finally:

'Very little can hurt her. She doesn't care about singers and musicians – once they've done what they're meant to. They themselves believe implicitly in the goals of the Prince's Men. You have no idea how deep their ethic of sacrifice goes.'

Silence lengthened.

Ferdinand clapped his hands, breaking it.

'If the Prince's Men are near the Anfiteatro Grande, they ought to be visible. Fabrizio, you have sufficient spare men to take a company out through Posillipo and examine the Flavian Amphitheatre?'

Fabrizio Alvarez smiled for the first time that Conrad had noticed; a slow, warm expression. 'I dare say I can dredge up a hundred men from somewhere, sire.'

'Take some of Enrico's people with you; they know the roads.'

Mantenucci re-buttoned his uniform jacket correctly. 'I'll come

447

with you, Fabrizio, if you like; I started as an officer in Pusilleco. Sire, Captain Esposito can stay in charge of security in the San Carlo; they know him. I could do with a ride to clear my head . . .'

Ferdinand's quick nod held amusement; clearly he suspected that Enrico Mantenucci's lack of sleep had been augmented over-night with bottles of wine.

'Be back before midday. Our guests will expect to meet the Commendatore of Napoli.'

Conrad clenched his fist, nails digging into his palm. He just managed not to exclaim *Figlio di puttana!* out loud.

When Tullio gets back, some time this morning! How do I explain that the world's changed – utterly – in the few days he's been gone?

Ferdinand turned a severe gaze on Roberto Capiraso. 'How long will it take to perform the black opera?'

'If *Il Reconquista d'amore* is performed without cuts – and I think they won't dare to cut it, without me – then, the better part of three hours. Much like *The Aztec Princess* is, now. I believe they must start when you do, when the sun and moon pull strongest, early this afternoon. By two at the latest.'

'And one must assume that they have preparations to make, if it is the Anfiteatro they're using . . . If the performance is inter-rupted, then there's no chance of a miracle?'

'I hope that's true, sire.'

Conrad glanced from Ferdinand's practised unconcern, to Roberto's bleak, elsewhere-stare.

'There's much I wasn't told,' the Count said. 'In the worst case – the very worst – then, once begun, the process of the miracle is also begun, and can't be stopped.'

The King paced a few turns by his desk. 'If that were true, the same would be true of the counter-miracle we perform, and what might result from such a paradox, God working against Himself – dear Lord, no!'

'Leonora could have explained it better.' The Conte di Argente spoke as if it cost him no pain or hatred to say her name. 'The forces under the earth don't stop being vulnerable at the moment the moon passes overhead. Volcanic earth is most easily made to erupt at the height of the earth-tides, but there's a certain amount of time after, while the moon passes over the Tyrrhenean Sea, in which the same effect might be forced to continue. With difficulty, but it's possible.'

He added, 'Apparently the same thing happened in the Dutch East Indies, when my brother died. Hence I listened when the other Prince's Men discussed it with . . . Leonora.'

Conrad heard the faintest hesitation. He met Roberto's sideways glance, and realised the man had censored the phrase 'my wife'.

Ferdinand began to pace and turn and pace. 'I know of no way to anticipate what might happen. I will put the matter in the hands of my Natural Philosophers.'

He halted, raising a brow at Conrad.

'Sympathising with the physiologoi, who always have the impossible questions to answer?'

'Impossible questions are always impossible until they're answered, sir.'

Ferdinand's eyes showed the amusement Conrad had hoped to call up.

'Regarding the practical matters we can deal with . . .' The King sighed, smile fading. 'If the Prince's Men have been planning a performance al fresco in the Anfiteatro – or, I suppose, elsewhere outside – they will have had time in which to shore up ruins, move in scenery, prepare places for the orchestra, make a stage habitable for singers. Because they appear nowhere else this morning. Unless they and their audience are on board ships.'

Conrad had an immediate mental picture of men – *perhaps with their wives and whores* – packing luggage for sea-travel, and coming by coach-road to every port in the Mediterranean. Ostia Antica, Marseilles, Istanbul, Cairo.

Conrad couldn't help a wry speculation. 'Which is worse? If Il Principe's singers are not on a side-wheel steam-yacht, as Enrico mentioned, but a five-thousand-ton three-decker war-ship? Or at the Anfiteatro Grande – big enough that the ancient Italians not only fought elephants and lions and men, but flooded it for mock naval battles?'

Ferdinand chuckled. 'You're a true bringer of joy, Corrado! If we have to fight the Prince's Men, let it be on land where I have an army. We don't have a ship other than the *Guiscardo*!'

Conrad recalled once hearing that, when the Two Sicilies had needed a warship, one had been loaned by the English Navy. *Doubtless since taken back.*

Down the far end of the chamber, bell-tower spies came and went, but no messages came over to the King.

Ferdinand seated himself behind his immense green desk, and signalled for an officer.

'Major Berardo, I want you to take another company of riflemen on the royal yacht. The *Guiscardo* will sail for Pozzuoli, and land you there, before it goes out to patrol the coast. You're to make your way back along the road and secure the Flavian Amphitheatre, and assist Colonel Alvarez there, or in the Grotto di Posillipo.'

The man saluted and left.

A long slow rumble and shake went through the Palazzo Reale. The ground grated, deep below. Conrad felt as if someone sharply nudged the chair he sat on—

Nothing was there.

Roberto glanced up from the score. 'I believe they are getting more regular.'

Conrad reached over and took the bound score out of the other man's hands. With cuffs restricting his wrists, Il Superbo's grab failed to retain it.

'You don't have time for that.' Conrad stood, and approached the King where the round-faced man rummaged through crumpled reports. 'Sir, we can't be sure of stopping the black opera before it's performed.'

Ferdinand grimaced. 'I know you, Corrado, you have some mad idea.'

Conrad held up the score of *Reconquista d'amore*. 'A lot of this is the music of *The Aztec Princess*. Here, it's composed as it ought to sound. Or with the sabotage removed.'

Ferdinand opened his mouth to interrupt. Conrad risked *lèse majesté* and didn't permit it.

'I realise we have no time! Sir, I want to call together the orchestra, chorus, and principal singers, and rehearse the new versions of key points—'

'New material now?'

'I've heard Nora sing.'

Silence spread out to occupy their end of the great chamber. A breeze from the open window ruffled at Ferdinand's brown hair. Conrad watched his gaze go inevitably to Vesuvius.

For the first time, the blue sky seemed flat to Conrad, rather than deep. *If I could see past it, I imagine I could see the darkened moon beginning to rise.*

The sun, the moon, and the earth all moving to line up; gravity's implacable pull stressing the dirt beneath his feet.

'All of this can still be coincidence,' Conrad murmured, too low for anyone but Ferdinand to hear. 'There's no proof – but evidence is stacking up for the "black miracle". You told me yourself, sir; when you rescued me from the Inquisition – if the Prince's Men can't be stopped any other way, we must have the counter-opera, and it must succeed.'

Ferdinand's expression hardened. 'If you try to rehearse new material and confuse the company enough that they fail in what they could have done—'

'If we change as little as possible, sir – the end of Act Two, the ultimo finale; maybe the Act One opening – I think we can do it.' Conrad added, 'Allow me to have Signore Roberto to assist, sir.'

He knows the material. For both operas.

'We're to trust Contessa Leonora's husband?'

If there was a way Conrad did not wish to think of his composer, that encompassed it in three words.

Ferdinand knows that, Conrad thought. *He tests both of us. In his place, I'd do the same.*

Conrad dug down into himself for honesty. 'Trust him, for this, because he feels more betrayed by Leonora than—' *I do.* '—Any man does. And we need a composer.'

A chink of shifting cuffs made Conrad look around.

Roberto Capiraso rose to his feet. 'I appreciate the compliment – and also the responsibility. If my guards can be unobtrusive, sire?'

Ferdinand Bourbon-Sicily appeared as struck by the other

man's composure as Conrad felt. 'This will not affect my judgement of you, or the Contessa, after this is over. However, I will remember it.'

The bearded man gave a short bow. 'I put myself in your hands, sire.'

Having assumed the Conte di Argente believed in the religion of his ancestors, Conrad now wondered whether it was that or a secular definition of honour that allowed Roberto Capiraso to sound so certain of his decisions.

Ferdinand inclined his head. 'Very well. Conrad, of necessity, Signore Capiraso's guards will be present at your rehearsals; is that acceptable?'

'Find men who go to the opera in their spare time, sir, and it might even be useful.'

'I'll tell the officer that! Meanwhile—' Ferdinand Bourbon-Sicily consulted his pocket watch. He caught Conrad's eye, and spoke in a tone of gallows humour. '—People put on an opera in – five and a half hours – every day?'

Conrad winced. 'Thank you for that, sir.'

'I told you they were words that would come back to haunt a man!'

'Consider me haunted.' Conrad tucked the score of *Il Reconquista* under his arm, made his farewells polite, and brief, and left the King's chambers with the Conte di Argente and two foot soldiers behind him.

They were not allowed through the indoor passage from the Palazzo to the San Carlo – it was still being cleaned in anticipation of the King's visitors – and so walked out of the Palazzo Reale by one door, and into the backstage area of the opera house by another. Conrad took refuge in one of the San Carlo's dusty, cramped side rooms.

'Ink,' he suggested to the troopers. 'Paper. Wine and olives. You need to watch il Conte, I suppose, but there's another room across the corridor; we can leave the doors open.'

Roberto sat on a rickety chair with as much dignity as he had on the King's furniture. He held his wrists up imperiously, and the other trooper unlocked his cuffs. 'Five hours . . . We should start!'

Conrad leaned his weight on the table, one hand flat on each bound score. 'You've spent six weeks telling me it's not possible to stage a real opera in the time we have. Now you think we can alter one in a morning!'

The dark man gave a tired, oddly warm, smile. 'I don't think it matters what I believe. If I've heard anything this past six weeks, it's from our professional singers: "How long does it take to learn a principal role? Ten days if a comedy, fifteen days if a tragedy!" Then they boast about how they'll also be learning the season's second opera, at the same time they're learning the first. And a back-up work, in case the first fails with the public. Nine hours in a day learning the part, and another four hours of rehearsal! Up at six and asleep at one in the morning! According to your singers, Conrad, they can do anything except walk on water – and Signore Velluti seems positive he could do that, too.'

'I believe he'd try if someone gave him the opportunity,' Conrad said absently.

The remaining infantryman chuckled.

I know what it is, Conrad thought, the illumination coming to him in a moment as he saw a likeness between the soldier and his prisoner that both would have denied. *Roberto's spent a month and a half in intense companionship with the opera company; they – we – are as much his comrades as would be the case in an army.*

'As for you, Conrad,' Roberto Capiraso said, imperturbably dry. 'They tell me Signore Rossini was locked in his rooms by the impresario Barjaba, with only cold macaroni to eat, until he composed *Otello*. And for Gazza Ladra's *Sinfonia* he was locked in a room in the roof of La Scala – and that was on the day of the performance! If a man can write music so quickly, surely you can compose a few new words?'

'I should have punched you more than once,' Conrad muttered.

The Conte di Argente choked back a loud laugh. It startled Conrad – and startled him even more to find he was glad of it.

The second of the guards entered with writing materials, wine, and food; Conrad took them with thanks. The riflemen took up station across the corridor. The room was so much less crowded without them that Conrad stretched his arms with a sigh of sheer physical relief.

He set about turning both scores to a matching place. He didn't sit down afterwards, but paced as much as the small room would allow: three steps either way.

'As soon as we have smooth transitions to new materials, we'll call people up on stage for rehearsals.' Thinking of what JohnJack, Sandrine, Estella and the others would say made Conrad flinch.

He pictured their faces and sweated at the danger of the next eight hours. *The rehearsal, then the performance, and if the Prince's Men have an attack in hand—*

Conrad came to an abrupt halt on the creaking floorboards, gazing around the dusty room as if it were the first time he saw it. 'I'm an idiot!'

The Count, all Il Superbo, murmured, 'If I refrain from the obvious remark, will you tell me why?'

'You've written Nora's role—' He deliberately didn't avoid her name. Roberto Capiraso showed a flinch in his creased eyelids, but otherwise didn't react. '—Her role as Isabella of Castile, for a voice that can apparently span the ranges of bass to high soprano—'

'Not apparently,' the dark man put in.

'As soon as we have them started on rehearsals – transpose!' Conrad ordered.

'Transpose? What?' Roberto sounded openly startled.

'Everything,' Conrad said with grim certainty. 'Begin with Act Four's finale ultimo. Go on to the opening chorus of Act One, and the finale of Act Two. If I remember, that's between eleven and thirteen minutes of music. Even with what we alter, the time won't be significantly different . . . I want all the principal singers, and as many of the chorus as are capable of it, to learn those thirteen minutes. All parts.'

Conrad thumped a fist on each score.

'Transpose as much as you can. Male to female roles, and vice versa. Tenor to mezzo, castrato to soprano, bass to tenor – hell, soprano to bass! My point—'

Conrad interrupted himself before the other man could stutter his outrage:

'—Is that the Prince's Men want us stopped. Ferdinand has a division of the army of the Two Sicilies in Naples, ostensibly to greet his Imperial Majesty. Your guards outside aren't just to keep you from deciding to run, they're here to keep you alive.'

'You think we'll be attacked.'

'I know we'll be attacked! We're not under your protection any more.'

Roberto inclined his head, acknowledging the hit.

In the uncomfortable quiet, the distant echoes of voices singing scales and phrases could be heard; and Angelotti's crew swearing blasphemously; and the noise of violins, cellos, and basses tuning up. The company, all unknowing, at what they think is a last rehearsal . . .

'You want me to transpose every principal role, where it's possible.' Roberto sounded both troubled, and oddly exhilarated.

'That's right. If one singer can't manage Nora's role, we'll divide it up between all of ours!'

Conrad sat, picked up his steel-nib pen, and drew his folder of the libretto towards him.

'And, besides that . . . By the time it comes to the finale ultimo, I don't know how many singers we'll have.'

✦

Luigi Esposito came into the San Carlo's auditorium, possibly attracted by the shrieks of singers given new material – so closely resembling the old material – so close to the rise of the curtain. Conrad caught sight of him leaning against the back wall, and left Il Superbo in the chaos of arguing with chorus and orchestra.

Having explained his situation, he raised a brow.

Luigi looked innocent.

'You always know what's going on.' Conrad didn't mind paying for his information with compliments. 'It's been an hour since I saw the King; what's happened?'

'I don't know much . . .' The police captain dusted off his white gloves. 'Word's come back from Commendatore Mantenucci. His men and Colonel Alvarez's troop, they couldn't find anything on the road out of Posillipo. Last I heard, they were going through the Grotto to scout out the Flavian Amphitheatre.'

Conrad didn't bother to ask how Luigi heard things; the police chief's network of informants rivalled the Commendatore's.

Luigi added, 'Colonel Alvarez sent orders for another company to join them. If it was me going after the Prince's Men, I'd have sent for more. But I hear the Commendatore's expecting "a handful of ruffians, conspirators, renegade gentlemen and their servants" . . .'

The impersonation was highly accurate. Conrad couldn't help a grin.

'Don't be too concerned,' Luigi finished. 'In the police, we're used to dirty fighting with the people we don't name. One has to hope that the Prince's Men won't be expecting Colonel Alvarez's troops.'

Conrad let himself think how badly he wanted to hear that the black opera company was found, captured – was not somewhere out in the countryside of Campania, threatening *L'Altezza azteca*.

He thought bitterly that the worry allowed him to avoid the one thing that tore at him with wolf's teeth. *Where is Leonora?*

A shiver of the earth penetrated the walls of the San Carlo, causing a sudden silence among the stage-hands and musicians. After a few moments it ended, and they returned to their work.

Glancing back at Luigi, Conrad thought – even in the dim lighting – that he looked unusually grim.

'What?'

'Oh – nothing about the opera, Corrado.' The reassurance fell from Luigi Esposito's tone. 'I just – don't like my orders. Naples is not to be evacuated.'

The sounds of tuning-up echoed from the orchestra. Conrad glimpsed Paolo with their father's violin, gesturing with the bow. His mouth went dry.

'I understand, I think. If you did give an order to evacuate, the city would be in chaos. People rioting, roads blocked by coaches . . . Most people still wouldn't get far enough away in time.'

Luigi looked down at his hands, and then up, meeting Conrad's gaze with a pained look.

'Corrado, doesn't it occur to you? If Ferdinand gives the order to evacuate Naples today, the Prince's Men would instantly know we're aware of their plans. He won't give away that advantage.'

To sacrifice Naples so as to have the black opera fail—

'I understand.'

Conrad exchanged a look with Luigi, seeing both how much the other man disliked necessity and bowed to it. There was nothing to say.

He left the police chief a short time later, and determinedly made his way down into the body of the theatre, where frantic rehearsals proceeded under Paolo's tyrant hand.

A voice that is Dead, that has no human restrictions, that can span bass to soprano—

'I am an idiot!' He said it out loud, just as he came up to the person he searched for. Taking Sandrine's arm, and momentarily ignoring her curious look, he escorted her to one of the boxes at the side of the stage. 'I need to talk to you about Contessa Leonora's voice.'

'Leonora's voice?'

It took a surprisingly short time to summarise what Roberto had told him. And would, he considered absently while he spoke, remove the need to make an announcement. *Sandrine will have it all around the company in ten minutes.*

She stared at him when he finished, absently adjusting her plumed head-dress.

Conrad took his copy of *Reconquista*'s finale ultimo out of his coat pocket. Sandrine studied the staves scribbled on a fresh sheet of paper by the Count.

'A woman can sing this?'

'Nora can sing this.' Conrad absently pencilled an alteration to one word of the libretto. 'She has no human limitations now. Sandrine, please. You could do this—'

He found a soft fingertip pressed against his upper lip, and stuttered to a halt.

'This is opera,' Sandrine said softly. 'If there was anywhere I wouldn't object to doing this . . . But it isn't possible. Corrado, it's true I used to sing tenor with a baritone lower range. Now I sing mezzo, with a contralto base – like Colbran, but without her soprano tessitura. It took a long time to train myself to use my upper range for speaking and singing. More to the point—'

She fixed him with a glare, as he tried to interrupt.

'—I've never trained for transitioning between the two voices! I have no idea how I'd go about finding my way through the passaggio between a baritone-shaded tenor and a high mezzo! And I'm not going to learn before two o'clock this afternoon!'

'*Merda!*' Conrad relieved his feelings. 'No, not you, Sandrine.'

He rubbed at his eyes, watching the Conte di Argente down in the orchestra pit.

'Il Superbo's never believed anyone could sing this but Leonora. He's re-scoring the last finale as a stretta, transposing it for all the principal singers, so everybody is singing part of it. I suddenly had the thought that you'd be the one who could sing it all.'

Sandrine Furino touched him gently on the arm, but didn't vocalise her sympathy. 'You may want to talk to Estella and Signore Velluti about anything above high B. You're thinking in terms of range, Corrado; not whether someone has the resonance, tessitura, flexibility . . . It takes a long time to train a voice, and a long time to re-train one.'

'I thought I'd solved our problems.' Conrad sighed.

Sandrine nodded absently. She couldn't keep her eyes off the scribbled page of score. 'Corrado, better get Il Superbo to make more copies of this *Reconquista*. Look at them over there, they're turning into a mob!'

'No one will have time to do more than learn their own part. The way we're going,' Conrad muttered, staring up at the rows of unoccupied boxes, 'we'll still be rehearsing Act Four while you're singing Act One!'

'They'll hang Il Superbo, and you too.' Sandrine snickered. She tucked the folded paper into the bodice of her costume. 'Oh, Corrado, don't look so worried! Our singers are very forgiving! Well, more than the Prince's Men would be, I think, Conrad?'

Conrad jolted out of his momentary daze.

'I've got it!'

Dropping Sandrine from his attention as if she were part of

Angelotti's scenery, he tucked himself into a corner by the proscenium arch, with a silver-point pencil and a sheet of paper, and engaged himself in six minutes of rapid-fire, utterly-certain, scribbling.

◆

Emerging, he found himself in the middle of singers on the stage, most of them waving either a short copy, or – in the case of Estella Belucci – Roberto's full score of *Il Reconquista d'amore*.

'I can't sing this!' Estella protested, waving her free hand at both Paolo-Isaura and the Conte di Argente. 'No woman could sing this! If I sing Isabella as it demands to be done, I'll burst a blood-vessel and drop dead on the stage. If I sang even part of it, my voice would be wrecked forever!'

'Who says you'll be singing Isabella di Castiglia's part?' Velluti glanced up from unbuckling his stage breastplate, and ran his hand through his dark hair – which gave him the look of a rather large Naples street-brat. The great chandelier cast bright enough candle-light that Conrad saw the acquisitive glint in the man's eye.

'No woman can sing that,' the castrato said. 'Not a mortal woman, anyway. But the soprano part of it is within my tessitura, and— I may lose my voice permanently, but all the same. Let me try.'

Velluti gave a sudden grin. 'If I succeed and I lose my voice, people will travel miles just to see the castrato who did it, so I'll still have fame and fortune! If I fail . . . If we fail, I don't think it matters whether I've got my voice or not.'

Roberto Capiraso looked up from where he sat at the upright forte-piano. 'I'm sorry to remove your chance of fame and fortune, Signore Velluti. Our finale ultimo is not to be one singer, nor the prima donna with an accompanying comprimario singer, or accompanying chorus. Conrad once said to me, "put the effort in that you would to the end of Act Two", so I'm scoring this the way an act would work when it needs to drag the audience back into the theatre after the interval. I'm scoring Leonora's finale ultimo as a sextet.'

A thunder of protest broke. Conrad put his hands up, gesturing for silence.

It fell only when Roberto Capiraso stood, by the forte-piano, his dark gaze picking them out one by one. 'Yes, I know it isn't done. The heroine or the hero sings at the final curtain. We'll be the first to do it differently.'

The silence deepened. Every singer and musician watched their composer. Conrad could see that all of them, by now, were aware that he had been one of the Prince's Men, and their enemy.

Roberto sounded both acid and grim. 'Leonora has the advantage of being able to sing this part – but one voice is one voice. It can't be six different voices, in unison, in harmony, in counterpoint . . . If you can't do what she can do, do what she can't. If her range and colouring are more than human – then we'll see what polyphony can do.'

Slowly, the singers began to nod agreement.

Conrad smoothed out the paper he had crushed in his fist and walked forward, his boots loud on the stage boards.

'Now you're all here, I want to confirm that there'll be libretto changes as well. No—'

He lifted a hand, quieting them.

'Nothing major except the finale ultimo, and there I've written a handful of new lines, and added one piece of stage business.'

Paolo groaned under her breath, evidently trying to figure out how she could adapt anything new into the tightly woven dance that was the staging and blocking.

Conrad held out the paper to her. 'If we can have copies for everybody? They don't have to be calligraphy, just quick!'

Her mouth curved into a reluctant smile, and she nodded, already reading over the slanting lines, crossed-out scribble, with its boxes and arrows that directed errant words and directions into their proper places.

'*Reconquista* . . .' Conrad widened his attention to take in the rest of the principal singers and musicians, and raised his voice slightly. 'We originally thought the Prince's Men would end with tragedy, being an easy emotion to evoke. Instead, the soprano Queen of Castile, Isabella, ends with her song of triumph over her

460

enemies. And I realised that doesn't matter. Only a few changes to our script, and we have an exact opposite to that vindictive triumph.'

Velluti looked unusually disgruntled. Conrad thought that would be because he had been denied his rondo finale.

'Meaning?' the castrato demanded.

Conrad voiced it softly:

'Forgiveness for all.'

JohnJack reached over Paolo's shoulder, as she followed the altered score, and made play of turning the page the other way up, and reading it that way. '*Porca giuda*, Corrado! How long did this masterpiece take you?'

'Less than ten minutes.' Conrad glimpsed words on Estella Belucci's lip and fixed her with a glare. 'I've had my head full of this opera for six weeks, night and day! I've had more opera than I've had food and sleep! Now, each of you tell me what you think I've written, and I'll tell you if you're right!'

The blonde woman covered her mouth with her fingertips, stifling a giggle. She leaned over Paolo-Isaura's other shoulder.

'All right,' she said cheerfully. 'All as before for Princess Hippolyta; I still leave the country . . . Ah, but the Aztec Princess Tayanna calls me "sister queen"! And we embrace: that's touching. And she requests that I bring the Amazon boy-Prince to meet his father now and again.'

Conrad turned from her shining gaze to the tenor. 'Lorenzo?'

'I, ah, as King Carlo, I forgive Signore Cortez for his rebellion against the crown—' The diminutive tenor interrupted himself to add, '—Although I really don't know why I should—'

'Natural forgiving nature,' Conrad said blandly.

Lorenzo Bonfigli gave him a look of disbelief. 'Says here, I understand the power of love, which even earthly rulers cannot conquer. And then Cortez and I, we embrace as brothers. Whether we want to or not.'

'Bonfigli!'

'We embrace as brothers, in a spirit of universal forgiveness.'

JohnJack looked up from his revised score with a snicker, subsumed into an enthusiastic beam. '"Universal" forgiveness is right.

I don't get killed, I get captured! Then I defend the Princess against *il Re* Carlo here when he tries to annex her kingdom – oh, and look: in the space of a couple of lines, Princess Tayanna forgives me for my rebellion, because love was at the bottom of it all, and sends Chimalli off in exile to the frontiers to guard the Aztec lands – but I shall be able to come home when I've expiated my crimes.'

Conrad subdued sardonic reactions with a narrow glare.

'This *lieto fine* is earned,' he emphasised. 'For each of them, there's as much happy ending as they deserve – after the punishment for their own stupidity has finished falling onto their heads!'

'Oh yes . . .' Brigida gave a surprisingly rich chuckle. 'I have to forgive my Amazon daughter for falling in love with a male – and tell her that, after all, that's how she got to be here in the first place . . .'

'That's not more than six changed lines between all of you.' Conrad turned to the tall mezzo beside him. 'Princess Tayanna's the one doing all the work. Double aria rondo finale cancelled, in favour of a new aria on the subject of love and forgiveness, leading into the new sextet.'

'With revised music from our composer . . .' Sandrine dropped Roberto Capiraso a demure little curtsey, much as she would have done before the morning's revelations.

The others just still think 'he's our composer' despite his actions, Conrad reflected, the illumination coming to him suddenly with her expression. *But Sandrine actually forgives him. I wonder what she's done, in her past, that makes her so understanding?*

Conrad clasped his hands behind him, feeling cold sweat in his palms.

One by one, the group around the forte-piano fell silent and fixed their attention on him.

They need to believe they can out-do the Prince's Men with a singer back from the dead; the Prince's Men with years to prepare; and who knows what other professional singers, what composer, or librettist . . .

'You're all professional singers.' Conrad found himself drawn up at attention, as Lieutenant Scalese of the Cacciatore a Cavallo might have stood. He looked from Sandrine to Lorenzo, from Velluti to Estella, JohnJack, Brigida . . .'We don't yet know if the way that Leonora sings even works in opera. We do know she's one voice, you're six. You can adapt. You're bel canto singers; you improvise as a matter of course! Use all the coloratura you know. Sing with each other, even where your roles are singing against each other, and it's going to produce something finer than any individual singer.'

Even Nora? some sceptical part of his mind put in.

He managed to keep the doubt off his face.

Reassuringly loud chatter broke out as he stepped back. Paolo-Isaura had her head together with one of the recitateurs; Conrad guessed there would be multiple copies of the new parts soon. *And then she has to brief the orchestra. It's a good thing the San Carlo musicians are close to the best in Italy!*

Conrad bumped against a thin, intractable obstacle. He glanced up to find himself standing beside GianGiacomo Spinelli.

'"Forgiveness for all"?' JohnJack queried mildly.

'Up to a point. The world is bad enough as it is, without humans making other humans' lives unbearable.'

'Cynical romantic?' Spinelli appeared to muse. 'Romantic cynic—?'

'JohnJack!'

They were interrupted by Paolo ushering them aside and calling the principal singers to the forte-piano.

The voices faltered at first, and then suddenly caught, as tinder catches, going up in a blaze. The first bars of the revised sextet soared in an unashamed anthem, as if it were part of some secular oratorio.

Conrad drew in a breath and forced his attention away.

If I sit and listen, I'll do nothing, and every word has to match what Roberto is writing—

He made himself turn and go towards the backstage maze, on the route to the upper work-rooms.

Some illumination shivered in his mind, almost ready to coalesce. *Some revelation about the nature of this music, this singing, and—*

A man stepped directly into his way.

Conrad lost his thought.

He halted, the words to flay the man on his tongue.

'Signore Scalese—'

It was a police officer of the Port district, Conrad realised; whose face he recalled, but not the name.

'—You were expecting a delivery at the dock, signore?'

Conrad flatly stared, his mind too tired for a second to catch up.

'Merda per merda!'

He shot out of the backstage exit of the theatre, barging past Roberto Capiraso and his attendant soldiers without even an apology, and left the San Carlo, heading for the royal dock.

45

Tullio Rossi followed the dignitaries off the yacht *S. Gennaro*, looking in his elderly greatcoat and tricorne hat like a guileless servant.

'Avoiding any secret police,' he murmured, straight-faced enough that Conrad was instantly reassured about what might have happened on the voyage from Stromboli.

The lackeys, court gentlemen, military escort, and King of the Two Sicilies made a fine display of colour on the quay, greeting his Imperial Majesty the (incognito) Emperor. The stocky figure of the Emperor bowed his greetings, and was given precedence by King Ferdinand as they departed for the Palazzo Reale on the way to an early lunch.

Conrad surreptitiously wrung Tullio's hand, in case it should be observed how glad he was to have his 'servant' back. 'You'll need to dress up if you're coming inside the Teatro.'

'Nah. My friends will be going up to the royal box with me, to check security, but we'll go in the back way.'

Tullio indicated by thumb two men in the uniform of Imperial Colonels, wearing the many colourful Orders of his Imperial Majesty.

Conrad recognised one of the Colonels as 'Philippe', whom he had met on Stromboli. And the other—

Conrad's head whipped round and he stared after the departing King and party.

'We got a message to his Majesty . . .'

Tullio's voice was a barely audible undertone.

'. . . That's Colonel Étienne wearing the fancy dress as his Emperorship. Won a game of mora. The other colonel will stay as his aide, and stick with him in the royal box. Never mind waiting for the Sinfonia – I've ordered a coach parked outside the stage door, now, and we'll be gone while Old Squeaky's still practising his entrance aria!'

'That's no way to refer to Giambattista Velluti.' Conrad with difficulty kept a straight face. 'You're checking the royal box because . . .'

'Because the big boss wants to know his colonels can get out of there when the shit starts flying.'

Conrad had met officers like that. *If the Emperor is one of them, it accounts for a lot about his rise to power.*

Turning back, Conrad discovered Philippe and his companion 'Colonel' gazing across the bay at Vesuvius. He made sure he greeted them with every sign of respect.

'You people of Italy, you are always mad!' The Emperor made a wide gesture, that seemed to imply approval, and concluded with a flourish at the distant crater. 'The earth turning crazy under your feet, and you don't even notice it. Bravo!'

Conrad couldn't help but follow the gesture. The haze that shrouded the top of the mountain might be catching light from the mid-morning sun, lifting up the arc of the sky – or it might be lit internally by some seepage of lava. From here it was impossible to say.

A jolt of the quay sent Tullio's coach horses half-rearing, the grooms at their heads clinging on and soothing them.

Wistfully, the Emperor said, 'I wish I could stay to see your opera.'

'Yes, sire,' Conrad agreed, dazed.

'We agreed, Imperial Majesty,' the other colonel observed mildly.

'We did, I know, Philippe; no need for all of that. I am your commander, not your Emperor. We have known each other too long.' The Emperor of the North hugged his subordinate.

Conrad suspected, from how the other man took it, that this happened quite often.

'We should go into the theatre, sire,' Conrad ventured.

'Of course!'

Conrad could see how difficult it was for the remaining colonel, Philippe, to avoid a subordinate position to his companion. Conrad ushered them towards the back entrances of the San Carlo, eyes alert for watchers. Tullio sidled up close.

Conrad muttered, 'If everything goes this much according to plan, this will be the first easy thing to happen today!'

'So what's been happening?'

'Luigi can fill you in on the details. I can't stay away from the dress rehearsal now – shouldn't be doing it for even this amount of time.' Conrad braced his mental strength. 'Briefly: we found our traitors. Roberto, Conte di Argente. Leonora, Contessa di Argente.'

Tullio Rossi stopped dead.

A momentary glint of light made his expression unclear; either fear or fury. He jerked back into motion, approaching the back-stage doors.

'And you believe it, padrone?'

Conrad's thumb found a small scar left on his hand by flying glass. It still bled slightly when rubbed. 'I was the one who discovered it. You won't believe how much has changed here in the last twenty-four hours.'

He passed significant details on to Tullio while they infiltrated the cramped wooden corridors in the upper floors of the San Carlo, entered at the rear of the royal box, and the two colonels – one indefinably in the lead – examined it from a tactical viewpoint.

'So . . . Let me get this straight,' Tullio said thoughtfully, removing his tricorne hat and scratching at his shaven head. He squinted at Conrad's face, where – Conrad hoped – Sandrine's stage make-up covered the black eye.

'So, Il Superbo came in and found you two kissing like two hogs eating the same banana—'

'Tullio!'

467

'—But it's not the composer who's the main traitor, it's the composer's creepy dead wife?'

'Leonora is not creepy!'

Tullio looked him up and down. 'Padrone – you're a lunatic.'

'After all these years, this comes as a surprise to you?' Conrad wryly quoted the Latin tag he had adopted as his own at the age of sixteen. '*Aut insanit homo, aut versus facit!*'

Tullio glared.

'The Roman poet Horace.' Conrad smiled. '"That man's either mad, or he's composing verses!"'

The ex-soldier watched the two colonels arranging lines of exit from various seats. He shuffled forward, towards the front of the box, and Conrad realised Tullio was looking out into the empty auditorium. But not at the gilded coat of arms of the King of the Two Sicilies, or at the chandelier, quivering from tremors too small for the human body to feel.

Tullio's intent gaze picked out the figures on stage, where a slim figure led one of the chorus singers to her correct mark by the hair.

He wants to speak with Paolo, of course.

'Minute or two, now,' Tullio murmured, his tone all business. 'My friend and me will be going down to the coach, and leaving Napoli. You sure you won't come with me? What you told me about Il Superbo . . . We been out-paced at every stage, it looks like. You and Paolo ought to come.'

Conrad gripped the other man's hand hard.

'If I could, I would, I promise. I need to stay here. Paolo's conducting – I wouldn't leave that to the second violin, or Roberto.' He winced. It remained natural to call the Count by his given name. 'And it looks like I'm going to be fixing the libretto and rehearsing them past the point where the curtain goes up.'

Tullio folded his arms, glaring sullenly down at the figure behind the forte-piano.

'I still don't like it that I'm leaving you behind – still less so now we know Il Conte di Argente is one of the Prince's Men. Bloody arrogant bastard! If the man has betrayed his cause, you can't trust him!'

'You can trust him to do everything a betrayed man would do.' Conrad hoped his hot neck and ears were not visibly pink. 'Take a minute while the Colonel gets settled in his coach. Come and see Isaura.'

It took very little time to be done with the royal box after that. The Emperor was escorted outside by Philippe, and Conrad indicated to Tullio the young man in a brown cutaway coat and dishevelled linen cravat, walking away from the violin section.

Tullio deferentially approached the opera's first violin and conductor, and Conrad took up a place further down the wall so that they might finish in peace. Paolo gave his cherub-blush, after a few minutes, and slipped back off into the auditorium.

'He says he has to conduct,' Tullio Rossi murmured, rejoining Conrad. He gazed after Paolo, seeming perplexed as she joined Roberto Capiraso at the forte-piano.

For a man who changed sides in a fit of pique, the Conte di Argente appeared to be working the others – and himself – to death rehearsing the new material.

Does he now hate his wife that much?

'We've arranged a rendezvous at the coast a bit north of here,' Tullio remarked quietly. 'Don't know if I can make it back before the end of *L'Altezza.*'

That bothered him, Conrad could see.

'I'll do my best. Corrado . . .' Tullio's questioning was discreet. 'Will we know what's happening at the Anfiteatro before I go?'

Conrad shrugged, digging down into himself for hope. 'They must have stopped her. Surely. If that was the right place. It's been nearly two hours.'

'Touching faith in humanity you got there, padrone.' Tullio couldn't restrain a grin. He looked resoundingly like some *masnadiere*.

Conrad accompanied him back to the coach. It was not entirely surprising that they found Luigi Esposito in conversation with the colonels.

'Luigi will know.'

'Yes, but do we have anything to barter for gossip?'

Conrad gave an acknowledging smirk.

469

With a civil-seeming farewell, Luigi Esposito left the foreigners and ambled back across the yard, all apparent ease.

Conrad suddenly realised that the police captain's white-gloved hands were clasped behind him, almost clenched into fists.

Conrad abandoned any idea of joking. 'News?'

Luigi Esposito swept the open back yard of the San Carlo with his gaze – Colonel Philippe and the false 'Colonel Étienne' tactfully stood discussing the coach horses, as men will – and came back to Conrad.

'Nothing. Nothing, Corrado. In the past hour, everything's gone dead.' If Luigi's expression seemed untroubled, his eyes were deeply uneasy. 'No rider from Commendatore Mantenucci. No messengers from any of Alvarez's captains. Nothing observed from the campaniles. Since they passed through the Grotto of Posillipo, it's as if over a hundred men have just vanished.'

'*Che cazzo!*' Conrad found himself patting the dapper man's shoulder in unaccustomed consolation. 'If they have got into a fight – it's far more likely that messengers have gone astray. The roads are bad out that way. Give it an hour before you panic.'

Luigi Esposito raised a groomed eyebrow. 'I'll panic when I please, thank you, Corradino!'

He nonetheless returned the clasp of Conrad's hand.

Tullio Rossi gave the police captain a respectful nod as Luigi left. 'Speaking of time, I need to be going.'

Conrad consulted his watch. '*Merda!* Three hours at best before curtain up! I have to get back inside.'

He put his hands on Tullio's shoulders, aware of the tension through the older man's body, and knew it to be partly the Emperor's arranged escape, and partly the same thoughts that Conrad found himself subject to, too often now, about any of his friends.

Is this the last time we'll see each other?

He embraced Tullio, with all his strength; the other man thumping him on his back like a brother, with a force that left Conrad breathless.

'I don't like leaving you here!' Tullio sullenly muttered, breaking free. 'And you can't trust her, wherever she's gone. You know that, don't you? *Minchia!* Why am I bothering—'

470

'I know I can't trust her!'

Tullio Rossi turned and walked towards the front of the coach. He picked up his coach-whip, and threw a handful of coins to the boys holding the horses. Conrad widened his strides to keep up with him, and grabbed Tullio's elbow before the older man could climb up into the box.

'I know,' Conrad protested. 'Trust me!'

'I trust you to do what I'd do if it was Paolo.' The older man rested the loop of his whip against Conrad's shoulder. 'Fight it tooth and nail, and keep looking for something that doesn't make her the cunt it looks like she is. Right?'

A tremor ran through Conrad's body, as if the distant caldera echoed his emotion.

'You know me far too well.' He managed to look Tullio in the face. 'It's gone beyond not trusting her. Every word that she's said to me since she came to Naples is a lie. Every word in Venice.'

Tullio Rossi smiled, almost wistfully. 'If you do meet her again – don't let her lie to you again.'

Quite how unlikely he was ever to speak to Nora hit Conrad with the force of knuckles in the kidneys. He was wordless. Then:

'Tullio, if you're able to come back here in the next few hours, then do. If not, run. Either way, I trust you to end up in one piece.'

Tullio wrung Conrad's hand with emphatic strength, and mounted nimbly up to the driver's box. The boys loosed the horses's heads; the tip of the whip cracked at the leader's ear. Conrad watched through the skirl of dust as, with a creak of the wooden coach-frame and the scrape of iron-rimmed wheels, the Emperor of the North began his escape from the Kingdom of the Two Sicilies.

Tullio grinned crookedly and shouted back to Conrad:

'Be well, Corrado! Don't forget! If you die doing this, I'll hurt you.'

◆

He missed curtain-up.

He had slipped out of the rehearsal rooms fifteen minutes

before, into the uplifting brilliancy of the San Carlo's auditorium. The tiers of opera boxes overpowered him, all six floors full of the nobility and important officials who owned them. Not a few had snuffed out their candles to see the bright stage the better. The blue and gold interior of the royal box filled up fast; Ferdinand shaking hands with nobles, dignitaries, and ambassadors; their wives in jewel-coloured dresses and white diamonds curtseying to show off their plump shoulders.

Conrad, down in the pit with the ordinary citizens of Naples – who gambled, gestured, and conversed at the tops of their voices – looked up at Colonel Étienne, beside King Ferdinand. Étienne appeared to be producing an excellent, over-emotional impression of his sovereign. Colonel Philippe looked as if he saved up the experience for recounting (with appropriate satisfaction) to the true Emperor.

Before anyone could ask Conrad what he was grinning at, he had pushed his way through the crowds and back into the theatre's private areas.

Tremors now ran irregularly through the building. The nerves of the principal singers appeared to respond in a similar manner. Principals, chorus, and those musicians chosen for the on-stage banda flowed through the narrow corridors and tiny staircases, past Conrad. In and out of dressing-rooms, with curses, trips, and panic kept down to a sacrilegious murmur.

'Corrado!' Sandrine squeaked. 'Hear that romanza? I have seven minutes before my entrance; I need you to hear the variations on my first aria!'

'You'll be fine, but of course.' Conrad stepped into one of the ancient rehearsal rooms with the mezzo.

He discovered his attention was not on Sandrine (true-voiced; holding back two thirds of her intensity for the performance) but on the Prince's Men.

Where are they? What are they doing? Do we have anything else to fear, over and above the black opera?

I'm waiting for the Prince's Men to make a significant attack on the San Carlo theatre.

A mechanical clock and a percussion cap would make a bomb.

472

Although as likely to blow them up as us—

Conrad tore his mind away from speculatory conversations in the cavalry mess, years ago. Sandrine – and then Estella, and then Lorenzo – needed his assistance, and he functioned as an amateur recitateur, hearing lines; and adjusted any part of the new verses that turned out to be unsingable.

JohnJack mastered the new stage business of breaking free from his guards – rather than being led off to prison – and springing between the Princess and King Charles of Spain. He still dropped his sword every time he drew it.

'*Merda!*'

Sandrine practised as the costumiers gave up and sewed her into her green and gold serpent-embroidered robe, since the buttons couldn't be set right in the time.

Brigida and Lorenzo fell out spectacularly and there was no opportunity to set it to music.

Like a sudden wave, an unexpected silence swept through the dark, crowded, cramped backstage areas.

Conrad's mouth went dry. He heard, in the distance, front of house, Paolo bringing the Sinfonia's first bars soaring up.

Dio! How could I miss it!

Soprano and mezzo chorus voices joined the intensity of the music. With a jolt, Conrad realised Velluti was gone from the rehearsal rooms – must already be at the back of the stage, mounting the placid white mare that would give him his *coup de théâtre* entrance.

Despite the muffling distance – stage flats, half-open doors, corridors stacked with ancient boxes there since Nero's time; the stifling warm bodies of the all-male chorus, tenor and baritone, massed to go on as Hernan Cortez's army – the audience's roar was clearly audible all through backstage.

'*Cazzo!*' Estella Belucci broke her costume's sword belt as she yanked it up a notch, proved that one can scream sotto voce, and strode off to prepare for her own entrance – in six minutes and thirty seconds – with her blade carried in her left hand.

'They'll just find her more convincing as an Amazon slave,' Lorenzo Bonfigli remarked as he shrugged the High Priest Mazatl's robes on over Captain Diego's mail shirt, ready for the quick change between Acts One and Two. 'Conrad, are you all right?'

Conrad put his hand on the wooden partition beside him, to keep himself aware of where he was.

The walls swam in his vision.

He staggered forward between stored stage flats, heading for the nearest door to the outside.

Lorenzo, following, called, 'Conrad?'

'*Minchia!*' One of Angelotti's crew swore them away from the ropes and creaking wood waiting in the deep backstage.

The cluttered storage areas seemed to go on infinitely. Conrad pushed on a heavy door, blind with pain and hope, and felt the warm air of the outside world flood over him.

One hand on the trunk of the umbrella pine growing in the yard supported him. He bent over and vomited up an interminable string of bile.

'Conrad?' Lorenzo looked garish out in the afternoon sun. The maquillage that would make him seem both South American and sinister on-stage was reduced to blotches of soot and rouge.

Conrad wiped at his forehead.

It was warm, damp, and, to his fingertips, oddly squashy.

That illusion gave him the answer. He blinked. Sliding diamonds of light still blocked much of his side vision. The warmth of growing pain crept up his neck and over the muscles of his skull, and began to pull inexorably tight.

Hemicrania.

Conrad put his hand down and touched dirt.

He was sitting on the dusty ground.

The sun filtered down through the pine and focused pain in the corner of his eye socket.

He had only the dimmest muscle memory of backing up against the outside wall of the San Carlo, and sliding down the peeling plaster facade to the earth.

Speaking made him wince. 'You needn't stay away from rehearsal—'

'Curtain's up so I'm done with rehearsing!' Lorenzo declared. 'Besides, I've got no new material until the finale ultimo. I'm on as Mazatl in ten minutes; until then – can I help? You look half dead, man!'

Conrad wiped his hands down his trousers, leaving dust on them as well as his tail-coat, and slid his fingers behind his neck-cloth, loosening it.

'There's nothing anyone can do.' He clenched his fist. *Of all times, why now—!*

Likely because it is now. This is the test. If the Aztec Princess *plays out uninterrupted, if it works in disrupting whatever the Prince's Men are trying to do, then this is when we win.*

Six weeks of effort and we win . . . if we win. No wonder I'm feeling the tension too.

If the fresh wind, with the city scents on it, was some relief, the light in the sky was anything but analgesic.

'At least come in and listen. It'll take your mind off it.' Lorenzo Bonfigli didn't say take your mind off your hangover, but his suspicion was easily read on his face. He still offered Conrad a hand.

Conrad closed his eyes briefly, feeling he wanted neither interruption nor pity.

'You go in. Tell them I'm recovering from some form of self-indulgence. I'll be in shortly.'

Lorenzo's expression showed relief, when Conrad looked up at him. *At hearing what he thinks is the truth.*

'Oh, lord knows we've all done that!' Lorenzo looked both kind and forgiving. The tenor cocked his head, listening, and nodded to himself. 'I have to go; I'm almost on. I'll send one of the lads out if you're not back in by the end of the aria. You're all right here?'

'Yes.' Conrad forced a smile, though he dared not nod. 'You – scene six, the chest high C, remember—?'

Lorenzo beamed at the encouragement and proclaimed his creed: 'For the tenor, the note of the future!'

The felt-lined heavy door closed behind Bonfigli.

Conrad was aware of all the men and women he couldn't see, through that door, moving at a dangerous half-run in the dimness. He would have given much to be in the cool, with the draughts blowing through the back stage storage areas. His body feared the pain of collision more than the afternoon sun.

More than the intrusive sounds from beyond the yard wall: the sound of the sea, human voices, horse-drawn coaches – even with straw put down in the street outside, to muffle the noise of the wheels during performance.

Conrad put one hand up to soothe the left side of his face. The ball of his eye flickered behind his fingers, the eyelid feeling hot and dry.

I can ignore this; work through it! I need to see L'Altezza azteca *play on stage – through to the finale ultimo . . .*

Frustration vied in him with nausea. He leaned over behind the pine and vomited, twice more.

The first – the only – significant performance of The Aztec Princess *and I'm out here!*

Self-contempt washed through him, and frustration and shame. His body must have tensed.

All emotion and thought vanished. Pain jerked exponentially higher, as if all the joints and ligaments of his spine were washed in fire. Heat forked and infiltrated along the top vertebrae of his spine: the Atlas, and then the Anvil—

To be able to name the site of pain is no help, when one only wants it to stop.

He was aware that faces appeared periodically; members of the backstage crew who had evidently been asked to check on him. *There is nothing to do with pain like this but endure it.* He cupped his hands over his eyes and watched the shadow of the umbrella pine move across the dust.

He had been through hemicrania with the pain untreated before, and was not surprised that he missed the first easing of the sensation. He was surprised – as much as he could muster surprise – when the pain did not drain away as it usually did, but only dropped to a mid-level.

The Aztec Princess, *for which I have worked like a man besotted for six weeks—*

—Is a faint crescendo of voices and orchestra. The only loud noise Conrad heard in the San Carlo's deserted back yard was a periodic roar from the audience.

Is it possible we're succeeding?

JohnJack shot out through the stage doors, all false dark beard and flashing bronze armour. 'You're missing it!'

A second man followed him out, also bearded, but genuine; slightly more self-restrained. Roberto Capiraso, Conte di Argente, composer of *L'Altezza azteca, ossia il serpente pennuto*. He frowned. 'I can hardly believe that you, of all people, could be late for— Oh.'

'Oh.' Conrad managed a sardonic echo, if in a somewhat creaky voice.

He forced away self-pity and contempt. *You're hardly the only one involved in this opera, Scalese.*

He gazed up at the two men. 'How are we doing?'

JohnJack dropped to sit beside him in the warm dust, hands linked over his knees, his position neither Aztec nor soldierly. 'You should see it!'

Roberto, still on his feet, blinked in what he evidently found to be startlingly bright sunlight. He put his head back in the cool air, inhaling. 'We have a success!'

Conrad frowned. And winced at the pain from that. 'It's too early to tell.'

'No! It's not.' JohnJack waved a hand at Roberto for confirmation. 'I heard them!'

Roberto Capiraso nodded, slowly. 'Two encores for Sandrine's trio with Velluti and GianGiacomo, here. All three of them made it gripping.'

Spinelli inclined his head in appreciation of Roberto's compliment. 'And Brigida and 'Stella! The pit stood up and cheered *"Onore e gloria!"'*

Roberto Capiraso's sombre features altered into a schoolboy grin. 'And they were *singing along* to the Amazon duet!'

JohnJack was all but shaking hands with himself. '*Dio!* I thought they were going to storm the palace when Belucci started singing for her liberty! I saw journalists, Corrado. We might yet see a review in *Il Giornale del Regno delle Due Sicilie*. For the singers, the composer, the librettist!'

477

All these factors are essential, Conrad thought dreamily. *But would be nothing without the great beast that is the audience's attention – charmed, enchanted, aroused, and made desolate and ecstatic, in turn.*

I need to be in there – to be part of it.

He put his hand against the wall for support, got to his feet, and straightened up.

Nausea overtook him immediately with the blackening and swimming of his vision. His abdominal muscles cramped up, sore with the effort of vomiting. Pain swamped all else.

When he could think again, JohnJack and Roberto were one each side of him, supporting him under the arms.

'Last time I saw him like this, he was in bed for three days,' JohnJack said absently. 'I wish I knew where Rossi was. He can usually make him comfortable.'

Conrad heard his own voice scratchy and faint. 'I'm not ill!'

Identical voiceless looks met him from JohnJack and Roberto.

'Right,' Spinelli said, after a pause. 'My dressing room is just about big enough to lay down in. There's bound to be a doctor here; I'll find one as soon as the interval comes.'

Their efforts to help him brought sickening pain. Conrad managed, at last, to walk unsupported, allowing himself to be guided inside and towards the dressing rooms. Because it would have required argument – painful argument, on his side – to prevent it.

'Fuck!' JohnJack exclaimed as they came into a better-lit area of the theatre's backstage. 'I'm going to miss my cue if I don't go now—'

'Go! Go!' The Conte di Argente released Conrad's arm. He took hold of the tall bass's shoulders, turned him towards the wings, and gave him a push.

Conrad leaned one shoulder against the wall. It gave him little relief, but it allowed him to look as if it did.

Roberto smiled crookedly. 'Can none of you remember I'm a traitor?'

That's right. Conrad was confused, but only for a moment. *Roberto's technically still under arrest.*

When the composer's introduced at the royal box, in the interval, all

478

the social highest and greatest will be flattering a criminal and a traitor without knowing it.

Here, in the opera house, while L'Altezza is taking them towards victory, it's almost impossible to remember that.

'The singers don't care,' Conrad got out through a jaw held stiff by hemicrania. 'Six weeks ago, they'd have lynched you for any hint you were associated with the Prince's Men. Now you're their composer. They trust the music. They trust you.'

'Trust!' Roberto gave a steadying grasp to Conrad's elbow.

'It'll be different once the opera's over.' Conrad hadn't realised he intended to speak that aloud. He caught Roberto's gaze.

'I know.'

Everything was plain in those two words. Conrad couldn't vocalise it, with pain blotting out his capacity to think, but he heard the man's willingness to be held accountable.

Roberto shook his head, as if he pushed the matter aside. 'Spinelli's right, you need to lie down. I think, however, that you need to see your work more.'

'Yes.' Pain made it difficult to manage more than the essential words. 'Thank you.'

Il Conte led the way, walking slowly enough that Conrad could keep up. He halted them between two of the stage flats, just out of sight of the audience.

Several of the stage hands were gathered there, watching. A good sign, Conrad thought.

'You don't know which side I'm on,' Roberto Capiraso muttered, in a voice that didn't carry beyond the two of them. 'Whether I want *L'Altezza* to work, or *Il Reconquista*. I don't know which side I'm on—'

'Hers.' Conrad pushed past the fiery discomfort to murmur. 'Nora. If she turned nun tomorrow, you'd be applying to be one of the Holy Father's Cardinals the day after.'

Roberto's lips twisted. He seemed not to know if he were amused or outraged.

A score of armour-clad men swept off stage, Velluti at their head; passing Conrad and the composer as if they hadn't seen them – which, in the dark between the flats, they very well might not. Fifteen feet away from the audience's sight-line, they began to struggle into the leopard-kilts and obsidian spears of the Princess Tayanna's guard.

Applause for their previous singing swept up over Conrad like a wave up shingle. He had to close his eyes and put his hands over his ears. Pain whited out the world.

Breathing raggedly, he uncovered his ears.

Beside him, Roberto Capiraso looked utterly bleak.

'Scalese, I don't know what could happen if Nora succeeds in "raising the Prince of the World", "changing the mind of God", whatever she meant by that. I can't help thinking she'll be a lot safer if she *doesn't*.'

Roberto's eyes glinted in reflected light.

'I find myself hoping that the King will capture her. That would be kinder than the Prince's Men, if they decide that she's failed them.'

I'd like to reassure you, Conrad found himself feeling, to his own surprise. His thoughts were as slow as mud. *To say: 'a company of expert riflemen are on the Burning Fields, along with Commendatore Mantenucci and the police; they'll have her safe as a prisoner—'*

But then I'd have to tell you what Luigi said. That no message has come back from them, yet.

'I hope Ferdinand's men do have her.' It was all Conrad could manage, through pain and confusion.

Movement snagged his eye.

From this angle in the wings he could just see Isaura, beyond the tin cones shading the candles on the music stands. Paolo-Isaura shook back her short, shaggy hair; white cravat and dark blue coat setting off her pale face perfectly. He made out the profiles of violinists and oboists, all turned towards her; the stage's candle-light reflected in the percussionist's cymbals, and glimmering on the coils of French horns. Each man – and they were all men – looked to Paolo for guidance.

If they knew she was Isaura—

How dare any man think less of my sister because she's not my brother?

She raised her baton.

The light made water gather and run down Conrad's face. He

clapped a hand over his sensitised eyes. The orchestra struck up a melody of winding complexities for the woodwind – the first bars of which they had messed up for weeks now – and performed it flawlessly.

Every ligament and tendon stiff with pain, body held perfectly still against the agony of movement, Conrad still found his mind prompting him with the exact score. *We're coming up on the other extended trio: JohnJack, Lorenzo, and Estella.*

Very carefully, he took his hands from his face. He saw, through wet eyelashes, the converging brilliant figures of the conspiring High Priest and seduced Lord General, and the eavesdropping Amazon slave-girl. Only a dozen yards away on stage, where dust lifted up from between the boards at every step – *and, at the same time, half a world and five hundred years distant.*

A sound too loud to be heard splintered the air.

✦

Something blazing and thick with black smoke smashed down through the ceiling of the auditorium. It vaporised the legendary chandelier of the Teatro San Carlo.

The missile exploded against the far wall of opera boxes.

All the space inside the auditorium shuddered, with the shock and violence of artillery-shot. Men and women in fine clothing spilled out of the opera boxes, into the empty air – falling—

Clothes, and the curtains of the boxes, caught fire.

Flame leaped up the tiers of seating, up to the galleries exposed to the air—

Conrad seized at his head, pain blazing along every suture of his skull. Human sound cut the smoky air, ripping into him. The squeal of benches forced across floors – the pounding thud of feet pushing past their neighbour – voices going up in shrieks, shouts—

As if every one of three thousand men and women struggled, shoved, fought for the exits—

Plaster sheeted down. Splintered wood bounced down and hit the stage.

Internal and external pain met.

481

The stage floor shook under Conrad's feet, lifting him. Floorboards flipped up over joists. He threw out his arms instinctively, catapulted forward—

Plummeting into agony, on his back, half-off the front edge of the stage—

High over his head, the domed roof of the Teatro San Carlo opened in a lethal flower of marble, brick, and rubble.

46

Everything under Conrad jolted and unsteadily vibrated. A grinding sensation reverberated in his bones.

Darkness slammed down.

Conrad clawed, enveloped thickly. Something blinded him; robbed him of air. He thrashed with unconstrained violence. Encumbrance, and the pain of migraine, sent him into true panic.

Sudden light.

The sear and crack of lightning iced the world with white.

Conrad rolled out of entangling, choking cloth.

He dropped a foot or so onto his back, hitting wooden planks with his shoulder-blades and the back of his skull. The blast of pain seared so strongly that he bit his tongue, and spat red, swearing blasphemously.

Dazzled, the sensation of touch told him the cloth in his hands was velvet.

The blue stage curtain that collapsed when the house shook.

Conrad broke out in a sudden, painful, coughing laugh. 'Fuck—!'

Scenery flats leaned crazily overhead. Ceiling and floor shook and jolted, in a series of violent knocks. The stage stood up broken – boards tilted crazily up – trapdoor entrances gaping blackly to the cellars. Sprawled bodies lay among rubble. Fleeing figures ran crazily here and there, screaming.

Pain filled his vision with black sparkles.

483

Noise stampeded past him. *Men making for the exit?* Fire and black ash leaped up drapes, scenery, a woman's long skirts. A boot landed squarely on his chest.

A choked-off scream took all his breath.

Squinting, he found he could see no more than ten or fifteen feet in any direction. A yellow-grey haze filled the opera house.

Is it fire?

Is something wrong with my eyes?

Everything hurt. Every part of his body.

But everything hurt before.

There was no blood.

As well as the hemicrania, his head and back felt physically bruised, as if beaten with clubs.

Conrad rubbed at his eye-sockets savagely, until tears ran and cleared dust out of his eyes.

Weak sunlight drifted in through the hole in the theatre's roof.

In the vast open air, where there should be song and music, something pale and grey sifted down.

In England, where it snows more often than here, they have long sunset winter twilights. Such a change from the latitudes where the sun drops into darkness in a matter of minutes. This light is exactly like such a twilight, on a day when it has snowed, and most things are lost in grey, but a few colours are resolvable.

Snow falls white, but, when thick, makes the air look yellow with its fall. This, that falls now, might be snow . . . or smoke . . .

Not a fault of the eye: something occupied the air. *But* – he managed to get up onto his knees – *not smoke either.* The gusts of smoke from the burning were black.

I can smell something . . . something else. No idea what. No, I do know!

A child, in Catania, scrambling up the moorland far enough to catch the taint of it on the wind. Sulphur, and lava, and a flat chemical tang. The smell of volcanic activity.

Conrad caught grey foam on his palm, feeling it dusty and warm – and it was ash, he realised.

Vesuvius.

The ability to form thoughts returned to him along with the access to memory.

484

Vesuvius.

Is this . . .

He reached automatically for the emotional atmosphere of musicodramma and it was shattered.

Whatever L'Altezza azteca *was doing – is gone.*

Is this the Prince's Men's victory?

Vaffanculo! *It must be! They can't have been stopped, or the eruption wouldn't be happening!*

Part of him demanded: *How much time since – this – happened?* The rest of his mind obsessively chanted: *We lost, they won, we lost, they won—*

Distant screams came from the upper tiers of boxes.

Brick and rafters exploded into the air.

The floorboards under him thrummed like a harp. A dissonant crash raised clouds of dust; black rocks sprayed across the floor.

Conrad staggered onto his feet. Tremors lost him his balance. He fell to his knees, swung himself violently back up into a square-set crouch—

I have to get out!

A swirl of air – *no, sea wind* – blew inside the desolate building, clearing the haze far enough that Conrad could see from the stage to the exits.

The further wall still burned. If there were people there, Conrad could not see them.

I'm not shaking.

It's the earth that's shaking!

Something partially collapsed, behind him, in the deep back-stage. Clouds of dust and ash pushed out into the air.

Conrad crawled out from under the remains of the velvet and stood up. A quake shook him.

He found that he was facing that part of the auditorium that housed the orchestra.

It was buried under rubble, planks, and the end of an avalanche of bricks stretching up to the first floor boxes. Dust swirled over it, and flickering fires.

His mind still moving like syrup in winter, Conrad only came up with . . . *Isaura?*

'Isaura! Paolo!'

For all his force, his voice didn't penetrate the ash cloud wrapped around him. He choked, his mouth dry and dusty.

'Isaura!'

Nothing.

He would have thrown himself on Roberto to strangle him, but the other man was not there.

The building shuddered.

Conrad staggered one step towards the auditorium, and froze.

He dared not cross that open space under the uncertain roof.

Stay away from the fire; go out the back way!

He turned.

Pain slopped around in him like water in a bucket. All he could do was clench his jaw and push himself onwards.

The broken stage shuddered under him.

He became conscious of distant roaring, like the looms in English manufactories. The boards trembled under his feet.

He lurched forward, in a zigzag to-and-fro, like a man on deck in a hard sea. He tripped flat onto more swags of the fallen stage curtain.

His shins hurt where he'd fallen over some concealed obstacle.

Michele Angelotti's magnificent step-pyramid, he realised. Fallen now. It must have come within feet of crushing him where he originally stood.

He knelt up, hauled up the thick dusty velvet, and realised he was staring across the stage – what had been the stage – at one end of a diagonally-fallen roof-beam. The other end still perched somewhere up in the rafters, who knows how precariously balanced.

Under the fallen beam lay the body of a slight man in an Aztec robe and bronze head-dress, half-hidden by the cubit-thick wood. The roof-beam had smashed down, one end of it embedded into his hip and chest. His white robe was sopping red. Bone showed under broken metal armour, and pink guts spilled out of a body-cavity.

His dead face was undamaged.

Lorenzo!

Conrad thought dazedly, *Leave aside the chest-voice high C and*

Lorenzo Bonfigli was probably the weakest singer among our principals. But he was generous when he sang; he never minded the person with him looking good. I never in six weeks heard anyone speak badly of him.

Conrad clamped down on his sensitivities and knelt – swaying – to examine the body. He checked for a heartbeat and wiped the man's face. A touch to his naked eyeball got no result.

It was a relief to find that Lorenzo wasn't breathing. *What in God's name could anyone do with him if he was still alive?*

Diego's medieval armour was visible under Mazatl's white robe, but it hadn't saved him.

Someone should take care of his body, but I can't move him.

Conrad climbed to his feet, not sure if he or the building swayed.

And . . . he won't be the only one.

I need to get out of here before all the roof falls in.

Two yards away, at what must be the very back of the stage area, the church-choir tenor who sang in the chorus of Aztec citizens lay with his head smashed open. Conrad pushed himself back up onto his feet. Texture warned him – he glanced back, and down.

He had one heel on Michele Angelotti's yellow curls.

Angelotti's body's head flopped back when he touched it, neck broken.

He balanced upright on the juddering stage, and saw Estella Belucci on her back. Still on her stage mark. A fine layer of yellow grit covered the mark, the stage, and Estella.

Surely one's alive. Conrad picked his way across the shuddering planks.

Her hand felt warm. Her stage make-up was covered in a layer of fine white ash.

So were her open eyes.

His hand came out bloody from under the back of her head. Her skull felt like shattered eggshells in a bag.

Something creaked above him – the sound of wood under strain.

He released Estella and straightened up.

It cracked and let go.

Conrad flung himself forward. Rafters thundered down from

487

the theatre roof. He fell into a backstage corridor and sprinted for the doors.

Knocking one aside, already half off its hinges, he tripped and pitched full-length on the ground.

The impact stunned him. He rolled forward. The ground trembled under his raw palms. He got up onto his knees.

'Corradino!'

A body hit him. He registered a soprano squeal; solid weight.

'Paolo? We have to get out of the building!'

Her frantic hands dragged him up onto his feet, still clinging to his coat. 'I thought you were dead! Where have you been? We *are* outside! It's no better!'

Conrad grabbed her shoulders – *for support*, he admitted, only to himself. Her blue tail-coat and breeches were uniformly dusty white. So was her hair, and her face, except where blood had run down her cheek and dried. He clutched at her. *No obvious wound—*

He evidently had tumbled out through the San Carlo's stage doors, into the yard at the back.

But it might as well be indoors!

A pale yellow-white ceiling swirled overhead. No sun, no clouds, no blue sky. The buildings close to the Teatro stood shrouded as if by snow.

Those that stood.

Continuous tremors shook grey snow from tree branches, windowsills, balconies.

The world looked as if it lay shrouded not in snow, but in drift upon drift of Pozzuoli's concrete. The road, under the bombardment of thousands of small rocks, might as well have been a stream-bed, black and steaming as if a dragon laired under it.

The thought of underground fire, of Pozzuoli, gave him an instant answer.

He seized Isaura's wrist as she raised her hand to her face.

She gave him a look of utter confusion.

'I saw this through the King's microscope.' Conrad coughed. 'He has samples from the Pompeii eruption. Don't rub your eyes. It isn't ash from a fire, the way you'd think of it. It's splintered glass.'

488

'Oh *Dio!*'

He didn't release her hand; the grip was familial and comforting.

The hiss and whoosh of artillery made him duck, pulling Isaura down with him.

The explosion landed too far away to be seen in these streets of high buildings, but he felt it.

Belatedly, he realised, *Not artillery. The volcano. Rocks.*

'Estella and Lorenzo are dead.' He scrutinised Isaura's face, feeling in her hair to discover where she bled. 'And Michele Angelotti. And, I forget his name, the chorus tenor who came from San Gennaro's.'

She could not be more white and shocked. She gripped both his hands. 'Corrado, come with me.'

'Where—?'

'Away from these buildings!' Paolo-Isaura pulled him towards the street. 'It's not safe anywhere in the streets! Buildings are collapsing! I've told anyone else I found to meet right out in the middle of the piazza. Away from everything.'

A riderless horse galloped past the San Carlo. Conrad caught sight of a team of coach horses dragging an over-turned coach. Down the street, another team pulled the shattered remains of a barouche; something trapped under it that looked like a bundle of old clothes.

Shouting and screaming filled the air: women, men, and children. Ash-fall flattened every sound.

'How long since—?'

His sister muttered, 'Vesuvius? I don't know—'

He no longer listened.

He staggered out into the wide piazza, away from the Teatro San Carlo and the Palace.

That will let me see.

'No, wait!' Paolo-Isaura clung to his arm, almost too heavy to be dragged, thin though she looked. 'We have to hide you—'

Conrad felt a sweat of cold fear on his neck, behind his ears, down his spine.

He had reason to be aware of every yard of the seven miles or so that separated Vesuvius's vast crater from the city. Twice that distance away at Cape Misenum, in the first century AD, Pliny had only been aware of a plume of smoke. Here . . .

He couldn't look away from the eruption cloud – black and purple, shot through with lightning, and appallingly *solid*. As if someone had turned on a powerful jet of earth and let it blast into the sky, *straight up—*

To look at the *top* of the eruption cloud, he tipped his head back far enough for his neck to crick, and his vertebrae to spurt pain across his neck, skull, and eye-sockets. Mesmerised, he stared up at the towering stream of cloud, ash and rock that jetted up towards the sky. Great cumulus clouds of ash rolled straight up out of the summit. The sun shone down on the black clouds and cast shadows of the eruption plume on the slopes.

Spills of ash ran down the steep sides of the cone. Black earth sprayed up in what must be titanic quantities, to be visible in Naples itself. The solid-looking clouds rolled up in a pillar of ash, red at the base, now, and white at the very edges.

Conrad craned his head back, staring up, heart in his mouth. Lightning zagged across the rising ash-plume.

At some certain height – he could not even guess how far above the earth – the thundering pillar of ash ceased to jet upwards, and began to spread out. Tendrils of cloud reached across the sky, groping towards Naples itself. The spreading umbrella cloud would be invading villages and towns all around the slopes – but for some reason he could not take his eyes off the monster invading the coastline and sea between himself and the mountain. The shape of an umbrella pine – and its furthest reaching arms were shedding a black rain that became a white snow where it was backed by buildings or hills. *Falling ash . . .*

The earth continually quaked and shuddered underfoot. He wrapped his arms tightly around his sister, his chin resting on the top of her head.

'We can't stay here.' Isaura's voice came muffled from his jacket.

The last remnants of snow showed white on the mountain's summit, despite the late spring day below in Naples. Thunderheads of fluid rock rolled up from the mouth of the crater. Great bolts of Galvanic power arced from one part of the rising plume to the next – so loudly Conrad swore he could hear it over every scream, sob, and shattering quake that shook down churches and tenements alike. He felt it more in his chest and gut than heard it with his ears.

He felt a twist of cold fear. *How am I supposed to protect her from this?*

'We failed,' he said bleakly, hugging Paolo closer, and feeling her grip on him tighten. 'This is what they wanted. Naples is their blood sacrifice.'

47

Paolo took her face out of his coat. Tears left runnels in the grey ash sticking to her cheeks.

It will at least sluice the volcanic ash out of her eyes, Conrad thought.

She put both hands to his coat collar and yanked it up.

He hissed, knocked her arms away automatically, and swore at the fire of hemicrania stiffening his neck and skull with pain.

'What are you doing!'

'We have to hide you!'

Standing under the spreading eruption plume of Vesuvius, Conrad wondered, mundanely, *Have I gone as mad as I feel?*

'Hide? Me?'

He couldn't help equal sarcasm landing on each word.

'Out in the piazza, they're fighting – the men that came out of the pit are just a mob! Some are terrified and some are furious—'

Her voice rose. She made a visibly arduous effort at control.

'Corrado, for Our Lady's sake, don't let anyone know you're the poet of the opera!'

Pain made him sharp. 'What?'

'I heard them talking. They're all saying it was you that made this happen!'

Conrad stared, so taken aback that he forgot to be terrified.

Paolo-Isaura gestured at the ruined Palazzo.

'They're saying that your *Terrore di Parigi* got the Teatro Nuovo

492

struck by lightning and now your *L'Altezza azteca* has made Vesuvius erupt!'

'But— But!'

'First the Teatro Nuovo and now the San Carlo— It makes sense to them!'

'But—! But the black opera—!'

'They don't know there's another opera!'

Irony left him temporarily speechless.

I'm to be blamed for this. For what the Prince's Men have done—!

Paolo tugged at his cuff. 'I saw some of the others get out. Keep your head down! I can get us to them without being seen.'

Conrad flinched. The volcano's eruption grew louder and more violent. A sound like artillery split the air.

Before he thought, he was crouched down behind the wall at the back of the San Carlo, Paolo held in his arms and sheltered by his body. Two, three, four explosions sounded. He tilted his head up and caught sight of a burning rock hurtling down. It buried itself somewhere streets beyond, but he felt the shock of its explosion.

'Sweet Jesus!' Paolo yelped. He looked down to see her eyes wide. She muttered, 'Now it's throwing rocks at us! Let's go!'

Conrad scrambled up. He put his arm around her shoulder and gave her a quick squeeze, and then turned his coat collar up as high as he could, his cravat pushed up over his chin.

The ash in the air smeared his fingers—would be in his hair, he realised. *I probably look fifty if I'm a day!*

No one will recognise young Signore Scalese.

'Let's go.'

'This way!' Paolo caught his hand, and pulled.

Conrad followed her, running over the rock-strewn, uneven earth towards the front of the Palazzo Reale.

His feet thumped against the stone paving. Rock-bombs detonated above him: air-bursts that made him flinch, and swear at the fire of migraine inflaming every nerve in his body. He bashed his shoulder into one running man, and almost tripped over another.

'Cor— Brother!' Paolo corrected herself.

Conrad pinched the wing of his nostril, and the sharp, different pain did what he hoped. His eyes watered and ran, and he blinked away tears and ash. 'I'm with you.'

A skewer of pain pressed into his right eye, and made him absent from the world of fire and black smoke. He followed Paolo, her coat grey now with falling ash. He felt the continual vibration of the ground, and the rattle of falling brickwork. Skirting the edges of the crowds took him closer to the Palace, under the second-floor balcony from which the Kings of the Sicilies gave their speeches.

A decorative stone pilaster separated from the balcony and smashed down on the piazza. Conrad grabbed Isaura around the body and hurried her forward, at moments lifting her off her feet; coughing as they kicked up almost weightless ash.

He glanced back once, at the San Carlo's roof, cracked open like an egg.

In numb realisation, he thought, *Whatever we created – it's gone.*

With all the irony of a fourth-act reversal, Conrad's betraying body eased. He felt his muscles unlock from frozen spasm. A warmth of relief spread through his nerves, and left a sluggishness behind.

Vaffanculo! *Why now? Why not before?*

A gust of hot wind met him as they ran out into the open space of the great square.

Conrad clamped his handkerchief to his mouth. He heard Isaura wheeze, trying to breathe in the choking air. *And I hoped it might be better close to the water!*

Paolo abandoned his side, pounding forward across the unpaved earth.

Conrad's heart jumped in his chest.

He raked the bedraggled, bright group of people with an instantaneously encompassing gaze – Sandrine, green and gold costume covered in ash, handing something over to Paolo—an instrument-case, he saw—and JohnJack in close discussion with Brigida Lorenzani and Velluti. Brigida's plump face shone purple with exertion. At her shoulder – *wonders!* – the Conte di Argente.

Roberto caught his eye. Under his neat but dusty beard, his lips moved in a small cynical smile.

Yes, I thought you'd run, Conrad mentally admitted. *Yes, I thought you'd be with Nora by now, no matter what—*

It was actually good to see Roberto, Conrad realised, dumbfounded. *I suppose I'm – well – glad he's not dead.*

He was dimly aware of Giambattista Velluti, babbling apologies for his truncated performance. Seeing Brigida, JohnJack, Sandrine, and Velluti – Conrad found he couldn't help but look around for Lorenzo and Estella.

His eyes stung, and not with the ash.

With the skill learned on battlefields, he pushed the thoughts aside, mopped his streaming eyes, and looked up.

And up.

Now he was clear of the buildings, he could see clear across to the volcano – or as clear as the ash allowed. He could not see the top of the eruption cloud over Naples. It was over his head, for all they must be seven miles from its base. Spikes of lightning shattered back and forth across the black column, lighting up great cavernous mouths in the clouds—

Miles above him – miles above whatever heights the French military Observation Corps had reached in their balloon-flights – the black and violet cloud mushroomed out.

Red lightning flashed in its depths.

Smoke and ash thundered up from Vesuvius, still climbing, still shaking the earth and the sea like a terrier shakes a rat—

Nothing much of Naples beyond this piazza was visible. He could just see through the white ash-fog, to men and women screaming through the streets, pulling their children and wagons containing their lives behind them.

Conrad felt his palms sting. He realised his nails had bitten into the skin.

He stared back at the root of the huge black column, ash and smoke and fire still rising, darkening the afternoon sky. Soft whiteness sleeted down on the waves.

Air rasped in his throat, smelling of stone. His ribs felt heavy. He took a hand away from his mouth, and saw blood and ash on his knuckles.

'Corrado! Paolo found you!'

Ferdinand strode across the square in a thunder of bright uniforms: his personal guard of riflemen. The singers let him have precedence.

'I was afraid you'd died in there, Conrad.'

'Is it safe for you to be out here, sir? I'm told I'm responsible for this, and you hired me.'

'You, responsible? Oh! After the Teatro Nuovo . . .'

Ferdinand looked amused, for a moment, as Conrad had hoped he might.

The weight of desolation came back into his expression. The King of the Two Sicilies glanced around. 'Some of my bell-tower spies might be able to find me if they can see me . . .'

Conrad had an idea he knew exactly what the King thought. *We've lost Naples, and we don't even have the consolation of beating the Prince's Men . . .*

Paolo popped up beside him, instrument case clutched to her chest. *Alfredo's!* he realised. Conrad brushed dust off the case of their father's violin. He rested his arm around Paolo's shoulders.

The thought that insinuated itself into the shock of the last hour made its way into speech, without him having to think about it.

'Sir, do you think the Prince's Men have won what they want?'

Nothing but darkness rose in the east. Ferdinand turned his head to look west, towards the afternoon sun, and Pozzuoli, and the Burning Fields. The golden light showed every crease in the skin around his eyes; far too many for a man not yet thirty-five.

'Conrad, after this—' Ferdinand squinted at the desolation, where the houses of Naples ran out towards the Posillipo road. The sun made something beautiful of the ash-cloud sleeting down.

'But I expected worse.' Conrad didn't know the truth of it until he said it aloud. 'Yes, this is bad. It's the end of the city of Naples, like Pompeii, but . . .'

Conrad gazed west, in the direction of the Campi Flegrei.

No eruptions there.

'Have we won?' he suggested cautiously. 'Because of us, is this all the black opera could do?'

'"All" is hardly the word,' the King snapped.

Like the first silence of snow, ash flattened the distant roar of the eruption plume. Naples emitted no sound at all except human voices, and collapsing and burning buildings.

'I expected worse,' Conrad repeated. 'When Nora said she was going to call up the Prince of this World . . .'

Roberto gave his old sneer. 'I assure you, if you had won, you would know about it! As for "gods" . . .'

Another quake of the ground made Conrad almost lose his footing. Something deep in his gut insisted the earth should not move. He tried to ignore that primitive part of him that spilled fear all through his body. 'Have neither of us succeeded, then?'

Roberto Capiraso chewed his lip. The man gazed towards the unseen Burning Fields, as if he did not stand in a city of fleeing thousands, with an opera company around him, and the King of the Two Sicilies glaring to demand an answer.

Conrad blinked dust from his eyes, wincing as an arc of afternoon light slashed through the eruption cloud. The sun in his eyes triggered realisation.

'It's still afternoon – not much past three, by the sun—' Conrad met Roberto's dark gaze, and saw confirmation there. 'The black opera's still playing! Aren't they? They haven't reached the end!'

'Assume that Leonora began at much the same time as the San Carlo—' Roberto finally nodded. 'They can't yet be beyond the start of Act Three.'

'Why are we debating this?' Ferdinand demanded.

'We can still stop her!' Conrad was not aware, until he found himself staring the angry monarch down, how desperate and determined he felt that – whatever it was Nora did – it should be stopped.

Ferdinand Bourbon-Sicily glared at Conrad; at the aides and theatre crew surrounding them. 'I want to know why Enrico and Alvarez haven't blown them to shreds, yet!'

This burning city has been Ferdinand's responsibility since he came to the age of reason. Conrad bit back a snarl.

'They may be dead,' he said gently. He suppressed the hacking cough that ash wanted to produce. 'Sir, I understand that you'd prefer arrest, or military action, but we know that, for some reason, that's already failed. What I'm thinking . . . We still don't

497

know what the black opera might do. But we do know where they are. Or Enrico and the Colonel wouldn't have disappeared.'

He pieced it together slowly and carefully, looking around at JohnJack and the others as he did.

'The black opera may do nothing – but we think it's done this.' He gestured at the great plume of liquid rock that blasted into the sky. The admission was bitter on his tongue. 'They did it to Tambora, in Indonesia. But they haven't done more. Not yet.'

Ferdinand rubbed his hand over his face, looking puzzled, and leaving a trail of grey ash across his skin.

Conrad spoke carefully. 'The San Carlo's gone. But the opera – the operas – aren't over. If they're still singing *Reconquista* . . .'

Ferdinand glanced over his shoulder, at the cloud-shrouded chaos of Naples. 'There are no other houses—'

'No, sir,' Conrad interrupted. 'You want to break up the black opera and arrest the members of the Prince's Men: if that's possible, then all well and good. If not, we have four of the best voices in Italy here. So let's go to the Burning Fields. If we couldn't out-sing them at the San Carlo – let's go to the Flavian Amphitheatre and out-sing them there.'

✦

Conrad met Ferdinand's gaze, and understood the man's rigid pallor.

I'm frightened for me and a handful of others. He's frightened for every person in the Two Sicilies.

The King ignored the exploding rocks that shattered in heat and ash, breaking the windows of the Bourbon-Sicily palace. 'This— You prepared for this. You had the Count, here, transpose the voice parts . . .'

'I didn't prepare for this, exactly. I thought there'd be trouble, and that—' The faces of Estella and Lorenzo shone clear in his mind's eye. '—And that there might be casualties.'

Ferdinand glanced over at the bedraggled singers, costumes dropping pins and strips of fabric, tawdry in the outdoor air. Conrad felt as if he were on the verge of a cavalry attack; all nerves, excitement, fear, and exhilaration.

Casually, even insolently, Conrad called over to the group of singers, chorus, and musicians that had collected around them on the piazza. 'He says, will we go sing il Principe into the dirt?'

Some of the answers were in thick Neapolitan, some were in the pure Italian of Tuscany. JohnJack said it best:

'Fuck, yes!'

Paolo almost danced from one foot to the other. 'We were having a success! You heard them, sire! Right up to the minute we started seeing a version of Pliny the Younger, the audience was in South America with Hernan Cortez and the Aztecs. We've lost the stage. We've lost most of the instruments – but they'll be playing the same music. So long as we have voices, we still stand a chance. *Cazzo!* It doesn't matter if it's a concert performance so long as we sing!'

Ferdinand's gaze turned distant with calculation. 'I'll send messengers for ship's marines, sailors, and the rest of our own riflemen, we'll collect up any other members of *L'Altezza*, and go down to the royal quay and aboard the *Guiscardo* to Pozzuoli. That'll be far quicker than any roads to the Anfiteatro.'

Conrad remembered the morning as if it were centuries ago. *That's right. He sent a patrol down to Pozzuoli.*

The officer in charge of the King's yacht would have ordered it to return, in case the King should have need of it.

Conrad faced about to take a head-count of singers and crew. It was some minutes before he had a group collected.

'Follow me!' the King called. He broke out coughing himself, and strode off through the ash-fog.

Conrad followed Ferdinand around the end of the Palazzo Reale complex of buildings, and down a private road, busy shepherding members of the company. Halfway down the once-white marble steps to the King's private dock – a perfect nightmare imagining of Adriano Castiello-Salvati's death before his eyes – something bumped his arm.

He glanced up. Ferdinand, shading his eyes with both hands, stared out at the ash-darkened Bay beyond the King's Dock.

The dock was bare.

It had occurred to Conrad not long after he began the libretto

499

– in fact, while he was in prison – that in the event of the Prince's Men having a genuine ability, the central administration of the Sicilies would have to be evacuated.

Conrad had thought cynically that, among the things that needed to be saved from Naples, there would be a significant amount of the Treasury, which could not be moved before, in case it gave things away to the Prince's Men.

Has someone made off with that?

Ferdinand faced about. 'There she is!'

The King sounded unusually relieved. He led off, back towards the piazza. His troops encompassed the San Carlo singers, making an arrowhead of purpose among thronging, panicking crowds.

Conrad took advantage of his height to crane over their heads, as they came to the edge of the square. Swirls of ash and smoke rolled in and a sea wind caught them, blowing Conrad's vision clear.

From the road running around the Bay, he could see as far as the yacht *Roberto il Guiscardo*.

The white yacht didn't move—*Must be anchored out in the harbour*, Conrad realised.

'Why hasn't it come in to moor at the King's Dock? —*Merda!*'

He couldn't help rubbing the heel of his hand across his eyes. Leaking tears, and the wind off the sea, cleared his vision.

'*O ciel!*' Paolo whispered, at his side.

Hundreds of small boats surrounded the *Guiscardo*.

Men – and women, and children – scrambled frantically up the yacht's curved wooden sides, over the rail, in through the gun-ports, up the rigging—

All of them refugees from Naples, all terrified of the black column searing into the air over the city. Even at this distance Conrad could see that the ship's rigging shone white, covered in a layer of ash.

The *Roberto Guiscardo*, top-heavy with people and volcanic ash, rolled over and sank.

48

Conrad stared, open-mouthed.

I did not just see a ship disappear!

I did not *just see our last chance to get to Nora disappear.*

Ferdinand shouted urgent orders to his men. Conrad was dimly aware of him arranging a rescue, rationalising the efforts of all the small boats paddling and sailing about, picking up swimmers.

'Horses.' Conrad spoke aloud. 'We might still get through by road.'

'Have you seen them!' Roberto Capiraso kicked at the ankle-deep layer of ash and coughed. 'If you mounted up and fought through these mindless idiots, it would only be for the beast to break a leg a hundred yards on.'

Grimly, Conrad realised: *The man is right.*

He looked to see if there might be other ships the King could commandeer.

Nothing.

Everything that has the ability to float has put out to sea.

The Prince's Men survived Tambora that way. Those that survived.

A glance over his shoulder showed him the streets around the Palazzo Reale crammed full of people, shrieking and running. They wanted their King's help; so much was evident.

'Every street around here will be blocked. We won't get a carriage out of Naples by any road. If we make it to the harbour, we won't find more boats than there are here. Without the *Guiscardo* we're stuck here.'

Conrad refused to look up over the roofs of buildings at the searing plume of Vesuvius's eruption. *My knees are weak enough as it is.* Seeing it again might rob him of all ability to act. He concentrated his vision on the shoreline of Naples harbour – seeing how the water pulled back a little, exposing the beginnings of mud – and on the thronging fishing boats and small craft.

Even if we could use them, we can't get them.

Conrad turned to speak to the King.

Ferdinand's expression changed.

It brought Conrad's head around in the direction the King was looking, so fast that his neck cracked.

The shape became clear on the water, emerging from sleeting yellow ash. *Masts, with topsails set; prow, gun-port, sail—*

A lean, rakish forty-gun frigate curved into the Bay of Naples.

'*That* ship.' King Ferdinand snapped his fingers at one of his lieutenants.

Conrad blinked furiously. The frigate coursed directly towards him as it lost headway, men sprinting round the deck to pull on ropes; some at the rail, with boat-hooks, fending fishing-boats and swimmers away—

Not directly at me, Conrad realised. *Straight at the King's Dock.*

The young lieutenant squinted through his spy-glass. 'The ... *Apollon*, sire.'

The flag the ship flew became clear – the colours of France.

Conrad put a restraining hand on Ferdinand's arm. "Sire, you don't need to use force."

Ferdinand Bourbon-Sicily gave him a look incandescent with incredulity.

Conrad reached out without looking and seized Paolo-Isaura's arm. He marched her with him, in their wake.

The *Apollon* moored, letting a ship's boat down almost before the sails were furled. It rowed in to the King's dock.

Conrad, keeping pace at Ferdinand's shoulder, didn't recognise the ash-covered naval officer in the bows, beyond the oarsmen.

The other figure, sitting beside him, was completely recognisable.

'Tullio Rossi!'

49

Sailors threw mooring ropes. Conrad overheard the King being rapdily and informally introduced to the unknown man – one Captain Bernard of the *Apollon* – but all his attention was on the broad figure shaking ash off his greatcoat, and avoiding (after the first glance) looking eastwards, seven miles, to where Mount Vesuvius thundered its erupting cloud into the darkening sky.

Tullio Rossi descended the gangplank – carefully enough that Conrad did not at first realise he was limping. He turned his head.

Conrad followed his gaze.

King Ferdinand's soldiers formed a cordon to keep the frigate's boat isolated. On the *Apollon*, sailors used boat-hooks to push refugee boats away.

Gives us very little time.

Conrad gripped Tullio once, hard, by the shoulder. Tullio returned the grip, and then reached out his hand and laid it momentarily on Paolo's arm.

'Well?' Conrad demanded, breathless. 'What happened!'

Tullio Rossi's dark eyes showed an appreciation of the San Carlo – the visible part of its roof open like a smashed egg – but he spoke with his usual composure.

'We put "our friend" on a ship a bit to the north – up the coast, at Castel Voltumo. One of his commodores is loyal. Had a frigate send its boats in, so we didn't have any idiocy trying to get the

504

coach to ford the river there—mind you, nasty place; if I get malaria, it's you I'm blaming.'

Conrad snorted. He found himself grinning.

Isaura demanded, 'You're limping?'

'. . . Coach horse stood on my foot.' Tullio's Sergeant Rossi look suppressed any mirth at his expense. 'In mud. Paolo, it'll be fine.'

Paolo looked concerned and bemused in equal parts. 'And this is the frigate? Is our friend with you?'

'Our friend is headed north to Marseilles aboard the *Charles Martel*, a 118-gun Océan class ship of the line. He's on his way back home, and he was having a lot to say about the wrath of God – and how his arsehole councillors were going to think he was it . . .'

Tullio shrugged, but more as if it eased his shoulders to be back on land, no matter the chaos of Naples.

'No, this one, the *Apollon*, it's a frigate under a junior captain that he's decided to loan us. For some reason he thought I might be planning to leap in heroically and rescue you. No idea why he thought "Monsieur Scalese" might have his arse in the fire back here . . .'

'Can't imagine,' Conrad said dryly. 'I'll tell you the precise nature of the fire as we go. When you have your arse well and truly in it.'

Meeting Tullio's gaze, he pushed Isaura forward a little, until she was standing almost pressed up against the burly man. Both looked happier for it.

'Well, our friend gave us the use of this ship,' Tullio remarked. 'Better move quick. Where are we going?'

Conrad didn't bother to consult with King Ferdinand and Il Superbo. 'Pozzuoli. Then the Burning Fields.'

Tullio rolled his eyes. 'Not one big volcano but a lot of little ones, much closer to us. That's . . .' A sufficient word evidently eluded Tullio. '. . . Charming. We've got a small marine complement, and the Emperor told off a number of the Old Guard to stay with us, but I still wouldn't want to face something bigger than a skirmish.'

Conrad's spine tightened, pulled muscles paining him as he

505

steadfastly ignored the looming clouds and lightning covering the eastern sky.

'Then let's hope it doesn't come down to guns.'

✦

The *Apollon* lurched on choppy waves.

Fiery rocks and boulders hurtled down around the ships, striking the waves and sending up spray and sheets of sea-water. Conrad found himself ducked down below the railing, clamped into the ship's side over the scuppers, his mind shaken with memories of rocket attacks in the night, in the war.

A warm body was pressed hard against his back, shaking – unless it was he himself who was shaking.

'Rocks! Fucking rocks!' Tullio sounded completely affronted.

Conrad's hearing stung. The slap of waves, shouts of sailors, and Tullio's swearing all sounded muffled. He slammed a palm against the side of his head, and then rubbed one knuckle as far as he could into his ear.

Sounds began gradually to come back.

Beyond the ship's wake, hills hid Naples now. This close to Pozzuoli, they would be seven miles from Naples itself; which put them – Conrad calculated – an extra six or seven miles from Vesuvius.

Still, the great tower of roiling blackness swelled, spreading out over his head.

The volcano pumped out ash and lava and gas, black fire and lightning. The spreading clouds darkened all the afternoon sky, seeming as solid in the air as coral-rocks do under the sea.

'How long till Pozzuoli?'

'Dunno!' The crouching figure of Tullio Rossi glared up at the red and black sky. An explosion made it too loud to talk. Conrad felt Tullio touch his shoulder. The other man pointed south.

Conrad squinted against the spray and shook his head.

Timing it with a lull in the seas, he shouted, 'We're too far north to see Stromboli or Vulcano, or Ætna! Remember they told us there were new volcanic cones near Marseilles, and down near

Messina? I think that must be the same thing – new volcanic islands in the Tyrrhenean Sea.'

'I heard an officer reporting to the Frenchie captain.'

Tullio looked wonderfully innocent for a moment, leaving Conrad to work out how the older man might have parleyed his commission from the Emperor into a licence to hear all news.

Tullio's mouth twisted in something between a scowl and an expression of disgust. 'There was messages from the southern heliographs. While they were still working. The southern volcanoes have started to erupt. Yes, Ætna,' he added, anticipating Conrad's concerns for Agnese and the rest of the family. 'They're evacuating Catania.'

Conrad nodded mute thanks. The spreading extent of catastrophe numbed him.

And bad news has to be told, and won't be better for being kept.

'We've lost two people.' He put his mouth close to Tullio's ear as the gale howled over them. 'At the San Carlo. We lost Estella and Lorenzo.'

'*Shite.*'

The ship tacked into the Gulf of Pozzuoli, knifing towards the small and ancient harbour. It lay past western headlands, in a Gulf of its own, with a fort or castle skylined on the high ground.

The fort, glimpsed through sea-spray and falling ash, began a train of thought.

'I wonder?' Conrad said. 'Could we use this ship to bombard the Anfiteatro . . . ?'

'Might be outside the range of a sea battery.'

Tullio Rossi buttonholed one of the junior officers, and managed to have the matter discussed between Captain Bernard and King Ferdinand.

A shot that left the gun-crew shaking confirmed the *Apollou*'s guns unable to bombard any useful part of the Campi Flegrei.

Out on deck again, Conrad found himself looking up thousands of feet into the murk.

In the west, the day's blue was now only a fringe at the edges of the horizon.

How long before blackness covers all the sky?

Paolo scrambled over to him, holding on to ropes and rail, to walk the deck.

'Tambora! Conrad, *Tambora*! If the singers from the Prince's Men could sing on a ship there, couldn't we do the same, here?'

JohnJack Spinelli appeared behind her, bedraggled in wet ash that left him the colour of concrete. He broke out into swearing, and the emphatic words halted on a cough. He doubled over, a cloth to his mouth.

Sandrine raised her voice to be heard over wind and wave, creaking oak and manila cordage. 'What he means is that this air is full of enough ash to choke a mule! One verse into an aria and our throats would be scraped raw and bloody.'

Conrad watched all three of them amusing themselves with black humour. He rubbed the heels of his hands over his face.

'Padrone?'

He didn't turn to see Tullio. 'I got you into this. You, Isaura there, JohnJack who was just dumb enough to want to save me from the Inquisition, Sandrine who's a good friend; even Velluti and Estella and Lorenzo were brought into it because I recommended them.'

He looked up, finding his vision blurring with the aftermath of hemicrania. Tullio Rossi exchanged a look with his sister.

'Tell your brother he's an idiot, Paolo.'

'You're an idiot, Conrad.'

Sandrine grasped the rail as the ship leaned over, and tacked into the harbour. Her eyes were bright, although red-rimmed. She reached out and put her hand on Conrad's shoulder, and squeezed tightly enough that it hurt.

'What he means, Corradino — every one of us volunteered. When this is all over, and you want to indulge in misplaced guilt, we'll indulge you. For now . . . you know who's really to blame. Make sure you won't flinch when it comes to dealing with her.'

✦

Pozzuoli stood deserted, under a cover of grey ash and the startling yellow of erupted sulphur.

Conrad narrowed his eyes, gazing around the harbour. Only a dead overloaded mule bore witness to the locals making their escape.

Paolo stared at the ship's seamen as they threw ropes to the quay-side and moored the *Apollon* temporarily. Conrad came to lean on the rail beside her. He saw her tiny frightened glance.

'Miseno.' He pointed westwards, to where they knew it would be. 'Called Cape Misenum in Roman times—'

'Corrado—'

'Pliny was there, at Cape Misenum. It was dark enough that they had to tie pillows and mattresses on their heads when they walked around, because of the falling rocks.'

Paolo-Isaura exclaimed, 'Mattresses?'

She pushed salt-stiff hair out of her eyes. Conrad saw her abandon interest in the frigate's preparations. The *Apollon* was to pull out into the harbour and wait for a signal, or else ride out the earthquake-waves, if that became necessary.

'Mattresses!' she echoed, sounding almost incensed.

Conrad kept a smile off his face with difficulty, pursuing his distraction for her. 'It's what Pliny wrote. Cushions, pillows, mattresses. It was so dark they couldn't see the rocks falling out of the sky, or tiles coming off roofs, or if they were walking into the walls of houses . . .'

'Oh, come on! Tying a mattress on your head—!'

A crack and ping echoed around the apparently deserted harbour.

Conrad found himself crouched below the ship's rail, one hand clamped around Paolo's wrist, her body dragged down with him. 'Musket fire!'

Paolo-Isaura's hand smacked smartly against his ear.

'*Cazzo!*' He let her go. She stayed crouched against him.

Minutes passed. The King's Rifles and the Old Guard, and the *Apollon*'s marines, went ashore in a quiet, businesslike way. There was no more shooting.

'Picket line.' Tullio ambled back along the deck, looking dusty, and approaching without using cover.

509

Conrad slowly stood. 'Put out so the Prince's Men will have warning of anyone's approach? They'd want some way to know if they've been followed.'

Under the ash on her cheeks, Paolo was stark white. 'They'll know we're coming.'

Tullio, unexpectedly reassuring, said, 'King's Rifles think they captured all the pickets.'

'Isaura. You won't come,' Conrad decided, abruptly. 'You don't have to be afraid—'

'I'm coming with you; I'm conducting. I'm not scared for me! You— Tullio— One of them just has to be lucky with a shot! . . . There's nobles in the Prince's Men; they'll have armed and drilled their own servants. And they're men who use hunting rifles as a matter of course!'

'And when was the last time a deer stood to arms behind a barricade and shot back?'

The young woman grinned.

Conrad didn't want to add to her fear by remarking that the barrels of hunting weapons are rifled to be accurate far beyond a soldier's musket.

'Besides,' he added with calculated scorn, 'The nobility were officers in the last war, not men who went sneaking around in the undergrowth, picking off officers as a matter of course . . .'

Paolo-Isaura gave him a far too knowing look. 'Someone made a company of Colonel Alvarez's soldiers disappear. And Commendatore Mantenucci's armed police officers.'

'If they are at the Anfiteatro – maybe the Prince's Men have numbers. Or only a good defensive position . . .' Conrad shrugged, knowing himself to be unconvincing.

Tullio shot a gaze that accurately analysed the two of them.

'Welcome to war.' He managed a sour humour, and acknowledged Paolo. 'This is what it's all about. Being afraid your mates will cop it.'

Paolo-Isaura's posture straightened, taking on the other man's bravado as if it were infectious. 'Somehow I imagined war to be more exciting and less terrifying . . . More adventurous?'

'Nope. No adventure. Bad rations, lots of walking, puking in a corner with fear, and then lots more walking. Any different in the cavalry, padrone?'

'Lots of riding. Saddle sores. Horses bite, have diseases, fall dead if you so much as look at them, and then they take it out of your pay. No adventure.'

Tullio took up a stolid position at the head of the gang-plank, arms folded, ignoring the men of the King's Rifles, and the opera company, as all prepared to go ashore. 'Paolo.'

Paolo-Isaura wrapped her neck-stock carefully over her nose and mouth. It didn't hide the determined expression in her eyes. Her voice came out muffled. 'What?'

'I want you to stay on the ship.'

Conrad snorted, while he wrapped his own neck-stock over his mouth. 'Tried that one! I've got a better chance of stopping Vesuvius by sticking my arse in the crater . . .'

'Please do try,' Isaura muttered sweetly.

Before Tullio could collect himself enough to argue, Paolo strode down the plank and off the *Apollon*.

Sudden afternoon light slanted in under the eruption cloud, making Pozzuoli's buildings stand out as if they were against the blackest rain-cloud. An unexpected roar sounded. Conrad startled.

A brick house at the far end of the harbour slanted, shifted, and the walls finally burst open, as if from some slow inside pressure.

From the ship's deck, Conrad could see black, earth-rimmed lava pushing over the lip of the foundations, very slowly gliding towards the next house.

'That must be from Monte Nuovo,' Sandrine guessed.

Conrad followed her down the gang-plank to the harbour.

Roofless buildings leaned, crushed under grey lava. Trees and bushes stood stripped of their leaves and branches. All white. The ground was hot underfoot. Conrad took it for an illusion, but lifting his feet and touching the underside of his soles showed him it was reality.

The stink of sulphur almost made him vomit.

He found himself – and Paolo – in charge of the opera people.

511

The small knot of people drew apart from the soldiers and marines. Most of them coughed – Brigida Lorenzani with both hands over her face, cheeks turning a purple-red colour.

Conrad climbed down the edge of stonework where the quay ended, and wetted his handkerchief in sea-water. He passed it up to Brigida, and repeated that for as many of the principal singers, chorus, and musicians as he could persuade. Breathing through wet cloth cut down on the dry choking.

One of the oboe players tripped over the stream of boulders that the road out of Pozzuoli had become, and screamed. His hands and knees were red with scalds when he was helped up. Conrad borrowed a water bottle from one of the riflemen and shared the water between the singers, before refilling it with sea-water to wet down kerchiefs.

He obsessively counted minutes.

'Act Three, scene seven,' a soldier observed.

Startled, Conrad saw it was no rifleman, but Roberto Capiraso, Conte di Argente, in a borrowed uniform coat.

Of all of us, I suppose he most needs a disguise against the Prince's Men.

Even covered in ash, without hat, cane, or cloak, Roberto somehow seemed impeccable. He cocked a dark brow. 'I told you your face was a book.'

Conrad kicked at congealed grey ash, that ought to look like snow, since it fell like it, but instead resembled rocks and rubble. The falling ash gritted between his teeth. He noted that the corners and rims of Roberto's eyes were red, like everyone else's; adding twenty years to his apparent age.

He glanced at Ferdinand, where the King stood with the French officers, apparently arranging the order of march.

'Will we get there in time, do you think?'

'I haven't been across here since I was a child. I liked Monte Nuovo, and Solfatara.' Roberto's smile tilted. 'If I ever visited the Flavian Amphitheatre, I don't recall it.'

'And you call yourself a Neapolitan Count!'

'Conrad!' Ferdinand waved him forward. 'Are your people ready?'

'Yes, sir.' Conrad couldn't help a frown. 'Are we certain it's the Flavian Amphitheatre we should be going to?'

Ferdinand gave a slow smile, that altered his bland expression to something rueful.

'A conversation I've just had with Lieutenant Baptiste of the Guard . . . If nothing else, it's the place where everything disappears. Commendatore Mantenucci, Colonel Alvarez, their men, and any scouts I've sent after them. And now we've met a picket line. They claim to be native Pozzuolans defending their town, but I know the local accent, and they don't have it.'

'Do we know what size force we'll be facing? My people aren't soldiers.'

'Nor should they be.' Ferdinand glanced around the ash-ruined town. 'The Prince's Men expect any attack in force to come from the direction of Naples. Their forces are concentrated at Posillipo, and north of there.'

'That's very specific.' Conrad found he didn't care about the etiquette of questioning a king.

Ferdinand gave him a look both practical and ashamed. 'One of the pickets was informative when tortured. Several of his compatriots confirmed what he said. I believe, if we have luck, we can get close up to the Anfiteatro before the Prince's Men realise we're here.'

'And then?' It came out as a demand.

I've never had to care for civilians before, in war; I've always been with other soldiers.

Ferdinand said sympathetically, 'That, we'll discuss as we go. We have limited time. Very limited.'

Conrad started off to gather up the opera people, and turned back. 'Can we be sure they don't have enough men to cover their rear, and the road from Pozzuoli across to Posillipo?'

'I would like to think I'd be notified of so many armed men in my kingdom. Sufficient bribes in suitable places, however . . .' Ferdinand's gaze sharpened. 'No, I have no certain information on that. Without word back from Enrico or Fabrizio, we're going into this completely blind.'

◆

They began to walk in ghostly quiet; everything muffled, not by snow, but by settling wet cement.

'We're walking across to the Anfiteatro,' Conrad advised the opera group. 'It's just as well we don't have horses, they'd break their legs on this ground. We can't go fast in any case. Everyone will be able to keep up.'

He deliberately didn't look at Brigida, but he saw in the corner of his vision how Sandrine hugged the fat woman.

The track – that, to be fair, had been a better road beforehand – crossed what seemed like moorland and wild scrub. The steaming yellow pools of Solfatara were fountains, in the distance; Conrad had no desire to approach the sulphur more closely. He glanced up and down the line, checking that all the cast members of *L'Altezza azteca* and the workers at the San Carlo were present.

'Act Three, scene nine,' Roberto Capiraso muttered, the surrounding silence forcing him to keep his tone low. 'Or if I'm wrong, they've just started Act Four.'

It would have been easy to ask Ferdinand or one of his aides how long it took to walk from the port of Pozzuoli to the Flavian Amphitheatre. Conrad didn't ask.

All the while I don't know it's impossible, I can believe we'll reach the Amphitheatre in time to disrupt the end of Il Reconquista d'amore.

We'll get there, even if it's only in time to applaud their finale.

He was afraid of the lava. What little he saw of it, though, nosing up through broken ground, seemed to move infinitely slow. Heat glimmered over the earth. He could feel it a surprising distance away.

He walked with Ferdinand Bourbon-Sicily past ash the colour of Roman concrete. Vesuvius continued to pump cubic tons of material up into the rising column. Every sound was muffled here, behind the hills that lay between them and Naples.

Scouts came in every so often, some wounded. Conrad sat down when the forward movement abated, sitting with his head in his hands, in inches of volcanic ash. He couldn't help rubbing at his chest. Breathing deeply didn't get him any more air. The stifling remnants of hemicrania refused to go away.

He untied the handkerchief over his mouth, and took off his

long neck-cloth. Soaking the linen in a murky puddle, he shook the long cloth out and wrapped that over his mouth instead.

The kerchief he tied around his head, covering his right eye. A search in his pockets discovered a second square of linen. He dampened and folded that, doubled and re-doubled, and tucked the pad under his blindfold, over the throbbing eye.

The reduction in light eased a degree of the hemicrania's disorientation. Ferdinand dropped down in a crouch beside him, Roberto a pace or two behind. The King waited with apparent patience until Conrad finished tying a knot in the cloth.

'The Count tells me we can't out-sing them,' Ferdinand said bluntly. 'Not with only four principals.'

Conrad caught Roberto's gaze, over the King's head, and tried to convey that he, had he thought such a thing, would not have troubled the King with it. 'There's been a misunderstanding, sir. It's not a matter of singing louder, or even more technically correct, or whether we don't have singers for all the parts.'

Ferdinand gave him a blank look, surprisingly plain for a ruler of two kingdoms.

'Talk to Sandrine, and Velluti, and Paolo.' Conrad put his hand over the damp cloth and pressed it against his eye. 'It's a question of whose opera it is.'

The other two men exchanged looks.

'But if you don't sing better . . .' Ferdinand began, helplessly.

Tullio and Paolo joined the group, Tullio silent, and Paolo respectfully addressing the King.

'It's what I was saying back at the piazza, sire. They're playing the same music that we would.'

She gestured to Roberto, as if she forgot her enmity towards the composer.

'The scores for *Altezza* and *Reconquista* are almost the same, yes?'

'Almost, but the final score of *Altezza* is far superior.'

Paolo waved him to silence.

'Sir, Corrado and I were talking, about if it came to us, and if we had to sing "against" the black opera directly . . . It isn't a matter of competition. The audience doesn't score one performance better than another!. . . The *heart* of it has to be ours. If our singing, our

515

interpretation of the score, is better than the Prince's Men, then when we arrive at the Flavian Amphitheatre and sing, our performance overcomes theirs. Whoever Leonora's got in the Amphitheatre to listen to her – her audience becomes our audience.'

The King stood docile as one of his aides attempted, unsuccessfully, to clean off the royal clothes. 'How can you be sure it will work that way?'

Paolo shot an appealing look to Conrad.

He stepped in to field Ferdinand's blunt question.

'The Prince's Men want this work for their own purposes, but we just want it to be opera. If the Prince's Men are singing *Reconquista*'s score, and we're singing *Altezza*'s score, then, essentially, we're singing the same opera. Words and scenes differ, yes, and the meaning – but the sound . . .'

Conrad stood, wet neck-cloth pulled down, finding himself gesturing firmly.

'Depending on whether we're the ones who move the audience more, our singers become the principals. The two operas are one, and the black opera singers will become comprimarios and accompanists to our primo uomo and prima donna.'

Ferdinand let out a small rasping chuckle.

Conrad bowed his head, acknowledging that. 'Theoretically, sire, at that point their miracle is taken out of their hands – and because we don't want it, it won't happen.'

'Conrad . . . I do like the way you think. Myself, I can't help but think of the Prince's Men and their black opera as evil, as an affront against God . . . That stops me from seeing what's obvious to an atheist mind – that we can "kidnap" their miracle for our own purposes.'

Ferdinand nodded, with no hesitation or vacillation.

'My scouts have brought back reports: the roads ahead do appear empty. I don't like to say it, but you need to move your people faster. We need to be inside the Anfiteatro before the Prince's Men know we're coming.'

Conrad wiped wet hands down his dusty coat, and glanced back at the singers. Determined to finish it, he spoke to Ferdinand in an undertone.

'The problem is . . . Sir, it could work both ways. They could co-opt us. If the bulk of their listeners are swayed by Nora, rather than us, then our – energy, if you like – our vital Galvanic power . . . that would becomes hers. We'd end up helping the black opera's miracle, rather than stopping it.'

50

'And then there's the other fucking question,' Tullio muttered under his breath. 'Where is this fucking amphitheatre?'

Conrad leaned down, massaging a cramp in his calf. 'Up ahead— The Old Guard's scouts—'

'They can't find their buttons to open their britches to piss!'

The broad-shouldered man leaned against the side of a dip in the ground that might have been where a road passed, decades before. He ignored the mud and ash on his greatcoat.

'Ground's not safe. Never mind all the shafts opening up all over the place, and the mines— There's great cracks in the earth over by Solfatara. Me and one of Alvarez's men swung out to take a look when we passed it. Are you sure we're not lost?'

Conrad felt all the irony of coming so far and being stopped by the terrain itself. 'I think we're not lost.'

The road crossed what might have been another path. Ferdinand and his officers halted, arguing, gestures becoming vehement.

The opera singers and musicians flopped down on the ash-grey turf, grateful for the smallest respite. Conrad dropped down beside Sandrine – who had acquired army boots, he noted, with a great-coat worn over her royal robe. JohnJack wore the Lord General's faux bronze breastplate, and appeared to be in conversation with Brigida about it – the fat woman in Amazon steel breastplate, over her rags. Towering a head over her, Giambattista Velluti sat in the exotic white robes that Cortez wore in the Aztec court. Velluti's dark gamin features showed strain at plodding through volcanic ash, the earth shaking under them.

Plodding to where? Conrad wondered. *Tullio's right.*

He pictured Rome's Coliseum. Another Flavian Amphitheatre. The towering curve of brick arches against the sky. A blue sky, not like this threatening black one, but still . . .

'If we're anywhere close, shouldn't we see it by now?' Tullio demanded.

The groaning earth would cover the sound of singing, Conrad guessed, unless they were on top of it. *But still, one shouldn't be able to miss a whole amphitheatre!*

Conrad got to his feet, wincing at minor injuries. 'I'm going to talk to the King.'

Ferdinand Bourbon-Sicily knelt in a clump of scrub, in urgent conversation with the commander of the *Apollon*'s marines, the major in charge of the King's Rifles, and the French squad from the Tyrant's own Guard.

Conrad covered his face with his hands, for a moment, risking removing the damp kerchief from his eye. The world was much brighter when he opened his eyes.

He took several brisk steps.

His chest didn't hurt, he realised.

The sensation of air moving easily in his lungs astonished him.

I hadn't realised how much it was hurting until it's no longer here.

'Corrado?' JohnJack called.

His tone brought Conrad back the few yards between them at a run.

He stopped dead.

Both Spinelli's and Isaura's open mouths breathed out something grey.

Sandrine's lips, just parted, exhaled a flow of black dust. *Particles almost fine enough to be a gas . . .*

But they were dust, Conrad realised; dust from the pillar that thundered over the hills ahead of them, filling every inch of the air with minute splinters of volcanic glass.

He followed the swirl and flow of ash between their lips. Saw

Velluti with his hand to his throat, and his mouth as wide as if he expanded a note to be heard through all of an auditorium—

Brigida sat, chest heaving, tears running down her cheeks.

Tears of relief. *At being able to breathe.*

Dust and pumice-stone and volcanic ash all drifted out into the air, removing themselves from lungs. Wisps of grey dust exhaled, impossibly, into clean air . . . Everyone Conrad could see had faces of wonder and joy, expanding their chests, breathing in and then out, as if to prove to themselves that they could. Singers, musicians, sergeants, riflemen . . .

Conrad licked his own lips, and found his teeth and the interior of his mouth gritty.

All fear left him for the moment, replaced by heightened sensation. Ribs expanding freely, air moving through his lungs . . . He coughed out the very last of the clogging obstruction, and saw it dissolve into clear air.

Air, on the Campi Flegrei, that should not be so free of volcanic detritus.

'We just – breathed it out,' Conrad said wonderingly. He hit his forehead with the heel of his hand. 'Of course! They need to sing. And how could they without some kind of "miracle"?'

Ferdinand stepped briskly up, his own movement increased. 'Conrad, you know what this is?'

'I can guess!' He stifled his excited pleasure, in case he should offend the Sicilian monarch by seizing his hands and dancing. He settled for a broad smile. 'I should have assumed this would happen!'

Ferdinand looked puzzled. 'How could you possibly know? And what is this?'

'You told me, when Tambora erupted, the ship had to be close while they sang? We tried, out on the Bay, just now, but the air was full of volcanic dust; the singers would have ripped their lungs to pieces. This *had* to have happened at Tambora, and it has to happen here. The Prince's Men have to have clear air to sing.'

Ferdinand turned his head, gazing around at the soldiers and singers, catching the last wisps of grey dust as lungs breathed them out.

'Tambora,' the King repeated. He slowly nodded. 'The Prince's Men must have made it part of their miracle, that this happen. Haven't they been singing since we started in the San Carlo? They must have sung first of all for this to happen.'

Conrad felt his ribs ache. Now he could breathe freely, he felt the bruises from the wreck of the Teatro San Carlo. It was worth it, he decided.

'Sir,' he put in, as the King turned away to start the march again. 'If they made being able to sing a part of their "black miracle"— what else might they have done?'

Ferdinand evidently did consider it. A small, amused, ironic smile tilted his lips.

'Or, Signore Corrado, we could just march on and see what pleasant surprises they have for us?'

Which is as kind a way as I've come across of saying 'We'll have to shut up and put up with it' . . .

The King moved off. JohnJack's hand closed over Conrad's shoulder.

'The air's clear enough for the Prince's Men to sing.' Spinelli sounded triumphant. 'Corrado, if they can sing, so can we.'

'Yes.' Conrad looked down the column. He gazed from the man with the oboe to a woman who sang mezzo in the choir; counted twenty in all, including principal singers, and all with the same expression of determination that JohnJack wore.

I'm used to soldiers being brave – when they're not being cowards – but I hadn't thought to expect it from civilians. Tullio's right: I am an idiot.

Conrad smiled. 'Then let's go.'

Spinelli managed a mocking, soldierly salute. 'Yes sir!'

Paolo stumbled up as they moved off. Conrad steadied her by her elbow.

'What are we left with?' he murmured.

The young woman shrugged a filthy shoulder and grinned. 'A prevalence of winds and the smaller horns. As for drums, cymbals, and piano – no chance!'

'We'll think of it as a small concert performance. Besides, the Prince's Men will have brought the orchestra,' Conrad got out, with a grave humour he saw they appreciated.

'I'll get it sorted.' Paolo grinned

The rough moorland of the Burning Fields grew more erratic as they trudged on. The road became a mere track, occasional ruts from cart-wheels visible. Conrad watched the undergrowth – scrubby rowan trees hiding much of whatever was in the distance. There was no visible lava now. He scraped his hand against what he thought was a bush, and stopped to pull some of the ivy off it.

It was a low, moss-covered stone wall.

'We must be close . . .' He lifted his head and gazed around, searching for the rising tiers of brick arches that made up a Flavian amphitheatre.

The eruption plume, now close on fourteen miles distant, dominated the sky. Conrad momentarily lifted his head from where he was putting his feet, studying how the column of fire and smoke rose up and flattened out, slanted smears of black sifting down from it. *Volcanic ash falling like rain.*

'There are more of these walls.' Tullio pulled more ivy away. 'Would this be a part of the amphitheatre?'

Conrad saw they had dropped behind the singers. He quickened his pace, Tullio with him; deftly avoiding other low walls.

'Maybe it's a part of the tunnels that the ancients had, to flood and drain the amphitheatre for naval battles?'

'I doubt it. If that had been excavated, it would have been noticed.' Conrad pushed through a clump of scrub, palm trees, and newly leafed rowan.

He caught both feet on an obstacle and pitched over on his face.

Tullio made a high-pitched wheezing sound, fist pressed to his sternum. 'Holes in the ground would be noticed, oh yes!'

Tullio didn't seem inclined to stop laughing. Conrad knelt up, and tore away ash-greyed creepers. Enough of this particular ancient brick wall remained that one could see it had once had a doorway in it.

A man's feet stuck out of the vegetation-filled gap that had once been a door.

'Corrado?' Tullio's low laughter abruptly stopped. 'That's a body!'

Conrad tore ash-piled greenery down. He found himself looking at scarlet cloth; and into the face of an elderly man, sprawled on his back.

'Blessed Mother!' Paolo gasped.

'Get the King!' Conrad leaned forward and put his hand on the supine man's chest, and took it away bloody. Blood soaked the scarlet robe and white linen.

He pulled down the cloth at the man's neck, uncovering a red-black puncture in the pallid flesh above the collar-bone.

A stiletto lay discarded a yard off, in the bent grass. Blood ran like water down the blade.

Done only a short time ago – and I'll bet he didn't do this to himself—

The man twitched. His features showed grey as pumice ash in the weak sunlight; cheeks hollowed, eyes bruised in their sockets. *But not quite dead.*

Ferdinand arrived with Paolo-Isaura, at a low run; and ducked down into the scrub beside them. Conrad couldn't help seizing his sister by the arm.

'It's Corazza. I recognise him. It's Cardinal Corazza. He's the head of the Inquisition in Naples. He exorcised our Papa.'

Paolo's other hand took hold of his and squeezed.

'He's been stabbed,' Conrad added, collecting himself and speaking to Ferdinand.

The King knelt down beside the older man. 'Gabriele?'

Corazza's old man's eyes had been bright as candles when he exorcised Alfredo Scalese. Now they looked sunk in, and blue as if he had cataracts.

'They killed my dogs.'

He muttered it barely audibly. Conrad couldn't tell if he recognised the King.

'My best mastiffs. Not a boar in Campania could come close to them. They hung up all my dogs. Hung them on pitchforks driven into my door.'

Bubbling blood ran out of his mouth, down his cheek, and onto the pumice-ash and moss.

'Rest.' Ferdinand caught the eye of one of his aides. 'Do we have army surgeons with us? Must I send him back to the *Apollon*?'

The Cardinal choked.

His once-red cheeks glowed pale with blood-loss. Conrad scuttled back, his sleeves sprayed with fine dots of blood.

The old man's hand closed lightly over Ferdinand's. 'They said, next time it would be Renato and Cesare. If I didn't co-operate in every way. It was no harm. Truly. Just to use the palace. Storage. I was doing no harm.'

'Renato and Cesare?' Conrad murmured.

'His nephews.' Tullio, as a man who collected gossip, didn't need to specify any potentially closer relationship.

'I thought they might have been more dogs . . .'

Tullio ignored that, his frown thoughtful. 'Why did they knife him? He might have lived through it. He nearly has. Why not shoot him?'

The Cardinal said something that Conrad could not decipher, and very slowly the blood stopped pouring into his sodden robes.

Ferdinand closed the old man's eyes with a wet, red hand.

He straightened up with a grunt. 'Wrap him in a cloak, here. We'll take him back for burial afterwards.'

If we don't, it'll be because we're *in need of graves.*

Paolo's nostrils flared as the King strode back towards the head of the line, as if she continued to smell blood above the stink of sulphur.

Conrad stood, and gave her his hand to help her up. 'I'll never know if he was warned that Alfredo couldn't keep his mouth shut for long, even about il Principe. Whether disposing of my father was just a priestly duty, or an order.'

Isaura said nothing.

Tullio caught his balance on rough mud and buried bricks. 'Looks like he wasn't a Prince's Man by choice.'

Paolo's voice went up into an outraged yelp. 'There's always a choice!'

Conrad exchanged a glance with Tullio over her head, and read the same knowledge in the other man's face – that some decisions are in no way choices, and any man who loves gives hostages to the wicked of the world.

'Seems the Prince's Men didn't trust him not to run to the King.' Tullio wiped his sleeve across his mouth and spat grey ash into the knee-high grass. 'Better watch your footing, Corrado; don't know how many more men they'll have got rid of today!'

A tremor ran through the grass and scrub, the new leaves of a mountain ash swaying. Conrad kept his balance superbly.

It was not easy to read the landscape here. An ambusher's paradise. Bushes, and the ash-fall, hid the distance. Uneven earth and grass made the ground untrustworthy.

His pistol was still in his coat pocket; a reassuring weight. He examined it carefully on the march, checking under the frizzen to see that the powder hadn't fallen out during the San Carlo's collapse. It was still there. *Ought I to call that a miracle?* he wondered cynically, as he replaced the flint-lock pistol in his pocket.

They walked up a shallow rising slope, Conrad realised, as he returned his attention to the ground.

At the top, we might finally get a sight of the Amphitheatre—!

Tension made his steps quicker. He passed the King – conferring with his aides and officers – and ducked down, cautiously approaching the brow of the slope, where it was screened by bushes.

He parted leaves and thin branches carefully, eeling his way into them. *In case we need to see and not be seen—*

Grass and earth gave way under his foot – gave way completely, pitching him into emptiness.

His stomach jolted. He skidded downhill and forward, grabbing at the saplings and bushes; gravity ripping his hands free of them.

He plummeted helplessly forward – and fell into the vast depth of the Flavian Amphitheatre.

51

He threw his arms up to protect his head and fell face-down on concrete.

He slammed into something that was not level. Pain blasted him at knee, thigh, rib, and shoulder.

He rolled.

Throwing out his hands halted his fall—

He lay face down on steps, he realised. Face down and head down, too—the great oval of the Flavian Amphitheatre opening out beneath him.

He noted in a fraction of a heartbeat that the far, eastern, side of the Anfiteatro was what he dimly remembered. Like Rome – rows of brick arches in a curved wall, the sky showing through, and on the inside, facing him, tier upon tier of stone steps for seating, with access stairs between them.

The ground behind him was level with this topmost tier of the amphitheatre seating. On this side of the Anfiteatro, the stone entrance tunnels topped with brick arches were choked black with earth and shadow.

It took his stunned mind a long minute to process it.

This *side of the Flavian Amphitheatre has been excavated. Recently.*

Who'd notice yet more archaeologists and tomb-robbers, digging up more relics than Ferdinand has in Naples' secret museum? No one. No one at all. It's not suspicious.

It just means that the Anfiteatro, which I vaguely recall I painted as only a few rows of seating and a part of the arena, has now been dug out to be a full working amphitheatre.

Conrad inched up onto aching elbows. The arena floor was divided on the long axis by a dark path or ditch. On the far side of that, a slew of people in costume milled around.

On the lowest front tier of the far side, musicians sat. Scenery looked minimal. A hundred or so men and women made a scant blot of an audience, halfway up the further side.

There were other men in the arena besides singers. Conrad picked one out of the crowd, urgently pointing up – at him. The attitude was unmistakable; any soldier could read it in their stances. *Intruders!*

He yanked his pistol out of his pocket, lifted it, barely sighting, and pulled the trigger.

Click.

Conrad lowered the flint-lock weapon. He got up onto his knees, knowing he presented a larger target, but needing to work on the gun—

Powder under the frizzen plate, charge in order, no reason why the weapon should not discharge.

He raised it again, shifting his body side-on to the men far below in the arena. Shooting down at an angle, at this range, made him uneasy for his aim. He took the closest man as a target and gently squeezed the trigger.

Click.

'What?'

Pulling the trigger again got the same result.

He looked up from his pistol, only then realising that no shot had been fired from below.

Two or three men waved their arms in urgent talk; Conrad could see that. The noise of a stretta – that, up here, came to him without difficulty – concealed if they shouted. One walked forward.

He stopped at the edge of the black line that crossed the arena floor from the north-west to the south-eastern main entrances.

It took Conrad a long moment to realise that it was a gap in the earth.

A collapsed underground passage?

It must be deep, Conrad realised. They made no attempt to scramble across it. The distance down was deceptive: it might have been ten feet across, or twenty.

None of the Prince's Men below raised a weapon.

Without bothering to aim, Conrad pulled the trigger again.

Click.

'Signore Corrado—' Ferdinand Bourbon-Sicily pushed through the bushes and saplings, two tiers above, sounding highly impatient. '—Oh.'

Conrad slowly and painfully stood up, as men from the *Apollon* and Ferdinand's own Rifles began to filter down from the bank of earth above onto the highest tier of seating.

They stared, each one of them.

Conrad kept his eye on the King.

'The black opera, sir,' he said, unnecessarily.

Perhaps I just need to say it.

Ferdinand Bourbon-Sicily gaped like a peasant.

'Don't bother,' Conrad finished, seeing the King about to collect himself and give an order. 'I believe I know what else their "miracle" is doing, as well as allowing their singers to breathe.'

The brown-haired man stepped carefully down until he stood beside Conrad, gazing down all the tiers.

'. . . That's a small enough audience. But I suppose they had a smaller one at Tambora. Corrado, what did you say?'

'I know why they stabbed Corazza. Rather than shot him,' Conrad corrected himself soberly.

Ferdinand apparently couldn't take his eyes off the current central figure among the singers on the arena floor – a tenor, singing what Conrad recognised from his brief acquaintance with *Il Reconquista* as the aria of oath-taking by King Ferdinand of Aragon.

The King of the Two Sicilies, at Conrad's elbow, prompted him. 'What?'

'They don't want to take the slightest risk of their singers being hurt.'

Conrad held out his flint-lock weapon.

'Try my pistol if you like, sir. I believe that – along with the clear air – they've used the beginning of their opera miracle to make it so that any firearms don't work within this amphitheatre.'

✦

Out beyond the amphitheatre, the furnance-roar of Vesuvius's ejecta had sent shockwaves through him, his body vibrating like water in a pan.

It isn't just the air and firearms they've quieted.

The world's loudest thunderstorm was muted; the architecture of the Anfiteatro had its effect. Soprano voices sounded in unison in his ears, as if they sang only for him.

Flawlessly voicing a chorus that he ought to be hearing in bass or baritone.

'If that chorus is in the same place, we're halfway through Act Four.'

Tullio folded his arms, staring aggressively down the stone tiers. 'Better tell his Majesty that.'

Ash-delineated lines deepened at the edges of Ferdinand's eyes. 'How long do we have, Corrado?'

'If the scores are identical, we have only twenty minutes to the end.'

Conrad looked away from the tiny figures – none of which was Nora, he could tell at one glance – to see Roberto Capiraso with two soldiers flanking him, all three in the blue and burgundy of Alvarez's Rifles.

'A few minutes difference, perhaps,' Roberto murmured. 'If they conduct at that tempo, then the finale ultimo will begin in – twelve minutes.'

Tullio rumbled, 'They think they've won.'

Conrad narrowed his eyes, taking in the men and women of the Prince, below. They appeared to ignore being interrupted, as much as they ignored the half of the sky now drowned in boiling cloud.

Down on the far front row, he saw the elbow of a violinist lift. A drum let go with swift beats. It should have been inaudible this far off. It was clear enough to make the hairs stand up on his neck.

'They think they'll win because they've succeeded so far.' Ferdinand sounded grim. 'It's up to us to see that they go no further. —What's that?'

The odd sunlight, filtered through the yellow ash that fell outside the Flavian Amphitheatre, meant detail was difficult to make out. 'Where?'

'Around the edges of the arena.' Ferdinand sounded disbelieving: 'Those are men in Colonel Alvarez's uniforms!'

Conrad reached for the small spy-glass as Tullio put it into his hand. Clumsily, he focused the lenses.

Men sat along the edge of the dividing fallen passageway, and at the base of the stone tiers. They had their wrists behind them – *tied*, Conrad thought – and their ankles together in front. What must be Prince's Men paced among their prisoners.

Conrad thought he recognised some of the faces in the Rifles' uniforms. They had come on their off-duty days to listen to rehearsals, and make comment.

Men in dark uniforms sitting, bound, among them were – Conrad turned the focusing wheel – from the Naples police.

'I think we found out what happened to Colonel Alvarez's company.' Conrad passed the spy-glass over to the King. 'And Commendatore Mantenucci's men. At a guess, I'd say there are a lot more Prince's Men than we can see.'

'If they could subdue a company of riflemen? Yes! They may be part of the audience.' Ferdinand spoke, telescope shifting as he studied the tiers in turn. 'Ah! Adalrico di Galdi. We were right to be suspicious of the man. And there's his son, with him, and—'

Conrad took the glass away, after Ferdinand was silent for a whole minute.

He focused on the audience – all of whose attention was only for the singers – and at last found the hawk-faced and silver-haired Conte di Galdi. And a number of young men with a family resemblance. And—

'That's Enrico Mantenucci!' Conrad said aloud.

He watched the telescope's silent circle of colour and light. Saw the police Commendatore throw back his head and laugh at something a younger di Galdi said, at the same time as he clapped his hands together, applauding the soprano chorus.

'He's not a prisoner.'

Ferdinand sounded stunned. 'No, he's not.'

'I don't see Fabrizio Alvarez – wait.' Conrad twisted the brass scope. 'Second row of men away from that ditch in the centre of the arena. He's bound hand and foot, like the rest.'

He took the spy-glass away from his eye, and the figures sprang back to become miniatures.

The King's voice sounded low and cold. '*That* will be how Fabrizio's company were taken prisoner. He trusted Enrico.'

Conrad saw the tiny figure of Mantenucci applaud again. Hate washed over him, hot and vomit-smelling.

The King's hands clenched. 'And for Fabrizio and his men to be taken by surprise— I'll make a bet that more than one of Commendatore Mantenucci's officers are Prince's Men.'

Ferdinand sucked in a breath, as if the air was impossible to take in, even without the volcano's dust.

'And so Fabrizio and his men are prisoners.'

He didn't say *sacrifices*. His tone implied it.

Tullio fell into place at Conrad's left shoulder; Paolo at his right.

For all her thoughtful tone, Paolo's voice shook. 'They must see us!'

'Plain as a red-headed whore in church,' Tullio agreed. His gaze studied the amphitheatre's tiers, scraped clean of bushes.

Conrad remembered, as a young man, seeing the few exposed tiers of seating covered in flowering shrubs, and bushes with late fruit hanging from their branches. Even the highest seats had a furry coating of grass. The floor of the arena had been home to swaying thin mountain ash trees, as well as long uncut grass.

Now, even the edges of the pits had been cleared: brick-lined open throats, with ivy and wisteria cut back to ground level.

Tullio glared at the deserted tiers around them. 'Why bother to clear this side of the Anfiteatro? Were they expecting more of an audience, maybe?'

'Acoustics,' Conrad guessed.

Isaura nodded.

'Well, it leaves us without any damn cover, guns or not!'

The King of the Two Sicilies gave a regretful smile. His voice held a roughness Conrad had not heard before. 'They'll have their victory in minutes. It will only take them as long as it takes to climb this side of the auditorium. They can overpower us without guns.'

Conrad interrupted. 'It'll take more than minutes. Look at that.'

He pointed at the apparent ditch, running from one end of the arena to the other. Shadows and ash might confuse the eye, but the gap was wide – and deep.

'A collapsed passage?'

'I'd guess, the central underground access corridor.' Conrad lifted the spy-glass, focusing it on the ditch that was no ditch. 'The amphitheatre is bigger, of course, but from one end of the arena to the other . . . is, what, seventy metres? And about forty across. That means that "ditch", the gap – that could be eight or ten metres wide at the least. And if it's cleared all the way down, it could go down two storeys.'

He made out sifting sunlight, gleaming on the wall furthest from him, where ancient brickwork went down into the dark. It had been split here and there by volcanic convulsions. Where the roof across it had fallen in, uncounted ages past, the edges were rough with loose dirt. Below sparse vegetation, it went down into stark blackness.

Ferdinand cocked his head, like an inquisitive sparrow, and Conrad thought he glimpsed the boy who had disappointed his father's louche political court by his interest in sciences and antiquities.

'The Roman amphitheatres were full of passages and rooms underneath, for the beasts and gladiators,' Conrad said, memories coming fluently from his reading in the secret museum. 'This Anfiteatro would have had a whole complex underneath, with quarters for fighters, and cages for animals, and trapdoors and pulleys that raised scenery—'

He waved an arm, that took in the shafts dotting the surface of the arena. A brief fear – that the Prince's Men might have excavated under the Flavian Amphitheatre too – died as he made out how they were choked with creepers and bracken and cacti.

Movement came from behind.

Brigida Lorenzani left the scrub and bushes and stepped down from the lip of the earth-bank, with a delicate precision, for all her roundness and short stature. If her cloak and helm were lost, she still had a rag of skirt and the shining steel of a breastplate.

'Are you thinking we'll sing here, Signore Corrado?' She halted beside him, gazing down at the singers of the black opera. She put her hands on her hips, supporting the steel armour, and kept it turned towards the enemy.

Conrad caught Ferdinand's eye.

The King inclined his head.

'I think we must,' Conrad confirmed. 'They're too busy creating their "miracle" – let's give them something to worry about!'

A smile quirked the corner of her mouth, giving her roguish laugh-lines. 'The rest of them sent me out first because I was best protected! I can't blame them. Now let all those brave men follow me . . .'

She fanned her fingers in a little wave, speaking loud enough for JohnJack and the castrato, above, to hear her. A moment later they emerged from the brush and saplings, scrambling down to stand beside her; Sandrine shuffling along behind in boots far too big.

'*Cazzo!*' Sandrine exclaimed in a whisper. 'I never felt so naked in my life!'

Conrad didn't own up to chills up his spine. He suspected he didn't need to.

He found himself speaking before he realised that he would, spurred by the look in JohnJack Spinelli's red-rimmed eyes.

'It seems they were so anxious their singers not be shot down, that they can't touch us, yet. They can't shoot us. That gives us a chance.'

A passage of recitative tinkled across the auditorium.

Paolo glanced up, caught his gaze – and seemed to realise instantly what he was leading up to.

'They'll hurt you!' Her clenched fingers locked on the cloth of his coat; grey eyes, so like his own, glaring.

Some instinct made him confident.

'Paolo, listen. The Prince's Men – they won't risk anything interrupting them now. If they fight with us, there goes their audience's attention, and bang!, their miracle's gone. Believe me, they want more out of this than air free of ash, and firearms that don't work!'

Paolo-Isaura's fingernails dug into his arm, through coat and shirt.

'Corradino, by the same reasoning, they can't let us sing.'

Tullio rested a large hand on Isaura's shoulder, but looked at Conrad as he spoke. 'Just because they can't shoot at us doesn't mean they can't overpower us.'

'They just can't do it quickly enough not to provoke an interruption.'

Conrad glanced away, discovering Ferdinand Bourbon-Sicily listening quietly beside him.

'We don't have long, Corrado.'

'No, sir. I believe I'm right. We only have minutes, now – less than a quarter-hour. I don't think they can reach us in that time, if they try. I think we can act before they do.'

Conrad took a breath.

'We need to be sure the singers will be safe, down on this side of the arena. Paolo, wait with the company up here. I won't risk the principal singers, or what chorus we have, or anyone necessary to L'Altezza azteca.'

She clearly couldn't speak.

'You conduct us.' Conrad stiffened his back, disregarding his aching bruises, and the throb of migraine not yet fully gone. 'Take what advice Roberto can give you in the next few minutes. When I signal, bring everyone down as fast as you can.'

He moved before he could be stopped, shaking off Paolo-Isaura's loosened grip. He walked down three of the steps between the tiers of seating before he heard her stifled cry.

Treading down the access stairs, step after step, he almost felt the walls of the arena rising around him, as if he descended into a well.

It was absurd, given how large the Flavian Amphitheatre was.

He wondered if what constricted his throat was terror.

Or if it's the thought that, any moment now, I might see Nora.

His feet took him down each step with a jolt, the seed of hemi-crania stirring in his spine every time his heel hit the stones.

Closer to the arena floor, he walked on steps cleaned down to the brick or concrete. The oval floor of the amphitheatre was ringed and lined with the mouths of shafts. Fallen fluted columns had been rolled aside against the bottom tier of seating, away from the audience of Prince's Men.

His steps slowed without him willing it.

Down here, it was clear eight metres was a conservative estimate of how wide the central collapsed passage was. *Twelve? Fifteen?*

They won't even try to cross that, Conrad reassured himself. How far would you fall into darkness, and what would you hit at the bottom?

Slowly, not looking back, Conrad raised his arm and gave the signal for them to follow him down.

52

Ten heartbeats. Twenty – agitated heartbeats though they are, he can still count them – and nothing happens.

The Prince's Men see us. But we're not worth breaking this fragile, breath-holding truce for.

The soldiers and singers and King Ferdinand reached the arena floor.

'Musicians up on the third tier, there. It looks the least crumbled. Choir in front of the bottom tier; principals on the arena floor. Can everybody see Paolo conduct?'

'I'll get it sorted,' Paolo grinned, one hand on the oboe player's elbow.

Nothing but empty air between the Prince's Men and the singers and musicians of The Aztec Princess.

'Are they going to let us do this?' He spoke aloud, not aware of Ferdinand Bourbon-Sicily beside him.

'And I thought you were convinced by your own argument, Corrado . . .'

The King clasped his hands behind his back, not stooping or shrinking away from the several hundred men of il Principe on the auditorium's far side. He stood like any officer Conrad had ever seen, when it came to stand-up-and-shoot at close range of the enemy.

Nothing broke the uneasy truce, not even a shout of surprise.

'They were expecting us,' Conrad realised. 'Nora will have warned them – that someone might come, at least.'

Sound suddenly burst on Conrad's ears, making him shy like a nervous horse. The plaintive call of horns and flutes, and the low rumble of a drum – all instruments that might be easily transported – mixed with the sound of a dozen voices, spiralling up into a stretta that Conrad recognised from Roberto's scribbled score.

With the outside world shrouded by ash, falling silent as snow, every sound was emphasised. Conrad heard voices ring out, soaring up in a stunning duet.

'We're coming up to the end of the penultimate scene of Act Four,' Roberto Capiraso said, in all of Il Superbo's pedantic tones.

Conrad noted the sweat sticking volcanic ash to his forehead. He glanced around, curiously. The tiers of seating were still high, even after having suffered two thousand years of wind, rain, and depredating peasants. A glint of metal let Conrad's eyes adjust to what he was looking for.

Figures low to the ground, crouched behind the edges of the entrance arches. Just visible in the darkness. Very difficult targets.

They do have men with guns. Gamekeepers, hunters, peasants from their own estates – and I'd guess there's more than a hundred of them that I can see just from here . . .

'Firearms won't be subject to the miracle for ever,' Ferdinand murmured, under the sound of their own singers testing voices on a line here and there. 'We're in an exposed position – we *need* to defeat them. And then, we have no idea at what point in the performance their "black miracle" is planned to happen. Signore Conte, you speak on the basis that it is during the finale, but I suspect Madame Leonora did not tell her husband everything.'

Conrad just managed not to observe how that was the understatement of several decades. Seeing Roberto's expression robbed him of the desire to make jokes.

Familiar faces in filthy torn costumes – singers walked out into the arena, until they took up the places familiar from the San Carlo stage, but here, only yards from the collapsed underground way. Conrad saw that ash had darkened their faces like actors playing devils in the carnival.

537

They swear and make the sign against witchcraft every time the ground shakes.

But they are still singers.

Conrad spoke so quietly that Ferdinand leaned in to hear him. 'Sir, we don't have much of an orchestra, but I've heard Sandrine and Velluti sing a capella. The acoustics should be good, given what this place was created for. Sound does carry – so let's sing against them, the way you intended, sire.'

Ferdinand Bourbon-Sicily looked up at the daylight sky, rapidly obscured by obsidian-coloured clouds.

'Not quite the way I intended,' he said. 'But yes. Tell them – sing.'

Conrad found Velluti approaching him. 'Giambattisa, is this sufficient for you to do what you can?'

Velluti wiped black ash from his face and swore in Neapolitan dialect, surprisingly fluently. 'You know if I sing *her* part of it, my voice will be wrecked for ever! Scalese, you would have no one else to blame but yourself if I resign!'

Conrad heard in his mind the dead Estella Belucci. *If I sing it as it demands to be done, I'll burst a blood-vessel and drop dead on the stage!*

He seized on the conditional. 'But you won't resign? Not with a chance to match yourself against—'

Velluti glanced across at the singers of the Prince's Men, and a light came into his eyes.

'That *fessa*? Signore, the castrato is *the* classical voice, it will never be bettered!'

Sandrine Furino ripped a torn swathe of lace free from the hem of her snake-coloured robe. 'The one time in my life I would have been grateful for a britches role . . . ! We're ready, Corrado.'

'Ready,' JohnJack echoed.

Conrad could overhear one of the captains telling Ferdinand, *Sir, at least sit in with the soldiers or the choir, where you don't stand out as a temptation to sharp-shooters!*, but he knew what the end of that would be.

Ferdinand gave an absent nod.

'Stop her,' Count Roberto hissed, ignoring the King's aides and everyone else. 'Or she'll wake the Divine and Living God of this world – and we'll be here alive for His wrath.'

Conrad could have said plenty about the God of the Prince's Men. He found himself frowning over a quite different problem.

'Paolo.' He waited until his sister emerged from among the musicians and chorus, and stepped aside with her. 'I know what you want – so tell me what you think. We *don't* have enough musicians on our side. Roberto could conduct this last scene of *L'Altezza*. Only you can play first violin. But I won't ask it—'

The corner of her mouth pulled up.

'I wonder if Papa would approve of his violin being played to get rid of holy miracles?'

'Of course not – there's no money in it.'

She snickered. 'I'll talk to the musicians; you tell Il Superbo.'

Conrad gave the composer no chance to disagree, passing the suggestion on to Ferdinand, and letting the King make it an order.

'We're ready, sir,' Conrad said, two minutes and twenty seconds later. 'The stretta of this scene. Then we're into the last scene of all.'

Ferdinand raised his kerchief in what was evidently a signal, and brought it down sharply. Conrad saw JohnJack, two chorus tenors, a flautist bringing his instrument to his lips . . .

Paolo-Isaura stood up, her back to the tiers of seats. She put her bow to the violin that Alfredo Scalese had somehow never pawned. Conrad, to whom her face was visible, thought he had never seen her look so happy.

'She thrives on this!' he muttered, he thought too quietly to be overheard but Tullio shot him a knowing look.

'Of course she does. The same way she loves tweaking the world's nose by how she dresses.'

There was no condemnation in the big man's voice. *If anything,* Conrad thought, *Tullio Rossi looks as if he were jealous. Or at any rate, as if he craved the same kind of life.*

'Have you asked her yet?'

'Hush,' Tullio said gravely. 'They're singing.'

JohnJack stepped forward first, walking right up to the edge where the roof of the lower floors had fallen in. Conrad saw him inflate his chest, and pick up the melody with a few soft notes. The music Roberto had composed both as Isabella of Castile's soliloquy to God as she plans the death of her husband, and as Lord-General Chimalli's madness while he was haunted by the ghost of his dead king. But the words— JohnJack brought his head up with the words of *L'Altezza azteca*'s Act Four, not what the members of the black opera were singing.

My words.

'We have a damn pitiful chorus!' Conrad whispered, beside the King—and found himself gripped above the elbow, and propelled just as he was, no costume, into the back line of the nervously grouped men of the chorus.

'Don't tell me you don't know the words!' Ferdinand snapped under his breath. 'I've heard you in the rehearsal: you have a perfectly serviceable drawing-room tenor. Use it!'

Conrad picked up the choral melody, and fitted his own voice in as a background body to support the other singers.

The chorus that had come with them were not all professionals; some came from Naples' many church choirs, one or two – as Roberto no doubt noted – from drawing-rooms. Some from the comic opera houses, where the singing was in Neapolitan dialect. And a handful who merely followed opera with the obsessiveness of devotees, and – possessing a voice – were pleased to have the self-discipline to be sufficiently good to pass the audition, and spend their evenings at the back of the stage, singing. As opposed to the front, where they might hurl criticism, cheers, and bad fruit with incisive critical insight.

I may not be so out of place after all, Conrad decided, between a butcher from the Vomero district, and one of Luigi's off-duty police officers. They sang, in a swifter pace, throbbing like the great steam-engines Conrad had seen in England and France, wrapping him in nothing but the soul of music and voice.

One voice rose over the rest, searching, yearning upwards; soaring in sheer coloratura bass genius.

JohnJack! Conrad lost the rhythm of his breathing, too anxiously following the bass's brilliance.

Over on the arena's far side, the end of the aria had been scored as a duet for soprano and tenor, Leonora's voice climbing high into the ash-scented air.

The villain's Mad Scene went on, held in JohnJack's hand, stolen from the singers of *Il Reconquista d'amore*.

The Principe's tenor, spurred by an evident threat, strained and managed a creditable chest-note C.

JohnJack's gloriously resonant voice swelled out to take in the upper tiers of the Anfiteatro, without any apparent effort, and then sank down again, all in one breath – only to soar again. Mezza voce, the heart of bel canto.

Conrad wiped his cheeks hastily with the back of his hand.

Leonora, and a bass he recognised from the Paris Opera, sang as *Reconquista*'s Queen Isabella and the Muslim King of Granada – sang of the loss of the greatest age of Spain, when Christian, Muslim, and Jew alike lived and thrived there, and how the fall of Granada would wrench them from each other, as surely as it split its people into warring factions.

Their tenor broke in, singing in the new fashion, voice now soaring like a trumpet, nothing on earth like the power of nine high C chest notes in a row—

Power against intensity, Conrad thought, nursing his own head-voice C-note as much as he might, knowing there was no use attempting to put emphasis behind the sound. *Not unless I want it to crack, right here.*

The two scores fell out of synchronisation. The lovers' trio quarrel in Spain rose towards climax, each voice yearning toward the other. A few yards ahead of Conrad, Spinelli rose from his pose on one knee, where he had ended the aria with his head on his breast. He rose up with a surge, meeting the music that – Conrad could see – Roberto conducted in strict time, ignoring the momentary cacophony.

The end of the penultimate scene was scored, not as an aria, but as a cabaletta. Energy surged out of the orchestra as they switched gears, and Conrad found himself at the back of the male chorus as they surged forward – the army meeting their leader. JohnJack swung around, skinny tall body believably impressive in a breast-plate and scarlet cloak, and sent his own voice out to meet them:

'"Shame held me down, but by your faith I am risen;

'"Let us rise up, all, and save the Principessa—"'

With Estella and Lorenzo dead, both the high soprano and the tenor were missing; Velluti and JohnJack sang their transposition of it, and – inspired – Brigida's mezzo transposes down to make the necessary higher notes.

Conrad caught at Ferdinand's arm. He whispered, under the glorious sound, 'We know the black opera doesn't need more of an audience than they had at Tambora. We need an audience. And we've got it.'

Ferdinand craned his head. Conrad could tell the moment when he caught sight of the soldiers taken prisoner – some of Alvarez's men barracking the Prince's singers as if they were in the Teatro Nuovo on a Saturday night, and others applauding JohnJack, even with tied hands.

'Soldiers! If they can't find one kind of trouble, they'll find another!'

JohnJack came to the reprise of the aria, and joined his voice to the others, a bass deep enough to seem responsible for the shaking ground.

Conrad turned his head to share a look of congratulation with Ferdinand – but the King stared off towards the south east, as if there were not an opera being sung within paces of him.

Conrad found his attention dragged bodily, painfully, away from the singing.

Something's wrong.

'Sire, what—'

'Look!'

The broken vee-shape, where the walls of the amphitheatre opened away from the shattered exit, framed everything beyond it distinct and clear as a watercolour miniature.

Rock thundered up from Vesuvius, the fissure ejecting a massive jet of earth. Boulders and cumulo-nimbus clouds of dust flooded up into the darkening sky, lit by the slash of horizontal bolts of lightning.

Ferdinand was not looking there.

He stared at the hills, where the Grotto of Posillipo cut through, and the sea beyond that.

Absently, as if Conrad were merely an aide or adviser, Ferdinand pointed at the choppy grey waters under sleeting ash. 'We can't see that from here.'

'Sir?' *Is he mad?*

'This land's too low-lying.' The dusty creases in Ferdinand's face deepened. He spoke quietly, under the penultimate scenes of *Reconquista* and *L'Altezza*. 'My natural philosophers warned me . . . If, one day, the lava beneath the Burning Fields should swell and lift the land, then . . .'

Then we're standing on Hell, about to be opened!

Conrad could make out the shape of Egg Castle on its tiny promontory, but not the Palazzo Reale, where they had found the *Apollon*, or anywhere around the headland into the old city.

I don't know the land well enough to guess at how many inches of lift have been needed before we can see, not just Vesuvius, but the Golfo di Napoli at its foothills – but it's happening! Impossible that the solid earth should lift under my feet? But . . . 'I remember Pliny writing something the same, sir.'

As before – when he had visualised the sun not rising, but rounding the curve of the Earth as a racehorse rounds a bend in the course – his perceptions shifted. The physical earth, a byword for permanence, became a thin skin over magma and sulphur-gas, swelling like one of Montgolfier's balloons.

Ferdinand turned away from looking at Sorrento and Amalfi. He gazed up at Vesuvius – and made a choking sound. Conrad felt the other man grip his arm hard. He winced at the bruise.

Far over the eastern hills, the lightning-threaded tower above Vesuvius faltered.

Its upward eruption *hesitated*.

—The smoke and ash column over Vesuvius dropped.

It broke only for a heartbeat.

Conrad saw the boiling clouds of magma forced upwards again, blasting toward the cloud-ceilinged sky, plume turned red with jagged bolts of Galvanic force.

The crater of Vesuvius flooded over.

Unimaginably-hot gas boiled out of the lip, and ran down the mountainside – surged down, faster than a cavalry horse at full gallop – faster than a thought.

Conrad felt the other man's grip tighten. The onrushing front of dirty-white cloud slammed into the outlying hamlets on the foothills of Mount Vesuvius. Obliteration happened in a moment.

'The Bay—!' Conrad's heart stuttered with a brief intensity of hope. Naples, across the bite that the Golfo di Napoli takes out of the land. *Surely it can't cross the sea—*

The pyroclastic surge did not die out on the lower slopes of the mountain, nor at the edge of the sea.

It flowed out onto the water.

The billowing front of the cloud shot out onto the waves without hesitation. White steam went up in gouts from the foot of the flow – steam that might even cushion it above the sea; buoy it up as it hurtled on.

Seconds away from the city.

Risen land or not, Conrad could not see around the headlands and down into Naples itself. He witnessed the blossoming grey cloud jet out across the waters of the Gulf, aiming directly for Naples harbour.

The hills towards Posillipo cut off his view. He could only imagine what was happening seven miles away.

Conrad shivered, picturing the boiling steam and rock surging up over the hills, towards the defenceless amphitheatre.

Ferdinand breathed the words, as if the mountain itself could hear him. 'We're too far from the eruption – surely?'

Will another six or seven miles save us from the volcano? Conrad wondered.

He doubted it.

Seven miles between Pozzuoli and Naples . . . Two hours or more for a man on foot. An hour or less for a man on a good horse. And for the edge of the cloud of ash and gas, rocks and fire, that has spewed out of Vesuvius—

Minutes, only. The few miles between Naples and the Anfiteatro Flavio will make no difference. Such a distance was nothing when it came to Pompeii.

'The Anfiteatro will be flooded by rock and gas before the

544

Burning Fields can blow up.' Conrad was amazed to hear himself sound calm, even bored.

It's wonderful what panic will do.

'We're going to die.'

53

Ferdinand Bourbon-Sicily, in filthy uniform and aged grey by ash, gazed towards the scarred, steaming flank of the volcano. Conrad thought he must be picturing the streets of Naples now: super-heated ash and molten rock racing over houses and streets.

Looks like neither side will get to finish the opera.

Neither the singers nor instrumentalists moved, all their attention on the shuddering plume of rock jetting up from the distant mountain. They froze, Conrad thought, as if they thought how the collapse of the eruption might be worse than the eruption itself.

He glanced swiftly at the opera of the Prince's Men. The white figure of Leonora busily went from one to another of the singers, and back to the conductor. No one but Leonora moved.

With a considerable amount of *Schadenfreude*, Conrad thought, *Yes, these things are different in performance than rehearsal!*

Stubbornly, something not optimistic enough to be called hope reasserted itself. *Survival, perhaps.*

The concrete and brickwork of the arena floor had been worn by hundreds of years of weather and dirt, before il Principe uncovered it, and footing was everywhere uncertain. The remaining captain of the King's Rifles came forward with a dozen men, who formed up around Ferdinand as personal escort.

Conrad scrambled towards Isaura. 'Paolo! If we can start again before they do—'

Paolo's gaze went past him. She pointed up.

'Look at that . . . !'

Light vanished.

The very top of the amphitheatre seating vanished into clouds of ash, like sea-fog.

Nothing so cool, so damp, as fog.

Conrad's flesh shrank, he felt; as if his bones could bodily cringe away from the extreme heat so few yards above. Only a handful of seconds until death – *a horrible death* – skin crisped and fat melted, like a cooked animal, but all too fast to realise; *a man's body will be steam and gas within less than a heartbeat—*

He sprinted out across the arena, no thought in his mind except reaching Nora. Even knowing that he couldn't reach her, couldn't cross twenty or thirty feet of open gap, he needed to get closer to her.

It's too much, even for her, she can't survive it.

The Prince's Men can't have intended this!

A running body cannoned into him.

Conrad stumbled over broken earth and fell, not so far from where the collapsed underground passageway split the amphitheatre. His hands smarted with grit. He pushed himself up onto his feet – and saw the Conte di Argente, equally stunned, scrambling up from where the collision had knocked him.

A shriek, half pain and half joy, came from Leonora. Her hands covered her mouth. She stood in front of the other singers, staring up the ranked tiers of seating, poised on her toes—

Conrad spluttered a hysterical laugh. She might have been a parlour-maid at a fair, entranced by exploding coloured fireworks. The incongruity of it made him choke.

Roberto stared, bewildered, first at Nora, then up at the top tiers of seating.

Still tasting blood in his mouth, where he had bitten his tongue, Conrad stared where Il Superbo did.

Surging waves of ash boiled down from the obscured sky, swirling around the top of the amphitheatre. Swirling faster. Ash and superheated gas rose as if it were a blinding snowstorm.

Lightning cracked through the Anfiteatro Grande, turning the clouds white like sunrise.

A hot wind blew down around him, tightening around his forehead like an iron band, and centring in his right eye with an abrupt burst of hemicrania.

One hand over his eye, sheltering it even from this light, Conrad watched the ash whip in wind-devils and tornadoes, circling lower, until he felt nauseous and dizzy trying to follow it.

Cumulus clouds of ash and sulphur and fire flowed up and over the broken lip of the Anfiteatro walls, rolling further in, and further down towards the arena . . .

Conrad barely noticed the musicians of the Prince's Men, on the far side of the auditorium, surging down to the bottom of the steps.

The white gases flowed in through every arched entrance, at every level of the Flavian Amphitheatre except the lowest. Any remnant of grass or scrub left after the Prince's Men scraped the tiers clean now crisped up into ash. Bricks cracked under intense heat.

Run! Conrad urged himself.

His rational mind threw back the counter: *Where?*

Nora didn't run. She held her arms out, as if she welcomed the flow of magmatic heat; as if she thought she could not be harmed by it.

A blast of air hit Conrad in the face, so sharply that he threw up both hands against it, uncovering his throbbing eye. Anticipation of scalding heat tensed his spine and shoulders—

The air felt cold.

No, not just cold, Conrad thought wonderingly.

Frozen.

It blew in his face for as long as a man might count five. A wind, cold as that in the passes over the Alps, chilled his outstretched fingers – and was gone. The air in the amphitheatre was only the warmth of early spring.

'I don't understand,' he breathed, barely conscious he spoke aloud.

A few yards away, Roberto Capiraso made an incoherent sound, and turned his head frantically, staring around the stone bowl of the Anfiteatro Flavio.

The great rolling clouds flowed in – and seemed somehow to clot.

Conrad frowned.

Clumps and clusters of ash grew smaller and more dense. Separating out, coalescing out of the storm. Smaller still: as if they were no more than the height of a man—

Vapour and dust flowed into the amphitheatre, last remnant of the pyroclastic surges that must have devastated Naples.

Out of it, now – created of its substance – onto brickwork that cracked as it cooled – the dead came walking.

They took up ten or twenty rows of the upper seating easily, overflowing further down every moment.

Lightning dazzled from the volcano's towering pillar of cloud. Seen by violent splashes of light, Conrad made out first one man, then a woman, then three children running, another man . . . a dozen men . . . a hundred . . .

Thousands, Conrad mutely thought.

Filling the amphitheatre. Thousands of people.

Precipitating out of the volcanic ash that has taken Naples.

Sweat rolled down his temples, collecting coldly between his shoulder-blades.

'Corrado! There—' Tullio's hand caught at his.

Grey gases crept to the lowest of the tiers, close by.

A figure emerged from the swirl of the pyroclastic cloud, all white and ash-colours, but solid; no ghost or apparition. He brushed himself off as he emerged, and ended still dusty with ash, but recognisably in the colours of human flesh. The man wore a smart police uniform with cape and gloves; his dead face white and his dead eyes lively with amusement.

'*Luigi?*'

It was impossible to say more. Conrad's throat closed up with immediate overwhelming grief.

Luigi Esposito seated himself on the lowest tier, one knee crossed casually over the other, as if he were still a living man. He

549

removed his hat with its cockade and carefully brushed it, dust-coloured as it was.

Conrad could not see what had killed him.

Heat, pressure, lava, gas – it could be anything . . .

Realisation hit him.

Every man, woman, or child that walks out of the ash-cloud has Returned Dead from Naples.

They walk so close together that their shoulders rub. Thousands—and still there seems no end of them.

'The first miracle was clear air.' Conrad heard Tullio grunt assent. 'And the second, freedom from any weapon that could strike them from a distance.'

'Suppose this is the third, padrone.'

'Part of it,' Conrad muttered.

There's whatever she plans to do at the last.

Conrad turned away from his dead friend Luigi and stared across the broken earth, open pits, and sprawled hostages on the arena floor. The earth was hot underfoot. A last wisp of cloud covered him, briefly; he had to cover his mouth, and hack a cough that felt like needles in his chest, but the ash whirled and lifted, and took the feeling of suffocation with it.

The Returned Dead, uncovered by the dissipating surge, occupied all the upper seats of the amphitheatre, and considerably further down the rows nearer to Leonora and her minimal scenery and other singers. In a theatre that is known to have seated forty thousand in its heyday, they made it a quarter or even a third full.

Conrad wished he was close enough to see Nora's face clearly.

Judging by how she stalked and gestured, driving her musicians back into place, there was nothing left now of the Contessa, or of the ferocious singer of Venezia. If she distantly seemed brought down to skin and bone, what was left was the stubborn, determined, charity-child, fire in her eyes to let her have her ambition's way with the world.

I wish I could get close enough to speak to her without shouting. Ask why she did this – because she has done this—

'They're her audience,' Conrad said aloud.

Ferdinand's mouth set in one hard line. 'My people!'

Roberto shook his head. It was obvious he'd been told nothing about it.

Economically making use of the people who formed her 'blood sacrifice', so that she can get emotional reactions to the black opera—

If that's so, why didn't she do it before now?

If Conrad walked across the arena and (supposing he survives) shouts and asks her what she plans to do – he knew she'd tell him what il Principe's men have always claimed. Change the Mind of God.

Is it for this she's calling the recently dead of Naples back—?

The ash-clouds flowed on down onto the middle rows of seating, and stopped. Luigi remained an isolated figure.

Conrad took in, at a glance, the small number of men on their side. Ferdinand's riflemen – those who were not prisoners – sprawled along the lower tiers, gabbling like old gossips as they stared up at the Returned Dead of Naples. That and the hostages formed any audience sympathetic to *L'Altezza azteca*.

Conrad tried not to despair at the pitiful number of singers and musicians. *It may not matter.*

Roberto made some urgent explanation and left the King's side; Paolo, violin in hand, strode with him back to their singers. Conrad followed. Sandrine and Spinelli stood hand in hand. Velluti absently dusted at his white robes, all his covert attention on Leonora, seventy yards away.

'Corrado?' Brigida Lorenzani looked up from pinning a length of borrowed green cloth around her hips – torn from JohnJack's robe, by the colour. It gave her a modest full-length skirt under her shining breastplate. 'What do we do? Is there anything we can do?'

'Pick up from where we broke off,' JohnJack said, with a wary glance down the arena. 'Corrado, we're stronger if we have her musicians too. If she can stop them panicking.' His dusty round face moved into a wry grin. 'If her people are having hysterics, what are we supposed to do?'

Conrad caught Paolo's eye. She put her violin to her shoulder, with an encouraging word to Roberto, Conte di Argente, and joined the oboist and flautist.

Conrad halted beside the Count, leaning to look at the score one of the King's aides held.

Roberto gave an odd smile. 'You trust me, then? Not to sabotage as I conduct?'

'I don't think you ever cared about the Prince's Men. You played spy for them, and saboteur, but that was all for Nora. Now she's—' Conrad spoke with all the control he could muster. He couldn't bring himself to use the word *betrayed*. '—Lost your trust, you'll do anything to see *Reconquista* fail. Tell me I'm wrong.'

The Count snorted in sour amusement.

'Besides,' Conrad finished, 'guns have to start working again sometime. And then Tullio Rossi can shoot you dead.'

'Not even killed by a gentleman. That will sting.'

Despite the desperate strangeness of the situation, Conrad couldn't help a snort of amusement.

He glanced over his shoulder, and saw the Prince's Men still stumbling about. Instinct moved him to turn, where he stood beside Roberto, and address the singers and musicians.

'I think it's simple.' Conrad spoke loud enough for the acoustics of the auditorium to let him be heard. 'The Prince's Men have brought an audience. Clearly, they think the Returned Dead are theirs. I say— I say we have to win their audience.'

Light and shadow danced on the rough earth: the shadows of the ejection plume, and its lightnings. Distance dulled its fierceness.

We're not so far from Misenum, Conrad realised, *where the younger Pliny saw the eruption merely as an umbrella-tree of smoke pouring up into the sky.*

Pliny didn't have to contend with what's happening outside at this moment.

And even so, Pliny the Elder went in ships to take off refugees, and met his death on those beaches.

Conrad gathered his thoughts and his resolution. He pushed the pain in his skull as far into the background as he could. He met their eyes as he looked along the row of them, sitting on the first step: JohnJack, Sandrine, Brigida, Velluti. Paolo's wide excited eyes, and the different but equally grave frowns of King Ferdinand and Il Superbo.

'You have to trust the opera.'

He began pacing again, not able to contain his energy.

'Not *The Aztec Princess*, in particular. I mean: trust opera. Trust bel canto. There must be no jealousy, no aggression and backbiting, no upstaging; nothing that makes them call us *la feccia teatrale*. Unselfish singing.'

One hand went over his eye to prevent the light falling in it. He was aware he must look a fool, but he went on without regard for that.

'No singer ever made a success of an aria on their own! Not even a solo. If there's no chorus involved, there's still the orchestra. I know what tricks people have in duets and trios and choruses, singing over the top of one another, showing off coloratura where the score doesn't call for it – the list is endless.'

A low rumble rolled up from the west, shivering through the earth – originating, not from Vesuvius, but from the Campi Flegrei.

'I've sat in the pit and listened to singers support each other. You've read the score: you know that if you sing to make your partner look good, they'll return the favour further on. You become part of something stronger—' Conrad fought for words, and gave Ferdinand a nod of acknowledgement. '—Something more intense . . . You trust bel canto itself—'

A long-drawn chord launched on the air.

Conrad halted, swinging round and staring down the long axis of the amphitheatre. The singers of il Principe clustered in a ruck, on the edge of the stage farthest from the Returned Dead. A low chorus began.

A few yards off, on the lowest tier, Conrad saw Luigi Esposito lean forward, one elbow on his knee, hand cupped to his ear to better hear the distant singing.

'That's it, right there. We have to get Luigi's attention. And everyone else's.'

Conrad couldn't bring himself to look up the tiers at the *lazzaroni* and corn-sellers and butchers and laundry-women who made up a proportion of Neapolitans present.

'And we need to do it soon. Or the Prince's Men will have won.'

Conrad turned away. Roberto gathered their attention with the lift of a hand. Conrad glimpsed the King's face.

I suppose I need not ask if he regrets, now, not giving orders to evacuate Naples before the eruption.

'You should sing.' Conrad put out a hand to stop Ferdinand rejoining his scant group of officers. 'Any of us who aren't professional, but can read music, will make an adjunct to the chorus.'

Ferdinand's bland face took on a smile. 'I admit to singing while Maria played the piano; I'm not hopeless. Very well. Some of these gentlemen may have done more than sing in the mess. I'll call them over.'

'Yes, sir—'

In the centre of the Anfiteatro, not far from the cleft in the earth, Leonora stepped forward, lifted her head, and – a capella – reprised the first two bars that began her final part in *Il Reconquista d'amore*.

'It's the finale ultimo!' Conrad snapped, ushering Ferdinand Bourbon-Sicily into the row of chorus singers, beside him. He pitched his voice to carry to all of the remaining company of the Teatro San Carlo. 'We've practised this enough to sing it asleep! We don't have—'

Estella and Lorenzo.

'—Soprano and tenor, but you know the roles transposed to your own voices. The Prince's Men haven't even had it all their own way so far! But it isn't decided until it's finished. Remember what we know – you can trust bel canto, and we can trust who we sing with!'

Conrad took a space, this time between a church-choir mezzo and a captain of the King's Rifles; the latter moving over to make room for Ferdinand.

A few yards around the shallow curve, Paolo sat with the oboe player and other musicians. At her feet, she had the case she had been clutching aboard ship; in her hands, Alfredo Scalese's violin.

JohnJack, Brigida, Velluti and Sandrine clustered on the arena floor, and Roberto Capiraso, Conte di Argente, some yards in front where all could see him.

They began to sing.

How long before ... before we stop what the Prince's Men have planned for so long? Or before what they plan to do – is done?

He barely noticed his audience. If he had been told that he would, one day, ignore the better part of ten thousand Returned Dead men and women, he would have laughed. Only a minor part of him kept any track of the Neapolitans, sprawled on the tiers as their ancient pagan ancestors would have, desperate for blood shed for entertainment. Only the absence of wine and bread and olives made it clear this was no usual crowd.

We're losing them.

He breathed, in respite from his role as the tenor shadowing what Lorenzo Bonfigli would have sung, and gazed down the amphitheatre. Sunlight still blazed beyond the western edge of the eruption cloud. The edge of shadow caught Sandrine and Velluti, singing hand in hand as if lovers were trusting children.

Across the arena, where the Sun was full, Isabella of Castile stood as her pages removed her bright armour, and gowned her in blue and gold. Her low contralto floated across the ancient, shattered stone:

'Di Dio più santo, io giuro!'

By God most holy, I swear!

The Returned Dead of Naples shifted in their seats, heads turning first towards Conrad, where Velluti spiralled a delicate harmony up beside Sandrine's mezzo, and then to the Prince's Men and the inhuman perfection of Isabella at the height of her conquest. Conrad cast a quick glance round. *What do we have here? Hundreds? Dozens?*

One of Alvarez's sergeants held out Isaura's scribbled-over score for Conrad to share. About to shake his head, Conrad caught Roberto's eye on him.

A stern jerk of the conductor's hand, and Conrad bent over the score – startled at what authority the man carried when he was not being il Conte – and found his place.

He straightened to sing, this time shadowing Sandrine.

Conrad waited until his rest came before he looked again. He climbed onto the lowest tier, shading his eyes against the brighter end of the amphitheatre.

'Oh, I think I see . . .'

He stepped down, threading his way between singers to where Roberto Capiraso conducted. The Count stood with his body twisted, attempting to both conduct from the score a rifleman held out for him to see, and listen to Brigida Lorenzani whispering urgently.

Conrad overheard her frustrated cry: 'They're trying to listen to both of us!'

Without wasting time, Conrad gave a sharp nod of agreement. 'The two operas share music.'

He kept all accusation from his voice.

'There are differences,' Conrad pressed on. 'Particularly in the finale ultimo, but I think we ought to have realised before now – as far as our audience is concerned, there aren't two operas. There's one.'

Roberto Capiraso scowled, went to speak, halted, and began again. 'If we're the "black opera" too—'

'—As much as Nora's singers are the counter-opera.' Conrad faced the bearded man and his dark, haunted eyes. 'You told me you thought the end of *Aztec Princess* was better than *Reconquista*. So it comes down to singing it to interpret it that way—'

JohnJack shook his robe, a few more sewn peacock's feathers abandoning it with the dust. 'But if we're all singing the same thing—!'

'You're not; not quite. And it wouldn't matter if you were. What matters—'

With time running out, Conrad found the words.

'What *matters* is whether those people sitting down there feel that you're singing in support of Nora's principals, or whether Nora and il Principe are singing comprimario roles to you!'

A moment succeeded, silent despite every note and every voice in the arena.

Sandrine patted at her hair, re-fixing a hair-pin. 'People's attention has to – shift. We have to sing well enough to make it apparent her voice is in service to ours.'

'Yes.'

'And this from the man who wanted none of the dirty tricks of bel canto!'

Conrad silently marvelled at what he was about to say. 'Trust your composer.'

The startled-deer look that Il Superbo shot him was almost worth it.

'Trust him,' Conrad repeated, 'because *L'Altezza azteca* is the most recently composed and revised of the two. *Reconquista* was written over the space of years. *L'Altezza* was composed over weeks in a white heat in *il mondo teatrale*. Which do you think is going to be better?'

It got a knowing chuckle from all of them, even Velluti.

'Places!' Paolo-Isaura called, not interrupting her playing.

Roberto Capiraso hung back a moment as the singers walked forward across the nominal 'stage'.

'Do you believe that to be true?'

'I do.' Conrad smiled crookedly. 'Under any other circumstances, of course, I wouldn't admit it.'

'No.' Roberto's lips twitched, in a smile darker and more self-knowing than Conrad had seen before. 'I don't suppose you would. Get into line, tenor. This is the finale.'

It's not up to me, to Roberto, even to Paolo. It's up to the singers. And chiefly, to those four men and women—

Conrad didn't move from where he stood on the arena floor, transfixed as they sang.

—Sang the wrong parts, but the right voices. Lines transposed – because every singer knew all the words of the scene. And it was not Velluti, but JohnJack, who sang, *'Mi perdono, perdonata!'* in his resonant, precise, passionate bass, holding Sandrine's hand as he sang, the General begging pardon of his Princess rather than the hero of his King.

Every word and note fell into place.

Velluti put his arm around Brigida's plump shoulders and sang with her the duet that should have been hers and her daughter's, 'We are strangers, you and I, in this land of stone and serpent,' and the emotion fitted both of them, Hernan Cortez so far from any familiar road or hill to walk down, and Thalestris utterly at sea

557

in a country that values no woman unless she fights for power like a man, and Conrad couldn't keep his eyes off Leonora.

He broke off his singing and whispered to Paolo. 'Move, go with them, she's doing it!'

He pointed down the arena, where Leonora walked up the centre of the arena, or as close as she could come while avoiding the sunken corridor, and her voice was sufficient without accompanying instruments – *which is just as well*, Conrad thought, watching her bewildered musicians already frightened by the Returned Dead, and the bemused other singers of the Prince's Men who stared after her from the stage.

Leonora walked on, fists clenched, and sang, and turned all the heads of the audience to her.

Roberto bowed his head to one side to hear Paolo and sharply nodded assent, and without ceasing to mark the time, said, 'We'll go down towards her.'

The instruments they had with them were of necessity portable, but he signalled the musicians to stay with their scores.

He knows he can depend on the Prince's Men for music, Conrad realised, walking down the arena behind the composer.

'Bring my music,' Paolo directed without ceasing to play.

She walked off, and the other musicians followed her anyway. Conrad picked her score up, holding it open so that she could see it; silently cursing at having a buffoon's part. He just managed not to fall over the rock-bombs that scattered the arena now, hot and spitting where they sat in small craters in the earth and brickwork.

Tullio took the score from his hands with a reassuring grin.

Leonora launched into improvised coloratura melody.

It was not in Il Superbo's score. For a moment the counter-opera clashed horribly to a stop.

Roberto bit out a sharp oath. '*Cazzo!* You sons of whores, keep playing!'

The handful of musicians began to play from the score.

First Velluti and Sandrine, then Brigida, and at last JohnJack, abandoned the known notes – and the rehearsed score – to soar with Nora's incredible voice; winding a coloratura quartet around

558

her because they can improvise like this, they know the shape of music and can follow her.

Conrad stopped, his serviceable tenor nowhere capable, and his mind leaped to catch the new melody.

This! Yes, this—

This is what I heard when I dreamed, weeks ago.

When I had hemicrania after *Il Terrore di Parigi*. What I was dreaming as I woke.

It can't be.

It isn't in the score, and it's not something I heard Roberto play, but I dreamed it, and only now remember.

Objections followed on the tail of that; thick, fast—

I only imagine I dreamed it; I had hemicrania then and now, it's a false similarity, or even a product of the illness. It must be like a part of the score that I've forgotten. Or something Roberto did once play. Or she stole it from another opera and I'll remember in what house I heard it . . .

He violently forced himself to believe the reasons of Reason. It did no good. All of him, heart, mind, and soul – *If there's any such thing!* – insisted that it was true.

Conrad's head throbbed, less for the pain in his skull than the painful puzzlement of knowing in his heart that he first heard this sound in sleep on a morning in February, on a day when he had no idea whether Nora was alive or dead, and no conception of what her voice had become now it had been through fire and ice. *I dreamed what she is singing now.*

Is there some link between us, since Venice, that I heard in my own mind what must have been in hers, rehearsing for the black opera?

Conrad's eye throbbed in time to his heartbeat. He stared at Nora. A faint unseeable disturbance in his vision warned him.

As it had in times past, a flickering defect appeared in the centre of his vision, expanding outwards until the whole world was fractured in planes of light. He stood blind, nausea rising in his throat, and the music and her voice seizing on him.

He felt himself listening so acutely that it was as if he joined with the music. He barely noticed the defects of light in his field of vision – did not note when they dwindled and shrank, as they so far always had, and freed him from the icy terror of remaining blind.

The conviction remained. *I've dreamed this; these are the notes I couldn't retain in my mind.* For all the reasons why it might be an illusion, a trick of memory, a wished-for thing; he could not divest himself of the absolute knowledge of the inexplicable.

It's something I can neither climb over nor go around, he thought, his now-clear gaze on Nora's face.

She looked as intent and silly as most singers do, finding the sounds within their body and giving them voice, and she leaned forward very slightly, as if she leaned into a gale that opposed her.

Something broke warm and fragile within him; he loved her with something that was not pity – *No one can offer such a force of nature pity!* – but might have included an empathy for another outsider who remained out of the pale of ordinary men's social lives, not from some romantic rejection of it, but simply because what she is – what Leonora Sposito is – precludes it.

And yet she's improvising.

Voice mounting by leaps, with no need for breath control, no weakness in the passaggio – though indeed she must be controlling the breathing she didn't need, to produce the sound.

Her voice lifted up, bringing half the Returned audience of Naples to their feet with her, stamping, whistling, cheering, crying *brava!, bella!, bellissima!*

At that moment, the four voices of Sandrine, Brigida, JohnJack and Velluti, and the musicians – the orchestra of the Prince's Men, too – dived into unison, and flew up, and missed four bars seamlessly together, all of them, without any sign to each other or from the Count. Missed those bars and came in together on the next phrase, their playing and singing all of a piece.

The principal singers of the San Carlo walked forward, their music lifting hearts; stood all in a line with hands joined, and began to sing the finale as Roberto had rewritten it.

JohnJack first, noble and immoral, loved once, corrupted by ambition but raised up now by remorse, swearing to go into exile as Sandrine bade him, but first to lay down his life for her against the white man's king.

And at this, the Aztec Princess gave him a wonderful smile as Sandrine came in, at lowest contralto, jumping two octaves and dropping down, swearing she would walk through a sea of blood to keep her throne, but she would not put her General Chimalli or her Consort Cortez in danger of their lives. Love is so easily frangible and comes so seldom that it is never to be wasted when it comes—

Brigida's voice broke for a second as she joined the bass and contralto, lamenting her daughter whose love she has lost to a man who no longer cares for her. *Now I will take Hippolyta home and soothe her hurts.* Brigida sang with the desperate knowledge that no hurt of Estella's can ever be soothed: she lies dead on the stage of the broken Teatro San Carlo.

To his utter amazement Conrad saw a tear slide down in the dust on Velluti's cheek.

The castrato added his voice to what should have been a sextet – were not Lorenzo Bonfigli laying with Estella, as dead as she – and Velluti brought his presence into the choir of voices, not ponderous, but young and energetic as his clear, dark face.

He sang first to JohnJack: that if they have been enemies and competitors before, they now meet equal on the floor of desiring what is the most best for the Princess, for that Tayanna whom they both love.

And then, to Brigida, the castrato sang that whatever happens to him, her family will always find succour among those who have loved the name of Hernan Cortez.

'Non sia spaventato!' Velluti's voice soars up, swelling, unencumbered by the thunderhead eruption cloud overhead. 'Don't be afraid! Proud defender of your nation, you will always find a friend in me.'

They ought to look comic, Conrad thought. The over-tall castrato singer in dirty robes and armour, his hands resting on the much lower shoulders of the round Brigida Lorenzani . . . but it only makes the words come with more sincerity.

They faced the singers of il Principe with utter defiance. Brigida

561

held a prop sword – Conrad couldn't begin to imagine how she might have clung to it through the San Carlo's destruction and the flight on board the *Apollon*; but there it is, wiped clean of dust – and it gleamed as she raised it.

The steel of her breastplate caught the light, and glowed with the colour of the dust clouds. Not a property armour, but one from Castel dell'Ovo made for a large man, and it fitted her; and Conrad saw at last why they call bright steel 'white armour', taking every bit of light and reflecting it the colour of milky ash.

Brigida sang, 'How long have I wandered – and to find my daughter so!'

They came up to the new lines that Conrad had talked her through as they scrambled over rock and ash, leaving Pozzuoli. He found himself holding his breath.

'*Solo una memoria, curò teneramente ed adorò* . . . Just a memory, cherished and adored.' She voiced it flawlessly. 'I will take home with me this token of your love, your son.'

The voices flowed in and about each other.

JohnJack lifted his head.

'*Fratello detestato!*' His deep voice reached every highest terrace of the amphitheatre. '*Nemico valutato!*'

Detested brother. Valued enemy.

Conrad caught a sideways glance from Roberto Conte di Argente, where the man conducted.

I never thought . . .

Conrad lost himself in the music, with the knowledge that very often one does not think; the applicability to personal situations is only apparent afterwards; and in some senses, a libretto is always a story that the poet tells himself, only to be truly read after it's finished and other people sing it back to him.

All four of the voices sang. Here and there a silent bar, where Lorenzo or Estella should have come in – Conrad found his throat too tight to give voice, reminded painfully of those parades after the war, in which the cavalry formations led a horse with an empty saddle, to mark all the fallen.

It is those silences that underscore the sadness of glory and joy that is the last stretta of *The Aztec Princess*. Far more than what

Leonora is singing, her coloratura moving as unnaturally far below the female voice as Velluti's is above the male, but it didn't matter, Conrad saw and heard.

The attention of the Dead is not divided.

They were not partisan between one opera or another. Inexplicable as it seemed, he thought—

The people of Naples regard both these operas as one and the same work.

But what else are they to think? Conrad realised. *All singers are on the one stage!*

They clap and compliment all equally. Leonora's is not the solo star voice. It is, Conrad hears, the accompaniment to what the quartet sing. JohnJack's 'I regret', Sandrine's 'I love'. Brigida's 'I grieve', and Velluti's 'I burn with the fire of ambition'. For a stanza, Leonora was the comprimario voice which threw all of theirs into sharp relief.

She realised it, he saw, but there was nothing to be done.

Conrad began to sing, very quietly, in the tenor which would never be professional, no matter how much as a young man he had tried. Sang softly enough that surely no one could hear him, but sang, because it was beyond him not to be a part of this.

He walked forward, finding himself behind Paolo-Isaura, who sent her bow over the strings in ferocious pursuance of the score. She whipped out notes as if the violin bow were a sword; reinforcing Roberto's control of all the singers of the counter-opera as she walked, as if all the gathered singers were one instrument, and could be played like one alone.

Tullio Rossi walked beside her with the score open in one hand, and an army bayonet in the other. He stared alertly from side to side for threats, acting as if he were the one man present not involved by the musicodramma – but Conrad saw his feet fell on the cinders in the rhythm of the major part of the music.

It changed.

From quartet and comprimario to an ensemble of all five singers – Leonora's superb unearthly voice winding in and out of the others, joining in unison now with Velluti, now with Brigida, now with JohnJack and Sandrine, until it was not possible to say whether she sang for the black opera or against it.

Even more troubling, Conrad found as he dropped his efforts to sing, blasphemous in the face of this kind of quality, there was no way to say if the San Carlo's quartet sang for the counter-opera or against it.

The stretta of the finale ultimo became something else with a life of its own. He lost his breath at the sound of it. Velluti and Leonora without hesitation and on the same note changed roles, so that Nora's voice rang out triumphantly on 'O Re, mi perdono,' and Giambattista Velluti portrayed more emotion in his voice than he ever had in acting, and sang at the lowest extent of his range, 'We will live as one, all together, as we ought.'

Nora sang coloratura improvisation around the melody that Conrad had heard when he dreamed of storm-riven sea-water sinking into sand. He couldn't recognise it – *should* not, because what does that say about the universe? – but he did.

He tried desperately not to be swept away.

He failed.

His heart clenched under his ribs with a sensation of emotional vulnerability as the chorus joined her, and soared up into air thick with destruction. He forgot that it was Roberto Capiraso – *husband to the woman I love* – who had created this music. Forgot that it was Nora singing – *lying treacherous bitch* – and felt something in himself aching, reaching out, gathering himself and his energy as the orchestra and singers began building by note and phrase.

The voices of il Principe's tenor and contralto joined her inhuman voice, making something – *heart, lungs, soul?* – swell inside his rib-cage until Conrad became breathless. *Not inhuman!*, he protested his own thought. *But not human either.*

Orchestra and other singers paused in an aching moment's silence. Nora's soprano rang out:

'*Non perdoni! Io non pento!*'

Isabella of Castile's declaration, when her plans of murder are irrevocably committed:

'Do not forgive! I do not regret!'

Her audience cheer, shout, loud enough to drown the instruments – the strings (and Conrad thinks that if opera has a soul, it rests on the strings) – the brass for emotion, and the drums are the heartbeat.

All of it nothing without the voice. *And now's the time to find out if that prejudice is true*, he thought. *Because, here, we have almost nothing else except the voice—*

Conrad would laugh if he weren't weeping. He stifled that, so he could feed even his own weak tenor into the chorus. A little ragged because not rehearsed, but forgivably human against Leonora's searing unbelievable accuracy.

Words slotted seamlessly into sound, the stresses falling on the important emotions and knowledge – the surge of the chorus coming to lift the whole body of the work up – he smeared tears from the corners of the eyes with his sleeve. The stretta shifted to a different level: words and lines repeating – he heard the distant drums and trumpets of war – the aching desire of love – the words carried beyond the music by one singing voice—

Music and choir crashed back down in a secular hymn, an anthem that sent shivers down the hairs of Conrad's nape.

Everything acted on his nerves, as if he had no skin: the interplay between soloist and crowd – the part the orchestration played in echoing back the words – everything complex and complete to the last decorated words and music. All the singers' voices lift up, and buttress the poignant voice of the soloist – desiring, balked in that desire, but searing up to completion despite all. Even the pain is enjoyable, or it would not be possible to leave a performance streaming with tears and yet searingly happy.

His head throbbed, hearing her melody and that of *L'Altezza* twine around each other, join and climb, all five voices lifting like the skylark that flies up and up into the hot skies of June, flies upward until it can sing no more and falls out of the sky – every effort given, every heart emptied, every exposed emotion naked and the dead of Naples stand up on the amphitheatre steps, where their ancestors cheered blood, two thousand years ago, and they shout, shout almost enough to drown the orchestras, calling in a confused mess for each of the singers by name, Velluti, Spinelli, Lorenzani, Furino – and *Contessa*!, too; *Leonora*!, Conrad heard; the audience giving their loud validation not to one or the other but to both, as if the only way to defeat the black opera were for black opera and white opera to become one.

'The finales are different!' Conrad shouted – going completely unheard.

The music passed without a break into the finale ultimo, that in *Reconquista* will be tragic death and then triumph: Ferdinand of Aragon's death, and the apotheosis of Isabella of Castile, free to rule and reign. And in *L'Altezza azteca* . . . will be forgiveness.

It felt like a physical weight on his shoulders. *Roberto composed both of these, so the difference is in the words—*

The thought was swept away in a moment. Dramatic soprano and male soprano clashed against each other, and Conrad thought, *No, I wrote the emotion, but it is how* they *interpret it.*

It is on Tullio's face that Conrad sees the first change.

Sees him soften, caught up without his own wish, as, a few yards away, Velluti began to truly sing.

Some of his voice was male soprano. Some down in the natural range that castrati normally sing: a rich and flexible contralto. Some of the notes dropped low enough that they must be out of Velluti's tessitura—

And they *are.*

'Sandrine!'

Conrad stared at the mezzo, hearing Sandrine picking up the role of the hero, to give voice to all that she is – both upper and lower ranges of her stupendous range. She did not risk jumping from one to the other, or finding some passaggio, but she sang in a mezzo that mirrored Leonora's flawless soprano, and then dropped to a strong tenor to out-sing il Principe's man, her coloratura brilliant enough that even the Prince's Men applauded.

Tullio said in deep appreciation, 'God *damn.'*

A soaring note rose from Leonora, up into the smoky air, buttressed by the male voices. Her coloratura roused Alvarez's shackled hostages to shout in appreciation. Conrad found his eyes free of volcanic dust as water welled up and ran down his cheeks.

No one has ever heard such singing, Conrad knows. Or ever will again. *Whatever power there is in musicodramma, this is the zenith of it.*

Rocket-showers of notes cascading into the thickening air, spangles, bright as thrown gold coins, joyful as bells – the unearthly sound bringing the taste of ash and char into Conrad's mouth, as she reached notes not attainable by the human voice.

A capella, Velluti and Sandrine and Brigida sang with the joys and pains that belong to mortality, love, and pardon.

The slim figure of Leonora, so still against the background of swirling ash and smoke; she sings with the joy that comes of being freed of the pains of mortality, Conrad knows.

No wonder she sings Non perdoni! *Who has a right to pardon her?*

Time doesn't constrain her any more: she has all the time in the world. Death isn't an end: death is endless life to her – endless existence, anyway. If she finds herself in pain, she need only wait, and sooner or later it will end. For all intents and purposes, she is immortal.

Her aria took what the others sang as joy, and transmuted it into a wrenching sorrow. Conrad couldn't help the water that ran down his face. Her words spoke of triumph, but the sound spoke of love denied—

Across the distance of the arena, Conrad met her gaze.

One of us.

The sadness in her song comes from looking at us: Roberto and Conrad. Two men she loves – *I think, still truly loves, despite being dead – and she weeps because she has neither of us.*

Watching her bright eyes and unbound hair, he thought, *She needs a lover who will love what she is, or she will mourn still when Naples is a city of brick and iron, far far in the future.*

The two sets of voices soared, and he was not certain, now, whether they fought, or whether they supported each other: Leonora's fire, Velluti's slender beauty, and Sandrine's pure open joy in singing. Their voices have all the joy and aching pain of being alive in them, heightened so it is more bearable than mere everyday living.

Leonora's voice soars, luring them to follow—

Velluti's voice broke.

567

It cracked and tore, with a sound no human throat ought to make.

Conrad had a split second to think *Velluti will be lucky if he ever speaks again, never mind sings—*

Leonora was still standing. Triumphant, opening her mouth, singing her coloratura victory at them—

Not higher, but more able to penetrate the dull everyday and carry the hearer away. Not louder, but more intense; soaking up every part of the one who hears it, and impelling emotion into them.

Leonora began to walk forward towards them.

Conrad glanced back – saw Roberto Capiraso stop conducting – and Paolo-Isaura flawlessly pick it up in mid-bar—

The Conte di Argente walked until he was almost at the crumbling edge of the gap. He and Leonora stood no more than eight metres apart, across the gash in the earth. Close enough to see expressions, even the most subtle; close enough to hear what is spoken, if not what is whispered.

Incalculably far apart; the gap cannot be bridged.

Conrad couldn't stop himself. He slipped out of the group of singers and went forward.

'Leonora.' The Count's ash-clogged voice could not have carried two yards, but she looked at him as she sang, her voice rising to pure notes that the human voice could not reach.

Her voice reached up, overcoming the ambient noise, even the thundering explosions of Monte Nuovo and Solfatara that miracle kept outside the amphitheatre. She lifted her head, as if the shrieks of applause from the rising tiers blew into her face like a warm summer wind. Her voice caressed pure notes that the human voice cannot sound.

'We can't win against that!' Conrad swore, frustrated.

Roberto's fists clenched at his side. He didn't look away from his wife's face. 'You've realised that, have you?'

The great stretta of the fourth act's finale ultimo swelled

up, soaring over the fumes and smoke of the Burning Fields, Leonora's voice going far beyond the mortal.

She prolonged the final note far beyond the ability of a living singer. Conrad listened and let it run through him, never staggered by Roberto Capiraso's work as much as he was now.

A silence fell, like no other.

Silence after the great anthem of the finale – silence padded by the volcanic ash that still sleeted down over the Burning Fields, covering the stone of the amphitheatre and the men and women who stood inside it.

The ash-born crowds of dead men and women turned as one, every head simultaneous; from those on the highest tier of the amphitheatre to those a dozen yards away.

'Padrone.' Beside Conrad, Tullio's whisper sounded taut. 'Why are they all looking at us?'

A crackle of friction-lightning echoed through the amphitheatre. The thunder that rolled around the eruption pillar of Vesuvius shook the stones.

The lips of the Returned Dead moved in unison.

The voice, from each ash-dry throat, spoke.

'You have summoned the Living God – and I am here.'

54

Conrad found himself speaking before he realised that he would.

'I don't know what you are, but I do know you're not God!'

Commotion. Many living voices speaking. Many Returned Dead speaking in unison, speech interwoven so that all – including the voices of the most distant – seemed to arrive simultaneously in his ear.

The unified voice demanded, 'How do you know this?'

'I don't know it, the way you mean "know",' Conrad said, surprisingly buoyed up by that conviction. 'Not to be certain. I've no proof. But it seems to me the most likely theory.'

Paolo-Isaura muttered, beside him, 'You mean you're positive that you're not sure.'

Conrad's declaration was drowned out by Dominicans – Luka Viscardo's voice the most vociferous. And by the remaining living Prince's Men, hailing the vocal apparition as the Prince of this World.

And by a number of the King's riflemen loudly praying; crying that they should have brought a priest.

Only Ferdinand looked amused at Conrad's willingness to debate theology and philosophy in the middle of something aching to turn into killing violence.

The throng of Returned Dead stood shoulder-to-shoulder in ranks on the tiers of the amphitheatre. They – or it – ignored the prayers, praise, and cries of heresy issuing from the Prince's men, to focus on Conrad.

'For all I know,' Conrad added, 'since you're speaking through all our voices, you're something that comes from our dreams.'

He half-hoped he might be given some clue to Nora's music.

Instead, the Voice of the Dead visibly pondered.

The risen earth shook under their feet.

Conrad eyed those of the Prince's Men with rifles – those he could still see. They had mostly abandoned the upper levels of the ruined amphitheatre, he noted, almost with amusement. As if guns would be harmless for all the future. The lower archway entrances seemed crowded with men who still carried guns, and who could cover King Ferdinand's small force without effort.

'Now it begins.'

Leonora's voice filled the air without effort. Conrad watched her, standing on the arena floor, gazing up at the Returned Dead of Naples.

'What is she doing?' Paolo asked.

Conrad turned his head, looking for Roberto Capiraso, and found the Count standing with his hands clasped behind him, as if he stood at the back of an opera-box like any gentleman, watching the finer points of the performance. 'Roberto?'

'They've given the Prince of this World the ability to over-ride the rules that the Creator-God set in place.'

Capiraso's lips quirked in a dark, oddly self-mocking, smile. To Conrad it said, *How could I ever have believed in this?*

'In a moment, the requests will begin. I beg your pardon: prayers. And then we see how different a world the Prince will make.'

Leonora lifted her head, gazing up at rank upon rank of the Returned Dead. Conrad expected to see more kinship with them. He thought she still outshone every one.

'You are free!' Her voice came as triumphant as when she sang. 'Prince of the World, you're free. Tell us how you've healed this world of its pain.'

Silence.

They're wondering what to tell her first.

571

Conrad surveyed row upon row of Naples faces. The kinship of being Returned was too subtle for him to see. What was plain – entirely plain – was that no mouth even intended to open to speak.

Leonora stared.

Only that motion, as her head came up, but he recognised the stillness in her.

Nora, when trapped, thinking rapidly and desperately for an escape.

'Of course,' Roberto rumbled quietly, his voice desolate. 'I should have seen it.'

'That there's no God to answer her?' Conrad prompted.

Before Roberto could answer, Luka Viscardo's corvid profile drew Conrad's eye.

'I believe I see the difficulty.' The Canon-Regular gazed at the collapsed subterranean passageway that separated them as if he hated every brick and clod of earth – and every foot of open air.

And especially those beyond it.

Conrad knew every singer and member of the San Carlo opera felt their dusty, gritty, dirty appearance to the full under that censorious gaze.

'The reason that God has not smitten this enemy, these heretics, this atheist—' Pure hatred illuminated Viscardo's last word. '—Is that it is our task. The Heavens have not smitten your heretic opera because our first task is to wipe you out.'

Before Conrad could respond to Viscardo, or let loose the anger that boiled inside him, Leonora stepped past the Dominican canon and surveyed the whole amphitheatre of the Dead.

'God is capable of making that known, if it's His will,' she said, deceptively quiet.

Conrad caught Roberto in a wince, out of the corner of his eye. *He knows that tone too, does he? Yes, I suppose he would.*

Lightly, as if he didn't feel that he bled to look at her, Conrad said, 'Your Prince doesn't seem to be saying much.'

The younger Silvestri, the Conte di Galdi's son, raised his voice, glaring at Conrad, Ferdinand, and all the group standing by the King of the Two Sicilies. 'You say this isn't the Prince – what else could it be?'

Ferdinand spoke up, surprising Conrad with his tense but urbane speech.

'Mass delusion? Like the mass Dancing Madnesses of the Middle Ages?'

The hawk-faced older di Galdi, Count Adalrico, turned where he stood, with an impassive slow dignity. 'There may have been delusions before. This, sir, is not a delusion. It speaks through *dead* throats. Thousands of them! Not just one man returned from judgement before the Prince – condemned as He is to follow the Creator's laws. Not one – not a hundred – not a thousand! Ten thousand men! Speaking in a unison that can be nothing else *but* God!'

'We know the desires of the Prince!' Niccolo di Galdi chimed in, 'Our reward is in Heaven, but our work starts here. We will rule at the side of the Prince of this World! As for you, sire, I regret to say that the theocracy of the Two Sicilies will have no room for kings.'

Conrad took a pace forward, putting himself in front of the group of singers and crew.

'To have a theocracy, you have to have a deity.'

Conrad waved a dismissive hand at the ranks of the Returned Dead.

'And to me, it doesn't sound as if you do.'

'He may.'

The interruption came unexpectedly from that quarter of the seating where Luigi Esposito sat among his fellow Returned Dead.

'We might be God. For example, we can tell you what happens now with Stromboli, Vulcano, Ætna. All of them break and send fire into the air. If I have such knowledge, am I not God?'

Conrad cast an eye up at the cumulus-cloud-and-lightning darkness of Vesuvius. 'Or that could be a very mundane good guess.'

Luigi's face has that alert light that means he's enjoying an argument – any argument, for the sake of an argument—

Conrad looked around.

—and that expression appears to have spread to others of the Returned Dead.

Of course it has! They may have come back from the Dead, but first and foremost, they're from Naples!

The gaze of tens of thousands of dead eyes was nonetheless unnerving. Conrad said, 'Suppose you do turn out to be knowledgeable and powerful – all-powerful, all-knowing, and for all I know, all-loving! – does that make you a deity? Or does that make you just a very powerful and old phenomenon?'

Leonora appeared in his field of vision, on the opposite side of the chasm, a few feet back from the edge.

If she seemed to address the Returned Dead on the north-western side of the amphitheatre now, still, Conrad felt the burning of her attention on him like sunlight.

'This shall be settled.' Leonora sounded grim. She stretched out her arms to the tiers of Dead. 'Tell us. Are you the Prince of this World?'

'No.'

55

Conrad barely caught the simple sound before it was gone.

No?

Did they say—?

Leonora, her own voice steady, demanded, 'Tell us. Have you broken the rule of the Creator-God? And cured the world's pain?'

'No.' The syllable fell into a waiting utter silence. 'No.'

They stared at each other, the Dead in unison and Leonora Contessa di Argente.

Conrad only looked at Nora. Her chin rose perhaps a quarter of an inch. Nothing but that, and the tightening of the skin at the corners of her eyes, told him how she took her utter failure.

'How could you do this to us!'

The voice was not one of the Returned Dead. Conrad recognised Enrico Mantenucci's accent.

'We are good men!' The police Commendatore held out his hands. 'Our hands are covered in blood for you!'

Leonora had the ability to make even the most ridiculous opera costume look like clothes: Conrad had noted it in Venezia. Now she walked around the arena, surveying both the Returned Dead and the Prince's Men, and she moved as if the gilded leather sandals and embroidered blue and gold robe of Queen Isabella were perfectly normal to wear, in the location of a Roman ruin, during the eruption of a volcano.

Roberto, beside Conrad, said, 'She's beautiful.'

His voice was choked by more than ash.

'She walks as if we were safe, here.' Conrad recalled being shown a layer of yard-deep volcanic ash cement beneath the foundations of the Angevin Old Palace, that showed Vesuvius had certainly not been idle for all its centuries, and had reached as far as Naples at least once before.

She turned her head, surveying the ranks of the dead, dusty in their glorious return to the world of the living. Conrad saw she didn't fix on any one face when she asked her questions.

'Some things are beyond your powers,' she speculated aloud, as if she wanted the voice of thousands to confirm it.

'They are.'

'And you have no solution for the pain of the world.'

'It's written into the construction of the universe,' the voices said, and Conrad could not help looking at the one face he knew.

Luigi Esposito now seemed to have as little individuality as a singer in a choir.

'Written heart-deep,' the voices in unison said. 'So that everything is either predator or prey; predator on what is below it, and prey for what is above. Disease preys on your children only so it can breed, as you do. Faults and mistakes and happenstance are embedded into the world, since in this world they are the only way to bring about change. If there were a God, to alter that—to do it, they would have to destroy the universe and begin again.'

'You think I wouldn't ask it?' Leonora muttered under her breath, as argumentative as Conrad had ever heard her. 'You're the god we *have*. What's your justification for the existence of pain?'

'Pain is a consequence. Pain is a protection. Pain is the thread that runs through all life, plant to animal.'

Conrad said, frustratedly, 'It's not that it won't answer. It's that we don't know the right questions to ask. Or we don't yet have the knowledge to understand what the answers mean.'

He wanted to step forward and put his arm around Leonora, as he always used to; leaving the choice to her of whether she accepted the touch or moved away. That he couldn't reach her—

The voices said, 'I don't have the power to end all the world.'

Leonora snapped, 'And you can't bring about a solace for the pain of it? Create a reward for us, after our suffering here? Give us the afterlife that the churches promise, so that what we've endured here will cease to matter?'

Conrad thought his heart stopped. Just the idea that all the tenuous dreams of the loved dead, alive again, an eternity in a world of beauty and no pain, had been for a moment in reach . . . His throat closed up so that, when he cleared it, the noise came out closer to a sob.

He thought there was a slight intake of breath, magnified through thousands of throats, as if the voice felt an emotion all too human, like regret.

'If I could do it, I would,' the voice said, 'but that's beyond me. The world has a billion of you, and I am strong in their strength, but it's not enough for me to create worlds for each of you after you go through the process of death. I focus all that I am to infuse a vital spirit into those few of you who need to Return. There's nothing else I am powerful enough to do.'

Leonora took a number of swift paces across the rock-starred earth, not tripping, her blue and gold robe whipping around her ankles as she turned. 'So you can't mend this world?'

'No.'

'And you can't make enough of an afterlife for us, to forget how much pain and grief and suffering we go through here?'

'No.'

'Then—' Leonora straightened, surveying the rising ranks of dusty figures. 'Then what *can* you do? *Vaffanculo!* What fucking good are you?'

The pause lasted long enough for Conrad to feel the stone amphitheatre floor shake under his feet with the first quiverings of an earthquake, and hear the distant explosions of rock-bombs plummeting down onto the Burning Fields.

Each mouth moving in unison with the next, the Returned Dead gave voice again: loud enough to be heard by all.

'I can tell you the truth.'

The silence was intense enough that Conrad heard the sulphur pools bubbling beyond the walls of the Flavian amphitheatre.

'What?' Leonora said flatly. 'You can what?'

'I can tell you the truth, as we know it. If I don't know, I will tell you so. No riddles, no prophecies, no revelations. Ask, and if I can answer, I will.'

The idea of such an opportunity had Conrad frozen, dumb.

Not God . . . but if it has the knowledge of something we'd call 'god-like'?

'Ask it *questions*!' Conrad exclaimed, words stumbling out of him. 'What sort of believers are you! *I* could do better—!'

He swung around to face Luigi.

'Are you *sure* there's no life after death? Do we have souls? Is there a Paradise? Do we end up twittering ghosts in a world of grey, hungry for blood? If our idea of a deity is wrong, is that true of all others – have you knowledge of Buddha, or the Muslim god, or the god of the Protestants?"

Conrad became aware he was gesturing wildly. He willed his hands to his sides.

"What is Right and Wrong? Why are we the only species that evolved to think? *Are* we the only species that evolved to think? If pain is how the deity teaches, what does it teach the mastiff or the donkey, when they're beaten daily?"

A beat of silence filled the ash-shrouded world.

Leonora, almost absently, said, 'Why are there so many subjects willing to be your mouthpiece?'

Lips moved in unison. 'That I can speak through them is convenient for me. But they returned because they each consider that, given the manner of their sudden deaths, they have unfinished business on the face of the Earth. They may be speaking for me now, but they're still the people of Naples, and they want their children, their fathers, their mothers, their aunts and cousins and god-parents; they want everything that you ripped from them with the eruption of the mountain.'

Leonora's pacing abruptly stopped. She didn't pale – for all he knew, Conrad thought, she couldn't – but she looked abruptly as if she were fifty years old. 'I . . . I didn't . . . I meant . . .'

'You did,' the unison voices said. 'You took them out of their lives, to give you a channel to the God who made the world. They're Neapolitan, and stubborn, so more came back than you planned for. I think they plan to stay.'

A voice from the side of the stage area, irritated, said, 'Why waste your time speaking with what's obviously a demon sent to mislead mankind? You—'

Leonora didn't address the man – one of the clerics of the Prince's Men, Conrad saw. She turned on her heel and gazed up at the ranked dead. 'Did *any* of them find a heaven waiting when they died?'

'No.'

It's one thing to be an atheist by rational conviction and experience. It's quite another, Conrad thought, to hear all the dead themselves tell you that the Heaven of which your parents, tutors, priests, and friends spoke so definitely isn't there.

Or at least, is not in the memory of those who have died.

Or seem to have died.

We know so very little, and each answer inevitably opens up more questions!

He missed the officers of the Prince's Men interrupting Leonora and her response to them. A touch against his upper arm proved to be Isaura, eyes dark, looking in her spoiled evening dress like a refugee on the return from Moscow, or a particularly debauched evening out.

'Corrado, I want to ask it. If there's no Heaven to be banned from, or no Hell to go to – why are there ghosts?'

To his surprise, she was answered. Dusty people sitting on ruined stone stands, thousands of different mouths moving with the same sounds:

'Some of the dead come back in bodies. Some come back only in minds. Through my focus, they form themselves as they wish. Or some, perhaps, as they feel they're obliged to.'

It would have been possible to ask which group Alfredo belonged to, he knew. Conrad deliberately let the opportunity pass. *There is nothing about my father that I have not had answered by the man's actions in life.*

He noted Leonora stood back and let him continue.

Conrad said, 'Are we capable of creating a god?'

Movement caught his eye, off to one side, where the stones of the Anfiteatro's stands crumbled, sliding in a cascade of dust down to the floor. A roll of heat came off the crack that opened, and he smelled the unmistakable scent of lava.

'God-like? Perhaps. A god in the sense that people mean the word? No.'

Conrad couldn't tell whether he was disappointed or relieved.

Was I asking because I wanted there to be a supernatural power for each of us? Or because I was afraid that the Prince's Men, if it could be done, would have no compunction in doing it?'

His gaze took in Luka Viscardo, among the Dominicans in the yet-living part of the audience.

And I suppose Signore Viscardo wouldn't hesitate to make doubly sure his god existed, and wasn't being impersonated by a devil or demon or heretic deity?

Or am I doing him a disservice?

Leonora broke off from discussions with her fellow Prince's Men and strode back across the stage area. This time Roberto stepped forward, as if he would intercept her, despite the chasm between them. Their gazes crossed like swords.

Conrad pulled Roberto back by the arm, until he stood in the same group with Tullio, Isaura, and the King.

'She has no idea what to do!' the Count whispered, sounding furious – with himself, Conrad thought, and not with Nora.

A waterfall of questions flowed towards the Returned Dead, every man present keen to question it – them – before it was time to leave. Entreaties and queries came from all sides. Thousands of voices produced a sound like a long roll of summer thunder, oddly distinct against the noise of the eruption.

Roberto Capiraso tilted his head towards Leonora, where she spoke with the officers of the Prince's Men 'She's making it up, now, as she goes along!'

We are the two men who know her best in the world—

'You're right,' Conrad said.

The Count shrugged. 'Well, I suppose, so would I, if I had that gang of jackals at my heels!'

Diverted, unable to hide amusement, Conrad said, 'Actually, I think you do.'

Capiraso made to speak, stopped, and folded his arms decisively.

A flood of questions came – from the Prince's Men; from singers; from troopers in Alvarez's regiment, gesturing with tied hands. *Why is the universe cruel? Am I damned? Is my wife, my husband, cheating on me? How do I avoid Hell? What is the secret of happiness? Is there a purpose to our existence?*

A Dead boy, no more than twelve, narrowed his eyes and demanded, 'Are You our Father? Why did You create this world?'

'Wrong question . . .' Conrad felt as if his head cleared.

He nodded to his sister, and touched Tullio's arm as he passed; acknowledgements, more than anything else, that he was glad to have them with him today.

Five yards back from the stands, he cocked his head and looked up at them, rank on rank of Returned Dead, right up to the skyline.

'Excuse me.' Conrad let what determination he had cut through the interruptions of the Prince's Men. Heads turned to look at him, all as one.

'I have a question,' Conrad said. 'If you're a deity . . . What exactly do you remember of Creation?"

Voices rolled like thunder.

'The beginning is hidden in fire and aether. In the time of dreams, creation was by beast-headed men, and ancient pantheons. Now that dreams are fading, you know of more time than I do, but the beginning is still hidden.'

'What?' Tullio said blankly.

Conrad frowned. "I'll put it simply. How far back into the past do you remember?"

An outraged Canon Viscardo snapped, 'Five thousand eight hundred and twenty-four years of humankind, that's the most that will be possible! The Bible tells all the generations of mankind!'

Adalrico di Galdi looked contemptuously at Conrad. 'Even your prehistoric-lizard-discovering Doctor Buckland can find no old human remains, as Darwin insists there *must* be. Even his "Red Lady of Paviland" is proved only ancient enough to have lived when our Roman Empire ruled over Britain!'

Luigi smiled. He spoke, and the echo of multiple voices sounded in his words.

'Those bones were not the skeleton of a lady, but of a young man – we dyed his bones with red ochre, and sang, and we laid his body in a cave for burial, because we loved him, three-and-thirty thousand years ago.'

A deeper silence fell.

'We drew his hunted animals on the cave walls, bull and cave-bear and aurochs—'

Conrad felt as if the answer hovered only just out of his reach. 'What *are* you?'

The dead features of Luigi Esposito composed themselves into his chess-playing expression – the one he wore in the game's autopsy, usually; explaining to Conrad where he went wrong.

'I understand that parables are traditional under these circumstances. Suppose . . . there was a world made all of water. And then suppose a part of that water separated off, began to experience, to think, to explore, and to grow. And eventually this individual made of water became old, and dissolved back into the water again.'

Conrad frowned. 'Are we water—?'

Luigi smoothed his gloves on his knee. His glance met Conrad's, and was deep and warm.

'Corrado . . . The water that's aware is transformed. At death, it ceases to exist. Its component parts fall back into the whole, but they're no longer the same as they were . . . Now, suppose more than one individual forms itself out of the water. All of them – those who made great discoveries, those who were superlative at love, those who inflicted atrocities on their fellow water-beings – all dissolved back, in the end. And this process went on for, oh, many revolutions of this world around the sun. *Many* of them . . . And after a time—the ocean itself became changed.'

The chess-player expression stirred Conrad – both spurred him to guess at the answer, and warmed him with the knowledge of Luigi's presence.

'I think I understand,' he said slowly. 'You're saying we don't exist until we're born; we don't exist after we die. But the ocean – that's *you*.'

Luigi's smile seemed ancient. 'I bear the same relationship to you as you bear to the material "sea". I'm made of you – and the memories of those who died before you. I emerge from your minds, all of you, as you emerge from the "sea". I remember what you experienced – all of you— Far more knowledge than I could ever tell you through these few thousand mouths! That would be like trying to force the ocean through the eye of a needle . . .'

Stunned into comprehension, Conrad thought *All the memories, all the experiences, all the pains and pleasures and discoveries . . . !*

'I remember the leaving the forests for the plains.' Luigi sounded agreeable. 'We can count easily back half a million years – although we looked and walked differently, then, but it was us, all the same. I remember when we grew weary of the hunt, and put seeds in the ground for harvest, and, because it was simpler than remembering to come back to those places each harvest-time, I built cities in those places – villages, you'd call them now. But that was only yesterday . . . ten or eleven thousand years ago.'

Dazzled by the vision of deep time, geological time, Conrad found himself smiling in wonder like an idiot – he thought – and groping for a sufficient question.

'Not God,' he said, 'whatever you are, and we shouldn't treat you as if you had those kind of answers. Not a deity. You're – the Library of Alexandria!'

He heard Canon-Regular Viscardo bellowing up at the ash-coloured mass of men and women. 'Are you a demon? '

The unified voice came back: 'Yes . . . and no.'

'There.' Ferdinand Bourbon-Sicily beamed in pleased amazement. 'Proof that the Prince's Men are wrong. The one true God would remember Creation, as would the Fallen Angel Lucifer; therefore this manifestation is no kind of Deity at all.'

'Heretic!' Another of the apostate Dominicans glared at his King. 'It's proof, on the contrary, that the Prince's Men are correct – the one true Creator-God has evidently departed from the world, and this is the Prince who has been left in charge to oversee the human race.'

King Ferdinand looked quizzically back at Conrad.

'It isn't *proof* of anything,' Conrad remarked. He added, 'But if it was an indication of anything at all, it would be that the Deity is a creation of man, rather than the other way around. Its knowledge only goes back to when man was beginning to be a conscious animal.'

'Heretic!' Viscardo hissed. 'Darwinist!'

'If two sides are calling me heretic, I have to be doing something right,' Conrad muttered.

Conrad looked at the faces of the Returned Dead, meeting their eyes. He found himself wondering what it might truly be like if human minds could be joined, in the way that human voices are joined in musicodramma, and if they might in the same way create something that is beyond themselves.

'Oh, I understand!' he exclaimed. 'It comes down to music, of course. And Aldini's work on Galvanic forces . . .'

Ferdinand Bourbon-Sicily sounded impatient – and intrigued. 'It does?'

Someone towards the back of the Prince's Men was still quietly singing. Conrad caught '*Quel'anima*—' '—that soul'.

'I was thinking of Monsieur Bichat,' Conrad said.

'Of course you were!' Tullio's mutter seemed to find an echo with both Paolo and the King.

'If you recall—' Conrad turned to the tiers of seats, making it evident he also addressed the Prince. '—Bichat said that he'd dug into the human body as far as it's possible to go.'

'Blasphemy!'

'—Thank you, Signore Viscardo. Monsieur Bichat theorised that the mind – or the soul, if you prefer to think of it that way – comes into existence because we're alive. Emerging out of some Galvanic force that animates the human brain and body.'

Ferdinand cocked his eyebrow, in much the same way he had done on the terrace of the Palazzo Reale, when Conrad first met him.

'And the relevance?' he asked.

'Luigi – our friend here calls it "the sea". If the Galvanic force of one body can produce a soul, a mind, then what can the force

584

of thousands – of millions! – produce? I wonder if what men call their God *emerges*, if you like, as a property of the millions of intelligent beings alive at the same time?'

'And you think that this—' Ferdinand struggled for a term that evaded him, and said, finally, '—this entity, is what? An emergent God?'

In the middle of chaos, Conrad smiled.

'I like that, sir. Yes. An "emergent God". It knows what we know, remembers what we remember. And remembers no further back, because we were not intelligent animals in the beginning?'

Adalrico di Galdi snorted. 'My family were never animals!'

Conrad ignored the Prince's Man.

'Not everything it knows will be true. In fact, most of it won't. If it contains the human body of knowledge, that includes true and false theories, mistaken knowledge, myths, fiction, and misunderstood truth.'

Luka Viscardo pounced. 'Mistakes! Fiction! This isn't God the Creator, or the Prince of this World – this is a beguiling demon!'

King Ferdinand waved the Canon to silence. Viscardo – out of habit, Conrad suspected – obeyed.

'And the relevance of this to music?' Ferdinand emphasised.

'Easy, sir. The Emergent God is susceptible to music because we are.'

Roberto Capiraso gave a snort. 'Does that *help* us?'

'It helps to know we've been asking it the wrong kind of questions.'

The King of the Two Sicilies glanced around at the chaos. 'Corrado—'

'I have a better question, sir.' Conrad ignored Viscardo, bellowing somewhere in the background, and faced the tiers that rose up in ranks of Dead. He couldn't help but focus on Luigi.

'What I want to know . . . is, how much can you affect the *material* world? – Can you control the eruptions of Vesuvius and the Burning Fields? Ætna and the others too, maybe, but, selfish as it sounds, *here* in particular. Is there anything you can to do to stop the volcanic eruptions before all of the Phlegraean Peninsula and Naples goes up?'

The Dead surveyed him. He caught a smile – Luigi's, he noted, seeming almost individual.

'I know what has been known – has been calculated and observed,' the voices said as one. 'Thick lava moves slowly, and sticks in the stone throats of volcanoes, and they erupt. Make molten stone *thinner*, and no such blockages occur. Lava will seep out onto the land, but there will be no eruptive explosion. And this . . . this, I can do.'

56

The Roman concrete felt gritty under his hands. Conrad sat down on the lowest tier of the amphitheatre. He leaned forward, hands on his knees, head hanging down. He drew in air slowly. His mind felt senseless as the volcanic stone. *Do I have no emotions left?*

'Wait a short while,' the voice that was not the Prince of this World echoed. 'Until it's safe to leave.'

Conrad heard a rumble, underfoot, that died away after a long moment.

He did not look in Nora's direction.

The vibration of the eruption could be felt through the skin of his hands, where he rested them on the scoured stone. Or it might have been that he shook, tension relieved.

Sandrine and JohnJack and the other singers made a bright knot of concern around Velluti, some distance away across the arena. Conrad wondered briefly why he didn't join them.

'Well then, Corradino . . .'

Conrad blinked, and rubbed at his eye on the excuse of the dust in the air.

Luigi Esposito rebuked him. 'Wash that out with water, don't rub it!'

'Yes, Mother.' Conrad snorted. And could not – for the thick heaviness in his throat – say another word.

The dead police chief smoothed his gloves onto his fingers; both grey with volcanic ash. His smile was no different to when he had been living.

A little wistfully, he said, 'I wonder what now, Corradino.'

Will he live as long as any Returned Dead? Or will he vanish with these ash-clouds, because they're the miracle that brought him back?

A strong shudder of the earth under Conrad's feet interrupted his attempt to put words together. Glancing up, he saw that the Returned Dead no longer all moved in the same unison.

'Go to the ship.' Luigi's pale hand rested briefly on Conrad's shoulder.

His smile was little more than a crease of the under-lids of his eyes, but it warmed Conrad clear through.

The pyroclastic flow formed again in swirls and retreating waves. Conrad watched as the Dead of Naples returned, man by man and woman by woman, to their own individuality.

If something ancient still looked out of some of their eyes . . . *Well, that's part of being Returned Dead*, he concluded.

Only Luigi Esposito of all the vanishing Dead lagged and looked back over his shoulder. His smile was not particularly altered by the ash that smudged his flesh, being as innocently sweet and wicked as the choirboy that he had once been.

His voice came low but distinct. 'Don't grieve, Corrado. We'll see each other again.'

Before Conrad could ask what he meant, the police chief was gone, lost in the dispersing crowds.

'What did he mean?' Conrad asked, out loud. 'Luigi of all people doesn't expect to see us in Heaven!'

Tullio snorted. 'I don't think we have time to worry about it right now—!'

The big man staggered as one of the panicking crowd of the living barged into him. He shouldered the man off effortlessly, and turned his body to shelter Paolo-Isaura.

The ash-cloud of the retreating dead began to move with something other than eerie unison. Conrad watched the animating principle that had spoken through them ebb, visibly, like the tide of the sea.

Scuffles of pushing and shoving broke out on the tiers. Prince's Men, churchmen, Ferdinand's soldiers—

Conrad shaded his eyes with his arm, looking up the rake of the steps to the silhouetted arches. Dust condensed there, hiding the upper reaches of the amphitheatre from view, and dulling the pearly sky.

'We're losing the arena miracle. This is our signal to move; we may not get more than one chance.' Conrad glanced around, searching for the King.

Movement snagged his peripheral vision.

He turned, at the same moment that Ferdinand Bourbon-Sicily fully raised his arm.

In the King's hand was an English duelling pistol, made with exquisite skill to be perfectly accurate.

Ferdinand Bourbon-Sicily took aim, pointing the pistol across the collapsed sunken passage, at Enrico Mantenucci's forehead.

With thirty feet between them, he squeezed the trigger.

The explosion came simultaneously to Conrad with the echo from the far side of the amphitheatre. He flinched automatically, as men who have been in war tend to. The officers immediately behind the Commendatore yelped and leapt aside from skull fragments and brain matter.

Ferdinand lowered the pistol.

His lips formed a name that might have been *Adriano*.

Wide-eyed, the top of his forehead blown away and his open skull scooped out bloody, Enrico Mantenucci's dead body fell over backwards and hit the concrete like a sack.

'After all,' Ferdinand muttered, 'guns had to come back into use at some point.'

A signal, and the King's Rifles fell into order, covering the retreating Prince's Men – most of whom were lost among the departing Returned Dead.

Ferdinand ordered, 'Now we leave.'

✦

Tullio's elbow caught Conrad in the ribs, jolting him back from shock.

'Padrone, *look*!'

Movement flinched into being at the far north western end of the arena.

The stone and concrete of the amphitheatre floor buckled on both sides of the collapsed access corridor, tearing apart like a book with a ripped spine.

'Shite!'

Dust stung his eyes. Through blurring vision he saw underground brick walls, and supporting subterranean arches. Chambers that might have been long-hidden gladiator-barracks and beast-pits exposed, at that far end of the amphitheatre—

Not far enough away!

The arena floor near the south-eastern entrance collapsed. A whorl of gases shot up from the corridor below – a gulf two storeys deep.

Light gleamed up. The edges of the broken amphitheatre floor stood out boldly black.

In the depths, something glowed orange and red.

Conrad took a step forward before he could stop himself; his stomach lurching with terror. Once experienced, the distinctive smell is not mistakable for anything else. *Sulphur and molten basalt!*

'*Scheisse!*' Conrad spun round.

No help to be had.

He instantly saw that. *Luigi, gone – almost all of the Returned Dead seemingly gone—*

He breathed in, unguarded. A throat-choking smell seared his gullet. He couldn't get out the oaths he wanted for coughing.

'I agree!' Tullio evidently took the tone for the meaning. 'Let's go!'

Paolo-Isaura nodded at the centre of the arena.

One single figure was not a part of the running, panicking crowds. She paced forward, almost at the lip of the sunken underground passage, and Conrad met her eyes without any sense of shock.

Of course. Leonora.

'What do we do about her?' Paolo muttered hesitantly.

Tullio snapped, 'Nothing. We can't reach her. You can see that!'

Conrad ran parallel to the edge of the drop.

True, we can't reach her. For the same reason we've been safe over here; she can't reach us.

No safe way over that gulf – but when did Nora ever care about safe?

Not knowing if he faced someone who might kill him, or someone he must rescue, he slowed and picked his way between rubble across the arena, completely focused. Men coughed on both sides of the arena as they shouted would-be orders. Two women from the chorus clung to each other and cried. A dozen men he recognised from the Prince's ranks sprinted for the north-eastern rake of stone seating, and were driven back by a whirl of volcanic dust. All of it existed before Conrad's eyes – and meant nothing.

Nora!

Footsteps scraped the stone.

Roberto paced beside him; matching him stride for stride. The bearded man's gaze was fixed on Leonora.

'Be careful of her.' Conrad couldn't find the right words that would not offend the proud man. 'She— This must have been a shock to her.'

'. . . Yes.' Roberto did no more than nod.

Conrad found himself slowing, despite himself. A mound of ancient fluted pillars lay to their right, rolled out of the way after falling from the rim of the amphitheatre, some time in the last two thousand years.

Picking his way between marble rubble, he had a momentary light-headed fantasy of using a pillar to cross the underground gulf like a fallen tree. *It would take a Titan's strength to even shift one!*

He looked up as the ground cleared and he could walk.

The impromptu stage-area on the far side was deserted now, except for Nora.

Her gaze was entirely inward.

An open pit broke the surface of the arena, not ten feet to one side of her; where the ancient Romans would have winched up wild beasts to loose on their gladiators. She took no apparent notice of her danger as she walked past it, towards them.

Towards the empty gap that divided them; the unguarded drop into the sunken access passage.

591

'Get away from there!'

He made fists, aching to shout but only daring to raise his voice slightly in case he panicked her:

'Nora!'

Roberto's voice came almost in unison. 'Leonora!'

Is she desolated that her 'god' has left her?

Conrad scowled.

Is she listening?

The earth jerked, laterally.

A fountain of bricks, stone blocks, earth, trailing grass, roots, and concrete flew up from the gap in the arena floor.

The ground grated underfoot. Debris thumped down with impressive bumps that could crack a skull, or a spine—

'Nora!' Conrad bellowed.

Pozzuoli concrete pushed up under his feet. It sent him sprawling down on his back in ash and gravel – away from the open access passage.

Conrad choked on sulphur, and dragged himself up on hands and knees. He could get no further.

Through streaming eyes, he saw lava glimmer in the underground Roman passage.

Something sheered, deep below; Conrad felt it through his grazed fingers.

Roberto Capiraso threw himself towards Leonora's lone figure, as if he could leap the thirty feet of open space between them.

'Roberto!' Conrad's mind chittered *No! Not possible! No!*

Vibration juddered through the ground.

The tumble of fallen pillars broke apart and rolled.

Marble cylinders skidded in terrible slow deliberation. Roberto lurched forward, rising earth pushing him into a staggering run. Fluted stone shook up ash from the arena floor, billowing in choking clouds.

Roberto vanished in the ash.

Conrad scrambled up. One foot twisted under him.

Leonora stepped up to the crumbling edge of the sunken subterranean passage, close enough that, if she held her hand out in front of her, it would be over the drop.

'Nora—' Intended as a shout, it came out a whisper.

The underground corridor split.

Cracks raced south-east, tearing across the arena floor. Tiers of seating shattered; brick arches exploded. It split north-west—

The arena floor ripped open under Leonora's feet.

She dropped like a stone statue into the depths.

57

Pain and grief wrenched at him so hard that he couldn't breathe the iron-tasting air.

Sweating, he tried to push himself to his feet, and failed. His belly twisted. He knelt. Furnace heat blasted up, half-blinding him.

Conrad stripped off his coat, and wrapped it around his arm to shield his face.

Holding it tight against his dry, burning eyes, he groped forward on hand and knees. Closer to the cleft splitting the arena floor.

His hands encountered nothing of Leonora, neither herself or – he swallowed, hard – *her body.*

Why should they? I saw her fall.

The sides of the cleft dropped thirty feet – to a heaving bulge of black lava. Rising gases made his eyes sting and blur.

The unbearable heat pushed him into a backward crawl. Conrad crabbed his way away from the cleft's edge, spasming with coughs.

His face was wet, he dumbly realised; although it dried almost immediately in the heat.

The pain of her absence reduced him to a dumb animal. If he could have bitten off a limb to free himself from its steel fangs, he would have done it instantly.

Stronger tears ran down his face, hot droplets trickling from the point of his chin and spattering in the grey ash.

He felt every muscle and ligament tense, pull taut – the impulse to spring up and run into the gap in the earth thrumming through him.

What would it be? The pain of a fall, moments of agony before molten stone burns me to death? That's nothing—

The earth buckled and threw him into the air.

He fell flat on rubble, breath knocked out of his chest. As he landed, his foot hit something that gave.

A deep male scream cut off abruptly, in choking coughs.

I recognise that voice! 'Roberto!'

Fallen stone cylinders became clear through swirling dust – ancient, lichen-covered pillars, all around him, tumbled like children's skittles.

Roberto Capiraso slumped against a section of fluted marble. Ash made his hair and beard all but white: he looked sixty.

That's not just ash. He saw it too.

Conrad pushed himself up into a crouch, the shaking ground making him stagger. Broken concrete scraped his arms. He was in his shirt-sleeves, coat discarded at some unnoticed moment, and now irrecoverably gone, he realised.

'Are you hurt?' He was not sure which part of the Conte di Argente he had stumbled over. *His leg?*

Conrad groped closer, supporting himself on the fallen pillar. At first glance the other man didn't look physically damaged.

His eyes were dark and stunned.

'She's dead.' Roberto Capiraso stared at the cleft through ash rising, now that the opera miracle lapsed. 'No one could survive – not even Nora . . .'

'The Dead don't come back a second time. Not even her.' Conrad tried to keep his voice level. It betrayed him, cracking on the last word.

A bead of light glinted on Roberto's face. Conrad saw water overflow, suddenly, and cut lines in the dirt on the man's cheeks.

The Count reached out and wrapped his square-fingered hand around Conrad's arm. Conrad gripped Roberto's shoulder.

He felt himself entirely understood: met and matched in searing grief.

Conrad coughed, inhaling sulphurous gases. Recovering, he lifted his head, squinting around. *There are the living, as well as the twice dead.*

'Tullio! Paolo!'

Two dark figures emerged from the sulphurous steam. Tullio thumped down beside him. 'There you—'

'He's hurt. Check him. Where's Paolo?'

'Here!'

Hidden behind Tullio's bulk, Conrad realised. The ex-sergeant began gently to feel Roberto's body for injuries – first the skull, then the trunk, then the limbs. Paolo made her own tactile examination of Conrad.

'Nora's dead!' Conrad blurted out. He buttoned his waistcoat with shaking fingers, and couldn't look his sister in the face.

I still have no idea if she thinks I'm a fool – was a fool! – for loving Nora.

Paolo stared over at the shaking crevasse, face whitish-yellow under the coating of dust. 'I saw someone fall— That was— Was that *her*? Oh, Corrado—!'

A cone of ash emerged on the lip of the chasm, growing visibly.

'We have to leave!' Wide-eyed, she caught Conrad by his torn shirt-sleeve. 'Or we'll die too!'

Tullio knelt back from efficiently removing one of the Count's army boots, and slitting the uniform trousers to the knee with his pocket folding razor. 'We got a problem.'

A raised bump low down on Roberto's exposed shin did not break the skin, Conrad saw, but it was already swelling.

'Fracture,' Tullio assessed. 'Other leg hurts him—'

Roberto Capiraso's head went back at the touch. Conrad saw the muscles at the hinge of his jaw knot.

'—But I don't think it's a break. Likely a crack partway through the bone. Corrado, he can't walk on either of 'em.'

Conrad managed to meet Roberto's desolate look.

Neither of us care about this, not at this moment, but—

'Did the pillars fall on you?' Conrad asked.

'One cracked against me.'

596

It would have been a glancing blow, or the man's legs would both be crushed. *Along with the rest of him.* Conrad swore.

'Leave me.'

The tone was uncompromisingly practical. Conrad did not have to look closely to perceive Roberto thought it a providential excuse.

He wants to die.

How ironic is it that I can't follow her because I have to help my rival?

And the others, the practical part of his mind emerged to say. *Paolo, Tullio, JohnJack, Sandrine, Ferdinand; the rest.*

He let the practical mind take over, splitting his emotions away with practised ease, like fissuring a rock. *Maida, again.* A battle is no place for complex passions. For grief over the dead.

That comes later.

There are others to be got out of this. And after— Well, that will be my decision.

He rested his hand on Paolo's shoulder, on her man's coat. 'You and Tullio splint his legs. I don't care what you use. I'll see who else of us is alive.'

Paolo's red-rimmed eyes held an oddly-aged understanding and gratitude.

Conrad turned away, to the clouds of yellow gases that swirled, parting to show the tiers of seating, and closing in again. He sheltered his mouth with his hands and called, broke down coughing, and called out again.

Velluti staggered out of the covering murk, supported by Sandrine and Spinelli. The castrato failed to form words. He bled from the corners of his mouth.

Conrad found himself torn between the memory of Velluti matching Leonora in the stretta, bringing the sextet up to overcome the solo soprano voice, and the knowledge that something irreplaceable had likely been destroyed.

He took refuge in practicality.

'Sandrine, JohnJack, find help for him. Collect as many people as you can. See who's missing. I'll talk to Ferdinand. No—' He held up a hand as they protested. '—We have to evacuate the amphitheatre. *Now.* It's too dangerous to run around like chickens with the fox in the hen-house!'

JohnJack wrapped one hand around Sandrine's arm. 'We'll call the roll.'

A handful of men appeared out of ash and gases. Conrad shouldered forward to one whose stance he recognised. Uniform and hair grey with ash, but unmistakably Ferdinand Bourbon-Sicily.

'Corrado!' The King's expression was sheer military exhilaration. 'Good! I have a refugee column; join your people to it— What?'

'Sire!' One of Alvarez's corporals interrupted, skidding to a halt. 'Scout report from the top of the arena. More of the Burning Fields is visible. They report big eruptions from Monte Nuovo and Solfatara. Lots of small lava floods everywhere. The Campi Flegrei can be crossed to the west, at the moment, but not east towards Posillipo and Naples.'

The corporal turned to a man Conrad recognised, with surprise, as Fabrizio Alvarez, much the worse for wear but evidently rescued from il Principe.

'Captain says, he thinks you ought to see it for yourself, sir.'

Colonel Alvarez saluted his King and departed in the soldier's wake at a ground-covering trot.

Ferdinand rubbed at his chin, apparently unaware that he smeared pumice and ash across himself as he did. 'The Burning Grounds are breaking up, I think. We'll be lucky to get our people out.'

Conrad blotted out everything but the current emergency from his thoughts. 'Land or sea?'

Ferdinand's blue eyes showed red around the rims, and at the corners. He stood foursquare, feet placed apart on the shaking earth.

'We'll go out the way we came in, where the top tier of seats is level with the ground outside. What concerns me is how many injured men I have.'

'I have two who can't walk,' Conrad supplied. 'There may be more to come.'

'Get your able-bodied to move them. We're leaving as fast we can. If we lose contact, make for Pozzuoli and the *Apollon*.'

'Sire.' Conrad touched his forehead in salute, automatically Lieutenant Scalese, Cacciatore a Cavallo.

He turned away as the King took other scout reports – and had a moment of complete blankness.

I forgot her!

Hot shame fought with practical survival:

I have to forget her now.

He staggered back across the uncertain earth. A larger group clustered around Tullio Rossi, in the ragged remains of costume or evening dress. Two Kings' riflemen appeared by Velluti, crossed wrists to make a cradle and scooped him up, heading for the southern tiers of steps.

'Go with him.' Conrad put his hand on JohnJack's shoulder, giving him a push. 'You too, Brigida, Sandrine. Quickly!'

The basso called his name. Conrad waved a hand without looking back. 'I'll be there! Go!'

He made his way cautiously out over the arena floor, sloped now. Red light flickered through the dust storm. The black ash-cone spurting from the earthquake-cleft, no larger than a loaf of bread at its birth, now stood waist-high to a man.

Nora. Leonora!

Tullio and Isaura moved almost as mirror images of one another, torn shirt-sleeves and cravats binding Roberto Capiraso's legs to a makeshift wooden splint. They had lashed both legs together with a musket between, the barrel and stock long enough to span from foot to pelvis, wood and steel a strong enough support.

Tullio stripped off coat and shirt, put his coat back on, and bit at the linen to tear it. Paolo added her neck-stock as a last binding over the others. The Count's legs resembled an Aegyptian mummy. She stood.

She's shaking, Conrad realised.

Paolo didn't seem to notice it. She said, 'He'll live if we can get him out of here before the broken bone cuts an artery.'

Conrad found himself curtly realistic. 'He has more chance of burning than bleeding. Are we set to go?'

Sandrine strode up. A dozen of the King's riflemen followed, with chorus singers, musicians, and the other refugees from the San Carlo.

Several stray Prince's Men trailed after the riflemen, their hands tied. At Sandrine's sharp command, they formed a column, escorting the staggering men and women through the smoke and gas, and on up the aisle towards the high exits on the southern side.

'Well?' Tullio demanded. 'I take it this muck in here is still better than what's outside?'

Conrad flicked a glanced at the exit stairs, and how many flights there were up to the amphitheatre's north-western rim. He didn't soften it.

'Out that way, then try to keep everybody together while we find Pozzuoli. Assuming the roads aren't blocked – make for the *Apollon* before the Burning Fields go sky high. It may get rough at sea, but there's worse to come on land.'

'*Dio!*' Tullio's expression showed what he thought of that.

Gaps in the swirling sulphurous murk let Conrad see the King's column moving up the steps, towards the rim of the amphitheatre. Ferdinand himself loomed out of the smoke.

He beckoned Conrad without breaking stride.

'Corrado, if it means saving the able-bodied, we will leave the wounded. But not until it's absolutely necessary. Are your people ready?'

'Yes, sir.'

The Count stirred. Conrad knelt, instantly, and gripped Roberto's shoulders firmly. Because he'll try to run, and make a cripple of himself!

'Leonora.'

Roberto's voice grated, acid with grief and disappointment.

Conrad stated it brutally and without tact. 'It's true. We both saw it. She's dead.'

The Conte di Argente made to move, and slumped. Conrad eyed the dirty bandages that wound him from hip to foot.

Self-evidently he can't stand on his own. So—

Conrad gestured for Tullio to help pull the man up. Tullio's powerful shoulder under Roberto's armpit heaved the Count upright so that his feet barely touched the earth.

Conrad caught Roberto's right arm and pulled it sharply forward. At the same moment he ducked his own shoulder under the other man's lower ribs and into his stomach, and pulled Roberto's arm over his shoulder. He braced, breathing hard. Tullio supported him from one side, Paolo from the other, and he lifted.

An in-breath made him choke. '*Che cazzo!*'

He stood with the man's body balanced over his shoulders, Roberto's head resting down his back, and splinted legs hanging over Conrad's chest and belly.

For a minute he thought they would both fall.

He got his feet braced squarely apart, and adjusted to the twelve stone dead-weight draped warm and limp over him. He steadied the bound legs with his hand. *One thrash and we'll both be on the dirt—!*

The other man hung motionless over his shoulder and back.

Is that the weight of the splints on his injuries?

'Has he fainted?' Conrad grunted.

'—Syphilitic son of a cock-sucking whore—!'

Tullio lifted his voice over Il Superbo's flow of raw insults. 'Uh, I don't think so, padrone . . .'

Isaura made a small snorting noise, part laughter and part distress.

Roberto Capiraso subsided into grunts of suppressed pain.

Might be better to let him curse.

His sister glanced at Tullio. Something in her expression brought another face to Conrad: pale and gamin, under clouds of soft brown hair.

Water washes the volcanic particles from the eyes. Water is good. And tears are water, aren't they?

It took three of them to carry the wounded man up the amphitheatre steps to the earth outside. Conrad shared the weight awkwardly with Tullio – the composer unconscious, now – and they eased him over the lip of the excavation.

Tullio grunted, reaching down, and lifted up first Sandrine and then Paolo, his hands encircling their waists, as if neither of them weighed more than a bale of straw.

Wild wind thrashed. A harder tremor shook the ground. It was easier to see, outside the amphitheatre, but more difficult to walk. Conrad took the Conte di Argente up over his shoulder again. Rocks and ash-camouflaged holes caught at his feet. Thin whips of scrub slashed his face. Tullio grabbed his elbow as he almost came down. He hit Roberto's legs with a flailing hand, and the Count swore.

'You can't carry me!' Roberto's voice protested thickly, close to his ear.

'I can drop you, if you'd rather!'

All his effort went into supporting the man; he had none to spare for politeness. Conrad tasted grit in his mouth, hauling in a lungful of air. He let Tullio steady him, made sure he had the Count's body securely over his shoulders, and a tight grip on the man's arm and splinted legs.

The air above was dark as snow on a midwinter afternoon.

The pathway down towards Pozzuoli passed in and out of vision, yellow-tinged clouds adding to the sleeting ash. Conrad did not think of the ship waiting, in the harbour. He plodded on, aware he must be ahead of two thirds of the column, conscious only of grey ash caking every bush and track, the wheeze of his breathing, and splinter-pains stabbing at his chest.

Roberto's voice sounded strained, weakened, but full of malice.

'I've seen Christ painted like this, carrying the one sheep that was lost back to the flock. Is this a newly discovered Christian feeling in you, to rescue your fellow man?'

'Purely altruistic—!' Conrad just stopped himself from adding *God knows why*! He winced, pulled muscles catching him. 'Read Plato – Socrates—'

'A few more minutes and we can ask them in person!'

The man's heavy weight shifted; evidently he was trying to look around at the rest of the straggling column of soldiers and operatic refugees.

'Stay still, *che stronzo!*'

'Put me down! I can walk.'

'Of course you can,' Tullio murmured. He strode beside Conrad, his right hand gripping Paolo's left. '. . . You got a clean break above the left foot. You want to shove it out of kilter and let bone splinters slash up the muscle, you go right ahead and put your weight on it.'

Conrad felt the man's breath increase, where he lay prone over Conrad's shoulder.

'I don't need to be carried!'

'Not sure what the other leg's got.' Remorselessly cheerful, Tullio continued. 'Cracked the bone, I think; it's swollen all to hell. You can go running around on that, too, if you want. Then you can see the rest of your life from a wheeled invalid-chair.'

Tension rolled through the composer's muscles; Conrad could feel it where the man sprawled helplessly over his shoulders.

'Leave it,' Conrad ordered sharply.

He'd rather be dumped here for the short time it will take him to die.

And so would I.

He wondered briefly if either Tullio or Paolo realised it – and almost missed his footing again.

Scheisse! *I have to concentrate!*

The earth juddered.

The concentration needed excluded all else but moving one plodding foot in front of the other. Rocks littered the heathland. Fireballs shot across the darkening sky: rocks hit scrub and it burst into flames. Lightning cracked, more deafening than thunder.

The shouts of Ferdinand's troopers, rifles at the ready now, drowned out the singers, and one or other of the musicians who would not be parted from his instrument case. Conrad staggered sideways to avoid the roped line of prisoners.

It isn't forgiveness.

If I didn't have to do this, I would have to think.

I would disbelieve that she's gone, even though I saw her die in front of me, because how can it be true?

The knowledge of other griefs and losses doesn't help. Conrad knows from war-time, and from when the plague is loose, that the shock of the news itself can mute the pain. Temporarily disconnect the grinding unhappiness that eventually sends other people away, leaving one waiting for the grief to pass.

And only Roberto can understand that this time it won't.

The wide track to Pozzuoli was a river-bed of rocks. The uncertain footing, and the unconscious man's balance across his shoulders, took all Conrad's attention.

He forgot, for long enough to take three easy breaths.

It crashed back down on him.

She's gone. I saw her die.

A shudder went through his belly, and he found his mind disconnected from the situation, coolly turning over ideas. *Whatever it is the Returned Dead do, they don't do it when so thoroughly destroyed, as by fire. But how long did it take for the lava to kill her? The same as for a living human, or – longer?*

Roberto Capiraso's body stirred. The injured man was not unconscious, Conrad realised. He recognised the shuddering breath, kept under iron control.

O Dio! I hate her for dying!

Grief and guilt took him between iron jaws. The unbearable dull agony of bereavement stretched ahead – days and years of nothing. Only the glance at a street corner, heart stopping because a chance woman looks like her. The hallucination of knowing he has just heard her voice, when there's no one there. And when all strength is expended just to get through a week, a month –knowing it's all to do again. And again. And again.

Rising tones of panic roused him.

Paolo slid ahead, through the head of the column of refugees. Conrad slowed his trudging pace, watching Paolo move into the mob.

A minute or two later, she reappeared.

She nodded towards Roberto Capiraso. 'You might want to put him down.'

The heavy weight had settled onto his body, compressing muscle and spine, tension and lung.

'If I put him down I may not pick him up again. What is it?'

She beckoned him a step forward. Conrad staggered, made it and was looking down a shallow curve of hill, at the sails of the *Apollon* in the harbour.

We've covered more ground than I thought.

Surprisingly close to Pozzuoli itself, he could see roofless houses, and roads full of rocks, under the black daytime sky scrawled across with lightning-bolts.

Between them and the port, a lava stream cut a wide red channel in the earth.

Conrad blinked the slow-moving scarlet brilliance out of his vision. It took him a moment to realise the extent of the flow.

We're cut off from the sea.

From the Apollon.

Tullio reached up, moving by instinct as Conrad did. He felt the older man's strong grip help him slide Roberto Capiraso down on the ash-covered grass.

A figure plodding through the ash-snow became Ferdinand Bourbon-Sicily, half a dozen aides and officers behind him.

'We're already cut off from the coast, down there. Too rough for a boat to take us off the beach anyway.'

He gestured south, over the rough scrub and rock, to the sea. Seeming to take Conrad as the authority for the San Carlo group, Ferdinand added:

'I've sent men to time both streams. The one behind us, and this one, ahead.'

Conrad turned his head stiffly, muscles cramping.

He had not even noticed the unobtrusive line of steam and sparks crossing the Burning Fields to their rear, he realised. The lava stream behind them was surprisingly undramatic. A smudge of black above the tufts of grass and scrub, a shimmer of air where heat sent the ash swirling . . . it might have been nothing.

The wind shifted. Conrad caught the hiss of steam, and the sparks of the lava flow behind; the stink of sulphur more virulent than at Solfatara or Monte Nuovo.

'The lava flow is wide, but I think shallow.' Ferdinand frowned. 'But that hardly helps us! We can't cross it.'

'How fast is it moving?'

Ferdinand gave a shrug that attempted to be careless. 'Walking pace. Or a little faster.'

He's terrified, Conrad realised. His own heart thumped.

Ferdinand is terrified we're going to be caught between that flow behind us and the lava in front.

'Alvarez's scouts say we're surrounded,' Ferdinand admitted. '. . . No one expected the flows to start moving at different rates.'

Frantic panic churned in Conrad's stomach. He pushed it out of his awareness, knowing it to be only the body's animal desire to survive.

Towards Pozzuoli, the lava looked no wider than a city street. The heat-rippling air above, and the charcoal where it touched anything but earth, made it obvious no man could survive it.

He elbowed his way to the front of the group of aides, where the King had the best view of what was before them.

Raw black earth.

A black surface with vermilion underneath.

And then – only a few yards in front of them, now – liquid orange-red lava slid down towards the harbour of Pozzuoli at the pace of a walking horse.

'My men have rockets and maroons, to send up as signals for the *Apollon*.'

Ferdinand looked back, letting his gaze linger on the thundering earth from the throat of the volcano, and the lightnings that continually sparked up and down the six-mile-high plume of cloud.

'If we get to the harbour, we'll still be extremely lucky if we're seen.'

More King's riflemen came back from all directions. *Sent out as scouts*, Conrad thought. He watched Ferdinand's face as they reported in.

Frustration burned acid-harsh in his belly. *No, no way out. We're surrounded.*

No way off the Burning Fields. The Campi Ardenti will have us in the end. Ahead, the stream of molten rock looks to be twenty-five, thirty-five yards wide . . . And anything we could bridge it with, will burn.

'This is my fault,' Conrad said aloud.

Ferdinand gave him a sharp amazed stare. 'Conrad, I'm aware you're over-responsible, but—'

606

Conrad rubbed both grimy hands over his face, as if the grit and stink of sulphur might wipe out the heathland in front of his eyes. It was still there when he stopped. He blinked furiously at floating ash, and watched as the wind shifted again, long plumes of smoke and gas obscuring all trace of Pozzuoli.

Ahead, lava flowed in visible torrents, coils of black soot floating on the orange surface and marking the currents in the molten basalt. It felt as if a giant held him up to a furnace door, face forced unrelentingly forward. His skin dried. He felt it pull tight over his cheekbones and nose.

He didn't turn away from the flow, aware of Ferdinand at his side.

'I asked for this. You'll remember, sir. Sticky lava blocks things up, and then unblocks itself in eruptions. With sticky lava, the whole caldera of the Burning Fields would blow sky-high. Thin, runny lava, on the other hand . . . means the Burning Fields and Vesuvius won't blow up.'

Conrad couldn't help a bitter smile.

'—Proof if you needed it that we didn't speak with an all-knowing God! Any idiot could have told me that, yes, it would stop the volcanoes detonating, and they'd just spill over. And any idiot could have told me that thinner lava flows faster.'

The thunder of Vesuvius made him raise his voice. He became aware he was waving his arms, and consciously clasped his hands behind his back.

'Any idiot but me . . . Thin lava will run faster. So it won't erupt. But it will cover this whole area, several feet deep. And the streams are fast enough that we can't out-run them. I didn't think! I asked for this miracle. And it's about to kill us all.'

Voices shouted, sounds muffled by ash; he thought it was the rear of the column coming up faster. Nothing was quieter than where he stood. The silence emanated from King Ferdinand.

Tullio's resonant snort fractured the hiatus.

'You have to excuse him, sir. He gets like this. Often.'

Conrad cut in. 'Yes, anyone could have asked for the miracle, but it was me, and I didn't think it through.'

Ferdinand gave a snort that was an aristocratic echo of Tullio's.

'You might as well blame me for not seeing it. Or not seeing a way out of it. Or for . . . not ordering the troopers mounted, so we could make better time.'

'On this ground? The half that didn't break a leg would have gone rump over ears—' Conrad realised Ferdinand's manipulation, and ceased babbling cavalry maxims. 'All right. Perhaps there was no way to win.'

'Bear to the left.' Ferdinand had a small smile, under the muck and ash. 'There's a parallel track to this one; it may get us across in front of the lava.'

Conrad hoisted Roberto Capiraso across his shoulders, again. The man, semi-conscious, was able – fortunately or not – to turn his head both behind or in front, see, and comment on what he saw.

It was not until Conrad had to come to a sharp halt to avoid crashing into a King's rifleman, in front, and heard the Count's sharp '*Vaffanculo!*', that he came out of the altered state induced by physical exertion.

The slope of land dipped down to the sea, and the muddy withdrawn shore of the Bay. The fort of Pozzuoli harbour showed silhouetted against an odd, violet daytime sky.

The vast, slow-moving lava stream cut its channel in the earth, flowing between them and any chance of a ship. Lava seared its way into the sea. Where molten rock hit sea-water, raging gouts of steam made everything invisible.

That flow must be thirty yards across!

Here we are between hammer and anvil, Conrad admitted to himself.

Tullio's welcome grip helped him lower Roberto Capiraso down on the ash-covered grass. Conrad stood over the slumped man, protecting him, and caught an elbow in the ribs. Someone trod on the back of his heel from behind.

From this height of ground, he could see the steam and hissing sparks of the lava flow behind them, stemming from Solfatara, or perhaps some rift in Monte Nuovo.

Where every other breakthrough of lava from under the Burning Fields moved so slowly as to be – *astonishingly!* – tedious to watch, the lava flow from behind was approaching them much faster than a man could walk.

Trapping us completely against the flow in front.

No way we can cross what's in front. And what's behind is coming up fast.

Paolo's hand tugged on his sleeve.

'Corrado! What's that?'

◆

Conrad turned in the direction of Pozzuoli again, following Paolo's prompting.

'—*Minchia!*'

Ice-cold rain slashed down into his face.

Conrad instantly threw his arm up to protect himself. Bitter rain stung his exposed hand.

No! Not rain! Hail!

'Hail?' he said aloud, in complete disbelief.

Tullio yelped and clapped his hand to his eye.

A hailstone stung Conrad's cheek and bounced, falling white to the dusty earth.

He saw a second one hit the lava and die with almost no time for a hiss.

A blast of air from above kicked up steam, ashes and dust. Conrad had to cover his face with his hands and blink furiously.

He straightened, and found himself bending forward into the wind. A slap of cold air in his face alerted him – a cloud of hail slashed down, and turned into rain as it came close to the lava.

Rain fell warm across his face, sending filthy black trickles of ash down to soak into his shirt.

Paolo's grip on his arm closed until it hurt. She pointed with her free hand. 'What *is* that?'

Ahead, where the wide stream of lava coiled down the Burning Fields towards the sea, Conrad glimpsed ice-cold air *pushing down* from above.

He blinked, disbelieving.

The wind roared, too loud to make himself heard. He caught Paolo's hand in turn and dragged her down to kneel beside the

Conte di Argente and Tullio, in hail-soaked grass and scrub.

Heat blasted into his face – but cold wind was on the tail of it, cold enough to be icy. He sheltered his face with both hands and managed to look up.

A slice of light cut down from the spreading eruption cloud, over his head.

The lightning-filled pillar still thundered up from Vesuvius. It rose a half-dozen miles into the air, flattened out, and spread everywhere over Campania.

Everywhere except here, Conrad realised.

Ice-white light blasted in from the west – from clouds that roiled and broke up and showed the faintest snatch of blue sky.

Not blazing blue-white, he discovered, while tears ran down his cheeks. Only the white-gold of an ordinary late spring afternoon.

He let himself think the water from his tear-ducts only cleared them from ash and dust, and did not mean he responded to the sight of natural light by weeping like a child.

By his shoulder, the Conte di Argente surreptitiously dragged a sleeve across his own cheeks.

Sandrine gasped.

'Yes, it's sunlight,' Conrad muttered, bemused at the smoking cold rain that fell with it. 'We're not going to see much of that when the clouds close in—'

'Corrado!' The mezzo pointed.

He broke off, silenced.

Twenty yards ahead, a figure appeared, framed in the fleeting light. Appeared out of a fog of steam and hailstones and cold—

On the flowing molten lava.

The heat from the earth made the air shimmer, but Conrad was certain the moment he saw her.

For a number of moments, his voice wouldn't function – lost to disbelief, wonder, fury, love, and a desire to both shake and kiss the approaching figure.

She is walking, naked and barefoot, over the streaming lava.

'Leonora!'

58

With her hair loosened and falling unbound, long enough that it curled against the backs of her knees, she might have been some Greek goddess in sculpture. But a sculpture that would inhabit the secret museum, given that the long slope of her thighs and the quick curve of breast and nipple were quite uncovered.

He fell down onto his knees, on the rough turf. His legs wouldn't hold him up.

The flow of lava crisped scrub and bushes black, at the edge of the molten river. The heat that rose over it swirled ashes into towering clouds. For the last quarter-hour, he had stood before an open furnace door. No place to turn away from it – turning from the one ahead only left him seared by the one behind. The faster the lava ebbed up onto the surface of the Campi Ardenti, the closer the land they stood on came to being an island at the confluence of two lava rivers. Inside an hour, the flow would join up; there would be only lava.

Conrad swayed, on his knees, the cold wind blasting into his face. Rain slashed down. Warm at first, but the nearer the figure came, the colder it became. Conrad blinked away hail and melting snow.

Wind struck down from above. The frozen air blasted away from her. Away from her no matter what direction one looked.

Roberto's grip startled him. The injured man had hold of Conrad's shirt, struggling to hold himself sitting upright.

His expression was open and utterly defenceless. 'You see her too?'

Conrad's heart beat once, as if it were some large foreign object that lodged in his throat. His pulse shook him down to his fingertips. He knelt with his gaze fixed on the roiling treacle-flow of the lava.

'I see her.'

'But the Dead don't return twice!' Roberto whispered.

Conrad echoed him, speaking in same moment: 'The Returned Dead do not return a second time . . .'

'But she has,' Conrad finished. He leaned his weight against Roberto's shoulder for a moment. The other man didn't move away. 'That's her. I know it's—'

'I know it's her. I thought I was hallucinating her . . .'

'It's Nora.'

Freezing air and light blasted in from high above, sucking out heat everywhere. A hiss and pop confused Conrad, until he saw hailstones hitting the surface of the lava.

His shirt flapped in the cold gale.

He wiped his hair out of his face, as the wind blew it there, staring fixedly at the magma.

Roberto Capiraso wiped his mouth, and Conrad saw the man's beard was white with frost.

The film of moisture on his eyes dried and Conrad finally blinked.

No, this will be gone if I blink!

He realised he was gripping Roberto's shoulder, in turn. The solidity of the wet coat cloth was a link to the reality of the world.

'She's still there.' He heard his own voice strained and croaking. 'Roberto, tell me what I'm looking at.'

The fire of the lava reflected in the man's dark eyes. Almost too quiet to be heard, under the hiss of lava and roar of Vesuvius's eruption, Roberto Conte di Argente breathed out, 'Leonora . . .'

The heat made her seemingly-black figure dance and shatter and come together again. She came closer, across the black and orange swirls of the lava currents. Liquid superheated stone fell away from her feet and ankles like the waves of the sea.

'Leonora . . .'

Twenty metres now, in the shaking heat and hissing cold that surrounded the human figure. Conrad saw her place her foot down for her next step—

Through the glimmering air, he saw the molten lava turn black under her foot.

Turn black—

Turn into islands of solid stone, he abruptly understood. *Parts of the flow cooled down enough to go from liquid to frozen basalt.*

He couldn't take his eyes off the figure in front of him. She was close enough for him to see her expression – close enough that every detail of her naked rangy body and little full breasts was visible, and he tried not to attend to that. *Of all the unsuitable times to want to lie with a woman—!*

Not 'a woman'. It's Nora.

He blinked rain out of his eyes, where he sat. Warm water dripped from his hair. He knotted his fingers tightly into the shoulder and collar of Roberto's coat, and the Count's left hand gripped his wrist in an iron vice.

One of us is holding the other up. I just wonder which it is.

Roberto looked as if he had forgotten the fractured bones of his shin and ankle; forgotten everything but the apparition in the snow and smoke. 'Is this your miracle?'

'No. Is it yours? No—' Conrad interrupted himself. 'If anything, it's her miracle.'

'Why is she . . .'

Conrad voiced his fear. 'To say goodbye? To one of us? To both of us?'

He feared that.

Feared she might be an apparition, as Alfredo Scalese had been; not Returned from death in the body, but merely an echo of the past.

The blasting wind whipped around her as she stepped closer, lashing her hair into a Medusa-whip. *Too far yet to see her face, but she carries herself like Nora*, Conrad thought. *Shoulders back, head high, unashamed.*

Somewhere above the mushrooming ceiling of the eruption

cloud, it's still late afternoon above the Bay of Naples. A knife-blade of light ripped down, cut by wind and cold, and terminated at her figure – Leonora Capiraso, Contessa di Argente; Leonora D'Arienzo; Nora Sposito of Castelveneto orphanage . . .

She came closer. The islands of black around her grew larger. Cold whispered on the air; ash-fall yellowing the air like snow.

Roberto's hand unconsciously closed around his wrist, digging in, beginning bruises. 'That can't be.'

Conrad narrowed his eyes against superheated air, so that he could bear to follow her footsteps.

Each time her high-arched narrow foot came down, basalt grew blacker and more solid under her. A few more yards and she walked on a bridge of stone – one that slowly disintegrated in her wake, basalt melting back into the coiling lava flow.

'She's singing.' Roberto Capiraso brushed white from his beard and moustache.

'She is singing . . .' Conrad did not dare speak loudly. Not and break the thread of sound that whispered over moorland and lava stream, and called up islands of stone under her feet.

Tullio shaded his eyes against the light that fell down the rising column of air.

A chin-point digging into his other shoulder let Conrad know Paolo leaned on her knees behind him, her arms around his body.

Tullio swore obscenely. 'The dead don't Return twice!'

'Ghosts don't turn lava back into stone!'

Conrad tried to choke down the heart that again threatened to fill up his throat, and wondered, quite idly, if he might drop dead of an attack before he knew what was truly happening here.

Roberto's voice sounded sudden and grim. 'It can't be her. She's moving.'

That was astonishing enough that Conrad registered Sandrine, Paolo, and Tullio all turn to look at the man as he did.

'When she came back – she was cold, at first,' Roberto said. 'Cold. Cold like marble outside in winter. She couldn't have moved around, then! It took her months to become warm—'

Until she ended up warmer than the human beings who haven't once died, Conrad filled in.

'If this was her,' Roberto said fiercely, 'she wouldn't be walking!'

Contrast made the slice of falling light look blue-white, against the sifting ash and the lowering eruption cloud. Conrad slitted his eyes against it—

'Look, there.'

He realised that what boiled up from where she trod was not white ash, but steam. Steam, rising to whirl about her in cyclonic disturbance.

Her wordless singing soared in the anthem that closed *L'Altezza azteca*'s second act, and *Reconquista*'s Act Three.

'I understand!' he exclaimed.

Roberto and Tullio gave him identical glares. Paolo's strong, thin arms tightened around him.

She chirped, exasperated, into his ear. 'What do you understand!'

Her coldness turns the lava into cold basalt beneath her feet.

'She's giving her cold into the lava.' Conrad felt himself willing to bet any number of experiments would support his instantaneous hypothesis.

Roberto snarled. 'What do you mean, "giving her cold"?'

'Fire is – movement. Heat is movement. Heraclitus said it. Atoms in movement. I don't know what death is—'

Momentarily, his situation returned to him in belly-churning reality: *trapped between lava flows that are closing together, and merging.* He swayed on the unsteady earth.

'—But I suppose death is the utter antithesis of movement.'

The objectivity came from the part of him that always observed, always took notes; was always the observing poet's eye.

'Cold is the opposite of fire. If she was as cold as you said, Roberto, when she first came back, then she would be if she came back a second time.'

'The dead don't come back a second time!'

Conrad pointed to the blazing white figure haloed in sun and steam.

'That is *Nora*.'

He stared into the murk and light. He searched out her face. A moment later he met her gaze, and fell back against Paolo before he could catch his balance.

'Corrado, what is it?'

How to explain that meeting the eye of another living being can send a charge of Galvanic energy from spine to belly to cock?

Conrad shivered at the trauma, even as he sought out her eyes again.

The slight figure held out a hand, beckoned sharply, and – *all Leonora!* – stamped her foot on the newly formed basalt.

The motion sent spikes of frost across the black stone.

'She's come to lead us out.'

Conrad heard a baritone echo of his voice as he spoke, and looked over in surprise.

The injured Roberto Capiraso hooded his eyes. 'Conrad's right. Whatever she's come back for – the first thing she intends is to lead us over the lava.'

The temporary opening in the clouds knit closed. Ragged edges merged together overhead, closing off the last of the day's light that they were likely to see, Conrad thought. Vesuvius's darkness infiltrated the sky and the air. Men and women formed up in a confused column.

Her naked body glowed like a beacon pearl.

'What aria did you come back for this time?' Roberto Capiraso snapped.

Capiraso was likely in considerable pain from the cracked bones in his lower legs. Conrad knew the viciousness in his voice had nothing to do with that particular injury.

He turned his back on Leonora as he stood. He had to do it at once and deliberately, or he couldn't have done it. *And if I look at her – I'll ask her—*

'Which of us are you going to say you came back for?'

He didn't recognise the voice that spoke, until both Capiraso and the woman looked at him, and he realised it had been his own.

'Well?' Conrad demanded aggressively. For fear he would weep.

'I don't care if I never sing. I had to come back.' The low, female rasp cut through the noise of shouting, explosions, eruptions, and the hiss of hot lava where it met low-lying water. 'You're going to die if you stay here.'

The cold came off her in waves. Conrad could have told with his eyes closed that he faced her. She was the antithesis of the searing lava.

The cold of the grave! he thought, and almost giggled.

Roberto demanded, 'Why would you care if he or I should die? What plans have we interrupted this time?'

She looked from him to Roberto, and from the Count back to Conrad. There was a desperation in her face.

'I suppose,' Roberto said slowly, despite the chaos around them, 'that neither of us will ever know if you're telling the truth. Lying perfectly was how you survived growing up.'

She stamped her foot.

Under her bare sole, the earth turned black, solid, and frosted over with crystals of ice.

'I just want you both to live!'

In the periphery of Conrad's vision, he could see Roberto's white, sweat-stained face. The Count watched his late wife too.

Leonora stood up straight. Every pretence dropped away from her. The lava slowed, congealed, and stopped where she stood.

'I can lead you,' she announced. 'The first to follow me will take my hand. I have to have human contact as well, while I'm still touching death, to follow the direction of life. Form a chain, take hands – use belts and kerchiefs, to make yourselves secure. Otherwise you'll get lost in the storm.'

Conrad looked at her face, that he had not ever thought to see again in motion. Her skin still breathed off cold. 'The further you get from that state of non-existence, the less you'll be able to cool the lava. So we don't have long.'

She gave one short apologetic nod. By the end of that first year in Venice, they had rubbed through sufficient of a young marriage's difficulties that many things went without words. This was one, he realised.

'Nora . . .' Roberto's voice lost its acid edge. It occurred to Conrad that she and Roberto were likely working through the same difficulties, at the same time.

He could see plainly that the column of soldiers and San Carlo people would need to be led. With ash, dust, rain and hail swirling in thick as gruel, trying to follow Leonora blindly through the worsening visibility would result only in half of them stepping into safety, and the rest lost to the lava-flow.

He wondered what it would feel like to take Leonora's hand, now. If any human could take her hand without irrevocable damage. *Her body must be beyond freezing. Cold so intense will burn. Especially, it will burn other flesh.*

'Which of us?' he said aloud, without meaning to.

Roberto scowled, puzzled.

Conrad explained, 'Nora will have to lead. Then . . .'

Leonora bit at her lip, and said nothing.

Neither of us can ask her to condemn the other.

Conrad caught Tullio's eye.

Tullio seized the Count's left arm, and Conrad his right.

Conrad bent and drove his shoulder into Roberto's belly, and with Tullio steadying him, he lifted.

A phenomenal effort and a grunt. Conrad balanced himself under the weight.

The Count di Argente hung with his splinted legs straight down, his body over Conrad's shoulders, unable to get free. It didn't stop his abrupt, frustrated cursing.

'I'll do it,' Conrad said steadily. 'Tullio, Paolo; see that everybody's ready.'

He said nothing while they and Sandrine were gone, or while a column formed on the shrinking patch of earth. He held Nora's gaze, watching her bright eyes and unbound hair. She sang under her breath – Conrad recognised Queen Isabella's aria on first meeting her beloved King Muhammed. Her words spoke of triumph; her voice of love denied.

Before he could fully realise a thought, Tullio shouldered through the fog, heavy grip locked around Paolo's wrist. 'We're ready.'

Conrad reached up and put his right arm over Roberto Capiraso's body, clamping the man to his shoulders in a tight grip. He felt Tullio pull the sleeves of his coat and shirt loose, and Tullio's broad hand wrapped around his right forearm, skin to skin.

Conrad looked down at the twice-Dead woman's pale hand, cold coming off the skin in skeins of fog. His guts twisted.

'Corrado,' she murmured. 'Why?'

He unearthed no words to describe all his reasoning; all the push and pull of instinct.

Conrad very clearly and decisively held out his left hand to Leonora.

✦

He bit through his lip when her twice-cold flesh enclosed his.

✦

The earth was hot under his boots. Leonora's step called up solidified rock – cold rock, under her feet, forming temporary 'islands'.

The first step onto lava was a terror to him, his balls crawling up into his belly at the knowledge of the heat beneath.

Out of the corner of his eye, he saw Tullio reassuringly tighten his grip on Paolo-Isaura's hand – Isaura grabbed Brigida's plump fingers; JohnJack, behind her, held Brigida's other hand – and so on for all the opera company, the King, the King's riflemen, and those of the Prince's Men taken prisoner.

The temperature of the surrounding lava could have blackened all of them to charcoal within seconds. Under Conrad's feet, the congealed rock was a shield.

If he would remember anything, Conrad thought, it would be this:

The living human hand of Roberto Capiraso gripped in his right hand, feeling the slick sweat of pain as his fractured leg-bones were shifted clumsily.

Leonora's fingers closed on his left hand like iron machinery, pulling him forward.

The pain of it overrode everything, even wondering if this would work, and whether he was about to step directly into molten rock.

His foot came down on frozen lava. He staggered forward, and her scorching cold hand held his as desperately as he gripped hers.

How else would her step bridge the lava-flow with instantly cooled rock? Miracles come with, if not a price, their own internal logic. And Conrad had been, for that very reason, careful to make sure that it was his left hand he offered into her world of miracles, and his good right hand that he used to hold on to Roberto, next link in the chain.

✦

Ten steps and he bit through his lower lip in another place, blood flooding down over his neck-cloth and coat. Twenty steps and he screamed, not sure if he had thrust his hand into a fire, or into the jagged metal jaws of a man-trap, spring snapping it shut through his flesh and blood.

He shouted over Roberto's back at Paolo for her to ignore him when he screamed.

He took good care not to look down at his hand in Nora's.

'Talk?' he got out. He refused to say *Take my mind away from this.*

The boiling steam framed her face, long hair blasted back in a banner towards the winding line of walkers behind them. Wind blew sharp off the frozen basalt. She walked at a slight angle, to study him. He found himself staring into those gentian-coloured eyes which are her facet of the world's beauty.

'Corrado . . . Why volunteer for this?'

He might have said something laying claim to heroism. He struggled towards something more subtle and difficult – the truth of what made him step forward.

'You were in Naples, six weeks ago.'

'Yes,' Nora said cautiously.

'And—rehearsing? The dress rehearsals for *Reconquista*?'

She had to turn again, to lead the cavalcade forward. Her voice sounded warm. 'That's a good guess on your part, Corrado.'

'It's not a guess.' He ignored her implicit question, that he read in the line of her shoulders. 'You knew I was in Naples.'

'. . . Yes?' She might have been frowning. In a clipped, hasty tone, she added, 'I didn't intend to seek you out.'

Conrad narrowed his eyes. The steam lapsed, giving a glimpse of the eruption cloud—it shut out all but the furthest western sky. The lowering sun caught him in the face.

'Do you know what hemicrania is?'

'*Headaches*?' Nora sounded utterly bemused.

Conrad felt the tension of Tullio's grip on his arm, and heard the low conversations from JohnJack and the other singers, the King, the riflemen, the local singers—none of them quite daring to believe what they were doing, he guessed. It let him turn all his attention to Leonora.

It's no bad thing if she's frustrated enough that she's only thinking of me. She doesn't need to be thinking about her responsibility, here. Or if the lava is too wide for her to cross before her coldness is dispersed.

'More than a headache. I've had the migraine since before the war ended. I went to some doctor friends of Monsieur Bichat, in Paris.'

A swirl of hail and grit caught him in the face, and he lowered his head, bulling into the wind, trusting Nora's grip on his increasingly-numb hand. He regained a grip on Roberto's weight, and his pace on the frozen ripples of basalt, but when he blinked his vision clear, the world was lost in thick fog and steam.

'Storms,' he said. 'If you listen to Signor Aldini's followers, migraines are storms of Galvanic energy in the brain, similar to *grand mal*.'

'Corrado—what are you talking about! And why *now?*'

He smiled. The fierce curiosity and frustration—*that's all Nora.*

'The last time before today that I had bad hemicrania, it was the morning after *Il terrore di Parigi* was such a success.' He drew the tale out, tempted by the cat-like irritation in the set of her shoulders. 'Everyone thought it was a hangover. I thought, well, exhaustion can provoke old wounds to act up. But later I realised, *Il terrore* made a success, people talk about the prima donna Fanny Tacchinardi, and the composer Persiani, and maybe even about the poet Conrad Scalese . . .'

Like a cat that has had a string trailed in front of it for far too long, she pounced. '*What* has this to do with you volunteering to be my link to these others!'

She unconsciously clenched her fingers in frustration, and Conrad flinched as if an engineered metal tool gripped his left hand.

He shifted Roberto's boneless body more securely over his shoulder.

'You were in Naples when *Il terrore* played. You knew I was there—thought of me, I believe. And in the morning, I woke with a score playing in my head that was no opera I ever knew.'

He sang a little, under his breath, voice ragged. Enough of it to bring a noise of speechless surprise out of her.

'This was before I ever *heard* of the black opera! And later on Roberto vanished off with *Reconquista*'s score to ransack it; I never saw the whole of it. When you sang . . . I recognised every note.'

Ridged lava shifted under his boots. She swung around, light-footed, as if waiting for the column to catch itself up. Her eyes fixed on him.

'What does it mean?'

Conrad spoke flatly, too frightened that she would reject the idea to soften it.

'There's a connection between us. Down deep—in the same place the Emergent God exists. We're connected. And I believe it's because I love you, and . . . you love me.'

The wind wailed between rocks, and the scrub and bushes off in the distance. Black smoke went up from the still-distant edge of the flow. The lava spat and hail and warm rain melted onto the roiling surface—the basalt 'islands' forming the bridge creaked under the weight of people, who screamed to each other, over the drowning noise of the volcano's eruption.

All of it sounded like silence to him, facing her lack of response.

'. . . You and Roberto, you're clearly connected.'

'Nora!'

Nora gave a surprising orphanage-brat grin. 'You fight like brothers!'

A rumble of semi-conscious gutter language came from Conrad's shoulders, where the Conte di Argente slumped.

'You and *me*, Nora!' Conrad forgot his physical pain.

Almost absently, she checked the line behind them. She spoke in a soft voice barely audible over slashing rain and snow, the explosion of distant lava bombs, and men shouting to each other.

'You're connected through me,' she said simply. 'All three

of us are connected. Me to him, me to you. So deep a connection that my music went to you when you slept? Oh yes, I believe you.'

She slowed her forward pace, looking up over her shoulder at him. Her Delft-violet eyes held unusual seriousness. 'Could we be connected through the Emergent God? The emergent mind of us all? Corrado, you and I – if that's true, our connection goes so deep that you and I can *find* each other through millions and millions of people, even if we don't know we're doing it . . .'

It left him breathless. *I hadn't thought of it in those exact words*.

Nora's smile dazzled against the brilliance of light and air sucked down by her chill. The wind blew from her into Conrad's face, lashing him with the wet tips of her long hair.

He took another few steps, labouring across the rough lava, keeping the rhythm of it; pulled back and forth by Tullio's grip from behind, and her beyond-cold hand. 'You came back from death for Roberto.'

She turned her head back and forwards continually, now, checking the staggering line of people on the basalt behind, and the narrowing distance to smouldering scrub and brush, yellow with sulphur; apparently not needing to look at where her bare feet came delicately down on freezing rock.

'Something important happened between Roberto and myself. Not over that year in Venice, but later, as time passed . . . I came to trust him.'

Conrad spat something inarticulate, that sent a spray of blood from his bitten lip. 'Nora, you don't trust anyone! I know you. You can't trust people!'

He couldn't mention her childhood. She lived with one eye open, he knew. Orphanages don't bring out the best in people. Not the children, cruel as all children can be, who fight for that one extra meal – fight even if the cost of it is a hand up the skirt, or worse; and the independent life of a whore begins to look attractive, because at least you get to choose who fucks you.

He moved his foot to avoid twisting his ankle as a chunk of basalt shifted. The far bank looked closer. The smell of lava was stronger.

He couldn't find a plainer way to ask. 'How did he make you trust him?'

'The same way he *made* you do it!' A shimmer of amusement touched her voice. 'You found out that he can be proud, insufferable, vindictive – but if he makes a promise, he keeps it; and if there are two choices about what to do, he'll pick the one that matches his morals.'

The last six weeks flashed past Conrad's inner eye. Yes, Argente is Il Superbo; he didn't get that name by accident. But there are moments, writing the score together, when the Count clearly forgot his claim to landed estates and ancient titles, and rolled up his sleeves to work in *il mondo teatrale*.

'He made me come to him for money. He made me beg, and then he turned me down, the bastard.' Conrad gripped the weighty body with his right arm. 'But . . . I think, now, if I hadn't been able to work in the debtors' prison, he would have got me out. For the sake of the opera.'

'Forgetting, as he so often did this last month, exactly *which* opera he was supposed to be supporting . . . Oh yes,' she said. 'Brothers.'

Grit and wet pebbles slid under his boots. Conrad almost lost balance between one step and the next – felt Tullio's fingers dig hard into his arm – and almost pulled Nora back off her feet. His hand blazed with pain.

'Why are we talking about him?' Conrad stubbornly demanded. 'You and Roberto don't have a fraternal relationship.'

'Nor will you and I.'

She glanced back over her shoulder.

Conrad gathered his expression must satisfy her.

She gestured with her free hand, forestalling his inchoate protest. 'You don't *need* to compete. I came back from my first death for Roberto. You and I – we have a link that no one else does; we're connected through the minds of all men, linked so tightly that we speak to each other's dreams . . . How many times I've found my way back from death . . . isn't important to me. That girl from the orphanage in Castelfranco Veneto, she trusts *both* of you. That didn't happen in a day, or weeks. When you tell me we

624

have a bond, you're only confirming what I've felt deep down for years.'

Conrad couldn't speak.

An ugly expression of threat appeared on her face. 'I left you alive, when I should have let the other Prince's Men dispose of you. They argued for it. It would be safer . . .'

She was clearly in the recent past. He didn't like the ugly expression – but not, he realised, because it might once have been a threat to him.

None of us are quite stable. What can one expect?

'I don't like to see you look afraid,' Conrad said. 'I want to make things better for you.'

'And now you see why I trust both of you.'

It might be the wind dashing steam in her face. Conrad listened to the roughness in her throat, and the thickness of her speech, and realised just how close she was to tears.

'No one but me has been dead twice! Dead once, yes – all you have to think of is light, movement, *warmth*, and how badly you want them. But the second time! When you recognise that cruel cold, and the rest it promises you can have – there's one moment, one *short* moment. You have to know yourself really well to get out of there. You have to know, deep down, in an instant, what you *truly* need and want.'

The agonising pull on his hand eased.

She paused, allowing the strung-out line of people on the basalt bridge time to close up.

'No one but me has died twice. And as I was dying in the lava, I had just enough time to know I've been a *fool*. To know what I abandoned when I left Venice—'

A groggy voice behind Conrad's right ear said, 'Tell the silly bitch she can *have* you!'

Conrad spluttered, 'What!'

The Count's voice rumbled through his bones. 'It's been obvious what she wanted ever since she left Venice. Go back to her, Corrado, and then maybe we can all get some peace!'

Conrad tensed his shoulders, preparing to heave the man to the basalt earth, splinted legs or not—

He froze as something else flashed into movement.

Of all of them, Nora had a free hand. It swung white in the mist's shadow; made Conrad flinch—

The yowl at his back let him know he wasn't the target.

A guffaw came from Tullio, behind, and a muffled explanation, evidently to Paolo: 'She smacked his ear!'

'Damnation, that hurt!'

'Serves you right, Superbo!' Nora's eyes flashed, and caught a glint of western light as she swung around to lead them onwards. 'You were awake and *listening* to this, but you weren't *hearing* it!'

Another yank at Conrad's hand made him add a snarled curse to Roberto's tirade.

'I'm sorry!' She shone a tired smile at him. 'We have to hurry. I don't know how much more cold I have in me. Pass it down the line to move faster!'

Conrad let her set the pace, adjusting himself to her steps, and Tullio's shifting grip on his arm. The Conte di Argente lay prone over Conrad's shoulders, but the tension in his muscles gave him away.

'*Were* you conscious for all of that?' Conrad asked, under the exchange of shouts down the line.

'Mostly.'

'And you couldn't keep your mouth shut for *one more minute*? I wanted to hear what she had to say!'

A muffled laugh shook the slumped body. 'I dare say you do, since it was you she was making up to . . .'

Under the apparent spite – and how many other times, in the past, has this been true? – the Count's voice carried a teasing reassurance.

Despite the growing pain from his hand, Conrad found himself with a wry smile.

The line of scrub came closer, blackened and flickering with little flames where the lava rolled over it, sparks spitting. On the surface of the lava flow, black currents swirled, delineated by soot. And black ice-floes of basalt jostled at the bank, rocking as Conrad and the line following him approached closer to the shore.

'*Here*!'

Nora stopped on the edge of the lava stream.

'Stay still,' she directed. Her brow creased, watching Conrad. 'Only a short time. Very short. Hold *on*, Corradino.'

The rising steam and smoke got into Conrad's lungs. Despite the effort to hold himself still, he all but choked, shaking. Pain flared in his hand and up his arm. He tried to straighten his body – and couldn't, not with Roberto's weight on it.

Nora's toes pressed on the edge of basalt.

She reached around past Conrad with her free hand.

He didn't understand what she did until Tullio passed him. He realised Nora was shepherding the long tail of people past them – like a gigantic *grande chaine* in the ballroom – and off the hissing, spitting, white-sparking earth.

A fang of pain bit nerves that ran up the underside of his left arm, into his neck, and made his whole spine spasm, the muscles locking tight. He shook, choking; tried to straighten up—and could not, with Roberto's weight over his shoulders.

Over the lava flow, the others passed by: man and woman, singer and soldier; Sandrine and Ferdinand and Paolo-Isaura; each stepping off the lava flow at Pozzuoli's first uncovered streets.

He concentrated on that, not on the pain that – *dangerously* – had numbed itself to nothing in his left hand.

Weight lifted. He made an inept grab, and then realised someone had prised Roberto Capiraso from his shoulders.

Another man caught Conrad as he fell forward—

He sprawled flat, face-down on the hot earth. One of his boots smoked, and scalded his foot; he felt himself finally dragged far enough from the lava to land on earth cool enough not to be part of the volcanic stream.

Looking behind as he fell, he saw Leonora step off the lava onto the rocks. The flow of molten basalt sprang up gold and red and searing as she left it. Her first two or three footsteps scorched the grass.

He guessed that, by the time they came to examine her, she would have exchanged her unearthly chill for the almost equally unearthly warmth of the Returned Dead.

Returned Dead twice.

Only then did he look down and let himself see a hand, whitened in places and blackened in others by her sub-arctic touch.

It doesn't look so bad. But then neither does frostbite.

Who will she go to first?

He hated himself for his doubt of himself and his doubt of her. The pain in his hand seared far worse than the visible injury seemed to justify.

Before he or Roberto Capiraso could be moved, the gloriously unselfconscious naked woman stepped between them, whispering something inaudible, and knelt down and reached out at one and the same time to catch Conrad's shoulder and Roberto's forearm.

'You can't bring yourselves to believe that a woman can love two men equally. I've had to face the truth to escape death, and I *know*! It was only a heartbeat, but I had time to see how stupid I was. What I abandoned. What I was *too afraid to want.* Why do you think I could never choose between you? I don't want to be made to choose! I *won't* choose! I came back for both of you. *I love both of you.* Believe me!'

She whispered again, as Conrad slipped into rising unconsciousness, this time clearly enough that he heard it.

'Both of you. Always. Both.'

✦

'The ship!' The King's voice was urgent. 'Every man to the *Apollon*, quickly!'

Drained utterly, Conrad heard the sounds as if through distant fog.

His eyes might have been open or shut. He thought he saw Tullio Rossi's greatcoat settled over a naked Leonora.

✦

He had not recovered from the feeling that he had been exsanguinated by the time they reached the harbour. They boarded the French frigate *Apollon*. The ship's rigging showed pale, thick with ash. The vessel heeled over as it cut across the waves, past the

628

ancient fort guarding Pozzuoli. Conrad, boosted over on to the deck with every other man in that last traumatic rush, sprawled on holy-stoned planks, until two or three of Alvarez's riflemen picked him up.

Blood ran down his chin again as he bit his lip against the pain.

They would have taken him below, but he rammed his other elbow in one man's ribs, and swore at the other, and he and Roberto ended up jammed into a corner by the wheelhouse, out of the way of the sailors, who ran across the deck in apparent confusion, raising what little sail the King evidently trusted on the mast.

Fever filled his head, slowing his reactions and leaving him staring in wonder at quite natural things, while the astounding passed him by. He felt dizzy. He felt as if they inched away from the great eruption column of Vesuvius, no matter how fast the sleek ship sailed out into the Bay, on course for the middle of the Tyrrhenean Sea.

He realised that he could still hear Nora singing.

She was by the mast, a military cloak bundled over her naked body, her hands clutching wood and rope. She sang at the full power of her voice.

Just as Conrad managed to wonder *Why?*, the *Apollon* lifted and fell down the long slope of a vast tsunami.

Water came crashing into the Gulf of Naples, stirred up by undersea volcanic detonations, he realised.

They rode it out – every man who could pinned to the port rail, straining to see what damage the tsunami might do to the land.

There was no way of seeing, through the murk and coil of ash, smoke, and spray, but Conrad couldn't blame them for looking. He kept his own gaze on the southern sky, knowing he could not see from here if Stromboli, Vulcano, and Ætna had also erupted.

The last thing he coherently heard was Ferdinand Bourbon-Sicily, worried about Palermo as well as Naples. He couldn't understand what answer the ship's master made. Leonora's now-hoarse singing filled his head and then faded away.

The heat of his hand swelled up like a tide, filling all his mind. He jolted back to awareness, recognising the faces over him but not able to put names to them. Something cold as ice and wet pressed against his left hand.

It was the last stress; he fell into the oncoming numbness with something approaching welcome.

59

He saw nothing except hallucination, trapped in the memory of fire and the pain of his frost-burns. Worse, hemicrania gripped him in an iron clamp.

Among excruciating shouts and crashes came the familiar bellow of Tullio Rossi.

'There isn't no other place to put them! Unless you want them below decks in the butcher's shop – surgeon's station, beg his pardon. The Emperor won't have them down there kicking the bucket. Clear out the captain's cabin!'

At *them*, he struggled for consciousness, but failed to disperse the fog on his drained mind.

If his mind – his *spirit*, for want of a better word – felt like a guttering candle-flame, his material body was only too present.

Held motionless, curled up around his hand, he begged under his breath that the physical pain should cease, knowing he addressed his pleas into a void.

It was on Conrad's lips to say *God help me*. He wondered dizzily if wishes counted as prayer – if wishing desperately that the world had returned to what it was so the Emergent God might heal his hand amounted to a prayer, and a betrayal of his principles through fear.

Is the mind that emerged from the human race still . . .'awake' . . . enough to hear? How easy it would be to call wishes, prayers; call it God!

He kept silent.

✦

Time passed.

✦

If it felt that it might be hours or days, some part of him suspected it was not more than fifteen minutes.

The air still rang with the orders of the crew, getting the *Apollon* under sail.

Without apparent interval, he found himself strapped into a narrow hanging wooden bed, close under creaking planks. It swayed in every direction.

'Am I in my coffin?'

If someone answered his question, he never knew.

Pain had him like a wolf by the hand. The world flung itself about. Dimly, he realised the ship's creaking and booming meant storm-waves. Gigantic waves, by how long it took between the crest and drop at the top of a wave, and the long slide down into the hollow.

Wind howled loud enough to block out the world.

Have we survived the eruption only to die in the aftermath?

✦

A man in a blood-stained apron jammed himself into the corner by the shuttered stern window. He harangued a dark-haired officer in a soaked woollen over-jacket, who bellowed back.

Conrad distinguished the repeated phrases – *Dread of a lee-shore— new volcanic reefs— Sardinia— such deep water sailing as the Mediterranean has to offer—* but his mind slipped away each time he tried to process them.

The deck heaved up and dropped down as one falls in night-mares, without end.

✦

He groaned, conscious only of a stink. Wooden planks creaked not far from his head – but a ship shouldn't smell so vile, unless he was down in the orlop, among the rubbish of a hundred voyages.

Air caught in the back of his throat, dry with volcanic gases. The odour of sulphur gas couldn't compete with the rotten stench that threatened to turn his stomach.

The lean of the ship spoke of it sailing swift, almost even.

Relief softened his muscles, relaxing from their extreme contraction. He felt the sensations of his body cautiously, not sure yet if he could confidently think it.

The hemicrania has gone. Or if not gone, eased to almost nothing.

The corners of his eyes felt wet with gratitude for the relief.

The absence of pain let him drift down towards deep sleep.

'Scalese!'

A known voice, but he couldn't put a name to it.

'Oh, *che stronzo!* Conrad!' The sound of anger altered to an unwilling kind of desperation. Conrad felt hands shaking him by the shoulders.

That doesn't hurt so badly . . .

He rose to wakefulness. If the hemicrania had left him, other pain remained. It was impossible to identify any one thing among the bruises, sprains and gashes.

His eyes opened for minutes before he focused.

The boards a few feet above must be the frigate's deck. The ill-lit space in which he lay, a cabin. Two or three men shoved past the man who held him, voices raised. Conrad glimpsed a bloody apron by the light of a lamp.

A surgeon.

'Corrado! Blast you!'

Not Tullio's voice.

Roberto Capiraso, Conte di Argente, lay in a hanging cot beside him. His legs seemed to be restrained. He leaned over awkwardly, shaking Conrad's shoulder.

Conrad tried to shrug free. Failed.

The movement sparked a fire in his left hand. It seared him so badly that tears leaked out of his eyes. The stench grew greater. He dry-heaved.

Roberto's dark, bearded face loomed and receded in a swinging lantern's light. Conrad had no idea why the man frowned. His blunt fingers dug into Conrad's muscles.

'Listen to me!'

Another – foreign – voice said, 'It's no good, he can't understand you!'

'He can!' Roberto's expression hardened. 'Conrad, listen! We— Your friends have waited as long as they can. If the surgeon doesn't operate, you'll die.' He hesitated, and added harshly, 'Your hand is gangrenous.'

Conrad found a voice. He was surprised at how weak it sounded, beneath the sound of straining wood and hemp. 'I would have thought you'd be happy enough to see me die of gangrene.'

The other man flinched.

'I'm not that ungrateful. You saved my life.' Roberto sounded extremely ungracious.

Before Conrad could get out a rejoinder that might have amounted to *Damn your life!*, the composer added, in an embarrassed mutter:

'I suppose I would regret it if *L'Altezza azteca* was the last opera on which we co-operated.'

Oddly and dizzily touched, Conrad admitted, 'I suppose I would, too.'

'Then be sensible enough not to die of this!'

Conrad bit down on his lip and winced. He must have been doing that before, when he was unconscious. His lower lip was gouged bloody. 'Are they proposing to cut my hand off?'

'The damaged tissue. It'll poison you. You can smell it yourself.' Dark eyes blinked. 'You, surgeon! Let him see it. Of all the times when we could have needed a god and a miracle . . .'

It wasn't clear if the last was spoken in jest or seriously. Conrad finally settled on 'wistful'.

One of the Frenchmen setting out instruments walked over and stripped the bandages from Conrad's left hand. The immediate increase of stink made him retch.

His hand lay on his chest, where they had propped his arm, but he couldn't feel most of it. What was not agonising was numb.

His thumb still looked human. His hand and first finger were swollen, waxy white and purple-black, under the swinging light.

The three lesser fingers were blown up like German blood sausages. Here, the worse stink rose. The flesh on the back of them was a dry, blood-blister black. The inside curve of the fingers shone wet and brown, swollen and split. Wet, like some creased and furled vegetable matter; no longer looking anything like human flesh.

He couldn't move his hand, to hide the vision. He turned his head to one side.

Roberto Capiraso flushed in the swinging lantern light. It was possible to see – past the aristocratic hauteur so long a part of his expression that it might have been grafted on – that he was not only concerned, but had been willing to sound clumsy and inept if it meant he could convince one stubborn librettist not to lose his life over this injury.

'Has prayer been tried?' Conrad managed to sound sarcastic.

'Certainly not by me.' A degree of sardonic humour entered Roberto's voice. 'God doesn't listen to men like me; nor does that demon we raised at the amphitheatre. Your hand won't wait. Drink down the brandy, and I'll make them find you a leather belt to bite on.'

The frigate must sail in a better sea: the wooden cots hung at shallow angles from the vertical. Calm enough for surgery.

Conrad's stomach turned over, sick from his chest to his belly with fear.

It means losing part of myself. I may die. If I die and return, that won't give me an amputated hand back . . .

A man – *a surgeon?* – shouted something towards the ship's apothecary-boys.

'Leonora?' Conrad demanded.

'They won't tell me! And she's my—' Capiraso swallowed the word. 'Before they banned your obstreperous servant from here, he said she's in the first mate's cabin. Under strict arrest.'

'I want to see her.'

Conrad knew before he asked that it was not possible.

He shuddered on the hard pallet. A swimming feeling in his head and the way his thoughts misted out at the edges decided him. He forced his mind to focus.

635

No false hope. I'll lose the hand for good. Men haven't always been healed – healed themselves – in the past. No reason to think they will in the future.

'Roberto.'

The man's head instantly turned. 'You're sure?'

'I don't want to rot by inches.' Conrad suppressed the reflex to vomit that surged in his stomach.

Roberto Capiraso hammered on the side of the wooden cot. 'Brandy, here!'

'See if they have laudanum.' He made knowledge of what the drug could do a block for fear.

A feeling for the integrity of his body still shuddered in his belly.

He took a last refuge in mockery. 'Do me one favour, Roberto. Make sure they take the correct hand . . .'

The Count snorted. With a startling frank honesty, he said, 'You can trust me.'

✦

If there weren't words to describe the absolute intensity of song and music, there were still less words adequate to pain. He bit through the leather belt, though it was folded over twice. The surgeon's voice rambled on above him – *explaining the operation to his assistants?* – and he lost all knowledge of the world.

Only pain remained. Pain: as if he were smashed up against the world's ultimate reality.

He did not pray.

He did beg.

The surgeon understood his mixture of Neapolitan, High German, and Parisian French.

'Herr Sertürner's recently discovered and much-lauded drug, morphine!' the Frenchman proudly announced. 'You'll find that we in the Emperor's navy are scientifically advanced—'

'Thank God for science!'

Conrad succumbed to the drug while ignoring the deep laughter of the Conte di Argente.

It did not precisely ease the pain, but it put him into a distant and preoccupied state where he could still feel it, but he didn't care.

◆

'You sure you want to look at it?' Tullio – who, reinstated, had taken over the bandaging of Conrad's left hand – shot him a concerned glare.

'Yes, I'm sure!' Conrad snapped.

The Conte di Argente muttered something in his sleep, shifted in his wooden cot, and groaned unconsciously. He must have accidentally moved his lower legs – both wrapped in the albumen-stiffened bandages which the French surgeon thought appropriate for, respectively, a clean break and a slight fracture.

Conrad waited a moment but Roberto didn't wake.

His bandages coming off pained him.

'I . . . can feel it again. That's good, yes?'

Tullio nodded. He unwrapped the dry inner bandages.

Conrad found himself staring at a crab's claw.

His stomach turned over. He spat on the planks.

A look back at his hand confirmed that the black blisters and waxy skin had diminished, mostly giving way to healthy-coloured skin. His thumb looked almost uninjured.

The first finger missed its top joint. Shortened, without a nail, and topped by bloody sewn flaps, it looked hideous

The three remaining fingers were not even stumps, taken back to the knuckle at the palm. Sealed over with snipped and folded skin, gruesomely red-black where stitches were healing – *No less hideous*, he thought.

The lowest joint of the little finger was gone. The knuckle too; leaving him deeply cut into down the outside of the hand, large parts of the palm gone.

'Says he saved as much as he could.'

'Wrap it up.' Had it been possible, Conrad would have run from the grotesque object as far as he could. The knowledge that he must carry this around with him . . .

'Saw worse in the war.' Tullio expertly swayed with the frigate's motion as he bandaged up the half-hand, and re-tied Conrad's

637

sling. 'Not that that's any consolation. Except . . . you were right to choose the one you did.'

Tullio finished. He scratched through his growing-out, cropped hair. Conrad had a problem identifying the other man's expression – and realised, startled, that it was admiration.

Conrad found that ironic enough to almost make him burst out laughing.

Except if I do, I'll never stop.

'I couldn't have been that . . . cold.' Tullio shook his head. 'Haul somebody out safe because you're in the right spot at the right minute, yeah. Doesn't take any thought. But choosing like that . . .'

He smiled, crookedly.

'I'd started to forget what you were like in the war, padrone. And you were the one who chose to walk in and pull me out of a building on fire. So, suppose this shouldn't surprise me. Just seen you do too much scribbling, that's all.'

Conrad couldn't prevent himself muttering, '"Scribbling" is all I'm going to do now.'

'Corrado.' Tullio punched him lightly on the other shoulder. 'You can walk. You can see. That puts you two up on the people we saw the day after the battle at Maida. You can write, you can conduct, you can fuck a woman – or if you can't, you got one hand to wank with, at least!'

Conrad would have interrupted, but choked instead.

'So stop looking like the world ended – before I show us both up by kicking your arse across the deck. You can get a glove made with wooden fingers in it. Or you can just let people see what you did. You imbecile hero!'

Conrad took a breath – and another, deep inhalation – and felt his heated rage defused by Tullio's entirely serious, affectionate gaze.

'I'm not a hero.' Anger gone, left grief and resentment behind. But neither of those were to do with Tullio Rossi, he thought, and could be withstood until he and Tullio could get drunk together, and talk the matter out to exhaustion.

'Trust you to beat up the cripple,' Conrad grumbled.

'I find it's safer. Able-bodied men might beat me up.'

The ex-soldier's remark was entirely separate from his warm smile.

Running feet thumped on the boards above his head. Conrad startled. He tried to guess, from shouts and hauled, creaking ropes, what might be happening. 'Tullio?'

The ex-soldier leaned outside for a moment, speaking to the guards at the doorway.

'We're back in sight of Naples!' he burst out. 'Finally! A whole fucking week upside down in a storm; thought we'd never make it.'

Conrad beckoned Tullio over, not leaving him an option of refusal. 'I'm not the one under arrest! Help me up on deck!'

The sling on his left arm unbalanced him. He did not need to add, *I'm not steady yet*. That was obvious enough fighting up companionways and steps.

The outer world burst on him in a flurry of white canvas, fresh wind, blue sky, men working at the sails, and a green and blackened land beyond.

The peak of Vesuvius touched the sky from here, seen from the level of the sea. Even its foothills towered. Conrad squinted against the blue sky, and made out great scars of black and grey ash on the south-east slopes.

The waters that had been blue and limpid were grey.

Conrad made his way cautiously towards the bows, where he should be more out of the way, and shaded his eyes with his right hand. Paolo-Isaura came over. She looked with concern at his sling.

'At least you're not off your head now.' She jammed an unexpectedly gentle elbow in his ribs.

'You can tell?' Conrad absently stared ahead, at the glowing pale stone of Napoli's buildings. Too far yet to see detail, and yet damage was apparent.

'Looks like it mostly hit the city itself . . .' Tullio said no more as they closed on the port.

All sails brailed up, the frigate glided on through the Bay of Naples, silent but for the groaning of rope and wood. Every man not occupied with the sails or the steering stood about on the deck, getting in the sailors' way. Conrad saw Ferdinand with a crowd of his officers and aides, Fabrizio Alvarez awkwardly unsafe on crutches.

'There aren't any boats coming out.' Conrad went to shade his eyes with his left hand, bit back a swear-word, and switched to his right hand. 'Not one.'

Tullio said, 'If the day's come when bum-boats don't come out to rook ships' crews of their pay, we have reached the Apocalypse!'

'No pilot's boat,' Paolo added anxiously.

If they're not sending a pilot out, something is very wrong.

There were no ships moored in the harbour, either, Conrad saw. No commercial ships with their sails going up to take them to Marseilles or Cyprus or Gibraltar.

A smart man in the blue coat and white breeches of the Emperor's navy passed behind him, where he stood at the rail. Conrad recognised him as the dark-haired, soaked man who had been berated by the surgeon. Officers followed him. The man bowed to Ferdinand and his entourage, a few yards further towards the prow.

'We have not been formally introduced, as yet, the weather preventing. Sébastien Bernard, Captain of the *Apollon*.'

The King wore a grey military cloak, his head bare, and the wind blew through his short-cropped brown hair. His attention was all on Naples; the rest of the world might evidently not exist. 'Can we come closer in without a pilot?'

'I have men who know the waters, yes, sire.'

'Come close enough to launch a boat.'

Smartly efficient seamen moved to obey almost before Captain Bernard ordered.

Conrad narrowed his eyes against wind and spray. The long shore of the Bay of Naples was silent and still. Wavelets lapped.

Tension pulled against tendon and bone in his arm. He relaxed the muscles of his shoulders, and attempted to ignore the fire in what was no longer a hand, no matter how much phantom feeling assured him it was.

Like the war, men in the surgeons' tents, staring at their injuries in disbelief.

After the surgeon's tent, there were men who healed and went back into battle.

Tacking again brought them on a slow glide past Castell dell'Ovo, apparently deserted, and along beside the blank broken wall of the Palazzo Reale.

The view of the King's Dock opened. The *Apollon*'s captain opened his spy-glass with a click, and swore under his breath. 'No use sending a boat in here.'

The dock lay under the hot sun, a hopeless shambles of broken spars and planks, mud, and small boats driven in and piled up on each other like driftwood.

Silence pressed down, somehow more terrifying than the wreckage. Even the sailors of the Emperor stared, only the wind audible in the sails.

'Take us into the harbour.' Ferdinand's voice broke the quiet.

The frigate tacked and came about, making its way back across the Bay, and rounding the promontory.

The whole landscape opened up east and south of the city. Conrad heard Paolo swear. The raw broken top of Vesuvius stood black against the horizon, lower now. Black earth, ash, steaming rock: all stretched down from the scooped-open crater, as far as the city.

The Gulf itself was smaller, clogged up on the shore beneath Vesuvius's foothills by sodden tracts of ash.

Two of Ferdinand's men, assumed courtiers, proved themselves to be Natural Philosophers as Conrad overheard them leaning on the rail nearby:

'—*Heavy* ash sank from the bottom of the avalance into the sea, as I premised! The *light* ash covers the city—'

'Here.' Tullio reappeared, nudged Conrad's shoulder, and handed over the old army spy-glass—

He took it back, opened it out, and handed it over again.

Paolo-Isaura slid between Conrad and the rail. He rested the glass on her shoulder. The focus was not optimum, but with an arm in a sling, he couldn't adjust it. Still, he picked out the Port district, the old centre of town, and the New Palace, where the volcanic surges had rushed into the city's buildings.

641

'There are people.' He lifted his head, finding that the ship's captain and King Ferdinand were in loud consultation over their own scopes.

He dipped his head back to fix on the town again.

Naples looked as crowded as it might normally be. From this position he could see there was activity from the Port District round to the Palazzo Nuovo's stern round towers, and the shattered walls of the Palazzo Reale. Up in the city, too. Men worked – and women. A few children played. Fewer than one might expect. And if there were old men and women, they were not visible to his eye. *But Naples is not a desert!*

He took a deep glad breath of sea wind, and opened his mouth to report it.

A murmur went through the ship's company. It began with those in the rigging, high enough to see best. It spread. Conrad heard Alvarez speaking anxiously to the King. He didn't take his eye from the glass.

In the magnified circle, Conrad looked again at the city full of people. People working – shifting rubble, clearing streets, even building new stone-work. They laboured with coats and waist-coats discarded, as if they were too hot. By the progress made in clearing the detritus of the eruption, and new walls rising, the men and women of Naples had been working without sleep, all through the long nights.

Without sleep because, even at this distance across the water, the eye picked out how they lifted chunks of stone too heavy for normal men and women.

Their indefinable too-smooth movement called Leonora inexorably to mind. Leonora, during those times when she was not pretending to be one of the living.

'The people who came out of the ash!' Conrad realised. 'The Dead who were used for the voice of the Emergent God. I thought they would have gone . . .'

Ferdinand's voice spoke beside him. 'It seems they were given a choice.'

Conrad straightened, aware of Paolo and Tullio making respectful bows. Beyond them, the captain was overseeing the lowering of the ship's gig into the calm water. 'Sir?'

'We may be wrong. Or there may be only a few . . . Can you accompany me—' Ferdinand Bourbon-Sicily checked himself. 'My apologies. And the Count incapacitated too. *Porca vacca!*'

He strode off before Conrad could formulate a response.

Aware of his face heating scarlet, he thought, *They'd have to rig a chair for me; there isn't time.*

He wondered if he would be able to use his left hand to grip anything, after it healed. Loss surprised him. The intensity of it blinded him for a moment with shameful tears.

The King led a number of men down into the gig. It was not until Conrad followed the progress of the last man that he realised it was a woman, in a cloak and man's borrowed hat. Two armed soldiers from Alvarez's company sat either side of her in the stern.

'Leonora—!' He choked off a cry.

A glance at Tullio and Paolo let him know he was not wrong; he had seen her.

'King must think she can help.' Tullio shrugged.

Paolo, severe, corrected: 'Taking her in to see what she's done.'

Oars dipped and rose, water flashing in the sun. She was out of sight before he could see if she were well.

Conrad leaned one arm on the rail and let the breeze cool his face. He ignored conversation around him, where all attention was fixed on Napoli. He saw the boat ground on the shore, and the small group vanish into the city.

An hour passed.

Time went past slowly enough to make him envy the sailors at their tasks – though he knew he'd bitterly regret any life that forced him up masts and yards, to furl and unfurl sails. Pain bit again. No use offering himself for menial tasks to take his mind off what might be happening in Naples, since few enough tasks can be done literally single-handed.

He was turning his right hand for inspection when Tullio came up to lean on the rail beside him. *Creased palm, fingers still stained with ink even after scrambling through Pozzuoli, capable manipulative fingers . . .*

'Anything?'

'Man at the top of the big mast says they went to the palace.'

'Look!' Conrad's focus abruptly shifted. The dark motion beyond Tullio's head became the lifting and scooping of oars, and the dark blob the ship's boat returning from the silent city.

Sling or not, he managed to elbow his way through the idlers waiting at the side of the ship, and hold his position there while the men came back on board.

Seeing a familiar profile, he shoved forward.

Alvarez's men hurried Leonora away before she could even look around.

King Ferdinand came aboard with agility. He shrugged his shoulders, brushing the wide lapels of his coat as if he could brush Naples away with the dust.

'We sent out scouting parties. Their reports are conclusive.'

Ferdinand spoke generally, gazing around at aides, sailors, the survivors from the opera company. By his grave expression, the emergency had him still in the frame of mind to speak openly to any man of the Two Sicilies, rather than with the reserve of a king.

'The city has been dug three-quarters out from under the ash in a week. The Returned Dead may have gone back into the storm after the god spoke through them – but they evidently didn't go away. There are hundreds, thousands, of them . . . If there are any living survivors, they've fled; likely out into the countryside. There's no living man, woman, or child to be found.'

Ferdinand rubbed absently at his dust-red eyes – and dropped his hand, his expression abruptly pained.

'Naples is a city of the Returned Dead.'

60

The *Apollon* ran south through the Straits of Messina, and south and west, around island-Sicily, rather than directly past Stromboli and the Aeolian Islands.

'Weather's still unsettled,' Tullio Rossi muttered, leaning unprovoked on the ship's rail beside Conrad, as they passed through the Straits.

Conrad stared out at land and sea for a long time before he identified the strangeness. 'It's wider . . .'

'They say that wave was something to see.'

Conrad tried to comprehend that, while he and his compatriots fled fire, a great flood of water had undercut both sides of this channel, widening it out in minutes.

The notorious current didn't seem less strong.

A distant yellow stone line of buildings fronted the sea, under sullen and black-sloped Ætna. Conrad wondered aloud, 'Think we'll make port at Catania?'

'The King wants to set up at Palermo too much. Don't worry, padrone.' The big man looked embarrassed. 'Your family are all right, I'm sure.'

It was a niggling pain, somewhere inside, that Conrad was content to wait for a communication from Zio Baltazar telling him his mother Agnese was well. *After all this, I don't want to be nagged for money I certainly haven't got! Even when I get paid for L'*Altezza's *libretto.*

Worrying about that enabled him to ignore the fang of pain chewing on his left hand.

The *Apollon* sailed on. The King of the Two Sicilies wished to aid his stricken country, shipboard rumour said – and since Naples was a city of the dead, to move his capital to island-Sicily, in the north of the island, at Palermo.

Day and night and day.

Conrad did not see Leonora.

Attempting to bribe his way past the door of the first mate's cabin failed. Even bribery with the request that he merely be allowed to talk to her through the barred door.

The sergeant in charge of the soldiers of Colonel Alvarez was sympathetic. 'We'd like to do it, signore. We wish we might do it for the hero of the Campi Flegrei. But you understand, it's duty.'

'"Hero"?' Conrad shook his head, stunned, and walked off, leaning against the slant of the ship. *Hero! All I want is to speak to Nora!*

He found himself turning it over and over in his mind.

This is not the woman I opened my heart to in Venice. Even without what has happened to her, how could it be? Five years gone: we are both different. She's . . . I don't know what she is. But I love her with her potential realised: all fire and ice and sword-blades.

Her arrest was strict enough that he temporarily gave up his attempts.

What does this imply for her future?

✦

He might have been given his own quarters below decks, but comfort and some odd feeling – that surely could not be any kind of loyalty – kept him in the makeshift sickbay that was Captain Bernard's cabin, with the Conte di Argente.

The Count's arrest was strict. Conrad still had visitors. Each allowed in by ones and twos, but visitors nonetheless.

JohnJack Spinelli came with an extra ration of crackers, and leaned against Conrad's cot making 'single-handed' jokes until Conrad threw him out, pleased to have got that initial hump over with.

Sandrine offered her protests about her plight having to live below decks, 'at close quarters with all those common sailors', but confessed that Paolo had hung up a curtain to cut the 'opera' section of the lower deck off at least from curious stares, if not from flirtation . . . Scurrilous company gossip followed.

Paolo-Isaura came with Tullio and a wordless, but beaming, Giambattista Velluti. Apparently all the officers and half the crew wanted to hear his story of what happened in the Anfiteatro, and needing Isaura to translate his whispers into her broken French only made it more effective.

'Oh, yes, brother,' Paolo-Isaura said innocently. 'I'm told we have to congratulate you on your new-found belief in God . . .'

'My what?'

Tullio snickered. By the look of him, he was not the source of any rumours.

That'll be Count Roberto that's flapped his mouth off, Conrad mused grimly. *Since he was the only other person here apart from the surgeon. He must have said something while I was asleep.*

Paolo cast her eyes up to the heavens (or, in this case, the underside of the frigate's deck) and murmured, '"Thank God for science" . . .'

Conrad managed to summon a lofty dignity. 'I was using the term in the cultural, *secular* sense of the word.'

Even Giambattista Velluti joined in the jeers in response to that.

'All right, I was out of my head with brandy and laudanum!' Conrad very carefully folded his arms, and sulked his way through an afternoon of teasing.

They haven't abandoned me.

He dared not look when the lob-lolly boy changed the bandages. He kept his head turned away, and at those times read what remained of his cut and de-boned hand in Roberto Capiraso's horrified gaze.

Conrad met with Ferdinand again only briefly, the King congratulating him on surviving surgery.

Now that it looks like the Apollon *and all of us will survive . . . there'll be arrest, judgement, and punishment of the King's enemies.*

647

Conrad could not have imagined, before, that it would give him a moment's concern.

◆

The two wooden cradles swung to an identical angle as the frigate heeled over, running west before tacking north again.

Roberto Capiraso's voice held no apparent emotion. 'I suppose it will be a matter of prison.'

'You deserve it.'

The bearded man lay back flat, his expression a curious mix of resignation and frustration. 'I know. I don't deny it.'

A laugh bubbled out of Conrad before he could stop it.

The Conte di Argente glared, and then heaved a sigh. 'What is it now, poet?'

'You can talk!' The most recent dose of morphine loosened Conrad's tongue, but didn't move him to speak anything but his true opinion. 'You out-poet the poets, Superbo! All for love . . . All for her . . .'

If the man had not been injured and in pain, Conrad wouldn't have seen the flinch, or watched the muscles of Capiraso's jaw tighten.

That hit home.

The Count said bitterly, 'I have half a mind to get out of this thing and find her—'

'—If you want to be on crutches the rest of your life.'

The man cursed like the dockside *lazzaroni*.

Conrad had no idea, now it came to it, why he should be warning Il Superbo of anything.

Because of her, Conrad reflected. *Because I understand him, and I can't help but sympathise, even with my rival.*

The surgeon made his rounds then, inspecting both men with a dour confidence in his own ability that Conrad found cheering.

Conrad caught sight of uniformed, armed men beyond the door.

'They must think I'm improving,' Roberto grunted. 'I'm under the strictest possible arrest.'

◆

The *Apollon* came into the north-west facing harbour of Palermo early in the morning, bows seeming hardly to disturb limpid water. March brought out green scrub and grasses on the great grey crags that cupped the city. The southern light, and the heat that soothed his skin, made Conrad physically at ease for the first time since the Burning Fields.

As they came into the curve of the bay, he looked beyond the town. A smalt-coloured haze went up into the heavens.

The grey-blue cloud gave way, halfway up the sky, to stark rock.

Not a cloud, he realised. The higher foothills of Ætna, on the far side of the island; whose white snow and eruption-blackened peak stood out precise and distinct. High enough that he must tilt his head back to take it in, even this number of miles away . . .

'Coming, Corrado?' Tullio reached down to the ship's boat, where they had been rowed into Palermo's keyhole-shaped medieval dock. His mouth twisted wryly. 'Shall I give you a hand?'

'Fuck you, Tullio . . .' Conrad caught the ex-sergeant's left hand with his right, and let himself be heaved up onto the ancient stones, feeling marginally less embarrassed at being crippled.

Palermo, between its granite hills, thick with palm trees, camellias, and every other flower, welcomed him instantly in. He was dazzled by the city whose arches spoke of the Moors, churches of the Normans, and mosaics of the Byzantine Empire to which the island briefly belonged. He was smelling scent-laden air before he realised, and the cooking of rice with saffron – listening to a thousand competing voices as he stumbled through the crowds.

'I'm here!' Paolo-Isaura slid in beside him, smart in borrowed French navy uniform. She helped Tullio shut him off from the shoving groups – it seemed every man and woman of island-Sicily wanted news of Naples, of mainland Sicily, of their relatives in Campania, of the likelihood of ships landing with provisions.

Tullio and Paolo manoeuvred deftly. Conrad realised they followed behind the litter in which the King had ordered the Conte di Argente transported, using that as shelter too.

He glanced over his shoulder, seeing the opera company trailing behind, spreading out. Sandrine Furino stopped to give her account of the Burning Fields – crowds gathering – and Brigida Lorenzani translated the whisper of Giambattista Velluti . . .

'They'll be a while,' Tullio commented. 'Might as well see where we're sleeping.'

Paolo, a ship's bag of belongings over one shoulder, and Alfredo Scalese's violin in its case under that arm, linked her free hand around Conrad's elbow. She sounded worried. 'Are we under house arrest, too?'

Conrad frowned, looking up the hill, past the Duomo, at the faded golden stone of the Palazzo dei Normanni – evidently their destination.

'I don't think so. They will want us to answer questions.'

✦

It was another week before he finished repeating, ad nauseam, what he had seen, heard, and said.

A week without ever seeing Leonora Capiraso, Contessa di Argente.

He asked to see Leonora. He was refused.

He demanded. He was refused again.

Conrad found himself in modest rooms in the Palazzo dei Normanni, along with Tullio, Paolo (who continued dressing as Paolo), JohnJack, Sandrine and Velluti; those dozen bedraggled chorus singers and musicians who had followed him across the frozen lava; the Conte di Argente, and – presumably – the Contessa.

'Good God!' Paolo-Isaura exclaimed, on her way out. 'Not another inquiry . . . !'

The King of the Two Sicilies convened a board – a number of boards – before which the witnesses of the eruption and the events at the Flavian Amphitheatre were called to give evidence.

Something to keep my mind off this part-hand as it heals, Conrad told himself sternly.

A week from the day they docked, he slumped into a chair on the balcony that overlooked an inner courtyard of the palace. Built first by Palermo's Emir, and then by Roger the Norman, the palazzo's fretted wood and pointed arches were lost on Conrad, for all they might make a wonderful backdrop for an opera.

The King's surgeon changed the bandages on his hand. Conrad preferred to look away when that happened.

'They still won't let me see Leonora,' he growled, when the man had gone.

'They won't let anyone see the Contessa.' Tullio sat down beside him, carrying two glasses of wine, and passed the second one over. 'You want to join the syndicate on Paolo and the boards?'

It was a worthy attempt to distract him. Conrad allowed it. With the di Galdis gone, he might have a little more income to play with; his original creditors would presumably be willing to go back to their old arrangements.

'Put me in for five soldi. On her continuing to get through every one of these testimonies without them guessing she's not a boy.' Conrad found a cause for sly humour. 'Anyone who suspects it certainly won't mention it – a woman couldn't conduct an orchestra, especially not in an opera house . . .'

Tullio gave him a grin for the mock outrage.

Isaura joined them at the inner balcony an hour later, cravat untied and waistcoat unbuttoned. There was nothing about her torso specifically female. Conrad supposed that she bound her breasts, like the heroines of adventure tales; certainly it was not a thing to ask one's sister.

'I did overhear, today,' Paolo-Isaura dropped into the conversation, as they sat gazing out at the Aeolian Sea. 'Leonora's still giving her testimony, but it's all done on her own, and only with one or two very secret boards of advisers. They don't even allow Il Superbo in on all of them. I saw him when I was coming back.'

'Moping around like a wet weekend,' Tullio said, opening another bottle of the wine. 'Like the padrone here. You and il Conte make a good pair, Corrado.'

Conrad pondered the responses that *vaffanculo!* might get, and chose to remain sullenly silent.

The following morning a page arrived to tell him he was called to the rooms which Ferdinand had chosen for his private office.

✦

Conrad made his bow in the tall, sun-shadowed chamber before he realised that another chair was occupied besides the King's.

Roberto, Conte di Argente, did not rise, as etiquette demanded.

It was not one of the palace's gilded chairs he occupied, Conrad noted, but a wheeled invalid-chair. The chair supported his stiffly bandaged, outstretched legs.

Argente gave Conrad a reluctant nod, and said nothing.

The King of the Two Sicilies wore the regimental uniform of his royal guards, golden epaulettes on the shoulders of his blue coat, gold frogging across the breast. The Order of the Golden Fleece hung bright in the spotless linen at his throat.

He seems very distant from the man struggling through the crevasses of the Burning Fields, with ash-clogged boots and torn breeches, Conrad thought. He would have greeted that man without hesitation. This distant pale-featured man, he momentarily had no words for.

'Corrado!' Ferdinand stood up from the vast desk piled all over with the papers attendant on commanding the kingdom, especially in this extremity. He beckoned Conrad further into the chamber. 'Come and speak with me for a moment.'

Tension left Conrad's shoulders at the lack of ceremony. 'Sir.'

All the windows and shutters of the room had been flung open. The morning was early enough to be fresh. Pots of cacti and palms shaded the balconies. Ferdinand drew him out onto one balcony.

It overlooked a fountain, in another courtyard, throwing light back up to the sun. The view of Palermo's roofs was beautiful, but irrelevant, Conrad realised. *We're out of earshot of the Conte di Argente.*

'Another board of inquiry, sir?'

Ferdinand gave his mild, compelling smile. 'We're near to concluding our business. I plan to give my final judgement this morning. I wished to speak with you first.'

Panic located itself under his sternum, and churned in his stomach. *This soon? Leonora . . . !*

'As for yourself . . .' Gazing at the bright falling fountain-water, Ferdinand continued. 'I had wondered if you might want to take on Adriano Castiello-Salvati's role.'

'Me? Sir,' Conrad added belatedly.

He couldn't bring himself to say *No! Look what happened to Castiello-Salvati!*

It was likely plain on his face.

'However, I realised.' Ferdinand looked warmly at him. 'You're not one of nature's natural spies, Corrado. Though it's true a man who speaks his mind bluntly, against the tide of society, might be unsuspected about passing on what he hears.'

'I'd make a mess of it,' Conrad said frankly and paused. 'If you want someone who can hear scandal, I recommend Signore Rossi.'

Because any preferment he can get, he'll need.

'Rossi, I had thought to reward,' Ferdinand said. 'Since he tells me he's getting married – although I'm a little confused as to whom – he should be welcoming of something from the Treasury. I hope to keep him in reserve, should I at any time need a private courier to the Emperor.'

'You won't insult him with money. The same goes for everybody in the company.' Conrad realised he might have implied something about himself, and fell silent in confusion.

'Very well; that all seems clear.' Ferdinand waved him back inside, towards the great desk and attendant chairs, that stood under a gilded and painted ceiling.

The Conte di Argente gave Conrad a look that was all Il Superbo.

The King seated himself, linked his fingers, and leaned forward.

'The Two Sicilies owe you much, Conrad. A great debt. It would be difficult to repay it. You won't be surprised, therefore, when I repay it by asking something more of you.'

Conrad sat down hastily, and hoped he didn't look as confused as he felt.

Given Ferdinand's amusement, that was a lost hope.

Ferdinand leaned back in his gilt chair, one outstretched hand on the desk turning a pen over in his fingers. Oddly, it gave him an air not of tension, but of relaxation.

'I wish you to consent to do one thing for me, Corrado. I'd like your services as chief adviser on a board I plan to set up. It's intended to plan a scientific institute for the Two Sicilies, along the lines of those in France and England and Germany. Admittedly we don't have the reputation of being up to date, here in the south, but I think that might be countered in time. We have studies of the recent eruption, which justify our setting up present inquiries. By natural stages, that leads to a permanent institute.'

Conrad sat stunned for sufficiently long that Ferdinand laughed out loud.

'I won't be insulting you with riches, but I think a sinecure such as that should carry some reward. Sufficient for you to regularise your financial situation, at least.'

Nine years, and the mind grows to think of certain restrictions as permanent, like ivy growing to match the shape of a tree.

Iron bonds, when they have been on long enough, leave heavy ghosts of sensation behind them.

I'm free of my father's debt, Conrad dimly thought. It didn't feel real.

But it will. Oh, it will!

'Corrado, do you want the position?'

'Yes! Sir,' Conrad collected himself enough to add. 'Thank you.'

'Oh, don't thank me. I'm giving you his Eminence Cardinal Filippo Gattuso, Corazza's successor in the Holy Office, and all the Dominicans, to argue with . . . Along with every reactionary old buffer who calls himself a courtier and claims an interest in the matter! If I say I want a single-minded man with no tact whatsoever, I hope you won't feel insulted?'

Conrad ignored the friendly insult. 'If this is some necessary part of court politics— Sir, is this intended to be a genuine scientific institute? The findings won't be watered down or censored?'

'Oh, it's genuine. So is the resistance to it. That's why I want a hard-headed man to break the rock-face for me.' Ferdinand gave him a very direct look. 'I'll smooth feathers and suggest compromises in your wake – and if my compromises happen to tend more towards your views than theirs, well, they'll think themselves lucky to escape every tenet of atheistical heresy, won't they?'

Conrad couldn't quite make up his mind between a smile and a scowl. By Ferdinand's entertained look, this must be apparent.

'I'm relieved,' Conrad said, his tumultuous thoughts quietening.

Ferdinand raised a brow. 'Relieved?'

'I was beginning to worry that you were the dangerous one

– likeable, rational-minded, and Christian. Forgive me, but, you're the enemy. Not Canon Viscardo, or—' Conrad closed his mouth on the name *Nora*. '—Or the Prince's Men. I'm relieved that your appetite for science is genuine, sir. And, if you'll excuse me being outspoken, I'm willing to bet that for every man you convince to be religious, there'll be two that your Institute turns into atheists.'

There was a light in Ferdinand Bourbon-Sicily's eye. 'Conrad, do you really want to talk yourself out of a job?'

Conrad smoothly matched him. 'I'll just hope that's a hypothetical question, sir.'

The King snorted.

'Well, I hope I shall prove a sufficiently convincing enemy, Corrado. You may as well know that I don't give up hope of bringing even you to an awareness of the spiritual side of life. I foresee interesting moments ahead with our Institute. Although, remember, I don't intend it to occupy all your time; you will still have librettos to write—'

A lackey interrupted at that point.

Conrad sat in a quiet daze while the King sent out several orders. Something that was closer to exaltation than happiness burned in his breast.

Oh God! He used the phrase mentally without shame, referring to that emergent voice on the Campi Ardenti that had proclaimed itself no god at all.

Oh, God, I'm free of all my debts!

No more delaying on paying the rent each month, until another tiny fee creeps in from the local opera board. No more fulsome apologies and sickening politeness, hoping that will gain me a day or two's grace. No more snatching up every piece of work that comes my way – no matter that there aren't enough hours in the day – because I daren't let any work go by.

A sinecure, he said.

If it's sizeable, I'm going to buy a mansion, and Paolo and Tullio will never be without a place to live.

If it's more than sizeable, I'll be buying Mother a cottage – and listening to her whine that it's not as nice as the house 'dear Zio Baltazar' loans her.

And if my pay is no more than reasonable, I'm going to live the way I do now, but without waking up at three in the morning in a cold sweat.

'Conrad?'

Conrad shook himself out of his daydream. 'I was thinking, sire – the "Institut Campi Ardenti"?'

'That seems fitting. Yes.'

Ferdinand rested his arms on the arms of the gilded chair, the diamond at his neck catching scintillating light. His expression lost its liveliness. A gravity of authority settled on him.

'Now, we come to the judgements. Conrad. Count Argente. You are two of the three most centrally concerned with this. The third will be joining us shortly. Conrad, you're here primarily as witness and adviser: you saw much at first hand that I only have through reports. If you hear anything that sounds mistaken or incomplete, you are to tell me.'

'Yes.' His breath came short. *If Roberto's here with me, then the third* must *be her* . . .

Some part of himself wanted to put off the hour in which he must see her.

He asked, almost randomly, 'What's been decided about the other Prince's Men?'

'Exile.' Ferdinand shook his head. 'If I send them to execution, I shall only have dozens more of their agents flooding over the borders. I'm sending them back to their countries of origin, except when they're Sicilian; those I merely intend to put a considerable distance over the border. Let the Prince's Men sort out their own confusion. They have massive losses in the Council of the North – our friend in the north is more ruthless than I am in putting down anarchy. With their erroneous conception of "the Prince" known, I suspect they'll be just another secret society that withers away once the first fanatics are gone.'

Ferdinand's round face, that could be utterly bland, altered very slightly, but displayed both pain and betrayal.

'Enrico Mantenucci is dead—'

Conrad's comment froze in his throat, recalling both the corpse in the Flavian Amphitheatre, and the trusted colleague in the map room of the Palazzo Reale. What is there that can be said?

'—It only remains to deal with the other leaders of the Prince's Men here.' Ferdinand pushed his gilt chair back. Standing, he restlessly paced the great chamber.

Conrad caught a creak from the invalid-chair as Roberto Capiraso shifted his weight. The bearded man gave no other sign of tension.

'Signore Conte . . .' Ferdinand Bourbon-Sicily halted, close to his huge desk. 'You conspired in a plot that would have had the Kingdom of the Two Sicilies destroyed. You turned your coat, and by that betrayal helped the process that saved us. Both these things for the same reason.'

Ferdinand rested his fists on the green leather, and leaned forward. He fixed a long weighing stare on Roberto Conte di Argente.

'You are easily dealt with.'

The Count drew himself up, as much as a sitting man can. 'Sire.'

Ferdinand laid his hand on a pile of papers heavy with wax seals.

'I'm taking over the estates belonging to Argente. Those here in the Sicilies. Those in Spain. The revenues they bring in will come direct to the Treasury of the Kingdom of the Two Sicilies. So also will the profits from your financial dealings. I confiscate any and all other properties you own: palazzos, farms, lesser properties in towns. Also horses, carriages, jewels, heirlooms, inheritances. Anything other than minor personal belongings I appropriate to the Crown, signore. You may keep the title.'

Roberto Capiraso stared, thunderstruck.

Lightly, maliciously, Ferdinand added, 'There's an argument as to whether the leisure of being a gentleman, or the necessities of poverty, better bring out the talent in an artist. I imagine as a composer you'll be able to settle that argument in my mind.'

Roberto's expression moved from bemused to bewildered.

Conrad wanted to put a word in, and could not imagine what it might be.

He's guilty, guilty of everything, but . . . But.

Roberto said, 'It is not to be prison, then?'

'That would be a waste.' Ferdinand's blue eyes had a cold glitter to them. They relented, a very little, as he added, 'You've composed for the San Carlo; I dare say other houses will give you a hearing just because of that.'

Moved by something closer to compassion than pity, Conrad put in bluntly, 'I can write the book. If I'm still wanted as a librettist, when rumour says I'm responsible for the destruction of two theatres.'

'Three! If we count the Flavian Amphitheatre . . .' Ferdinand smiled lightly. 'All of that will have been subsumed in what happened to Naples itself, Corrado; you're a hero. And you can always write for me.'

'Thank you, sir.'

'Justice is important.' The King's gaze swept over the Conte di Argente once more, as if he weighed whether the penalty that reduced the man to absolute poverty were sufficient. 'Despite his title and sex, the Conte di Argente was not the leader of the Prince's Men in the Two Sicilies. And so we come to the instigator of this thing: the woman Leonora.'

Ferdinand rang a small gold bell on his desk. Soldiers of the royal regiment entered. Conrad automatically rose to his feet.

The Contessa di Argente was hidden among the tall uniformed men, being a few inches shorter.

Their lieutenant saluted and left, with his men. Conrad saw her as servants took her bonnet, parasol, and gloves.

She dropped a curtsey, briefly enough that it did not seem like either sycophancy or insolence. 'Sire.'

She is unchanged.

Conrad remained standing, caught in everything about her. The reflected sunlight from the walls called out a bloom in her skin. Blue irises, so dark in the shade as to be purple, were echoed by the lilac shadows in her eye-sockets and temples. Thick ash-brown hair done up in a loose knot, as the goddess Athena might have worn it in classical sculpture . . . A white muslin dress, with a blue high-waisted tunic *à l'antique* over it – the creases in the fabric made Conrad realise this was the same one she had worn on the day he parted from her, in the Argente house in Naples; clearly saved for any interview she might be granted with the King.

He watched her profile. She would not turn to look at him.

She is wholly changed.

He couldn't identify anything that would make him feel that, but he did.

Ferdinand gestured to Conrad to sit down again.

There was no chair for Leonora.

She stood with the perfect stillness of the Returned Dead, not breathing or blinking.

Conrad felt trapped in that same frozen lack of motion. The dead woman fixed her gaze on the King, looking neither at her husband nor Conrad.

'Leonora Capiraso, that is—' Ferdinand turned over one of the papers on his desk, clearly unnerved for a moment. '—You are widely known as Leonora Capiraso, Contessa di Argente, but this is a courtesy title, your marriage to the Count having lapsed on your – first – death.'

Conrad realised he must have made some protesting noise.

Ferdinand gave him a direct look. 'The Church authorities have agreed and given their judgement. Marriage only lasts until death. "For when the dead rise, they will neither marry nor be given in marriage."'

Conrad's heart beat so hard that it felt as if it rose in his throat and choked him.

Leonora's husky, still-strained voice added, 'Matthew, chapter twenty-two, verse thirty, sire.'

'And that will be your Church orphanage upbringing . . .' The King of the Two Sicilies turned over a page upon which not much was written. 'Leonora D'Arienzo, in Venice; Nora Sposito, in Castelveneto.'

'That's the earliest name I recall, sire.'

Conrad found himself taken back to barely-lit rooms, as dawn lightened to a cold grey, and Nora woke from nightmares. Whispered, wept confidences afterwards . . . *Call it bad blood and be done*, she had snarled. He couldn't help contrast that fire and misery with her current polite meekness.

'If there's a family who should take responsibility for you,' Ferdinand Bourbon-Sicily said frankly, 'I can't find it. Very well. It's irregular, not having a father or uncle or brother here, but needs must. Nora Sposito . . . You understand that you are here to hear your judgement?'

Conrad's jaw ached. He made himself breathe. He watched her expression – impossible to read.

'May I be heard, first?' There was nothing conciliatory in her tone.

Roberto Capiraso made a cut-off movement, as if he would have warned or stopped her.

I think if he and I were not present, Ferdinand would instantly order her out of here in chains.

'Speak.'

Without asking leave, Leonora walked to the window, gazed out at the sea, and turned and walked back; exactly as a man would pace if he needed to think something out.

'I was a high-ranking member of the European inner circle of the Prince's Men. I still am a Prince's Man. Even having seen what the Prince of this World is . . .'

Ferdinand cut Roberto's stuttered exclamation off with one glance.

'I did what I was supposed to do.' Leonora turned, her hands a little out from her sides, as if she presented herself for the King's examination. 'But I wasn't supposed to come back twice! I wasn't supposed to rescue the enemies of the Prince's Men. I wasn't supposed to find the idea of the death of the traitor Roberto Conte di Argente unbearable – never mind the death of an unimportant librettist. I wasn't supposed to abandon my post – even though everything we were doing had just been proved an utter failure! – so that I could try to rescue the men I love.'

She and Ferdinand looked at each other as if they crossed swords. Her voice didn't waver.

Conrad guessed the King had attended the boards at which she was questioned, had heard her in front of examiners and advocates, without ever knowing what it was like to have her – a woman, born a commoner – speak to him as an equal.

Conrad hid in his heart that she had said *men I love.*

Ferdinand made a sign for her to continue.

'I defied the Prince's Men by coming back on the Campi Ardenti.' Leonora's accent drifted back towards the north and Castelveneto. 'And given that their code of honour is more strict than anything in Sicily, my life isn't worth the price of an old sock.'

The Conte di Argente, a dark flush across his cheekbones, demanded, 'What protection can the King offer you that anyone else can't?'

'It's not a matter of protection—' Conrad felt the glimmering of a realisation.

Regardless, he finally permitted himself the words he had planned all the week. 'Sire, I don't make *any* excuses for what Nora did. But don't execute her. Please.'

The first look she directed at him was a cutting glare that demanded silence.

Conrad saw her glare catch Roberto equally.

She took another set of steps across the wheat- and crimson-coloured chamber, and swung around, facing the King as if she challenged the whole House of Bourbon-Sicily.

'Remember, I could have just rescued Signore Scalese and Signore Capiraso. Nothing compelled me to wait for any other man!' Defiance flashed from her eyes – and vanished. 'That said, Signore . . . I'm a murderer.'

Air dried up in Conrad's throat.

The only sound in the room was the buzzing of bees outside, and the falling water in the fountain's basin.

Leonora's voice was barely louder.

'A murderer, dozens, hundreds of times over. Perhaps thousands. I don't know how many of the Neapolitans dead in the eruption were called to the Flavian Amphitheatre. Maybe all of them.'

She took a breath she didn't need.

'Yes, there was something in them that wanted to hear us, or else I couldn't have called them to come back and listen . . . But they were dead because of what we did – because of what I did.'

Ferdinand nodded. 'Yes.'

'It's useless to put me in prison.' Irony touched her lips. 'Your son or grandson would likely let me out, when it was forgotten why I'd been locked up.'

She's fey. Conrad could hardly bear to look at that smile. *How many legends of the fairy queen and mortal lovers have ever ended happily?*

She came forward from the window to the desk, until she was a mere yard from the King's chair. Ferdinand rose to his feet automatically, as one does for a lady. He did not seat himself when he realised his error. He extended a hand to Leonora, indicating that she should speak.

She had completely abandoned the pose of the lady of society. Conrad realised, *We're seeing her now as she was when she commanded the Prince's Men.* Her fingertips rested lightly on the desk, as if she measured out some chart or battle-map. She carried her weight balanced evenly, without the affected pose recommended to women in deportment lessons, and magazines.

Leonora said, 'I killed several thousand people. Men of Naples, their wives, their children. Even if I'd had a valid cause—'

She broke off, briefly.

'Men go to war and kill thousands more than I did, for a valid cause. In retrospect, this was not one. I consider what we learned to be . . . stupefying.'

Her dazed face had an expression Conrad recognised: someone who has been forced to reconsider everything they ever knew.

'But the price was too high, learning at that cost . . .'

The thin, too-tall woman whose plentiful hair and light-filled eyes were her only beauty gazed at the King. The two of them were almost of a height.

'All that said, sire . . . You have a task that only I can do.'

Her eyes blazed.

'Don't execute me. Put me into Naples, Signore – as your Governor-General in Naples.'

61

An intake of breath sounded; almost an oath. Conrad only belatedly recognised that it came from him.

Ferdinand Bourbon-Sicily stared dumbfounded at Leonora. 'How you can ask—?'

Leonora interrupted the King without hesitation. 'How will you govern in Naples?'

Ferdinand Bourbon-Sicily slowly closed his mouth. His expression was both outraged and bemused.

Leonora faced him without faltering.

'How can you, sire? Look at Naples – a city of the dead, now. You don't know what the people want, what they need. They won't trust the living. Not as they would one of their own.'

Her stare accused Ferdinand.

'They don't understand what's happened to them! You don't understand what's happened to them! I do. I can give them what they want and need, sire, if you let me! . . . I'll spend as many years doing it as are necessary. I can't make up for bringing back the dead. Nor for the eruption that killed them in the first place. I can care for them. If you appoint me as Governor of Naples, then the Dead will have someone on their side.'

Conrad waited, his chest tight with breathlessness, for Ferdinand to speak.

The King remained silent.

It burst out of Conrad, before he could stop himself. He snapped at Nora. 'You think they're going to welcome you?'

Leonora's lips ticked up at the side, in a secret half-smile that she had always reserved for him.

'I'll be lucky if I'm not hung up from the nearest lamp-post. Assuming I survive the *a la lanterne*, then they'll see that I can help. I want to help.'

Her voice dropped in power. She involuntarily lowered her head.

'I can tend to them, look after their interests, make the life they have – if that's the word – as happy for them as it can be. I don't know how long the Returned Dead survive, but I think it reasonable that I'll survive as long as the rest do.'

Her back was to the light from outside the windows. Warm air stirred the wisps of her hair. Conrad saw that she looked immensely sad.

Her head came up, her eyes dazed.

'It's not a thing one can atone for. Still, I want to atone. Give me this chance. You can watch me every step. I won't betray them.'

Ferdinand gave one great informal sigh. He flipped over a number of the folders on his crowded desk. 'Donna Leonora. You made them. The stubborn dead of Naples . . . You say, you're the same as they are, Returned Dead, and that you therefore understand their nature?'

Leonora made a quaint little bow, which reminded Conrad immensely of her appearances in travesti roles. 'Yes, sire.'

'Let me think on it. It can't be rushed into.'

'It can if the other option today is my – well – not execution. Destruction.'

Conrad remembered once dredging his mind for arcane rumour. Saying, *It's possible for the Returned Dead to, well, not die, but to be destroyed . . .*

Ferdinand made idle circles with the shaft of his dip-pen, running the wood over the leather top of his desk. He studied Leonora's face with the utmost keenness.

Difficult as it was to see against the light, Conrad glimpsed the wet streak of tears down her cheek. 'Nora—'

She made a sharp unfeminine gesture, waving him off. Turning

back to Ferdinand, she sniffed and achieved a shaky self-posses-
sion. Although her voice wobbled, her tone was shot through
with self-mockery:

'Consider, also, that if I'm your Governor in Naples, the Prince's
Men will be convinced all their secrets are spilled. Even if we
survive as a society, they'll think it will be a long time before it's
safe to resume their activities in the Two Sicilies.'

'And would their secrets be handed over to the Two Sicilies,
Contessa?'

Conrad expected a plain yes or no, and probably the former. He
realised that several moments of silence had passed.

Nora sighed.

'I still am a Prince's Man. There are men in the society to whom
I owe loyalty, even if I have betrayed them. Assure me of some
form of armistice – that they only suffer exile, not execution –
and, yes, you'll know whatever you need to know.'

Ferdinand's gaze swept over Roberto and rested on Conrad.

Belatedly realising he was being canvassed for his opinion,
Conrad exclaimed, '*Cazzo!*' And then, hastily, added, 'You can't
think I'm impartial, sir. Not about this.'

'I think you know this woman, well enough to know if she'll
keep her word.'

This is why I'm present here, Conrad realised.

*Yes, I'm intimately concerned with what's gone on. But from Ferdi-
nand's viewpoint, I'm the one who can tell whether Nora's honest, and
(unlike Roberto) be willing to speak about it.*

Conrad made himself think.

Words of assent must be bitten back, because what could be
easier than to say *Yes, I believe in Nora, I believe what she says.*

And yet, Conrad realised, *despite everything I've been through in
Naples – perhaps because of it – I do believe.*

He looked at Ferdinand, where the King waited.

'She kept her word to the Prince's Men until she died for the
second time. She kept more than her word to the Count and
myself—' Conrad was proud that his voice stayed level. '—When
for a second time she Returned from death. Yes, sir, you can trust
what she says. You can trust her.'

Negotiations concluded over two hours later, lawyers having been summoned, a contract drawn up in rough, and the King's seal and Leonora's signature attached.

Many times during that period Conrad thought, *I don't know what I'm still doing here.*

The same might be said for the newly destitute Conte di Argente. Conrad could see the same thought pass through the man's mind.

You might make a case that I'm here for advice because I do know Nora, but why is that needed, now?

Even if you could say the same for Roberto, the King can't imagine – even now – that he'd say anything to her detriment. So why is he still in the room?

Ferdinand sat back. 'The last point agreed, then. The dead of Naples will have a free channel to me, to tell me if they think they're well looked after, or oppressed.'

'Yes, sir.'

'This is only useful,' Ferdinand tapped the rough contract, 'in spelling out duties and responsibilities. It can hold neither of us. This is useless unless we exercise trust between us, donna. I think it will be apparent in – shall we say, a year and a day? – whether you and I are capable of working together.'

'I agree, sir.'

'Then the sooner you can take up your duties, the better.'

Conrad watched as Leonora rose from the chair she had taken, and walked to the window.

It was not possible to hear the city, here in this isolated part of the palazzo. The sun crept up the sky – the helioscope in the Duomo would soon mark noon – and the heat become great enough for everyone to retire behind closed curtains and open shutters. For a moment Conrad longed for the slant of the declining sun, when the citizens of Palermo would be out in the warm dusk; eating, drinking, gossiping; listening to the lap of the sea in the harbour, and watching the pulsation of fireflies.

His eyes on her thin silhouette, against the windows' bright-ness, he blurted out, 'What about her singing?'

Nora spun from the window with far more agility than any lady ought to have; all workhouse brat and opera donna. 'Corrado!'

Ferdinand tilted a hand. It invited Conrad's further explanation.

He's not angry, Conrad judged.

In fact, is he pleased?

Conrad let himself speak plainly to her. 'You still have your voice?'

Leonora's expression went from shame to anger to sorrow; dif-ficult to decipher against the light. Finally, she gave a small nod of assent. 'Strained, but it will recover if I rest it.'

Conrad turned back to the King. 'There are rumours going round, from the men who went with you into Naples. That the Returned Dead are rebuilding – and they appear to have begun with the San Carlo.'

Ferdinand slowly nodded. 'Yes, that's true.'

'Naples won't be wholly a city of the dead. Tell me you think that the living won't come to the San Carlo and the other houses, as soon as they re-open?'

He let the King think. And realised, *Yes, he did think that, as if being dead were like leprosy, to be shunned.*

He glanced over at Nora, as he had been used to do when they were together, and exchanged a look of silent understanding.

The dead who have Returned are those who want the world . . .

'The Teatro San Carlo should still be the best. If Nora's there, it would be—' Conrad sought the word. '—Would be shameful, for her not to be heard.'

The silence that succeeded could not have been more than two minutes long. Conrad felt every heartbeat of it.

Ferdinand's bland features gave away nothing of what he was thinking – whether he was wondering if forbidding this might not be an additional and better punishment for Leonora Capiraso. His eyes momentarily closed.

'Set the Governor's offices up in the Palazzo Nuovo—' Ferdi-nand's eyes snapped open. He seemed both sardonically amused, and sad. '—Naturally the old Angevin castle appears to have survived better than the Palazzo Reale. If you choose your officers well, Governor Capiraso, you may have one season of the year free of your duties to sing. Christmas to Lent, or the summer season; your choice.'

Leonora stumbled, sank down into a chair by the balcony, and looked up with her expression raw. 'Sir— Thank you—'

Conrad said something at the same moment. He could not have told what he mumbled, if it was not the same thing.

A similar rumble at his elbow was Roberto Capiraso, features white and startled.

Ferdinand sighed. 'I would not withhold that voice. I think, too, the dead of Naples will wish to hear it. If the Count di Argente and Signore Scalese agree, I dare say both of them will write for you, as Rossini wrote for Colbran.'

There was a light in his eye that proved not even the monarch of the Two Sicilies immune from the enthusiasm for opera that involved every man, from *lazzaroni* to count and cardinal.

'You sing for them,' Ferdinand added, 'not for you.'

Leonora had the proud look on her face that was Nora's shield against the world. *Behind it*, Conrad recognised, *is gratitude*.

Not for being allowed to sing.

For being given a way to make up for those lives she transmuted from living to Returned Dead.

'If there's more, we'll complete it tomorrow.' Ferdinand smiled. 'I'll make the announcement officially tomorrow, but if I know the court, it will be known now – say, within a half-hour . . . We'll have a reception in your apartments here, Donna Leonora, since at least that way we can control any rumour and gossip; always a concern . . . Shall we say, in two hours?'

The King closed his manila folders. He reached out his hand towards the bell, and paused, before ringing it.

'Corrado, I would have said this as your friend, in any case. Now I add Leonora, and you, Roberto.'

Ferdinand inclined his head with some civility to the Conte di Argente.

'Since it's now a matter that includes the efficient functioning of my Governor-General in Naples . . . I have no preference for how you do it, but I perceive it's necessary that it be done. For preference, before you, Donna Leonora, leave for Napoli.'

He gazed sternly around.

'The three of you – regularise your private lives.'

62

The few corridors between the King's apartments and the quarters of the King's new Governor in Naples passed in tight-lipped silence, breath inhaled through the nostrils and let out with almost audible huffs. A servant would have pushed Roberto Capiraso's chair, but the injured man waved him off, determinedly wheeling himself in her wake to Leonora's quarters.

Conrad followed the other two in.

We could go down to my quarters, but I think Tullio and Isaura are in; as for Roberto—

'Where *are* you staying?' he asked, before he caught himself.

The Conte di Argente shot a burning glare at Conrad, and then at the entrance to the apartments occupied by Leonora.

'If his Majesty had left me my pocket watch and rings, I'd be hiring rooms. As it is, one of his gentlemen-in-waiting is permitting me to share his cupboard, on the grounds that the Palermo opera house may offer a conductor an advance – always supposing Palermo needs a conductor!'

Conrad dropped back a pace as the servants opened up the rooms ahead. 'So, yes, let's meet on Nora's own ground,' he muttered.

The servant stood aside as they entered, with a respect that told Conrad rumour of the new Governor had already spread.

'You!'

Conrad looked up as the doors closed, hearing utmost venom in Roberto's voice.

He expected it to be directed at him.

Startled, he discovered Roberto staring across the room from his invalid's chair, at Leonora.

'You.' His tone was no less venomous for being quiet. 'You made me join the Prince's Men! And now my reputation is dog-shit, and you're betraying me with another man—'

'You joined il Principe before I even died!' Leonora's pale hands clasped together, knuckles white from pressure, if not loss of blood. 'You followed your brother into the society—'

'—Not the inner circle!—'

Conrad walked around the edge of the drawing-room, pushing the shutters open. White sunlight streamed in. Too hot, too bright, perhaps; but after the eruption pillar spreading across the sky above Naples, he found himself twitchy when there was no natural light.

A warm breeze blew the gauze curtains in, and he faced around.

'You—' He ignored the composer, pointing his finger directly at Leonora. 'You abandoned me in Venice where we were husband and wife – yes, we were! All but the ceremony – to go off with a rich man. Just because I had to pay off my father's debts—'

'And didn't that make a wonderful excuse not to marry me!'

Conrad stared across the room. 'I would have married you.'

'Would you?'

Taken aback by the aggression in the room, Conrad thought, *Why have we never spoken like this before?* – and the answer came to him instantly. *We were never free to until now.*

The sharp ring of a bell interrupted his thoughts. Roberto Capiraso gave sharp orders from his chair, and a few moments later the servant returned with a pair of padded crutches. The Conte di Argente got himself deftly up with the man's help, while Conrad was still suppressing an inexplicable desire to lend a hand.

'You still care more about what he says—' Roberto hitched himself closer to Leonora, all his weight dependent from the crutches. 'About what happened six years ago—!'

'You brought me back from the dead!' Her mouth momentarily

671

lost shape. Her heels rapped on the terracotta tiles as she paced. 'Yes, I think I came back because I wanted to, but . . . Roberto, how do I know that what you did didn't make all the difference? I'm still not sure if I love you or hate you for that. How can I pay off such an obligation?'

The composer stopped, more than an arm's length away from her. 'It's not a debt!'

Conrad watched the emotions that altered her features. The shifting light from outside called up purple highlights in her blue eyes, and gold highlights in her undistinguished brown hair. The line of her shoulders dropped.

She sat suddenly down on a satin-covered chaise-longue, nothing mannerly in her posture.

'I don't know . . .'

Her head came up; Conrad realised – his heart missing a pulse-beat – that she spoke to him.

'. . . I didn't know then . . . I have no idea how to love someone when I don't know if I'll be out on the streets tomorrow. I'm ashamed that I ran away from the opera life at the same time that I ran away from you. I wasn't brave enough for either.'

Conrad opened his mouth, closed it, and shook his head. He turned, on the point of reaching out for the door-handle. In the corner of his vision, he caught sight of Roberto Capiraso.

No, why should I leave him here with her?

'As for you, signore—' Even boiling with hatred, he could not infuse the word with the same contempt that Capiraso would have managed. Conrad was infuriated. 'As well as taking my woman, you betrayed *L'Altezza azteca* every day we worked on it! And I'd come to think we were friends—'

The admission was sour on his tongue; he burned with more humiliation than when he had had to beg for money for Adalrico di Galdi.

'—Yes, I admit it! You had me fooled too.'

Conrad waited for the whiplash response of scorn.

Roberto Capiraso manoeuvered himself a few troubled steps. He supported his weight heavily on the padded crutches. Conrad saw the older man lift his head, in the path of warm wind blowing from the open shutters, as if he too needed to see the sky in its natural state.

'I know.' Roberto glanced away from the open air, his irises seeming black as the pupils. 'It's been wearing on me since the first weeks we worked together.'

'But.' Conrad found he couldn't manage another word.

'When Adalrico and his son put their plot into action, I half hoped it would push you back to a distance . . . but then you came out of prison, and work pushed us back together.' His mouth quirked in his clipped beard, in an expression of sardonic humour. 'There have been great partnerships in the *mondo teatrale* before: Persiani and Donizetti, Romani and Bellini . . .'

Conrad noted the stain of pink high on the man's cheekbones. He thought, amazed, *Roberto is ashamed.*

Faced with that, he could do nothing but be honest.

'You still love Leonora,' he said.

Roberto's smile twisted into pain. 'Yes, I love her. You love her, too. Despite everything. And since I'm now the one who can't support her . . .'

Conrad felt every muscle tense. He held himself back. 'You don't get to call her a whore, Roberto!'

'I'm sorry, Corrado, I'm sure I've heard you say the very same thing—'

'*Che cazzo!*' One of the balcony shutters was drifting closed; Conrad slammed it back against the wall hard enough to flake off the plaster.

'Ask her!' the dark man demanded. 'You have a stipend as director of the scientific institute. I have nothing! She said it herself, a minute ago— Ask her which one of us she's going to choose!'

A high-pitched scream of anger split the air. Leonora sprang to her feet, the chaise-longue screeching back over the tiles. 'Neither! *I choose neither of you fucking idiots*!'

Conrad opened his mouth to shout.

The drawing-room door banged open.

Luigi Esposito strode through.

'Oh thank *God*! The 'thirty-eight!'

The Returned Dead police chief was holding a wine glass, Conrad saw. He swept over to the side-cabinet, and seized a bottle.

'Anatoile Vercel, bless him,' Luigi breathed, lifting the bottle, and filling his glass at eye-level with the yellow wine. He didn't look at any of the three people in the room. 'Ah, there's nothing like wine made from savagnin grapes and aged in oak casks . . .'

Conrad managed to recover his voice. 'Luigi?'

'I had to find a bottle of the 'thirty-eight. Maria will kill me, otherwise.' Luigi favoured them – all three of them – with a dazzling smile. 'When she and my second wife got together about me, they sent me out to buy wine and spent the entire night with this, trying to drink the other one under the table . . . And every hour until dawn, I came home, and I found Adelaide and Maria stone-cold sober.'

Roberto eyed Luigi Esposito with what Conrad thought, at first, was distaste – and then realised was an odd fascination.

'You have two wives?' Roberto said.

'I have three, now.'

The police chief took a sip of the wine, and closed his eyes, either in appreciation for the Vercel wine, or lost in memory.

'All the children play together,' he added, proving it to be the latter.

'Three wives?' Conrad blurted. 'And they all know . . . ?'

'None of the children call me "Uncle". Stefania is from Palermo, so I suppose we shall live in the house here, now, since our sovereign monarch wants me to be his liaison between the Naples and Palermo police forces. And in Naples, let's be honest, there's a lot of rebuilding to do.'

Luigi opened his eyes, his innocent gaze gleaming.

'You'll excuse me; Maria and Stefania and Adelaide will kill me if they don't get their share!'

He tucked his empty glass into the hand that held the first bottle of the Vercel, returned to the cabinet, acquired two more wine-glasses, and picked up two bottles by their necks.

'. . . What this wine needs is a fine quality cheese . . . By the way, you have guests.'

Not having a hand free, the police liaison between Palermo and Returned Dead Naples backed his way out through the doors.

There was a silence.

A long silence.

'So.' Conrad hoped his voice didn't betray him. 'So . . . What should we put on at the San Carlo next season?'

Roberto hurriedly said, 'I'd thought about a comedy?'

Nora lifted her head to look at both of them. 'I can have the rebuilding completed by November?'

CODA

CODA

Luigi Esposito left the drawing-room of the apartments in the Palazzo dei Normanni, letting the doors fall shut behind him.

A man, and a woman in man's clothing, hastily stumbled back from where they clustered outside.

'I couldn't hear anything!'

'What did they say—?'

'*SST!*'

Luigi beckoned them down the corridor towards the palace apartment's large central hall, and a rising babble of sound, where his Majesty King Ferdinand and a growing number of society's great and good collected, taking drinks from the servants, and waiting to greet their hosts.

Luigi made introductions between his three wives and Tullio Rossi – they amiably gossiped with him – and to Paolo Scalese, whose evening dress fooled two out of the three women.

The string quartet in the corner came to a subtle, quiet halt.

Flunkies flung back the double doors.

'Your Majesty!' the apartment's major-domo announced. 'Lords, Counts, ladies, gentlemen! I present to you – the new Governor of Naples!'

King Ferdinand of the Two Sicilies clapped his hands. '*Bravo!*'

Every man and woman present joined in the applause, polite at first, and then, as their hosts appeared, sincere.

'Bravo!'
'Brava!'
'Bravissima!'
All three of them walked into the room together, arm in arm.

The penniless Count leaned on his stout padded crutches. Leonora had her left arm tightly though Conrad's, and her right arm under Roberto's, ready to support him if he slipped. Conrad found himself poised in case he should be needed, good hand ready.

Roberto smiled as if a touch stunned – and Conrad as if he heard glorious applause for the production of some Neapolitan opera. Leonora might have been only beautiful, in a plain high-waisted white dress, with antique bronze ear-rings and hair ornaments, but neither the silk nor the metal shone as brightly as her smile.

Luigi discreetly passed wine-glasses to Tullio and Paolo-Isaura. He filled them, and his own, with the Vercel jaune.

Wordlessly, they raised glasses to each other:

Ting! Ting! Ting!

RUDE ITALIAN
FOR BEGINNERS

(Please note that rough modern equivalents have been used for early-nineteenth-century swear-words; it would take more of a linguist than I am to accurately portray Neapolitan, Sicilian, and other pre-Unification Italian of the period.)

cazzo – as a noun: penis, cock. As a colloquial interjection, used more as the UK currently uses 'fuck!'; the all-purpose transgressive exclamation.

che cazzo – lit. 'what penis'; colloquially 'what the fuck!'

che stronzo – lit. 'that asshole'/'what an asshole'.

ciel; 'O ciel!' – lit. 'heavens!' or 'sky!'; an archaic appeal to the deity.

cornuto – 'horned', i.e. cuckolded; a husband sexually betrayed by his wife.

Dio! – 'God!' (As appeal, imprecation, or whatever else this all-purpose oath can cover.)

fessa – lit. 'cleft', colloquially 'cunt'.

figlio di puttana – 'son of a whore', used similarly to 'son of a bitch!'

merda – shit; crap.

merda per merda – 'shit, shit, shit!'

minchia – southern Italian version of cazzo: penis.

porca miseria – lit. 'pig poverty' or 'miserable pig'; colloquial equiv. 'goddammit!'

porca vacca – lit. 'pig-cow'.

porco giuda – lit. 'Judas pig' (Adding 'pig' to almost anything can turn it into a swear-word; this hardly seems fair to a beautifully-natured animal . . .)

testa di cazzo – dickhead.

Vaffanculo – much stronger version of 'fuck off!', implies 'go fuck yourself', 'go do it up the arse'.

NB - *Scheiße* or *Scheisse* is, of course, not Italian but German; it translates as 'shit', with much the same vulgar connotations as the English word.